THE
IKESSAR
FALCON

Where do I begin with the violence and terror that follow my waking moments?

It will take me years to write it all down, and I don't have years. I must pick only the parts that fit the puzzle in the hopes of it forming a picture somehow. In retrospect, it is frightening to realize how easily the worth of our lives can be broken down. How easy it is to say words like *she lived, and caused sorrow*. Small things build up over time, and suddenly your legacy looks nothing like you imagined it to be. Not even a queen can live with the reassurance that her life will be of value. If my father had been alive, he would have never understood how his precious daughter is nothing but the sum of her mistakes.

"Staring at that won't make the words come any faster," Sayu says, looking up from her own work: that curved, elegant handwriting, so beautiful it ought to be preserved behind a glass case somewhere.

"A pity. I was hoping it would." I give her a small smile, considering my own messy scribbling. I still do not know how to talk to her about any of this— facing it myself is enough of a struggle. I am grasping for a word now, turning the thoughts inside my head for that one, perfect response if my father ever pointed that wrinkled finger at me again. *Why, child? What happened to the daughter I raised? What went wrong with you?*

Praise for K. S. Villoso and
THE WOLF OF OREN-YARO

"*The Wolf of Oren-Yaro* is intricate, intimate, and intensely plotted. Full of subtle poignancy and remarkably genuine characters—even the rotten ones. I loved this book"   Nicholas Eames, author of *Kings of the Wyld*

"A powerful new voice in epic fantasy. Villoso deftly creates an intricate and compelling world of high fantasy intrigue and adventure dominated by a crafty, whip-smart heroine determined to unite her kingdom at any cost"

Kameron Hurley, author of *The Light Brigade*

"Deeply compelling and wonderfully entertaining, *The Wolf of Oren-Yaro* feels at once timely and timeless. K. S. Villoso's lush and finely crafted world envelops readers from the first page, as she takes us on an adventure full of heartache, hope, and triumph. It's a fabulous read!"

Josiah Bancroft, author of *Senlin Ascends*

"A tale balanced on the blade's-edge between intrigue and action—and then Villoso twists the knife"   Gareth Hanrahan, author of *The Gutter Prayer*

"Delivers complex and intriguing characters, and an action-packed plot full of surprising twists, and deep, vivid worldbuilding"

Melissa Caruso, author of *The Tethered Mage*

"Intimate and epic. It compels you to read on, because it's a story about people not characters, civilizations not settings, and deadly power plays not sanitized throne-room politics"   Evan Winter, author of *The Rage of Dragons*

By K. S. Villoso

Chronicles of the Bitch Queen

The Wolf of Oren-Yaro
The Ikessar Falcon

THE
IKESSAR
FALCON

CHRONICLES OF THE BITCH QUEEN:
BOOK TWO

K. S. VILLOSO

www.orbitbooks.net

ORBIT

Originally published by Liam's Vigil Publishing Co. in 2018
First published in Great Britain in 2020 by Orbit

1 3 5 7 9 10 8 6 4 2

Copyright © 2018 by K. S. Villoso

Map by Tim Paul

Excerpt from *There Will Come a Darkness* by Katy Rose Pool
Copyright © 2019 by Katy Pool

The moral right of the author has been asserted.

A CIP catalogue record for this book
is available from the British Library.

ISBN 978-0-356-51449-9

Typeset in Garamond by M Rules
Printed and bound in Great Britain by Clays Ltd, Elcograf S.p.A.

Papers used by Orbit are from well-managed forests
and other responsible sources.

MIX
Paper from
responsible sources
FSC® C104740

Orbit
An imprint of
Little, Brown Book Group
Carmelite House
50 Victoria Embankment
London EC4Y 0DZ

An Hachette UK Company
www.hachette.co.uk

www.orbitbooks.net

To Conrad and Eirene,
this faint attempt
at piecing together these stories
to a world that will never
know how to listen.
Try, anyway.

THE STORY SO FAR…

They called me the Bitch Queen, the she-wolf, because I murdered a man and exiled my king the night before they crowned me.

So begins the story of Queen Talyien, daughter of Warlord Yeshin, a man who declared civil war on the ruling clan years before her birth, and who only accepted a truce on the condition that his daughter be betrothed to their heir and be crowned queen.

Or so the books might say. She herself is convinced of it; that her moment of failure began at the point when she could not hold her marriage together. Five years of unstable rule followed Prince Rayyel's departure, until the land could no longer utter the queen's name without a hint of sarcasm and more than a shred of anger. She fought back, retreating behind an armour of barbed words and threats. To them, Warlord Yeshin, the mass murderer, and Talyien, Yeshin's bitch pup, are one and the same; with Yeshin dead, Talyien took the brunt of their hatred.

But Queen Talyien and Tali are different edges of the same sword—one a mask, the other a woman. Tali, who grew up motherless in Oka Shto, whose only family was a frail old man who could be both terrible and kind at once, tried to seek solace in her betrothal to the indifferent Prince Rayyel. Initially rebuffed, later gradually accepted, she found her world shattered when she learned of her betrothed's relationship with another warlord's daughter. She, in turn, found comfort in the arms of her oldest friend. Afterwards, she resolved to put everything behind her and embrace her responsibilities, rendered bitter by reality.

Rayyel, however, abandons her three years later. And she doesn't hear from him again until five years into her rule as queen, when a message comes asking her to meet with him across the sea, in Anzhao City in the Empire of Ziri-nar-Orxiaro. Her eagerness to reconcile is mixed with her anger. Her general suggests she use the opportunity to declare war against her husband's clan, as he has been urging her to do for years; against his will, she travels with a handful of guards and her adviser, relying on political goodwill to carry them the rest of the way.

She is sorely disappointed when she realizes that the power of a queen of a small nation is hardly recognized by officials of the mighty empire. A deputy, Ino Qun, shelters her and insults her almost in the same breath; Qun's wife drops cryptic words. On the way to the meeting, chaos breaks out in the streets, and Tali finds herself separated—whether by accident or on purpose—from her guards. She wanders the streets and meets a con artist, Khine Lamang, whom she assists in swindling a shopkeeper. In exchange, he takes her to the restaurant where Prince Rayyel is waiting. Prince Rayyel is accompanied by a priestess and the governor of Anzhao City, Gon Zheshan.

The meeting goes nowhere; Prince Rayyel wants Queen Talyien to cede half of Jin-Sayeng to him. The treaty that put them both on the throne required that they rule together, but never laid out the circumstances. Before the meeting can conclude, they are attacked by assassins. Tali finds herself alone and without her guards in the slums, where her position matters even less. She finds one of her own guards in prison; before he is beaten to death by the city watch, he tells her that her own guards have been acting suspiciously and she would have been better served if she had kept her old captain, Agos. She encounters a gambling lord, Lo Bahn, and barely escapes being made into his whore; the only sympathetic soul she meets is Khine, whom she runs into again. She initially distrusts him—everyone she has met has only been looking out for themselves.

But Khine is persistent, and she slowly grows to enjoy his company, sharing what she can of her life, or at least what she feels she is allowed to. With him, she finds it easy to be herself, to drop the queen's act and be seen as she is, unjudged, with no expectations.

Lo Bahn catches up to her while she is recuperating in Khine's abode. She escapes and learns from her maidservant that Gon Zheshan is holding her husband captive. She also confirms the deaths of her adviser, Arro, and what appears to be half her guardsmen. The other half, including her captain, Nor, are missing.

Talyien finds herself trying to seek aid from the emperor's Fifth Son, Prince Yuebek, to save Rayyel. She is separated from Khine on the road, but is picked up by Governor Radi Ong—Prince Yuebek's father-in-law—and taken to Zorheng City, a fortress on the riverbank seemingly built by mages. It doesn't take long for Tali to surmise that Prince Yuebek is a madman. He offers to marry Talyien and kills his own wife as a show of solidarity. And because Talyien continues to refuse, he throws her in prison.

Months later, Tali wakes up in a strange room, where she encounters the ghosts of her brother and her father. Yeshin berates her, telling her she has failed because she fell in love with Rayyel. This confuses her, because she thinks her duty was to love him—her zealousness came from both her own feelings and her loyalty to her father. She realizes she is still being chased by an assassin and narrowly escapes. She finds a note on the dead assassin telling her that her husband was behind the attempt on her life.

She returns to Khine, but the comfort of his company is short-lived as she finds herself reunited with not just her guards but also her old friend Agos. She also learns there is an embargo preventing travel from the empire to Jin-Sayeng.

With Khine and the gambling lord, Lo Bahn, she sets in motion a plan to infiltrate Governor Zheshan's office and confront Rayyel. But here she comes face-to-face not with her husband but with Prince Yuebek, who reveals to her two things: that he is a mage with a strong connection to the *agan*, and that he planned everything, including the assassin, in order to convince her to fall for him and discard her husband. Because none of his tricks worked, Yuebek threatens her son, telling Talyien he knows the truth—that the boy could be a bastard whose life is forfeit if the rest of the nation finds out. He also tells her that it was Talyien's own father, Yeshin, who promised her to him first, in exchange for his power and his army; her betrothal to Rayyel was a sham. Warlord Yeshin's desire to win his war was too strong, and he undermined his own treaty in order to claim victory once and for all. Talyien's own men had betrayed her to deliver her to Yuebek.

Refusing to believe Yuebek's claims, Talyien delivers him a killing blow and watches as he runs into a burning room. She returns to Lo Bahn's, where Governor Zheshan commits suicide after confirming how Yuebek has attempted to blackmail him into betraying Rayyel.

Still reeling from everything she has learned, she receives a note from Rayyel asking for another meeting. Even though Tali is aware it might be another trap, Khine convinces her to go, as she is still holding on to the hope that somehow she can salvage her marriage.

Tali finally meets Rai, who confesses he has always loved her. The reader learns that it is the knowledge of his wife's affair, and that her son may not be his, that caused him to walk away; already damned by the politics that gave birth to their lives, their mistakes hastened the ruin. He swears to make things right, that he is seeking mages that will help reveal the truth, and that if the boy is not his, he will kill him himself.

The novel ends with Tali trying to grasp on to the last shreds of her father's rhetoric: *A wolf of Oren-yaro does not beg. A wolf of Oren-yaro suffers in silence.* But her downfall is just beginning...

ACT ONE

THE ROAD TO
JIN-SAYENG

CHAPTER ONE

THE PRICE OF
INNOCENCE

A thousand hooves trampled the sky the night my father died.

No words can describe what it feels like to gaze at the man you looked up to—a man you respected, and loved, and feared—and realize that somewhere along the way, he turned into a shadow of his former self. That he had, in fact, been fading for years, and was simply doing a remarkable job of pretending the world wasn't falling apart. Where there was once power, presence, and might, now there was only sickness and the stench of death: not yet the sweet-stink of a rotting corpse, but a moldy, urine-tinged scent, one that seemed to crawl away from his stiffening body and up the walls to fill the entire room.

The storm started with his last breath. I found myself sinking back into the chair, frozen in terror as the lightning flashed over his shadowed face, revealing the hollows under his eyes, spidered with black veins. Deep-green bruises, cracked lips, yellow-white skin, wrinkled as parchment. I had been instructed to inform Lord General Ozo first should my father succumb to his illness, but I couldn't even find the courage to stand, let alone look away from the withered image of the man who used to be strong enough to lift me on his shoulders. *You're alone now*, my thoughts whispered, a thin thread that sought to wrap itself around my heart. *You will no longer be able to depend on him. From now on, everything falls on you.*

The sobs stopped at my throat, settling inside my chest and wrenching the breath out of me. My eyes burned, but I forced the tears not to fall. What if one of the soldiers walked in and saw Yeshin's heir red-faced and bawling away like a child? The other warlords would think us weak, that they all made a mistake when they bequeathed the Dragonthrone to an Orenar. To an Oren-yaro. Would I let it all turn to dust after everything my father had sacrificed?

I slowly let go of Yeshin's hand, curling mine into a fist, before I reached up to plant a kiss on his wrinkled forehead. It was still covered in a layer of cold sweat. I wanted to say something, to utter a prayer or words of farewell for a man whose name carried a weight that could break the world. But silence seemed to be the only fitting poetry for someone who had lived as Warlord Yeshin had. So instead, I swallowed and murmured an oath that I would do everything it took to make his dreams become a reality. A united land, prosperous in the way the Ikessars couldn't make it, with the discipline and the ideals that made the province and the people of Oren-yaro stand head and shoulders above the rest. And so even if it meant facing my fears, if it meant walking the road laid out for me... if it meant becoming someone I was not...

He was dead and yet I still carried on in my head like he was listening. It started there; it never stopped. And there was never a time since that I didn't find myself carrying out my duties to the echo of his voice—to that sharp, lightning-like roar of it, the one that could crumple my very soul.

It was that same voice that reached deep into me and forced me to consider my failures the day I lost my husband. My quest for Rayyel was a twisted reflection of the turbulence around me, a lighthouse in a stormy sea. I was accused of blindness, of obsession, of allowing my love for a man to become the center around which my life spun. I hardened myself to it. Embraced it. Call me what you want—irrational, careless, an idiot, even—every name you can think of. I know. I've told them to myself for years. When you internalize such thinking, allowing it to settle into your bones so deeply you know your own weaknesses to be a fact, it becomes a kind of foolhardy strength. Make of that what you will.

So when the bitter truth came—when my husband declared that he *had* loved me after all, when I had long convinced myself that *I* was the one holding our marriage together—my world came crashing down. For the longest time, to hear those words was all I ever wanted. *He loved me*, but because three days before my wedding, I had fled from his ancestral city straight into another's arms, he could no longer be certain if our son was his. There is nothing worse to wash down anger than the taste of your own mistakes.

A just reaction, so many others will say. Rayyel deserved it after what *he* had done—after his own betrayal, his own languid affair with another warlord's daughter. But they don't understand. They don't understand that it was the kind of emotional reaction my father used to warn me against, proof enough to remind me that I was not what my father needed me to be, that I did not deserve to be Warlord Yeshin's daughter. What strength I thought I had was laughable—I *needed* to be more than this. Jin-Sayeng needed me to be more than this. Thousands had lost their lives to get me to where I was. If I faltered, thousands more would follow.

It was as if I had taken a sharpened knife and stabbed my father's dreams over and over. The worst part was that I didn't do it to rebel. I didn't do it out of spite. I did it because my position was an iron hand around my throat and I needed to catch a moment's breath. The failures of youth; Yeshin could've done better than to pin all his hopes on someone like me. A brilliant mind, but he was wrong about the one thing he couldn't afford to be wrong about.

To speak of my father has always left me hollow, and to write about his death is to scrape my insides out and smear them over this ink-stained paper. To speak of my failures to the land I was entrusted leaves me with the urge to rip my work apart and burn it on the candles. I imagine the sight of these in flames would give me a measure of satisfaction, if only because I cannot erase the details from my own memories. But I am not exactly in my own home, and Sayu would frown on that—if she doesn't throw me out first. She has also made it clear how much more expensive this paper is than what she uses for her own scribe work, and while I'm sure she won't lecture a queen, her sigh alone might cut me. The very presence of the woman shrivels me like a brush of shadow over a touch-me-not plant; I do not want to imagine what my father would say that a peasant's judgment of a queen should hold so much weight. The queen of Jin-Sayeng, worrying about paper?

But the thought only fills me with sorrow, that I know so little of my land after all these years. That crisscross in the grains of the paper, for instance, is supposed to mean the paper comes all the way from the mills in Natu, with trees from the low-lying lands there. This ink was made in a factory in Kai, one that has been with the same family since Reshiro's reforms that allowed merchants to operate outside of the warlords' influence. Sayu told me they are struggling now—ink is not as prized as weapons these days. They have asked for help before; I have a vague recollection of those papers on my desk somewhere, fully intending to get Arro to take care of it at some point in the future. Arro, who now lies in a mass grave somewhere in the empire—the land of his birth, but not his chosen home.

I pause, blots of ink dripping from the end of my pen. I wonder if maybe I should proceed forward—to talk about the events that transpired immediately after my bitter separation from my husband in Anzhao City. Should I talk about how Agos tried to chase him down to the docks and was blocked by Zheshan's men? Maybe I can speak instead of when I returned to Lo Bahn's mansion just in time to see him dragged out by officials in chains, face as hard as a rock. He had seen me on the street, and for a moment I was afraid he would betray me. But as soon as our eyes locked, he looked away, and I heard him say, "I don't know anything, you sons of bitches."

They set him free a day later. "None the worse for wear," he hissed through bloodstained teeth. He was covered in bruises, one eye swollen so shut it left only a thin crease behind, and when he tried to wipe the blood from his lips, I saw that his fingernails were torn out. "I hope you're enjoying the hospitality, Queen Talyien." His servants led him away to see a healer, and I didn't see him again for days.

Where do I begin with the violence and terror that follow my waking moments? It will take me years to write it all down, and I don't have years. I must pick only the parts that fit the puzzle in the hopes of it forming a picture somehow. In retrospect, it is frightening to realize how easily the worth of our lives can be broken down. How easy it is to say words like *she lived, and caused sorrow*. Small things build up over time, and suddenly your legacy looks nothing like you imagined it to be. Not even a queen can live with the reassurance that her life will be of value. If my father had been alive, he would have never understood how his precious daughter is nothing but the sum of her mistakes.

"Staring at that won't make the words come any faster," Sayu says, looking up from her own work: that curved, elegant handwriting, so beautiful it ought to be preserved behind a glass case somewhere.

"A pity. I was hoping it would." I give her a small smile, considering my own messy scribbling. I still do not know how to talk to her about any of this—facing it myself is enough of a struggle. I am grasping for a word now, turning the thoughts inside my head for that one, perfect response if my father ever pointed that wrinkled finger at me again. *Why, child? What happened to the daughter I raised? What went wrong with you?*

Ignorance—yes, that's the word. Because only an ignorant woman would willingly swallow a vat of poison in the hopes of finding a cure. Maybe another would have been allowed the mistake, but I was the lady of Oren-yaro, future queen of Jin-Sayeng. I was supposed to understand the significance of my every move. My father had drilled these things into me the moment I was old enough to know my name was Talyien aren dar Orenar. I was the Jewel of Jin-Sayeng, a symbol of peace, a double-edged sword. I wielded enough power to send men running for the door or falling at my feet—an army of ten thousand, my father's bloody legacy around me like a shawl.

But in those moments of my mistake, I had dropped all trappings and left behind a girl of eighteen. Old enough to know better, but still too young to understand the nature of the world, the pitfalls that could open up and trap you. I remember the rain, the lightning across the sky and the thunder that followed, pounding against the glass windows of the inn. The smell of mint and beeswax candles, the ringing of wind chimes spinning with the storm. The hollow sensation of loneliness, of broken illusions and dreams disappearing rapidly, like a bucket of water upturned into the sea.

I cranked the door open and called for Agos. In crowded inns, he usually slept in front of the doorway by the hall, refusing to get his own room. I had long stopped insisting. I heard him stir from the shadows at the sound of my voice.

"Princess," he said, stepping inside with the surety of a beast stalking through the night. "Do you need something?"

"I'm frightened of lightning," I blurted out, forgetting whatever excuse I had planned to give.

A puzzled expression drifted over his face. "Lightning," he said evenly. "Not thunder?"

"Lightning," I repeated. "The flash, the crackle. Not the rumble."

"*You.*" He didn't sound like he believed me.

Almost as an answer, another flash of lightning lit up the sky, and I cringed involuntarily. His eyes widened, as if he had only just realized I meant what I said. A few moments later, the thunder broke through and I felt the tight grip of fear loosen itself around me. I was able to breathe again.

"Do you want me to make it go away?" he asked, a hint of laughter behind his voice.

"Could you?"

He was still wondering if I was serious or not. "I could ask around for the nearest temple..." he started.

I sighed. "I didn't mean...I *am* joking, Agos. Partly." A third flash, another cringe.

Agos continued to stare. "I can't tell, sometimes."

"Really? After all these years?"

He nodded.

"Just sit with me. Talk." I placed my hand on the mattress.

Agos took the furthest edge. He looked uncomfortable, like he was about to fall off. He placed his hands on his knees. "Are you all right now?" he asked. "You didn't tell me why we left the Dragon Palace as quickly as we arrived."

"Tell me about training," I said, ignoring his question. "I've heard General Ozo is a bit of a hard-ass."

"A princess shouldn't speak like that."

"A princess hangs around long enough with soldiers like you, she's bound to pick up a few things. Come on, Agos. We haven't seen each other in *years*." I had been fifteen the last time he had visited Oka Shto. "Surely you have some amusing story to tell."

"I don't..." he began. He scratched his cheek. "Nothing I could repeat in polite company. Especially not in front of a *lady*."

I punched his arm. I used to do that often when we were younger. His reaction now was more subdued than I remembered.

"You've got to act like one, too," he murmured, rubbing his skin as if I'd actually hurt him. "You're going to be a wife soon. What would Prince Rayyel say?"

The smile I had pasted onto my face disappeared. Hearing my betrothed's name felt like a blow to the head. I dropped my gaze. "I don't want to talk about Rayyel."

The fourth flash of lightning, and then thunder almost immediately after. And then the rain, pouring so hard around us that I scarcely noticed I had thrown myself at him. I *was* afraid of lightning. It wasn't something Warlord Yeshin's daughter should readily admit. If my father had known when he was alive, he would've locked me in a shed during a storm to try to knock it out of me, or at least numb my senses to it.

"Princess Tali..." I heard Agos grumble.

My hands were wrapped around his shirt. "I'm sorry," I whispered, glancing down so that I didn't have to look at his face. "I'm..."

"What the hell did Prince Rayyel do to you, anyway?"

"Nothing," I quickly said. "He did nothing." *He did nothing while letting that woman do whatever she wanted with him. Chiha, Warlord Lushai's daughter.* I didn't see her face, but it had to be her. Her father had wanted to undo everything mine had worked so hard for while maintaining a pretence of friendship.

I let my hands fall to the side. "I'm sorry," I repeated. My own weakness disgusted me. I could almost feel my father shaking my shoulder, telling me to stand tall, to *think* clearly. I was better than this. I took a deep breath. "Please. You may go, if you want."

He quirked an eyebrow. "If I want?"

"I don't know anymore." I could hear his shallow breathing, and I looked up to catch sight of his flushed face, of the rise and fall of his broad chest. What had happened to my childhood friend, the older boy who didn't think twice about indulging my harebrained schemes? I was acutely aware that this was now a *man* beside me. I tried to shut the images of the last few hours from my mind, the sound of Chiha moaning on my betrothed's bed.

"Would you stay with me tonight?" I asked. I could barely recognize my voice.

"If I want," he repeated. His own had dropped another octave.

I hesitated, and then nodded. I noticed his hand had been on my elbow. He now slid it up my arm, testing my reaction. I didn't flinch, allowing him to touch my bare shoulder.

He started to kiss me, but I twisted my head away from him. I wasn't exactly sure what I wanted at that moment, but I knew what I *didn't* want. I didn't want that sort of intimacy—I didn't want to play at love. He took the hint and let his lips fall on my neck instead.

There was a clicking sound. I watched in horror as the door opened and the innkeeper barged in. "Your horses are—" he began. He saw us on the bed and his face turned as white as his beard. "I'm sorry, my lady. I'm..." He walked out just as quickly, slamming the door behind him.

I cleared my throat. Agos got up. At the doorway, he turned to me. "Are you sure about this?"

I almost said *no*. Wasn't this the sort of thing I was supposed to iron out with my betrothed first? I knew in the back of my head that I could approach the council with evidence of Rayyel's wrongdoing, which would discredit him without the blame falling on me. It was the kind of thing that would strengthen my support among the warlords, too—in a land as idealistic as Jin-Sayeng, adultery was seen as a great affront. It was true we weren't married yet, but there was protocol about these things, small subtleties I could've taken advantage of.

But I didn't have a template on feelings. I was aware I was acting irrationally, but I didn't know how to handle it. And so I didn't stop Agos when he locked the door and returned to me. One hand on my knee, he paused long enough to take his shirt off. I had seen him naked before, but five years in the army had transformed his stocky body into something unrecognizable, one of hard muscle and scarred flesh. His skin, which had once been as pale as mine, had tanned considerably under the sun. I made myself touch him, half curious at the sensation stirring within me, but also half wishing it was Rayyel there instead.

Agos moved like a man possessed, as if he was afraid I would change my mind at any moment. He untied my shirt, sliding it off my shoulders, and pushed me back onto the bed, rough fingers running over my skin as if it were made of glass. Lips on my neck again, and then down on my breasts, one after the other, hot mouth hungry for my flesh. I lay still, unsure exactly of what I was supposed to do, what was expected of me. No templates, like I said. I had them for everything but this.

I could feel his hardness on my leg. A slight attention to it was all it took, and now he was unbuckling his pants and spitting on his hand. He slid into me, hard enough to make me gasp in pain, and only then—*only then*—did it occur to him exactly what was happening. I could see it in his eyes, the horror on his face as the blood began to run down my thighs. This was not a thing I just did, a thing I had picked up for fun in the few years since we had last been friends together. He had just claimed my maidenhood.

"Gods help us both, Princess," he exhaled. "What are we doing?"

What, indeed?

But he wanted this; he wanted this more than he knew how to say. Even before I could answer, he drove deeper, wrenching his manhood into me like a knife. I questioned what pleasure women could derive from this act, but I didn't interrupt him. The smell of the candles, the surrounding rain, the salt of his sweat on my tongue—they worked together to create a heady atmosphere that wasn't entirely unpleasant. After a few minutes, the pain numbed down, no more than what I had to suffer through with my monthly bleeding. He bucked his hips against me—I felt the ache turn into something else momentarily, rising as he sped up, a hint of what this was *supposed* to feel like, but before I could think about it any more, he stopped, spent.

Agos pulled out, his seed spilling onto the sheets. The numbness was spreading throughout my body, up my fingers and deep into my heart. I craned my head to look at him. He was on his back, his arm on his forehead.

"They will kill me for this," he grumbled. I didn't have to ask who *they* were. If word of this got out, the entire nation would be running to avenge the future queen's lost honour.

I pulled my knees up, covering my legs with my robes. I was sore and confused and, more than anything else, exhausted. Which was surprising, given

I had done nothing at all. Was that it? All that trouble and fuss for something that was over in a few minutes? I still didn't know how I was supposed to feel and wondered, perhaps, if I was the one at fault. Perhaps I had expected too much from everyone—from Rayyel, especially. "Then why go through with it?" I found myself asking, hoping the conversation would drive my restlessness away.

"You don't know much about men, do you?" He looked up at my face and frowned. "No, you don't. I shouldn't be surprised, after…that."

"I'm sorry." I had lost track of how many times I had uttered the phrase.

"Don't be. I'm not." Agos turned to me now with his dark eyes, his brow furrowed. "But you're marrying Prince Rayyel in three days. You know what this means, right?"

I had gleaned enough from hearing gossip from the maidservants. Losing one's maidenhood was supposed to be a moment of great importance. Belatedly, I wondered how much blood there was on the sheets and if I would have to burn the damn bed before we left. This—none of this—was how I imagined things would turn out. "I don't think he'll notice."

"And the innkeeper?"

"Threaten him. Bribe him."

"Wiser if he was dead."

"I won't kill a man for *that*, Agos. He didn't do anything wrong." I shivered, pulling the sheets up to my chest. My insides felt bruised. There was comfort, at least, from the torrent of rain outside. I wanted it to keep falling. I wanted it to flood the whole town, to carry me away and drown me.

"Can I sleep?" Agos mumbled. "I can protect you right here."

"Go ahead," I replied. "We can deal with the innkeeper in the morning."

He hesitated. I think he wanted to try to kiss me again. Instead, he sank back to the pillows and fell asleep almost immediately. I watched the lines on his face ease away, and only then remembered that we had been on the road since early that morning. I had taken for granted all the things I'd asked from him, and a pang of guilt took seed inside my heart. I had no name for whatever I felt for Agos. I liked his company well enough—I didn't love him.

How could Yeshin's daughter make such a grievous error, one that would follow me all the way across the sea? There I was in Anzhao City, having been given one last chance to unite my people, with my husband—my king, the man I *did* love—bearing heart and soul at last. A moment's error shattered it to pieces, casting a shadow over my son Thanh's very being. A moment's error in which I failed not just as a daughter, but as a mother to a child not yet born.

But I didn't know, I didn't know, I didn't know.

Ignorance can be the sweetest sin.

That is, of course, old news, enemies I would have been glad to bury in the dust once and for all. I did my best to move past them. What more could I have done? I had no right to complain—not everyone gets the chance to live out a fairy-tale dream.

But mistakes beget mistakes, and fairy tales turn into nightmares. And what would've been challenging in more capable hands turned into a catastrophe in mine. Now I was dealing with the knowledge that I had been betrayed by the very people who were supposed to be serving me, all to lead me into the arms of a mad Zarojo prince. That it was my own father who might've conjured such a plot. And that my husband, amid all of this, had every intention of killing Thanh if he learned he was not his after all.

I didn't even know what got me out of bed every morning. My love for my son. Responsibility. Habit. What else was I supposed to do? I had to save my son. It seemed like the simplest thing to latch on to, with everything falling apart. And yet I didn't know how to do it. All I had were half answers and two guards to my name. My son was being guarded by people who had no reason to be loyal to me—by Ikessars, my husband's people, in a sea of Oren-yaro, many of whom still claimed loyalty to my father. And he was all the way back in my castle. It wasn't a distance I could easily cross, even without the embargo on ships travelling to Jin-Sayeng.

A part of me was counting on the chance that thwarting Rayyel in his wretched quest to prove my son's legitimacy would somehow stop all the other bricks from falling, like damming a bursting embankment with your hands. So I had spent the last few weeks in Han Lo Bahn's house, wedged deep in the slums of Shang Azi, while trying to find out exactly what the man had planned.

All I knew was that he had gone in search of mages. Mages, whom he planned to bring to Jin-Sayeng, where we have outlawed the practice of magic. And if the land found out exactly why he would allow this madness into our midst? If they found out what I've done?

I would lose my crown, and the only thing keeping my son alive.

I closed my eyes, willing away the twinge of fear that crawled up my bones, before making my way down the steps of Lo Bahn's house to where my Captain of the Guard was waiting for me. These weren't thoughts that I needed to enter-tain on what already seemed like a dismal day. Grey clouds covered the sky, which filled the air with a damp chill. Even the garden felt cheerless—withered leaves curled along the branches, as if they had long given up on the promise of sun.

"You have children, too, don't you, Nor?"

Nor paused from the doorway of Lo Bahn's mansion. She was a tall woman, a match for many of the soldiers back at Oren-yaro; I always wondered what she felt having to look down on me to talk. Even now, she hesitated, as if unsure why I was asking her such a thing. "A daughter," she said, at length. "Beloved Queen. You were at her last nameday. You brought a wooden sword for her."

"Akaterru help me," I grumbled. I had no recollection of this. She was my cousin... her child was my niece. I fulfilled my duties to my clan well enough if the gift sword was any indication, but I couldn't put a face to her daughter. I couldn't even remember her name.

I chewed over this as we walked through the gardens, past metal arches thick with leafy vines and bloated seed pods. Lo Bahn kept an impressive orchard behind stone walls, with no fewer than twenty fruit trees arranged around stone benches and decorative stones. He claimed to like nature, that the smell of a fresh breeze—an uncommon occurrence in the crowded, dirty streets of Shang Azi—was good for a man's circulation. I looked back at Nor. "I apologize," I said.

Her firm face remained unyielding. "There is nothing to apologize for, Beloved Queen."

"You would be back home with your family if not for me."

"We're trapped here because of an embargo. My duty is to remain by your side. There is nothing to apologize for," she repeated.

I didn't have the courage to correct her. She had no knowledge of what trans-pired in that dockside inn between me and my husband, only a faint inkling of rumours best kept away from prying ears. She didn't even know I had gone to see him that day. As far as she was aware, we were still trying to find him, still trying to piece together information we could glean from his activities in Anzhao while we remained hopelessly stuck, unable to board a ship home. It had made for a very dismal three months. I wasn't sure how she would react to the truth. She was a wolf of Oren-yaro, too, one still reeling from the bitter taste of her men's betrayal. The silence from back home was unnerving. It almost looked as if our people just went and abandoned us overnight. Where was Lord General Ozo and our army? What was stopping them from sending ships after us, Anzhao City politics be damned? Did they know about my mistakes, and had they all but abandoned me because of them?

No. Nor would kill me if I told her. That the rumours were true—I had faltered, I had sinned, and the heir to the throne was possibly illegitimate, a scandal waiting to explode. It felt ridiculous even to think about how I had let it come this far. I, foolish woman that I was, had never thought to question it. Thanh came out looking every inch like Rayyel and was growing up to follow in his footsteps, much to my dismay. A quiet, serious boy who liked books and had to be reminded to hold a sword the right way—how could he be Agos's son? Agos, who had once pretended to read in front of me with the damn pages upside down?

I opened my mouth to say something in an effort to drown out the silence, but it was overtaken by the sound of the gates opening. Agos's tall form strode past Lo Bahn's guards, but my eyes settled on the figure behind him. Khine Lamang, Lo Bahn's right-hand man, of whom I hadn't seen hide nor hair for a good long while. I felt a lump in my throat.

"The hell are you doing here, Lamang?" I called out. I was hoping the famil-iar banter would ease the beating of my heart. The sight of him brought sol-ace, which was immediately followed by shame—emotions my father would've frowned upon. I had already asked for too much from him.

"Your language has been improved by your time here," Khine said easily. His voice had that cool, polite detachment that he used with people like Lo Bahn—people he disagreed with but didn't want to confront. An easygoing tone, swathed in ice. He nodded towards Agos. "I heard you people have been asking around for a Gasparian merchant by the name of Eridu. What do you need from him?"

"We were told my husband paid him a visit a few weeks before he left."

"Your method of questioning leaves people on edge," he said. "I'll spare you the trouble. This time of the day, he'll be at the hawker's hub in Dar Aso."

"Why have you decided to help me now?"

He looked past me. "Captain Nor," he said, greeting her with a smile. "You're looking lovelier these days. I think the Shang Azi air is starting to agree with you."

"Are we just going to stand around here listening to this idiot, or do we have a merchant to find?" Agos barked.

"This idiot knows his way around the neighbourhood and wants to assist you before you cause more trouble," Khine replied. "Let's go before he changes his mind."

"Stay here, Nor. No sense scaring the man if we can help it." I spoke as nonchalantly as possible, but I could see her regard me with a look of suspicion.

"My queen," she replied. "As Captain of the Guard, I insist on being at your side at all times."

"She doesn't need two captains," Agos broke in. "I did the job just fine before you, Nor."

Khine's eyes flickered towards Agos when he spoke. *There*, I thought. Khine had heard everything my husband had said the last time we saw each other, and then some. Khine had never spoken to me about it, but he'd started making great efforts to avoid me ever since, as if he despised the thought of having anything to do with me again. I couldn't blame him. Khine was an idealistic man—why would he tolerate the presence of a woman who would jeopardize an entire nation because of her personal affairs?

Nor steeled herself for what looked to be another argument with Agos. I intervened before it began. "We'll be all right, Nor," I assured her. "Please."

I could see the protest in her eyes, but she stepped back with a bow.

Khine pretended I didn't exist as we left Lo Bahn's. I was at a loss for words, the first time I had ever felt that around him—a chasm of silence that grated at my nerves like rusty hinges. It put me at odds with everything that I was, that

I knew I was meant to be. Since when did queens walk behind con artists or care what they thought? Yet ever since that day at the docks, nothing felt right anymore. My righteous anger at Rayyel had been a crutch...without it, I was crawling and I didn't know how to get up.

You wouldn't. You've done nothing right since the moment you became queen.

I turned away from those dark thoughts, spoken in my father's voice, and focused on not tripping on the sidewalk.

CHAPTER TWO

THE MASSACRE AT DAR ASO

τῦϙ

Dar Aso was the immigrants' district in Anzhao City, bordering Shang Azi. The majority of the population consisted of Jinseins—many second or third generation. I had since come to learn that Khine was comfortable around my people, and that he spent most of his spare time in Dar Aso among Jinsein friends. He spoke Jinan easily enough, with a slight accent that stood out—he emphasized every word carefully, instead of allowing the syllables to become a rolling mess the way others tended to do. Our conversations—back when we had more of them—were split between Zirano and Jinan, lapsing towards whatever felt more comfortable at the time.

I am still not sure why Khine was drawn to a place like Dar Aso. It was just as dirty as Shang Azi, with the noticeable presence of the city watch. In exchange, there was the absence of big houses like Lo Bahn's—everything was small, narrow, cramped, hovels on top of hovels. That told you that the people in Dar Aso were barely getting by and that nobody had the money to bribe the watch to look the other way. The price to pay for Zarojo citizenship. I had to wonder, though, what was so awful about living in Jin-Sayeng that people were willing to brave the sea and live out in dirt and grime *here* instead. You'd think the ruler of Jin-Sayeng would know.

The one shining glory of the neighbourhood, as it turned out, was the hawker's hub. It was a small, covered marketplace—about half the size of the one in

Shang Azi—with a dozen restaurants and a common dining area that could probably sit a hundred people at a time. The building itself was an assault to the senses—drapes with all sorts of patterns hanging above each food stall, the sound of people chatting, pots clinging, and oil sizzling, and the smell of smoke and every type of roasted meat there was.

It seemed that the man we were looking for, a Gasparian, liked to have lunch here. We had found out about him after backtracking through Rayyel's contacts. Khine had explained nonchalantly, and mostly to Agos it seemed, that he ran a store by the Eanhe, the river that served as the border between Dar Aso and Shang Azi. It apparently had a reputation, but he didn't say exactly why.

It was only after Agos had left our table to see if he could catch a glimpse of our target that Khine finally managed a soft sigh, one that he seemed to have been holding on to since Lo Bahn's.

"Come, now," I said with a half-cocked grin. "The food's not that bad." I picked up a piece of the steamed chicken in front of me with my chopsticks, the bright, golden skin jiggling, and swirled it around the ginger-and-scallion-infused oil before popping it into my mouth.

Khine rubbed his chin, which had the shadow of a week-old growth of hair—too sparse to be called a proper beard. A far cry from the groomed courtiers that used to surround me, but he was typical of the sort of man I kept company with now.

I frowned at his silence. "Khine," I said, my chopsticks hovering over the bowl of soup: a conflagration of bobbing fish heads and strips of carrots, oyster mushrooms, jicama, mustard greens, and tomato. It smelled of coconut cream, curry, and enough pepper and spices to knock a bull out. "It's all right to talk about it, you know. We've been so busy the last few weeks—between me following my husband's tail and you with Lo Bahn's affairs. I believe the last time I've had the chance to talk to you alone was on the way to the docks to see Rayyel. Are you not in the least bit…" I struggled for the right word, even as I scolded myself for it. My father's daughter had no business trying to explain herself to a commoner. She'd just pick herself up, shake it off, and move on.

He played with his rice with a chopstick before he finally set the bowl down. "I'm not sure what there is to talk about. It's none of my business." His voice remained cold. It was painful to hear.

"That hasn't stopped you before," I said, trying to lighten my tone.

"Mmm," he said. "I'm trying to learn restraint." He turned towards the other tables, pretending to look for Agos.

"Khine..." I began.

"Yes, Queen Talyien?"

"What's going on here?"

"We are waiting for Agos to find Eridu. Now, I know for a fact that he prefers fried pork, so you may find him at Uncle Josi's Pork Skin stall, but on occasion..."

"Khine."

"Yes, Queen Talyien?"

"You're avoiding the conversation."

"Which conversation?"

I gestured around us. "This. About Rai, and Agos."

"Like I said," he murmured. "It's not my business."

I felt a well of dejection open up inside of me. I considered begging him to speak his mind, an idea that resulted in mocking laughter in my head— laughter that sounded so suspiciously like my father that I found myself looking around to see if he was behind one of the tables. Ignoring my rising panic, I regarded him with what I hoped was a neutral expression. "It is, actually. As queen, I need to know how much *you* know."

"If that was an issue before, you would've brought it up on that day. Or killed me within the hour."

"If you are judging me for... what transpired..." I began.

"Not judging, *Beloved Queen*," Khine said, using the Jinan words. He stopped there, hesitating. He scratched his cheek and took a deep breath. "I've let my mouth run ahead of me in the past. I'll hold my silence."

"You *are* judging me. You might as well say something instead of letting it eat away at you." He was staring at the edge of his plate a little too much. The buzz of conversation around us seemed to fade away.

Khine sighed. "It's nothing. A nagging thought, but you know I have many." His voice rose. "But have you ever considered the people who get caught up in all of this? How *they* feel?"

"I'm not sure I understand what you're saying."

"You were born a princess, into a world of politics and appearances and deceit. And I have seen you try to live up to your name more than most. Queen Talyien aren dar Orenar is a strong, capable woman who needs no one, a true daughter of Warlord Yeshin—"

"Keep digging at it," I drawled.

He smiled thinly. "But I think perhaps that you are taking for granted how people react to the things you do. Being someone in your position means every single decision, every single error, is amplified."

I took a deep breath. "I'm aware."

"I disagree," he said. "I don't think you are. Naivety is…dangerous for someone like you. Dangerous for others. Han Lo Bahn, for example. Has it occurred to you that the man has been trying to bed you for weeks?"

"I know *that* part," I said, a little embarrassed that he would bring it up. "Gods, Khine. I'm not some half-wit maiden, and he's not exactly subtle with the hints. Do you know I caught him picking flowers a few weeks ago? Lo Bahn, *with flowers*. Put that image in your head for a moment. I had a hard time keeping a straight face during our conversation."

His face barely flickered. "But you see? He wants you, but he knows he will never get anywhere, and so his patience becomes more brittle as the days go on. You can't offer him anything more than empty promises—he doesn't know how hopeless your situation is. Who knows what he will do the longer you string him along? Your indecision can harm others, people who might not even know you exist."

"You haven't told him?"

"Of course not. But it doesn't matter. He'll know soon enough."

"If he's planning anything…"

Khine gave a pained smile. "I wouldn't know about it. He knows what you are to me."

I felt a moment of distraction as I tried to piece together what he just said. "What *am* I to you, Khine Lamang?"

"A responsibility."

I bristled. "That's—"

He avoided looking straight at me. "Maybe I'm using the wrong word."

"*You are forever responsible for a life you save.* You told me this once. And I told you that I will not hold you accountable."

"It's not you I worry about," he said. "It's everyone else. I saved your life—you, a person whose very existence makes others suffer."

He was an honest man outside of his cons. It would have hurt, except I agreed. "I don't think about those things, Khine," I muttered, my irritation fading. "I know I'm supposed to. The gods know I was trained to. But politics disappear when I think of my son, and he is all I can think of these days. I've been gone for months. I missed his nameday. Do you know how fast children grow? Thanh will be taller now. Thinner, I know that much. He was never a good eater and the servants wouldn't have tried hard enough to feed him without me there. I'll never get these days back, and the longer I'm gone, the more time I lose. I have to fix this—whatever I did with our lives. I have to stop Rayyel. And I don't *care* what it takes, if I have to deal with men like Lo Bahn or risk myself or bleed—I'll do it if it means protecting my son from harm. Is *that* naivety? Probably. Did I claim to know all the answers when all I really wanted was to keep the people who mattered safe?"

We fell into an uncomfortable silence.

"I wonder where our friend has gotten to," Khine murmured. "It's well past lunchtime."

"Maybe the rich food got to him."

"Making the queen of Jin-Sayeng wait while he's bent over an outhouse pit. That's quite an image."

I had to smile at his attempt to lighten the situation. "Didn't your mother ever tell you not to raise certain images in front of a meal?"

"No. Raised by rats, remember?" He looked at me now. Goosebumps prickled my skin.

"Agos is…" I started.

We heard the sound of dishes clattering to the floor. I looked up and saw a man in full city watch regalia standing on top of a table, a half-strung bow in his hands. He was scanning the dining hall for someone. More guardsmen were filing into the hawker's hub, causing the staff from the food stalls to stop in the middle of their duties.

The guard turned to me.

I realized something in a heartbeat: I was *not* just enjoying an afternoon meal with a friend. My reflexes handled the rest. I grabbed Khine by the wrist and dropped to the ground just as an arrow flew past us. It buried itself into a post behind the table.

"Shit," Khine said.

People were fleeing for the exits. I looked around for the archer, but he had disappeared. Did I just imagine that I was his target? I briefly wondered about Agos, but I didn't have time to mull over whether he was safe or not. I caught Khine's eyes before dashing towards the crowd. After a moment, I heard him huffing behind me.

We burst through the doors. In the distance, I heard someone screaming, a sound that felt like it had been ripped from deep inside someone's body. I also thought I could smell blood. "We have to get out of here," I heard Khine whisper.

"Agos is still back there."

"Nothing we can do about that now."

I stepped to the side of the street just as another wave of people broke through. There was the terrified wail of a mother who had lost her child in the stampede.

"Monsters, all of them!" the woman cried. "They're killing everyone!"

I felt a hand on my shoulder. I steeled myself, expecting a fight, but when I turned around, it was only Agos. "Oh, Blessed Akaterru," I gasped. "I was starting to think the worst."

Agos turned to the thin dark-skinned man beside him. "Eridu," he said. "I had just found him when the soldiers arrived. They started killing the shopkeepers."

"This city's gone mad," Eridu grumbled. His Zirano had a heavy accent.

"And going madder still," Khine broke in. "It's best we get to a safe spot."

"You," Agos said, pointing at Khine. "Did *you* have anything to do with this?"

A thin line appeared over Khine's brow. "Why would you think that?"

"Three months without incident, and then I leave you with the queen for half an hour and *this* happens. Some hell of a coincidence." He turned to me. "Leave him here. Or I can gut him now, if you wish."

"Don't be ridiculous, Agos," I said. "We're staying with Lo Bahn, and Khine's working for him. Don't you think it's in his best interests to assist us?"

"Who knows what his best interests are?" Agos snarled. "The man's been sniffing around you for the past three months. I told you to keep away, Lamang. I told you—"

Khine didn't reply. He wasn't even *looking* at Agos. "What do you mean you *told* him to keep away?" I asked.

Agos's face tightened. The boy I had grown up with had changed into this bearded stranger. He used to be so easygoing, with a golden laughter that never failed to set my heart at ease. I had once asked him to jump into a pit full of dragon bones. He complied, soot on his face, and dared me to do the same.

Now...

I swallowed. Not a day went by that I didn't blame myself for what Agos had become. Perhaps he had been eager enough to participate, but then again, he was sworn to me. Everyone knew he would die for me without a moment's notice. Was refusing Warlord Yeshin's daughter even an option? I didn't understand then how power worked, how easy it was to blur those lines when you run along the edge like that. Arro did, which may have been why he was so against Lord General Ozo's promotion of Agos as my guard captain in the first place.

Now I understood a little better. One night's mistake had cost him his reputation and a good career. He would probably be a minor general by now, under direct command of Lord General Ozo himself, or at least well on his way to climbing the ranks of the Oren-yaro army. He wasn't even an official member of the Queen's Guard anymore. And I had little clue about what he had been doing the last six years—he remained tight-lipped about his activities.

All I knew was that this sullen, tightly wound man was not the boy I once knew, the one who did whatever silly thing I asked, who listened to me talk about Rayyel for hours on end. I wondered if he would ever return to the way he was. I missed my friend, not this constant reminder of my poor choices. If only wishing could turn back time...

Agos turned away. He had known me long enough to recognize when I was baiting him into an argument, and it was clear he wasn't going to have any of it. Khine cleared his throat to break the silence and led us down the alley. The chaos behind us was getting louder. Before we left the shadow of the building behind us, I noticed that the sewage water in the gutters was streaked with red.

"What do they have to gain from all of this?" I said out loud, trying not to think about where the blood was coming from.

The man called Eridu cleared his throat. "I have only a guess," he said. "It is a purge."

"A what?" I asked. His use of the word was surprising. I had only ever read it from a book before. "What would they be trying to *purge*?"

"Acting Governor Qun is most insistent that there is a plot that resulted in Governor Zheshan's disappearance," Eridu replied. "It is no secret that Qun holds no fond feelings for us folk in Dar Aso. Perhaps he is trying to spread fear among the people, hoping it will get someone to talk."

I gave Khine a look before taking a deep breath. "Nobody knows what happened to Gon Zheshan." It was a well-practiced lie, one I had been saying for weeks. "There's more to this than that." I tried to drown out my fears with a nervous laugh; Khine turned sharply at the sound, his eyes searching. I closed my mouth, wondering what he saw. Maybe I didn't want to know.

We reached a quiet corner a good distance from the butchery behind us. I could see a line of soldiers still marching towards the hawker's hub, heavy boots pounding on the muddy cobblestone. People gathered outside their houses to stare at them, whispering amongst themselves. Even from afar, the terror was plain on their faces.

"Should we speak at a better time?" Eridu asked.

I tore my attention back to him, taking a deep breath and reaching inside to become queen of Jin-Sayeng once more. "No." I drew him aside, pushing him to the back of a stone fence, well away from prying eyes. "You've eluded me long enough. You will talk. *Now.*"

———

There had been a faint smile on Eridu's lips this whole time—a gesture of appeasement, as if he had somehow convinced himself in the minutes since he had met me that I was not the woman they said I was.

Most days, I wasn't. I loathed the reputation that came with being my father's daughter. To hear people talk, you would think that the streets of Orenyaro often ran red with blood the way the neighbourhood of Dar Aso's did now. But it was convenient sometimes, especially after Agos had already gotten started on him. He grabbed him by the shirt collar and hauled him onto a nearby bench. I stuck a dagger into the wood, a hair's breadth from his leg, and brandished another. "Agos must've told you what we came for," I said, running my finger along the blade.

Eridu swallowed, his throat bobbing as he did. "You want to know about your husband, Lord Rayyel, and his whereabouts. You think the information I gave him will help you."

I gave my best impression of a wolfish smile. "You're a smart man. I like dealing with smart men."

"He wanted to know about mages. I'd traded with some of them before, goods from Gaspar. They're very interested in them."

"Goods?" I asked, glancing at Khine, who had given me his name in the first place.

"He's a smuggler," Khine explained. "Artifacts from temples. The *mandraagar*, the Gasparian holy mages, have a bounty on his head."

Eridu gasped. "I'm only doing it to feed my family."

"He's got no kids and five whores," Khine added.

I clicked my tongue. "Lying already. Smart men know when to tell the truth. What did I do with the last man who lied to me, Agos?"

"Cut his tongue out," Agos said, eyes gleaming. "With a saw."

"And then I fed it to my dogs," I said.

"You don't—" Eridu started. But he was starting to sweat.

"I don't have dogs here, is that what you were about to say?" I smiled. "I can make do. I saw a stray pup on the way here. Maybe he'll appreciate a new plaything."

"Mangy thing like that, he'll just swallow it whole," Khine commented wryly.

"A man came to my store and wanted to know how to contact some of my clients," Eridu quickly said. His hand flinched, as if he wanted to wipe some of his sweat away but didn't dare to in front of me. "I told him to go away. My clients don't trust me just so I could rat them out to anyone who came jingling a bag of coin in his hand."

"Rayyel wouldn't do that," I said. "Jingling a bag of coin—honestly. You really don't get this whole not-lying part, do you?" I threw the other dagger at him. It buried itself on the bench between his legs, which was a better shot than I had anticipated.

Eridu shook his head, rivulets of sweat running down his face like tears. "I'm telling the truth. I don't know if it was this Lord Rayyel who came to see me. *Someone* did. I sent him away. Later, my store was raided—ransacked. My clients' records were missing."

"You kept records of clients who wanted to be kept anonymous?" Khine asked. He looked amused.

I wasn't. I drew my sword now, watching with some satisfaction as the merchant wilted from the blade. "Now you're implying that Rayyel *robbed* you. I dislike your tone. I'm trying to decide whether I dislike it more than your pathetic limbs. Maybe I'll hack one off before we start on your tongue with that saw."

"The *truth*," Eridu gasped. "You wanted the truth. That's the truth. Why ask and then accuse me of lying?"

"Because you're scrambling. I'm losing my patience, merchant."

He coughed. "All right—I ..."

"Ah! All right?"

"It wasn't a man. It was a woman. Jinsein, like you. Dressed like a priestess."

"Sounds like my husband's friend," I said. "You're doing great. I'm less annoyed now. Go on."

"She wanted to know where I sent most of my shipments to. I didn't remember, so I made her go through the records herself." He shook his head. "Not that it made a difference. She didn't get the chance. When we returned to office, we found it had been ransacked. She had to leave empty-handed."

I swore.

Khine placed a hand on my arm before glancing at the man. "I have a hard time believing she left without anything. Don't tell me this woman wasn't persuasive at all." Eridu glanced away.

"Come on. She's Jinsein," Khine continued. "She would've pressed further. For your own sake, you must've tried to salvage what you could for your business. Scribbled something down off the top of your head, maybe. That's what I would do. She would have asked for ... I know. The courier service you used. They'll have the exact addresses of where your clients wanted the goods delivered. You sent her that way, didn't you?"

"Fuck you, Lamang."

"Which one was it?"

Eridu swallowed. Khine's grin grew wider. "You know she's not going to want to leave you alone unless you give us something. Her husband's on his way to—"

"Lamang," Agos warned.

"—kill her son with the help of those mages. Do you really want to stand between that?"

Eridu shook his head.

"So talk!" I rarely heard Khine raise his voice. In that instant, I caught a flash of the rage he liked to say he kept in check.

"Hatzhi and Sons. They've got an office by the Eanhe."

"Good man. Start running," I suggested.

Eridu carefully extracted his legs around my daggers. Without another word, he fled down the street. He didn't get very far before Agos bore down on him and cut him from the back. "Stop!" I screamed, but it was too late. The man tumbled forward, his back spread out like an untied robe. Agos walked up to him.

"What are you doing?" I hissed, grabbing his arm.

Agos's mouth was a thin line. "Lamang gave him too much information."

Khine's face had gone sheet-white. "I was only feeding him enough to get him to speak," he murmured. On the ground, Eridu groaned. Khine dropped to his knees beside the merchant, his fingers curled over the wound. I think he was trying to figure out how to help, but he didn't know where to start—there was blood everywhere.

"He's already dead," Agos commented. "Let me finish the job. Unless you want to leave him here to bleed out."

"I'll do it," Khine whispered. He held out his hand. "Get me a dagger."

"Are you sure?" I asked.

"I can do it faster."

"Killing is killing," Agos spat.

"To a fucking butcher, maybe," Khine said. His voice was cold rage, now.

"He would have told someone else about her husband and the boy," Agos replied. "It wouldn't take much to put two and two together."

"The dagger," Khine repeated.

I pulled out a dagger from the bench and pressed it into his palm. He wrapped his fingers around the hilt, holding it more firmly than I thought he would. Khine bent over the groaning man, placing his hands on both sides of Eridu's cheeks. "An-albaht guide you on the road," he said before stabbing the side of the man's neck. He hit the artery on the first try; blood squirted down his arms, splattering on the ground. Eridu's body fell limp.

"They'll think he's just another victim of this," Agos said. "But we have to get out of here before we're seen."

"I didn't know participating in a massacre was part of the plan," Khine growled.

"If you're going to insist on tagging along with us, then you better learn to keep your mouth shut," Agos barked.

"Enough, Agos," I broke in. "We have other things to worry about."

Agos sheathed his sword. "Perhaps we should return to Han Lo Bahn's while everything settles down. We can go to the courier later."

Khine was still looking at Eridu's prone form. "You knew him," I said.

His face flickered. "He was a patient of mine a few times when I was still a student with Tashi Reng Hzi. A rash he picked up from the whorehouse, and then a broken hip bone when he tried to chase a woman down the street."

"Good riddance," Agos sniffed.

Khine looked up, staring back at Agos long enough that I thought he would hit him. Instead, he pulled out a handkerchief from his pocket and draped it over the dead man's head. "Gods, Tali," he murmured, his voice dropping down to its familiar softness. "Rivers of blood, everywhere you walk. Now do you understand?"

He said nothing more, but the accusation was enough to make my ears ring.

CHAPTER THREE

RIVERS OF BLOOD

ᒍᛏᏆᎫ

I could hear Khine's breathing as we walked, loud enough that I started to measure the rise and fall with every step. *Rivers of blood.* I could already guess what history books would say after this. I landed in Anzhao City and heads flew. What else did they expect from Jin-Sayeng's Bitch Queen? Once upon a time, I might've been able to manage a smirk at the thought, even carry it with pride. Now I could only feel exhaustion, a candle burnt at both ends.

I know that I made for a poor queen. If nothing else, the last few months here in Anzhao had taught me that. I didn't know how to respond to situations as *befitting* a queen, as Arro had warned me so often. Which was something that didn't used to bother me when I was younger——I was convinced that I was upholding my father's name, damn those who thought otherwise. Even after Rayyel left, I could pretend that it was all on him, or the Ikessars, or Chiha Baraji, his woman—that I was following my father's path with every ounce of my being. But as time went on, the crown grew heavier, Thanh grew older, and...

My son's resemblance to Yeshin is remarkable. Which is odd when you consider that I only knew Yeshin as an old man, and Thanh was still so very little—black hair instead of faded wisps of grey, smooth skin in place of wrinkled flesh, bright eyes that had yet to see a broken world wherever he turned. I remember the first time I ever noticed it. It wasn't long after Rayyel left. Thanh was playing with a paper ball in the gardens, throwing it in the air and laughing as it floated down for him to catch. I realized it against the sunlight—it was there in the turn of his eyes, the shape of his nose. My father's ghost. It almost made me scream.

From then on, I couldn't look at him without seeing a glimpse of my father, which always brought with it a mess of conflicting emotions. This boy that *looked* like Yeshin was heir to the Dragonthrone. The Ikessars never said a word about it, but I could feel the gazes turn to him whenever he toddled through the halls, as if they were measuring how much of him was falcon and how much was wolf.

Every time their judging eyes fell on him, I felt the urge to shield him from them and tell them to go to hell. It didn't matter *what* he was—he was my son. These laws, these tenets, these words, I wanted to strip them off him and throw them into the nearest fire. *You will* not *be governed by the same shackles that brought me here*, I wanted to tell Thanh. *When you're Dragonlord, you will rule as you see fit*.

But I kept my silence. He wouldn't have understood—he was still a child, and the things he cared for had nothing to do with clans or laws or kingdoms. What he loved were books and animals, and flowering plants and the bugs that paid them a visit. "Do you think the flowers like it when I water them in the morning, or at night?" he asked me once, and I had to turn the question over in my head, because how could he ask those things as he gazed back with my father's eyes? How could these words come out of a mouth that had ordered the deaths of thousands?

The Ikessars blame me, of course. At every turn, they accuse me of indulging the boy, of making him as carefree as it looked like he was becoming. But I knew that I could never foist so heavy a burden on him as my father had on me. To me, he was just a child. He was just my son. And I needed Rayyel to see that, even if it came at the risk of confronting the truth. Why did it matter whose seed planted the boy in my belly? If I should not be blamed for my father's sins, my son should not be punished for mine.

"What's this?" Agos called out. I noticed smoke curling from the rooftops on the street ahead, black tendrils shooting to the sky.

"Gods damn them all," Khine whispered as we reached a store at the end of the street. The door was in splinters, the decorative jars smashed, and the curtains ripped to shreds. He turned to me with a grimace. "Jien Hatzhi's shopfront. I don't think there's anyone in there, but..."

"Should they be open this time of the day?"

He nodded.

"Then someone got here first." I frowned. "Eridu said his shop was ransacked, too. Someone else is looking for Rayyel."

"Or maybe someone doesn't want you to find him," Agos said. "Maybe you should listen."

"This isn't like last time."

Agos crossed his arms. "Isn't it? I told you we need to focus on getting home. You need people—you can't do this alone. And if someone wants that asshole dead? They can go right ahead and save us the trouble. They're more than welcome to his corpse."

"This is Thanh's life we're talking about here," I murmured.

"So what will you do once you find that man?" Agos asked. "Beg him to reconsider? You tried that already. Ask him to return things to the way they were? Even after everything he's done to you and Thanh..."

"*Prince* Thanh," I reminded him. "And we *can't* get home, not with that embargo still in place."

"We could try to find passage elsewhere."

"While Rai's trail grows cold, and we might be left stranded anyway. No, Agos. *This isn't like last time.* The man threatened my son. The man who was supposed to love and protect us threatened to *kill my son*. Do you think I'm going to let that bastard go free after that? He has to answer for this."

"So at the end of the line, what then?" he asked, nostrils flaring. "If I have to kill him, you won't stop me?"

"We have to find him first."

He turned away, his face red.

"Agos," I repeated, walking closer to him.

Agos finally glanced up. "If anything happens to you..." he began.

"Nothing will happen to me," I replied.

"You say that now," he said, drawing his brows together. To his credit, he didn't raise his voice this time. "Look at how this empire has chewed you up. From the moment you stepped foot here, you've been nothing but a tool in everyone's political games. You're the queen. This is supposed to be *your* game. They're supposed to be grovelling, every single one of the bastards."

"And you think you can break their knees to make them do that?"

He sniffed. "I can try."

"This isn't like when we were children," I reminded him. "These aren't young recruits looking at me the wrong way."

"It kills me that you don't get the respect you deserve," he grumbled under his breath.

I wanted to tell him I didn't need him worrying about such things for me. But it was exhausting being in this position at all. My own father had no faith in my abilities; why should anyone? That Agos remained at all still surprised me. I once took loyalty for granted, but in the wake of every betrayal since I'd arrived in the empire, I was starting to re-examine my relationships under a different light. Out of everyone in the world, Agos had all the tools to betray me. He was a fixture of my childhood, a remnant of my life before I ever truly understood what I was supposed to be—before my father's death, before Rayyel. Even his scent was pleasantly familiar, reminding me of home as it had been. Of hot afternoons chasing after dragonflies, stuffing them into glass jars and watching them whiz around before letting them go by dinnertime, and childhood games played with sandals and chalk. Even the way he breathed, the sound of it, brought back memories of his mother's cooking—sour fish stew with red onions and tomatoes, my father's favourite, or cubes of pork belly with green chiles, coconut milk, and shrimp paste, or her specialty: squash and fish patties, fried to a crisp perfection.

Agos could hurt me. He hasn't. At a time like this, it was all I needed. I knew it was a sorry position to be in, and years ago I would've scoffed at the idea of embracing such a thing. But being kept in a dungeon for months by your father's *chosen prince* could really put things in perspective. I wanted to tell him I appreciated his presence, and then wondered how much of it he would take the wrong way.

Or maybe you shouldn't care what a cook's bastard thinks.

I cringed at the internal rebuke. In that same instant, I caught sight of a familiar figuring sauntering towards us from the bridge.

Lo Bahn was not an overly huge man, but it was difficult to describe him as anything but *substantial*. Equal amounts of fat and muscle covered his tattooed body, and when he walked, you couldn't help but pay attention. He kept his thick beard neatly trimmed, a sharp contrast with the rest of his rough appearance. "What the hell are you doing, Lamang?" he barked. "I don't pay you to run around with her in the middle of the day. Look at this godsforsaken neighbourhood."

He glanced at the trail of blood in the river with the sort of distasteful look you would give a dead rat before turning to me. "And you. What the fuck did you do this time?"

"I didn't—" I began.

"It was me, Lo Bahn," Khine said. "I killed someone. Eridu."

"The Gasparian merchant with the garlic breath? I always did find the man offending, but whatever for?"

"Her affairs."

"You'd kill for her, but not for me?" Lo Bahn looked amused.

"What do you know about all of this, Lo Bahn? We were led to believe it was done under Governor Qun's orders. Something to do with the former Governor Zheshan's disappearance," Khine said.

"Right." Lo Bahn's eyes flickered. "I need to speak with the queen, Lamang."

"You're free to do that any time you want."

"Without you." He huffed. I had heard my dogs make that sort of sound before.

Khine smiled. I think he wanted to refuse, but Lo Bahn had too much power over him. He seemed to drag his feet as he walked away, the sort of man who played at being a fool when he despised the idea of authority. "Why do you keep him around?" I asked. "He clearly doesn't like taking orders from you. I'm sure you'll find more compliant henchmen."

"Don't let him hear this, but he's the smartest man in Shang Azi and I need that more than ever. I can have the insolence beaten out of him if I want to. I'm still deciding." Lo Bahn craned his head towards me. "Come," he said. "There's something I need you to see."

Agos started forward. Lo Bahn snarled, holding a hand out. "She needs to come with me alone."

"Lord Han, no offense, but…"

"You don't trust me. Bah! As if that hasn't been clear to me since you pumped me full of wine and pretended you slept with me. Lucky for you, my old woman's coming back in a week's time. If I were you, I wouldn't even mention how we met." He snorted, as if not quite believing he had uttered such words.

I didn't, either. "You, Lo Bahn? Scared of your own wife?"

"I've got my reasons," he retorted. "Are you going to come or not?"

"Where to?"

"Just outside the walls." He looked calm enough, but I noticed his whiskers twitch a little, as if trying to snort away a foul scent that persisted on clinging under his nose.

"If it's all the same to you, I'd rather not," I said.

He sighed. "I was hoping you'd be more cooperative." He clicked his tongue.

Agos lurched forward, but before he could draw his sword, four spears appeared around him, held by guards in full uniform. He gritted his teeth. "Bastards."

"Qun's?" I asked. "Sleeping with the enemy now, Lo Bahn?"

"Qun's not my type."

"He had you tortured after what happened with Zheshan. Your fingernails haven't even grown back." I saw his fingers twitch in reflex, and his mouth twisted into a grimace. "They all warned me this was going to happen. They warned me, and I didn't want to believe them. I thought we had a deal, but I guess deals are flexible for some."

He looked almost embarrassed. Almost. I have since learned that those who betray you know exactly the sort of knife they're plunging into your back, and though they might feel shame—they might even feel pity—nothing short of a better offer will stop them from twisting the blade. "I have to look out for my own. I have children, too, Queen Talyien."

"And I guess you don't seem to care that what you're doing is going to jeopardize my own child."

"No," he agreed. "I don't. But I'm giving you the courtesy of being honest about it."

"Thank you for such a warm and unexpected compassion," I growled.

He snorted and called for the guards to escort me.

Six months ago, a betrayal from Lo Bahn *wouldn't* have stung.

That was before Zheshan's untimely demise in front of us, before he had slid a blade into himself and bled all over Lo Bahn's pristine wooden floor. It was the first time I saw fear in Lo Bahn's eyes. A man like that, breaking his mask— the only thing more surprising would've been the sight of my own father shitting his pants. You don't forget a thing like that easily.

Once we were able to shake ourselves out of our stupor, we rolled Zheshan's body into the closet and wiped the floor before anyone else arrived. We left him there for over a day—there were too many people walking in and out of Lo Bahn's house, and I had to leave early in the morning to meet with my husband by the harbour. Much later, Lo Bahn woke me in the dead of the night to help him drag the stiff, blue body of the governor to his garden, where we buried him in an oversized jar. He insisted on no servants—we were the only ones who knew. I marvelled over how I could feel so much guilt over someone I didn't kill.

The image of Lo Bahn holding out that shovel to me in the moonlight hovered between us like a shadow as he led me down the street and to a road cresting the outskirts of the city. A queen who dug her own graves was not a good omen, no matter how you looked at it. I wondered if Zheshan might've been the lucky one.

By now, a steady rain was beginning to fall, strong enough to flatten my hair as soon as I heard it dripping from the rooftops. I immediately regretted not taking a warmer cloak. Lo Bahn strode ahead without flinching, as if he was unaffected by the cold. It was not the first time that I felt cowed at the thought that a gambling lord could somehow act more noble than a queen.

We reached a slope by the end of the walls, at a low, crumbling portion unmanned by the city watch. Patches of grass grew through the cracked ground, interspersed with black soil. A man with a torch was waiting for us beside a headless statue of a *rok haize*. I recognized Ben Taey, one of Lo Bahn's. He gave me a small nod of acknowledgment before accompanying us past the walls and out of the city.

We walked alongside the ditches for some time before Ben Taey extinguished the torch into the running water, allowing the darkness to cover us. I opened my mouth, but Lo Bahn pressed a finger to his lips before pointing. I followed the gesture and saw a mass of shapes on top of a gorge, the black gap as ragged as the side of a dog's jaw. I blinked. When my eyes adjusted, I saw a long line of soldiers along the rocky cliffs, their armour slick from the rain. They walked in pairs while holding a body between them. Once they reached the edge, they braced their legs and tossed the body over the boulders and dead brush.

"Remnants of the massacre," I said in a low voice. I watched as another body tumbled with a spray of loose gravel, swirling into the blackness below.

"There are many Jinseins among the dead. You knew that, didn't you?"

"I suspected as much."

Lo Bahn sneered. "It has nothing to do with you, believe it or not, though it's true that *Acting* Governor Qun has no reason to love you. He knew you were involved with the attack on the governor's office. And you killed his wife, which he has chosen to take very personally. I'm not sure why—the woman was a hag. I'd have just gone and picked another. Plenty enough healthy spinsters in Anzhao."

"Let's not speak of the dead that way."

"Hag she was, and hag she will remain in my memories and the afterlife. She can haunt me if she wants. Of course, Qun always knew you were staying with me. He's not an idiot." Lo Bahn gestured at the bodies. "All of this—this is just a show. Your meddling has quite clearly been the best thing that's happened to him in his life."

"So what's all this for, then?"

"A *pretence* at flushing you out, to make it seem like he's doing *something* about Zheshan's disappearance. Why not get rid of a few pesky Jins along with it? As for Qun, better for him if Zheshan remains missing. If word gets out that the man is confirmed dead, there'll have to be a re-election immediately. But while Zheshan's whereabouts remain unknown, he's in a good position to maneuver things to his benefit, make sure that the vote falls to his favour when the inevitable re-election occurs. This *purge*—this is just the beginning of many. It's Qun's way of positioning himself right in the heart of Anzhao City's politics."

"It's almost as if you admire his daring."

Lo Bahn smiled. He liked it when you followed his train of thought—not many people did. "Look there, Queen Talyien," he said, drawing my attention back to the mass grave.

I squinted against the rain, towards the spot where body after body was being grabbed by the limbs and swung into the open crevice without a care. I could see the gaping wounds where the soldiers had hacked at them, ripped flesh and bone. Merchants and shopkeepers and dishwashers—people of no importance to anyone but themselves and their families.

"You helped with this," Lo Bahn murmured.

I bit back the inclination to disagree. "My son's life is at stake."

"Children," Lo Bahn said, "are easy to make." He sneered. "But I suppose you're not that much different from me after all. Come. We've made him wait long enough."

"I'm not just going to give myself up to him without a fight."

Lo Bahn smiled. "I don't blame you. He's the type of two-faced snake that you wouldn't want to ally yourself with."

"As opposed to you?"

"I told you that I'm an honest man, Queen Talyien. Honest enough, anyway." His eyes hardened. "I *am* sorry, for what it's worth. What would you have me tell my wife? That I lost our fortune because I let some woman get to me? The blood money I've had to cough out for the families of the men who died at the governor's office, my assets that were confiscated because of my involvement in the first place…"

"Illegal assets, I was led to believe. Apologies don't mean anything, Lord Han. And here I thought we were doing so well in our newfound friendship."

"Not as well as I had hoped for."

"Sleeping with you wouldn't have changed a damn thing. You know that."

He laughed. "A man's whimsy."

"An old man's whimsy."

"You know how to cut into a man's soul. You really do."

"And you of all people know how badly I react to force."

"Don't think you have to remind me. It's why you've got me by the balls in the first place." He sniffed and fell silent, forehead creased as he continued to watch the bloody burial—if you would even call it that. The bodies were being discarded like animals. To the soldiers, these were carcasses, not people.

I remembered, with a hint of shame, how much I had admired the way the Zarojo ran their cities when I had first arrived at Anzhao. It was the sort of prosperity that Jin-Sayeng had once enjoyed. Perhaps it was better if we lingered in poverty if this was the price to pay. Every upheaval, every shift in power, seemed to come at a cost. I looked back at the limp bodies, drenched in mud and rain, unseeing eyes staring at the godless skies, and imagined I could feel my father's hand on my shoulder. His own actions, nearly thirty-two years ago, had resulted in tens of thousands of deaths. This . . . this would've been nothing to him.

The soldiers parted in the distance, and I recognized the straight, narrow-shouldered form of Ino Qun as he strode in. Qun was still wearing the same sombre clothes that I remembered, with the same pencil-thin moustache over his lip—at first glance every bit the government official, the sort people trusted. I made that same mistake in the first place, months ago when I had first sought shelter in his household. He was speaking to the soldiers, heedless of the pelting rain.

I felt Lo Bahn take hold of my elbow and, with one last snort, lead me down the path.

Qun was still speaking to his soldiers when we arrived. Two guards stopped us in our tracks, spears crossed to block our way. Qun tipped his head forward, rain dripping over his square hat. He looked like he had been expecting us to appear from the darkness all along. "Queen Talyien of Jin-Sayeng," he said without a hint of surprise in his voice. "You honour us with your presence."

It was a thinly veiled insult, especially considering that *he* was the one who had me brought here. "Well, but how can I miss your promotion?" I asked, responding to smooth affront with my own practiced words. "Well-deserved, I hope," I added.

"Why wouldn't they choose me?" Qun asked. "I've served faithfully. There *was* a vice governor, but he was struck with an unfortunate accident the same week our dear Governor Zheshan disappeared. The gods can be most unkind sometimes." His eyes darted to Lo Bahn. "Lord Han. I don't think I've ever thanked you for sheltering the Beloved Queen. You've done the empire a great service."

Lo Bahn spat to the side. "Spare me the pleasantries, Qun."

"Lord Han is angry. Rightfully so—the law can be very *specific* at times. He is, however, lucky to still be alive. The Zarojo Empire rewards good service quite appropriately. You know this, of course, Lord Han. I truly hope that it was a mere slip of the memory that caused you to try to convince us for months there was no queen of Jin-Sayeng in your safekeeping, that you didn't even think Jin-Sayeng had a queen, and that, furthermore, if you met her, you would...and I quote, fuck the living daylights out of her first before handing her over to us." He smiled, a true politician's smile that was better than my own.

Lo Bahn didn't even looked embarrassed. "I say things, so do you," he said. "What of it?"

I strode forward. "We need to speak, Governor Qun."

"We are speaking already, are we not?"

I gave a grim smile and glanced to my right, where the soldiers were still tipping the bodies into the gorge. "This is all a bit too much, isn't it? These are my people."

Qun shook his head. "Drop the false concern. These aren't yours anymore. The empire gave them full citizenship and allowed them to live as if they were born Zarojo all along. They, unfortunately, chose to conspire against our beloved Governor Zheshan. This manner of death is pretty lenient, as it stands. We could've rounded them all up and cut them to pieces in front of a crowd."

I wasn't sure how he could say such things with a straight face. The difference between an elected official and one like me who had no choice, I suppose: he was a *lot* better at pretending. "Perhaps Lord Han is right," I said. "Let's get to the point, Governor Qun. You and I both know what's going on. I'd like to find a solution we can both benefit from. My precarious situation prevents me from offering too much to you right now, but as soon as I'm able..."

Qun held a hand up. "Queen Talyien, I don't think *you* are aware of your situation."

I rubbed rain from my eyes. "What do you mean?"

Qun clicked his tongue. His soldiers parted, revealing two bound men on their knees. I looked back at Qun in confusion. "You probably don't know them," Qun said, a faint smile on his face. "So let me introduce you: Jien Hatzhi, and a son. I'm not exactly sure which one. The other one, er, died resisting arrest." He made a mocking bow towards the two prisoners.

"You're a bastard, Qun."

"Mmm," Qun said. "Did you think you could slink around Anzhao City without your activities being documented? Come now, Queen Talyien. Surely you can't be *that* naive. But we can't have you leaving the city, now, can we?"

"This is a personal matter between my husband and me. It has nothing to do with Anzhao's politics."

"I beg to differ, Queen Talyien. Your husband was last seen on a ship leaving the docks with a retinue of Governor Zheshan's finest soldiers. A thing like that, happening *so soon* before dear Zheshan was found missing? Suspicious, mighty suspicious. Of course, we *had* to know where they were headed. It was a chartered ship; it left no schedule."

A thought drifted into my head. *Let Qun catch Rayyel. Let the snakes take care of him, and be better for it.* But I quickly realized the danger of such an arrangement. Did I want them learning about what my husband was trying to do? About troubles that were better kept behind Oka Shto's doors, where they belonged?

"Rayyel didn't conspire against Governor Gon Zheshan, you bastard," I found myself saying. "He..." I felt Lo Bahn's hand on my elbow. I turned to him. "The man committed suicide, Han!"

"Now, now," Qun said. "You can't really be running around the city letting everyone know that. Whatever would they think of us?"

I heard a loud cry, and turned in time to see one of Qun's soldiers stick a spear into Jien Hatzhi's son. Blood spurted out of the boy's mouth, but he didn't die immediately. The soldier kicked him away, sending him rolling along the dust. His father crawled along the ground after him, sobbing. He picked up the crumpled body.

"I think it's time to talk, Hatzhi," Qun said, kneeling over the wrecked man. "Someone came by asking about shipments you've made to mages from a certain Gasparian's shop. You had no reason to lie to them. You would've told them exactly where."

"You should have killed me," Jien groaned. "Me, not my sons." His Jinsein accent was unmistakable. Jinsein—and Oren-yaro. I felt a twinge of shame. This was someone who had grown up back home, who had to learn Zirano as an adult, who probably felt like he had to take a name that wouldn't stand out so much in the empire. If he had assisted Rai and his priestess friend, he would've done it from the goodness of his heart.

Qun patted Jien's face. "Now, why would I do that? They would've clammed up. The young are admirably foolhardy, but it's also terribly inconvenient."

"Go to hell, *Governor.*"

"You have a couple of young daughters somewhere, with your mistress. Don't you want them alive to inherit your shop?"

Jien's son began to convulse. Jien wrapped his arms around the boy's body, his face shadowed with resignation. "The featherstone mines in the Ruby Grove," he finally whispered. "That's where the merchant sent his wares. I recommended the woman take a ship south, to An Mozhi, and take the road from there."

"Now, was that so hard?" Qun asked. He turned to one of his soldiers and nodded. A spear struck Jien Hatzhi from the side. He would've seen it coming, but he made no motion to avoid it. My people embraced doom like warriors, but I wondered inwardly if it was still something to be proud of. Pride can only get you so far.

"Cleaning up is such a messy business," Qun said, breaking my thoughts. He seemed amused by his own observation. He turned to me. "We have, of course, sent men to bring your husband Rayyel to justice."

"He didn't kill Zheshan," I said. "If you've been watching us this whole time, then you'd know . . ."

"*Woman!*" Lo Bahn warned.

I took a step towards Qun. "You don't really believe that about Rayyel and Zheshan, do you? It was Lo Bahn who attacked the office. Yet despite dragging Lo Bahn in for questioning—*torture*, even—you haven't tried to arrest him. Why not? Is it because an arrest will mean an investigation, and an investigation may lead you to Zheshan's body, the one we hid in Lo Bahn's garden in a jar?"

Lo Bahn began to swear. I ignored him. A flaw in my personality, I suppose—I felt very little remorse for people who betrayed me first. A loyal friend, a bad enemy—all I did was borrow a bit of his poison. Just like he said, I had to look out for my own.

Qun stared. His eyes were cold. Hard.

I smiled. "Such an investigation would be bad for you, Qun. Confirmation of Zheshan's death by his own hand means no conspiracy. No conspiracy means a re-election. It'll mean—"

A guard grabbed my shoulder and struck me on the jaw before I could finish speaking. I tried to strike back, but another had his hand on my wrist and twisted it, driving me to my knees.

"Enough," Qun said. "I don't know why you think you have the upper hand."

On the ground, I laughed. "Qun, you snake. Anything happens to me, word will get out of what *really* happened to Gon Zheshan. Once his body is discovered, you'll lose this cushy position of yours."

"Did you think such a thing worries me?" Qun asked. He turned to the soldier behind him. "I want both of them detained."

Lo Bahn roared and charged the guard nearest to him. The blow barely rattled the armoured man, who brought an elbow down on the back of his neck. More guards stepped forward, crowding him.

I lifted my head towards Qun. "You fool. You think you can hide this and somehow pin the blame on Rayyel? He is a Jinsein monarch from a respected clan. You'd risk stirring the wrath of every warlord in Jin-Sayeng and bring war to your doorstep?"

"War will happen, Queen Talyien, whether we want it or not," Qun said in a low voice. "My only concern is preserving what little I can." He turned around. "Send men to intercept Prince Rayyel in the Ruby Grove," he told his attendant. "If we can catch him on the road, all the better for everyone. If we don't…they'll take care of him from that end. The fool doesn't realize he's heading straight to his death."

CHAPTER FOUR

THE GOVERNOR'S GRAVE

ᏗᎣᏥᎢᏗ

I barely had time to process what he said. A soldier came with iron manacles, jerking me to my feet to snap them on. "We're all aware of your penchant for violence," Qun said easily. "But I wouldn't try anything if I were you. You'll just hurt yourself again."

My first instinct was to tell him I didn't give a damn, but the lump forming in my jaw made it difficult to open my mouth fast enough. Qun clicked his tongue and stepped towards me, hands folded behind his back. "The queen and I will take a walk," he called out.

A few guards appeared to escort us away from the gorge. I limped after him. The rain had stopped. Over on the horizon, the sky was turning red, with a slight purplish haze that crested along the city's silhouette. I could already see the faint impression of a few stars appearing behind the clouds.

"So is this normal around here?" I asked, raising my voice. "You go around killing people for a few pesky votes?"

"No one will miss them," Qun said simply.

I made a sound.

He smiled. "Protesting. *You?* Considering who your father was?"

"My father never..."

He lifted his head up high, a smug grin on his face as he waited for me to finish my sentence. I trailed off, mumbling under my breath. Yeshin *had*, actually.

More times than I cared to find out. Never people he was responsible for, of course—always the enemy's—and he never crowed about it. But I supposed that someone like Qun wouldn't be able to tell the difference.

"You could've made this so easy," Qun continued, "if you had just let the assassins kill Prince Rayyel and Governor Zheshan in the first place. We would both have what we want now, without the fuss."

"What do you mean, what *I* want?"

He sniffed. "You wanted to get home, didn't you? With a husband? So you can go back to ruling your despicable, backwater nation?"

"You meant Yuebek," I said dryly. "I didn't know you liked jokes, Qun."

"A prince who could trample your pathetic nation with a flick of his little finger is hardly a joke," he said.

I shrugged, chains and all. "Perhaps. Too bad he's dead."

"You know who else is dead?"

We stared at each other for half a heartbeat. I knew what he was getting at. I smiled—slowly. "You order the death of hundreds of innocents, but you'll hold the death of your wife against me? Come now, Qun. You play the game—you *must* know the stakes."

"Do you know yours?"

I licked my lips.

"Do you know," Qun continued, his voice dropping an octave, "how often I've dreamed of tearing you to pieces, limb by limb, over the last three months?"

"I've been told that obsession isn't healthy. You should try meditation." I gazed up, realizing he had led me back to Shang Azi. We were standing right in front of Lo Bahn's gates.

"We'll see if you can learn to keep your smart mouth shut." He turned to his men. "Burn it down!" he cried. "Kill them all!"

"What do you want, Qun?" I snapped, straining at my chains. His soldiers were marching ahead, drawing their swords as they met Lo Bahn's guards. It wasn't even a fair fight—the soldiers had them pinned to the ground in mere moments. I reeled back from the scent of blood and tried to slam into Qun. A soldier pushed me away.

Qun wiped his hands in distaste. He nodded at the soldier, who dragged me through the gates.

The servants fled at first sight of the soldiers, who mercilessly bore down on them, hacking and stabbing like they were nothing but stalks of wheat. Some of them stared at me as they died, pleading for me to do something. *Anything.* I was queen, wasn't I?

"Governor Qun," I started.

The man smiled from the corner of his lips. "Are you going to beg me to stop? Do it well enough, and I might consider it."

I jerked my head back. "Why are you doing this?"

"You said it yourself," he said. "An arrest will mean an investigation. So I'm getting rid of all the evidence."

"You can just let us go."

"Your persistence is astounding." He pushed back on his heels as his soldiers appeared, carrying two of Lo Bahn's sons and his youngest daughter. They deposited them in front of us. The children's faces were streaked with dirt and tears.

"What," I repeated, my voice rising, "do you want?"

He smiled. "You've got one of your own, too, don't you? Ah. I can see it in your eyes. That panic. I knew you were a mother, but to see the Bitch Queen of Jin-Sayeng raise her hackles over something like this is . . . surprising. I would have imagined such maternal concerns are beyond you. You show your hand far too easily, Queen Talyien." Qun snapped his fingers.

"Stop!"

I didn't expect him to listen to me, and steeled myself for the sight of the children's heads rolling along the dirt with the rest of them. But then he turned halfway, his lips pulled into a grin. "Show me where you buried Gon Zheshan," he said.

I didn't even hesitate. I led them deeper into the garden, down into the orchard of star-apple trees in the furthest corner, near the fences. I indicated a spot between two benches, half-hidden in the shadows.

A soldier arrived with a shovel. Qun took it from him and held it towards me.

"Dig him out," Qun said, teeth gleaming.

I realized something at once: that he had no intention of killing me, but *wanted* to, and that the best thing he could do at the moment was humiliate me. It was a chilling thought. But the joke was on him. His Zarojo propriety didn't understand Jinsein pride. I took the shovel from him without a word and sank it into the soil, pushing it down with my foot. It was awkward with the manacles on, but I wasn't going to give him the satisfaction of complaining about it.

Three months of rain had done its share of packing the earth down. I sweated in silence while the soldiers watched me in confusion, wondering, perhaps, why a queen would sink so low. What would their own officials have done? Gone down on their knees and begged for fear of getting a little dirty? I would've laughed if I wasn't exerting myself. The darkness didn't help, and I struck my own toes more than once, but I soon unearthed the lip of the clay jar. Fingers shaking, I worked at the soil around it until I uncovered the lid.

"Open it," Qun said. He was enjoying this too much.

I struck at the lid once, and then another time. It shattered.

The stench of rot exploded in the air. I staggered back, my arms burning, and caught sight of the tip of the corpse's head, hair stiff with dirt. Qun wrinkled his nose as he took a few steps forward to peer into the jar.

"That's the bastard all right," he said. "Poor Gon. Bit off more than he could chew. I warned him this was too much for someone like him." He whistled to the soldiers. "Take the corpse and throw it in the gorge with the others."

Sweat poured down my face. "The children—" I began.

"How old is your son, Queen Talyien?"

It was my turn to smirk. "Threaten my child, Qun. That's right. Give me a reason to make you bleed. Not that I don't have enough already."

"Biala and I never had children," he mused. "Probably for the best. She wasn't fond of them—thought they screeched too much. And they can be such unnecessary complications, don't you think? How much does your son screech?"

"Fuck you," I told him.

He broke into a wide grin before he glanced at the soldier behind him. "Do you have her men?"

"Not yet, Governor," the soldier replied. "They escaped."

Qun's eyes flashed. "Incompetent fools." He took a deep breath. "Consider yourself lucky, Queen Talyien. Since I need your compliance, Lo Bahn's children may live for now. Try not to make this needlessly difficult for us."

I was dragged back into the city, straight to the dungeons of the governor's office. Lo Bahn was sitting in the cell next to mine. He glowered at me, eyes hard. He must've heard the rumours.

I slumped down, feeling like I'd been dragged between horses. "Your children are safe," I said.

"This wouldn't have happened if you'd kept your mouth shut," he replied.

"Do you honestly think the kind of shit you were trying to pull wouldn't come back to haunt you? You forced my hand." I sidled over to the bars to examine them. They were made of wood so thick it might as well have been iron. I tested a bar with a kick and frowned—it barely shifted. There was no forcing my way out of this cell.

"I was kind enough to warn you before my own hands were forced to wring your little neck," Lo Bahn spat. "The soldiers said they burned down my house."

"You slept with snakes, Lo Bahn. Did you think you wouldn't get bitten?" I resisted the temptation to dig at his sorrow further. There was a limit to my anger, and I had reached it. "You can ruin him, Lord Han. You're aware of that, aren't you? One word, and you can undo him."

Lo Bahn paused for a moment before he began laughing. "I don't know what to think when I'm talking to you," he said after he caught his breath. "You've got a tangled mind, worse than all the gambling lords and whorehouse mistresses in Shang Azi combined."

I ignored him. "That Qun. He's very good at pretending. Too good. It's almost like he's a puppet in a play. So everything up to that point..." I trailed off, falling into deep thought.

I heard Lo Bahn swear under his breath. "Well? Keep talking, woman. I've got no other entertainment in this blasted hole you've dragged us into, and unless you're planning to show me your tits over the next hour—"

"Do you talk like that in front of your daughters?"

"Hardly. My sons, though..."

I looked away. "There's two threads to this. Qun's personal ambitions are clear enough. But he's also working for someone else. It's conflicting with his desires, *complicating* things for him—especially since he's technically still in office and has to abide by all the rules of the empire. What does he have to gain from wanting Rayyel dead, for instance? My husband is nothing to him. He…" I felt myself grow numb as soon as the last few words left my lips. *No*, I thought. *It can't be. To want Rayyel dead, while leaving me alive…*

"What?" Lo Bahn asked.

"Nothing," I whispered. Lo Bahn didn't know about Yuebek. He didn't have to. Yuebek was dead. He had to be dead. I had stuck a sword into the fucking bastard myself, and he had nowhere to go when that whole chamber went up in flames. I had assumed there was no official announcement because the whole situation was an embarrassment to the empire. The Esteemed Emperor's son, going to the lengths Yuebek had gone to obtain power… it was despicable.

Yuebek was *dead*. Mage or monster, he bled easily enough, and anything that could bleed could die.

He was dead.

Wasn't he?

Doubt crawled up my senses. Leave it to me to be so unhinged that I couldn't even tell fact from fiction anymore. I had to keep ahold of myself. The dead remained dead.

Just like me, child?

I placed my head on my arms and willed the darkness to go away. It seemed as if I had been doing nothing but that over the past few months—awake or dreaming, I was begging the shadows to recede and reveal the walls of my home on Oka Shto Mountain, that I may stumble towards my son's bed and curl beside him before dawn came to light the windows on fire. It was only in the past year or so that he had started sleeping in his own room—he used to sleep beside me in the years after his father left us. The *aron dar* Ikessars, distant relatives who acted as his guardians, didn't like this, claiming it made the child too clingy, but it was the old way and I dared them to say otherwise. "The king will hear of this," they liked to grumble whenever I told them off.

"So go find the bastard," I would reply. "And while you're at it, make sure to ask him what kind of parent abandons his child. If I'm the one at fault, why hurt *him*, too?"

I opened my eyes back to the prison cell. Lo Bahn was throwing a pebble at the wall, hearing it clack in the darkness before getting up to find and retrieve it. A restless man, Lo Bahn; it wasn't surprising how he had gone so far in his forty years or so of existence.

"How long has it been?" I asked.

I heard him huff. "An hour or so. Moon's up."

"No word from Qun?"

Lo Bahn snorted. "The man isn't the sort who'd come down and taunt his enemies. Not in his blood. I can respect that about him, if not much else. Certainly not his taste in women."

"You make your bed..." I started.

"Yes," he snapped. "I get it. You don't have to lord it over me."

"He taunted me. Played with me. But I was nothing to him—there was nothing he wanted from me other than to see me shamed, just like when I first arrived in this damn city."

"Obviously, he's keeping you locked up here for someone else."

I felt my senses crawl.

Lo Bahn chuckled humourlessly. "You'll be all right. This is all just play to you, isn't it?" He gestured at the bars. "Half the women I know would have wept themselves senseless by now. The others would be calmly waiting for the tide to turn, or else be trying to figure out how to get out of here. But you... you're enjoying this, almost. I saw it on your face when we played *Hanza* the day we met."

"You're severely misreading me, Han. Do I look like I'm enjoying myself?"

His grin looked like a snarl. "Maybe you don't enjoy it, then. But it's all you know. This dance, this looking at people, deciding what *piece* they play in your little game. Is it a pawn? A priest? A soldier?"

"You just have to look at the dots on the pieces," I said sardonically. "Get your eyes checked, old man."

"Don't play coy. You know exactly what I'm talking about. Born to be queen—I know that much, anyway. You'd have your entire nation feeding off your hand except for one thing: your zealous dedication to your king."

"You can't win a game of *Hanza* without the king. It's the rules."

"Can't you?" He laughed. "Then rewrite them. It's just a damn game. This whole thing—it's all in your blood."

I wasn't sure how to respond to that. We fell into an uneasy silence. Lo Bahn returned to his stone throwing. It became a little irritating to hear the pebble clattering over and over again, but he was the sort of person who would continue to do things if you told him not to, just to spite you, so I kept my mouth shut, hoping he would tire of it soon. The shadows shifted, cast from the moonlight that steadily grew stronger behind us. I thought of the pregnant bitch dog I had left back home, how many pups she had. I had been looking forward to that litter.

Somehow, I managed to fall asleep, which was surprising—I had expected to dream of the corpses in the gorge under the falling rain, the dead servants at Lo Bahn's mansion, and Khine's voice, thick as the fog. *Rivers of blood*. But it is difficult to grasp the weight of our own actions, to make sense of the ripples our every decision makes. It is why we hurt and continue to get hurt; how we can plunge a knife into someone, wash the blood off, and pretend it didn't happen. Even when your entire world turns upside down, you carry on like it didn't.

I woke in the dead of the night to the sound of the wind beating at the windows. I blinked against the darkness, which was followed by the sensation of being forced underwater. There was a hand on my mouth.

My body reacted even before my brain could fully wake—feet flung forward, hands grabbing for the sword I had forgotten Qun's guards had confiscated. The figure tapped my shoulder before pulling back to point at Lo Bahn. There was a dart sticking out of his neck.

My eyes widened. But before I could even worry about him, Lo Bahn began to snore.

The figure placed a finger on its lips. "Queen Talyien," a raspy voice greeted me. A woman's. "Beloved Queen." She spoke in Jinan.

"Who are you?" I asked.

"A servant to Jin-Sayeng," she said. She was dressed completely in black, tight clothes that hid her well in the shadows.

I wiped my mouth, grimacing with distaste. Her hand had stunk of herbs. "Which lord sent you?"

"Jin-Sayeng," she repeated. "You are her queen, are you not?"

"The last time I checked. Why did you drug Lo Bahn?"

"Certain things have to remain discreet, for all our sakes."

Realization dawned on me. "You're an Ikessar agent," I said, sitting up. My husband's clan had used such tactics in every civil war and unrest that had reared its head over the years. On the surface, they pretended to be passive and peace loving, a clan that valued progression and ideas above power and force. They even claimed to refuse to maintain an army on the grounds that they were expensive to maintain. It took a long time for the nation to learn that it was all a show—that they found other ways to silence those who disagreed with them. I wouldn't be surprised if they did have an army, as hidden as their assassins.

Her lips twisted into a half smile. "I am not, Beloved Queen, though I do not blame you for thinking so." She cleared her throat. "But if you so insist on knowing, then very well. I was sent by the Shadows."

"Do you take me for a fool? The Shadows served the Ikessars. Was it my husband?"

"The Shadows were once the Ikessars', and never again. It's been twenty-eight years since we broke ties with them, my queen."

I pulled away from her, resisting the urge to rub my temples. "The war ended nearly twenty-seven years ago."

"Indeed."

"Are you telling me the Ikessars continued to fight without the Shadows' aid? I thought it was a Kaggawa who convinced Princess Ryia to consider a betrothal to end the war. Sume Kaggawa, if I recall correctly."

"I do not know the details, Beloved Queen. Sume Kaggawa took over the Shadows in the last half of the war, and led it better than Magister Ichi rok Sagar ever could. I am here under the orders of her nephew, Dai alon gar Kaggawa, servant of Jin-Sayeng."

I had not heard that name in years. The memory of my chance meeting with the man sixteen years ago came rushing back to me. He had saved me and Rayyel from a stray dragon, lecturing us like the children we were. I knew of his family and their contribution to Jin-Sayeng over the decades, and that he was involved with both the rice merchants of the Sougen and the Anyu clan who had seized control of the plains from the merchants. Beyond that, I knew nothing else. I was queen of a nation with so many clans and families to keep track of; I had very little patience for petty intrigue.

I slowly pushed myself up along the wall, staring at this woman who had somehow sneaked her way into a well-guarded cell. What *did* I know of the Shadows beyond what my father's scribes had written about them?

"I think it's time you tell me what you came here for," I said.

The woman's face was expressionless as she spoke. "I've come to take you home, Beloved Queen."

"Home?" I repeated like a half-wit. The word had almost lost all meaning.

"Master Dai sent us as soon as we heard of your disappearance. He was convinced none of the warlords would act, and he was right. They have all but abandoned you. We, on the other hand, know where our loyalties lie. We have a ship waiting for you in An Mozhi."

CHAPTER FIVE

THE SHADOWS

ᘿᔓᔑᔓ

I stared back at her. A ship—after all this time… "I've been here for *months*," I hissed. "Why you? Why just now? An Mozhi is all the way south—I thought everyone knew I was trapped in Anzhao."

The agent looked amused at my attempt to remain calm. The most disappointing thing about this whole excursion—more so than my soldiers' and handmaiden's betrayal or my husband's indifference—was the silence from my own people. Was it too much to expect someone, *anyone*, to send an army on my behalf? They could've gone and trampled my enemies while they were at it. It would be nice to see Qun's smug head on a spike.

I knew it was wishful thinking. A show of power of that magnitude could result in retaliation from the mighty Zarojo Empire, one that my tiny nation would have no power against. My warlords would sooner see me dead than risk their lands and people—a basic truth in Jin-Sayeng, one I had known since birth.

"We received reports that Anzhao City's officials are not to be trusted, Beloved Queen," she said. "We also heard that the Oren-yaro are aware of your exact circumstances, but they've been tight-lipped about it. The others, of course, accuse Lord General Ozo aren dar Tasho of blatantly refusing to send aid. He insists he has."

My ears were burning. "One man came, *against* his orders."

"They think Lord Ozo is seizing control of the Oren-yaro. He's got the blood, and with you the only living, direct heir of the Orenar, your bannermen would allow it."

"*I'm* still alive! And my son, Thanh…"

"Is an Ikessar," she reminded me.

"Madness," I murmured. "The world is falling apart and they've resorted to *finger pointing*. So my general doesn't send help. Can't the others spare the people themselves? Am I not still queen of Jin-Sayeng?"

"Queen or not, you're still in prison. If you'd rather stay and talk here…"

I swore under my breath.

"We are your servants come to fetch you, Beloved Queen, not drag you back home like a trussed chicken for slaughter," she said. "But even you should see the sense in running now and asking questions later." She vaulted up the open window before turning around to offer me a hand.

I ignored her and crawled up the windowsill myself. We found ourselves in an empty courtyard.

"My men took care of them," she said, to my inquiring look.

"Rather efficiently, I see."

"Everyone in Anzhao can be bought as long as you have enough money."

She led me down the street and through an alley, eventually emerging on a wide road in what appeared to be a business district in the city. At this time of the night, everything was quiet. A blanket of stars twinkled overhead, and I could smell wet grass and wet horses. In the distance, I could see the silhouettes of the saddled beasts.

The woman whistled to the horses. They came trotting towards us, snuffling. She handed me the reins. "They burned down Han Lo Bahn's house," she said. "I wouldn't go back there now."

"I know. I was there." I pointed at the three horses. "You know the exact number of servants I have. What else do you know?"

"Your people have congregated at an inn near the outskirts, the one with three cherry trees and a fountain near the street. Your guards and the four siblings that go by the name of Lamang."

"Next you'll be telling me what I ate for breakfast the day before."

She looked unamused.

"You probably do know, you smug bitch. What do your people want in exchange for all of this? Dai Kaggawa saved me from a dragon once when I was a child, but he holds no love for me or my father. This all seems far too much trouble to take as a mere sign of goodwill."

"The world of the Jin-Sayeng royals," she said. "You've stabbed each other so much in the back that you can no longer tell good intentions from bad."

"Can't I?" I replied. "Maybe you want me to guess. Let's see—Kaggawa, playing the hero, sends you. The common man breaks his silence and comes to show us how it's done."

She ignored the insult. "Kaggawa's businesses are based out of Ni'in and Nalvor, well outside of Jinsein politics, and they are all doing well enough for themselves. We have nothing to gain from this service, Beloved Queen. But I understand that you are not one to give your trust so willingly—in truth, I would think less of you if you were. The city of An Mozhi is some distance to the south. You intend to travel that way, don't you? To the featherstone mines in the Ruby Grove?"

I stared at her. "I thought Qun was the one who ransacked Eridu's establishment. But it was you, wasn't it?"

"The ship, *Aina's Breath*—you can't miss it. It's the only Kag ship on the docks." She was an expert at deflecting questions. "We will be there once you've concluded your errand."

"And you're going to give me time to think about it, just like that?"

"I want to give you a reason to trust us."

I gazed at her. She was young, this woman, no more than a few years past girlhood, but there was a gravity to her voice that made her seem older. She must've noticed me sizing her up, because she suddenly took a step back, as if keenly aware, for the first time, that she was on a quiet street with the Bitch Queen.

"How much do you know of my errand, exactly?" I asked, making a great show of looking at the dagger on her belt. I outweighed, outmuscled her; if we both made a grab for it, I would probably win.

"You're asking the wrong question," she replied, pretending not to be nervous.

I smirked. "I have to start somewhere."

"Start with what we know of what's around you. How many people we took care of who had been watching you, as we have. Shadows follow you wherever you go, or at least they did. For now, you can rest assured you are safe."

"From other shadows," I said. "But not *yours*. You say you have nothing to gain from me. But doesn't your family own land in the Sougen? You're the people who fancy yourselves the true royals of the west, aren't you?"

"You are," she said, "really quite perceptive."

"Empty flattery. Tell me what you want."

"Your ear."

"Which one?"

Not a joker, this woman. She gave me the same glare my tutors had whenever I opened my mouth. I pressed my lips into a grim smile.

"You were once the Ikessars'. You're telling me that you want to pledge your allegiance to *me* instead?"

"We are pledged to Jin-Sayeng," she said, "of which you are still the Dragonlord."

"See, my concern is that when I hear the word *Shadows*, I am reminded of the people you so willingly assassinated in the Ikessars' name. There's quite a list."

"The past is the past. You bedded with the Ikessars, too—not that you need anyone to remind you of that." She cleared her throat. "All Master Dai wants, Queen Talyien, is the chance to speak with you about the plight of the west, which *your* Jin-Sayeng seems to have so easily neglected the past few years."

"*My* Jin-Sayeng? Is there any other?"

"The rest of it, Beloved Queen." I was impressed at how she could be both informative *and* insulting. "The rest that has fallen into shambles after over five years of your rule."

I considered going for her dagger, now. But she made another step back before I could commit. *Too slow, Talyien*, I chastised myself. *You've ceased to become a wolf. You're a pet dog, good for nothing but a jewelled collar. No wonder everyone is convinced you need a better master.*

"The land is suffering, but you can still turn the tide," she said. "It's a fair trade, Beloved Queen. Pay us heed, and we will give you the support and the tools you need to rule better, to change the pattern that has plunged Jin-Sayeng into ruin."

"And then you'll ask me for favours I can't refuse, because by that point, I'll *owe* you," I said. "A fair attempt. You might think this is a game, but it's one I've been playing since I was a child. I know what you people are trying to do. You want Yeshin's daughter indebted to you. That's a power you can't resist. You think you can trap me that easily?"

"Not easily," she said. "But do you have any other choice? You *do* want to go home, don't you?"

I fell silent. I could tell from the light in her eyes that she knew she had me. She gave a quick bow. "We will wait for you once you've changed your mind. May the gods bless you, Beloved Queen," she said, leaving me to my thoughts.

———————

Most people speak of the idleness of childhood. I suppose mine had been, too, if you consider that my earliest memories consisted of sipping tea with the warlords and pretending to be interested in everything they had to say. Lo Bahn was right, at least, when he said that I had made a habit out of judging men and their intentions. From the moment I was old enough to sit quietly, my father had brought me to every meeting and bade me to observe. Once, I had fallen asleep—my father stopped the meeting long enough to strike my arm with his cane. "You missed Lushai licking his lips," he told me later. "You don't close your eyes in front of the enemy, Talyien."

"Enemy?" I remember asking. "I thought he was your friend, Father."

"You *thought*. Never assume." Yeshin's voice could cut deeper than a sword.

There was even a game he taught me, one that was supposed to amuse me during formal occasions or meetings with warlords, though clearly his intentions went beyond. The object was to look at the people around you and strip them of everything—their expensive clothing, their weapons, their lands, their titles, their people—before putting them in a precarious situation such as a famine or war. And then you tried to imagine what they would do next if you wielded the answer to their problems. Would they bargain with you? Work together with you? Kill you at first light?

Now, staring at the inn from the street, the one where the Shadows' agent said my people were staying, I felt my insides twist. Judging others was all well and good when nobody's life was at stake. Lo Bahn had accused me of seeing this as nothing more than a game. What stung was that he wasn't wrong. What else was I, if not queen of Jin-Sayeng, if not Yeshin's heir? The wind had more substance.

The moon was a deep red that night, as if someone had lit a paper ball on fire and stuck it onto the black sky. It gave the empty streets an eerie glow, reminiscent of a candlelit hallway. I left the horses by the cherry trees before hefting myself up to the rooftop like a common thief. I wasn't sure that striding into the inn and announcing my presence was the wisest thing in the world. Memories from the last few months—of escaping one situation after another—had left a bad taste in my mouth, and the thought of more was enough to make my hands shake.

I caught sight of Agos from one of the windows. He was sitting on the edge of the bed with his elbows on his knees, a lantern burning merrily on the table beside him. Even at the late hour, he was wide awake, staring at the wall with red-rimmed eyes. I hesitated, fighting against that old instinct to go running to him first for help.

The guilt was like a fire, spreading. I remembered my wedding day, listening to the priestess say, "Love carries us like a river…" and looking away from her and the sea of solemn faces to my new husband, running ahead with my own thoughts. *And then with a hand around our neck, tries to drown us in our ignorance.* Harsh words from a young woman standing beside her young, handsome prince. I remembered uttering my vows while my gaze skipped past the statue of Kibouri's Nameless Maker and towards the silent, austere Agos, who stood near the altar, ready to throw himself at anyone who might dare interrupt such an important occasion. The night we had spent three days before felt like a bad dream. I was resolved to put it behind me, just as I had asked him to: "Never speak of this again," finished, erased.

Easier said than done. The shame of my moment of weakness had haunted me for years. It was true he was mine to command, but indulgence was not the sort of ruling my father had raised me for. But where did indulgence end and respite begin? Was I *never* allowed to breathe?

My thoughts took me away from his window to another a few rooms down. This room, too, was well-lit; I spotted Khine with his back to the wall, arms crossed, as if he had fallen asleep mid-conversation. He was alone. I drifted towards him with every intention to watch him for a few moments, to settle into my thoughts over how he made me feel before I whispered my goodbyes. *Just a few moments.* But as soon as my hand touched the wooden shutters, his eyes snapped open.

"Tali," he said, the way he had the first time he said my name after he learned I was queen—with that tinge of surprise, as if he was amazed I had one at all. That I wasn't just the Bitch Queen.

I found myself staring into Khine's eyes—Khine, ever the enigma. If I took everything from this man, what was left? Already he had nothing, and yet he remained the same unwavering, idealistic man I had first encountered on these streets. I, with all my father's training, could still not decide what to think of him. Another person born in the midst of complex relationships, rather than observing from afar as I had my whole life through, might have an easier time untangling the threads. But in Khine's presence, I felt as if I was the one stripped of all the trappings that gave my world reason and meaning.

He blew my father's game out of the water.

I stood aside as he unclasped the window, silently chastising myself. *Three horses*—one for me, two for my guards. What was I doing here? It was his employer that had betrayed me. He stepped out onto the rooftop. He was barefoot, unshaven, clad in a thin jacket that looked far too cold for such a night. "You escaped," he breathed.

"Did everyone else?"

"Cho and Thao are with their friends. Inzali went with Lo Bahn's steward—they're working on filing a report to gain custody of his children. The whole thing reeked of an illegal arrest…I'm not sure why Governor Qun thought he could get away with it." Khine paused from his rambling. "How did *you* escape?"

"The Shadows," I found myself murmuring.

"You mentioned them before. Don't they work for your husband's clan?"

"They insist they don't, anymore. That they're pledged to *me* now. They have a ship in An Mozhi waiting to take me home."

He paused. I wondered if he was thinking over the details.

"I don't want to accept it," I continued. "The thought of asking for aid from people who once worked for the Ikessars makes my stomach turn. What would my father say? I am drowning in my own mistakes, and to willingly make another when I've yet to fix any seems one too many. I've already lost support from too many of my people. After this? The Oren-yaro would never forgive me."

"The Oren-yaro…" he began. He cleared his throat. "*Your* people are not just the Oren-yaro. You're responsible for a whole nation."

"I—"

He cringed, as if regretting what he'd just said, before he settled beside me with a soft sigh. "Are you afraid there's no other way?"

"It's been months, Khine. We've done all we can. Even without the embargo in place, we don't have enough coin to hire a ship. Telling people who I am is dangerous. And then there's Qun. The bastard's got it out for me… I don't even know what for. But he's not just going to let me sail off here." I curled my hands into fists and took a deep breath. "First, I have to stop Rayyel. There's no point going home with *that* hanging over our heads."

"You still don't know where he is."

I glanced back at him. "Qun had Jien Hatzhi arrested, too. The Ruby Grove. The mages Rayyel seeks have been sending shipments to the featherstone mines there."

"The Ruby Grove," Khine repeated. "Interesting that they would. I didn't think those mines were still active. How *is* Jien Hatzhi?"

"I'm sorry, Khine."

The expression on his face changed. "Fucking Qun," he whispered, turning away. I wondered if his tone of voice was meant for me. "The featherstone mines. I could've sworn those were abandoned years ago. Nobody lives in the towns anymore."

"Which means it's a good spot to hide illicit activities."

Khine frowned. "Maybe. Featherstone helps enhance connections to the *agan*, which mages value. At least, that's what was explained to me once. It *is* a dangerous substance. It gets into the lungs and has the habit of staying there. Breathe too much of it and you can go into shock and die in a matter of days. Even just getting it on your skin can cause rashes and sores. I've treated patients afflicted with featherstone ailments… it's never pretty. It's probably not the best place to travel to."

"It's not like I'm planning to start digging for it with my bare hands."

"It's more than that. Just being in the area is dangerous. Featherstone *isn't* just in the mines—it's everywhere. Patches on the ground, along crevices on the cliffs. People learned that too late."

"What choice do I have?" I asked.

He sighed. "I know. It's dangerous, not having a choice."

We were silent for a few moments. "I have to go see Agos and Nor, now," I said, my insides knotting. "Thank you for everything, Khine. For what you've done for me since the beginning. I . . . I came here to say goodbye."

He coughed. "What if I went with you?"

"We only have three horses."

"What if I travelled with you? Alone?"

The weightless feeling dissipated.

"I know the area very well," he continued, unaware of how his words made me feel. "Alone, we're not risking anyone else. Your guards don't know yet, do they?"

"No," I mumbled.

"We'll leave a letter so that they don't worry. Tell them to stick with Inzali so we know how to reach them afterwards."

"And you're sure you're a competent guide?"

"As sure as I'm a con artist, Beloved Queen. The Ruby Grove lands border Lay Weng Shio. The mines themselves are an hour north of Phurywa. After people started dying, they left the mining towns. The few that couldn't afford to go further ended up staying in Phurywa." Khine rubbed his chin. "My father was a miner. Got us out safely, but not even a year later, he started coughing blood and it killed him in the end. It's why I had to be a physician in the first place."

My body moved even before my mind could finish forming a proper response.

We crossed the yard as cautiously as two lovers on their way to a tryst. I realized for the first time that my mind was vacant—almost startlingly clear. I wasn't aware of much else except my racing heart and the starry sky above. The destination didn't matter. He could've told me he was leading me back to Yuebek and I would've followed, anyway.

Deadly thoughts. My father's logic told me I needed to bring Agos and Nor with me; that if I had to risk their lives, then so be it. I needed to put the mask back on and *order* Khine to guide me as queen, his moral quandaries be damned. Instead, I took all three horses with us, and we went down the street to buy supplies from the one store that answered Khine's belligerent knocking. Dried fish, rice, and sweet potatoes made up the bulk of our food stock, with some dried fruit and bread. He also bought blankets, though he said he wasn't too worried—it was summer and the nights were unlikely to be cold.

And yet I found myself shivering as I watched Khine exchange words with the shopkeeper. No—this had gone far beyond my father's logic. I was turning things over in my mind too much, wondering why he was doing this, if this was all merely guilt from his involvement with me or his way of stopping me from causing any more harm. Irony of ironies—that a man who couldn't be a physician would instead find himself helping the daughter of a murderer. I wished I had better answers.

In retrospect, I should've at least asked my father about all the people who had died for him, all the people he had killed. Contrary to what people believed, Warlord Yeshin was not a mindless murderer—he had a reason for everything he did, twisted as those reasons may have been, and he was always ready for a conversation about them with the right people. He wouldn't have denied me such a request.

I could imagine, for example, that he would have a ready answer for the massacre that happened at the Dragon Palace in Shirrokaru, when he marched his army through the butterfly gardens and the elegant ballroom with all its imported furnishings and down to the throne room to seize control from Regent Ryabei. Everyone from Ryabei's council was dragged up to Yeshin in chains. I was told they begged for their lives, that many of these high-ranking officials instantly pledged their support of the new Dragonlord. The heads of Jin-Sayeng? Mere heads on the floor, as far as Yeshin's blade was concerned. My father disliked disloyalty, even when it wasn't directed at him. There was no way he would trust men who gave up on their lord—dead or missing as Rysaran the Uncrowned was in those times—so easily.

And killing innocents didn't trouble him; he once set an entire village on fire. It belonged to a bannerman of the Ikessars, who was planning to do the same to one of our own. Better to strike first than allow the Ikessars to kill *his* own to save theirs. There was nothing more dangerous than a man with conviction, one who could rationalize his way out of everything. If someone had asked Warlord Yeshin how he could look at himself after everything he'd done, he would've broken every mirror in the palace as a response.

Khine…must detest me. For my husband's confession, for the stench of death that followed me like a loyal hound, for the things I had done to preserve what little I had. Discomfort wrestled with the exhilaration of my newfound freedom.

After we had loaded the third horse with supplies, we cantered down the southern road. Even with the lanterns hanging from the saddles, I couldn't see much, but the horses were used to the road and didn't seem to mind the darkness. A confident horse is always a comfort—it at least tells you he doesn't think there is anything lurking out there that will eat him.

We didn't follow the main road all the way. An hour or so later, we turned onto a dusty footpath that slowly rose uphill. Now the horses balked, confronted with a new thing. Khine's horse was better than mine—when he dug his heels in frustration, she lurched up the switchback, loosening bits of rocks and pebbles as she crossed the path. My mount tried to scramble out of the way, but when he saw Khine and his horse widening the gap between us, he decided that the wisest thing was sticking together and clopped up the trail to join them. I patted his neck in encouragement.

We allowed the horses to walk at their own pace the rest of the way, bathed in red moonlight.

"Khine," I said, testing him. Cold air and dust stirred with my breath.

"Yes, Tali?"

The *queen*, I realized, was for the others' benefit, not mine. My heart lightened. I urged my mount faster so that all the horses were nearly nose-to-rump. "You've never told me what you think about all of this. You've been quiet after what happened down at the docks."

"I didn't think it was my place to comment," he grumbled.

"I'm asking you now."

"What do you want me to say?"

"You used to speak to me honestly about my husband. Was that before you knew what I had done?"

He didn't reply.

I smoothed my horse's mane as I lurched after the thing that had been nagging me for months. "It *is* about that," I said. "You want answers, is that it? Yes—I slept with Agos three days before my wedding night. Yes, I made an error. Yeshin's daughter was never as strong as she made herself out to be. All these years, I thought I could fix it. That if I just got the chance, I could make it all go away. I was wrong."

Khine hesitated. "I suppose I just didn't take you for the vengeful sort," he finally managed. "Or the sort who would discard a man after she was done with him." He glanced behind for a moment, as if to see if I was still there, before looking away, brow furrowed. "I'm sorry. You asked for honesty and I—"

"I didn't discard Agos," I replied. "I was trying to protect him. I can't take it back now. And..." I swallowed. Where was this conversation going? "It wasn't vengeance. I would never... hurting Rayyel, I mean..."

The rustling of the leaves sounded like applause. My own words felt hollow, hypocritical. Pretending didn't undo the past. Ignored like a festering wound, it had grown only bigger. It didn't seem to matter before. But under Khine's scrutiny, I could feel myself wilt. Around *him*, my father's name felt like a mantle of shame. Bitch Queen or frightened girl? What kind of gods would decree such an insurmountable battle for someone responsible for thousands upon thousands of lives?

"It wasn't vengeance," I repeated, my voice cracking.

CHAPTER SIX

THE RUBY GROVE

M y father had four sons before me: four sons who died during the rampage of Rysaran the Uncrowned's mad dragon in Old Oren-yaro.

People have not always been sympathetic to my father's sorrow, even before he decided to have his revenge against the Ikessars with the War of the Wolves. Rumours say that it was his own fault; that it was Yeshin who sent men to seize the caged dragon from Dragonlord Rysaran's clutches. Our nation had sunk to a point where our leaders believed mastery of a dragon would make all the difference.

The details of what happened on that day had been lost over the years—my father was the only living survivor, and his accounts had a tendency to turn into rambling nonsense if he was prodded about the issue too long. Something about a soldier—*not* a dragon—turning around and cutting my eldest brother Taraji's head clean off. Other times, he would say it was in fact the second eldest, Senjo, who was responsible for the deed before Senjo himself ran towards the dragon, straight into its gaping maw. Later, I would learn about how dragons were connected to the *agan*, and how Rysaran's dragon used it to create madness in the air, turning people into something like beasts themselves.

Whatever truly happened, one thing remained clear: I was Yeshin's first daughter and was raised the only way my father knew how to raise a child. I was four years old when he gave me my first sword, a wooden one that was too heavy for me to wield properly. Then he dragged me down to the barracks at the base of Oka Shto Mountain, where I joined Agos in training.

I wasn't fond of the training. I kept up a good pretence because my father wanted me to—because to defy Yeshin would be to face down a dragon myself and I've never had the strength to do that, especially not at four years old. I went through the exercises with the precision of a newborn calf and then, for the next two days, lay sick in bed from the fever brought on by sore muscles. The servants took turns rubbing me with hot compresses and spooning chicken-and-papaya soup down my throat, all while criticizing my father behind his back.

That, for many years, became the shape of my life. At least once a week, I was required to sit with the soldiers and taught how to wield a sword properly, how to read an opponent, how to take a blow. Not every swordsmaster in the army was eager to send a young girl flying across the yard, but eventually, Yeshin was able to secure the services of a skilled sellsword from Darusu. Anong Garru we called him to his face—Sharkhead to his back. He was an awful man with a temper that matched his hideousness. Agos hated him so much that he once dipped the man's boots in cat urine, which meant we had to sit through an entire lesson pinching our noses with our fingers. The prank was discovered and Agos spent that entire summer carrying two sacks of rice up and down the mountain steps.

Not exactly an idyllic childhood, but the sweet note was there all the same. I remember chasing after Agos in those days, laughing with him as he sweated up the mountain and cursed poxes on Garru and all his children, or clapping with the young recruits while we watched Agos decimate his opponent during training rounds. "Agos the Crusher!" we'd yell. I was the youngest, with a shrill voice that ran with the wind.

The lessons stopped in my tenth year. Yeshin hired Sharkhead as my private instructor, and I was no longer allowed to spend time in the barracks without an escort. The turning point had been an argument between Yeshin and my tutor, Arro. "A lady!" my father had fumed at Arro's retreating back. He caught sight of me stumbling into the hall, witnessing the last of the exchange. His face contorted. "You..."

"Yes, Father?" I walked up to him, thinking he was calling me.

Trembling hands grasped my shoulders, but he lifted them as soon as he made contact, like he was afraid he would break me with his touch. "I *know* you're my daughter," he said. "I *know* what you are." His eyes were red, and his lower jaw was shaking. This frightened me—I had never seen my father near tears before.

I struggled to maintain my composure. "Yes, Father."

"They brought you those dresses, didn't they? Your grandmother's... I asked them to. That silk survived the Zarojo sack from Dragonlord Reshiro's time."

"They did, Father. They're beautiful."

He nodded, as if this reassured him somewhat. "Wear one to the next meeting. The blue suits you best, Tali."

I bowed. But because he didn't dismiss me, I stayed standing in front of him, straight and true—a soldier's stance. After a moment, he drew me in for a hug. One hand came up to pat me on the hair once. And then he pulled away, that hard expression returning to his face. He would die in that same year.

My father's daughter, my father's soldier. They were one and the same as far as I was concerned, and it used to help whenever things became unclear. I tried to remind myself of this over the next few days, which was harder than I thought it would be. I couldn't seem to cross whatever it was that lay between Khine and me. The journey felt disjointed, days of going through the motions rolling into each other. We never stayed at the same place longer than a night, arriving in inns late and waking up long before the other patrons in an effort to remain hidden. Three times we ran into Qun's men, who were looking for me. But they didn't know what I looked like, and they didn't know I was travelling with only one companion. Each time, we managed to slip past them unnoticed.

It came as a relief when we finally left the towns behind and came upon the first strip of wilderness. The Ruby Grove was named for the forest and the unusual growth of a variety of bright-red-leafed deciduous trees and shrubs. By sunrise, the brilliance was dazzling, giving the hills the appearance of a rolling sea of fire. I felt like we had been transported to a magical land—to Sheyor'r, perhaps, what the Zarojo called the land across the *agan* fabric. I saw a gecko of some sort sunning itself on a rock, and even its skin was red, with bumps of bright orange.

"Anjishing isn't far from here, you know," Khine said. It was the first time he had spoken in hours.

I blinked, remembering the name of the village he liked to use for some of his cons. "I thought the red cliffs were to the north, past Anzhao," I managed.

"Yes. Up there is a village called *Anjishing*," he said. "Which *is* a hub for craftsmen peddling rare and valued jewellery. You hear about it often enough, you think it's the same thing."

"You tricky bastard. They sound almost the same."

"That's the whole point. If a guard catches up to me for fraud, I could always tell him that I *did* acquire said item from Anjishing, yes, at the base of the red cliffs in the Ruby Grove... what, you don't call them red cliffs over there? But *everything's* red..."

"Any other trick you want to tell me about?"

"I have one that involves a suckling pig. You need..."

His voice was drowned out by a rush of wind from above. I looked up just as an enormous shadow crossed the field. A giant shape, rather like a ship in mid-air, blocked the sun. I had read enough about airships to know what it was, but it was my first time seeing one.

Khine whistled. "That's a new route," he said. "Looks like it's heading east for the Inland Sea."

We watched it drift off into the sky. The wooden sides of the ship were marked with brightly coloured carvings of lionbeasts and *rok haize*. The rest of it was dominated by green and blue paint, with red tassels attached wherever they could fit. Dageian airships, from the drawings I had seen in books, were more sombre in comparison. "They run on *agan*, too, don't they? Just like the Dageians'?"

"I think so," Khine said. "I don't know much about it myself. I've read about these channels they've made along the ground, and how the mages draw from them? I'm not sure. They copied the system almost entirely from Dageis."

The ship continued to bob up and down until it disappeared into the horizon. I realized that my horse had drifted right beside Khine.

"I'd love to ride one," I mused. "How does the sky look from above?"

"You've never?" He made a sound. "I thought, being a queen..."

"Politics is my whole life, Khine. It's always been one meeting after another, the warlords' complaints, my bannermen's requests, laws to pass over to the council... I once thought if things got quiet and Thanh was older, maybe we could travel and see the world." I swallowed past the lump in my throat. "You've been on one?"

"Tashi Reng Hzi once took us to the southern coastal cities. The route only went so far back then. That new one, though—that's going to bring you to the capital at Kyan Jang. The things they can accomplish with the *agan* are nothing short of amazing."

"What's it like?"

"Like you're soaring on the back of a bird. I was frightened at first—nauseous. Tashi Hzi made me chew on a piece of gingerroot until it passed. And then—it's nothing I can describe. You feel like you can see *everything* from up there." He gave me a look, and the smile died on his lips. "Maybe someday, you and I…"

I turned away, wishing he wouldn't say half the things he said. I clicked my tongue and urged my horse forward, trying to ignore the feeling of dread welling up inside of me. If I wasn't dead by the end of the year, I would be back in Jin-Sayeng, back on the throne. I, who had grown up with so much, who had every need taken care of before I could even realize I was wanting, had no right to ask for more. I was content with these red trees, the way they bowed over the worn trails; the ride through them was a pleasant excursion on what was an otherwise wretched quest. And Khine…

The uncertainty of what awaited me had the effect of slowing down the passage of time. From the hills, we dropped down to a path running along a river, where I could see steep mountainsides from across. Mounds of sandstone scree gathered in the valleys between the ridges, while pink and white wildflowers blossomed around the base, so many that they looked like snowfall on the first day of winter. I caught Khine staring at them, a faraway look on his face.

"I haven't been through here in so long." He shook his head as soon as he had spoken. I wanted to ask him when the last time was, but something in his voice stopped me—it felt like I was stumbling onto a stray thought, one I wasn't supposed to hear.

"Did you know they would be out this time of the year?" I asked, gesturing at the bloom.

He gave a wry smile. "Impressed?"

"Not unless you braved the death-defying rapids to plant the seeds yourself."

The relatively calm river continued to trickle past us. His horse slowed to a walk, but Khine's usual chatter was gone. A hot breeze came to tease my hair, which was followed by a bug that made clacking sounds by my ear. As I tried to brush it off, I caught sight of a mousy-looking deer, one with tusks the length of my thumb. It stared back at us, unafraid, and waited until we had passed by before it hopped back into the bush.

Sweat trickled down the grime on my face. As I wiped it off, I heard him clear his throat. "I'm sorry if I've been scarce the past few weeks."

His words caught me by surprise. I smacked the bug just as it landed on my arm and flicked the carcass off. "You've been busy. I understand. Lo Bahn isn't exactly an easy employer."

"You can't imagine," he said. "Everything was a downwards slide for him after what happened at the governor's office. Partners turning on him left and right—I was at my wits' end trying to help him salvage what he could. I wasn't even sure I was going to succeed. He very nearly had me beheaded for tricking him at one point—I'm going to spare you the details—but he *needed* me and Inzali, and so I lived to scheme another day."

"What did you do for him?"

"Everything I could. Set up meetings with his partners, spoke on his behalf. A good percentage of his operations were illegal, so without the muscle to back him, he was grasping at thin air."

"He didn't have money to hire new men? Anya Kaz could've provided them to him."

"I don't think Anya would risk her men just to save Lo Bahn's assets—not in a million years. You caught Lo Bahn at a bad time—he had sunk a fair amount of his fortune in some new investments, and paying the blood money all but crippled him. He's put up a commendable show in pretending it's nothing to him, but I don't think the man's getting out of this any time soon. His only chance is to start all over."

I looked down past my mount's ears to the ground. There was a new insect buzzing at my ear, and I let it. "I didn't know any of this was going to happen," I murmured.

"I didn't, either. I would've found a better way to help you if I had known what would come from it. Perhaps I wouldn't even have helped you at all." From the corner of my eyes, I saw Khine gaze out at the horizon again. "I used to walk along this river with my father when I was younger. Not all the time—only if the overseer would spare him a few days. He used to tell me about his dreams for me—how he wanted me to be *more*, do more, to get out of that mining town and carve a life for myself. 'Khine,' he would tell me. 'Some of us, me included, can only live for ourselves for today—to scrape to survive, only to wake up to scrape again. But I want you to be the sort of man who can live for tomorrow, who can dream of something better.'

"When he died—not long after Cho was born—I stood over his body for the seven days and at the end of it my mother came with a box. She showed it to me—it was half-full of silver. 'This is not for spending,' she said. 'Father had been saving to send you to Anzhao City. He had been corresponding with Tashi Reng Hzi of Kayingshe Academy. He wanted you to be a physician, Khine, and I think if we can save a bit more, you can go.' I remember staring at that box, wondering how we were going to be able to do that without my father, without the mines, with a new mouth to feed. I was only nine years old."

"Khine…" I reached out to touch his arm.

He remained still. "I don't know what to think, Tali. About you, about all of this."

"I thought you had an opinion about everything."

"I've always known I've been on a downwards spiral, but back then, I was harming only myself. Only me and what I could have been. This is different. I knew some of those men, Lo Bahn's guards. I went to their funerals. Their families fed me. I couldn't bring myself to say how I had caused the deaths of their husbands…their children…their fathers."

"You didn't."

"It was my idea in the first place."

"We didn't know Yuebek would be there."

"There are patterns we can observe to prevent such things, and we owe it to the people around us to take heed of them."

Khine was looking at me while he said this. I felt my ears ring. "That's why you wanted me to ride alone with you. You wanted me away from your family."

"Among other things."

I struggled against the disappointment in his voice. "Then why not just leave me be, Khine?"

"I take you to your husband, this all ends."

"You know it's not that simple. Walking away, on the other hand..."

"It's not that simple, either," he said. And he left it at that.

Some time later, we laid out bedrolls beside the river in the dark. I watched him talking to the horses, rubbing them down and scratching their chins, and tried to imagine what my father would think about him. They shared, if nothing else, that stubborn, idealistic streak. Yeshin would've enjoyed talking to him, at least before killing him for overstepping his bounds.

He came up to join me by the fire. "Dealing with me is tiresome, isn't it?" Khine asked.

I stared at him, my cheek on my knee. "Sometimes." I wanted to ask if he thought the same thing about me, and then decided against it; I didn't know how to deal with it if he said yes.

"We haven't even known each other all that long."

I nodded, smiled.

"Tell me what's on your mind."

I pretended to mull over his words. "It's..." I began, before changing my mind. "If you had a choice, what would you have been? Not a physician. Anything else. If you were free."

"You'd laugh."

"You know I won't."

Khine looked embarrassed for a moment, which was an odd expression for a man usually so brazen. "I suppose I'd have been a soldier."

"You," I said. My lips quirked into a smile. "But you don't like killing."

"I told you you'd laugh."

"Sorry. Tell me, then. Why a soldier?"

"I had this dream once that I could maybe rise up the ranks and become a general. If you did well enough in your studies and did your best to get noticed, it's not a far cry. Do you know how much influence a general can wield? Being a soldier isn't all about killing. You can stop deaths. March an army elsewhere. Save people."

"You could do that as a physician, too."

"A physician's reach is limited. You're controlled by the guild, by what you have to charge people, by the fact that you couldn't stop them from getting hurt in the first place. And you can see how well *that's* turned out for me. In any case, it's better than being a con artist and a hired thug from Shang Azi, don't you think?" Khine turned to me. "What about you? If you could be anything else but a queen? If you were free to walk away from all of this, what would you be?"

I stared at the fire for a long time.

"I'd be free," I murmured.

There are no words to portray how I felt over those next few days—none, at least, that wouldn't be misinterpreted by a historian with a better overview of how my life turned out in the end. I can write what I remember, but I feel my words are a poor substitute for the truth—that somehow in that wilderness, with the company of that one man, I found the shackles of my life loosening. I knew only the sound of the hooves clip-clopping on the trail, the feel of my sweat running down my back from the heat, the swaying of the bridges we needed to cross—something the horses, I was pleased to find out, were used to—and the endless, unreachable blanket of the clear sky above. We chewed on dried mangoes and flatbread along the way, boiling rice only when we camped for the night. Khine would explain the forks in the road, and tell me stories about the villages and towns that existed out in the expanse of this dusty wilderness. I listened with rapt attention as we fell back into the pattern of our early acquaintance, before the baggage, before he knew I was queen.

The trail followed the banks of the Tanshi River. The river itself didn't just run in a straight line—it swung out like a serpent, making long loops and winding around itself so often that it sometimes felt like we weren't making any forward progress. Parts of it were calm and shallow enough to tempt you to walk across—elsewhere, it was loud and rushing, full of foamy water and rocks and battered driftwood. The colour changed, too—it was usually a deep green or grey, reflecting the amount of brush around it. On the third or fourth day, it turned to a brilliant blue, so wide and calm that it very nearly seemed like a rock-fringed lake. The only disturbance came from a waterfall on the other side. There was a cave underneath where the water gathered, forming a small pool that seemed deep enough to swim in.

Khine broke into a grin. He urged his horse across a narrow part of the river, where scattered rocks formed a loose bridge. I didn't need a second bidding and tugged at the reins to follow him, the third horse snorting behind.

The bank led around the waterfall and into a crack in the cave, where a small ledge jutted over the pool, forming a platform. We found a spot where thick roots formed a lattice across the ceiling and splotches of sunlight were sprinkled over the damp moss. As I worked to tie the horses to the roots, Khine stripped down to his loincloth and waded into the water first. He yelped.

"Is it cold?" I asked.

He wiped water from his beard and swam up to me. The pool was bright blue, a sharp contrast with the red rocks. "You stay there," he said. "You'll hate it."

"Really," I drawled.

"Really. It's not for queens." He leaned over the ledge with his elbows, water dripping down his tanned skin.

I gazed at the pool. It *was* tempting, particularly after days of hard trudging through heat and dust. I dipped my toe in the water and then, after a moment's deliberation, pulled my shirt off.

"What—" Khine started, before turning away. "Warn me first, dammit!"

I removed the rest of my clothes and dropped into the water up to my chest. "Oh," I said softly as I imagined the layers of dirt falling off. I turned to see him begin swimming away. "What, Khine?"

"Nothing," he murmured.

"You're allowed to, but I'm not?"

"I didn't say that," he bristled.

"If my lack of modesty offends you…"

"Just…just keep away. About an arm's length or so." He flailed about in the water to show me exactly how far. His idea of "an arm's length" came out to about five.

I couldn't stop myself from grinning. "Afraid of what Rayyel will say?"

"And Agos, and your whole damn nation while we're at it." He took a deep breath. "You, being with you…isn't *safe*, as I think you're well aware."

"That didn't stop you from wanting to ride with me alone." I dipped my hair in the water and began running my fingers through the strands to wash it.

Khine grinned lopsidedly. "Not one of my wiser choices."

I paused, staring at the water so I didn't have to stare at him. "How are we, Khine?"

He hesitated. "What do you mean?"

"When we left Anzhao, I felt like... like we weren't how we used to be."

"I wasn't aware we had a history."

"You know what I mean."

Khine cupped the water with his hands and stared at it as he replied. "I just... I don't know how to feel about you lately. Learning you were a queen was one thing. We were running from Lo Bahn then, and you were still... you. Tali, the same woman I met on the streets of Shang Azi. But then your guards found you, and you put on this mask of authority and arrogance that I don't know how to deal with. Queen Talyien of Jin-Sayeng, with her carelessness and devil-may-care attitude and blatant disregard for others... she makes me angry, Tali. And I don't even know if it's fair to put that on you."

"You know it's all an act."

"If it's all an act, what lies behind it? Do you even know? Have you discarded who you really are because you're not who you think you're supposed to be?"

"You wear lots of masks yourself," I said. "Those cons you pull, or when you pretend to fawn over Lo Bahn and the rest of them when anyone can look at your eyes and see what you're really thinking."

"A big difference," Khine said. "I can apologize and pay back what I took, maybe laugh it off the same day. Can you bring people back from the dead?"

I grimaced. It was not a subject I really wanted to discuss in detail. "Kora was a traitor. Biala Chaen..."

"These words hold no meaning for me. What about Eridu?"

"I didn't *want* him dead."

"Agos thought it was necessary to kill him to protect you. You could've seen that. You *should* have." Khine sighed, water dripping down his chin. "I'm sorry," he grumbled. "I've upset you. I'm... this is exactly why Jia left me. Tashi Reng Hzi made a diagnosis. Diarrhea of the mouth." His eyes looked distant.

"I've heard there's no cure for that."

"None that I know of. I'm still looking."

I heard my father's voice in the back of my head. *You do not owe this peasant an explanation. The Ikessars surrounded themselves with peasants. Do you want to know how well that turned out for them?*

"Thank you for your counsel, Khine," I said. "I will consider it."

"That mask again," he mused.

"Doesn't it suit me?"

His eyes were dancing. "No."

I smiled. "But it's all I know. What else is there for me?"

"Can't you discard it? Bury it. You're fine without it, you know."

"You make it sound so easy, like I can just walk away from the world my father had built for me even before I first drew breath." I looked away. "My grandmother was his wife, too, you know. His second wife, the one who bore him no children. My mother's mother."

"What?" There was a note of disgust on his voice.

"It's not what you think. My grandmother left him for another man. During the War of the Wolves, he caught up with her and found that she had been keeping a daughter secret all this time—this man's daughter, born long before Yeshin married her. Yeshin seized her by the time she had her first blood—a *tribute*, he called it, recompense for my grandmother's lies. My mother wasn't even sixteen by the time I was born."

"Spirits," Khine breathed.

"This isn't common practice," I said. "Not in Jin-Sayeng. There are no rules forbidding it, but everyone else thought—in secret—that it was a crime against the gods. But Warlord Yeshin had a vengeful streak, an anger that ran deep. He could wield it like a weapon, and he wielded it well. I think my grandmother died not long after my mother died of childbirth. Died in grief for her daughter, for the sorry fate she had fallen into. Even now, people won't speak of it, not where I can hear anyway." I paused. "I don't believe I remember my mother's name. I must've known, once."

I turned to Khine. "I'm not trying to gain your sympathy," I continued. "I just wanted to show you the construct of my entire life, how I'm still dancing to the tune made by a man who has been dead for sixteen years. I can't stop the music. I wouldn't know how to, not without throwing away the few things in the world that are dear to me. My husband, once. My son, Thanh. I can play the part of a queen well, Khine, but deep inside...I don't know. I've always known I'm not Yeshin—not half of what he was—but I couldn't even be some-one who could erase the pain and sorrow he brought to the world."

"Then abdicate."

I took a deep breath. It ached to admit how beautiful the word sounded. "My enemies would love that," I murmured. "I bare my neck and half a dozen warlords will come running to tear my jugular out before turning on each other. And they certainly just won't let my son, the heir of *two* clans, walk away." I swallowed. "You see, Lamang, I do know how things *are*, as opposed to the way I think they *should* be. I've always known. I stopped dreaming of a quiet life with my husband and son years ago."

The cave echoed with our words. I shook my head, hating how much I had spilled over the course of a few minutes. He didn't need to hear all of that. "Are there no village girls waiting for you in Phurywa?" I asked, trying to change the subject.

He sniffed. "Between the ones I scared off and the ones related to me..."

"It's a serious question."

Khine paused for a moment. "You know the answer to that. Jia was...the first."

"And last." I swallowed, sliding deeper into the pool until my jaw touched the water. I watched the surface ripple with my breath. "You never tried to find her?"

"I don't think she would appreciate seeing me again. Not after the things I've said. Besides," he mused, "Kyan Jang is very far from here."

"Is that why you were happy about that airship route?"

My question caught him off guard. Khine looked startled. "I didn't consider that," he admitted. "To be honest, when she said goodbye, that was it for me. I knew we could never go back to what it was. I recall saying *good riddance*. The last thing I would ever say to her. And not the worst, by far."

His voice sounded so broken that without realizing it, I had forgotten his request and started swimming up to him. He turned towards me; this time, he didn't try to keep his distance. He allowed me to approach him, drawing both of us deeper into the shadows.

"Let's stay here forever," I said. I meant it lightly, teasing. But somehow it came out just as broken as his voice. Here we were—two rejects trying to run away, at least for a time. Was even the talk of escape so unforgivable? Could I sink the shackles of my life in this pool, and not drown with them?

I expected him to laugh at my words. "Why not?" he asked instead, echoing my thoughts. He looked straight into my eyes as he said it, with a gaze so intense I felt a shiver run through me. I was close enough that he could reach out with both hands and pull me to his chest if he wanted to. I think I wanted him to.

The water rumbled. I turned around in time to see an enormous scaled jaw, filled to the brim with razor-sharp teeth, smash along the mouth of the cave.

The horses panicked. I swam up to the ledge to reach for my sword and the thing slammed into the cliff behind the waterfall. It gave me a moment to see a gigantic fish-like form slide past the cave opening, half in and half out of the water. Wet feathers dotted the creature's scales, which formed into a crest above its head. The creature reminded me of a shark crossed with a bird, a thing that looked like it could both swim and fly. I cursed my luck, imagining what the warlords would say when they learned I'd been found in the belly of some unknown beast. Yeshin's legacy, indeed.

The beast made no sound as it dropped to the bottom of the river. I didn't know if the pool was deep enough for a creature of its size to follow us into the cave; I couldn't see into the thickness of the blue water, and I didn't want to wait to find out. I sidled along the ledge with my sword in hand, past the screaming horses, and paused, waiting. I could feel the water gurgling around me, shadows moving where they ought to be still.

"Tali—" I heard Khine call.

"Get back!" I screamed.

The horses strained on their ropes just as the enormous shadow rose from the surface. It struck the mouth of the cave, making the walls vibrate. I caught a flash of its throat, with black gills covered by a fringe of feathers. As it dove back into the water, I stabbed right into its gills, feeling the blade catch on gnarly scale and bone. I twisted the sword, and was rewarded by a hiss and dark blood spreading through the water like a cloud.

I pulled back and the creature lashed out, its teeth snapping once on empty air.

I readied my sword a second time. The beast returned; two sets of yellow eyes gleamed like piercing candlelight. It slammed straight into the granite, its massive jaws scraping along the edges before pressing against the mouth of the cave, dislodging a flurry of rocks from overhead. I was afraid for a moment that the whole cave would collapse on top of us.

But the creature had other plans. It pushed its tongue out instead, through its rows of jagged teeth, like a child trying to lick the last bit of honey from a pot. I drew back as the tongue went past me, straight towards the closest horse. The frightened creature tried to bolt. The appendage wrapped itself around the horse's neck and pulled, dragging the horse into the water.

I sank my sword into the base of the creature's tongue, where blood vessels spread like a pulsating spider's web. The creature turned its head away from the cave, but it didn't let go of the horse. The horse stared helplessly back at me. I reached out of the water to grab the ropes, but the bridle snapped as the creature began to beat its feathered fins like wings. Little whorls of air appeared above the water—a moment later, it was soaring through the clouds, taking the horse with it.

I walked past the trail of blood for the other horses. "There, there," I murmured, the words meant to soothe myself. The shaking was starting. I dropped the sword so I could place both of my hands on the warmth of the nearest mottled neck.

"Tali," Khine breathed.

I turned. He was still in the water, and there was a look on his face that went beyond terror over what had just occurred. I realized I was still naked, with blood all over me. Modesty returned. I felt my cheeks burn as I slowly slid back into the water. The attack had lasted barely more than a few heartbeats, but I was suddenly so exhausted.

"How many more of those out there?"

"Probably just the one," Khine started. He cleared his throat and turned away from me. "It's, ah...a rare and solitary creature, or so I've heard. Never seen one until today, actually. It's extremely territorial. I doubt there's another in the area. Are—are you hurt?"

"I don't think so," I said.

"You're shaking."

"Nerves. I'll be all right. It happens all the time."

"You've a gash…on your arm there…" He gestured, but made no movement to come closer.

I looked down. I didn't notice it before. "It's not serious," I said. "I think I got caught on the rocks there. It could have been worse. Did you see the size of those teeth?"

"Yes. Teeth. I was looking at the teeth." He swallowed. "We should get dressed and pick another spot for the night. The blood might attract other beasts."

He scratched his cheek before getting out. I turned away. There was rustling as he put his clothes on, and then footsteps. I looked up and saw him place my own clothes closer to me. "Before you catch a cold," he grumbled.

I felt embarrassed all of a sudden—whatever spell I had been under in the water was broken by the gesture. "Thank you," I managed to croak out.

Khine mumbled something I couldn't hear before walking out of the cave.

With only two horses left, and one burdened with supplies, we decided to walk the rest of the way. Khine had wanted to ride double, but I wasn't going to do that to a horse, not with at least another day ahead of us.

The added complication meant another one or two days of delay. It was a good thing, at least, that the fish-bird beast—Khine said they called it a *kunuti* in Lay Weng Shio—didn't drag the saddlebags with it. We still had enough rice and dried fish to last another week. But Khine didn't seem worried about the supplies, and I found that I didn't mind the idea of spending a few extra days with him. After months of trying to track my husband down, I was starting to dread the thought of seeing Rayyel again.

It was a far cry from how I had been three months ago.

"What are you going to say to him this time around?" Khine asked me as we bedded across from each other that night. A fire crackled merrily a few paces away.

"I haven't thought that far ahead."

He chuckled. "All this time I've known you, I thought you've got every step figured out like some brilliant tactician. Lo Bahn's convinced of it, too."

"Is he, now? Is that why he made the effort to stab me in the back before I could get one in him?" I smiled softly, knowing he couldn't see it. "I know how to look like I do. It's part of the act I've played all these years. That first time... I thought I could get Rayyel to listen to me. That I could somehow explain everything, holding on to that thin thread of hope. And why shouldn't I? He was my husband, no matter what else we were. We had shared a bed together. A life. I was convinced for the longest time that there had to have been something in that, that it meant something." The painful thoughts resurfaced. I pushed back at them with expert ease.

"What was it like after he left?"

I thought about the question, biting back every sarcastic thing that came to mind. "Hard," I finally admitted.

"I thought you were adamant that you didn't need him around."

I stared at the dancing flames, my chin on my knee. "I don't know if having him would've changed anything," I said. "But it would've made things more tolerable. Rayyel and I... we are little more than puppets, propped up between the warlords to stop them from tearing into each other. Those first few hours were chaos. We thought he went straight to Warlord Lushai—they'd seen him hire a carriage to take him east. As soon as we could, we rode out there with every intention of accusing the Baraji clan of treason. But Lushai welcomed us with open arms. We ransacked his castle from top to bottom, searched every room and larder. There was no sign of Rayyel."

"What did Chiha say?" Khine asked.

I didn't even think he'd remember her name. Akaterru knows, *I've* tried to forget it often enough. "That bitch," I said. "She was there. Her room was the first thing I searched. She just stood there while I threw the sheets aside and looked under the bed, smiling ever so smugly."

"That's suspicious of her."

"I thought so, too. She *was* hiding something, but whatever it was, I couldn't find it. 'Missing a husband, Queen Talyien?' I remember her asking me. 'Hard to imagine how you could misplace a man.'"

Khine started to laugh, and then thought the better of it when I stared at him. "It was all I could do not to strike her," I continued, as if I hadn't been interrupted. "She *was* still Lushai's daughter and an affront like that would've been hard to justify, at least not without revealing what I knew."

"I've wondered about that," Khine said. "I hope it's not too forward to ask you."

"We've come this far."

"You would've saved everyone a lot of trouble just telling everyone what Rayyel did. Yet you kept it to yourself, allowed them to blame you instead."

"There would've been more trouble had I accused Rai of anything. The way it played out, they only *thought* the worst of me—they couldn't prove it."

"But see, *he* doesn't even know that *you* know. Or else how could he stand to accuse you as he did? Why didn't you tell him?"

"A wolf of Oren-yaro..." I began.

"Ah, right. This ridiculous notion of your people that you can bear more than others because of your bloodline or who you serve. You Jinseins are so hard to understand sometimes."

"You have ideals, too."

"But they're my own. Not anyone else's. Certainly not passed down to me by ancestors who don't care a lick about how they would ruin my life."

"It's so easy for you to say. You don't—"

I stopped. I could hear something moving in the dark, and thought for a moment that perhaps the *kunuti* had returned. The trees rustled and I heard it again—a deep, low groan, rather like a dog who couldn't decide whether to growl or bark.

I gathered my bedroll and plopped down beside Khine. Evidently, he thought this was too close and tried to inch further away.

"You've got to stop acting like that, you know," I said. "I'm not going to order you to sleep with me. I just thought it would be safer if one of us was close enough to stop the other from getting dragged off into the woods."

"The thought never even occurred to me."

"Never?"

He stared as I began to spread the bedroll on the ground. "Er, *order* me to?"

"That's what everyone thinks happened. They think I deliberately sample my guardsmen every turn of the moon. There was a time after I was crowned that every single meeting would devolve into these accusations. Not to my face, mind, but you could see them *thinking* it when they spoke to me. They—and some of them were *friends* of my father—sometimes hinted I could...widen my tastes, perhaps add *warlord* to the menu." I shook my head in disgust.

"I've underestimated you. You knew how to handle Lo Bahn from the beginning."

I gave a small smile. "That's why Nor was appointed as my Captain of the Guard. Magister Arro made the call, insisted it was better I was shadowed by someone related to me instead of another whose name they could drag to the dust like they did Agos's. I shouldn't have asked Agos to disappear that night. But I was afraid Rayyel would find him and that one of them would get killed. Would Agos stand by and just let Rayyel run him through with a sword out of devotion to me? Or would Agos crush my husband's skull with his bare fists? I didn't want to find out. I cared for them both. I don't have a lot of people in my life, Khine. I don't want to lose either.

"But it became clear to anyone that his disappearance meant something. He had been by my side ever since *he* was appointed Captain of the Guard at Oka Shto. He had a house in Oren-yaro—they tore it apart and torched it. I never could find out who was responsible—I suspected the Ikessars, but I didn't have proof. I was told later on that it was done *for love of the queen*. Like I would ever order such a thing. He couldn't show his face again, could never enter the service of another warlord—not with me as queen of Jin-Sayeng. Everything he was…gone overnight."

"So you keep him around because of guilt," Khine said, like he had stumbled onto a rare realization.

I shrugged.

"On the other hand, he would've done a commendable job back in the cave," he continued.

I glared at him.

"I meant with the *kunuti*," Khine stammered.

"Some soldier you'll make. Those nerves…"

"My nerves are fine. It's running across monstrous beasts I'll have to get used to. You seem to have a knack for attracting them." He shook his head. "It *was* cowardly that I didn't do anything. I wasn't sure what I was supposed to do and then it was over really fast."

"I see. The true reason Jia left you."

"I walked right into that one."

I closed my eyes. "I'll need to teach you to use that damn sword Lo Bahn gave you one of these days."

"All right," he said.

"I was expecting you to protest."

When Khine didn't reply, I cracked open one eye. I realized he had fallen asleep, arms crossed over his chest, the back of his head on the tree trunk behind him. I stared at this man and wondered when my fear of him had turned to trust. After a moment, I placed my head on his shoulder. He shifted slightly and cleared his throat, but he didn't pull away this time.

The night wore on. The sun came up. We broke camp and went on our way.

CHAPTER SEVEN

THE FEATHERSTONE MINES

ᛏ♀

We spent another day through the woods before the mountains flattened, exposing roads on the horizon that seemed invisible before. The illusion of solitude ended, and I felt the chilling reality of what awaited me. I was lost in my thoughts as we followed the trail away from the riverside and up an overgrown path, blocked by hedges and brush. Khine swore repeatedly for the next while as we pulled out our swords and cut our way through. We reached a marshy meadow, in clear sight of the closest road. Swirls of dust rose from the surface at the first blast of wind.

"That's the mining road," Khine said, covering his mouth with his hand. "They closed it when the mines were shut down. If you follow it north for a few hours, it should take you to the southern border. We're in Lay Weng Shio now."

"I can't believe you made me take the long way," I sighed.

"It's the safer way. Do you think we would've gotten this far with Qun's men at our backs?"

"I beg to differ. The *kunuti* was anything *but* safe."

"I think you had fun."

"I think we should examine your idea of fun, Lamang. Your head, too, while we're at it. Do you have any physician friends? One who isn't a quack?"

"I'm going to pretend that didn't hurt. You could at least admit it was the scenic route. And we didn't have to worry about Qun's men the whole time."

I slowly exhaled. "That's about to change, isn't it?"

He said nothing as we crossed the road. The sky above was orange with a hint of purple, marked with a faint scattering of stars. Khine looked up, squinted, and then turned to wrap a scarf around my neck. The movement was so swift it caught me by surprise; I stood still, feeling self-conscious as he pulled it over my mouth. And then, almost as an afterthought, he tucked my hair behind my ears. "Don't go walking into any white, fluffy patches on the ground or on rocks or wherever you see them." He lifted part of his shirt collar to cover his own nose.

We arrived in the first town: a run-down settlement of abandoned buildings, just as Khine said. Most of the houses had become little more than piles of moss-covered debris. Some still stood—mostly the ones with stone walls. I paused at the doorway of one such house, noting a broken bed and an upturned table.

"So Hatzhi delivered goods to these mages *here*," I said, glancing at the tattered curtains on the windows. "That must mean their settlement is somewhere close. Are there any other villages nearby?"

"None that I remember," Khine mumbled. He was staring at one of the houses.

I came up to him and paused. "Yours?" I asked, noting the wistful look on his face.

He nodded.

It was a small hut. Only the frame and the roof remained, but I could see an outdoor kitchen with a stone stove and the rusted remains of a water pump. "Sixteen years," Khine said. "But I still remember it like yesterday. I remember…"

His eyes darted down the street and then up to one of the buildings. "The priest's son was a miner. I was playing out here with my friends when he collapsed right there. Bleeding from the mouth and eyes. They thought he had a run-in with an evil spirit, a forest nymph of some sort, so they wrapped him up in cloth from head to toe and uttered prayers over him all night long. The healer from the next town arrived that morning, but he was dead by then.

"A huge argument erupted when my father said the boy had stumbled into a patch of featherstone the day before. The priest's son had laughed and brushed it off, but started feeling ill after lunchtime. The overseer thought Father was making mountains out of molehills. Said we had been mining featherstone for years and no one had died yet. Except of course people had been falling ill for *years*, too... no one made the connection until then.

"I'll spare you the details of what happened after. It ended with my father packing our whole family and what few possessions we had on a cart for Phurywa. Some of the miners followed, weeks or months later. My father died before the actual mines were closed down. People remembered that about him, that if he hadn't insisted we leave, everyone might've fallen ill and died."

"Your father was a hero, Khine," I said.

He fell silent, as if the thought embarrassed him more than it pleased him. "There *is* the mine itself," he murmured. "A dangerous area, for more than one reason. White dragons are attracted to featherstone. They're immune to its effects and like to use it for their nests. It warms up their eggs, I think."

"White dragons," I repeated. "Gods, it's never anything fun, is it? Don't tell me—you wouldn't want to meet one."

"They're savage. Hornless, not like your Jinsein fire-breathers, and they don't fly so much as they hop around and glide. When the mines were running, the men scared them off the ore piles at least once a month, more often during the mating season. A doable task if you have enough people and spears surrounding the creature. Still, sometimes they'd bring a man in ripped to shreds, guts everywhere..."

"And with the men gone, it's a good chance the mines are overrun with these things. Wonderful. So where *else* would the mages be? They couldn't possibly just whisk themselves off into thin air every chance they get."

I paused as Khine stiffened. I followed his gaze and saw figures in the distance. Taking a deep breath, I reached for my sword just as the two silhouettes drew closer: a broad-shouldered man and a tall, well-built woman. Agos and Nor. My own relief at not having to fight was quickly replaced by anger—not at them, but at the reminder that I was still Queen Talyien, a woman who needed to be followed and guarded and watched. The last few days suddenly felt like a blur. I glanced at Khine. Already I could see him crawling back into that wretched hole of these past months, the one where he didn't have to confront the same issues that plagued my waking moments. He could do that easily enough. I, on the other hand...

My guards approached, their dirt-streaked faces betraying both delight and disappointment at the sight of me. "Beloved Queen," Nor said. "Thank the gods. We thought the worst."

"That's a rotten trick, running off without us," Agos added. "Lo Bahn arrests you in Qun's name and then suddenly you're *not* in prison and all the guards are gossiping about your escape and all you leave behind is a fucking letter that could've been left by anyone. '*Went with Khine, don't worry.*' Did you really expect us not to? You should've gone straight to us!"

"We had to leave as soon as possible, and I didn't want to risk you both," I said. "Khine told me the featherstone in this area is dangerous, and I know you wouldn't listen even if I asked nicely."

"You *never* ask nicely," Agos said.

"You would've disobeyed a direct order, too. You see why I didn't have a choice? I don't want either of you to get hurt."

"Since when was that a problem?" Agos snarled. He turned over to Khine. "And Lamang, this was *your* idea? Who the fuck do you think you are?"

"Leave him out of this," I said in a low voice.

"With all due respect—what would Magister Arro say if he was alive to see this?" Nor broke in.

Her mention of Arro, instead of my father, caught me off guard.

"I understand it is not my position to scold you, but in the absence of your advisers, I feel like I have to say something," she continued. "You are not a young girl anymore, Queen Talyien. This—what you did... running off with this man..." She turned to Khine, narrowing her eyes. He'd been silent the whole time.

"It's not what you think," I said. "Khine knows his way around here. My only goal is to find Rayyel. If you both serve me, then stop questioning my every move. None of this is easy for me. I haven't forgotten my responsibilities. Captain Nor, if protecting me is the goal, then get started. Look for signs of Qun's men."

"We've been here since this morning." Nor said. "We've seen nothing."

"Then look *harder*," I grumbled.

She placed her hand on her sword. After a moment of deliberation, she bowed and stepped away.

I turned to Agos. "And you," I said. "You're not in the guard anymore, but that doesn't change anything. You're here now. Either you leave and you get to do what you want, or you follow protocol. Start deferring to Captain Nor, for one thing."

He crossed his arms. "Haven't killed her yet."

"Good for you. Are you going to help find Lord Rayyel or not?"

Agos glanced at Khine before staring at me with a look that reminded me of the night I slept with him: that of defiance. Was that why he agreed to it? As if in the moment, he wasn't following an order, but going against the grain and the nature of who he was, the limitations imposed on him. Maybe I was overthinking it. Enough men wouldn't think twice about bedding a future queen.

But Agos wasn't *just* a man. Agos was the only person I knew who understood my prison in and out. We had both grown up with others defining every corner of it, every iron bar. Once in a while, he would risk the elders' punishment and wrath to indulge my little acts of rebellion. "The princess doesn't need *another* dog, Agos," Arro had said more often than once, whenever we returned home with a mangy puppy Agos had caught for me in the streets. "Every time it rains the whole place smells like wet dog, and the rugs have more than enough fleas." We would beg and beg until eventually he agreed, calling a servant to take the shivering ball of fluff down to the kennels for a bath.

Was Agos angry because I chose to approach Khine instead of him that night? I wondered if perhaps Agos didn't know what to think of himself without me, the way I couldn't reframe my life without Rayyel in it. We'd been told what we would be before we could even make the decision ourselves, and Agos had been entrusted with the task of protecting me from the moment I was born. He took pride in it once. Maybe he wasn't sure what he was now. He had come here against General Ozo's orders—never mind that he didn't belong in the army anymore. The things that once gave meaning to his life, that gave his world sense, were all gone. I wanted to free him, to tell him it was all right to move on with his life, but I knew he would take it as an insult, a patronizing attempt at masking his failures with pretty words. Of course he would. He was

Oren-yaro, too. The day he abandoned his beliefs would be the day I abandoned mine.

"Since we have everything cleared up..." Khine broke in.

Agos turned, and for a moment it looked like he would hit him. My muscles tensed as I prepared to intervene. But Agos simply stared, his jaw clenched. He would know there was no turning back if he went down this road. He could defy me with words, but I wouldn't let him get away with open treachery—not even *him*.

"I was just telling the queen we need to go down to the mining road," Khine continued. "Believe it or not, I was quite pleased to see the both of you after our talk of white dragons. That greatly increases the odds of us walking out of those mines alive."

"Should've considered that in the first place," Agos snorted.

"Well, since you're already here insisting you die of suffocation with us..." Khine gestured and began to walk. I folded my arms over my chest and turned to follow him.

Agos whistled to Nor and they caught up, their shadows as tall as prison towers behind me.

As we walked, Khine explained that featherstone was popular in the cities as a building material, that it didn't catch on fire and was useful for a variety of purposes—from making warmer walls to mixing with water as mortar. It was particularly valuable to builder-mages, because it offered micro-connections to the *agan*—not enough for large spells, but it did the trick to enhance runes in order to stabilize buildings and bridges, among other things. After word of its danger got out, some of the mines got shut down, but not all. Work continued in the mines that had good road connections to towns far enough not to feel the side effects, and builders continued to use the material, reasoning that mixing it with cheaper alternatives rendered its unique properties inert.

People die. The world turns.

My father had tried to show the commoner's world to me when I was little— visits to the rice terraces and farms on the foothills, or to the small fishing villages along both sides of the River Agos. I remembered enjoying the fresh air and the marked contrast with life at court, and sleeping at the crook of my father's arm, one of the few times I remembered him as my father and not Warlord Yeshin. But listening to Khine's stories made me aware of how fabricated those experiences had been. How much did I really know of people's hardships, I who could return to a palace where I would be clothed and fed without anyone losing a finger? The gift of perspective, to a woman in my position...

I tried not to think it over too much. I was too far away from home to do much about it. But I did resolve to examine the conditions of the iron mines up the mountains where our lands bordered the Ikessars' and the villages that relied on them. Ruling Jin-Sayeng was supposed to mean more than simply juggling the warlords' whims. It was too easy to forget that sometimes.

We reached the entrance to the mines. There were upturned carts with missing wheels and mounds of dirt piled along the sides of the narrow road. "Don't turn around," Nor said, before I could take a step into the darkness, "but I think we're being watched."

"Mages?" I asked.

Nor grimaced. "Qun's men, I think. A scouting group."

"I wonder how long they've been here."

"The rest must be in the other town," Khine said. "It's closer coming from An Mozhi, about an hour from here. This one's closer to Phurywa."

"We came from Phurywa," Nor said.

Khine looked up in surprise.

"The road led straight to there," Nor explained. "We travelled with your siblings, Lamang. With news of Queen Talyien's escape and you gone from the inn the next day—we had no choice but to ask for their help. They decided to come with us—Anzhao didn't feel safe anymore, not with Qun rampaging like a madman."

"Are they well?"

Nor nodded. "We saw your mother, too."

Khine's face tightened. "Did she look healthy?"

"We didn't stay very long," Nor said. "We left as soon as we knew how to get here." It wasn't really much of an answer, and Khine looked lost in thought as we strode deeper into the tunnel.

"How did you know we were coming here in the first place?" I asked.

Agos snorted. "Lo Bahn."

"Inzali filed a complaint over Lo Bahn's arrest," Nor said. "Qun had no choice but to let him go the next afternoon."

"Came up to him, then," Agos added. "Threatened to beat the shit out of him so he would tell us where you went."

"That must've worked well," I remarked.

"He deserved to have his skull bashed in for what he did to you."

Nor scowled. "I told Agos that violence leads to nowhere. You're right, my queen—Lo Bahn didn't flinch. What he *did* ask for, in exchange for this information, was if he and his children could travel with us. He didn't think he could trust anyone else in the city."

"He's there, then? In Phurywa?" I asked.

"I believe he's planning his next move with his steward."

Agos cleared his throat. "So what are we looking for, exactly?" he asked, waving the torch. His voice was muffled behind his shirt, which he had pulled up to cover his mouth at Khine's insistence.

"Anything that stands out," Khine spoke up. "Your Rayyel—"

"He's not *my* Rayyel," Agos growled.

"Her Rayyel, then," he corrected, "is looking for mages. But the work here stopped a long time ago, so what we need is something that says otherwise..."

"I think we have to talk about Qun's men first," I said. "A more pressing concern."

Agos snorted. "Bastards. Think they know it's the queen?"

"I don't think so," Nor replied. "Didn't seem like they were at all interested when we passed by. But someone's bound to figure it out soon enough. We have to act before they do."

"Ambush them?" Agos asked, cracking his fists.

"There's only four of us. I counted six heads."

Agos snorted. "That a yes or a no?"

Nor smiled. "I suppose if they're not expecting it..."

We split. Khine whistled before I could walk a step and pointed at a white patch on the ceiling. I nodded and made a wide berth around it. A few steps ahead of us, Agos dropped the torch and stepped on it, covering us in near-darkness. Daylight was dying, reduced to a thin, pale shaft by the entrance.

I breathed against the scarf while I gripped my sword and waited. It didn't take long. I heard voices deep in conversation, echoing through the tunnels. I was starting to wonder if maybe we should've agreed on a signal before Agos rushed straight for the last man who walked in. He cut him from behind before I could blink. Nor appeared a second later, dropping the one next to Agos's victim. This left four very alert soldiers, who swarmed them.

I picked the smallest target in the hopes of felling him just as fast as my guards did. No such luck; the man turned on me with such speed that I completely forgot my plan of attack. It was all I could do to defend myself. I heard Agos yell at me to fall back, but I couldn't even do that. From the corner of my eyes, I saw Khine follow, as if waiting for an opening.

"No!" I found myself screaming. "Don't—"

The soldier turned. Another soldier moved towards us, but Agos grabbed him by the shoulder and struck him in the face with a closed fist.

I turned back to my opponent, who had smashed his elbow into Khine's belly. He had decided to get rid of Khine before me, which was almost smart of him. Almost. The momentary distraction was all I needed. I slashed low, catching him across the thigh. He realized I was the one he needed to worry about and pushed Khine away to get to me.

I stepped back, smiling.

"Fucking bitch thinks she can fight," he said.

"Think you can prove the fucking bitch wrong?" I crooned.

He laughed, brandishing his sword as he approached. I detected a swagger in his step and kept walking backwards. If I could lead him into the darkness, I might have an advantage, if my eyes adjusted before his did. I had been in the dark longer and was confident they would.

I heard footsteps. The soldier opened his mouth to speak, but he could only utter a grunt. A blade appeared through his belly. I was about to praise Khine for his efforts when I realized that he was too far away. Nor and Agos were still busy with two soldiers near the tunnel entrance.

The soldier made a gurgling sound, spilling blood as he was kicked away from the blade. I saw a torch, and then the figure holding the torch, and then my husband's face.

CHAPTER EIGHT

VILLAGE OF THE DAMNED

ᛏᚢᛗ

"Rayyel," I tested, unsure if I was seeing a spectre. The rush from the battle was still pounding through my veins. I'd had too many dreams like this before and I didn't know if I trusted what was right in front of me.

His jaw quivered, his eyes dancing with that same, unreadable expression that had plagued me in the life we had shared together. I couldn't tell if he was surprised to see me, if he had been expecting me, if he had been waiting in fear or anticipation or anger. The familiar irritation returned. I had failed as a wife as much as I had failed as queen. When it came to him, I had chosen emotion over reason, and he continued to prove that I was wrong. And yet...

The clashing blades faded behind me. I took one step forward.

He turned, and ran.

"No," I found myself saying. "Rai—wait!" I hurtled down the path after him.

"Tali!" Khine's voice. I pushed it away from my thoughts. I was focused on the torchlight, the faint outline like a distant star. My eyes watered.

Stop and turn, Rai. Stop and turn, why won't you stop and turn? You said you loved me. And I loved you, for so very long I loved you. Why can't that be enough?

Faint echoes of the narrative I had repeated to myself all these long years. I wasn't sure I believed them anymore, but I tore after Rayyel like my sanity depended on it, not caring that the movement dislodged the scarf. I screamed his name, hoping the echo would carry it further than my feet could take me, that somehow it would rip us back through time, before he left, before our marriage, before I had made my bed.

I felt the ground begin to shake.

"Above you!" Nor screamed. My reflexes kicked in. A dark shape dropped down, blocking the path. It unfurled its wings before turning to me, red eyes gleaming, hooked mouth open.

I headed straight for the gap between its tail and the wall. Even after my eyes had adjusted to the darkness, I couldn't see much except the dancing shadows cast by Rai's torch. That he had *stopped* gave me renewed hope. I drew my sword up as the creature slammed its head into the wall, missing me by a hand's width.

The tunnel shook.

I struck its front leg and felt my sword bite into leathery flesh. I pulled back and tried to aim for its neck.

Footsteps. "Watch out!" Khine cried. "White dragons spit—"

The beast's neck arched. I dropped my head just as a wad of venom smacked above me.

The shadows danced. Rai's figure turned around in the distance.

"Now, Queen Talyien!" Nor called. She threw a rock at the white dragon's head, hitting it in the eye. It turned towards her.

I tore my eyes away from the battle and started down the path again.

"Rai!"

I had never heard so much desperation in my life. That it came from my own voice was a clear sign of how low I'd sunk. I could hear Yeshin's booming retort in my head. *What are you doing, child? Steel yourself! A wolf of Oren-yaro would never…*

But I didn't care about all of that. I didn't care about the anger or those tired old quarrels. All I could see was my chance to save my son disappearing into the darkness, and it was all I could do not to shred the shadows into pieces.

My boots landed on wet rock. I skidded, tumbling down a short slope. I tried to catch myself with my hands, but I fell at such an angle that my shoulder slammed first. My head spun as the pain erupted around the socket; the last I noticed before I slipped into darkness were the feathery wisps of dust under my nostrils.

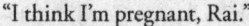

"I think I'm pregnant, Rai."

It was sunset and we had just walked out of a meeting that had started before lunch. I had also just finished vomiting into one of the flowerpots in the garden; Rai was politely standing a few paces away with a look that verged on horrified. I got up to wipe my mouth, and that was when I told him.

His expression changed, but not by much. I had come to expect that. "So soon?" he asked.

I wanted to smack him. "Apparently, it works that way."

It was like he had never considered it before. "Our coronation is still three years away. Would having a child before that violate the priests' plans? I had wanted to consult with them after the wedding, but there's been so much going on and I didn't have the time…"

I came up to him. "Rai," I said. "Are you not happy about this?"

"I'll have to go to the temple tonight. And send word to Shirrokaru. And to the Citadel—my mother will want to know."

"Rai."

His eyes snapped back from its usual haze and turned to me. "Beloved Queen."

"We're having a *child*."

"Yes, you said. You have visited the healer, of course?"

"That's how I found out." I reached for his hands, both of which had been hanging loosely at his sides, and squeezed them. "I asked you a question."

Rai blinked. "What question?"

"I asked if you were happy about this. You seem distracted."

"I'd have preferred if this happened with the priests' blessings. The eyes of the entire kingdom are on us. I am Ikessar by name only—my father is a minor noble from the Hio clan, and with my uncle dead, exceptions had to be made to name me an Ikessar. A child of mine…"

"Akaterru rot your priests," I hissed. "I wanted to know if you were happy about this. For *us*."

"I don't understand your question," Rai said.

I looked into his eyes and saw the truth in that. He really didn't. Inwardly, I asked what I *had* been expecting. Clearly more than what I got. It didn't have to be much—something that told me I was more than an obligation, that I could give him something that rivalled whatever it was Chiha Baraji offered. A fraction of the depth of my feelings for him.

But he had the perfect mask on, that unbreakable wall. I didn't want to admit it, but he was always much better at it than me, and I couldn't see beyond his blank eyes. He *was* thinking about something, but I didn't know what it was. "Are you trying to decide on names?" I asked, trying to keep my voice light.

"The priests..." he started.

"Right," I murmured.

He was now staring at the pond with such intensity you would think the fish in it were more interesting than his own wife. Knowing Rai, though, they probably were. "I suppose," I heard him whisper, "that there will be no problems. But I must write to the Citadel at once. Beloved Wife..." He pulled his hands away from me and bowed.

I watched him walk away, counting his steps. He stopped at the first garden archway.

"I am partial to Thanh, if it's a boy," Rai said.

"Thanh," I repeated. "The first Kibouri priest. But wasn't he a commoner?"

I knew, as soon as I said the words, that it was the wrong thing to say. I meant nothing by it. But there was a slight tremor in his voice when he replied. "A servant to the people, through and through. As we all are."

I reached for him to apologize and saw him crumble. I turned, and my surroundings were swirling back, fading into darkness. My first instinct was to wrap my arms around my belly to protect my child, but something told me that my womb was empty. Barren. I dropped to my knees to scream.

Silence. I opened my eyes. I was still in the garden, but it was nighttime and there were crickets in the grass. Rayyel was still there, but he was wearing different robes and his beard was longer. I slowly rose and saw that he was sitting on a bench by the fishpond. There was a soldier's helmet on his lap.

I recognized the falcon crest of the Ikessars. The last time the Ikessar clan had an army was when the mountain clans lent their men during the War of the

Wolves. Rayyel's father, Shan aron dar Hio, had been a high-ranking general. *Had* because my father killed him, of course. Rayyel never spoke of him. It was understandable, because all things considered, Rayyel was a bastard and the less said about that, the better.

He looked up, but not because of me. A servant came to announce a visitor, and then I saw him standing there, wringing his hands together. An old man, the innkeeper from that damn inn.

Rayyel set the helmet aside and beckoned for him to come closer. The man began to talk.

I stepped towards them. They both turned at the sound and the innkeeper raised a crooked finger to point at me. "She was in bed with that man," the man gasped. "The one she is always with, her dog, her guard's captain."

The words sank in. For a moment, I wondered if Rayyel would get angry. And then—a stray thought... I *wanted* him to be angry. I wanted him to react. I wanted him to do something. He was always so quiet, so rigid, expression-less. Was it too much to ask for a spark of love from a man I would so willingly die for?

He did nothing. In the meantime, the innkeeper was babbling, talking about his debts, his inn going bankrupt, and if only we could lend a helping hand he would forget he had ever seen anything. And then my sword ripped into his gut, the wound like a broken smile...

Snakes began to crawl out of it.

I reeled back. Called to Rayyel. But like the falcon that marked his clan's crest, he had flown from my sight, leaving me to pick up the pieces.

The memories repeated like a never-ending play. The details would change once in a while: in some, Rayyel *would* turn, but his face would distort into a demon's, forcing me to run my sword through him as well. Or the snakes would crawl out of me as soon as I announced my pregnancy, ripping their way from my belly and out through my mouth. I could *feel* them, too, the way they stretched my throat as their scales slithered past my lips. Terrible, wretched dreams. They still haunt me to this day.

I finally opened my eyes, waking from what felt like the longest sleep in my life. The first thing that caught my attention was a fan on the ceiling, turning gently with the wind from what was probably a weather vane on the roof. Pain shot through my neck and down my spine, and I had the distinct sensation of glass shards being shoved down my eyeballs. "Water," I managed to croak out, not even knowing if there was anyone there who could hear me.

But someone *was* there. I heard footsteps, voices. I saw Khine beside me, a cup of water in his hands.

I propped myself up against the wall. Breathing was painful. I took the water and drank all of it before I handed the cup back to him.

"Damn you, Tali," Khine whispered. "We thought we'd lost you."

"I'm hard to kill," I managed to croak out. I tried to gather my thoughts. "Was it the dragon? I remember fighting that ugly bastard."

"Agos and Nor killed it. No—you fell into a patch of featherstone. You also tore your shoulder."

That explained why it felt like it was wrapped in iron. I resisted the urge to look down, because every single movement was painful. "Where am I?"

"Phurywa," he said. "We . . . we dragged you back here. Got help. This went beyond what I was capable of." He scratched his head.

"Qun," I managed. "Did we escape the soldiers?"

"So far," Khine said. "I don't think they saw us head out here. No sign of them since the mines."

The door slid open. An older woman stepped in. She shuffled inside softly, as if she was afraid of disturbing me. "If your patient is awake, Khine, shouldn't you feed her?" she asked.

"Ma—she's not really my patient," Khine said.

The woman made a snorting sound. "You're too modest. He's always been too modest, this son of mine." She patted his shoulders before drifting to the foot of the bed. She tapped the window with a closed fist to prop it open. "I hope the bed isn't too hard," she continued. "I wanted you brought somewhere more comfortable, but Khine didn't want to bother anyone. You wouldn't think he's a big-city doctor from the look of him."

"I'll get you food," Khine grumbled. "If you feel like eating, that is."

"I feel like there's knots in my stomach, but I guess it can't hurt."

He fled before his mother could get another word in. As he stepped out, I turned to observe her. On second inspection, she wasn't that old—there were barely any lines on her face, and her greying hair had yet to give over to white.

She had Khine's eyes. Hers were even softer than his, the softest eyes I had ever seen on anyone.

"Thank you for your hospitality," I said, bowing to her. "Please accept my utmost gratitude."

She looked taken aback. "My home isn't much, but I hope you're comfortable."

"I am." If you didn't count the sensation of cats crawling up my gullet and lungs, but she didn't have to know that. I glanced around my surroundings. I was in a small room, cramped enough that the shadows cast from the fan reached from one side of the wall to the other.

I turned back to Khine's mother. "Did Khine and his siblings grow up here?"

"No. We had another house back then. I've been living here since the children left." She noticed the blanket had fallen off me and pulled it up to cover my legs before patting my knee. "The children say they know you from the city. If it's not so forward, may I ask how they are doing? Are they well?"

I opened my mouth, but it was Khine who answered for me from the door. "Well enough, Ma. I told you." He was carrying a steaming bowl. "Can I speak with Tali alone, please?"

She flicked his ear with her fingers before walking out. "Why are you smiling?" he asked.

I tried to straighten my face. "I'm not."

He set the tray beside me. I could see noodles in a thick, red broth. Bamboo shoots, leafy cabbage, and boiled eggs bobbed amid a sheen of oil—sesame, probably, from the smell of it. There was also a new cup, one filled with a drink that almost made me recoil when I sniffed it.

"Better you don't ask what's in that," Khine said with a sheepish grin.

"You're trying to poison me again."

"When have I ever?"

"You keep making me drink weird things."

"It'll help with the pain. An old recipe I got from an apothecary in Shang Azi. Runs a bookshop, too—roundest eyes I've ever seen on a woman. There's poppy extract, and herbs..."

I grimaced. "An apothecary? Or a tavern?"

"Well, there's also gin in it."

"I knew it. You want me drunk."

"It helps stabilize the infusion but yes, you *are* less snippy when you're drunk."

"If this is the extent of your powers of seduction, I can see why you don't have anyone waiting for you here." I took a sip. The concoction wasn't as bad as he made it sound. It was fairly sweet, with a hint of sourness and spice mixed in with the earthiness of the herbs. I felt my senses blur; along with it, the pain began to subside, and it was suddenly easier to breathe.

He was staring at me now. "You almost died," he said, his voice growing serious.

"Why didn't I?"

"Rayyel's friend."

I pushed the cup away. "He's here? It wasn't a dream?"

Khine nodded.

"I remembered chasing after him, and then the dragon..."

"It is as you recall. Rayyel was in the mines trying to obtain featherstone samples for the mages in the temple."

"A moment," I said, trying to wrap my head around his words, because it still felt like someone was punching me with a brick. "Mages? Temple? I thought we were looking for a school of some sort."

"It seems that the temple of Shimesu in the mountain has been taken over by mages the last few years. This may have been the *academy* pointed out to him. It seems that they are not entertaining visitors, and he has been here for weeks trying to convince them to speak with him."

"*Rayyel*," I repeated. "You talked to him?"

"Not exactly," Khine said. "When you fell into the featherstone, his companion Namra stepped up to assist us. She's a mage. She's also a Kibouri priestess, as it happens."

"That's impossible," I said. "We don't dabble in the *agan* in Jin-Sayeng."

"I thought so, too. But this was how she introduced herself. I didn't argue. We took you back here. Your husband stayed in the mines."

"Qun's soldiers..."

"He knows about them. He's a smart man—he's been hiding from them the past few days and didn't seem concerned. And he's safe from the featherstone,

I've been led to believe. A spell. Namra's been studying how to protect oneself from the worst of it." Khine scratched his chin. "She helped me flush it out of you, actually. Without her, you'd be dead by now."

"Do I want to know *how* you flushed it out of me?"

He grimaced. "Water and spells and..."

"Never mind. This Namra." I paused, remembering a priestess of Kibouri that evening I met with Rayyel in Anzhao City. I remembered calling her by my horse's name. I bit back a moment of indignation—I had been so angry that night. "I suppose she's been with Rayyel this whole time."

"She returned to the mines yesterday after the worst was over. She wanted to give him a full report on your condition. They *will* be back, Tali," he quickly added, noticing my restlessness. "They've secured lodging here, paid for in advance. Now please, eat before you talk again. You were asleep for three days."

I lifted the rim of the bowl to my lips. The soup was sour and creamy, the noodles thick and soft. My hunger made me finish the meal, but my mind was in a daze. Khine bent forward to take the empty bowl.

"When I fell..." I began. I struggled to find the words. "What did he do?"

"You mean, your husband? I didn't notice. All I cared about was you." Khine took a deep breath. "I think he ordered the priestess to follow us. It was very dark there, Tali."

"But he cared enough to send her."

He hesitated before nodding.

"So why does he want to kill our *son*?" I turned to him helplessly.

Khine's face softened. He placed his hand on my arm. "I can't answer for him," he murmured. "I can tell you that for a man to go through such lengths as he has for hate seems...a bit too much. Not with what you have told me about him, with the kind of man he seems to be. You wouldn't have loved him in the first place if he wasn't a good man."

Choking down the tears felt like swallowing nails. "That doesn't tell me anything. Love. Love is meaningless in our world. We move to the beat of our ancestors, of our clans. I need to know if he thinks he is doing this because he has to or because he *wants* to. My child's life is at stake here."

"I never said I had a gift with words." His eyes turned to the door. Agos was standing there, arms crossed.

"I heard you were awake," Agos said. "Welcome back, Princess."

"She still needs to rest," Khine replied.

"I *know*," Agos snapped. He nodded. "There's one inn in the village, if you could even call it that, and it's full. The rest of us are staying at the mayor's. *He* insisted on having you in this hovel."

Khine made a sound in the back of his throat. "She needed peace and quiet."

Agos ignored him, his eyes fixed on me. "So you've found him. Prince Rayyel. He doesn't want to see you, seems like, or he'd be here now. What do you want me to do?"

I folded my hands over my knees. "I want you to let me figure it out."

"You said you'd give the order to kill him if it comes to it."

"I haven't decided yet."

Agos snorted. "*Talking to him*—you've already tried that. He's dead set on getting rid of Thanh. You know why, don't you? He wants you and Thanh out of the way so he can sit on the Dragonthrone alone."

"Rai's not like that."

"The hell he's not," Agos hissed. "The Ikessars are sneaky. They know how to act and what to say, but to trust an Ikessar—his mother did *everything* she could to get her hands on your father. She would've wrung the life out of War-lord Yeshin if she could—she was just as ruthless as he was." He sighed. "I know you're not going to listen."

"Good. You're learning."

"What if you let him have it?"

"I'm sorry?"

"The Dragonthrone. Let Rayyel have it."

"I already brought that up," Khine broke in.

Agos barely glanced at him. "We can pretend to cooperate long enough to get home. And then take Thanh and just run. To the Kag, to Dageis, away from the rest of them. I know you don't like this half as much as you pretend to."

I felt Khine's eyes on me as I considered Agos's words. The image of me taking my son away from all of *this* filled me with the same mad longing I experienced when I saw that airship in the sky. But the thought passed as quickly as it came. "I can't do that," I found myself saying. "I wouldn't deny my son his legacy. He will be Lord of Oren-yaro someday. My father's grandson..." My heart ached, hearing the words. I imagined Thanh's face, so clearly Yeshin's shadow with nary a trace of his own father. Did my father mean more to me than my son? "Don't speak of this again."

Agos took a deep breath, a clear sign that he wasn't going to argue any further—at least, not for today.

"I'll stay here," I continued. "Keep an eye for Rayyel. Send word as soon as he returns to the village."

"Beloved Queen." He bowed and strode out. I fell back into the bed.

"Would you?" Khine asked. "Give it all up?"

I stared at the fan as it skipped with the breeze. There were a hundred answers in my head, all very surprising. I settled on one.

"My father fought too hard for this."

If people were sensible, after all, the War of the Wolves would've been over in an afternoon.

Instead, the Ikessars responded to my father's call for parley with hidden knives and poison. *Support Yeshin*, their actions said, *and your livelihood dies, your family dies, you die.* That something good was able to come out of that tangled mess was still seen as a miracle by historians and common people alike.

If I stepped down, who would take over?

Rayyel?

Like Rayyel could rule anything that couldn't be shoved into a bookshelf or folded into a desk. If I handed the throne over to him, I would be giving it up to the hissing tongues and venomous fangs in the shadows. Who else lay hidden in the dark? His mother Ryia had not even *left* the Citadel in the mountains for over twenty years out of fear for her own life. My own mother-in-law, whom I've never met—not even during the wedding she had agreed to. I don't think she had ever even formally acknowledged me—some of my advisers claimed it was because I did not take the Ikessar name, which was ridiculous, because it was one of the terms my father had demanded: that we rule equally, the way our people used to long before the Ikessars came to power. All my brothers were dead; I was his only heir.

It wasn't as if I was expecting open arms and warm embraces. The acceptance Khine's mother offered, for example, was something beyond my experience as queen. She had been unprepared for the sudden arrival of all her children and coped by doting on *me* instead. When she learned I was to stay in her hut during my recovery, she looked thrilled. She even gave Khine a layered look, the message quite clear in her raised eyebrows.

"I liked it better when you thought she was my patient," Khine grumbled.

"Well, she's *someone*. I thought the next time you came home it would be with Jia."

"Thao already told you—Jia was years ago." Khine looked like he wanted to be anywhere *but* there, having this conversation. He wouldn't look at either of us, and he answered as if out of habit.

"And you never thought to tell your old mother when it ended? I had guessed, of course—for you to fall silent after so much excitement could've only meant the worst—but I would've still appreciated the news. Are you *ever* going to get married, Khine?"

"The way she goes on," Khine told me a few days later, when I was strong enough to take a few steps out of the hut, each one bringing us further away from the shadow of the tight houses, "you'd think she didn't have two eligible daughters to worry about."

I paused to catch my breath. "Can I please see you tell that to Inzali's face?"

He grimaced, as if the thought terrified him. "I'm not saying anyone *has* to get married. I'm just saying it would be more fair to spread our dear mother's judgment around."

I pretended to narrow my eyes. "I see."

He scratched the back of his head. "Feel free to call me an idiot, as my sisters readily do."

"I'll save it for later. But you don't think you're an eligible son? You're *clearly* her favourite."

"We all have our own opinions about that. Thao never gets any trouble from her and Cho gets away with *everything*. No—she expects more from me as the eldest. Everything I do must be...perfect." He smiled. "I know how that must sound, especially to you."

I shook my head. "I am starting to learn that commoners and royals share more troubles than I've been led to believe."

I had been told before our journey that Phurywa was a village at the edge of the sea. I had imagined some sort of fishing village like the ones I had been to back home—small clusters of huts and hovels along the side of the road. But the houses here were built along a narrow peninsula and a few small islands, connected by wooden bridges that swayed with every gust of wind. We were on the peninsula itself, overlooking a bay filled with pebbly red and grey sand. I could also see a deep-blue lake the shape of an hourglass in the distance. Grass-covered cliffs rose sharply from one end of the lake.

On the other end, I saw the remains of buildings and broken rubble, more than the mining town in the Ruby Grove. It reminded me of Old Oren-yaro—of the abandoned section of my city that had been torn apart by the last Dragonlord's mad dragon.

"You said this was a village," I pointed out.

"What else is it?" he asked.

"It looks like it used to be a city."

"It was," he said. "Long before my parents' time, when Lay Weng Shio was its own nation and not the shadow it is today. The empire burned the city to the ground to teach my people the price of defiance. To remind ants that a giant is not easily toppled."

"Your people must have other cities."

"Maybe," he said. "Further down south, the empire left a few still standing. If you destroyed everything, after all, you'd have to deal with the people coming in, and I'm almost sure the empire doesn't really want that. But I've never been to them. For all I know, they're caricatures crawling with the empire's officials, as bad as the seediest depths of Anzhao."

"You've got no desire to find out?"

He shrugged. "I don't know. It's not easy to think about what could have been when you know very well it won't do a damn thing. We fought against the empire, and they won. What you are looking at is...the spoils of war."

I had to pause, listening to his words. Old Oren-yaro alone was painful enough to look at on the best of days. Imagining the rest of my nation falling into such shambles was more than I could bear. What if my people started speaking of Jin-Sayeng with the bitterness on Khine's tongue? Burdening them with a history marked by nothing but loss seemed almost too cruel.

"Nevertheless. It's beautiful here, Khine," I said, to distract myself from my thoughts.

"There's a path up there that leads to the mountain temple," Khine said. "I've asked around. The villagers . . . don't want to talk about it."

I tore myself away from the scenery. "Is that odd?"

"Let's just say the people here aren't like the ones in Anzhao," Khine said. "I haven't been home in years and they already consider me a stranger. So I can't tell if it's because they won't speak with me or they have something to hide. Bribing them doesn't normally work, either."

"What makes you think they're hiding things?"

Khine didn't reply immediately. He led me to the end of the settlement, where a low rock slope led to a tidal pool. Waves bubbled over the sharp edges, which teemed with barnacles and mussels. I also spotted a crab daintily making its way along the shoreline.

"I asked my mother," he said, when he was sure that we were out of earshot. "Asked her if she's heard about these mages, or anything happening up at the temple. Everything I learned came from Namra. But Ma only wanted to talk about you. And I figured maybe she was just frightened for your sake, because she was convinced you were Jia at first, and I never really found the time to explain to her until we knew you were on the mend. I brought it up this morning again and instead of replying, she announced she was going to visit Inzali and the others.

"I tried the others and they were all tight-lipped. I'm still not sure if it means anything—they're mostly old folks, these ones who remained in Phurywa. Fishing is poor in this region and the road is badly connected. Almost everyone who grew up here has left. I'm not even sure we have young families around anymore. I haven't seen any children."

"It's possible there's pressure from the mages," I said. "They went through quite the trouble of keeping their location secret."

"That's what I thought, too."

"Will you bring me to where everyone is staying? I'd like to speak with them."

"It's by the bay. You sure you can walk that far?"

I nodded. "I think I'm strong enough, and it'll get the blood running."

"You're such a good patient. And I'm not just saying that for my mother's benefit." Khine held out his hand. I stared at it. A week ago, I would've taken it without a problem.

He must've noticed the look on my face, because he dropped his arm to the side before I could reply. "I've forgotten—your husband could return to the village any moment."

"I don't want to make more trouble," I mumbled. "At least, no more than what we've already had."

"We'll walk really slow, then."

There was an eerie silence as we returned to the street. I tried to ignore it and focused on the furtive glances the villagers threw our way. I saw what Khine said about the village population—our black hair stood out in a sea of grey and white. Many of the residents were much older than Khine's mother. Some were so gaunt they looked like skeletons as they gathered around their outdoor stoves, fanning the flames while they waited for the evening's pot of rice. They were also grilling thin strips of fish over the charcoal.

"If there is not much around here," I found myself whispering, trying to catch up to Khine, "how do people live?"

Khine hesitated before he answered. "Sons and daughters send money. Once every few weeks, the elders use it to hire a wagon to buy supplies from the next town."

"What your mother's been feeding me, that didn't come from her pantry, did it?"

"The mayor's daughter is Inzali's friend. They've been providing everything." He paused. "Why did you ask?"

"Did you see what they were cooking back there? There were five pieces of fish—one for every elder. My thumb is wider than those things. Surely you know what starvation looks like."

He swallowed. "Ma never said anything."

"How long have you been away, Khine?"

"Nearly ten years," he croaked out.

Too long, I found myself thinking. If an entire ocean could come between me and Rayyel in five...

Not that it was the same thing, and I needed to learn to stop bringing my personal issues into everything. I grabbed the ropes as we made our way across the first bridge, built over a rocky cliff that separated the peninsula into two. A man passed by us, carrying steaming bamboo baskets. He was dressed in the blood-red robes that marked him as a priest of Shimesu, with the beaded belt that went twice around his waist. I smelled the scent of cooked rice with lemongrass.

"I guess someone else has been feeding them," I said, turning around to watch the man saunter down the street. A crowd was beginning to gather around him.

Khine paused. "Perhaps," he murmured. My words must have struck a chord. I of all people should have known the hollow echo of failed expectations.

"I apologize if I made you worry," I said. "Your mother seems perfectly healthy." In the distance, the priest was unwrapping the contents of his baskets and handing them out to people. "You see? The fine priests of Shimesu..."

The priest grabbed the first outstretched hand and stabbed the arm with a needle-like implement. There was a vial immediately under. I was too far away to see what else was happening, but I heard a low groan.

Khine was gone from my side before I could blink. The bridge swayed with my efforts as I hobbled after him.

"What is this?" he thundered, approaching the crowd.

Blood was trickling from the end of the implement straight into the vial. The priest pulled away to cap it and wiped his hands on his robes. He handed the woman a rice ball wrapped in lotus leaves, and only then got up to face Khine. "Who are you?" he asked. Behind his hood, I caught a glimpse of a hooked nose and thick, brushy eyebrows.

"It doesn't matter," Khine said. "I'm asking what you're doing to these people."

"That's Mei Lamang's son!" someone called from the crowd. "Let the priest be, boy!"

"Khine Lamang," the priest said, his eyes lighting up in recognition. "You're

Inzali's famous brother, the physician we've heard so much about. You don't remember me, do you? Why should you? You used to be such an arrogant son of a bitch. But I suppose anyone would be, the way your family goes on about you. A boy from this village making such a big name in Anzhao City—and to have studied under Tashi Reng Hzi himself! It's been all Mei could talk about for years. Which reminds me—I haven't seen Mei all last week. I hope she's well."

Khine took another step closer to him. "You haven't answered my question."

"Your hostility is—"

Khine grabbed him by the shirt.

"I would listen to him if I were you," I said as I reached them. "Make this easy for all of us."

The priest's eyes darted to me before falling back on Khine. "I'm taking blood samples," he finally grumbled. "Nothing wrong with that. Half of these people are sick."

"Sick from what?"

"Featherstone exposure. You'd know that, being here and all." The priest licked his lips. "We're doing a study on the effects of it on the local populace. Purely for...future incidents."

"There won't be future incidents unless you're planning to open up the mines again."

"Not my concern. I was just asked to do this."

"You're bleeding them in exchange *for food*." Khine's voice was shaking. I found myself reaching for his elbow.

"Let's not stir up trouble," I said.

The priest nodded. "Listen to the lady. They're *letting* me do this. I'm not forcing anyone."

Khine looked like he wanted to throw up.

CHAPTER NINE

SLAVES OF SHIMESU

ᴵ╤ᵠᵛ

The priest had uttered one truth, at least: there was no resistance from the crowd. They knew exactly what they were there for. They fell in line, baring their arms as they reached the end and looking away as the horrifying procedure took place. When they received the paltry amount of food in exchange, they looked almost grateful—one man even kissed the priest's hands with tears in his eyes. It took a lot of effort to pry Khine away from them. He had the decency to let me, at least; I would have gone straight for my sword and asked questions later. The crowd's acceptance seemed to have shocked him into silence.

We reached the street leading up to the mayor's house. Here, Khine's eyes lit up with rage, like he was just seeing something for the first time. I tried to understand what it was. The mayor's house was bigger than the rest of the hovels, which by itself wasn't a strange thing—it was exactly the same in Anzhao City. Lo Bahn himself had a mansion in the slums. People always found a way to rise up among the downtrodden, or at least benefit from them.

Inzali met us at the gate. Khine grabbed the rails with his hands before she could even open it, tugging hard enough for the hinges to creak. "Tell me you didn't know about this," he hissed.

Inzali regarded him with an expression that hovered between irritated and unamused. "Maybe you should calm down first."

"Don't treat me like an idiot. You were here long after we'd all left for Anzhao. What's going on down there? A priest of Shimesu is *bleeding* the elders and everyone looks at me like *I'm* the one going mad. Inzali…"

"Let go of the gate," Inzali said. He stepped back, and she pushed it outwards. "I'll speak with you about it, but you have to keep your voice down."

"I don't know if I can..."

"*Promise me*, Khine."

He made a sound that could've meant anything.

Inzali's eyes flicked towards me. "I see you're well enough to have walked all the way out here. The last time I saw you, you looked like a corpse."

"Your mother has been most hospitable."

"It's a family trait, I'm afraid." She snapped her fingers in front of Khine, who was pacing impatiently. "Stop it. You're acting no different from the rest of Lo Bahn's thugs. Men, I swear—let's go find a quiet spot before you hurt yourself."

We took the stairs from the end of the street down to the beach. Thousands of shells lay strewn amongst the pebbles, glistening in colours of cream and mother-of-pearl. A muddy seagull came by to peck at the detritus.

"This started right before I left," Inzali said, drawing a quick breath. "The priests gave out the food for free at first. Their civic duty, they said. Some of the elders—their children don't always send money, so they've learned to share what little they have amongst themselves. The food was a welcome thing, and who was I to stop them? We barely had enough for ourselves as it were."

"I tried to send money as often as I could," Khine murmured.

Inzali gave him a look. "Are we here to talk about this, or are we here to talk about you? Because this has nothing to do with your problems, Khine. When they first asked for volunteers, no one wanted to step up. So the priests stopped giving food. And then the supply wagons were late again, so you can guess what happened afterwards."

"The villagers volunteered," I said.

Inzali gave a wry smile. "They drew lots."

"So they forced each other?"

"Easiest way to get food down here. Mother..."

Khine grabbed her arm. "Don't tell me you've *let* her do this, too."

Inzali pulled away. "Do you think I could stop that woman from doing something she felt she was obligated to do? The way I can stop *you*? Where did you think you got it from?" She snorted through her nose.

"We're not talking about me right now. You said as much. You were supposed to take care of her!"

"The nerve of you to put this on me—"

I left them to argue and made my way back to the mayor's house. Thao stood by the doorway. "Are those two biting each other's heads off again? You would think they would have outgrown it by now. They used to fight all the time when we were children."

"You probably heard everything."

"Enough to know I shouldn't step in," she said. She beckoned. "I'm glad to see you well. My brother was hysterical when they brought you in. I don't believe I've ever seen him so frightened in my life. Your face was all black and blue."

I walked past the gate and into the door. "How are you acquainted with the mayor?"

"Inzali stayed behind to tutor his youngest son after we all left Phurywa. His daughter was a childhood friend of ours."

"Could I speak with him?"

Thao wrung her hands together. "He's not here."

"His daughter?"

Her face tightened. "Please, Queen Talyien. You understand we're simple folk, don't you? We've tried to help you as best as we can, but the troubles you bring... they're beyond us."

Thao's response was unexpected. I opened my mouth to protest, but she drew away before I could get a word in. I awkwardly stood there, wondering if I should chase after her and explain myself. I would've never considered such a thing seven months ago. How easily we forget a lifetime of decorum. Set a horse free and it will resent the saddle forever.

But I didn't have time to indulge in such thoughts. Thao soon returned with the mayor's daughter, a certain Iri Feng, who knew nothing about me other than my position as an unfortunate tourist who discovered the dangers of featherstone. She didn't know my real name; Lo Bahn had introduced himself as a businessman looking to make investments in Phurywa. The rest of us were referred to as "road companions," whatever that meant.

Inwardly, I wondered at how long that story would hold with Qun's men at our doorstep. I berated myself for my clumsiness. I was so close to my goal...

and yet here I was, struggling to keep upright. Even the faked pleasantries were starting to get exhausting.

Drawn by the sound of our conversation, Lo Bahn appeared just as I asked where Iri Feng's father might be. He looked amused.

"He's away on a trip," she stammered.

"Any chance he'll be back soon?" I asked.

She threw Thao a look, mumbled an answer about it being sometime *soon*, told me to make myself at home, and excused herself. Thao followed her, and they left for the main door.

"So," Lo Bahn said, turning around. "You're alive."

"*You* are," I quipped. "Why shouldn't I be?"

He snorted, casting a quick glance at the door Iri Feng had disappeared through. "I heard your husband's nearby," he said in a lower voice. "And that he isn't Qun's prisoner, at least not yet. I'd congratulate you—"

"Spare me your attempts at civility."

"—but I'm preoccupied with our current situation, as *you* should be. You're aware that woman just lied to you, of course. Bah! Of course you are. Her father's not on a trip. The weasel's up in that temple. Whatever's going on up there—I want no part of it. But it seems like I'm already balls-deep, anyway. Where's Lamang?"

"Speaking with Inzali. The priests are getting involved with the villagers."

"Why am I not surprised? The whole thing reeks of mage-work."

"I thought you knew nothing about mages."

"Never said that," Lo Bahn said, heaving his bulk into a cushioned chair. He grimaced. "I know enough to keep away from them. I don't know what got into your husband's head about this whole business, but I can see why you're so enamoured with him. You're both the same. Obsessed. Persistent. Going to have a hard time explaining Lamang to him though, aren't you?"

"I don't know what you mean."

A smile. "Of course you don't."

"Get to the point, Lo Bahn."

He pressed his lips together. "I suggested to your guards that since you're awake and out of danger, they can help bring an end to this madness. They agreed. They left for the temple right after lunch to see what they'll discover. Of course, as soon as Iri Feng found out, she looked flustered and started avoiding me. Wasn't sure why she even fed you that line about his business trip with me standing there. Village folk, pah!"

"How far is that temple?"

Lo Bahn looked irritated. "How should I know?"

"Come with me back to the bridge. I need to talk to someone and you're the most levelheaded person around at the moment."

He thought I was joking. When he realized I wasn't, he made a soft sound of acquiescence and allowed me to lead him out on the street.

The priest was still there when we crossed over to the southern end of the peninsula. Lo Bahn watched silently as the priest carried out his procedures. He filled another vial, corked it, and placed it back inside his baskets before holding out another rice ball. "Last one!" he called out.

I heard Lo Bahn grunt. "He didn't bring enough for everyone."

"No," I agreed.

"Keeps everyone bickering. And not everyone's eager to volunteer. What he's doing seems harmless enough, but…"

"But what?"

Lo Bahn cocked his head. "You can forge a connection to the *agan* through blood. But the spell you conjure from it is forever linked to that person; I've heard of the vile things that have happened to such donors. Tales of people turning into twisted monsters and walking amongst their neighbours to snatch children from their cribs to eat. Foul things."

"Bedtime stories," one of the men behind us broke in.

Lo Bahn laughed. "So why don't you go raise your hand, then? Come on. I dare you." He bared his teeth.

The man looked flustered. "Don't need to. Have enough to eat back home." He stepped back, looking ashamed.

"Fucking coward," Lo Bahn sneered.

I drew my attention back to the crowd. An old woman had stepped forward. I recognized Khine's mother. The priest himself broke into a wide grin. "Mei Lamang! What a surprise! I was just speaking with your son."

The look on her face reminded me of Khine from earlier. Even their eyes were the same. "Just get this over with, Belfang," she said, exposing her arm.

I moved to stop her, but Lo Bahn grabbed my shoulder. "You don't want to cause trouble," he said in a low voice. "A crowd of unruly elders is the last thing you want to see."

"But..."

It was too late for me to do anything. The priest Belfang stabbed Mei's arm. She sat back, gritting her teeth without a sound, not even a whimper. The priest set aside the vial and handed her the rice ball. She barely looked at it. She gave it to the woman next to her, got up, and began to make her way back through the crowd.

I reached out for her shoulder. She didn't recognize me at first and started to pull away. And then her eyes fell on me. "You should be in bed," she said in a low voice.

"You have to explain what's happening," I told her. "Khine saw the priest when he arrived. He's upset."

She smiled softly. "He would be. He's arguing with Inzali right now, isn't he?"

"You know your children well." I realized she was struggling to walk and allowed her to lean on me, which had a poetic sort of irony to it. We both stumbled past an open gutter, stinking of raw sewage. Here, she paused to catch her breath.

"We are old," she said.

"That's obvious," Lo Bahn replied. I shot him a look.

Mei smiled, ignoring him. "Not so old that we are dying, but old enough not to imagine a life away from all of this. The effects of the featherstone..." She looked me in the eye. "It's different for everyone. A lot of us who have lived in that mining town for years, some since birth, have been breathing the featherstone for a long time. It didn't kill us, but it's made us too weak. I get tired just walking to the lake.

"Some of the others have it worse. Coughing, itching, vomiting in the middle of the night. When those new priests arrived years ago, they asked for our blood in exchange for food and claimed they were trying to study how to cure these ailments to prevent future deaths. Our blood—our tainted blood—could tell them things, they said. I was a miner before I had my children, so I knew I'd been exposed to more featherstone than some of the villagers. I give when I can."

"Yet you can barely walk," Lo Bahn said. He gave another snort of derision. "You *are* Lamang's mother. Don't you fools realize what's truly happening here? Those new *priests* are mages in disguise. They're using your blood to help enhance their connection to the *agan*."

"There are healers who specialize in the *agan*," Mei replied.

Lo Bahn sneered. "That man back there looked nothing like a healer. Your son's not even a real doctor and he does a better job."

"Lo Bahn—" I started.

Mei's eyes were wide open. "I'm not sure I heard you correctly. My son went to Tashi Reng Hzi's school. Of course he's a real doctor."

"He didn't tell you?"

"Lo Bahn!" I snapped.

"He failed his examinations." I clutched at Lo Bahn's arm in an attempt to get him to stop, and he turned to me with a sour expression. "How am I supposed to know you've been keeping the old woman in the dark? All of you? Bah." He jerked away from me. "It doesn't change a damn thing. These *priests* have been fooling you and you've been letting them. What dark spells have you unleashed into the world because of your ignorance? What abomination? And for what, a paltry bite to eat? You're no different from the scum in Shang Azi, begging from the streets and wailing about their misfortunes..."

"We did this so we could lift our children's burdens," Mei whispered. "One less day for them to worry about feeding us. Do you know what helplessness feels like?"

"I don't," Lo Bahn snorted. "Give in to helplessness and you've got nothing left."

I pushed him aside. "That's enough, Han. I didn't ask you to come here to criticize them. All I wanted was your opinion."

"You're getting it. Waging war on the empire, trekking through the wilderness, and now mingling with mages. What else do you have in store for me?"

"I told you I'll fix this."

"*When?*" Without giving me a chance to answer, he waved me aside and walked away.

I turned back to Mei. She was shaking from head to toe. "Let's go back home," I said. I offered her my arm again, and after a moment's hesitation, she took it.

She didn't talk until we reached her house. I helped her climb the stone steps, feeling like I would slip myself with every tread. But even with the headache that was threatening to consume me, I couldn't tear myself away from the expression on her face. "Lo Bahn made it sound worse than it really is," I finally said. "Khine is earning as much as he can so he can go back for his last year. He's found work in the meantime."

"You don't have to lie to me," Mei murmured. She slid down against the wall. I tried to offer her a cushion, but she refused it. "My children's stories did not line up. Cho is out there somewhere, drinking himself to a stupor. He hasn't been able to look me in the eye since they arrived. I knew something was wrong. It was my fault—I chose to ignore it."

"They're only concerned about you."

"They shouldn't be!" she gasped. "I don't even know why they're here. They've all been busy up at the mayor's house. Could they even afford this trip? I've asked them not to come here because I knew money was tight. I thought, since Khine was already a physician... *if* he was a physician..."

Mei's face tightened, as if the thought that he wasn't was more painful than she imagined it could be. She turned to me. "Do *you* know what happened?"

I shook my head. I wasn't about to admit anything else to the woman.

"Inzali wrote a few years ago about Khine having some troubles. But I didn't want to pry. I had faith that he could handle whatever the gods decided to throw his way. Was I wrong?"

"No," I said. "Khine's a good man. You know this."

"He is..." She gazed out of the window. "Full of anger."

"That's not how I've come to know him."

"Not towards the world. I think he loves the world. Too much. But down, deep in his heart..." She swallowed, grasping for words. "When he was young, he would get into these fights."

"Most boys do." My son didn't, but I wondered if any of that had changed since I'd been gone. Thinking about him was becoming more painful with each passing day.

"Vicious fights. Not mere scuffles. Cho would get into scuffles. Khine...he would come home with a bleeding ear and smashed fists, and I would have to talk to the other boys' mothers because they always came out looking worse. It is not in his nature to want to hurt someone—not unless he felt like he had to do it." There was a shiver in her voice as she spoke.

"He isn't that boy anymore," I said, trying to lighten the mood.

"If he failed his examinations...gods, it all makes sense now. Why he wrote less and less over the years, and the letters that used to be full of hope had turned sour. I sent Inzali to Anzhao for his sake. She didn't want to leave me in the first place, but I told her that there was nothing for her here anyway, and her brother needed her more than I did." She turned to me. "That anger, turned inside...he would die trying to make things right again. Is this what he's been doing? What has he gotten himself into, trying to fix this?"

Almost as if he heard us talking about him, the door opened and Khine barged in. "What did you do?" he asked.

"I didn't..."

"I saw Lo Bahn along the way. He told me everything."

"Son—" Mei began.

"Tali," Khine said carefully, his eyes blazing, and I had a sudden glimpse of what his mother had spoken of. "Please—give me a moment with my family. Go outside and worry about yours."

"I had no intention of bringing Lo Bahn to see your mother. He was the one who opened his mouth. And anyway," I added, my own temper rising, "*you* wanted me to stay here in the first place. I didn't..."

"You're not listening to me," he said. "Outside. Lord Rayyel is waiting for you outside. Are you going to speak with him or not? Isn't that the reason why we're all here?"

CHAPTER TEN

SON OF THE IKESSARS

ᏖᎾᏂᎦᏖ

My head was spinning as I clambered down the steps. Khine's words still rang in my ears, along with the shame that the rejection of a con artist could be so upsetting. I barely even saw Rayyel at first—only his faint outline as he stood in the middle of the street with his arms crossed. He wore a loose grey tunic that rippled slightly with the breeze.

My first thought was that he looked every bit like an Ikessar should.

Not, of course, that men from the Ikessar clan didn't come in all shapes and sizes. But reading history books can give one the impression that an Ikessar scholar needed to appear a certain way: a royal bearing even in threadbare clothes, a thin face with a soft jawline, long hair tied high, a well-groomed beard—if they could grow one—and a seemingly permanent vacant look on their faces.

Rai was not a true *aren dar* Ikessar. He carried the name, but that was only because his mother was the last of her line and they needed him to secure the throne. Contrary to popular belief, the Ikessars were one of the few who clung to the rubrics of their clan and religion with near-zealousness, so I've always wondered how they were able to undermine custom in Rayyel's case. Regardless of the specifics, there he was, with the sort of bearing that would make you hard-pressed to imagine that his father was a mere soldier. His clan had nothing to fear.

"You are a persistent woman," Rai said as I strode up to him.

"You knew that," I replied. "You've always known that." I stopped a few paces away. My heart was beating very fast, and I realized I was holding my breath. I considered that with a measure of detachment. Was it because Rayyel was there, or because Khine was angry with me? Maybe it was both. I tried to imagine how Rai and I had been in our youth—a gilded prince and princess, worshipped and loved by so many. Looking at us now, with our unkempt hair and filthy clothes while we stood in the middle of those dirty hovels, you wouldn't know that.

"Perhaps," he said. "I'm not sure I know you as well as I thought I did."

"We have that in common, at least." I paused, trying to figure out where I wanted to stand on that line between anger and resignation. "You...you have to stop this madness, Rai. You have to come home with me." *Have to*. Once, Queen Talyien might have told him in simpler words. *Stop this now. Come home*. But I didn't feel like a queen anymore. I felt like a woman trying to grasp at the last strands of her power, a wife going through the motions of what she felt she was expected to say. It was as close to begging as I was capable of, and it made me imagine my father's hissing breath on my shoulder as soon as I stopped speaking. *Who is this? When did my daughter die and leave you in her place?*

Out of reflex more than anything, my hand dropped to the sword that wasn't there. I was suddenly grateful for that.

Rai shook his head. "My mind is made up."

I steeled myself. "Made up to what? To *kill* our son? Or at least get him killed? You're creating problems where there are none."

Rai cocked his head to the side. "Did you think the innkeeper was alone in his knowledge, Talyien?"

I swallowed. "If he wasn't, we would've found out by now."

"His entire family knew. His wife, his three daughters. Their husbands."

I realized what he was saying. "Gods, Rai—you didn't..."

There was barely a flicker of emotion on his face. "Had to be done. The last thing you needed was one of the warlords catching wind and interrogating true witnesses. This isn't even about the boy anymore, but maintaining order."

I swallowed. "Who did it? The *Shadows*? You?"

"It doesn't matter."

"It does. You've kept me in the dark far too long, Rai!"

"There's a reason for that," he said, bristling. "It worked, too. You accuse me of making trouble, but the truth is I stayed away to protect you and your rash, impulsive…" He drew a quick breath, checking his temper. "Because I was the one who walked away, they couldn't very well blame you, could they?"

My ears were still ringing, but for a very different reason now. "But they did, Rayyel. They all did."

"Not officially. That makes all the difference. Do you think the Ikessars would've kept as quiet as they did if they found out first?"

"So you're telling me that this—*all of this*—is just political maneuvering?" I reached out to grab his arm with every intention of yanking it out of its socket. "You told me you intend to kill Thanh if he isn't yours. I didn't just dream that, Rai. You said…"

"I did," he said in an even voice. "I meant it, too." He slowly removed my fingers from his sleeve.

"Princess Ryia must've dropped you on your head when you were a child. If you really think I'm going to just *stand by* and let you—"

"Don't be dramatic, Talyien. He is an entire ocean away from us, surrounded by the best guardians the Ikessar clan has to offer. Anything I say will have to be backed with proof, which the council will first examine and then deliberate over. None of this will happen in a day. I don't intend to murder a child in cold blood. I think you should know me better than that." He cleared his throat and stepped aside as a man passed by, giving us a curious look. We had been conversing in Jinan, completely oblivious to the rest of the world.

"It won't come to that if I stop you now."

He frowned. "If you feel that is necessary. You're the one with guards, after all. And we both know I'm no match for you in a fight."

"What happened to the men you inherited from Zheshan?"

"I was given an escort to An Mozhi and no further. I only have Namra." He paused. "I'm not a fool. After everything, I knew it was only a matter of time before you came rushing after me. You were never one to let an insult go by without action."

"Ah hah! So you *do* learn."

"I was…the things I said…" He turned red, slightly. "I may have erred in that." He shook his head. "Do you know what the Ikessar clan will do to the boy if he is found false? What my mother Ryia will subject him to—her enemy Yeshin's grandson, and not her own? Think for a moment, Talyien. A clean death by my hand will be the most merciful thing I could give him."

"You're an idiot."

"And so I am. And thus, you follow me all the way out here." Rai held his hands out, showing me both of his palms. "I am at your mercy, Queen Talyien."

I flushed. "You saw I wasn't armed."

"I wasn't paying that close attention. Would you like to go and fetch your sword now?"

I didn't answer.

"I thought so. I don't have to remind you that killing Thanh is not the only option. The boy *could* be mine, yes?" He gave me a look of appraisal.

"I can't be the only one who remembers our wedding night," I mumbled. "Or the nights after."

He flushed and glanced away. "A most ideal situation. Should we find a way to prove it, we can put all of this behind us."

I met his eyes. "Explain."

"Zheshan's suggestion to split Jin-Sayeng was sound at the time when I thought there was no hope in making you see sense."

"Now *I'm* the unreasonable one?"

He sighed. "Yet you followed me, risking your life in the process. I apologize if I have questioned your loyalty to the nation. If Thanh is mine, then believe me, Beloved Queen, the whole land will know. Such a declaration will silence the warlords once and for all. We will forget that accursed meeting in Anzhao and resume our duties side by side."

"*If* he is yours," I said dryly.

"Yes."

"Can we not just…" I started. *Just go home. There's a ship waiting for us. Our son is waiting for us. Our son.* But I had no energy left. Something had changed. A shift in the wind. I wasn't throwing myself into his arms. I wasn't trembling with joy or hope or all of those feelings I once longed to have. *Too many years, Rai.*

"Too much has happened," he said, echoing my thoughts. "To do so would be to walk through a battlefield blindfolded. In order to put these rumours to rest, we need to face them head-on—pretending that nothing has happened will only weaken our stand. Uncertainty has served us very well for now, but for how long? How long will Jin-Sayeng remain happy with this uneasy peace?"

Gods be damned, but I hated it when he made sense.

"All right," I said, after a moment of deliberation. "I will call a truce for now."

"It was all I ever asked for, Beloved Queen."

"But if you talk about *killing* my son one more time, I swear to Akaterru and the rest of Jin-Sayeng's deities that nothing will stop me from spilling your guts. I'll use a kitchen knife if I have to."

He was used to my threats. Without a flicker of reaction, he gave a small nod.

I turned, my eyes skipping down to the street and the house at the end of it, where I imagined Khine arguing with his mother. I stared longer than I should've. I forced myself to turn away. *Worry about yours.*

Rayyel, unaware of my disquiet, gestured for me to follow him. I tore my attention back to my husband. "When Namra and I arrived, we encountered one of the priests in the village, a man who goes by the name of Belfang."

"I am acquainted with the bastard."

Rai pretended not to be bothered by my language, but I could see his face muscles twitch. "I asked him if he knew of a settlement of mages around, and he immediately blurted out that visitors to the temple will not be entertained unless there is a reason. Namra, of course, pointed out that his reaction meant the mages *were* there, which was when he started speaking of the featherstone, of trying to cure the villagers of this common ailment. The mages, he said, were sent by the empire to help the villagers."

"Namra. This is the priestess you were with during our meeting in Anzhao?"

"She is a devoted servant of Kibouri, as well as someone who has been study-ing the *agan* in the west for years."

"A risky endeavour."

"Mages in the Empire of Ziri-nar-Orxiaro are sanctioned by the Esteemed Emperor himself. This is one of the few ways they keep them under control—similar to how Eheldeth functions in the Empire of Dageis, for example. Or—"

"Yes, I get it, Rai."

He flushed. "Namra pointed out that serving a small hamlet that has other-wise been forgotten by the empire seems a bit—out of touch. Yet we had observed him gathering blood from the villagers, so that much at least was true.

Blood magic is outlawed in most places for a reason—including here, as far as we're aware. It is volatile, dangerous; in Dageis, where it is practiced, there are precautions set in place. For instance, they tattoo slaves with runes that imbue them with a spell to keep the *agan* fabric intact. Was he gathering the blood for this reason? And why these villagers, in particular?

"To speak with these mages, to get them to entertain us, we needed leverage. Namra suggested we investigate the featherstone itself. A hunch, she said. It's been said that featherstone can enhance a mage's connection to the *agan*. It is one of the reasons it's prized, despite the ill effect on anyone who works around it. We wanted to find out why these mages would choose to come here."

"So you went to the mines. Did you find out anything?"

He folded his hands into his sleeves. "They are creating moving effigies using the *agan* and the villagers' blood," he said, in the same voice one would use to announce that it was, in fact, starting to rain.

"You're ah—going to have to explain that a bit more, Rai."

"I explored the tunnels for days. The remains of the mining are evident, but so are remnants of other things—things that have nothing to do with such an operation. Broken vials and burners. Mage equipment, as Namra pointed out. And there, in the deepest section of the mines, I found them—wrapped effigies that *breathed*, like insects caught in a spider's web."

What Rayyel lacked in basic conversation sense he more than made up for in memory and a gift for description. We walked slowly along the streets, our past animosities seemingly forgotten in his fervour to explain exactly what he had seen in those mines.

"They were effigies," he said. "Things that appeared to be corpses wrapped in linen at first sight. They lined one of the tunnels like clutches of frog eggs, one on top of another. I cut one open from the thin membrane that encased it. Its chest moved to simulate breathing, but it didn't look like it had lungs or needed air—it was like a reflex, one that created a bubble around its mouth as it pressed against its casing."

He wasn't really looking at me as he spoke. He was going through this tunnel in his head, seeing everything unfold once again. *Look at this man*, I imagined my father would say. *More interested in his own boots than his estranged wife. This is what you've wasted the last few years on?*

"My knife had nicked the effigy's belly, which is when I realized it was not made out of flesh at all," he continued. "The blade slid through as effortlessly as if it was clay. A thin, black liquid poured from the cut, followed by globs of congealed blood and wet sawdust. The effigy itself continued to make breathing movements while it flopped along the ground like a dying snake."

"Just like you to inspect these things instead of worrying about getting attacked," I said.

"I suspected the effigies weren't self-aware and went as far as to spend a whole night near them to see if there was any activity. Later, when Namra rejoined me, I showed her the entire chamber."

"Did she scream?" I asked him.

He didn't answer. By this point, we had reached the house that had agreed to provide lodging for them. Dogs wandered along the low-lying bamboo fence, attracted to the smell of cooking food. Rayyel absently walked through them. "She can explain the rest to you," he said, gesturing.

Namra was sitting near the single table propped out on the deck. I recognized her immediately.

Her reaction was the same. "Beloved Queen," she said, rising before giving a deep bow. She had tanned considerably since our last meeting in Anzhao. I couldn't recall anything else about her from that time. Back then, the anger had consumed me like wildfire and I had considered them all enemies, Zheshan included. If I could turn back time, even only until then…

Perhaps if I had swallowed my pride, swallowed enough at least to take my tongue along with it, Arro would still be alive. Or perhaps I would be in the bottom of the Eanhe with Rayyel. What does regret accomplish beyond making us obsess over things we cannot change? We had gotten that far without killing each other. And she did save my life, if Khine's words were anything to go by. I didn't have to like her, but I could be civil. I accepted the bow and allowed myself to sit on the other end.

"I was explaining the effigies," Rai said. He strode to a spot near the table between us, and because there were only two mats, decided to stand.

"*Agan*-wrought creatures. Do you want to know how they work?" Namra asked.

I nodded.

"The *agan* can be used to mimic life in certain cases. The common belief is that the *agan* inhabits the souls of living things. Imagine a current of water that runs through everything alive, all stemming from a single source—Sheyor'r, they call it here, the place across the fabric. We are all part of it, though most are blind—unable to feel or trace the various connections that allow people you call mages to manipulate it for their own uses. Someone extremely skilled in the *agan* could draw on that current and pass it on, imbuing life where there was once none or where it has long fled. A doll, a dead body, even skeletal remains.

"The thing, of course, is never truly alive. For it to act on its own, it must continuously draw on the source of *agan*. A skilled master might be able to use his own connection, his own soul if you will, but these creatures will be little more than puppets dancing on a string. I've heard of others who have been able to create a shielded well—a fabric—around their creation in order to block the *agan* flow and trap another, forcing *that* soul to be its rider. This requires tremendous skill—in all of history, I've heard only of one who was able to accomplish such a feat."

"I might've read about that," I broke in. "A Gasparian witch, wasn't it?"

She nodded. "So for most, a medium is necessary. The mage, as I mentioned. Or, if you need an entire army..." She gave a cursory glance at the street. An old woman was toddling by.

"You mean the villagers?"

"Yes."

"They're using the villagers' blood... to give *life* to these things? To connect to their souls and make them move?"

"That's my guess," Namra said. "The *agan* is difficult to study, and even the most educated scholars and mages will disagree with each other. But it is as good a guess as anyone can make."

"An army," I mused. "What would they need it for?"

"Dragonlord Rayyel had a number of suggestions. None mean much in the grand scheme of things—begging your pardon, my lord," Namra replied.

Rai made a motion that was as close to a shrug as he was capable of.

"What *is* important is that this sort of practice is outlawed in this empire," she continued. "It's the kind of thing you could get executed for. They won't be pleased to hear about this in Kyan Jang."

"Blood magic. Rai mentioned that. I see what you're planning—you're going to threaten to expose this entire operation. In exchange, they grant you a simple request: send a mage who can reveal who my son's father is. I'm sorry, but I have a problem—one of many, actually—with this whole scenario." I placed my hands squarely on the table. "Of all the mages in this bloody empire, why pick someone who practices *blood* magic?"

Rai cleared his throat. "Working with blood is *exactly* what they've been trained for. Not all mages are the same."

"I certainly wouldn't be able to do it," Namra added. "You need someone with certain skills. These were the first mages we've encountered who could do this, based on what Eridu had been shipping out here."

"Which already tells you the whole thing *stinks*." I turned back to Namra. "How do you know so much about the *agan*, anyway? You're a priestess of Kibouri. Last time I checked, this isn't something your Nameless Maker embraced, as harebrained as Ikessar ideas tend to be."

"I grew up in Dageis, Beloved Queen. I trained as a mage."

"You wouldn't have been allowed to without a citizenship."

"I have one, Beloved Queen. My parents were refugees during your... during the War of the Wolves. Your father was... not kind to children like me."

I didn't react. I've built up an immunity to that sort of comment over my life. My mind has learned to detach from my feelings as soon as I hear someone utter the words *your father* in that tone so that nothing will stick. "Why did you come back?" I asked. "I've heard the Empire of Dageis is a marvellous place. With a citizenship there, you could do anything."

"Why did I go back... to *your* nation?" she asked, amused.

"I know what you're implying," I said. "But I've never once fooled myself about Jin-Sayeng. I know its struggles. I know we can't offer what Dageis must've been able to give you. Why did you come back, priestess?"

She smiled. "My father was a devoted servant of Kibouri. He taught me the texts, and I grew to love the Nameless Maker since childhood. After my father's death, I decided that the best way to honour his memory was to dedicate myself to the Nameless Maker and the principles of Kibouri. I made my way to the Citadel and took the rites, spending two years in complete silence in one of the temples."

Two years of silence was the process that created a priest or a priestess of Kibouri. Ryia, Rayyel's mother, had gone through it, I believe, and so had her sisters. So had Rysaran the Uncrowned. Unlike other deities in Jin-Sayeng, servants of Kibouri were not bound to the temples and could live out the rest of their lives as they saw fit. That Namra still wore her priestess's robes was a good indication of how devoted she was to her cause. But to have gone through all of that in the memory of her father?

Well, and what have you done for yours?

"Did they know about your special…skills?" I asked, to drown those thoughts away.

"I have spent enough time in Eheldeth, the Dageian school for the *agan*, to know how to control it," Namra said. "It was easy enough to hide, Beloved Queen, especially around those blind to the *agan*. I entrusted Dragonlord Rayyel with the knowledge after he sought my assistance with…this entire matter."

She had propriety, at least, which was more than I could hope for these days. "So you've been with him this whole time."

"The better part of three years now, Beloved Queen."

We were interrupted by the arrival of the old woman who owned the house. She placed two bowls of fish head soup and a pot of rice on the table before walking away, grumbling something about extra people.

"When do you plan to go up to the temple?" I asked as Namra ladled out scoops of rice, the fragrant steam a sharp contrast with the cold air. She slid her own plate over to me.

"The sooner, the better," Rayyel replied.

"It's too late now," Namra said. "I've been told it's a three-hour walk up the mountain, and I would rather not travel in the dark."

I hadn't even noticed it was close to evening. I gazed up at the grey sky and had an uneasy feeling over Agos and Nor's plight. They should've reached the temple by now—would they be spending the night on the mountain? Or were they on their way back? It was unlikely the priests would've let them in if they were all as unfriendly as Belfang.

"Tomorrow morning, then," I said.

"You intend to travel with us?" Rai sounded surprised.

"Is that a problem?"

He turned to Namra. "If her doctor thinks she can make the trip..." Namra began. She peered into my face. "You *were* at death's door. I'm surprised you're as talkative as you are now, considering."

"I'm sure he won't try to stop me. I've been walking around the village the whole day, and the exercise will be good for me." The innkeeper arrived with a third bowl of stew and a plate. I thanked her profusely before ladling the contents over my rice. This wasn't food I knew how to eat with chopsticks, and with no Zarojo watching, I felt confident enough to begin eating with my hands, scooping enough wet rice and thick, white fish meat onto my fingers before placing them in my mouth. There was a smoky sourness to the food, with a hint of garlic, red onion, and ginger. It was almost Jinsein, and I wondered if our host was accommodating our particular tastes.

After a moment of awkward silence, Rai pulled a wooden box closer to the table to sit on and turned to his own meal. To my amazement, he followed suit and picked at the rice with his fingers, too. After years of servants and giant tables with more food than we knew what to do with, it was strange to be sharing such a simple meal elbow-to-elbow. Without the trappings, without the ceremonies, we were just people. It was suddenly difficult even for me to believe the fate of an entire nation rested on our shoulders.

Night came, followed closely by mosquitoes. The innkeeper lit lanterns and scented candles to drive the insects away. I took a deep breath and turned to Rai, only to see him rise. "We should sleep soon if we are to be up before dawn."

Namra nodded. "I'll get our things ready. Dragonlord Rayyel—will you and the queen be sharing quarters?"

I felt the blood pound against my ears and found myself unable to answer. If he said yes...

I had wanted this. I had wanted this for so very long.

Six years, Rai. Six. In that length of time, a young dog becomes old, a sprout becomes a sapling, a baby becomes a child, a girl becomes a woman...

I swallowed my misgivings and that memory from the Ruby Grove, when

Khine asked what I would be if I could be anything in the world. Freedom was…a luxury I couldn't afford.

"I think," Rai said, breaking my thoughts, "that we are not yet ready for such an arrangement." The discomfort was plain on his face. Despite myself, I felt a wave of relief, followed closely by guilt.

"Then you may have my room, Beloved Queen," Namra said with a bow. "I will not be sleeping until much later, anyway, and I think the common room will suit me just fine. Is this suitable?"

"It is suitable," I found myself automatically replying. I got up. Namra reached forward to support me. I didn't need the help, but it was difficult not to like her now. I had been hasty in my previous assessment of her. Rai stayed in the garden, mumbling about needing to speak with our host.

The room was extremely small, no bigger than the bed, but I had grown accustomed to such arrangements and sat cross-legged on the rice mat without fuss. "I apologize for my behaviour in Anzhao," I said, looking straight into Namra's face. "My separation from my husband wasn't easy for me. Seeing him again after so many years was…difficult. I would've lashed out at anyone."

"Beloved Queen, there is nothing to forgive. The circumstances were not ideal. You were tired, and we had your back to the wall. A part of me knew it was not the best plan—I didn't expect less from Yeshin's daughter."

"I must be the worst queen Jin-Sayeng has ever seen."

I heard her take a deep breath, the sign of someone who knew how to hold back criticism. "If it's any consolation," she said at last. "It's not like there's anyone else to compare you with."

"There is that," I mumbled. "Thank you, Namra."

She bowed once before she left.

The one good thing about my exhaustion, at least—it was easy enough to push away my desire to get up and return to Khine and his mother. I pressed my head on the pillow, fingering the cotton seeds inside the fabric before falling asleep to the hooting of an owl outside. Sometime during the night, I woke momentarily to the sound of my husband entering his bed from the other side of the wall. The floor creaked with his every step. Perhaps if he had come to me, proving the words he had uttered back in Anzhao when he had kissed me and told me he loved me before expressing his distaste—all nearly within the same breath—it would have changed everything. I could still, at least, convince myself it would. I might have allowed him back into my life, all uncertainties be damned. It would offer me a semblance of progress, that I hadn't come all the way out here for nothing after all. If I had spent the last five years with my eyes closed, well, couldn't I just simply shut them again?

It would keep my son safe, for one thing.

But he didn't. The memories were real, but they must have been nothing more than the outburst of a man who had dammed his emotions his whole life. I wouldn't be surprised if he found his actions shameful and would never speak of them again. That same old unease that had marked our marriage returned. What were we, really? What was I to him, what part did I play in his life? Briefly, I considered going to him instead. I could use what he claimed he still felt about me to my advantage. If my memories of our time together were correct, Rai was still a man, and one not quite dead yet. He would respond. If one kiss could open up possibilities, more might change his mind. But the thought of seducing a man I had chased an entire sea and half a coastline for felt like a step too far. I had done all this work; couldn't he do the rest? I was one door away. One door, to close the gap.

There is nothing worse than grating silence where love ought to be.

Do you see your weakness now, Talyien? I heard my father ask. *How you hold a sword, and yet refuse to drive the blade?*

I slept again, and dreamed I was back in the outskirts of Anzhao, in a quiet shed with Khine's arms wrapped around me. Outside, the rain drummed a symphony that drowned the world, strong enough to wash the bitterness and regret away. Silly dreams, ridiculous dreams, the sort that had no place in my life. I forced myself to forget them as soon as I woke up.

CHAPTER ELEVEN

THE HOLY BLUFFS

ᶦᶩᶠᶦᶜ

The sun rose behind a drizzle of rain as we broke our fast with toasted rice coffee, dried fish, sticky rice, and more conversation about the *agan* and the effigies. Namra looked eager to have someone to talk to other than Rayyel. Given that she had just spent the last three years with him, I couldn't really blame her. I wondered if it was truly devotion to their shared god or penance for some unimaginable crime that drove her to serve him. A bit of both, probably. Afterwards, she left to see if she could borrow oiled cloaks from the villagers, which gave me time alone with Rai in the covered deck. A moment with my husband, watching raindrops dripping along the shingled roof before they plopped to the ground, where they gathered into furrows in the soil…

I sipped at the scalding coffee before glancing over the rim to stare at Rai. I knew that I had to start with him somehow. He was both a threat, and a solution. I went through the options as I blew on the coffee to cool it down. I could kill him—

And yet you haven't.

—but it was as good as declaring war against the rest of Jin-Sayeng, because to explain *why* would be to announce my son's supposed illegitimacy anyway.

I could let him do whatever he wanted while I made my way to An Mozhi, to that ship. I could accept Kaggawa's help, which of course wouldn't come free. Nothing did. And then I still had two choices: I could accept his terms, or pretend to accept his terms. My father would've done the latter.

Your father wouldn't have sunk low enough to have no choice but to be at the mercy of people who used to work for the Ikessars.

And then there was that last option: I could give our marriage a chance.

Rai had made a good enough argument, after all. If my son was also his, and if he could prevent the rumours from escalating with facts—and if we didn't get deposed by the council for the way we would choose to present those facts— then maybe we could rule together at last. But that was more *if*s than I was comfortable with. It felt like wildly swinging into the void, hoping to catch my enemies unaware. I'd been in enough fights to know they don't work like that.

I heard him clear his throat, and realized I had been blowing at my coffee long enough to make it tepid. I swallowed half of it in one gulp before returning the bowl to the table. "How…did you sleep?" I asked, before chiding myself. *With my eyes closed,* is what he would probably say.

I was wrong about that. He merely grunted in response.

"The air here smells wonderful, at least."

"We're by the sea."

"Yes."

"The salt—"

"I know."

He stared at his food, and I stared at mine. I wondered which of us was worse at small talk. It would be a close contest between a man raised by monks and a woman raised by dogs. Eventually, I couldn't get past the awkward silence and excused myself to take a walk. Another person would've commented on the weather, at least, or asked me if I was feeling well; Rai just grunted again.

My body, surprisingly enough, felt better than yesterday. Apart from my sore shoulder, my legs were starting to move with ease—a sharp contrast with my frayed mind. I went through the gate and turned at the first alley. There, I stopped to stare out at the sea. The waves were unusually rough that morning, crashing against the rocks into a spatter of mist and sea foam. It reflected the state of my nerves, of what the last few hours had reduced me to. Without realizing it, I began to make my way back south to the bridge. I hadn't even gotten that far when I saw Mei walking towards me.

I called to her. She turned. Her clothes were soaked, as if she had been walking under the rain for some time. "Have you seen Khine?" she asked.

"He didn't spend the night at home?"

Mei shook her head. "I was hoping you knew where he would be. His sisters don't. I'm worried about him." Shaking, she reached out from under her sleeves to grab hold of my hand. Her fingers were deathly cold. "He seems to think highly of you. Please, if you see him, tell him—tell him it's not too late to start over. A chipped sword...still has an edge."

"I will."

"Because he thinks that he's done for—that he's used up everything he could have ever been and that I and his sisters and his brother are paying for his mistakes. But perfection is only for the gods. We have to keep going even if all we have left are pieces of what we thought we were." She looked like she was going to start crying.

I almost didn't want to talk about what I had learned last evening. But I had to—there wasn't much time left. I led her to the alley under the shelter of the overlapping rooftops and waited for her to calm down before telling her everything. Of the mages in the temple and how they had been using the priests as a front to get the villagers' blood, how the featherstone mines now housed an army's worth of things that would use the blood to draw power from them.

"Warn the villagers. If they begin acting strangely, it's because the effigy with their blood is being used, and until it is destroyed, the link to them remains. Try to keep them safe until then—they haven't gone mad, it's all the mages' doing. We're heading up to the temple now, where I intend to get to the bottom of this."

She took this news better than yesterday's—in fact, she became almost calm. When you've made it your life's goal to pass minute judgments on people and their character, you start to recognize that look of resolve and strength. Mei Lamang was someone who knew how to crawl through life, someone who had weathered enough pain for several lifetimes.

I heard Namra calling for me from the other end of the street. I turned back to Mei and pressed both of her hands together. I kissed them. "You have nothing to worry about," I said. "Your son is a good man."

"You told me that already."

"And I don't just say these things. I have a son, too. He's only eight, but I understand your fears. I am so far away from him—I don't even know if I'll

ever see him again. But if he can grow up half as compassionate as your son..."
I trailed off, hearing my own words. *Compassionate?* Compassion was for the
unencumbered. My son was both Ikessar and Orenar, a seed of two warring
clans. He needed to be strong to survive—to be unyielding, ruthless. Because if
I had proven anything, it was that the smallest crack could bring a whole building down.

"The man on the street yesterday," Mei said, her voice raspy. "He's your
husband?"

I nodded.

"I see."

"What—what do you see?"

She reached up to touch my face and gave me the ghost of a smile, one that
made it easy enough for me to admit how much I envied Khine for his mother.
"My son is a restless soul," she said. "And he thinks he is somehow equipped
to deal with the injustices of this world. Or maybe he's already learned that
he isn't, and that is why he is so angry. When he is angry, he will do reckless
things. I had hoped love and marriage would calm him down."

"My experience has been the complete opposite."

"Perhaps. But that is why I was so sad when I heard about Jia. My son needs
an anchor, or else he'll let the sea wash him away." She squeezed my hand. "Will
you stop him, if you can?"

I should have said no. Instead, I nodded. The light in the woman's eyes
drowned out all my doubts.

I rejoined Rai and Namra by the gate. She had found cloaks and wide-
brimmed hats made of dried reeds, which did a decent job of keeping the rain
off us. Not that it helped much in my case; my clothes were already damp from
my walk. We made our way past the streets to the lake, and the narrow, rocky
trail that wound around it. The lake looked more grey than blue through the
torrent of raindrops—a grey, broken mirror with a thousand cracks.

We continued up until the lake was a dot below and the midsummer air
became thick fog, an impenetrable blanket. I could barely see Rai ahead of me.
The sound of rainfall was soothing, at least... the trickling of countless small
streams was a welcome distraction from my roiling thoughts.

My luck ran out with the first crack of lightning in the sky.

"Well," Namra said, looking up. "That was unexpected."

"Midsummer rain," Rai replied. "Lightning is expected."

"Could've told us that," I whispered, wondering how they kept each other company in the last three years with such dull conversation. The sky began to rumble. "We should stop while there's still cover."

Rai made a noncommittal sound that indicated he was comfortable either way, but Namra agreed. We found a small alcove under an array of tree roots and boulders. I sat with my back to the soft soil and buried my face in my lap. I heard movement and saw Rai settle next to me.

I gazed at him from the corner of my eye. He had grown thinner than when we shared our lives together. Life on the road was a stark contrast with the one in the palace, where entire days revolved around shuffling in and out of meetings. For perhaps the first time in my life, I understood that I didn't know much about him at all. I knew about his interests, but not what he thought of the world. I knew about his life, but not his hopes for the future. I had incorrectly assumed it was all the same as mine. It was an odd conclusion to come to about the man I claimed to love.

"You understand why I have to do this," he said in a low voice.

I blinked. I didn't realize he had noticed me looking at him. "I don't, Rai," I murmured. "You know I really don't. Everything you do confuses me."

"I am not truly an Ikessar."

His words caught me off guard. "They changed your name in the books," I said, wondering what he was getting at.

"A name means nothing," he replied. "Names do not change the truth of things. They can call me an Ikessar as much as they want, but it doesn't change that I spent my whole life proving it. Why me, when they had so many others to choose from? The father I never met was married to another woman, and my mother never loved him. Sometimes I think she had me just so she could maintain her power." He lowered his eyes, as if ashamed of his outburst.

I simply stared back, unsure if the man I was listening to was the same man I had married all those years ago. I thought they had raised him the same way they raised me—irrevocably the future Dragonlord, without a shred of doubt. *You* will *rule the land*, my father would say, with certainty. What did his mother tell Rai? That he could have Jin-Sayeng if he didn't roll over for the wolves?

"You can understand why I do not want it done a second time," he said in a lower voice. "A lie on top of an untruth. Is this the basis for which you'd want us to rule?"

I digested his words while I held back the familiar anger. I didn't know what to tell him. It is difficult for someone who had grown up with so much to consider it from the perspective of another who had to earn the very same things I took for granted. It felt like listening to a new language, or viewing the world upside down. "And so you refused to be crowned," I managed.

"My uncle Rysaran, the last true Ikessar, thought he needed a dragon in order to rule. Calling himself a Dragonlord when he had no dragon was something that went against his beliefs. He disappeared before they could crown him, too. When I found out about...about all of that...I needed to do something. I didn't want to be an imposter setting another imposter forward as heir. Imagine how my clan would react. I left you to be crowned as queen because I didn't want to fracture the land."

"Your proposal with Zheshan would have accomplished the same thing. What would splitting Jin-Sayeng have done?"

"My clan's concerns would have been divided. The boy remains heir to Oren-yaro and would be safe, for a time."

My throat tightened. No—I understood nothing at all.

"If..." I found myself saying. "If Thanh isn't yours, couldn't you just let us be? I'll...I'll step down." Agos's words came back to me. *Take Thanh and just run...*

"Escape the Oren-yaro? Or his guardians? Neither of us has enough people we can trust for that. The boy will die by my hand, Talyien—peacefully. Need I remind you how brutal my mother was to your father's supporters? I am afraid that she will consider the boy an appropriate tool for the vengeance she couldn't exact." There was hardly a flicker on the expression of the stone wall that was my husband. I thought a wolf of Oren-yaro was unyielding; I had no idea how deep the Ikessars' own tenets ran. I thought all they did was preach about the things the rest of us were doing wrong. I had always known Rai was stubborn, but not to what extent. That he had asked a *priestess* for assistance, among all the people he could've turned to, spoke volumes.

A thought occurred to me. "What did you do for the two years before Namra joined you?"

"A vow of silence," he murmured.

"Akaterru be damned. You're a *priest* now?" It shouldn't have come as a surprise.

"As was my mother, and Rysaran before me."

"It was Rysaran's selfish decision to stick to his ideals that caused the War of the Wolves in the first place. Self-made ideals—I understand how important these are for everyone who follows the texts of Kibouri, but they're not practical. These ideals made him abandon his duties, just as . . . just as they made you abandon yours." I realized how badly I wanted to ask him about Chiha. But it was not the sort of question I could think about without getting irrationally angry, and I chose to leave it at that.

"I am not Oren-yaro, Tali. But you are. I knew you would try to hold things together, that you would be queen to the best of your abilities. I wasn't wrong."

No one else but Rayyel could irritate while offering praise, all in one breath. I turned away in time to see a figure emerge from the fog. No hat for this one, not even a cloak—his clothes were soaking wet. I lifted my head from my knees when I recognized Khine.

"Doctor," Namra greeted.

"I'm not, really," Khine mumbled, dropping into the shelter of the alcove without waiting for an invitation. He looked at me, and then at Rai. "I'd like to go up to the temple with you."

"Go back to your mother," I said. "I'll speak with Belfang on your behalf. I—"

"I wasn't asking for permission." He sat on a rock, a good distance from the rest of us. "No sign of your guards?"

"None. I'm sure they're fine—they're probably stuck under some tree or rock like we are." I wasn't sure when I'd become a nervous chatterer.

He nodded, swallowed, and gestured towards us. "And you're not killing each other."

"For now," I said. I smiled at Rayyel. He didn't reciprocate.

"That's progress." Khine began coughing.

"You're drenched. Was it too hard to find proper clothes?"

"Would've taken too long. I wanted to catch up to you."

"And where did you spend the night, anyway?"

"If I had known all you were going to do was pester me..."

"You *knew* I was going to pester you. You came anyway."

"You allow him to speak with you thus?" Rai broke in, in Jinan.

"He can understand that, you know," I said.

Rai looked embarrassed for a moment, but he recovered swiftly. "I believe that as queen, you should know to remind people not to overstep their bounds."

"Akaterru, when did you morph into both Magister Arro and Yeshin? Fine—Lamang, this queen wishes to remind you that you are not allowed to speak with me thus. Happy, Lord Rayyel?"

Rai frowned.

The thunder stopped, the rain ceased, and we returned to the trail. My heart was racing again, and I was trying very hard not to look at Khine. I tried not to compare how he was nearly of Rai's height but with thicker limbs and broader shoulders, or how he shuffled through the drizzle like a wet dog, unlike Rai who strode forward as if he was on some death march—eyes hard, face expressionless. Two men couldn't have been more different.

We reached the base of a cliff. The trail split, winding around both sides. Perched above was the temple—a grey, moss-covered building that shot straight into the sky. It had two narrow towers on each end, marked by stained-glass windows on every floor. Rainwater from the faded yellow roof dripped into a pond, which overflowed and spilled over the rocks like a small waterfall.

The trails both led up a flight of steps carved right into the mountain before joining once more in front of the gates. There were two priests waiting for us at the top of the shared landing.

"Beloved Queen," they said in unison. They bowed. Before I could reply, they turned and tugged at the iron rings of the enormous wooden gates.

We entered a vast courtyard, past a grove of fruit trees, most of which were flowering at that time of the year. Clumps of moss grew from the cracks in the stone footpath—some had flowers on them, too, red and purple capsules shining with dew. One of the priests led us up the path while the other closed the gates behind us. Another man waited for us between the arches that marked the entrance to the temple. He was clad in regular clothes, not priest robes. He bowed when we approached, so low it looked like he would tip over.

"Let me guess," I said, before he could speak. "You're the missing mayor."

He blinked. "Missing? I don't—"

"Feng, isn't it? Your daughter was most insistent that you were on a trip. Of course, since she couldn't be bothered to lie properly, we all thought you'd be here. We were right." I patted his shoulder. "That's all right. I understand the need for secrecy. Maybe you just wanted a vacation, maybe you've got a lover up here…"

He turned red. "It's nothing of that sort."

"I don't know what it is you've heard about me, but believe me, I don't take heads off for no reason. Speak truthfully and you've got nothing to fear." I dropped my hand to my sword and cocked my head at him with what I hoped was an innocent-looking expression. "Would you happen to know where my guards are? They came up here yesterday. They haven't returned since and we didn't see them on the road."

"They were—"

"Ah hah!" I exclaimed. "So they *were* here."

"We were told you don't accept most visitors," Rai broke in.

"We—we didn't accept them," Feng stammered. "We caught them spying. The priests brought them in."

"Spying?" I pretended to look surprised. "They came here to speak to you on my behalf. What would they be spying on? Is there something you're hiding?"

"Such a violation of Holy Shimesu's sacred grounds…"

"Enough of this," Rai said. "You know the queen. Do you know me?"

"Lord Rayyel, of course," Feng replied, turning to him. "Forgive me if—"

"*Lord?* Not Dragonlord? Not even *Prince?*" I wondered out loud. "Whoever told him about us doesn't acknowledge Rayyel's position."

"You don't, either," Khine whispered behind me.

"That's not the point," I hissed back.

"Considering that Lord Rayyel was never officially crowned…" Feng stammered.

"Yes, yes, we know all about *that*," I said. I walked past him and started up the steps.

Feng turned around. "What are you doing?"

"Isn't it obvious? *You're* not in charge. And the fact that you're here means it's not the priests, either. I promised I'd look into this and I will."

"Could it be Qun?" Khine asked.

"Qun's soldiers were still near the mines," Rai answered.

"That's because they were looking for *you*," Khine replied.

"I wasn't aware I was the object of their investigation."

"You just slipped by them without even realizing—oh. I think I get it, now."

"Get what?"

"Nothing."

I held my hand out to silence them both as we strode into the antechamber. Even though we were indoors now, the damp smell of moss and clay pervaded the air, strong enough that I could feel it on my skin. We walked past small alcoves lit with white candles and reached a large, circular hall, where sunlight streamed from three windows on the domed ceiling. The multiple light sources made our shadows jump with every motion.

Feng's sandals clicked on the floor as he caught up with us. "Queen Talyien, I must insist that you not go any further. Lord Rayyel has it right. The priests do prefer not to entertain visitors, but they made an exception in your case and it would be best if we respected the sanctity of these halls."

"Sanctity," I said dryly, turning to face him. "Tell me, Mayor Feng, what sanctity is there in allowing your villagers to be drained of blood by power-hungry mages?"

He looked back in shock. "The blood—it's to help find a cure for the feather-stone ailments. Surely one of the villagers would've told you."

"Notice he didn't deny the power-hungry mage part," Khine said.

"You're right." I stepped towards him. "You're housing mages here. No sense denying it, Feng—Belfang has already admitted as much. Also, another interesting thing... Lord Rayyel found the effigies you've been keeping in the mines. Maybe you can explain that, too, before we write a strongly worded note to your Esteemed Emperor in Kyan Jang. Your involvement won't be overlooked."

"What?" Feng stammered. "I didn't know—I had nothing to do with what you're saying."

"He didn't know," Khine droned. "So what *do* you know?"

"I told you—the cure..." The skin on his cheeks jiggled in his confusion.

"These effigies, these dummies, are full of the villagers' blood," I said, taking one step towards him. He backed away. "Blood that offers a connection to the *agan*, which allows a mage to control these things using the villagers as a source of energy. How do you think the villagers are going to react when they find out you've sold their souls in exchange for—what? What did they give you, Feng? Money to build that nice house? Promises of safety, maybe a nice cushy position away from this hellhole? Do you know how bad this is going to look if the empire finds out? Blood magic is outlawed."

I heard applause—each clap loud and crisp as it bounced through the hollow halls.

"Excellent, my queen," a voice called out. "Excellent. I didn't expect less from you."

The blood left my face. The voice was familiar—but not the sort of familiar that came with meeting a long-lost friend or even a friendly acquaintance. It was a sound that sent a chill through my bones, with a timbre that came from the depths of hell.

A figure appeared from the end of the hall. Distorted and misshapen, it ambled slowly towards us before stopping underneath a shaft of sunlight. It turned to me and grinned.

"Yuebek," I said. I had not intended to speak it out as loudly as I did. I was hoping the word alone would break the dream and I would wake up panting back in an inn or the side of the road somewhere. But I could hear Khine's shallow breathing behind me as he swore under his breath, which told me that he was seeing exactly what I was. I realized why Qun's soldiers had stopped chasing us the moment we reached Phurywa and why he hadn't killed me back in Anzhao. What was in front of me was real—somehow, despite my insistence, my worst fears had come true. Yuebek was alive, and I had walked into one of his traps yet again.

The grin on the figure's face widened. "So," he said. "You *do* care."

"Fuck you," I said, because that voice, his voice, was proof enough this *wasn't* a dream. This wasn't a dream. I was staring at the bastard I was sure I had killed, the bastard whose body had swallowed the tip of my blade, who had squealed like a pig in a slaughterhouse before running straight into a fire that engulfed a whole chamber. Why wasn't he dead? Had they updated the textbook on death, and somewhere along the way someone had failed to inform me?

But it was him. If I couldn't believe my eyes or ears, then maybe I could listen to the terror that crawled up my skin. I could feel the cold sensation slithering past my pores, all the way down to the tips of my fingers. *Of course he isn't dead. Why did you think I chose him for you?*

I didn't know what part of him I should look at. He looked enough like the Yuebek I knew, the mad prince who had attempted to manipulate me over the past few months. It was the eyes—that fixed expression of sheer delight, as if he found *everything* about this situation amusing. I knew no one else who could seem so perpetually out of touch with reality as this man. If you could even call him a *man* anymore. Part of him was covered in burnt skin, all shades of black and flesh and purple. All of these were interspersed with a substance that appeared to be lumps of red clay, stuffed into holes, as if someone had hastily tried to fix him after he had been chewed up by a dog.

The rest of him—which included most of his forehead, the lower portion of his mouth, and the entire right side of his face—looked *clean*, untouched. He didn't look like any of the burn victims I'd encountered before, where you could see the natural transition between scarred and uninjured flesh. Yuebek looked like an unfinished doll, and moved with all the jerky imprecision of one.

It would be pointless to ask how he had survived. He had; that was all that mattered. If Namra had used the *agan* to prevent me from succumbing to the featherstone, what more could a group of mages under control of a prince do? It probably didn't hurt that he was a mage himself, too.

"We have to stop meeting like this," I said with a smile, counting on the calmness of my voice to carry me through the rest of the conversation while I made note of the quickest exits. The walls of the courtyard were very tall— could we climb over them? Could we break down the gates? If he attacked, could I use Feng as a shield?

"Explain this abomination." Rai's voice brought me crashing back to reality. I felt my palms begin to sweat. I had led Rai right into the heart of this mess.

Yuebek began to laugh. "This . . ." he said, shambling closer. From this distance, I noticed that the untainted parts of him were well-groomed—his beard was oiled and trimmed, and despite his horrendous appearance, he was dressed as befitting a prince. He peered at Rai, his eyes growing even wider. "The famous Prince Rayyel!" he exclaimed. "Son of Princess Ryia, the witch that was ever the thorn in Warlord Yeshin's side. How excellent! They told me you had arrived with her, but I didn't want to believe it."

Unaware of his own awkward movements, he jerked himself into a bow. I stepped back, revulsion stirring in the back of my throat. Liquid was oozing out of the holes, along with globs of coagulated blood. *The villagers*...

"You have to forgive me," he said, picking himself up. "I'm not at my best right now. The circumstances of our last...unfortunate meeting..." He casually dabbed at the liquid with a handkerchief, as if he were wiping away mere dots of sweat. "I've been in recuperation the past few months. Hiding out here, ahh—such glorious mountain air is good for the lungs. Especially ones as badly damaged as mine."

"Good for you," I said. I was still wondering if I should attack him or run. He would have other traps laid out for me.

"*Good?*" Yuebek replied. He took another step closer, and I could smell him now—a curious mixture of rotting flesh and moldy earth. My stomach curdled; I struggled to keep my senses. "I wonder if you think flattery will get you somewhere. I know how I look. Don't worry—my mages do good work and they're just getting started. You looked surprised. *My* mages—of course they're mine. They've been mine for years. Consider this my summer home."

"Well—" I struggled for anything coherent I could say. "It's lovely. I'm sure the breeze is refreshing."

"I don't understand what's happening," Rai broke in.

"Right," I said. "Lord Rayyel, meet Prince Yuebek, Fifth Son of the Esteemed Emperor Yunan. I believe you are acquainted with the name, if not the man."

Rai looked outraged. "This isn't a prince," he said. "This is an abomination."

"I was going to get to that. We had, ah...what was it you said? An *unfortunate* meeting the last time?"

Yuebek nodded eagerly, oblivious to our insults. "The queen does know how to reject a man."

"My lord husband is aware of your offer to me. We have also discussed how your involvement has resulted in the current state of affairs. So you can understand why neither of us looks particularly thrilled." If I didn't have years of training in diplomacy, I would've found it very hard to talk to him without spitting in his face.

"I see," Yuebek said. "Did you tell him everything?"

"What does he mean?" Rayyel asked.

Yuebek turned to Rai. "I did ask the queen to set you aside and marry me." His holes dripped fluid with every word. I was afraid his eyes would pop out and fall to the floor—I didn't want to step on them while he was speaking. "Did she tell you why?"

"An army of twenty thousand," I said. "I told you that's not quite enough to sway me. My husband and I have obligations to fulfill."

"So you didn't tell him," Yuebek said. Evidently, he found this hilarious, because he started laughing so hard I thought he was going to hack out a lung. Considering the way his body seemed to be assembled, it didn't look impossible. He finally caught himself and grabbed for Rai's shoulder.

Rai knocked his hand away before it could touch him. "You've got the nerve..." Rai began.

The grin fell from Yuebek's face. "No. No, *Lord* Rayyel, though I shouldn't even call you that, should I? You—a bastard." He spat. "In this empire, we throw infants like you in the rivers. Or raise them as kennel boys and the only royal blood they'll ever get to fuck is if they decide to do it with one of the hounds. Warlord Yeshin knew that. He never wanted her to marry you for that reason. Oh, he went through the whole pretence of the pact and your betrothal to buy himself some time, but did you really think Yeshin would've allowed your grubby hands on his precious daughter if he'd been around? He hated your mother. Hated her so much he would've strangled her with his own hands if he had ever been given the opportunity." He lifted his finger and jabbed Rai in the chest so hard I expected the appendage to fall off. "I was promised to her *first*, bastard."

Rai's face tightened. "Explain this." He wasn't talking to Yuebek.

I wanted to tell him we didn't have time for this. But that was the sort of thing that wouldn't work with Rayyel. "He's convinced my father had betrothed his unborn daughter—if she should be a daughter—to him during the War of the Wolves. My father wanted *his* mother's help to get rid of yours. He says that Warlord Yeshin made this elaborate plan to remove you from the picture before our wedding so that I would marry him instead. But that somehow, it didn't work, and so instead..." I lifted my eyes to meet my husband's. "He infiltrated our plans to meet up in Anzhao City and orchestrated this farce that resulted in my men betraying me. In me being left all alone in this country so that he could swoop in and save me. He wanted me to be grateful for it, too."

"Him," Rai said evenly. "A Zarojo." Even after hearing all of this, he remained calm.

"A Zarojo," Yuebek repeated, "with royal blood. As detestable as I'm sure Warlord Yeshin found it—I am not blind to what he thought of the empire in those times—it was still *vastly* preferable to having his daughter given to a penniless bastard. I am the Esteemed Emperor Yunan's *trueborn* son, with the blood of a long line of emperors running through me. You, on the other hand...didn't your father peg your mother in the back of the stables during the war?"

Rai's hand flew to his sword. I grabbed his arm. "Don't," I whispered. "He's a mage."

"He looks like he's about to fall apart," Rai said in a low voice.

"The queen is right, my lord," Namra spoke up. "I can detect an enormous connection to the *agan* within him. It would be wise to avoid violence."

Rai gritted his teeth. "Is this true, that this was Warlord Yeshin's desire?"

"It's not," I said.

"I have proof." Yuebek grinned.

"Choke on your proof. My father would've never lied to me."

"*Never?* Such words, my lovely queen...and yet—Yeshin was never known for his *honesty*, was he?" He turned to Rai. "Step aside. Let me marry the queen and you can walk out of here alive. That's all I want. It's all I ever wanted. You are so unimportant that even your death would be more of an inconvenience than anything else."

"This is insanity," Rai whispered. "To think that we would just let Jin-Sayeng fall under Zarojo rule after we have narrowly avoided it for *centuries*..."

"Zarojo rule is inevitable," Yuebek said. He drew away from us and began to glide back to the middle of the hall. "The way you both ran it to the ground, Jin-Sayeng is teetering on the edge of a war bloodier than what your mother—" He pointed at Rai before glancing back at me. "—and *your* father could have ever conceived. Queen Talyien, your people love *wolves*. Do you still have wolves in Jin-Sayeng? Didn't your dragons pick them all out centuries ago?"

"You're starting to bore me," I said.

He giggled. "*We* have wolves. You know what they do, don't you? They go after the weakest of the herd." He curled his fingers and gnashed his teeth. "If the herd is Jin-Sayeng, who is the weak, the blind, and the cripple? Could it be any of your warlords, sitting in their castles and keeps while their soldiers sweat and train for the inevitable? Is it Dai alon gar Kaggawa, with his army of sellswords growing stronger by the day? Or could it be these two bedraggled figures before me: this lovesick queen and her bastard king?"

He extended his arms and snapped his fingers. I heard footsteps and saw hooded figures dragging two captives behind them. My heart leaped to my throat as the light revealed their faces.

"Your servants," Yuebek said as his men pushed Agos and Nor to their knees. "Such loyalty. Such devotion. This one, in particular…" He grabbed Agos's chin and stroked it. "Perhaps I was wrong about Rayyel. Wasn't it *this* one's cock that you prefer?"

I threw caution to the wind and lunged at him.

An unseen force smashed into my side, sending me sprawling across the floor. As I struggled to regain my balance, I turned and saw my guards on the ground, their hands clutched around their necks. Something was sliding its way out of their jaws. I realized, with horror, that it was snakes, exactly like in my dreams.

"Don't worry," I heard Yuebek whisper next to my ear, just as his death-stench hit me. "When I put a child in your belly, it won't look like that."

I smashed my elbow backwards. It caught Yuebek in the chest. I felt something begin to swallow my arm, which made me jump to the side in shock. There was a gaping hole on Yuebek's body where I had hit him.

He looked down at it and smiled. "Still a work in progress," he said. "In time, I will be whole again."

"What *are* you?" I gasped.

"The sweetest dream," he crooned. "Or your worst nightmare. *It's up to you.*"

"Fuck you."

"So you've said. While that honestly sounds quite delightful, I don't think you understand your position here, my queen," Yuebek said. "Or your lack thereof, as it were. I was only trying to show you my courtesies. Any future husband ought to, in my opinion. But you don't have a choice. Your father gave you to me—and the Oren-yaro know it. Haven't you wondered why no one has come for you all this time?"

I tried to strike at him with my sword, but for a misshapen lump, he seemed to move quickly when he wanted to. I missed him by a hair's breadth. He laughed and clapped his hands, and the ground began to shake. The snakes wriggled out of my guards' bodies completely; as soon as they were free, Agos and Nor turned white and crumbled into dust.

The snakes flopped once before they stood up and grew limbs.

"Blood magic is outlawed," Yuebek said, echoing my words as I watched the snake-men take form. "For a reason. My father would rather put a lid on something he doesn't understand. But I've spent my life studying it, *living* it."

"Your father will *never* let you have your army if he finds out," I gasped.

Yuebek snorted. "He may not let me have all of it, but I have enough. And you know about my *reserves*. Let me show you what they can do." He drew his hands back. The snake-men began to walk towards me.

I readied my sword and went for the closest one. Its flesh was surprisingly soft. My blade cleaved through it like butter, sending a spray of black liquid. The body fell to the ground, twitching.

"Sorry," I said. "I'm not impressed."

The two split halves got up and slid back in place. Only a thin line remained where my sword had struck it.

"How about now?" Yuebek asked with his usual child-like eagerness.

I didn't have time to respond. The snake-men hissed and attacked me all at once.

CHAPTER TWELVE

FOLLY OF A FIFTH SON

ㅜ工⑪

You would think I should've known better. Should've been more careful, should've anticipated what a man like Prince Yuebek was capable of. But I had thought he was dead. I *wanted* him to be dead.

Before our desperate flight from Anzhao City, I had spent some time reading up as much as I could on Yuebek. It was difficult, given my limited knowledge of the Zirano script and the fact that I didn't want my guards realizing how worried I was about the whole thing. It took a few weeks of harassing shady book dealers outside of Shang Azi and visiting public archives near the governor's palace, but I was able to gather some knowledge of his past. Enough knowledge. Enough to worry me.

Yuebek grew up in the capital in Kyan Jang and was the only living son of Emperor Yunan's Fourth Consort. He was the younger son until his ninth year, during which it was said he strangled his elder brother to death during a schoolyard fight before setting him on fire.

An inquest deemed it an accident. An unfortunate thing, but a thing boys sometimes did. It wasn't as if Yuebek's brother was a saint. The boy was cruel to him, a bully who would smear his face into the dust and call him names. There was also the possibility of sexual abuse. But the most important part of the whole incident, aside from Yuebek assuming the position of *Fifth* Son from there on out, was that Yuebek's skill in the *agan* surfaced. He was sent to study with mages at a nondescript location before he turned ten.

His connection to the *agan*, it was said, came from his mother's line, not the emperor's. A connection to the *agan* was deemed a useful skill when put in service of the empire, but it frightened them to see it within the nobility. It implied a potential to tip a power struggle their way, and it was commonly suggested (though not within polite company) that such children ought to be silently whisked away to be raised by mages without knowledge of their status.

The imperial court, of course, kept silent about the whole affair, although questions were raised. How did Yuebek make it to his ninth year without anyone noticing anything about the boy? The Fourth Consort's servants were taken, grilled—some, it's said, under torture. The empress was livid; attempts were made on Yuebek's life over the years. Somehow, he survived them all, and returned to Kyan Jang as a young man, fully intending to take his place in court.

There was a massive outcry. The empress and her sons wanted him gone, but the Esteemed Emperor refused to banish him without reason. And Yuebek was—for all his eccentricities—a devoted enough son. That was when they arranged for his marriage to Zhu Ong. It wasn't exactly *banishment*, but it wasn't an ideal marriage even to someone who didn't know much about Zarojo bloodlines. The Ong family was at least five steps away from the imperial dynasty. Bottom-feeders, as far as everyone was concerned.

That the Fourth Consort even *agreed* was the greatest mystery. Sure, there was the gift army, Yuebek's Boon, but in such a vast empire, they were drops of water in a rolling sea. Yet she made no comment and even praised the Esteemed Emperor's foresight for such a marriage—at least, according to the texts I read. She had been more vocal in the past when her elder son was alive.

Sometime after Yuebek had first gone to live with the mages, the War of the Wolves happened.

I could deny my father's involvement with Yuebek when I thought the man was nothing but ashes in the governor's building in Anzhao. No one else had heard him say it, or read with their own eyes the letter penned by my father's hand. The knowledge had gnawed my insides, but I was convinced I could make it mean nothing in time. That if I could unite my kingdom, that would also somehow undo my father's treachery.

I suddenly remembered his ghost laughing over my marriage to Rayyel back in Yuebek's dungeons. "You fell in love with the brat," the hallucination had accused me.

Wasn't I supposed to, Father?

A snake-man bore down, hot breath on my ear as it gave a smile reminiscent of Yuebek's. I saw my father's decision in its eyes, saw the power that tempted him to hand me over to a man like that. And I never proved him wrong, did I? I couldn't prove that Yeshin's daughter was enough. I roared as I parried the snake-man's attack, my blade nicking an arm. With every passing moment, their limbs seemed more solid, actual muscle and bone in place of clay. Their attacks gained in speed. I realized that I was still alive because they weren't trying to kill me—Yuebek was just trying to wear me down. He was laughing like a little boy who had just discovered a new plaything.

I missed a step. A fist smashed into my cheek. I dropped to the ground and tried to get up. Rai was charging Yuebek. Namra was—doing something, creating a spell, I didn't know. Khine was nowhere in sight.

I threw an arm up and stabbed the nearest snake-man in the throat. It contorted immediately, black blood gushing out of the wound. I rolled to the side before I got drenched, grabbed the limp arm, and threw its body into the path of the next one. It didn't recover. Yuebek was now preoccupied with defending himself against Rai.

I tore into the second snake-man with renewed vigour. With Yuebek distracted, its movements had become imprecise. I slid my sword into its belly and yanked it up, right through its rib cage. The bone parted. Torrents of black liquid oozed through the gap, running down the blade and onto my hands. I kicked the body away and turned, breathing through my mouth, my fingers tingling.

Shadows emerged from every corner of the hall. Hooded figures. Yuebek's mages.

A strangled cry pierced the air. I craned my head in time to see Rai's sword explode into pieces just as Yuebek stabbed him in the gut with a dagger. I realized the cry came from my own throat.

The chandelier near the antechamber suddenly crashed right on top of at least two mages. Someone hurled an oil lantern into it from the shadows. There was an explosion, and the curtains and tapestries caught on fire.

"To your left, Tali," Khine called out. There was another lantern in his hand. He walked up to Yuebek before throwing the lantern straight at him. As Yuebek tried to dance away from the flames, Khine lifted Rai onto his shoulders. "I've got him!" he screamed. "Clear the way!"

Smoke was engulfing the room. I tore into a mage who tried to block my path, my blade sinking into his thigh and then his shoulder, as if he were nothing but a hunk of meat strung up in a butcher's shop. The man stood no chance. I pushed the convulsing body to the side just as another dashed up to meet me. I dodged, slashed again, gutting him. His innards decorated the garden walkway, spilled across the flagstone like a sick dog's breakfast.

Somehow, I made it to the far side of the courtyard. Two figures were tied to posts in the middle of the square, their bodies bleeding from a dozen lashes.

"My queen," Agos gasped.

I hesitated. I had just seen him explode minutes ago. But there were probably more mages behind me and I didn't have time to think things through. I struck his bonds with my sword. He fell forward into my arms. He was alive—warm, breathing, and reeking of sweat. He scrambled to gain his footing. "I saw him make dummies of us," he managed to whisper. "That man—he should be buried alive. What's happening back there?"

My relief at learning they weren't dead after all was overtaken by the urgency of the situation. "No time to explain," I said. I turned to set Nor free. She looked disoriented as I helped her to her feet.

"Beloved Queen—it is as you said," Nor whispered. "That man believes he is doing this according to your father's will. He says there are others back home who support this claim. Prince Thanh is in danger—we have to return to Oren-yaro at once."

I had never wanted to agree with her as fervently as I did that moment. But my next thoughts were drowned out by the sight of Khine dragging Rai up the steps to the square. Blood dripped on the ground with his every step, so much of it that I was afraid he would slip. I didn't know where it was all coming from. How could one man bleed so much?

Yuebek appeared behind them like a ghost, eyes glowing blue. I pushed Nor towards Agos and sprinted back to the archway, raising my sword as I ran. I could feel my heart pounding; I didn't think I was going to reach them in time.

Flames exploded. Yuebek rolled to avoid them, and Namra began to cast another spell. I readied myself to strike at Yuebek. He lifted his hand, which was glowing blue. This time, I was prepared for it—I sidestepped just as his spell reached me. It slammed into a sapling several paces away.

Khine was on him before he could recover, having dropped Rai to clumsily swing at him with a sword. I took advantage of the distraction. My own blade caught Yuebek's arm, just above his elbow. Yuebek grimaced like a man who had just been bitten by a fly. My attack didn't seem to hurt him, even when I could see his skin swallowing the bit of sharp edge.

"Do me a favour," I hissed. "Just *die* already."

Yuebek grinned. "Not before our wedding night. Don't you want to find out what you're missing?"

He turned to meet Khine's next attack. I tugged my sword loose from his flesh and launched myself at his exposed back with renewed vigour. Right before I reached him, the wound on his arm closed itself.

I struck him on the thigh, just as his spell sent Khine toppling back.

Yuebek glanced back at me. "Maybe you need more convincing."

"I'm pretty sure I've already made up my mind," I said.

A blue glow began to seep from the cracks in his body.

"My queen," I heard Namra call out. We were surrounded—mages who had survived the fire in the antechamber and priests clad in Shimesu's robes had caught up to us. One of them had a blade at Namra's throat. I recognized Belfang.

"You're pathetic," I said, directing my gaze at him.

"You're fighting the wrong battle," Belfang replied. There was an edge on his voice.

I rounded on him. "The villagers trusted you for a reason. You grew up in Phurywa—this is your home, the villagers are your family. Gods—do you understand what he's done to them? To your elders?"

"He—" Belfang stammered. He loosened his grasp and pushed Namra away. In the distance, I heard the gates creak open.

Yuebek walked past Khine. "What do you know about me, Queen Talyien?" he asked.

"I know I wouldn't marry you if you were the last man on earth," I replied. "I know I'd rather stab my eyeballs with bamboo skewers. Dull bamboo skewers dipped in vinegar—"

"You do have a gift for imagery."

"—while mountain lions gnaw my feet to the bones."

Yuebek smiled. "You can write poetry when we're back in Oren-yaro. You won't be doing much else when I'm Dragonlord. Your father didn't promise you to me because I was Fifth Son. Truth be told, he thought the position was too low for someone who would be the first queen of Jin-Sayeng, which already tells you what he thought of the paltry offering the Ikessars gave him."

He glanced at Rai's unmoving form. I was too far away to see if he still breathed. "No, Beloved Queen—I was given the task because your father knew that bringing your nation back together required a lot more than just warlords nodding in agreement. You needed a leader who knew how to take care of the little things, who had not only noble blood but the power to make things happen— quite unlike that husband of yours. Someone with a wit as sharp as his and who would prove a better bearer of his legacy than his inept, wayward daughter."

The hair on my arms rose. I could feel cold sweat dotting my forehead, trickling down my cheek. The way Yuebek spoke—I caught a note of my father's own words, the way *he* liked to pattern his speech. He must've been studying my father's writing for a long time. Knowing what he had done so far, I wasn't surprised. But could a person learn so much just by *reading*? And how would he even get his hands on my father's writing? The only copies of his journals that I knew of were in my father's locked study in Oka Shto.

I remembered the ghosts I had seen in his dungeon, my father and my eldest brother both. For the past few months, I had convinced myself that they were illusions conjured by a fevered mind. Now I wasn't so sure. I could feel myself sinking, dread and outrage combining with the ache of the thought that perhaps he was right. Perhaps my father *did* choose him after all. I wasn't worthy. I never had been.

"You know you're not capable," Yuebek said, echoing my thoughts. "If you were, you wouldn't even be here right now. You would've anticipated the moves his enemies made, made your own traps before they knew what was happening." He pointed at Rai. "You would've had *his* head on a spike before those hands ever touched you. No—but I think your father expected that. He wasn't going to leave his legacy in the care of a young, foolish girl. He had fought *too* hard for it."

Somewhere in the back of my mind, I remembered saying the exact same thing.

The truth straddles the line between lies and expectations. Arro told me that once. Arro had told me a lot of things over the years that I, wilful child that I was, had tried to shove away as quickly as they left his lips. What I had once thought were the inane ramblings of an old man suddenly seemed more precious; the world made more sense back when Arro was around. Did *he* know about all of this? Was he trying to shape me into a better ruler, knowing what would happen if he didn't? Mistakes, for a woman in my position, were drops of blood in a sea of sharks.

"You know exactly what I mean," Yuebek continued. "I can see it in your eyes, Beloved Queen. You knew enough about your father, at least. Who else did he trust in court? Why would he leave Jin-Sayeng in the hands of an Ikessar brat and his mother? He told me himself."

"He *told* you," I drawled.

"What can I say, my queen? The man had known of me since my return to the court of Kyan Jang—he had been observing my progress, watching the speed with which I rose in responsibilities in my father's court. He saw what perhaps even my own father didn't—a potential that would be wasted on whatever paltry position my brothers refused. It was then that Warlord Yeshin started corresponding with my mother. Later, I was forced to marry Zhu Ong while *you* were handed over to that bastard. What was that he called it? An unfortunate predicament. I read you his own thoughts on that matter, didn't I?" He laughed. "He visited me in Zorheng before his death. He had heard good things about what I was doing there and wanted to see for himself. He was not disappointed."

"My father never left Oren-yaro."

"Are you sure?"

"He—" There *was* a summer I spent in Lord General Ozo's keep near the rice fields two years before Yeshin died, but I had been led to understand that my father was in Oka Shto that whole time.

"Proof, you say. I have more than plenty. But for now…" Yuebek lifted his hands. I saw dark shapes moving by the gates, like a forest drawing closer by the minute. My eyes focused. I recognized the effigies from Rayyel's stories, the shaped forms pumped full of the villagers' blood and whatever foul substance the mages used to keep them moving. I could see it, too, running along veins that popped along the sides of their necks and down their bare shoulders, throbbing as it filled the vile, dead things with life.

"There are people here who mean something to you, terribly misguided as the sentiment may be," Yuebek continued. "Perhaps their imminent death may make you a bit more cooperative."

I felt the anger take life inside of me. Yuebek had missed something vital: studying my father, even a chance meeting with him if that were true, didn't make you his child. Perhaps I couldn't live up to my father's expectations, but that didn't change that he raised me never to accept defeat.

I went for the closest mage. He tried to shatter my sword, but I dropped it and stabbed him in the belly once with my spare dagger. I dragged him backwards as he struggled in my grasp. "Do you want another?" I whispered into his ear.

I felt him shake his head fervently.

"Cast me a spell."

"This is futile, my darling," Yuebek called out.

I grinned, turning the mage over to face the ones behind Nor. He flailed. Maybe he was trying to cast a spell, maybe he wasn't; it wasn't important. The mages turned to prepare themselves; Agos struck one in the back of the head with his fist, grabbed his sword, and stuck it into the others so quickly it didn't even look like he broke a sweat.

The sound of bodies plopping on the ground broke the standstill. Nor claimed a sword for herself just as the effigies reached us. They began to fight their way through the figures, whose bodies were sufficiently hardened, unlike the snake-men's.

I stabbed my mage a second time and kicked him away for good measure before rushing in to join the battle. The effigies weren't fighting back at all, but the sheer number was making it impossible to cut through them. I saw Yuebek making a hasty retreat to the end of the courtyard; behind him, the temple's roof was engulfed in flames. "You have to admit, at least, how wonderful this all is," he called. "Imagine these in Oren-yaro, with my twenty thousand soldiers. Imagine!"

Yes, I could. I could imagine his madness back home and Jin-Sayeng burning to the ground like the temple. I could imagine the death and destruction that would come from someone who not only wanted to revive Yeshin's legacy, but believed himself worthy of it. I kicked a figure away and fought to reach Rai's side while blood—not my own—ran down my chin. He was pale, but not blue. I touched his neck and felt a pulse.

I regretted any past romantic notions of dying together in a battlefield. His eyes flickered, but they didn't open. "Wake up, Rai," I grumbled.

"Not sure if you want him to be awake for this," I heard Khine say behind me. "Let the man have his sweet dreams." He kicked an effigy away.

"Is it not enough, my lovely queen?" Yuebek cried. "Do you want more?"

"Not particularly," I said. I didn't think he could hear me.

His laughter sounded like the creaking of a horse-cart. I saw a blue flicker in the effigies' eyes. They turned towards us, and I had the sudden, sinking feeling that they could see us.

"He's drawing completely from the villagers now," Namra gasped out.

The words had barely left her mouth when the effigies began to attack. They had no weapons, no clothes, even. But they rushed forward with outstretched hands, teeth snapping. One grabbed Khine by the arm and bit down, hard enough that I could see blood spurt from the wound. As Khine tried to dislodge it with his sword, another came to grab his leg. I reached out to help him, but I found myself preoccupied with two of my own.

I was able to hack off one's arm with my sword. The limb flew back and didn't reattach itself; the effigy lay on the ground, leaking curdled blood and fluids as it groaned helplessly into the wind. I turned my focus on the other one and saw hands grabbing Rai's body, pulling him into the horde. I dropped my attacker as quickly as I could and rushed over to cut him loose. My sword was starting to feel dull—I was hacking at the flailing limbs like a woodcutter with an axe.

In that tangle of old blood and fake flesh, mixed with the scent of mud and rotting meat and my own desperate anger, I thought of my son, of his sweet laughter, of love that still existed in this world. And then the effigies fell.

I didn't understand it at first. I kicked the last of the limp hands off my husband's legs before I saw them all collapsed on the ground, like sacks of rice gathered at the end of harvest season. None were moving.

My first instinct was to turn to Yuebek. His expression had gone from delighted to furious.

"Khine, help me," I said, grabbing Rai's body from the ground. Khine sheathed his sword and rushed in, taking him from me without hesitation. I stepped away from them both and turned to fight our way out of there.

Yuebek's mages were trying to step over the fallen effigies in a rush to shut the gate. It slammed shut just as I got there. I slammed my elbow into the closest mage and managed to stick my sword into a second before the first could recover. My companions arrived and I turned and slit the first mage's throat, his warm blood covering my already sticky fingers with yet another layer of red. Agos grappled with his own mage before the man could cast a spell—he managed to pin him to the ground, where Nor disposed of him with a quick stab through the heart. We turned to the gate, which was glowing faintly blue along the corners, as if it had been sealed shut by a spell.

Agos tried to rattle it open, but it held firm. He stepped back and smashed against it with his shoulder. Nor followed suit.

Khine caught up to us, half carrying, half dragging the still-bleeding Rayyel. The sight of his drenched clothes made me nauseous.

I tried to keep calm as I surveyed our surroundings. I spotted two more mages in the distance, their hands as blue as the edges of the gates. They were keeping it shut.

"Nor!" I called. We were both the closest to them.

She came running to me.

"Keep smashing it!" I ordered Agos, who remained behind.

He turned to comply.

Nor and I tore through the garden, towards the mages who must've realized they couldn't keep the gates closed and defend themselves at the same time. One couldn't seem to make up his mind; Nor took care of him without even blinking. The other dropped the spell immediately and drew another one, throwing a ball of fire in my direction. I barely avoided burning my face off. As he stumbled over with another spell, I slashed him from shoulder to hip, sending him spinning straight into the bushes. He fell facedown and I stabbed him from behind, straight through where his heart would be from the other side.

I pushed the body off my sword just in time to see Agos break the gate open.

"You know this is nothing to me," Yuebek called from across the courtyard. "Run! Run if you think that will do anything! Where would you go? Your husband is dying. Shall I kill your son, too? What you want and what I want are in the exact same place. Jin-Sayeng awaits us, my queen! Shall we set a date? Maybe I can have our wedding ready by the time you return!" He started laughing.

I gazed back at him as I let everyone else run ahead on the path. He stood like a beacon behind the flames and crumbling temple, a demon that ought to slink back to where it came from. I should have gone back there to finish him, or die trying. But all the strength had left my body; even if I did reach him, I wouldn't know where to start.

"What are we going to do about the freak?" Agos asked.

"We're pawns in his game," I murmured. "We have to get to Jin-Sayeng before he tears everything apart." With a last look at Yuebek's crooked form, I pulled the gate shut behind me.

CHAPTER THIRTEEN

THE FORGOTTEN

M y husband's blood continued dripping, like rain from a hole in the rooftop during a typhoon. I knew his life was fading with every step Khine
took. And the worry on Khine's face was palpable; I had known him long
enough by that point to understand what his silence meant.

We hadn't gone very far when Khine dragged Rai to the side, leaning him on
the ground with his legs on a tree root. "Watch for Yuebek's men," he told Nor.
The exhaustion was plain in his voice. He turned to Namra. "My apologies,
priestess, but I will need your help once more."

"Last time, you said you didn't like a mage touching your patient," Namra
said.

"I'm taking it back now," Khine snapped. "He's dying. He's your lord, isn't
he? So help me."

The words made me light-headed. I drew my sword and walked up to join
Nor and Agos.

"I don't think they followed us," Nor said. "You can go back and sit beside
Prince Rayyel, my queen."

"I can't," I murmured.

"How did the pisspot get himself stabbed?" Agos asked.

Nor jabbed him with her elbow.

"I'm just saying . . ."

"Respect," Nor grumbled.

Agos took a deep breath. After a moment of silence, he said, "Can I look at your sword?" His voice was softer now, reminding me so much of how he used to talk to me when we were children.

I handed it to him without a word. He wiped the blood off with his shirt and held it up to the light. "It's chipped," Agos continued with a grimace. "About as useless as a wooden stick now. I knew that merchant was lying through his teeth. Best Jinsein steel my ass. You can have the one I stole off those bastards." He all but shoved the new sword into my hands. I tried to look at it, but I couldn't really see anything beyond a sword—an object, a tool for killing. *Rivers of blood.* Funny I could still remember Khine's voice saying that while he was now yelling at Namra behind me.

"It's a Zarojo double-edged," Agos crowed. "A lot better than the ones I've seen the guards carry. See the nice engraving on the hilt? Consider it your nameday present."

"But that's not until..." I blinked. I had lost track of time.

"Yesterday," Agos said, cocking his head to the side. "I wanted to get back to the village in time with good news for you. Wasn't counting on your deranged suitor waiting for us back there. Not that you could blame me for that. We thought he was dead."

"I didn't even realize," Nor broke in. "My apologies, my queen."

"It's not like we could've had a celebration like we do in the palace," I said. Banners and drums and parades, in addition to the feast. My birth marked the end of the War of the Wolves, which meant a time of celebration. Twenty-seven years of peace. *And here I'm about to end it soon. If Rai dies here... gods. My son. What will happen to Thanh?*

"Always thought it was a waste of money," Agos started. "That roast pig, though, always shuts me up. Crackling skin..."

I almost laughed at the irony of discussing food while my husband was dying. But my expression must've lightened a bit, because he lifted his hand and very slowly placed it on my shoulder. "I wouldn't worry if I were you," he said. "The Ikessars are hard to kill."

"A well-known fact," Nor added.

"They're like insects. It's why they lasted so long. There's a joke in the army, you know. How do you fight an Ikessar? Well, if they don't bore you to death first..."

"No, you're saying it wrong," Nor said. "I think it starts with an Ikessar and a Jeinza walk into a bar..."

Agos rolled his eyes and handed me the scabbard. I sheathed the sword before sliding it through my belt. It was built for a much bigger person, and I had to tighten the belt to the last hole. I uttered a quiet thanks.

"Princess—" he began.

I heard Khine call my name and quickly turned away from Agos. I held my breath before I walked back to them, expecting the worst. Rai's colour was still alarming, but I caught sight of the rise and fall of his chest.

"He's bleeding from the inside," Khine said. "We did what we could, but I need to get him back to the village. I...I don't know how."

"Does the lord need a litter?" Agos broke in, sarcasm lacing his voice.

"I can walk," Rai mumbled.

I dropped to my husband's side and watched as his eyes flickered. He took several deep breaths before he finally opened them. "I can walk," he repeated, forcing the words out, as if he wasn't quite sure we'd heard him.

"Should he?" I asked Khine.

"It's not like anyone can carry him all the way down the mountain."

Agos gave a smug grin and reached out to help Rai to his feet. Rai ignored him and pushed himself, his face contorted in pain. "I can walk," he said a third time. "I'm not an invalid."

"Good that you know," Agos spat. "Stop holding us back. *She* may let you get away with everything, but if I'm going to have to wipe up after your perfumed royal ass—"

"This can wait for when we don't have people at death's door," Khine snapped.

Namra drew close, carrying a long stick. She whittled off the last branch with her knife and handed it to Rai. "I know it must be hard, my lord, but we should get started or else we might never get there at all. We shouldn't spend a moment longer than we have to on this mountain."

Rai took a step. Blood seeped through his bandages, but he pushed himself forward without a word of complaint.

No, I found myself thinking. *I don't think I ever knew him at all.*

I knew my husband, the scholar; his love for obscure topics, his perpetual cluelessness with a sword. I knew that he grew up in the shadow of the Citadel in the mountains, protected by no less than five guards at all times. It was generally accepted that my father would do to him exactly what he had done to General Shan—the torture, the public decapitation, the indecent burial (the man's body was never recovered for a proper funeral). I knew that despite being a bastard, they had found a way for the priests to name him an Ikessar—something to do with his father dying before he was born and the Hio clan's rejection of Princess Ryia's claim that Shan was the father, as if somehow that made it possible for Ryia to have created him *on her own*.

Everything else I had supplied from the knowledge my father had passed down on the Ikessars and their strange ways. I had never stopped to consider it from his point of view. Not a true Ikessar by blood, but he was—in every way you looked at it—Rysaran the Uncrowned's direct heir. My father may have been a mass murderer, but Rysaran was the weak ruler who allowed that murderer's power to go unchecked in the first place.

I had my burdens; Rayyel had his. Bleeding from the inside, Khine had said, but Rai walked like it wasn't just a piece of cloth holding him together. The silent way he struggled gave me a glimpse of what the past six years had looked like for him. I had kept myself busy nursing my injured pride; he, on the other hand...

Was all of this just an effort to find ways to assure his worth? That he was not everything my father had accused his clan of? Yuebek's words must've stung, but I didn't know where to start with that. I didn't think to mention it at all—Rai was too busy not dying, and everyone else was worrying about Yuebek's men on our tail. Small problems overshadowing larger concerns... it didn't matter what Yuebek had planned for us if we didn't make it back to the village in one piece.

It was on the long, winding sloped road near the lake that Rai finally collapsed. He crumpled to the ground, one knee awkwardly bent under him, and his body slid along the mud until Khine and Agos caught him. The bandage had come loose, and he was beginning to bleed again. "You got this far," Khine said, wrapping my husband's arm around his shoulder. "Don't die on me now, Rai." I wonder if anyone else had noticed how he neglected his honorifics, calling my husband by his familiar name. For a man who had once lectured me on them, he seemed completely oblivious to his own quirks.

"Akaterru-damned Ikessar can't even take a stab wound," Agos snarled. "Maybe we should just leave you for the dogs. You know how much I'll enjoy watching you get ripped apart after all the trouble you've caused the queen? Brain ground to a pulp, entrails on the dirt..."

"Enough, Agos."

"Why? Is he going to cry? Did I hurt his feelings? Come on, you bastard. I know you hate me. Come and take a swing. She went all this way for you—you're going to die on her now? Get up and prove me wrong, you fucking waste of air."

Rai didn't reply. His face was ashen. But I could see him struggling to maintain consciousness, his face flickering.

I held on to hope and rushed ahead to see if I could get help from the village. But before I reached the first bend, a man came running up to us. "Khine!" he called out.

"We're busy at the moment," Khine said.

"The elders—Khine, you've got to see..."

"Let me take this man back to my mother's house first."

"I don't think..."

"I have to take care of this man first," Khine said, walking past him. The hint of anger in his tone was enough to make the villager fall back, but he followed us all the way to the streets before disappearing by the bridge.

The village was eerily silent—not a single elder was in sight. Agos dashed off as soon as we crossed the first bridge, but I was too distracted over Rai to give it much thought. We reached Mei's house, where Khine called for his mother, asking if she could get some hot water ready. There was no reply as we dragged Rai into the common room.

Khine began stripping Rai's shirt off. I caught sight of the flesh around the wound, purple and black at the edges. The wound itself was small, which was the worrying part. Khine grabbed a metal case from the shelf and then, as an afterthought, turned to me. "Outside," he said.

"But—"

"I need Namra to assist me. But *you* step outside. You can't see this." He turned to Nor. "I need to open his wound up. Captain, please, take her away..."

"My queen." Nor grabbed my arm and led me through the door. From behind, I heard Khine asking Namra to hold Rai's legs.

Rai started to scream. Khine covered his mouth with a piece of cloth, and the sound dropped to a groan.

Nor led me to the street, where I slid to the ground, closed my eyes, and counted stars in my head. The sound of footsteps distracted me and I looked up to see Agos return from the alley. There was a strange look on his face.

"Did you see Mei?" I croaked out.

Agos shook his head. "Not a sign." He nodded towards the hut. "Bastard going to make it?"

"I don't know."

He snorted. "Good riddance if he doesn't."

"Agos," I said. "You know it's not that simple."

"Because you still love him?"

"Agos!" Nor barked.

His words gave me a headache. I struggled to keep my voice low, because I felt like screaming. "Because in case you haven't been paying attention, Agos, Yuebek has both his hands deep into this mess and likely won't back out any time soon. If we lose Rai right now, what do we tell his clan? *There's this Zarojo prince who claims my father wanted me to marry* him *instead and oh, by the way, we got your heir killed, so there's that.* No, that doesn't look *bad* at all."

"There's that," Agos grumbled. "It's always been a mess."

"Of course it has."

"There must be a way that doesn't involve allying yourself with the Ikessars *or* your father's wishes."

I turned to him. "Have you become a politician all of a sudden?"

Agos smirked. "Not in a million years. I've seen what it does to you." He paused. "There's something you should know."

I sighed. "Out with it."

"Before we left Anzhao, someone…came up to me. An agent of the Shadows."

Nor's eyes widened. "This is the first time I've heard of this. What have you been doing behind my back, Agos?"

"She was the one who helped me escape Qun's dungeons," I said.

"So she told me," Agos replied. "She must've also spoken about the ship, then."

I frowned. "I don't know whether to trust her or not. I'm almost sure I don't want to."

"About that…" Agos started.

I narrowed my eyes.

"She's here," he continued. "She…she tailed us from Anzhao. She was concerned that you chose to be alone with Lamang instead of taking your guards."

"Someone's been following us this whole time?" Nor snapped. "Agos, you've gone too far!" Her hand dropped to her sword.

Agos's eyes flashed. "Don't you want to get home at all? What other options do we have?"

"Do you even know what dealing with the Shadows means, you thick-skulled excuse for a soldier?" She turned to me. "My queen…"

"We *do* have to get home, don't we, Nor?" I asked. "We need to know what's happening back there, how many of the Oren-yaro are under Yuebek's control as he claimed. And no matter what happens with Rai—" I swallowed. "So she's here?"

Agos nodded. "They've got a boat docked somewhere on the east shoreline. She said they'll meet you there when you're ready."

From inside the hut, I could hear Khine swearing under his breath. I could also smell the sharp, iron-tinged scent of blood, enough that I could've sworn I was soaked in it. I didn't want to spend another moment there—I didn't want to see Khine walk out shaking his head.

I got up. "Bring me to them."

From afar, the boat looked like a simple fishing vessel, moored near an outcrop of jagged rocks where it rose and fell with the waves. It seemed abandoned, but when Agos placed his fingers in his mouth to whistle, a woman emerged from belowdeck. She pulled herself onto the closest boulder and made her way to the sand, where she dropped to one knee in front of me. A Kag-style bow—I made a note to remember that.

"My queen." It was the voice of the agent who broke me out of prison.

I was stunned by how much younger she was than I had thought. Fifteen, perhaps sixteen—you would've taken her for a fisherman's daughter in a heart-beat. She was short and thin, the sort of person who could probably fit in a wine barrel with the lid closed, with a plain face fringed by shaggy black hair that would be hard to pick out from a crowd. I had severely overestimated her; this mere mite of a girl wouldn't last two heartbeats in a fight. "It's about time you tell me who you really are," I said as she rose. "If Dai Kaggawa is as smart as he believes he is, he would've sent a formidable warrior. Instead, *you're* here. There must be a reason for that."

"I am Lahei alon gar Kaggawa, my queen," she said.

"Kaggawa's eldest?" Nor spoke up.

Lahei nodded. "My father wouldn't entrust this task to anyone else. He would've come himself, but the Sougen is...well. We have many, many problems in the Sougen, the sort we were hoping the queen could lend her assistance with."

"What sort of problems?"

"Well, to start with, we have mad dragons, and the Anyu clan..."

"I know about all of that," I said. "We've done what we can. What else would Kaggawa want from me?"

"That's not for me to say," Lahei replied. "There will be enough time for talk later, I think. Your...business. Is it finished? We can bring you to the *Aina's Breath* in no time."

"What will you do if I refuse?"

"My queen..."

"I've been betrayed too many times in this godsforsaken land," I said in a low voice. "You know I have nothing else to fall back on. My husband is hurt, I'm down to two soldiers, and there are Zarojo politicians after me. You're using my situation to your advantage."

She looked surprised at my honesty, enough to be speechless.

A log drifting out on the horizon caught my attention as I awaited her reply. I stared at it for a second longer than I should've before I realized it was a body, float-ing facedown. Something clicked, followed by a harrowing thought. Without a word, I waded into the water to get a closer look.

I saw three more bodies as soon as I reached the edge of the rock outcrop. They bobbed silently underneath a mass of shrieking seagulls. In the distance, the sun was beginning to set.

"What the hell is happening?" I heard Nor gasp. A body drifted close enough for me to grab. I pulled and with some effort, managed to flip it over. The body was bloated, its face black and swollen, but I thought I recognized one of the elders from the village, Mei's neighbour. Underwater, her white hair spread out like tendrils.

I bit back against the prickling sensation in my stomach as I dragged the body to the sand. There was no sword mark on it, nothing except a gash on the head, like someone had smashed her with a rock, hard enough to tear the flesh open down to the skull. I also noticed that her arm was twisted unnaturally, as if it was ripped from the socket. And as I stared at her, I thought about what had happened up in the temple, how fast the effigies fell. My heart dropped. Nor turned to say something to me, but I ignored her and sprinted back to the village, to Mei's house.

The man that had met us at the trail earlier was talking to Khine by the doorway. Before I got within earshot, Khine's eyes widened.

"No," Khine mumbled when I reached them. His sleeves were soaked in blood.

"I was trying to tell you earlier—" the man said.

"It's Mei, isn't it?" I broke in.

Khine didn't answer, nor did he look at me. It was as if he had been jolted out of his senses and into a world of his own. I followed him from the elders' compound all the way to the southern bridge, which ran across the sea towards a small island. A handful of people were on the shore below it. I caught sight of Thao.

"The elders started acting strangely earlier," she said without bothering to greet us. Her eyes were red, her face white and tearstained. "They started fighting amongst themselves, said they felt empty—hollow. Like someone was pulling at them with invisible strings. Mother came to try to calm them down, and then..." She turned to me. "You told her it was the priests' doing. That they've been working with mages, that the villagers are being *used*."

"It's true," I said.

"You told her this. You told her they were *tainted*."

"I didn't—"

"What else did you do?" The accusation bubbled from her throat.

"I said I was going to fix this. I told her—" *They haven't gone mad, it's all the mages' doing...*

"She said she could see *you* and Khine and that you were in trouble. She couldn't explain what was happening, but she said she couldn't let this go on any longer, she said she was done being a burden to us all, and that if the other elders were wise, they would..." Thao shook her head. She was beginning to cry again.

"Thao," Khine said blankly. "Where is she?"

Thao pointed. "She jumped off the bridge. The others followed. *What did you tell her?*" She grabbed me by the shoulders. Her words tore a hole through me. Worse, though, was the look on Khine's face, that stricken expression of someone whose life was flashing right before his very eyes. He started for the edge of the shore. I glanced back at Thao, who dug her nails through my shirt before pushing away in disgust.

Wordlessly, I stumbled after Khine. More bodies were strewn across the shore, but none were what Khine was looking for. With barely a glance at them, he plunged into the water, heedless of the waves. I called for him, but my voice fell on deaf ears. He was too busy searching, calling for his mother. Every wave that came washed my husband's blood off him... I could imagine the drops spinning into the distance, the current carrying them to the ocean the way it did his mother's broken body.

Somewhere in my memories, I remembered my father telling me that life wasn't fair; that for everything you were ever given, somebody paid a price.

There are many things I have carried to this day, no matter how painful the process of recollection might be. Call it respect, call it penance—a twisted way of punishing myself, though others might tell me I'm not responsible for it, not really. I know only that I burned every moment of that evening into my memory, that even now, all I have to do is close my eyes and I will be there again, watching the circling seagulls and listening to the waves while Khine falls apart in front of me.

Some of the details, of course, have faded since. How many times did Khine call out for her, and was I only counting to drown out my own panicked thoughts? Was there hate in his eyes when he looked at me, or did he simply decide I wasn't there at all?

I know that I stayed with him there the whole night, even after the other villagers had taken away the few bodies that had washed ashore. That he argued with Cho when the boy tried to tell him there was no point, he'd tried to look himself as soon as Mei jumped and would Khine just stop pretending like he could control everything *for once*? Khine sent him flying across the sand once he had finished speaking. Cho got up with a split lip and a bruised nose.

"Mother's dead and you're still a fucking ass," Cho hissed. He pointed at me. "You know this is all *her* fault, right? You're the one who brought her into our lives! If you'd known to leave it alone from the beginning…" His words were garbled in his grief, and he stomped off before he could finish what he was saying.

Inzali—Inzali was nowhere to be found. I didn't have the heart to ask. Something told me that the only reason I stayed was because I didn't have it in me to leave Khine to grieve alone. Perhaps my guards understood this, because no one came to bother me except when Nor arrived with rice balls wrapped in lotus leaves. Despite everything that had happened, my stomach gurgled at the smell.

"Prince Rayyel is still sleeping," she said. "You should, too."

"He won't want to." I nodded towards Khine.

"You'll catch a cold out here."

"Then bring blankets," I suggested.

She didn't argue any further and left me alone. I ate a bit of the rice and saved enough in case Khine wanted any. I didn't think he would. When my father died, I forgot to eat for two whole days.

The moon came up. After everything that had happened that day, it seemed almost serene—a shadowed grey, waning. Clouds drifted past, not enough to block the light completely; a few wispy white ones along with the odd black, bloated with rain.

"Khine," I called out to him. "We have to go inside. It's getting cold." I took in a lungful of damp air.

He didn't answer. He had been crying, although the dark did a lot to obscure the tears.

"Khine," I repeated, hoping the sound of his name would bring him back.

"They did that," Khine finally said, holding his breath for a moment. He returned to sit a few paces from me. "Most of us would be dead in Yuebek's courtyard if they didn't... sacrifice themselves. I don't think they even knew what they were doing."

I wanted to hold him. I tucked my hands into my arms so I wouldn't give in to the temptation. I didn't think I wanted to find out if he was going to lash out like his siblings had. It was not the most important thing at this time, but I didn't know if I could give him comfort if he was of the same mind as them. "Your mother knew," I whispered instead. "Thao said she had a glimpse of us in the temple courtyard. A link, perhaps, to the dolls. And the others must've seen it themselves, or else they wouldn't have believed her."

"If I had actually managed to become a doctor..." Khine fell silent, the rage plain on the angles of his face. I suddenly remembered what his mother told me about him. *A chipped sword still has an edge.* But I couldn't say it out loud—I felt like I was incapable of saying anything that wouldn't come out ragged and hollow. What right did I have to intrude on his sorrow, to pretend like I knew anything about his life or that my words meant anything?

It did hurt to understand that even a queen cannot change the ebb of a single life. Perhaps that was why people like my father spoke in multitudes and generalizations. We cloak ourselves in power as if it could make all the difference in the world, but it changes nothing. My father had the largest army in the nation when my brothers died. I knew he would've torn himself apart to save them.

I heard footsteps. I looked up and saw Inzali. She was followed by Namra.

Inzali bowed. "You must forgive my family, Queen Talyien. My brother and sister sometimes let emotions get the better of them." There was a slight tremble in her voice, but she was calm compared with her siblings. She handed me a blanket.

I glanced at Namra. "Is Lahei still there?"

"Yes. She's been getting acquainted with the whole situation."

"She shouldn't be. You're aware she's from the Shadows?"

"I am," Namra said. "Which is why there's no point trying to hide this from her. The Ikessars may no longer have the Shadows' loyalty, but we still know how they operate. She claims to be a servant of the Dragonthrone, which at this point in time may be all we have to hold on to; we don't have the privilege to be suspicious of everyone." She cleared her throat. "I left out the part about Yuebek's involvement with the Oren-yaro, of course. As far as Kaggawa knows, you followed your husband out here and stumbled upon these sinister events entirely by chance."

"Thank you."

"Not that it will do you much good if any of his men or Yuebek himself decides to talk. I'm...forgive my candour, Beloved Queen, but I think it's best that I offer you my advice."

"What's on your mind?"

"Dragonlord Rayyel is still unwell. We've stopped the bleeding, but Khine says he will need to stay in bed for a few weeks, at least. I know you want to bring him home as soon as possible, but there is wisdom in taking Kaggawa's offer and heading to Jin-Sayeng *now*."

"I'm not going to leave my husband on his own," I said. "Yuebek may come for him at any moment."

"With all due respect, Beloved Queen, the only thing this man wants is *you*, and the further you are from Prince Rayyel, the safer he is." She gave an apologetic nod. "I'm not proposing that we stay and leave the doors wide open for Yuebek to just come striding in, of course. I have secured Belfang's cooperation. We can head east and find an inn where my lord can rest undisturbed."

"Belfang? The priest?"

"He came limping in tonight. He will not speak of what happened back there, only that he is done with Prince Yuebek. He believes that Yuebek will try to rally more men and come for you as early as tomorrow. He says that he will raze the entire village and leave no stone unturned."

"I don't know if we can trust the man."

"I'm aware he could be a rat. But a watched rat is better than one lurking in the shadows. Trust me on this, my queen."

"But that's...I can't leave *now* if you put it that way."

Inzali cleared her throat. "I've spoken to Iri Feng about all of this. We're leaving with what remains of the village, hopefully before Prince Yuebek arrives. Belfang's words were enough to sway her—her father died up there, you know." I tried to pretend that didn't bother me. "With you heading back north, Prince Rayyel east, and the rest of the villagers scattered, this monster will be welcomed by nothing but empty houses. We'll return when it's safe, perhaps find time to bury our elders."

"Why are you doing this for me, Inzali?"

She paused before glancing towards Khine.

I curled my hands into fists and followed her gaze. He was staring at the sea as if we weren't there, transfixed by the odd shape the moon made on the water's edge.

"I wonder if you could take him," she said. "If it's not too much trouble."

My heart leaped at the words, but I fought to suppress it. "It's too dangerous."

Inzali grunted in acknowledgment. "There is nothing for him here but painful memories and lost dreams. It was difficult enough for him when our father died. I still remember how deep he fell. I didn't think he'd ever come out of it. And now this…" She tightened her face for a moment, choking back her own grief. "I…I will ask Cho to go with you, too. I am not trying to foist a burden on you. You're a queen, we're nothing. But I know he can be of some use to you, and you seem to enjoy his company."

"It's not a burden," I said. "But…"

"Please, Queen Talyien. I just lost my mother. I will not lose my eldest brother, too."

"You know the troubles that follow me," I said. "You'd entrust your brother to that? To what I am and what I'm about to face?"

Her voice was like cut steel.

"He's got nothing else."

ACT TWO

THE RUBRICS OF RULE

CHAPTER ONE

AN MOZHI OF THE CLIFFS

ᛏᚢᛗ

The woman who sat with my husband's hand in hers that early morning before we left for An Mozhi was not the same one who ventured to Anzhao City all those months ago.

That one had her life all figured out, her father's daughter without question. She had suffered an insult and was acting as best as she knew how. She belonged in the history books, the pillar on which Jin-Sayeng's peace depended. There must still be a tapestry of her somewhere in Oka Shto, overlooking a crowd of bent warlords in the shadows, a ray of sunlight over her. In the tapestry, she is wearing a wolf headdress instead of a crown, a blatant attempt by the artist to hint at Oren-yaro superiority.

That woman would've known what to do. She would've ordered her ailing husband home—dragged on a litter if she had to, to hell with the consequences. She wouldn't be sitting there in confusion, her fear overriding all sense. To trust an agent of the Shadows, among all things…

Frayed minds lead to frayed decisions, or so my father liked to say. Mei's death was the last straw. If we hadn't gone to the temple at all, I would've fought like a mad dragon for my desire to bring things back to the way they were. I could even still hold on to my denial of my own father's involvement in the events. Whispered to me in the dark, it could've been a lie. Said out loud in front of my husband, with such conviction and display of power…

Even the words *my husband* had lost all meaning. I stared at Rayyel's unmoving form, the after-effect of an herbal infusion Khine had forced into him during his procedure. He would sleep for another day or two, I was told. I went over his features as I must've done more than a hundred times in the past, trying to place him against the man in my memories. He had aged in the last six years. There were lines where there weren't before and splotches of white hair along his temples. He had just turned thirty, too. The Ikessars greyed prematurely— another mark of the line he carried as surely as if he wasn't a bastard. His elders ought to be proud.

I took a deep breath. I had defied counsel to go to Rayyel and bring him home, and here I was on the verge of abandoning him, half-dead, to strangers. As faithful a servant as Namra had been, as reliable as Inzali had proven herself to be, *I* was his wife. That meant something once by itself, didn't it? Once, it meant the whole world.

I squeezed his hand. He didn't squeeze back. I fought back a grin. No difference, then; if he had been awake, he would have reacted exactly the same way.

Agos appeared at the doorway. He paused as he looked at me, head slightly bent. I studied his face at that angle, contrasting it with Rayyel's. I was trying to find my son in either of them.

"You saw Lord Ozo before you left to find me," I said in a low voice. "Did you see anything that will verify Yuebek's claims?"

"Nothing that will ease your mind," Agos replied. He shuffled his feet. "I'm not exactly his confidant."

"How did he react when you said you were going after me?"

"Like he couldn't give a damn," Agos said. "He expected me to abandon my quest just because he didn't agree. Showed the old wolf, didn't I?"

"He would have known you would follow me."

Agos rubbed his nose.

"Which means he was sure you wouldn't have found a way. Did he know an embargo was coming?"

"I don't know," he said. "Finding a ship wasn't easy."

"How *did* you get here?"

He glanced away, mumbling something under his breath.

"Was it Kaggawa?" I prodded.

"Yes," he grumbled. "I met an agent of theirs at the shipyards in Fuyyu. I rode with them to An Mozhi and took another boat from there to Anzhao."

I sighed. "I knew it. You just didn't want to admit it in front of Nor, did you?"

"You know me better than anyone."

"No, I don't. Why didn't you tell me sooner? You never would have hidden something like this from me when we were young."

"We're not children anymore," he said with a rueful glance at the floor. "General Ozo thought we were. Maybe he was waiting for you to admit you've made a mistake before he came to save you."

"Or Yuebek was telling the truth, and Ozo is working with him to trap me into this *marriage*." I nearly spat the last word out.

Agos's face was twisted in confusion. "You know I don't give a rat's ass about your politics," he said. "All I want is to see you home safe. You don't have to worry one way or another who put me up to it. I'm here because I want to be. Because I belong—" And here he stood up, chest puffed for a moment before his eyes darted away. "—with you," he finished with a mumble.

"And I'm thankful for that, Agos. More than you realize." I wasn't sure why I felt like I needed to reply. The Talyien of seven months ago wouldn't have. She would've taken him for granted. She already *had* taken him for granted, more than once. "But you know," I added, "that you're not my Captain of the Guard anymore."

"A title doesn't change what I was taught all my life," he said, pointing at me. "*You're* my responsibility. My princess, my queen." He looked embarrassed at his own admonition before glancing at Rai. "I could tell them this is all useless," he continued. "Like they could *force* you to marry anything, especially whatever the hell that thing was. They can't even force you to keep a dog you don't like. It's like whoever made all the effort to plan this out didn't know you very well. Call me shortsighted, but you'd think they would at least have considered that, especially if this all started with your father. He knew you best."

"I don't know," I murmured. "I mean, I married that one, didn't I?"

Agos's face broke into a grin. "Yes, well, you wanted *that*. Don't think I don't remember you simpering after him like some lovesick fool."

"Simpering fool," I repeated. "I don't disagree. All the years I wasted in anger..."

The smile left his face. "We do stupid things for love."

I swallowed and turned away. Khine had said the same thing once. I had never examined my relationship with Rai under that light before, never stopped to think about how pride and duty had muddled something that ought to be so straightforward and clear. Well—the dance had come full circle, and I was here now. And love? Did I ever really know what love meant in the first place? Did I love Rayyel only because I thought my father ordered me to or because *I* wanted to, desperately, because to love meant to feel something and I was tired of being alone? It didn't used to matter—there was no room for such uncertainties in my life. Back then it was all I knew, and I had held on to it like the very air from my lungs. But now that air was gone, and I found myself . . . still breathing.

I placed his hand back on the sleeping mat and pulled the blanket up to his chin. And then, conscious of the fact that Agos was watching my every move, I bent down to kiss him on the forehead.

"You've decided, then," Agos said with a deep breath, chasing away the disconcerting silence.

I frowned. "Whatever Lahei wants from me will be a blade meant for my own heart. To have the queen in their clutches . . . who knows what they will do with such power? It would be foolishness to accept. More than foolishness."

Agos sighed. "But going home—"

"I'm not finished," I continued, turning to him. "It would be *suicide*. All the lords of Oren-yaro would laugh themselves into a stupor if I fell for such an obvious thing. But then after what happened out there, with Khine's mother . . . I realized that it doesn't matter. I need to get back home to protect my son from whatever hell Yuebek has planned. I don't care what happens to me. Khine's mother—if a woman who thought she had nothing else to offer could still save her own child, why not me?"

Tears welled up in my eyes. Angrily, I wiped at them and continued. "It will bring me closer to my son. The bastards know it. They are all but telling me: *Drink the poison, Beloved Queen*. Yeshin's daughter would throw the cup at their faces. And if I knew what that still meant—if I wasn't scrambling for a scrap of hope and had strength enough to carry my name . . ."

"You're not Warlord Tal," Agos murmured. "None of us are."

I clenched my jaw, pretending that hearing those words from someone else didn't hurt. For all my life, I had tried to make myself a personification of that name in an attempt to make my father proud. I used to think I was doing a remarkable job of it.

"Who else cares for my son for who he is, and not what he embodies? I learned that yesterday. So I will drink their poison willingly, damn them all to hell. If I have nothing else, my son has even less." I took a deep breath. "One good thing, at least. I highly doubt Rai will want to continue with this ridiculous notion on the boy's parentage. Even supposing that the idea of working with one of Yuebek's mages isn't as despicable as it sounds—preventing Zarojo rule is more important than clan politics. There's nothing quite like a common enemy to unite two parties."

"If you say so," Agos breathed.

"You don't believe me?"

"The bastard is more stubborn than you are. A feat in itself, don't get me wrong."

"When we get home, I intend to launch an investigation. Rai may be stubborn, but he's also a sensible man. In the face of Zarojo invasion, our united effort may make all the difference."

"There you go with the speeches again." He snorted. "If the Oren-yaro is found to be behind all of this, nothing will ever convince the rest of them you weren't in on it, too. The entire nation will be killing each other for a chance to cut your throat."

"Akaterru," I murmured. "There is that, isn't it? All the more reason that we can't be at odds now, not with this looming over us."

"Tell him that," Agos said, nodding towards the still figure. He didn't look all that convinced.

———

Lahei steered the boat past the rocks just as the first rays of dawn spilled over the horizon. She had one man with her and claimed the others were with the ship. Lo Bahn, Khine, Cho, Nor, and Agos made up the rest of the group; Inzali stayed behind to assist Namra with Rai, along with Lo Bahn's steward and children. It felt strange to have both my fate and my husband's in the hands of strangers—the very notion made me bristle. But as much as this new reality went against every fibre of my being, the thought of Mei Lamang gave me courage. If she could do what she did, this was nothing. I think without that to hold on to, I would've fallen apart.

I glanced at Khine, who was staring long and hard at the water as if the answer to his own questions could be plumbed from its depths. I had heard the villagers say they had seen his mother's body by the mouth of the river, that it would take at least a day to recover most of it. I hoped none had tried to tell him this, things a son ought not hear. When my father died, he had a proper funeral pyre and a public mourning...my father, who had murdered thousands, dressed like a king and honoured like a hero. Mei had never hurt anyone in her life as far as I could tell.

The winds were in our favour, at least, and called for fair sailing. Staring at the wide expanse of ocean to our left, salt breeze on my hair and face, I allowed myself the luxury of anticipating my homecoming for the first time in months. If I had known what lay on this side of the sea, I would've never left at all.

We reached An Mozhi that afternoon. I was told that the sight of it unfolding from the sea was an experience in itself. From the road, you would've been fooled into thinking it was a small town built haphazardly above a handful of rocks that rose like sturdy spires. But from this side, with full view of the beaches and the stepped cliffs, the ocean yawned to reveal a city that engulfed the horizon. An Mozhi was not so much built on top of the cliffs as it spilled *around* them; there was a bustling harbour along the shore, with more ships than I have ever seen in one place at one time. This sprawled past the shoreline, spreading into low stone buildings and houses as far as the beach would allow. Wooden steps and bridges appeared where the cliffs began, the layered rocks stacked like coins on a taxmaster's desk.

The city continued from the top of the cliffs. There were buildings built right at the edges, accessible only by wooden decks nailed to the side of the cliff. What seemed to be a horrifying and ill-advised feat of engineering appeared to be perfectly normal to these people. As the boat drew closer, I spotted children hanging off the ledges and laughing as they leaped along, like little monkeys, as if unaware that one wrong step or handhold could cause them to smash against the boulders and down into the gaping maw of the sea below. Or maybe they knew, and didn't care. The foolhardiness took me aback. None of the royal children I grew up with would dare such things—even I, the epitome of recklessness as a young girl, would've balked at the idea.

I turned my attention towards the impressive sight of the airship towers, built right at the top of the tallest cliffs and attached to the rest of the city by bridges. They reminded me of the dragon-towers back home, except these ones were wide enough to dock four or five airships at once. Steam rose from the vessels as they drifted to the docks. None were leaving—Khine had told me once that they ran on a schedule, and never at night. We were probably seeing the last trips for the day.

"Can you pick her out from the herd?" Lahei called out from the end of the boat. There was a note of pride in her voice.

I made my way towards her. "Your ship?" I asked.

Lahei whistled. "Over at the harbour. Come on—there are plenty of things the Zarojo may have done right, but *one* thing they don't quite understand: shipbuilding."

I didn't want to offend her, so I made the pretence of squinting. I was born inland and lacked the real sense to tell one ship apart from the other, but I caught sight of a merchant's ship that lacked the elegant flourishes of the Zarojo vessels. Instead, it favoured straight lines and dark, heavy wood from the bow all the way to its masts. It gave the impression of a ship that could last for months out at sea, one that could break through ice or weather a storm without problem. I made a small sound of surprise at how majestic it looked.

Lahei must have expected me to react with such amazement, because her normally placid face broke into a grin. "A beauty, isn't she?" We drifted close enough that I could reach out and touch the side of *Aina's Breath* if I wanted to. Lahei gave another whistle for her people waiting for us there.

No one responded. Lahei cursed, the grin quickly replaced by a frown. Without even waiting for the boat to come to a full stop, she grabbed a post from the closest dock and heaved herself over. After a moment's hesitation, I jumped in after her. The boat creaked past us. I followed Lahei to the platform leading up to *Aina's Breath*. It was blocked by two guards.

"What's happening here?" Lahei said, shoving her way past a crowd of sailors disembarking from one of the ships. "Where're my men?" Her Zirano sounded almost as natural as a Jin-Sayeng royal's, which meant she had been studying it since childhood, as we had.

"Your ship?" one guard asked, pointing at *Aina's Breath* with a spear. "Word got out that you were sailing for Jin-Sayeng. Governor ordered it seized."

"Why would anyone think that?"

"You're Jinsein, aren't you?"

"You fools," Lahei said. "We're Kag."

"You look Jinsein to me."

"We're *Kag*," she repeated, voice rising. I'd missed it before, but in this light, the angle of her nose and her hard jaw, along with the pale tinge of her freckle-dotted skin, made her claim true enough: her mother was a foreigner. "We're merchants. We were loading up the ship and travelling back to Ni'in."

"Take it up with the harbour master," the guard suggested.

Lahei bristled, but she gestured before walking away.

"The empire has no trade agreement with any of the Kag nations," the guard added to our retreating backs. "You're not protected."

"Idiots," she said under her breath, as soon as we were out of earshot. "We had all the papers in order."

Inwardly, I wondered if it was Yuebek. The bastard wasn't a representative of the empire, no matter his claim. A *Fifth* Son didn't have that much power. If he had Governor Qun and his predecessor Zheshan under his influence, then it wasn't a far cry that he might also have the governor of An Mozhi, a man by the name of Hizao, in his pockets.

"This embargo," Lahei continued, breaking my thoughts. "It was meant to keep you on this side of the sea."

Not a question. I shrugged. "How am I supposed to know?"

She stared back. "My queen, you need to be truthful with us."

"I'm cooperating with you, aren't I? What more do you need?"

"We've done as much investigation around you and your activities in the empire as possible. You've been rubbing elbows with the officials, earning the ire of people like Governor Ino Qun. We even heard of an attack in Governor Zheshan's palace—a friend of Prince Rayyel, it seems. An attack *you* were apparently involved in. What happened there?"

I tugged my ear, choosing not to answer.

She frowned. "You think being silent will prevent us from learning every-thing eventually. You remain so naive, Beloved Queen. Did any of it have to do with Governor Zheshan's attempt to present his daughter to Prince Rayyel as a potential wife? I believe he had advised him to set you aside and split the nation in half."

I pretended to laugh. "I must seem so scatterbrained."

She pursed her lips. "You lacked the proper advisers, my queen."

"You're supposed to say no. *No, my queen.* Gods, you people have a way of making a woman feel good about herself."

She smiled. "If it's any consolation..."

"I hear that so often these days..."

"It's not as if we've ever had a proper leader. From the very beginning, our nation has been tormented with turmoil from within—warlords up at each oth-er's throats, and the only time they ever agree to anything is when they want to point out what someone else is doing wrong. A change needs to happen if we are to progress from here, one that goes beyond choosing *who* gets to be blamed the next time around. A proper upheaval."

We fell silent for a bit while I tried to absorb what she was saying. I recalled what Khine told me once, about how much I had not considered the snakes around me. I was well aware of them now, but the knowledge that you have enemies does very little in teaching you how to defeat them. If my father's army would choose Yuebek over me, how was I supposed to gather another in order to protect Jin-Sayeng? Do I offer myself to the highest bidder? What was the price for a woman a touch past her prime, with neither the backing nor the respect of her own people?

"The damn throne's not even that comfortable," I said, at length. "Ever wonder why I stayed in Oka Shto? Sitting on that thing, surrounded by glaring Ikessar supporters..."

Lahei gave me the sort of smile that could've been sympathetic if I wasn't aware what we were both doing. Another snake, this one, and here I was danc-ing with her. *Only a bit more,* I told myself. *Go through with this and you'll see Thanh again.* But the uncertainty made me want to claw my own face off.

We reached the harbour master's office. Someone called out to us in Jinan, and I stood to the side as a young man approached. He was stocky but not overly tall, with a sparse, curly beard that went underneath his round cheeks and a moustache that seemed to be nothing more than wisps of cat's hair. "You were gone too long, Lahei," he grumbled. He turned to me. "My queen. I was there when you were crowned, and watched the uproar when Prince Rayyel was nowhere to be found. Royals and their pride, pah! But you contained yourself remarkably well. Forgive me if I don't bow. I don't want to draw attention to us."

I nodded, keeping note of the thick loathing in his voice when he mentioned *royals*. I watched as Lahei took him aside. "What's the situation, Torre?"

"Bastards said we meant to violate the embargo, even after I showed them our papers and tried to explain that jumping from Ni'in to some other port in Jin-Sayeng wasn't explicitly forbidden. Their embargo only indicates *direct* travel—they don't fucking own the whole world, now, do they? I told them I'd report this to the governor's office and they all but laughed in my face."

"I'm sure we can fix this," Lahei said. "Did you secure a meeting?"

"We've got an appointment three weeks from now. They assured me at the office that it looks like a misunderstanding, and that clearing it up won't be a problem."

"Except," I broke in, "three weeks is far, far too long to stay in one place." I wondered if Yuebek wasn't on his way as we spoke. I knew he intended to travel to Jin-Sayeng anyway, but I'd feel safer once we were in the open sea.

"Where are the others?" Lahei asked.

"In an inn. They're not letting us back into the ship until we have this all straightened out."

"The ship that brought me to Anzhao smashed through the dock to get out," I said. "We could sneak in and make a grand escape."

Lahei looked like I had just suggested we kill her firstborn. "I am not," she said, "going to *smash* the ship into anything. Do you want to sink halfway across the ocean?"

"I don't know. She looks like she can take it."

"Let's file that under *desperate measures*," Torre said with a grin.

Lahei didn't look amused.

"Ask your friend to figure a way out of this," Agos said, drawing me aside.

"You mean Khine?" I asked.

"That's what he's good for, isn't he? Making plans? I thought that's why you keep him around."

I frowned, wondering what he was accusing me of. "This isn't the time," I said. "The man's mother just died. I'm not going to be bothering him with any-thing, Agos."

"It doesn't matter. He's just a peasant. You're—"

"Enough." I walked past him to rejoin Torre and his crew. My stom-ach turned when I saw Lahei watching me. She must've seen the interaction, must've heard what I told Agos. Did she see what I feared she'd seen? It had barely been a day; the elders' deaths were still fresh on my mind, too. But a part of me was aware that this was not the way to becoming the kind of queen that could turn the tides of war. I had not worn my crown in months, but I needed to pretend it was on my head once more. I had no way of knowing what these people truly wanted from me, and only my name and my position as queen protected everything I loved.

From the furthest crevices of my mind, I heard my father laughing.

CHAPTER TWO

SIGHTSEEING

ꗁꔤꖬ

Despite the illusion of safety the presence of the Shadows gave me, I didn't find the energy to do anything but rest for the remainder of the night. Phurywa weighed on my mind more than it had any right to. I had known Khine's mother for only a few days, but the sorrow of her passing filled me with as much sorrow as if she were family. Later that evening, I asked Nor to purchase two black candles, and we took Khine and Cho to the beach to light them for her. Cho looked torn, managing only to grunt his gratitude for the gesture, eyebrows drawn together in a seemingly permanent scowl. He still wanted so badly to hate me, and I couldn't blame him. After everything that had happened since I landed on these shores, I hated myself, too.

Khine didn't say anything. He hadn't spoken since we left Phurywa. He hadn't cried at all since that first day, either. He had taken to Inzali's request that he accompany me as simply as if she'd told him the sun was in the sky.

"It's not like you knew her all that well," Lo Bahn told me over lunch the next day: fried rice with sweet garlic shrimp, seaweed salad, jellyfish, slivers of pig ears braised with cashews, and thick, dark mushrooms cooked in duck fat, washed down with a thick, dark ale imported from Gaspar. "She wasn't even your mother, for spirits' sake. Not like you're fucking Lamang on the side, either, so I don't see why you'd feel the need to do anything about it."

I reached over to his plate and stabbed one of his pig ears with a chopstick. He rolled his eyes as he set his rice bowl down. "Like that means anything. I think if you wanted to kill me, I'd be dead now."

"Maybe you need to start keeping your opinions to yourself," I said.

"You know damn well I don't work that way."

I sniffed as I pulled the ear onto my own plate. "I've never seen him upset before. This... is all new. Grief I've seen in others, but Khine—"

"That boy," he said with a sigh. "I'm still not sure why the gods have cursed me with him. Thought I had my hands full. And then *you* came along."

"You ever wonder if it's because of all your sins?"

"I'm hardly the worst scum the streets of Shang Azi have produced. And yet I'm the only one stuck with the two of you."

"You've known Khine a very long time, then."

"Too long," he sniffed. "Knew him since he was a whelp running around with Reng Hzi and his group of pissants with lofty ideals, freshly arrived in Shang Azi with not a penny to his name. That first day, my men found him sleeping on the street all torn up and bloody, his pockets picked clean by thieves. They took pity on the boy and took him back home, and I gave him shelter for two days."

He held two fingers up. "Two days, Queen Talyien. Pay attention. By the end of those two days, I learned that three bodies were found floating in the river. Known robbers, of course. Were they the same ones Lamang encountered? I don't know, but he packed his things that same evening and told me he had found lodging. There was a look in his eyes that was different from when he came in—something that told me this boy could be useful to me if I put him on the right track. I offered him work, but he refused. That whole physician thing, like it's some sort of noble pursuit." He frowned at the thought.

"You're convinced he killed those men?"

"I don't know if *killed* is the right word. He maintained that he had nothing to do with it. But I later heard that one of the bridges had fallen, and that was how those men fell into the river in the first place. And the bridge was tampered with. He used himself as bait. Risked his life for revenge. He was younger than Cho."

"I think that shows courage."

"Courage! Pah!" Lo Bahn chuckled. "*You* would think so. I suppose my warning is just going to fall on deaf ears, then. But I'll give it, anyway. You take Lamang with you back to Jin-Sayeng the way he is now—who knows what he'll become? He's even more irresponsible than you are, hard as that may be to believe. Did he think he was doing me a favour by finally allowing himself to fall under my employ? I was doing *him* a favour. If you'd seen how he was when he lost both that woman of his and his beloved Reng Hzi's approval…"

I had to pause to consider what he was trying to say. "I'm sorry, Lord Han, I'm not sure I heard right. You actually care about him? *You?*"

"Wipe that disbelief off your face, woman. I care about a lot of people in Shang Azi, Lamang included. Maybe even *you*." Lo Bahn snorted. "Back there, all we had was each other. Maybe that's hard to believe for a queen. You've seen how little respect the likes of Qun have for the people around me. Even Zheshan wasn't without his faults. We made it our business to pay attention to people in the neighbourhood, including the more inconvenient ones."

"Which Khine was, I suppose."

"You have no idea. I don't think I've met anyone who could cause as much trouble as he can—until I met you, that is." He gave me a scrutinizing glare. "What piece do you think he'll play in your little game of *Hanza*? He's not a pawn, I can tell you that much. A soldier, then? Do you see him bowing to you out of loyalty? I can't even ask him to open a door without at least a grumble and an argument." He slammed a fist on the table. "If you want him to do work for you, it's simple. Give him a challenge. He'll latch on to it, if only to get his mind out of his grief."

"That seems manipulative."

He snorted. "And that's a problem for you?"

"It's easy enough with men like you, Lo Bahn."

"You're a heartless woman. You don't even try to hide it." He got up, pushing his empty plates out of the way. "Meet me at the An Mozhi government office in an hour or two. Maybe we'll find something Lamang can't refuse."

"I feel like you're going to betray me again," I said.

"Even if I'm not, it's nice to know I've found a way to curl your toes somehow." He laughed before walking away.

Back at my room in the inn, I watched Nor peer through the windows to view Lahei's men below. "They're still trying to straighten things out at the harbour master's office," she said. "Three weeks. What a joke. So much for Kaggawa's show of power."

"It's still more than I have now," I replied.

"What do you know about Dai Kaggawa, Beloved Queen?"

"Well, his family…"

"Which family? *Kaggawa* is an old name from Akki, one of the more influential families on the island back in the day. I believe this one's grandfather had assisted Reshiro Ikessar in his time. His grandmother is a royal—an *aron dar* Seran, I believe." She cleared her throat. "Old history. The important thing is that the Kaggawas became bankrupt a little less than half a century ago. Dai Kaggawa's resources are coming from elsewhere. His mother married into the Shoho clan, a rather important farming family in the Sougen. His younger half-brother defers to him. And his aunt married a Dageian lord, a powerful merchant in his own right. She has a daughter with the man, from what I recall—this woman is his heir. What does this tell you?"

"I don't know, Nor."

She gave me an impatient look. "Without Magister Arro here to guide you, you need to start putting yourself in his shoes. Think about what this means. You're not running around like a vagrant in Anzhao anymore, Beloved Queen. We may not be home yet, but you're with our people again—everything you do will be remembered in history."

"I hate that."

"What does it mean that Kaggawa has all of this, without any of it truly belonging to him? This is a man who knows how to wedge himself between cracks to get exactly to where he wants. This isn't a spoiled brat flaunting his riches to impress a queen. You said you've met him before?"

"He saved me and Rai from a dragon. He said he tracked it from the Sougen."

"They have plenty of dragons in the Sougen. Why would he track *that* one, specifically, all the way to Oka Shto?"

"You think he brought it with him? It was a dragon, Nor, not a lapdog you can just carry around."

"Your brothers were killed by a dragon from a box. This Dai's dragon doesn't seem like it's even a quarter of the size of that one. I believe you're being used, Beloved Queen."

"I think I'm aware of that," I said. "With any luck, all I'll do is disappoint him. What use is a powerless queen?"

The sound of knocking interrupted us. Nor slid the door to the side, revealing Agos in the hallway. "Let's head out," he said, stepping through the frame.

"To where?" Nor asked. She blocked him at the door.

Agos didn't look at her. "Could you just tell her not to get in my damn face all the time?"

"It's my job to get in the damn face of anyone I deem a risk to the queen," she said in a low voice. "Do you want my knife in your throat?"

"I thought we were getting along," he finally said, turning to her.

"That was before I learned you've been conspiring with Kaggawa."

"Listen to yourself. I haven't been conspiring with anyone. They tracked me in Anzhao!"

"And where exactly are you *headed*?" Nor turned to me. She didn't even try to hide the scowl on her face.

"The governor's office," I said. "You know how dearly we love visiting these Zarojo politicians."

"You're not going without me."

"I am. I need you to stay here and keep an eye on Kaggawa and her men. Unless you'd rather I leave Agos behind instead?"

It was clear she didn't want that, either. She swore. "And what are you hoping to find up there, anyway?"

"Maybe nothing," I said. "But maybe I'll find a way for us to get back home and have Lahei Kaggawa in our debt. Let's go, Agos." Without really waiting to see if Captain Nor had agreed to the arrangement, I strode through the door. A few moments later, I heard Agos stomping behind me, without Nor in sight.

We walked in silence through the streets. With both me and Agos in commoner's clothing, and Agos freshly shaved, we could pass for a couple who had just gotten lost during a stroll. There were enough of those out that afternoon that no one even gave us a second glance.

"What do you think Lo Bahn's got up his sleeve?" Agos asked, looking slightly unsettled with my arm hooked around his. His hair, cropped short at the top, ruffled slightly with the breeze.

"Qun's men," I said, leaning close to him as casually as if he had just asked me if my shoes were too tight. "I heard there's an entire group of soldiers from Anzhao waiting in the barracks. They're obviously looking for us."

"So he's leading you to them?"

"I don't know. Maybe he just wants to show them to me."

"Sometimes I tell myself you really *can't* be this trusting of people, and yet time and time again you prove me wrong."

"Just be quiet," I said. "Follow my lead."

"This sounds suspiciously like when we were kids."

"You see? When was the last time I got us killed?"

"If you want to count all the near-misses..."

"Now, that would be cheating."

"Still got us into trouble more times than I can count." He sighed. "Which way?"

We passed the markets and made our way towards one of the long stairs that wound around the cliff towards upper An Mozhi. Partway up the flight, I belatedly caught sight of the lifts that would've gotten us there faster. They were suspended on thick chains, swaying with the wind as they hung between the cliff ledges. Going all the way to the top meant a good four or five trips, depending on which platform you started on.

Agos must've noticed my look of longing, because he burst out laughing. "Are you kidding me? You need the exercise!" He was sweating rivulets.

"Because getting chased by mad suitors and dolls from hell isn't exercise enough," I said. But to make a point, I sprang ahead of him, taking two steps at a time. I had always been faster than him. I used to joke that since we were always together, it was all I needed to ensure my survival. The wooden stairs creaked under the strain.

"I've missed this," Agos blurted out loud when I reached the next landing.

I paused, running a hand over my damp forehead. "I'm not sure I know what you mean."

He gestured. "This. You, like this. That whole queen business never sat well with you, you know? It used to be easier. You had your responsibilities, but you left the hard part to the regents, left *ruling* to the old fucks who don't have much left to look forward to. If an Ikessar looked at you the wrong way, you told them to fuck off. But then coronation day loomed closer, and you...changed. Hell, I think you changed the day you got married to him."

Agos now had the same look on his face as he had on my wedding day. I tried to push the memory away from my mind. "You make it sound like the worst thing in the world," I said, starting back up the steps. A hot wind sweltered past us, drifting towards the sea where it was greeted by a symphony of seagulls.

"Watching a wolf slink into a falcon's cage and slamming the door shut herself, and then learning how to live like an Ikessar, as if it wasn't bad enough you had to share your bed with one."

"It's not like I dropped everything to embrace their customs."

"No, but you entertained the bastards and the sticks up their asses. Maybe you didn't bend all the way, maybe you grumbled under your breath the whole time, but you bared your neck, you let them get close enough to hurt you. You were trying so hard to turn into an *Ikessar* queen instead of doing things your way. Going to the Kibouri temples, letting their priests tell you what to do… you even let them dictate how Thanh was raised. No, Tali—you forced yourself to be this queen who looked nothing like the woman you used to be. And I don't know what for, considering *he* wasn't even there for the entirety of your rule."

I tried to consider his words without getting angry. "It's more complicated than that, you know," I managed to whisper.

"I suppose," Agos grumbled. "Told you I don't know much about politics. They tried to teach me—heavens know they did. I know you, though. Know you're trying to break loose, even when *you* don't realize the chains bringing you down. The bastard Rayyel, for one thing."

"You're wrong." I paused with one hand on the rail and turned around to look at him. The sun was casting directly over us, which had the effect of darkening his face, deepening the scowl on it. "I know about the chain. I've known it all my life."

"Then why tolerate it?" There was a snarl underneath his voice.

"Because I will not court civil war to indulge my whims."

"There you go again. That queen talk," Agos said smugly, as if he'd just proven a point.

I bit back the retort in my head. We reached the third landing, and I paused to stretch my legs. He caught up to me.

"So that's your lifetime excuse. You force Rayyel into your life because you *have* to, you have to love him, it's your duty and your father wouldn't have allowed it any other way. Don't know if you've been paying attention, but that ship sailed a long time ago. You're dancing the dance, but the music's stopped. I don't even know who you're trying to impress. Yeshin's dead."

I placed a finger on his lips, silencing him. We had reached a small street. I could see the barracks in the distance, an enormous walled keep within the city that stood across from the governor's office. Banners from the towers streamed with the wind. There were soldiers on the rooftop deck, marching to drumbeat as they practiced for a parade. Lo Bahn had wanted to meet on this very street, but he was nowhere in sight. Not that I expected him to show up. I *was* surprised that an army wasn't waiting for us.

I sniffed the air. "Well, I suppose this is the part where we pretend to be tourists."

"I'm not a royal, in case you've forgotten. My Zirano is horrible," Agos grumbled.

"As is your acting, so just close your mouth and nod along." Without waiting for his assent, I dragged him towards the gates.

———

Calling Rayyel a chain wasn't fair. He couldn't help that he was raised by people who believed you could find virtue by not talking to anyone for months on end, who were convinced that you could find the meaning of the universe if you stared at a flower long enough. But I was aware of what Agos meant. Striding up straight to the enemy's lair after all we had just been through was a thing *I* did, the sort of thing Rai's people frowned upon.

Growing up, I had the run of Oka Shto without even really knowing it. My father took great pains to ensure I was sufficiently disciplined, that nothing was ever *easy* for me, but we both took for granted that I was still in an environment that bent itself around my actions. *Foolhardy* was a word Rayyel liked to use. I took chances when it was wiser—sometimes even when it was easier—not to, because I was used to things going my way and I wasn't the sort of person who liked to sit around and wait for things to happen. I was told such rashness was not appropriate behaviour for a leader, so after we got married I tried to step back, tried to act strong and decisive like they said my father was, but also demure and proper and dutiful like a wife ought to be.

I've had horses who fought like demons when you put on one rope too many. They are fine with one, but the perception of being trapped by another drives them on edge. I felt like that more these days than ever before. Too many ropes, too many handlers. But if I ever broke free, where do I run to? This was the only world I knew.

"Hey," a guard called out to us before we could even step past the threshold. "You lost?"

I looked around. "I don't think so," I said. "This *is* the way to the barracks, yes?"

The guard walked towards us, his spear leaning over his shoulder. "We don't usually let civilians in."

"Oh, I know *that*," I said, waving a hand over my nose. "Don't we, Aggie dear?" I glanced up at Agos, who grunted.

"Then what—"

"We came here to sightsee. I was told An Mozhi was quite the city, and of course, everything is absolutely magnificent, but one thing I couldn't get off my mind was how you kept the peace and order. In Anzhao City, for example—that's where we came from, Anzhao—it's so chaotic you can't even turn a corner without getting your pockets cleaned out by thieves. Isn't that right, Aggie?" I elbowed Agos.

The guard looked bemused. "I don't believe I've ever heard Anzhao being described in such a way. If anything, An Mozhi could stand to learn from Anzhao's city watch."

"No!" I said, loud enough that the guard looked almost embarrassed for having said anything. "That's—why, we were at the docks all day, and not once, not *once* did I ever feel unsafe. Are you telling me this is out of the ordinary? But I have heard such good things about An Mozhi. Are you saying you let, even invite, tourists up here while deliberately letting thieves run rampant through your streets?"

"That's not . . ."

"Despicable," I said in a low voice. "Absolutely despicable. I demand a word with your superior."

"You really should go."

"No. *No*, I won't. You just *told* me that An Mozhi lacks proper measures to address thieves. We paid good money to travel here, which included some very heavy taxes on your city's part. If you can't take me to someone, then I need your name at least so I know what to tell the governor's office when I file a complaint."

The guard gave me the look of someone keenly aware of having placed his head on the chopping block. I had been counting on it. Perspiration dotted his face, and not just because it was hot. Very few people knew how to respond to an unexpected figure of authority; the usual reaction was complete avoidance. In this case, the faster he transferred us to the next higher up, the better.

"I'll... see what I can do," he mumbled. "Wait here." He gestured at another guard, who was watching us from the gatehouse with an expression that bordered on both terrified and amused, before walking away.

I glanced at Agos. "You..." he started.

"I just want this trip to go well," I said out loud, patting his cheek. "Of course it's worth the fuss. I want this all to be *perfect*."

"Bit too much," he grumbled. I wondered if he meant my acting, or if he was trying to play along himself. It was hard to tell.

The guard eventually arrived with someone in a crisper uniform. The guard saluted once before returning to his post. I craned my head at the new arrival, judging him to be an officer of some sort. "I'm told you have concerns about the city's security," the man said, making a sweeping half bow.

I felt at ease at once. The man was being polite, and I could use polite. "My husband here was just telling me I might be overreacting. Your guard says the city watch in Anzhao City is more efficient than your system here, which I find hard to believe because we just *came* from Anzhao. Did you know they have an entire neighbourhood of *thieves*? Dar Aso, I believe it was called. I couldn't believe it when I heard it."

"You're referring to the massacre a few weeks back?"

I pretended to shudder. "To think that the Anzhao city watch would have let a whole neighbourhood become overrun like that. I'm glad they got the people, don't get me wrong, but the very thought that it got that far still sends shivers down my spine. I get nightmares about it."

The officer's lips quirked into a smile. "I'm sure."

"I *do*," I insisted, stomping my foot. "So you can see why such a blatant admission from one of your guards, of all people, would send me into panic. I thought An Mozhi was safe!"

The officer held out a hand. "Rest assured, madam, it is. I do believe what you're referring to was localized to a particular problematic neighbourhood, and it's been taken care of, to my knowledge. Our own city watch may not be as rigid as Anzhao's, but we do our best. In fact, we have some of Anzhao's finest with us here right now. I believe they are giving us pointers on how we can improve our system here."

I blinked at him. "That's not very impressive. If you have to take pointers from *Anzhao*—I knew it, Aggie, dear." I made a big show of tugging at Agos's arm. "We should've gone to Kyan Jang. I don't want to be *murdered* in my sleep."

"Kyan Jang is worse, to be honest," the officer mumbled helpfully. "Madam, rest assured, An Mozhi is no less safe than any port city this side of the empire. Keep your wits about you and you'll be fine."

"You said Anzhao's city watch is here."

"I believe so."

"Since when?"

"A few weeks."

"How long are they staying?"

He scratched his head. "I'm not exactly sure, madam. I'm not in a high enough position to be told—"

"Because I'm wondering what they're doing *here* if they're supposed to be keeping Anzhao safe," I said. "You said they're helping you improve your own watch?"

"Among other things."

"Ah." I crossed my arms. "*I see.*"

"I'm sorry?"

"I may inquire with the governor's office, after all. It doesn't look good when an officer can't even tell a tourist what's happening in his jurisdiction."

It was now the officer's turn to sweat. Rayyel would've probably pointed out how shameful it was that I was manipulating innocent people just carrying out their duties, but I rather enjoyed seeing the effect of rank without the title to back it up. My father liked to say that all you needed to do sometimes was to act like you belonged, like you were in charge, and most people will naturally follow. "I'm not really that high up," the officer blurted out. "If you want, I can call my superior, but I'm not sure what he can tell you that I haven't already said. If you think you really want to complain at the governor's office, I can't stop you, but…"

He trailed off at the sound of commotion in the street ahead. I narrowed my eyes and felt a rush of panic when I noticed Anzhao City's flag perched on top of a covered litter in the distance. It was carried by servants dressed in Anzhao government livery.

"Make way for Governor Qun!"

I felt Agos grab my shoulder just as the guards stepped aside and the officer rushed forward to help pull the gates wide open. I heard the rustle of the servants' footsteps, but couldn't see them because Agos drew me in for a kiss.

"Agos—" I began, trying to shove him aside. I stopped when I realized what he was doing. With his head over mine, he was blocking my face from Qun's view. His eyebrows quirked up as he pushed me back to the wall, hand on my cheek. I stiffened, aware of nothing but my racing heart. And then I caught the shuffle of movement in the corner of my eyes and saw that the litter had stopped at the main door. Qun got out and clambered up the steps, the servants crowding behind him.

I pulled away from Agos to catch my breath. The kiss left me feeling light-headed and confused. I knew it was expected after nearly six years of being apart from my husband, but I couldn't stop feeling guilty over how easily I responded to his touch. I struggled for words. "That was sudden," I managed to whisper.

"You said *act*," Agos hissed back, with the faintest shadow of a smile on his face.

"That wasn't acting. And warn me next time."

"So you want a next time?"

I shoved his shoulder and pointed. Qun's arrival had distracted the officer from earlier, but another guard was making his way towards us, and he didn't look very happy. I didn't want to wait around to find out what he wanted. Together, we darted around the corner, hoping to lose him before he called for an alarm.

CHAPTER THREE

THE DEN OF SNAKES

ᗷᗝᘏᔱᕐ

There were two more guards at the far end of the garden, with their backs turned to us. I grabbed Agos's wrist and dragged him to one of the side gates, which led straight to the alley. Just as we reached the shadows behind the stone fencing, we heard one of the guards whistle. "Did you see anyone come through here?" I heard him ask.

I swore under my breath and began to look for an escape. There was scaffolding along the side of the alley that went all the way up to the rooftop, where workmen had been repairing the tiles. It was the middle of the day now, just in time for lunch, and none were in sight.

I grabbed the scaffolding rail and clambered up. Agos didn't waste time and began climbing from the other side. Even with our weight distributed, the lumber creaked with our every step.

We reached the roof just as the shadow of two guards crossed the street below. I leaned against the tiles, heart pounding.

"They must have gone..." a guard called out, before his voice was drowned out by the hum of conversation. I looked up and noticed vents between the eaves of the second rooftop above us. Glancing at Agos, I made my way further up the roof until I reached the wall. I pressed my ear against it, but I couldn't make out any words from the vibration of their voices. I frowned before crouching down to pry away one of the freshly installed tiles, where the mortar hadn't dried yet. It revealed a small hole where I could now see a straight figure dressed in silken robes. I didn't recognize the man, but assumed by the official's hat perched on his head and the servants' uniforms that he was Governor Hizao. The presence of the smaller, thinner Qun across from him confirmed my suspicions.

"Who?" Agos mouthed.

"Hizao and Qun," I whispered.

He started to say something like *We don't have time for this*, but I turned back to the conversation beneath me. I wasn't about to pass up the opportunity to catch a glimpse of Zarojo politics at work, especially if Qun was involved. If the bastard was still out to get me, I needed to know.

"You'll have to speak up," Hizao was saying. "My ears tingle in the presence of usurpers."

Qun smiled thinly. "An unfair accusation, my dear governor. I *was* voted in…"

"After you killed Zheshan. Yes. I know that much."

"I think you're sorely mistaken. There *were* rumours of Zheshan's death, spread by a certain businessman by the name of Han Lo Bahn, but we've scoured his property and found no traces of Zheshan's body. Han Lo Bahn himself disappeared almost immediately after."

"Everyone who crosses you disappears, Qun. It's amazing why you think the rest of the empire is blind to such tactics. You wonder why I had your men detained? Is it not plain enough? I'd sooner lick a dead whore's ass than trust you, and if the emperor could just see sense he'll have you stripped off your position before you can say another word." His expression was stern. I immediately pegged him as the sort of man who upheld laws even when they were inconvenient—the type that formed the backbone of governments, people like Rayyel. I've always appreciated the hard work of such men, even if they are difficult to deal with.

As I wondered how much of my analysis was correct, I turned my attention back to Qun. He looked unfazed. "Without proof, your accusation holds no grounds," Qun said. "I would like my men back. For what reason are you keeping them from carrying out their duties?"

"For the reason that they failed to carry documentation on *exactly* what these duties are," Hizao said. "We are not friends, Qun. We don't gamble together. I don't remember inviting you to my mother's funeral or my daughter's wedding. I don't see why you'd think the arrival of your men in such large numbers wouldn't go amiss."

"But as one governor to another…"

"As one governor to another," Hizao said, "I have taken the courtesy of not announcing that your men have breached An Mozhi regulations. Give me proper paperwork, and I will release them with no one the wiser. The men will continue to believe that this was all just a friendly visit and that you came by only to see how they were doing. Barring that…" He tucked his hands under his sleeves. "I will have to file a complaint with the council. This is not Anzhao City, Qun, for you to just walk in and do whatever you want with. Not that Anzhao City was rightfully yours to begin with."

Qun smiled. "I'll forgive your tone, since you're allowing your temper to get carried away by *gossip*. The entire issue with Zheshan is more complicated than we've allowed to show—in part because we needed to keep order in the city. I came all the way out here to speak to you about this in person."

Hizao's face never once flickered. "Indulge my curiosity."

"Gon Zheshan was conspiring with Jin-Sayeng for political power. He used a pact, signed ages ago, to lure the wayward king of Jin-Sayeng to his abode. Our belief was that he meant to marry his daughter to Rayyel, who has been years separated from his wife—a good enough reason to have their marriage dissolved by their priests. Zheshan comes from a lower-ranking family—such a move, had it worked, would've elevated his position quite considerably. And Zheshan's daughter is quite lovely, as I can attest with my own eyes. I can't see why Lord Rayyel would've refused. The light of her father's life—he was quite fond of her when he was alive."

"A fine story," Hizao said. "One that any old fool can come up with."

"I knew you'd say that," Qun said. "We've got documentation, gathered from both Gon Zheshan's office as well as that of his conspirator, Han Lo Bahn, who—if you must know—held Queen Talyien of Jin-Sayeng against her will when she arrived in Anzhao and right before she disappeared."

"Another important figure you've so conveniently misplaced," Hizao snorted. "My grandfather had better luck keeping track of his chickens."

"Ah, but you see…" Qun lowered his voice. "If you want to know the reason, the *true* reason I sent my men, you'll have to understand all of this. We believe Queen Talyien is hiding out here."

I nearly laughed. Of course. Qun didn't strike me as the kind of man who gave up easily.

"Is that right?" Hizao asked. He sounded bored. "That's the Jin-Sayeng queen, isn't it? The one they call the Bitch Queen?"

"She distrusts us—and rightfully so, after what my predecessor did! But we only want to clear things up with her, to assure her we had nothing to do with Gon Zheshan's ambitions. Her time in Anzhao City has been most...unfortunate, and we are only trying to make it right. The last thing we want is the Jinsein warlords deciding to declare war against us. They've already sent such threatening words."

"Why?" Hizao asked. "I say let them come. We'll crush them fast enough. A paltry nation can't withstand the might of the empire. Jin-Sayeng is nothing but a shadow to the great Ziri-nar-Orxiaro, and a poor one at that! You people have severely mismanaged your affairs if what you say is true. I'm surprised the Esteemed Emperor hasn't intervened."

"The Esteemed Emperor has bigger concerns. But I've brought all the proof with me, Governor Hizao. You are free to peruse it as you wish."

"Gon Zheshan conspiring with the Jinseins...I have never imagined one of our own could stoop so low. A mere governor, and someone *not* from the upper nobility as Zheshan was, having such ambitions? It is treason. To put oneself over the entire realm is despicable." He glanced at Qun while he said this, as if he wasn't really thinking about Zheshan at all.

Qun seemed unaware of his scrutiny. "You can understand my desire for secrecy, then. I am telling you this because you are an honourable man, and I trust that you care about the good of all involved, not just An Mozhi." He pressed a scroll into Hizao's hands.

Hizao unrolled it and carefully read the contents. I held my breath—I would've given anything to see what was written inside it. But I could tell from the look on his face that whatever proof Qun offered about Zheshan's activities was convincing enough.

Inwardly, my mind raced back to events from a few months ago. Qun, of course, was a lying dirtbag, but suddenly Zheshan's suicide didn't seem so out of place. If he was doing something that the empire would see as treason, then a sword through the belly was the Zarojo way of telling people you regretted whatever it was you did, that your family had nothing to do with it. I couldn't really know for sure. Zheshan's motivations had been the most elusive to me, including his misplaced loyalty towards Rayyel. If his own daughter was involved, it made sense to try to protect her once his plans—that strange proposal to have Jin-Sayeng split into half—failed. To protect his daughter with his own life was admirable. I doubted even my own father would have gone so far for me. I itched to ask Rai if he knew anything about it. It wouldn't have been surprising if he didn't.

"This was how Yuebek blackmailed Zheshan," I murmured.

Agos wiped sweat from his brow. "Who else does he have by the balls?"

"At this point, I'm willing to guess everyone. The man is easy to dismiss, but *we're* the fools if we don't take him seriously." I glanced down at the sound of wood scraping on tile, and realized too late that at least one workman was making his way up the scaffolding.

"You!" the workman called, pulling a towel from around his neck and waving it at us. "What are you doing up there?"

I didn't reply immediately. The faintest sound would send the guards running back for us.

"I said—" the workman started. He had a Jinsein accent.

"Hey," Agos broke in, his voice low. "Countryman?"

The man's brows furrowed. "What about it?" he asked, switching to Jinan.

Agos clapped him on the shoulder. "Sorry about that. My wife saw the governor come in and was curious. We're tourists, you see. We've been travelling around the empire."

The man spat. "Good for you. Now leave my worksite before my masters come around and blame me."

"It's like we were never here," Agos said. He clambered down the scaffolding first. I followed from the other side.

We had barely gone a few rungs when we heard the guards below. "Stop them!" a guard screamed from the other end of the street. They were still far enough that if we jumped the last few feet we could make a run for it.

The workman looked confused.

"Stop them, or I'll get the foreman to replace you!"

His eyes darted to us. Agos was closer to him.

"Don't—!" I cried, but it was too late. He attempted to grab Agos's arm. Agos countered by yanking him back, a movement that dislodged the scaffolding from the edge of the roof. It tipped, and with the added weight of three people, it began to spiral to the ground.

The stone fence from the next-door building saved us. Us, at least—not the poor workman. Agos tried to wrap his arm around him, but he slipped and crashed on the cobblestone at such an angle that I knew he died on impact.

I didn't even have time to contain my horror. The smell of blood was in my nostrils as we dropped right into the yard of the other building, past a throng of confused women out for a stroll. "There!" a guard pointed from the street.

"Straight for the motherfucker!" Agos roared. "He's alone!"

I drew my sword and gained speed, reaching the guard first.

He didn't know who I was. I could always tell that by the way they seemed surprised that I had a sword in my hands—anyone looking to detain Queen Talyien would've been warned to be careful. I slashed him across the chest and, before he could recover, stabbed upwards. I had been hoping to get him in the gut, but his armour was in the way. The end of the sword went straight into his armpit.

He recovered from his shock and swung his own sword, catching me on the left arm. I groaned as I felt the blade slide straight into muscle, fighting back against the searing, hot pain. I twisted my sword deeper in response, blood coating my fingers as I tore through his ligaments and struck bone.

Agos appeared a moment later, and the fight was over. He tore the guard off me by hacking through his neck several times. As the body dropped to the ground, he turned to my wound in disgust.

"You're right about me being out of practice," I said.

"Too much rich Zarojo food," he agreed.

The other guards appeared around the corner. There were too many to fight comfortably in the narrow street, and my left arm was starting to tingle. We turned the other way, straight down a row of tree sorrels with trunks dotted with green fruit. The alley opened up to a wider road; as we paused to let a carriage pass, we heard an ear-splitting whistle from the far end.

"Spirits, you're incapable of walking anywhere without causing trouble," Lo Bahn snarled, catching up to us. "I heard the guards screaming about intruders."

"There's more heading this way."

"Fucking hell." He glanced at the carriage, which had stopped to let its passengers off at the side of the road. Without hesitation, he strode over to the confused driver and punched him, before grabbing him by the shirt and throwing him off the seat. "Get in!" he called as he took the reins.

I got into the other end of the seat while Agos swung up the back of the carriage. Lo Bahn flicked the reins, sending the horses galloping down the road. I caught a glimpse of the guards' panicked faces as they emerged from the alley, too late to catch up to us.

"Where the fuck were you?" I said, turning to him.

"You're starting to sound less and less like a queen these days."

"This isn't the time for jokes, Lo Bahn."

He snorted. "Can't tell a joke from an observation, can you? I ran into Qun's men. Didn't know the assholes were staying in the barracks. Recognized me on the spot, the bastards." He tugged his shirt down, revealing a gash along his neck, as if he had narrowly escaped being decapitated. On closer inspection, I also noticed black bruises below his right eye.

"I thought you wanted to bring me *to* them."

"Even if I wanted to, the bastards aren't very amenable to me anymore. That's the problem with double-crossing everyone. Eventually they all stop trusting you." He sniffed and flicked the reins, urging the horses to go faster. "Except you, it seems. Woman. *Queen.* Do you know how hard it is for me to remember who you are? What you are? I sometimes wonder what I lost my entire fortune for, every time I look at you and the things you do. I know I betrayed you once already. You're right—I *would* have handed you over to Qun again in a heartbeat, except you've shown a surprisingly better sense of obligation despite everything. I helped him and he repaid me by burning down my house and throwing me in prison. I betray *you*, and...nothing. You're still here, talking to me like I'm a human being."

"Get to the point."

"I have a contact in this neighbourhood. An old business partner. I was going to introduce you to him. He's got some pull over at the harbour master's office."

"Let's head there now."

"With the guards on our tail?"

I paused for a moment, thinking.

"Double back," I said. "Head to the barracks. To where Qun's men were."

"Back to those assholes?"

"Trust me, Lo Bahn."

"Shit. I *hate* it when you say that."

"No, really. I have an idea."

"Fucking *dammit*, of course you do." But he tugged at the reins, swinging the carriage around. I peered to the side.

"They catching up to us, Agos?" I called.

"I can hear hooves," he replied. "What's that you were telling him? Something about a plan?"

"Your Zirano is improving."

"Well, whatever your plan is, it better be sound. We can't fight them all."

"I'm no Khine, but it's all we've got."

We reached the gates. I whispered something in Lo Bahn's ear, and his eyes lit up. He leaned over the side of the carriage. "Open up!" he called, waving over to the guards on the gate. "Hey, you!"

"You're the asshole the Anzhao soldiers arrested earlier," one of them said. "Didn't we just save your skin?"

"That's fucking Lo Bahn again," a soldier behind him said. "I think he really wants to die!"

"Come out here," Lo Bahn snarled. "See what I've got."

The soldier's eyes skipped towards me. He recognized me, too. His mouth dropped open. "Shit. It's..." But he didn't say anything else. He screamed for the guards to open the gates. They looked amused, but they did just that and stepped aside.

About five Anzhao soldiers came out to arrest me, swords drawn.

"Five!" I said, clicking my tongue. "I'm flattered."

The guards from the government building were right behind us.

"Hey, take care of these assholes!" Lo Bahn yelled, just as they came within earshot. Nobody knew who he was talking to. The Anzhao soldiers turned in surprise, swords still drawn. The An Mozhi soldiers came tearing down on horseback and drew their own swords, thinking the attack was meant for them.

Lo Bahn maneuvered the carriage around the street right as the carnage began.

CHAPTER FOUR

LO BAHN'S CONQUEST

ℐℱℴ℈

"You're right," Lo Bahn said as we ditched the carriage and made our way through the alleys on foot. "You're not Lamang. He manipulates with subtlety. You just smash into things. It's a wonder your head's still glued to your body."

"I got us out, didn't I?"

"Barely," he grumbled. We reached a small house on a quiet street. It was what you would consider a nice house in those parts, with a wooden door that opened up to a small courtyard before revealing the main entrance. Lo Bahn glanced at me before knocking.

A woman with greying hair tied in a bun came out and met us a few minutes later. "Quiet down!" she screamed over the barking dogs before staring at Lo Bahn with a frown. "Han Lo Bahn," she said, a flicker of amusement on her face. "I've heard rumours you were dead."

"That's an improvement. Last time they said I was fucking goats."

"Oh, we took that one for a fact. What the hell are you doing here?"

"Where's your husband?"

"Answer my question first."

Lo Bahn sighed before stepping aside.

The woman turned to me. "Who the hell is this?"

"You don't recognize your queen?"

"How the fuck am I supposed to know what she looks like? She's never attended any parties *I've* hosted."

"The invite must have gotten lost in the mail," I drawled.

She peered at me closely. "She *could* be the queen. She looks old enough."

"Wait a second," I said.

"And you've got an Oren-yaro accent, all right," the woman continued. "Well, I'll be damned. You're actually trying this time, Lord Han."

"I'm not here to trick you."

"You said that the last time."

"Even *I* didn't know those scrolls were fake!"

"Penned by the great scholar Biu Song himself. I should've known you fart just as well from your mouth as your asshole." She rubbed her temples. "Out with it, then, before I call the guards."

"Your queen wants to go back to Jin-Sayeng."

"Right. And you want me to lend you a ship, I'm assuming."

"And jump at the chance to renew our partnership while you're at it. This is a great opportunity here. How profitable do you think it would be to have the queen of Jin-Sayeng owing us a favour?"

"Not very," she said, almost politely. "I've heard she's a terrible ruler."

"That's two insults, now," I mumbled.

She gazed at my arm. "Well, come in, anyway," she said at last. "I'll get some bandages for that wound."

"You're not going to ask where I got it?"

"You're with Lo Bahn. That's answer enough."

Agos remained by the gate, arms crossed, as we took our shoes off in front of the door and followed the woman inside. Two small dogs came charging ahead, but she shooed both away with a sandal. They ran up the stairs and waited at the top, yapping and shivering, their eyes bulging out. The woman bade us to sit on the floor of the common room while she went into the kitchen. She returned a moment later with a plate of fried plantains and shoved it into Lo Bahn's hands hard enough that it was clear what she really wanted was to smash it over his head. With a sigh, she went upstairs.

"Someone hates you more than I do," I said at last. "Amazing."

"She's upset I lost them a lot of money. But I lost money on that transaction, too. That's how business goes." He clicked his tongue. "You, though. I wonder. I've seen you hesitate more than you did when I first met you. *Two* insults Mistress Daos has dealt you, and you didn't tear her face off with your bare hands."

"I've never done anything remotely like that in my life."

"But you're more than capable of it. You're learning restraint."

"I'm not half as strong a queen as I want people to think."

He sniffed. "Restraint isn't weakness, and neither is levelheadedness."

"Wait. *You're* telling me this? You? Shang Azi's Han Lo Bahn?"

"Han Lo Bahn has been a lord of Shang Azi longer than you've been alive. You think I'm just an old man—"

"Don't start with the self-pity, now."

"—but listen when I tell you that you're not completely hopeless." He crossed his arms. "Well, maybe just a little bit."

"I'll keep that in my mind."

"No, you won't. You'd rather I kept it to myself. It's clear from the way you deal with me that you've had enough of old men telling you what they think." He paused as Daos began to descend the staircase. "If you won't listen to me, maybe you'll listen to her. She'll tell you the same thing. She's kept their business afloat all these years, corrupt officials be damned. Not easy for a Jin around these parts. Know how she did it? By not stabbing everyone still blinking, even when she has every reason to. She *gave* us her hospitality."

"We still don't know that. Maybe she's poisoned those plantains. You haven't touched them."

He gave me a weak grin.

"Gossiping about me again, Lord Han?" Daos asked as she reached the bottom step.

"On the contrary, I was praising you."

"That's new. Next you'll be telling me you've got a terminal illness."

"If I've got to be at death's door for you to take a compliment, woman…"

"Shut the fuck up. Give me that arm." I realized too late she was talking to me, and she yanked it up impatiently. She began to wrap the bandage, not gently, but it helped with the pain.

"Since we're here," Lo Bahn said, putting the plate of plantains on the floor next to him, "we might as well talk about that ship."

"I am not lending you our ship."

"You're Jinsein," I suddenly blurted out. "That means the officials are aware you conduct business back home. Did they detain your ship, too?"

"The embargo to Jin-Sayeng doesn't apply when you know whose pockets to line," Daos said casually. "Not that we've done anything of that sort," she added with the faintest shadow of a grin.

"Who *do* we bribe?"

"You don't look like you have the money to bribe anyone," Daos said. "And I know Lo Bahn doesn't anymore."

"Fucking crone," Lo Bahn grunted.

"A crone *with* money," she cackled.

"Kaggawa could afford these bribes," I said.

"*That's* who you're travelling with?" she asked. "Well, that changes things. If they detained Kaggawa's ship, then it's one of two things. Either they're really out for *you* somehow... but that would mean they should have made arrests on the docks. Did they?"

"No. They just told us they've confiscated the ship. We'll get a chance to make a petition a few weeks from now."

"Kaggawa's ship must be that pretty thing that's been at the harbour for a few months," Daos mused. "I should've made the connection. The only *Kag* ship. I always found it funny how Kaggawa is a Jinsein family but they've chosen to do business in the Kag, as if—"

"You're rambling, old woman."

She slapped Lo Bahn on the arm. "It's a beautiful ship. Sturdy, well-made. They're trying to squeeze money out of you. I wouldn't be surprised if they stretch this out for months. They're going to force you to sell the ship for a low price, so they can turn around and sell it later on for much, much higher. Or else tack on a fee of tens of thousands of *rean*, which would take longer to process. Even Kaggawa can't cough that amount up on a whim."

I shook my head. "I don't have months."

She finished tying the bandage. "Why go back home at all? Money's easier to come by here, and as bad as it is, at least the warlords aren't all up in your face all the time. Jin-Sayeng is a shithole nowadays. What've you got waiting for you back home, anyway?"

I think she wanted me to explain Lo Bahn's claims, because I saw a glimmer of doubt in her.

"I just want to see my son," I said.

The sun was setting by the time we returned to the inn. Khine was waiting for me outside. I knew that because he strode up immediately, his eyes on my bandaged arm. "You should have told me. I would have come." His voice had a deathly chill to it, but it was better than the last two days, when he didn't respond to anything that wasn't a request to eat or stand aside or follow somebody.

"Let me tell you the rest, then."

I talked as we walked down to the beach. He absorbed every detail of my story with that same deathly silence from the past few days, a frown growing underneath his sparse beard.

"I think you're crazy," Khine said as I finished.

"You've always thought that. When has it ever stopped you?"

"That was before." There was a finality to his tone, one that hinted he was done with cons. I understood. They were all a reflection of his lies to his mother, of the life he was wholeheartedly ashamed of.

I struggled to set my feelings aside. "Khine, if we wait around too long, Qun will be two steps ahead of us."

"I don't think I can do this. Not anymore."

"You need to distract yourself."

"Distract." He chewed around the word as if it was the most insulting thing he had heard all day. "This is how you think I should deal with sorrow—with distraction."

"Khine…"

"You're asking for too much. I am not—how I was." He slumped down on the sand, his fingers digging into it.

I cleared my throat. "Consider this an order, then. Not a request."

He gave a hollow laugh. "You don't have that kind of authority over me."

I stared at him, waiting. One moment, and then two. And then I said, "Please, Khine. I need your help. You know I have to do this so I can go home to my son."

He licked his lips. "Fucking woman."

"I'll forgive you for that, only because I know you're not yourself right now."

"No," he grumbled. "This is exactly who I am. This is the man who ruined his family's life because he can't be damned to swallow his pride. Whatever I had to be after that was . . . a mockery. And my mother went to her grave knowing that." He closed his eyes. After a few moments, he cursed once more under his breath and ran his hands through his hair.

"Bring me to Lo Bahn," he finally said. "If you want this done right, we need everybody's cooperation." He got up. I grabbed his sleeve before he could take a step.

I could feel my heart beating in my throat as I spoke. "For the short amount of time I knew Mei, I . . ." I blinked back the sudden flood of tears. Khine stood silently while I attempted to compose myself.

"I do," he finally whispered, "appreciate it. But this isn't something you can fix in a day with a speech, Tali. This isn't your court." He pulled away.

Despite his words, Khine cornered Lo Bahn with very nearly the same efficiency he used to, and we spent the rest of the evening crafting a plan over mugs of rice wine. I couldn't help but observe that Khine seemed at his brightest when he was working on something. The deeper we got into our talk, the more animated he became, the more like his old self all over again—though a thinner version, one with dark hollows under his eyes and whose humour was biting, without a shred of joy.

"Are you sure about this?" Lo Bahn asked me later that night when Khine briefly stepped out of the room.

"If it works, it'll bring you one step closer to claiming back all you've lost because of Yuebek."

"All I've lost because of *you*, you mean," he said with a snort.

"Come now, Lo Bahn. We've been through this. Both our hands were forced."

"Pah! Don't I know this. You're lucky I have my children to think of. I don't know how long my steward will remain loyal without coin. Let's just hope this Hizao is both as intelligent and as foolish as you've predicted."

"Qun claims he is an honourable man, which is even better. People will go to great lengths to preserve such a reputation. We've got little else to work with, Han."

Lo Bahn snorted. "I know that, too. Both on a knife's edge, you and me. But that one—" He pointed in the direction of Khine's room. "That one is past that edge. The whole bloody blade is up his throat. I had hoped this distraction would be sufficient, but I know that look in his eyes. I've seen it before, when he lost that woman. Are you sure you want to take him with you to Jin-Sayeng?"

"You said you would cede his service to me."

"You don't want *that* as a servant. Foolish woman. You've been in this business as long as I have, you start to learn that people have their limits. Haven't you seen a broken man before? Ground to the dust with nothing to live for... if he gets himself killed, he won't care. Gets us killed, what's it to him? And yet you want to take him along."

"Would you rather he stay on with you?"

"Before that whole debacle with his mother, I would've said yes, without question." Lo Bahn scowled. "If the gods smile on us tomorrow and this whole thing works out, great. Qun ends up in chains and I'm back home trying to get my business started again. I could use him then, especially without you to distract him from his duties. But look at him now. He's like a half-empty wine barrel and everything inside is soured. And you'd take him with you? All the way to your nation? Whatever for?"

"Inzali asked me."

He laughed. "*Inzali* asked you. Oh, I grant you, she can be persuasive if she puts her mind to it—frightening, even. But surely you can come up with a better excuse than that."

"She did, though."

He held a hand out. "Listen. I may not get a chance to say this. But that boy—treat him right. Don't get him killed."

"What happened back then? With Jia? He never really told me."

Lo Bahn sighed. "A child was involved, or what would've been a child had the woman's pregnancy carried through. She approached Reng Hzi to get rid of it. Reng Hzi agreed, thinking he was doing Khine a favour. He only found out long after the fact, and started an argument with his teacher. The old doctor swore never to grace Shang Azi with his presence again. And the rest—shall I say—is history."

"History best left in the dredges of time, Lo Bahn," I heard Khine utter from the end of the hall.

Lo Bahn gave me a look before shuffling away slowly, like a bear who couldn't be bothered to fight for his dinner.

Khine crossed his arms as he approached me. "Isn't it too late to be sticking your nose into the issues of peasants, Queen Talyien?"

"Unfair," I said. "I'm worried about you. And you're one to talk."

"I promised I would do my part and I will. Know that much about me, at least. Go to sleep, Tali. Tomorrow will be a long day."

"Queen," I repeated, my voice rising. "Pick one. I'm either a friend, as you once told me I was, and you will let me help you, or I'm a queen whose authority you *do* recognize—in which case I will not suffer insubordination. You have to decide one way or the other before we get to Jin-Sayeng."

I expected him to argue, to tell me why he thought I was insane to assume he would follow me all the way back home. But he didn't. Neither did he give me an answer to my question. He simply dropped his head in resignation and left.

I closed my eyes, my head pounding. If this was how it felt to be queen again, I wasn't sure I wanted it.

———

We were greeted by yet another foggy morning, which I was told was not so unusual for summer in that part of the empire. Not that the weather was the topic of conversation at breakfast. Revealing our plan to Lahei was not met with as much enthusiasm as I had hoped. But she wasn't confrontational about it, and I went over everything and what I expected her men to do, where I needed them to be by the time I gave the signal. I noticed her observing me while I spoke, with a thoughtful look that was odd for a girl her age. It bothered me more than it should; I strove to focus on the task at hand.

Surprisingly enough, the one person who seemed almost calm about everything was Han Lo Bahn. He ate the simple inn fare of fried bread and dried fish with more relish than I had seen him eat anything in days. When he caught me looking at him, he laughed. "Just stocking up," he said. "They'll feed me worse in prison."

"They may not imprison you at all," I reminded him.

He snorted. "Somehow, I doubt that. But it is preferable to having my head on a spike—not that it isn't also a possibility with what you've asked me to do."

I closed my eyes for a moment before nodding.

"You're not going to say *You don't have to do this*, are you?"

"Lord Han..."

"Pah! Woman, I'm teasing. You should know me better by now."

"I have to admit, I really can't tell one way or another with you."

He took a long drink of tea before getting up. "Well," he said. "No sense putting it off. Either this happens, or it doesn't. Lamang!"

Khine looked up from his table. Lo Bahn gestured, and we both followed him out onto the street. There, Lo Bahn squinted at the dark sky and grumbled, "*The cicadas grow silent in the presence of a dead man.*"

I blinked. "I'm sorry—what?"

"He's quoting last-century poetry," Khine said. "They can't kill you, Lo Bahn. They have to believe you for this to work."

"*Can't* is a very different word from *shouldn't*. Striding up to Governor Hizao's office and proclaiming that Governor Qun ordered *me* to kill Gon Zheshan is believable enough, I grant you," Lo Bahn sniffed. "It's what they're going to want to do to me after that's the question. How will Hizao treat a self-confessed murderer? We know Qun *won't* be happy, though I'm sure he's going to have himself to worry about in the next little while. Ah, Gon, I would've throttled the life out of you myself if I knew it was going to come to this. Getting me into this mess... didn't think he had it in him. The softheaded fool should've asked me for help. I would've found a way."

"I could ask one of Lahei's men to shadow you," I said. "If things go sideways, it'll give you a chance to escape."

Lo Bahn squinted. "I'm not like you, Queen Talyien. I'm not young anymore—I don't have a stomach for these by-the-skin-of-your-teeth adventures of yours. Even a man like me knows his limits." He rubbed his jaw. "Let's just hope it doesn't come to that. I can deal with prison. A quick word to my wife, or business partners who have not yet given up on me, and I'll be back on my feet in no time. As long as Qun is out of the way..."

"He will be. Hizao won't let him get away with it—you should've heard him."

"I don't have to. I can believe it. Hizao's and Qun's families have always been at odds. But I won't bore you with our oligarchies." He straightened his sleeves and reached out to clasp Khine's shoulder with one hand, squeezing it hard. "You."

Khine looked up at him. "What about me?"

"Ten years I've watched you grow up."

"The hell are you starting on, Lo Bahn?"

"Stop yapping for a moment and let me get a word in. Ten years I've watched you fawning over Reng Hzi and then that woman of yours. And now..." His eyes flicked from Khine and then back to me. "We both get out of this alive, you know where to find me. I know what you think about what I do for a living. I know you think it's beneath you. But a man has to make something out of this life or else it consumes him."

"Lo Bahn..."

"Yes, I know. I'm starting to sound like you. Pathetic. Maybe we do need time apart." He slapped Khine's shoulder away and turned to me. "And you..."

"Lord Han." I bowed.

"You insult me and then you honour me. I don't know what to think about you. I suppose given what I am and who you are, it doesn't matter what *I* think." He returned the bow awkwardly. "You've probably met your fair share of fine, well-spoken men, so I'm not going to try to embarrass myself. I hope this makes things even for us."

I gave him a wolfish grin. "I hope so too, Lord Han."

"Should've given me at least one night, though. I could've blown your mind." He smirked. "Then again, perhaps I wouldn't have been able to keep up with you."

"Might've thrown out your back," Khine mumbled.

"Best we just leave it to the imagination," I agreed.

Lo Bahn chuckled and started walking away. "Even if they kill me, your little ruse might still work," he called, waving as he strode down the path like a soldier bravely walking to a battle he was not hoping to win. "Good tidings, Queen Talyien!" He caught up to the crowd, and then just like that, he was gone.

CHAPTER FIVE

THE LEGACY OF SHANG AZI

ᴛᴧᴍ

We spent the rest of the morning shopping for clothes, which was not an activity I enjoyed while wondering what was transpiring over at the governor's office. I resisted sending men to keep an eye on things—the last thing I wanted was the guards picking up Jinseins in case of a mass arrest. It would make our situation more difficult, make Lo Bahn's claims less believable.

So I tried to focus on nodding along while the cheerful shopkeeper described the cut of the silk dress I was buying. It was Zarojo-style, and rather expensive—a detail that didn't seem to make Lahei blink at all. She had not lied about the Shadows' *vast resources*. I left the shop looking nothing like the plain-clothed woman who had been running around the empire the past seven months. It was suddenly easy to remember that I was a royal, that begging and hiding and sneaking were not elements of the world I had been raised in. Agos's eyes widened at the sight of me, and he looked like he was having trouble breathing. "Beloved Queen," he murmured. "Princess. You look—"

"Streak of dirt on my face?" I asked brightly.

"Now that you mention it…" Lahei said. She leaned forward to wipe my cheek with her thumb.

"Are your men ready?"

"Let me worry about them, my queen. You focus on the harbour master."

"We don't have room for error. One slip, and…"

"My men are capable, my queen. As I assured you."

I heard someone clear his throat. The Lamang brothers appeared at the end of the street. Cho was dressed in plain clothes, but with a servant's hat on his head and the usual scowl on his face. I drifted from him to Khine, who, like me, was dressed in noble's clothing—black silk and satin. Perhaps it was the contrast with how I had always seen him, but his appearance gave me pause. He looked... almost lordly.

Khine came up to me. "They're already talking," he said in a low voice. "The tailor's son was gossiping about a commotion in the upper district."

I held my breath. "Any word on Lo Bahn?"

"Nothing that I could make out. Qun's been arrested for conspiracy, though. And people are talking about the embargo, about how Gon Zheshan used his connections to ask for it and force Lord Rayyel to stay in the empire."

"Lo Bahn followed through," I said. "And I doubt Hizao will have him killed if he can be a witness. What did I tell you, Lahei? The man may not look like it, but knows his way around these people."

Lahei gave me a nod of acknowledgment. "Now for your part," she said.

"The easy part," I replied, hooking my arm through Khine's. "Shall we pay a visit to the harbour master, my love?" I asked sweetly. I could see Agos glowering in the corner.

Khine grunted. We walked down the street like this, with only Cho following us a good distance behind. I caught a glimpse of us from a shop window and was pleased to see that we looked like a proper Zarojo nobleman and his wife. Of course, the expression on Khine's face said something else entirely—I had heard the phrase "a walking dead man" uttered more than once, which I found fitting to describe him now. I hoped it was enough to fool people with... if I didn't carry such an obvious Jinsein accent, I would've gone alone. I needed his craftiness, needed the old con artist who *revelled* in this sort of thing. It grated that I was asking this from him at such a difficult time.

We arrived at the harbour master's office. It was quieter than I expected—there was a single receptionist fanning herself and picking at her teeth in the corner. She looked at us as we entered.

"My dear, are you *sure* we're at the right place?" I asked, pulling Khine close to me.

I felt him take a deep breath, and for a moment, I was almost sure he was going to give up and walk away. And then he leaned over the desk to look the receptionist in the eye. "My wife and I saw this ship at the docks. We were wondering if you could point us to the owner."

The receptionist set her fan aside to stare at us. "Why?" she finally asked.

"Why, to buy it, of course," Khine said. He sniffed. "Have you been drinking?"

"I . . ."

"It's not even noon yet, woman! What a despicable way to run an administrative office. I demand to see the harbour master *at once*. Bah!" So—he *was* worried about Lo Bahn, too. It was almost a convincing depiction.

My hand found its way to his. His fingers tightened around mine in return, a brief gesture that he didn't even seem aware of. He pulled away quickly to slam his fists on the desk. The receptionist jumped back, glaring at us with a vehemence that must've been honed by years of dealing with foul-tempered sailors. But the display worked. She pushed herself away from the desk and fled to the end of the hall, where we heard her pound against a door.

The harbour master arrived, a stooped woman who stood as high as my shoulder, with sagging jowls and a puckered mouth. "What's this?" she demanded. She looked at us, and after a moment of consideration—us in our expensive clothing, while Cho stood quietly in the corner with his head bowed—her expression changed. "That foolish girl didn't tell me we had such distinguished visitors. You may call me Manshi Gwe. Come in, come in. Forgive the mess." She bowed and gestured at us to follow her into her office. We left Cho behind.

"Now," Gwe continued, rubbing her hands together as soon as the door closed. "How can this old woman be of service to you?"

"My wife and I have been looking for a ship for our business," Khine said. "There is one at the harbour that fits the bill. We were wondering if you could point us to the owner so we could make a transaction. It's a Kag ship, white sails . . ."

"Yes," Gwe said, trotting to her desk to pull out a piece of paper. "The *Aina's Breath*. It's the only Kag ship in our registry."

"And the owner?" Khine asked, letting the impatience seep into his voice, just as it would've if he were Lo Bahn.

Gwe gave the appeasing smile of an experienced bureaucrat. "It doesn't matter. The ship's not allowed to sail by orders of the governor."

Khine's face tightened. "Direct orders?"

"No-o…" the woman intoned. "There's a temporary order preventing Zarojo ships from heading to Jin-Sayeng, you see, and the crew let on that they intended to sail to Ni'in. Ni'in isn't too far from Jin-Sayeng. We had to make a decision."

"*We*." Khine seated himself on the mat without invitation and motioned for me to do the same. I knelt, rather demurely, straightening my skirts like a proper wife would've. Khine folded his hands over the harbour master's desk. "You mean *you*, of course."

Gwe leaned on the desk with her elbow. "It *is* my job."

"I don't see what part of your job prevents you from at least putting me in contact with the ship's owner. Unless…" And here, he pulled out a purse from his sleeve and slid it across the desk. His face remained stern. "As it happens, I've just heard that this *embargo* is under suspicion as a ploy created by the late Governor Zheshan of Anzhao for his own personal affairs."

Manshi Gwe's face didn't change much except for a slight upturn of her lips. "A grave accusation."

"Very much so."

"But we are only following protocol. We had nothing to do whatsoever with this Zheshan's affairs."

Khine snorted. "Obviously. But I don't, either, so you can see why your refusal to cooperate is grating my nerves."

"There are other ships in the harbour that I can direct your attention to. I'm sure their owners will be more than happy to discuss a sale with you."

"Those flimsy things? I need something I can sail around the continent, something that won't break in a storm." He nodded at the purse, which remained untouched on the table. "Consider that a gift. As it happens, I'm aware of the protocol surrounding seized assets. After a certain period of time, you're allowed to sell them to free up the harbour space and keep a certain percentage of the profit in fees."

Gwe sat back and began to fan herself with her hand. "Perhaps this is true. Perhaps it isn't."

"This situation is not going to resolve itself in a day, or a month, or perhaps even years if I know how these things go. There'll be inquiries, hearings. And in the meantime, what's going to happen to the ship? Will you allow it to fall into disarray?"

"Of course not."

"Bah! You don't know. Don't even pretend, mistress. But I can tell you this: if you can help me convince the owner to sell, I will be very generous. I want this ship. I *need* this ship."

"The embargo still stands."

"The ship does not technically fall under it," Khine snarled. "Do you want me to go over the details? You're detaining it *illegally*, and if this embargo is found out to be illegal as well—do you see how badly this can go for you?" Then he gave a quick grin. "It doesn't have to be, of course. If you cooperate with both me and the ship's owner, I'm sure we can sweep this under the rug. Tell me, how useful would transfer fees, fattened up a little, be for your drab little office? Some drapes for your windows, a better receptionist..."

"You know definitely how to sweeten a deal, sir," Gwe said. "But I'm an honest woman. If what you say is true, I can maybe pen up an inquiry for you, say... in four weeks?"

Khine pretended to think. I knew he was pretending because his movements were too swift, too angry. But Gwe had no way of knowing that. All she saw was a man on the edge of temper, a rich, obnoxious fool who wasn't being given the chance to part with his money.

"Four weeks," Khine said, returning to the desk. "Draw up an inquiry."

Gwe hesitated.

Ah, I thought. I hadn't noticed that Gwe had been haggling. But the hesitation told me she had nothing to gain from a *legal* transaction. Khine picked up the purse again, almost thoughtlessly, and I saw a sort of panicked light in Gwe's eyes. He pretended not to notice her reaction and crossed his arms, his fingers tapping on the embroidered cloth.

"Look," she finally said.

"What was that?" Khine asked.

"There might be a way for me to make this happen. But, er—any discrepancies in transfer fees will be noticed immediately. The fees are set each season, you see, and they will find it very odd if you overpay."

Khine narrowed his eyes. "So what are you saying?"

"You can, right now, pay for something like…" She quickly glanced at the documents on her table. "The taxes on the goods brought in by a ship that isn't scheduled to dock until next week. I'm sure the owner will be most pleased you took care of it for him."

"Right. Until he learns the money has been misplaced."

"Such is business, after all."

"How much?"

She took out a scroll and unrolled it. I didn't see the number, but even Khine's eyes flickered enough for me to know it was substantial. He hesitated for a moment before emptying the purse on the desk. And then he strode out, whistling for Cho.

He returned with more money, dropping rings of coins along with the rest. Gwe gathered them all, before depositing them in a yellow silken bag that she slid inside a drawer. I wondered why she didn't just take the money out-right, before realizing that this must not be a onetime thing. If she took bribes straight-out, sooner or later someone would talk. But the way she did things, it would be harder to prove whether she had pocketed the money or the harbour master's office had just made a clerical error.

"I can tell you where to find the ship's owner," she said, after she finished with the paperwork. "I'm told they're staying at an inn near the harbour."

"Thank you," Khine said. "My wife and I will want to take a look at the ship, too. I trust your guards won't be trouble?"

"I'll draw up an order right now." She pulled out a piece of paper. "Anything else I can do for you, Lord…?"

Khine kept up the act for the rest of the afternoon. I had never seen him go so long without breaking character before, and it worked so well that Mistress Gwe went as far as taking us to the inn herself to find Lahei. The entire exchange kept me on my toes—Lahei had not expected Gwe to show up herself and kept her answers short. She would've folded under scrutiny.

But Khine took over the gaps and the long pauses, and we soon found ourselves boarding the ship while Gwe gestured for the guards to unchain it from the piers. I felt the thickness of the wooden deck under my boots and had a sudden glimpse of Lahei's love and pride for the ship. Even the rails were polished and oiled.

"Once I buy this vessel, will you allow my crew to take the ship to Anzhao?" Khine was asking.

Gwe tapped her shoes together. "When all the papers go through, I don't see why not."

Khine walked to the base of the mast and looked up. "How long has this ship been docked here?"

"A few months," Lahei replied.

"Is that typical for you? I would assume that you'd want to get your goods and get out as soon as the weather is fair. Several months at the harbour seems suspicious."

Lahei looked confused. "I don't understand—"

"Is the ship seaworthy?"

The anger that crossed her features was real. "Of course she's seaworthy. I've never known a more seaworthy ship in my life. She's gone all the way to the frozen Shi-uin Sea, if you can believe it."

Khine made a sound and glanced at me. "I'm starting to change my mind, wife. There must be a reason why the ship hasn't left harbour in so long."

"It's indeed been registered since last spring," Gwe said, looking down at her papers with a measure of uncertainty. "And the ship was detained only two weeks ago. Perhaps..." She trailed off as Khine stamped his foot on the deck.

"What are you doing?" Lahei asked in shock.

"If I check the hold, will it have your goods?" Khine replied.

Lahei stared at him.

"You're a merchant. If they only detained you two weeks ago, right before you were about to leave—as you said—then your hold should be full. If I go there now, what will I find? Will it be as empty as your lies?" He crossed his arms smugly.

Lahei didn't reply. We had no idea Khine was going down this road. He had only asked us to follow his lead, and...

"Husband," I said out loud. "It doesn't matter whether she's lying about their business or not. I'm more interested in whether *we* can use the ship. Perhaps a test run...?"

"I was about to suggest that," Khine said without a note of humour. He turned to Gwe. "Can you ask your men to lift the anchor? I would like to sail around the harbour."

"I'm not sure I can allow that," Gwe said. "With ahh, a limited crew..."

"Bah! Don't be an idiot. Of course we can't go far with a limited crew. But I'm sure my man there can manage." He nodded towards the silent Cho before glancing back at Lahei. "What do you think? Can she make it to the end of the harbour, at least? We have a fair wind blowing."

"Of course she can make it," Lahei said. Her face was very red—she hadn't expected this line of inquiry. "There's nothing wrong with my ship."

"I don't have the authorization," Gwe said.

Khine stared at her, as if wondering if she was lying or not. He must've decided she wasn't; the quake in her voice was real enough. He glanced at Cho, a quick signal.

The boy reached down and began to work at the chains to pull the anchor up.

"Hold on a moment," Gwe said. "I told you we can't do that. You—hey!"

"Is everything all right?" a guard called out.

"It's nothing," she replied. "Just a misunderstanding. Just—"

I looked at Khine, who looked at Gwe. "Are you sure you'd rather not stay at the docks, mistress?" he asked. "You've already been quite helpful."

"I'm not going anywhere, and neither is the ship."

But it was, because Lahei was at the wheel, cranking the sails to catch the softest brush of wind. The guards, realizing the ship was moving, began running to the edge of the docks, screaming for us to stop.

"This is too far," Gwe broke in, still not realizing what we were doing. Or maybe she knew; she was just holding on fervently to the hope that we hadn't outwitted her. "Off to the left some more. Hey, you!" She turned to Lahei, who ignored her.

Gwe's face turned pale. "Tell her to stop," she said, grabbing Khine's arm. "This won't do! If they find out back in the office..."

We heard the ship creak. Four guards from the dock had leaped onto the side and were climbing up the chains. The only sword I had was strapped to Khine's belt—it had seemed better there, with his character's arrogance and disregard for the law. I pulled him to me so I could draw the sword, just as one of the guards came bearing down on him.

I shoved Khine out of the way. The guard's blade struck the deck with such force that he was stuck there for a split second. I kicked his jaw, sending him toppling away from his sword. He landed on his back with a dull thud.

The other guards appeared over the railing. Two, realizing I was the threat, grabbed me from behind, twisting my arm until I dropped my sword. The last one had his blade at Khine's throat. I caught a trickle of blood making its way down his neck.

The hatch from the lower deck creaked open. Lahei's men stepped out, followed by Agos and Nor.

"Drop your swords or we'll kill them!" a guard snarled. He tightened his hairy arm around my neck, threatening to crush my windpipe.

"You're outnumbered," Khine broke in, looking all the more like the arrogant lordling he pretended to be. "Even if you kill us, they'll kill you anyway. Are your lives worth a small embarrassment?" He was playing a game of chance; Zarojo officials doled out harsh punishments, and the guards might choose to die heroes to save their families from their wrath. But I was starting to realize that Khine didn't care about any consequences right now. Lo Bahn was right. This was a game, and he didn't care if he lost it.

"Drop your swords," I managed, before they could make a decision that would end us. "There's enough chaos in the city for today. Blame it all there. You can still leave, alive. Nobody ever needs to know about this."

That one glimmer of hope was enough. The guard holding me relaxed, and he pushed me away before dropping his sword. The others complied. Agos kicked the swords away from them.

"I'm afraid we're heading out to sea after all," Lahei announced as her men came to subdue the guards. "Mistress Gwe... the ship's not for sale."

She dabbed her perspiration with a handkerchief.

"We'll give you a boat," Khine said. "I don't expect you to swim back."

"This is..." Gwe started. "The governor will hear from me. He'll—"

"Be too far away to do anything," I broke in. "I'm sorry for the trouble. But you'll be home by dinnertime, don't worry." I patted her shoulders. She stared numbly at the deck, shaking.

The men started to work on the sails. In no time at all, the ship was finally headed full-speed across the Zarojo Sea.

CHAPTER SIX

THE WESTERN CRAWL

There are no words that can describe the feeling of having shed a burden and facing the winds that would bring me home. If I could write poetry, if I at least knew how to create imagery meant to evoke the beauty of emotion and all these things that make people clasp their hands and gasp in awe, I might be able to find the pretty words for what I felt as I stared at the fading shoreline on the horizon. If I was a poet and not simply a woman whose memories were bursting from her heart and onto paper, I might have found better ways to describe the trail of foam behind the currents against the setting sun, or the stars that crept along the edges of the grey sky above that swollen sea. Or the shadows that danced on Khine's face as he dropped beside me on the deck—a faint ghost of the proud, arrogant man he had appeared earlier. Perhaps I don't need words. Perhaps the reminder that joy and sorrow went hand in hand is enough. No laughter without at least a few tears. No light without the dark.

I reached out to cup his cheek with my hand.

He made no sign, no motion, of having noticed me. His eyes were dimmed, as if he wasn't even looking at what was in front of us. Maybe it was just that all he saw was water and sky. The horizon that called me back home held no meaning for him. Not that he would ever have anything of that sort waiting for him again. To have your home tainted with grief—my father would've known that feeling.

I pulled away, leaning back against the railing as the salt breeze played with my hair.

"Can't believe it actually worked," he croaked out after what felt like forever.

"You're good at what you do, Khine."

"At tricks? Lies? Cheating?"

"Making plans. Executing them."

"Maybe I'm glad my mother died." His face tightened. "At least she didn't have to know I've been using my talents to hurt people."

I didn't reply. The sorrow in his voice was so thick that I didn't know if I could find the words to remove it.

"Let me be alone, Tali," he said at last. "I need to be alone."

"All right," I whispered. "But when you're done, remember that I'm here for you."

He nodded without really looking at me.

I left him and went up the ladder to join Lahei. She was still at the ship's wheel, staring at the spread of maps and a compass on the table. "I don't really think they'll send anyone after us, but I'll rest easier once we're in Kag waters," she mumbled.

"How long?" I asked.

"Twenty days, if the weather stays like this."

"I suppose there's no sense trying to convince you to take me to Fuyyu instead. It's closer to Jin-Sayeng."

"My father wants to speak with you as soon as possible. He is waiting for us at Ni'in. To dock at Fuyyu would mean dealing with authorities."

"*My* authorities."

She smiled.

I took a deep breath. *Not even an hour in and it's already started.* "I was under the impression that we were working together."

"Are we not, my queen?"

"You tell me. It almost sounds like you're going to detain me against my will. Tell me, Kaggawa—am I your queen, or your hostage?"

She dropped her head. "It may seem like it, but believe me, this is merely a precaution. We do not know the sort of ill intention that lurks through the streets of Fuyyu."

"There are no warlords in Fuyyu. The city officials answer directly to the Dragonthrone."

"The Ikessar-appointed officials?"

I smiled at her. "Are you suggesting the Ikessars are not to be trusted? You people *worked* with the Ikessars once, did you not?"

"I'm not implying anything, my queen," Lahei replied. It sounded honest enough, although the knowledge that she couldn't act her way out of a wet paper bag probably helped. "That said, your husband is an Ikessar and didn't seem to trust them, either. Else why would he be alone out here, relying on the Zarojo almost as much as you?"

I paused, considering her words, before pulling myself into the chair next to the table. "Be straight with me, Lahei."

"How straight, Beloved Queen?" She leaned over the ship's wheel to face me. "Shall we talk about the situation back home *now*? Are you sure you're ready to hear it?"

"I thought we'd discussed this before. You've as much as implied that *you're* the only people I should be trusting. Did I get it right? Every single one of my warlords are only looking out for themselves, and my own general and lords, it seems, are no better. Tell me something I don't know, Kaggawa."

She smiled. "The queen is wise. But also a lot less concerned about this situation than I feel she should be."

"Must I stomp my feet and scream? Run around like a headless chicken?" I leaned across the table to glance at the map before turning back to her. "I know what the warlords feel about me, Lahei. It's not news to me. I wouldn't be surprised if half of them decided not to send help because they were hoping I would just die out here. As for Lord Ozo, I have every intention of having him answer for his actions while I've been away. If he is indeed involved with Yuebek, he will not go unpunished."

"My queen," Lahei said. "You seem to believe that you can return to Oren-yaro uncontested. That all you have to do is sit on your throne once more and the warlords will slink back to their dens like nothing happened."

I tried to hide my amusement at the prospect of a girl trying to school me on how to rule. "Tell me how I'm mistaken," I said.

"You? No, Beloved Queen—you are only acting as expected. You were ignorant, perhaps, but that is something we can all be accused of once or twice in our lives."

"You're lucky I don't know how to steer a ship, or else..."

I was losing my touch, because she merely continued to smile. "The ignorance is not yours, either. Not entirely. It lies in your father's misjudgment. He sparked a war to wrest control away from the Ikessars, because he believed that the Ikessars lacked the strength to maintain order in Jin-Sayeng. It is not a difficult leap of logic to make: the Ikessars valued diplomacy, sometimes over common sense. And without the army to support them, they've had to resort to cheap tactics to be heard. The Ikessars have always been aware that they are little more than the balance of power in the kingdom."

"Cheap tactics," I repeated. "*You* say this. Those cheap tactics were your family's, weren't they? Didn't they result in bloodshed, too?"

"We don't pretend to be more than we were. We served. My family did not always agree with what needed to be done, but the Ikessars were our masters at the time, and so..." She drifted towards the table and took a seat next to me. "Warlord Yeshin forgot to consider one thing. The problem with Jin-Sayeng did not lie with the Ikessars or how they managed—or mismanaged—their power. The problem lies with Jin-Sayeng itself. The word *royal*, for example."

I pretended to sniff. She said the word with about the same amount of loathing as her man had back in An Mozhi. "What about it?"

"The warlords believe they own the people, which stems from the idea that the nobles are at the top of the ladder. Why should a man be worth less because his name is *alon gar* instead of *aren dar*? The *aron dar*? A single letter, an entire world away. The *aron dar* serve the *aren dar*, no matter that they are also royals. My great-grandmother was an *aron dar*, Beloved Queen—of the Seran clan. They detested her for marrying a merchant."

"I believe I know that part of your history," I told her. "I'm told that Reshiro Ikessar became involved at some point."

"I'm not trying to reopen old wounds, only giving examples. Your own husband's father was an *aron dar*, too, and look at the trouble his mother had to go through in order to legitimize him as her heir. Is there a difference? They all come from the same blood. But I'm told there's a map you people follow, that it's different for every clan..."

"Yes. The *rules for lineage*," I said. "As Jin-Sayeng lost its dragons and its dragonriders, we had to resort to mapping out the bloodlines. It used to be easier. You were a royal if you had a dragonrider in your family. It signified service to your lord, sacrifice."

"It's like you're saying commoners don't know these words."

"That's not what I meant and you know it. I didn't come up with the rules, Lahei," I murmured.

"You're a queen," she said. "*The* queen."

"Even queens must follow the law," I reminded her. "Even if I wanted to change the way things are, they won't let me. The warlords hold on to what scrap of power they can like greedy dogs worrying over a bone. My father knew this, which was why he knew a stronger Dragonlord was needed to keep them in line."

"A stronger Dragonlord... we don't disagree with that, Beloved Queen. But not to keep the warlords in line—no. I believe you keep dogs. If you have weak lines in your pack, what do you do? Do you let them continue to run during hunts? Or do you keep them behind, cull them from the work and the breeding?"

"Cull the warlords," I said with a small grin. "This is what your father would talk to me about?"

"My father wishes to discuss many things with you, Beloved Queen. He has wanted to for a number of years, but we never found the opportunity... until now. We want to show you what's truly happening to your nation—the flames crawling at the edge of your map."

The way she said it, I had the sudden impression that if I outright refused, that if I demanded she turn this ship *towards* eastern Jin-Sayeng instead of the west, she would do something about it right then and there. Kill me, perhaps. The look in her eyes—I wouldn't put it past her. I reminded myself of the stories about the Shadows during the war. They were more than just spies and assassins; there was talk that they manipulated the war into ending the way it did against the Ikessars' will. Dai alon gar Kaggawa was just a young man in those years and I didn't know what role he played, but it was not an organization to take lightly.

Still. Cull the warlords, indeed. There lay the offered blade, and they didn't even have the courtesy of wrapping it in golden silk first. As if I needed a reminder of what I was getting myself into. But I smiled at her politely as I walked back out to the deck, and replaced every ounce of weariness and anger in my heart with an image of my son. A dangerous image, that. It brought me one step behind Mei, one step away from the edge of that cliff, and I didn't think I cared.

The winds were fair the first few days. The third or fourth day of our journey, I stepped out of my quarters very early on to catch the sunrise. Nor, who must have been standing outside the door all night, followed me silently as I made my way to the end of the ship.

"Agos cannot return with us to Oren-yaro," she said once we were well out of earshot of anyone who might already be awake.

"That's a distant worry, Captain," I told her.

"It isn't. He needs to know it now—that his task is to deliver you safely back to Jin-Sayeng. Once we are with people we trust, his services are no longer needed. Pay him, to make it official."

"People we trust. Who exactly, Nor? You two are all I've got, it seems."

She paused, as if considering her words. "I am your Captain of the Guard," she finally said. "A task assigned to me joylessly, as if I was the lesser choice. I am an Orenar, too, Talyien, lest you forget. A royal's daughter. My father owns a small estate in the Oren-yaro foothills, where I was heir until my elders decided I need to join the guard instead. They meant for me to serve you directly. The Orenar clan is far, far too small to maintain itself; we have always gotten by with support from the others.

"But who do they truly serve, Beloved Queen, if not their own interests? Lord General Ozo is a Tasho. He chose Agos—a bastard—over me. An untried young man, as hotheaded and impulsive as you. I had the credentials, the experience—I served as part of your father's guard for years before his death, and in Oren-yaro after that. Yet when it was time to officially assemble the Queen's Guard before your coronation, my name never came up. Did you ever wonder why?"

I hadn't. I gazed back at the older woman, gazing at the lines on her forehead between her eyes, the clear mark of someone who spent her days scowling. Scowling, or thinking.

"You can trust Agos," she said, when I didn't reply, "or you can trust me. To trust us *both* is foolish. We do not serve the same thing. To me, you are the Dragonlord, the queen of Jin-Sayeng. To him, you are..."

I turned my head away, the conversation filling me with discomfort.

"Beloved Queen..."

"No."

"Talyien."

"I don't need to hear it, Nor."

"I think you do. Sometimes I forget how young you are."

"I know he thinks he loves me."

"Well," Nor said with an exhale, "at least you're not *that* blind."

"I'm a married woman."

"You know full well that doesn't make much of a difference. The man doesn't act like a guard. I don't think he ever did. He thinks he owns you."

"He wasn't always like this."

"Well, something's changed. He hangs around you like a lovesick puppy, and I think if you don't find a way to get rid of him soon, you'll regret it." Her face tightened. "If you've been lonely the past few years, there's establishments where you can get—"

"Oh, gods. No. I am not talking to you about this, Nor." I was starting to miss the days when we *didn't* feel the need to have conversations.

"I gave you the chance to come clean the day we broke into Governor Zheshan's office," she said. "Or to kill me, if you'd rather not deal with my opinions. But you have, for whatever reason, kept me around. So I'll say this: he needs to go. His presence is a problem. If you're keeping him for sentiment, or quite probably something more, then fine—I won't be judging you as a woman. I will, however, be judging you as our ruler." She pointed out at the sea, where Jin-Sayeng lay. "That there is the land of our ancestors. The land of our *children*. Use this..." she said, now jabbing my forehead with her finger. "And not this." She pointed at my heart.

I wanted to tell her it wasn't that easy. Nothing was. But I chose not to answer, and we left it at that. Later, after she and Agos had switched shifts, I sat with him in the mess hall for lunch, sharing bowls of rice porridge with dried oysters, ginger, and green onion, covered by a dusting of fried pork rinds, and thought about what she'd said.

I didn't take any lovers during my separation from my husband. Certainly I was tempted to, especially given the anger that seemed to be a constant in those days, and I had more than enough suitors arriving on my doorstep as soon as it was clear Rayyel wasn't going to return. Nearly every province—apart from Bara—sent a representative, and at least five eligible men from minor but well-off clans came courting. I entertained them long enough to get the gifts, at least. Jewels, silk, and perfume did nothing for me, but it was hard to say no to the horses and the dogs, especially when they took such great pains to get ones that would catch my attention.

But I took no one to bed. Once or twice I may have allowed a fleeting kiss at the end of a long evening of banter, but my experience with men revolved solely around that one night with Agos and my brief marriage to my husband. I knew very little beyond that—nothing but glimpses of a world where passion was allowed and you didn't have to go to battle to feel the warmth of somebody's arms. And anyway, it wasn't as if I had the time. The demands of my position and my son left me little room for anything else.

It made me wonder about those who dared gossip about me, who would throw the words *whore queen* around without a second thought. Would they be surprised if they knew? Perhaps they'd find it too hard to believe—I played the part of indifferent wife too well the past few years. They have no reason to suspect that I spend almost half my time disassembling social norms, that the very idea of *romance* filled me with panic.

The memory of the kiss back in An Mozhi unsettled me. It didn't help that it was the second one Agos had unabashedly offered since our reunion. A more experienced woman would've been able to make a decision right then and there about what it meant and what to do about it. I could only fall on one thing: after years of not knowing where I stood in my husband's life, of waiting for his approval and trying to understand the meaning behind his terse words, it felt strange to know I was wanted.

"When you're quiet like that," Agos broke in, "it always makes me unbelievably nervous."

"How come?"

"Because I never know what you're planning next."

"Afraid I'll say something like, *Let's go hunt some whale-sharks?*"

"It's not that funny when you've said worse things."

"Like?"

He scratched his head. "I vaguely recall gathering stray cats from the city and bringing them up to the castle."

"That! I remember that. It was a brilliant plan. They're good for getting rid of mice. We were overrun, and the dogs were too fat and lazy."

He frowned. "The other boys caught me shoving cats into a basket."

"You should've explained why to them."

"Tali, have you ever been around boys?"

"Uh, yes?"

"When you're also a boy? I just grabbed the basket of cats and ran as fast as I could and—why are you laughing? Stop laughing. I told you, it's *not* funny."

I wiped a tear from my eye. "Gods, you're right. I'm sorry." I let out another snigger.

"You're horrible."

"What are you saying? Everyone tells me I'm a perfectly lovely queen."

"The most well-mannered, too."

"Absolutely, and not at all a bitch." I absently stirred the porridge with a spoon.

"Remember the crispy chicken in that place near Old Oren-yaro? Deep-fried whole and covered in garlic?" Agos asked, after a few moments of silence. "They sold them wrapped in banana leaves, with little bowls of soy sauce and vinegar."

The memory made me smile. "I'd come home smelling like oil and Arro would go into hysterics," I said.

Agos laughed. "I remember what he used to say. 'I will not have the Jewel of Jin-Sayeng die of dysentery on my watch.' Bless the poor man—you didn't, at least."

"Not yet." I paused. "I miss home."

Agos set his spoon down. "It won't be the same when you go back, you know."

"Gods, I know that. It's not like it has since...since that night." I looked down at the bowl, at the globs of porridge.

"You mean when Lord Rayyel left?"

"Rai. You." I met his eyes. "It's different being *queen* of Jin-Sayeng instead of just lady of Oren-yaro. You said I changed, but the truth was everything changed around me, too. It was hard enough growing up the way I did, as my father's daughter, but suddenly the entire nation's eyes were on me. The Ikessars… recorded everything I did. What I ate. Who I spoke to. How many times I hugged my son. They lectured me about staying in Oka Shto instead of moving to the Dragon Palace in Shirrokaru at least once a week, if not more often."

"It would've been worse if you had stayed in Shirrokaru," Agos agreed.

"But of course that meant that Oka Shto ceased to be the Oka Shto of our youth. At least half of the servants were switched around on a regular basis, and I stopped keeping track of who was who. That's how Kora slipped by. You remember Rai's spy?"

"How can I forget?" Agos said grimly.

"Rhetorical question." I took another bite of porridge and washed it down with hot tea. "Nothing," I continued, "will be the same, because the world that we knew was a lie. My betrothal to Rayyel was a fabrication."

"Warlord Yeshin's reach goes beyond the grave."

"You want to know something? When I was little, I used to wonder about that, about all the things people said about him. I knew he was firm, that his anger could tear through the walls of Oka Shto if he willed it, but I still couldn't see him as anything but a frail old man who instigated a revolution. I couldn't accept him as Yeshin the murderer, as the man who would willingly order his soldiers to slay innocent people—let alone sink a sword into a child himself. He wasn't that cold tactician, that man who could ruthlessly make decisions that changed people's lives. He was just… my father."

Agos took a drink and didn't say anything.

"You saw him differently, I suppose."

"I don't know," he admitted. "I know what you mean about him just seem- ing like nothing more than an old man. The rest—people said it about him, so I believed them. I didn't see a reason not to."

"All these things Yuebek says Yeshin planned… if they're true…" I swal- lowed. "What am I supposed to do, Agos? Do I continue to deny these allega- tions, even as the evidence mounts? I know now what my father was capable of—I've known for years. Or am I supposed to be a loyal daughter who will stop at nothing to carry out her father's will, and deny my husband and my own son in the process?"

"I'm not the sort of person who should be advising you."

"Arro would know. Oh, Arro... I'm sure the old man is pleased at how much I wish he was with us right now." I placed my hands over my head and was silent.

I heard Agos clear his throat. "Is this why you brought Lamang along?"

I glanced up.

"It just seems like you two get along, is all. He seems like an intelligent enough man—though you have to be careful about taking counsel from a Zarojo. At least Magister Arro's mother was Jinsein. Who knows where this man's allegiance lies? I just don't understand why you'd take him on now. He's not really of any use to you the way he is, is he? He hasn't left the sleeping quarters except to piss. Unless..."

"What are you saying, Agos?"

He crossed his arms and mumbled something under his breath.

"You know I've *killed* men for implying similar things?"

"You haven't. And anyway..." Agos coughed again. "When you went off with him back at the Ruby Grove, I thought for sure there was something else. And then you saw Lord Rayyel and near-killed yourself going after him again, and Lamang didn't seem to care at all about any of that..."

"I didn't realize you've been thinking these things *or* that it's your business to think about them at all."

He lowered his head. "My apologies."

"You're not sorry. You wanted to see my reaction."

"My queen is free to think whatever she wants."

"*Now* it's 'my queen.' Fine. I'll humour you, Agos, just because I want to make things clear. Lamang isn't my lover." It was true enough, in any case. Agos's gaze flicked back towards his food, as if he didn't quite believe me. "Do you really think I have time to entertain such notions? Especially while chasing after my husband?"

"The husband who abandoned you..."

"I thought you knew me better than that."

Agos's eyes flickered. "I've seen you in love," he said, after a moment's hesitation.

We were interrupted by the soft sound of a child's laughter. A little boy—the cook's son—toddled over towards us, hands held out in a plea for one of us to pick him up. He was an extraordinarily friendly child, with long curls that went down his shoulders. I turned around to greet him.

The ship lurched to the side.

The boy gave a small cry as he knocked his head against one of the tables, where a large bowl of still-steaming rice porridge sat. Agos grabbed him just as the porridge slid off the surface, crashing on the floor where the child had been. The ship righted itself again and the boy began to cry.

"Ah, there now," Agos said, setting the boy on his lap. He patted his back in circles, trying to get him to calm down. "That was nothing. You're a brave fellow, right? Look, it's over already." He wiped the boy's tears with his thumb before giving him a soft bun from our table. The boy hadn't finished crying, but he tore into the bun without hesitation, which made Agos chuckle. "Look at this little beast, eh?" he asked, a grin on his face.

I had a flash of memory from when Thanh was little, a year old, maybe two. Agos always held him the same way, with more affection than Rai ever did. Thanh cherished the attention. He wouldn't remember Agos now, but for a time there, he considered Agos a treasured friend. I wondered if Agos thought my son was his from the very beginning, or if it wouldn't have made a difference. How could I explain any of this to Nor? *I belong with you.*

He noticed my glance and placed the boy back on the ground, to shoo him back to his father. "We'll get to Thanh before those bastards," he said. "Trust me, Princess."

I gave him a cursory nod before excusing myself.

CHAPTER SEVEN

NI'IN

TŪṂ

I woke up to the sound of Nor's voice the morning we arrived in Ni'in. "We're at the docks, my queen. The mainland, at last!" She seemed almost excited, bursting at the seams, which was not typical of her. I rolled over to get dressed and put my boots on, pausing long enough to untangle my hair with my fingers. Not having a handmaid to take care of my grooming was liberating.

The sound of seagulls greeted us as we stepped into the harbour. There were more than I was used to—a result, probably, of the vast amount of refuse bobbing along the shoreline. I struggled against the stench, trying to find air to breathe that didn't send my eyes watering, and eventually I gave in and covered my nose with my hand. I caught sight of Lahei, who had a handkerchief wrapped around her face.

"You'll get used to it as we go along," she said.

I doubted it. The streets were covered in muck that threatened to crawl up my legs. It smelled like both human and animal feces, ground into the mud. The remains of a dead rat sat in the company of the stiff body of a cat, its lips curled upwards in a death-snarl. "Doesn't anyone clean around the harbour, at least?" I asked. I had to raise my voice a bit so I could hear myself above the din. The streets were too crowded, more than any street in Jin-Sayeng or the empire. Vendors seemed right on top of people, selling their wares by shoving them right in front of our faces. I turned one away, and she started screaming in a foreign tongue.

"The towns and villages in Kago have no government," Lahei said. "Power lies with who can afford it, and so typically the merchants rule, in what limited way they can. You can see why cleaning up may be the last of their concerns."

"Not really," I grumbled. "Think it'd bring in more trade if they did."

"The prices are low enough and the goods from the region are sound," Lahei replied almost cheerfully. "It works. It may not look like it, but it works."

I focused on watching my footing. I didn't want to slip, but maintaining my balance with one hand on my mouth was harder than it looked. When we reached the corner of the street, I tested the air with a sniff and found to my relief that the smell here was almost tolerable. I flicked my boots in the air like a high-stepping horse and heard Agos trying to choke down his laughter.

"What's so funny?" I asked him.

Nor gave him a glare, but he ignored her. "It's still amusing to see you like this, is all."

"You should remember to start respecting the queen again when we get back to Jin-Sayeng," Nor said. "If I had guardsmen with me, you wouldn't be allowed to talk like that."

"Give it a rest," Agos said. "Stick up your ass like that, can't imagine how you can even walk."

"She does have a point, Agos," I replied. "We're very close to home now. We *will* have to fall back to our usual routine, whether you like it or not."

"Our usual routine involves me in exile, remember?" Agos asked.

I glanced at Nor, who stiffened her lip. "We have to talk about that," I said. "You know you can't go with me all the way to Oren-yaro."

There was a long pause. Too long. After the last few months, I had expected him to be argumentative. Instead, he strode forward, pushing a man who ventured too close to me out of the way. He kept his eyes down.

"Agos."

Agos tilted his head towards Khine and his brother, who were walking some distance behind us. "What about them?"

"Their sister entrusted them to my service," I said. "You've seen how Khine was able to get us out of An Mozhi. It would not be the first time a royal took on an outside adviser. Arro was half Zarojo, if you recall."

"Ah—adviser. That's what you're calling him now."

"Akaterru—at least say *Beloved Queen* once in a while," Nor hissed.

"Beloved Queen," he said, gritting his teeth. "You may dispose of me however you see fit, once you and Prince Thanh are in safe hands. Believe that much. I obeyed you the first time. I can do it again." I couldn't tell if he was showing restraint at last, or being sarcastic. Or if he was talking to himself, checking to see how the words felt on his tongue, testing the truth of it.

Lahei turned to stare at me from the distance, and I walked faster to catch up with her. As I came up to the intersection, I noticed two men walking down the street towards us. I recognized Dai Kaggawa immediately. The image of him facing down a dragon to save both me and Rai was burned into my memory. He still had the same stern expression, a stark contrast with the turn of his mouth and the dimples on his cheeks. His curly hair, completely black when I was young, was now peppered with grey.

He was still built like a man who could cleave a dragon in half. Not tall—we were probably of a height if I stood on tiptoe—but stocky and well-muscled. Lahei came up to greet him, dropping to a bow and placing her hand on her forehead.

"Queen Talyien," Dai said. "It is good to see you again."

"I am honoured," I replied. "I still remember what you did for me and Lord Rayyel. I never did get the chance to thank you properly." I bowed to acknowledge his presence. Respect. My father taught me that in certain circumstances, you can never give too much of it, no matter what position you hold. Even queens still have to follow rules.

Dai turned towards my companions. "Is this your guard?" he asked. "I was told you went up there with an entire retinue."

"We ran into some unfortunate circumstances. Half of my men were killed."

"What happened to the other half?"

"Father," Lahei broke in. "Perhaps not out in the street."

"It is a simple question," he bristled.

There was no point in hiding it. "A Zarojo bribed them in order to get close to me."

Nothing seemed to skip past Dai. "Your guards were Oren-yaro. They are, I've been led to believe, not easily bribed."

"The matter has been taken care of." I hoped my own voice sounded convincing enough. It was becoming more difficult to pretend to be confident after all I had been through.

Dai considered these words with a grunt and gestured to us before striding ahead. We followed him around the corner, where the streets were wider, fringed with buildings—mostly storehouses from what I could see. There was also a brewery, which emitted a stench noxious enough that I immediately made a mental note never to drink anything they offered me.

We soon found ourselves in a small building overlooking a wide ditch. The stench was less prominent here, though that probably had something to do with the thick smell of incense they must've been using to mask it. I was still struggling to breathe, but felt less nauseous. My people stayed in the main hall while Lahei escorted me into a narrow office after her father. She closed the door behind us before standing in the corner, straight and stiff as a soldier. It reminded me of how I was in Yeshin's presence.

With a measure of discomfort—and without waiting for Dai's invitation—I made myself comfortable in one of the velvet-lined chairs. "You didn't strike me as a man who liked his luxuries," I said, rubbing the solid wood armrests, which had been polished to a fine sheen.

"Well-made things pay for themselves over time," Dai said, with one eye on the drapery. "You don't have to keep replacing them."

I laced my fingers together. "Is this the beginning of some drawn-out metaphor about the Ikessars?"

He snorted behind his beard. "Your husband isn't a well-made man?"

"Please don't tell me you're going to propose. I've had enough of those in just one year."

Dai frowned. "I'm not sure why you would think that. The luxuries, as it happened...when you grow up poor, you're made to understand the value of things as they are. It is amazing what people will put a price to. Some things are expensive for no reason. Which is the life and blood of a merchant, of course— a few years ago, purple rice became popular with the royals, and the demand for it increased beyond comprehension. Purple rice is tough and grainy, cheaper to produce."

"Good for the bowels, though," I said brightly.

He grimaced. "Value is worth what you pay for. I believe those drapes have been there since before my eldest daughter was born. My wife picked them out when she was still alive."

"My condolences."

"She died a long time ago."

I laced my fingers together and cleared my throat. "Tell me what I'm doing here, Kaggawa. I didn't want to argue with your daughter, not when she was my only chance to cross the sea, but you could have very well taken the short way around and taken me straight to Sutan. I would be sitting on my throne by now if you didn't insist on bringing me *here* instead. So. Talk."

"You're unbelievably arrogant for someone with only two guards and such a long way from home."

"I'm closer to home than I've ever been," I said with a half snarl. "Imagine what I would do to get closer."

"You mistake me for one of your warlords. I'm not interested in trading sharp words with you, Queen Talyien," Dai replied easily. There was a quick knock from the door. He nodded towards Lahei, who strode up to open it.

A girl in a silk dress stepped inside. She was probably ten or eleven years old, with hair that gleamed deep brown against the sunlight. She walked over to Dai and reached up to plant a kiss on his cheek, which struck me as odd. I always greeted my father with a kiss on the back of his hand.

"Bow to the queen," Dai said.

The young girl did so in a Kag-style curtsy. Other than her fairer features, she looked a lot like Lahei. I returned the greeting with a smile. "Your younger daughter, I presume?"

Dai gestured at the girl. "Let me introduce Faorra alon gar Kaggawa, our daughter."

Our daughter. He had said his wife was dead. I noticed his voice had shifted there, too, and the glower on his face seemed to disappear, replaced by something brighter, unlike the warrior I had just met. "A beautiful girl," I replied, trying to piece my thoughts together. It must've only been his pride over his daughters that caused the abrupt change. "I don't think you've ever taken her or Lahei to Oren-yaro during the festivities. You should. It would amuse them."

"Take Lahei to court?" He chuckled, glancing at his daughters with another odd smile. "Perhaps if you wanted trouble and a scandal or two..." He tapped

Faorra on the shoulder. "I would like to speak with the queen in private now, my dear."

Faorra bowed again, her cheeks dimpling. "I'm pleased to make your acquaintance, Beloved Queen." Lahei took her aside and led her back outside.

"What do you think?" Dai asked, as soon as Lahei had closed the door.

"About what?"

"About Faorra." He crossed the room and settled into the other chair. "For Thanh, your son, to marry when he comes of age."

I was still smiling, but could feel my heart sinking. The blade wasn't for me at all. *Oh, Thanh, my love. What have I done?*

I watched Dai carefully, trying not to betray what I was feeling because a single stone could cause a landslide, and what he had just said made want to kill him with my bare hands. "Thanh is only eight," I said. "And regardless—Faorra is your younger daughter, isn't she?"

Dai smirked. "Do you prefer Lahei?"

"I didn't—"

"Would you marry the prince, Lahei?" he called out.

"If the queen desires it," Lahei said. "It would be a poor match," she added.

Dai cleared his throat. "I can see the look on your face, Queen Talyien. I understand what this sounds like. A commoner—no matter how well-off or respected in these parts—asking you to consider his *younger* daughter for your son. And yet you have not made a marriage match for Thanh as far as I'm aware, and none of the other warlords have stepped up with their daughters, either. The presumption is not unwarranted."

"Master Kaggawa," I said, taking a deep breath as I considered my words carefully. "My desire has always been to give Thanh the freedom to choose his own bride when he is of age, without the pressure of politics or position to worry about. My father's agreement with Princess Ryia includes the notion that we will from now on always have two Dragonlords—a king and a queen. To leave the throne open for manipulation…"

"As it has ever been, the moment this agreement came to pass."

"My son will know love, Master Kaggawa."

He paused. "I never expected Yeshin's daughter to utter such words."

"I guess this day has been a barrel of surprises for everyone."

"It's a noble enough idea, except you seem to forget the sort of precipice your position has thrust you and your heir onto. Have you told your council about this? Both your clans have agreed?"

I bristled. "I was hoping, in time…"

"I didn't realize you were this naive."

"They're less likely to agree to *your* proposition than mine."

"Fair enough," Dai remarked. "But let's pretend we don't live in a land where the Ikessars' ways become law. Supposing these dreams of yours come to fruition—if Thanh grows up to adulthood and is allowed to fall in love naturally, and choose his queen among the selection of approved royal clans' daughters, then Jin-Sayeng remains where it is. Stagnant, unable to move in one direction or the other out of fear of her quarrelsome warlords. Dragonlord Thanh will just be another Ikessar, parroting the Ikessar ideals, and his wife will be a queen backed by whatever ambitious clan was smart enough to put her in his path. Let me tell you, Queen Talyien, that it is remarkably easy to put a desirable young woman where a young man can't resist her. I think you know what I mean."

"I don't—" I began.

"Chiha Baraji…"

Akaterru be damned, but he meant it when he said he knew *everything.* I tried to act as if hearing the woman's name wasn't going to send me into a fit of ungodly rage. "What about that bitch? She's yesterday's news. Yet unmarried, quite possibly fawning over another woman's husband…" Too late. I sucked in a breath of air to calm myself. "If Rayyel wanted her, why didn't he consult with the priests to absolve our marriage and take her? He'd already thrown away everything, so it can't be that he's holding on to this marriage for the crown." I rubbed my forehead. "This has nothing to do with my son. My son will have a life away from all of this."

"The land is not stable enough for this dream of yours," Dai replied. "It is an admirable thought, but one that has no place in a land as divided as ours. You need to secure a marriage alliance for the prince, and you need to do it in a way that will keep the warlords from tearing you apart the moment you announce it."

I laughed. "All right, Master Dai," I said. "Let's pretend I can entertain this notion of yours. I return to court and announce that Prince Thanh will be marrying an *alon gar* when he comes of age…"

He chuckled. "It will require a bit more finesse than that, obviously."

"Obviously," I snorted. "What do you have to gain from all of this?"

"With this sort of marriage announcement, you would be abolishing the rigid rules that separate royals from commoners," Dai said.

"Let's pretend I can do that. What then?"

"Such an announcement will give me the power I need to drive the Anyus off the land."

I almost slammed my fists on the table, but I didn't—it would have been too insulting, and I was still a guest in his household. I curled my fingers over my knees and gave him a dog's smile. "This was what you wanted the whole time," I said, keeping my voice low. "I have to admit I am disappointed, Master Kaggawa. After all your daughter's talk about the *common man*…" From the corner of my eyes, I saw Lahei flinch.

"I'm not sure I follow, Queen Talyien."

I shook my head. "You'd dangle your daughter as bait to get me to overthrow centuries' worth of tradition just so you could seize power in this region. What's next? Warlord Dai aren dar Kaggawa? Dragonlord Dai?"

He started laughing.

The smile on my face grew cold, but I kept it there until he stopped for breath. "Don't tell me I'm not too far from the truth," I said.

"Very far," he replied. "Though I can't say I blame you for making that leap of logic. It is, after all, the very foundation on which you royals have built your legacies."

"I'll cram your words back into your mouth, Kaggawa. I'm not sure *you're* clear about what this sounds like *at all*. This will cause war. Is overthrowing the Anyus and seizing power for your little corner of the map reason enough to risk it? We have barely recovered from the last one—you'll do that to our people again? Are you really *that* shortsighted?"

"It isn't shortsightedness, Beloved Queen," Dai said. "I would risk it all simply because our lives at our stake. *All* our lives."

CHAPTER EIGHT

THE MAP'S EDGE

ᒐᕐᑭᐄᐧ

What are you saying, Kaggawa?" I asked.

Dai pressed his hands along the side of his desk as he stared in silence, chewing on the corner of his lips. I took a moment to consider how different he was acting now than when I had first met him out on the streets. Out there, he had been more sombre, stiff; here, he seemed more pensive, expressive. And the light in his eyes looked different—I could've somehow sworn they were brown out there. Now they appeared blue, which I didn't think was possible. Based on what Nor had told me, his father was Jinsein. Even if his mother was Kag, his eyes should still be brown. "I think I will let you sit on my words first," he said with a grimace. "You'll have plenty enough time to think them through during our trip to the Sougen."

"I am *not* going to the Sougen," I hissed. "This little side journey *just* to see you has already cost me too much time. Our lives *are* at stake here."

He narrowed his eyes. "What do you mean?"

"The events in the Zarojo Empire…" I started.

He leaned back. "You made enemies out there, didn't you?"

"You could say that."

"You made enemies, and suddenly your people refuse to help you," Dai said with a heavy sigh. "I've been wondering why the Oren-yaro never went after you. It's worse than I feared."

"Da—" Lahei began. I glanced at her in confusion. *Da*, not *Father*? *Da* was a Kag affectation.

"My son's life is at stake here. I will not allow Thanh to be feasted on by vultures," I murmured. "You need him alive, too, don't you?"

"Tell me what's happening. You're going to have to trust me, Queen Talyien."

"My son is in danger. That's all you need to know."

His nostrils flared. After a moment of silence, he inclined his head to the side. "She sounds sincere enough. Frightened, even. Not what I expected from *her* at all. What do you think?"

"The queen, indeed, had her fair share of troubles in the empire," Lahei agreed. "I suspected there was more to it than she let on."

"And Faorra can't very well marry a dead boy, can she?"

"No, Da."

Dai pressed his hands on his desk, blue eyes gleaming in the shadows in such a way that it felt unreal. Inhuman. That, and the expression on his face, sent a chill up my spine. "A proposition, Beloved Queen. Consider it a token of goodwill so that you can begin to trust us."

"I'm listening," I bristled.

"I have men," Dai continued. "Something we're both aware *you're* short of. I'll take care of extracting your son from Oka Shto and his Ikessar guardians, away from this danger you claim he's in. In exchange…"

"I go with you to the Sougen," I finished for him. "You bastard."

He smiled. "If you remain this compliant, then we don't have to be hostile at all, do we? Our daughter *did* tell you we are your servants, did she not?"

"Servants who blackmail their queen," I grunted. "I don't know your men, Master Dai. I don't know if I can trust them so easily, even if you give me your word. You seem to be forgetting that my son is surrounded by both Oren-yaro soldiers and Ikessar retainers. Do you think you can wrest him from them so easily? The safest way is for me to be there, to get him out myself."

"I disagree. I believe your presence there is problematic. The Ikessars already mistrust you—who knows what will happen once they know you've returned to Jin-Sayeng?"

"The Sougen is still Jin-Sayeng."

"In that you are wrong, Beloved Queen. The Sougen *was* the heart of Jin-Sayeng, but that was a long, long time ago. Your forebears have neglected it, and you nailed the coffin shut yourself."

"How do you plan to get him out?" I asked.

"Your city has a network of sewers," Dai said.

"None lead to the castle. Our sewage is dumped straight to the river."

"The forest, then. The cliffs."

"Your people cannot possibly have the plans for every nook and cranny in Oka Shto. You worked for the Ikessars, not my father, and my father kept Oka Shto's construction a secret. Even *I* don't know everything there is to know about the castle, and I can tell you this much: every entrance you can think of *will* have guards."

"We can find a way, Beloved Queen. Our daughter got you out of the empire, didn't she?"

"Then send her," I said.

He grew serious. "No."

"If you won't send your daughter, then I know for a fact that an escape attempt will also be dangerous for my son. You don't have a deal, Kaggawa."

"You talk like someone who has a choice."

I tapped the desk before letting my hand graze the sword on my side. "I do. I can choose to kill you where you stand, or die trying. Either way, you lose something."

I felt those blue eyes grow cold. For a moment, I had the distinct sensation of standing in front of a beast that wanted to mow me down, and my fingers wrapped themselves around the hilt of the sword. But then his eyes changed colour, turning dark again. Brown. He slowly sat back against his chair.

Lahei leaned over to him and whispered in his ear.

"You know Torre," he said at last. "If I send him to scout the area and keep an eye out for your son, will that suffice? We will not intervene until you can personally make a decision yourself." His voice was different again, back to the same old firmness from earlier. "You can stay in the Sougen with the assurance that if there is any danger to your boy, we can do something about it."

I sucked in my breath.

"We are being gracious here, my queen. Acknowledge it, or let's all end it here." It sounded like he meant it.

After a moment's reflection, I nodded.

Lahei bowed and stepped out of the room.

I didn't know if it was relief or dread now running through me. "What happens when you have both of us in your custody?"

"Worries for the future."

"Don't play coy, Kaggawa. We'll become your hostages, won't we? You'll want me to announce Thanh's betrothal to your daughter right after, I'm sure. Between the warlords and the Zarojo army..."

His eyes brightened. "A Zarojo army?"

"I am *not* in the mood to play games. This is more serious than you realize. Do you have enough sellswords to stop the nation from burning?"

He laughed. "Sellswords! And where did you hear that from?"

I smirked. "I have my ways."

"The warlords will not attack us. This land's concerns go beyond your royal squabbles. But come—we've talked enough. The day grows shorter, and we have a long road ahead."

I followed him out of the building, where I saw my guards, Khine, and Cho on the street with Lahei. I wasn't sure what she told them, but Nor gave me a look as I passed by. "Later," I grumbled. "I'll explain later."

We continued down the street, which led to the outskirts of town. A low wooden fence surrounded one of the buildings. There were horses tied in a row along the street. Dai whistled and a young man ambled up to us, a straw hat set at an angle on his head. He was thin, more bone than flesh. "Your horses are ready, Master Dai," he said, speaking in Kagtar, although he looked Jinsein from the distance. On close inspection, I could see a brown sheen to his hair. His eyes were quite light, too—almost yellow. I wasn't surprised. Children of mixed lineage were common in that region.

Dai walked towards a large bay horse, the kind with a light feathering along its forelegs, and his face broke into a grin. He greeted the horse with the sort of fondness you reserved for a special friend, then turned back to the stable hand. "We've got company. I brought my daughter's horse, but please find something for the rest of them. Put it on my tab." I noticed his eyes were glowing blue again. He glanced at me, as if unaware I noticed it. "Perhaps the queen will want to pick her own horse. I've been told she's fond of them."

The young man bowed. "Everything outside is spoken for, but maybe something in the stables?" His face muscles twitched. He quickly slapped at it, as if it was an affliction he was used to. And then, wringing his hands, he led me down the path, straight to the run-down building. He indicated the available horses with haphazard flailing, and I went down to inspect them. I wasn't looking for anything particularly special, but I wanted to keep an eye out for the sort of horse that might be able to outrun Dai's mount if I needed it to. I caught a couple that looked like they had the legs for it, though they were flightier than I liked.

I heard the young man clear his throat. "Have you decided?"

"A moment," I said. I patted the nose of an amiable dappled grey before moving on to the next stall. A shaft of sunlight from the window crossed my path. As I glanced away from it, I noticed the stable hand's shadow on the ground. It looked like a forked tree branch, the edges hard and angled.

It gave me pause. I felt my skin crawl as I took a second look. The shadows where his fingers should've been ended in points, like claws. Higher up, his hair looked like it was standing on end, and the head was twisted, the silhouette of his mouth and nose upturned.

"Well?" he asked. His shadow opened its mouth. I saw fangs.

I looked up at him.

Maybe it was the expression on my face, or maybe because my hand had dropped to my sword, but his eyes grew bright. The thin line of his lips turned into a sinister smile.

Without another word, he *changed*.

I felt my hair prickling as it happened, the feel of the air before a lightning storm. His mouth split open, revealing long white fangs. His body contorted, ripping through his clothes. His flesh darkened, and patches of hair appeared all over him, like a flea-bitten dog's fur. His arms grew longer, lean muscles and veins popping through throbbing skin. There was a thick, oily sheen over him that smelled like rotting blood.

My observations ended there. He lunged.

There was little room to flee between the stalls, especially between the panicked horses and thundering hooves. I dodged the first attack, watching in horror as the creature crashed into the gate. The wood exploded into several pieces. A frightened horse raced past us. I was almost expecting the creature to go after the hapless beast, but it only had eyes for me.

It reached out again with claws the length of my arm. I ducked a second time and managed to wrench my sword free from the scabbard. I struck its leg. It howled and smashed me with the other leg, and I quickly realized my mistake in engaging something strong enough to send me flying to the wall.

I hit a board, my left shoulder taking the brunt of the fall. My head spun. I tasted blood from a split lip and spat out straw. Before I could even think about getting up, the creature was on me, claws dancing above my skin. I gazed up to its slavering jaws and stabbed it in the roof of its mouth with my sword.

It threw its head back with a roar. I pulled my sword back and struck it across the chest several times. The blade went through a thick swath of hair and muscle before the edge struck bone, sending a spray of black blood hissing through the air. The creature responded by pressing back until I could no longer swing my sword, until my blade was the only thing standing in the way of it squeezing the breath from my lungs. Blood mixed with saliva dripped down my face, making it harder and harder to see.

I heard Khine's voice call for me. "Get out of here!" I screamed as I removed my left hand from the sword. Before the creature could crush me, I pulled the smaller dagger from my belt and stabbed it in the neck. I was hoping to hit its jugular, but I felt bone instead. The creature roared and tossed me to the side like a rag doll.

Both blades slid out of my grasp as I hit a bale of hay. I coughed as I got up, and then found myself retching at the stench and feel of the creature's blood. When I finally caught my breath, I wiped my eyes and returned for my sword. It was half-hidden under clumps of straw and congealed blood. Slime coated the hilt. I wrapped my fingers around it as tight as I could and blindly rushed forward.

The creature had left me for Khine. He was keeping it at bay with a pitch-fork. Before I could reach them, the stable doors slid open and Dai's thundering voice broke through the air like a whip.

"Out here, you piece of shit!"

The creature hissed as sunlight struck it. Small pockets of burning flesh appeared on its skin. Unfazed by its injuries, it bounded through the door. I limped past Khine just in time to see Dai take it down with one clean upwards stroke.

The creature's body shrank under the sunlight, cracking like a wilted flower as it slowly turned back into the stable hand—a stiff, grey, desiccated shadow of him.

I managed to swallow. Somehow, my own saliva tasted vile—some of the blood had gotten into my mouth. "How inconvenient," Dai said. "I suspected he was one. Had hoped I was wrong." He had on the curt voice and brown eyes. There was no ounce of surprise or regret in his expression.

"What the hell is happening here, Kaggawa?"

"Knowing your reputation, you would've fled from me the first chance you got. I had to *show* you what was wrong here. My apologies if I had to use you to bait him to reveal himself."

I wiped my face. "Explain yourself."

"This is an unstable region," Dai said with a snarl. "Right before your father's war, Rysaran's mad dragon was destroyed in the mountains. The act ripped through the fabric."

"What does that have to do with that… *thing*?" I gestured at the corpse.

"Didn't your tutors teach you anything?" Dai snapped. "Ah, they wouldn't have. I forget how stuck up you royals get over these things. The *agan*… look…" He made a ball with his hands, oblivious to the blood that dripped down his arm—the creature's, not his. "A fabric separates our reality from the other side, which they say is the source of the *agan*. Rysaran's dragon created so much damage that it began spilling from that side into ours, causing instabilities. Dageian mages came to stop it. They erected spells around the mountains near Cairntown to contain the spill.

"But they couldn't repair the fabric and restore it to the way it was. Instead, their spells created a blockage, stifling the flow and creating a lake. A stagnant cesspool. I don't know much about it myself, but… we are all part *agan*. Do you know that?"

Khine cleared his throat. "I've been told it flows through every living thing. People who train as mages are more connected than most—they can see and manipulate these threads."

"So they can. When we die, our souls travel through the *agan* stream and return to Sheyor'r. Who knows what happens after?" He paused, then, his face contorting. His eyes glowed and turned blue. "Maybe some of us don't want to know. Those souls linger near the surface like rats at a pantry, waiting for the door to open. Those who found themselves at that torn fabric? They went through, straight into the dammed lake of *agan* the mages had inadvertently made. Something went wrong with the *agan* inside of it, as if it was tainted. It changed them. It changes..." He stopped, his face tightening. "What do you mean I'm not explaining it properly?" he asked with an irritated expression. He wasn't looking at me, or anyone, and his eyes were rapidly switching between blue and brown.

"Father," Lahei called out.

"It's not a problem," Dai replied. I wasn't sure if he was replying to her or talking to himself again, but his voice had changed once more. He turned back to me. "She has to know. How long will we pretend this isn't a problem threatening to consume us all?"

"What by all the gods are you both going on about?" I asked.

"Souls travel on the *agan*," Lahei said softly. "The creature you have seen was a man who somehow attracted the soul of a corrupted thing. We've been trying to understand how it works, to predict what causes possession, but all these years, it seems to be completely random. A neighbour can be masquerading as normal for years and later be discovered eating babies and children in the night."

"And this sort of thing only happens in these parts?" I asked.

Lahei nodded. "It caused the mad dragons."

I paused, letting that sink in. "They appeared right after the demise of Rysaran's dragon."

"During your father's war, yes. We believe the flow of *agan* through the tear in the fabric was enough to attract a few dragons back to the northern mountains. We think that the mages' botched repair attempt drew them straight into the cesspool. These corrupted souls came through and possessed them, causing them to turn into vicious, mindless beasts who kill beyond the need to eat. A second group of mages contained the area soon afterwards, and for the first few years only that first group of dragons was afflicted."

"The dragon that attacked me and Prince Rayyel as children," I broke in. "It was young. It wasn't one of those."

"No," Dai said. "I brought it with me. I wanted to *show* you that you had a growing problem out here. But you were a child. What did you know? How could I have explained all of this to a mere mite of a girl who had been far too busy worrying about her prince?"

"You could have tried."

"Like I didn't try with your father, girl," he said. "It's too late for regrets, now. It was bad then, and it's getting worse. We think the spells the second group of mages made are wearing off. The corrupted souls are escaping. Now they're possessing people, too."

I felt my fingers begin to shake, and carefully crossed my arms so it wouldn't be so obvious. My eyes darted towards Dai. "Are you saying that Jin-Sayeng will soon be overrun with mad dragons *and* these bloodthirsty monsters?"

His face broke into a smile. "You catch on fast. Perhaps we have hope after all."

On the road, the Kaggawas gave me the sort of education on the *agan* that my tutors had denied me all these years.

They spoke of its abundance in another realm, the one the Zarojo called Sheyor'r, and the fabric that separates it from our world. Across this fabric, *agan* flows freely, and everything there is made of this substance, which has resulted in a world of *agan* attempting to mimic a solid form—the trees, the water, the ground, and even the people.

It was like hearing a story, a fairy tale. Amusing enough coming from someone like Agos's mother on a cold winter's night with cups of hot ginger tea in our hands. To listen to it out here, among grim faces, with the knowledge that what had attacked me in that stable could very well be among us…

It seemed that when we died, our souls would slip into a stream and make their way to the nearest hole in the fabric, where we would then make our way to an afterlife in Sheyor'r. Our souls were made of *agan*, too, the exact same substance, only different enough to retain wills of their own. Dai and Lahei's arguments gave me a glimpse of how little people really knew of it and why there were different schools of thought and interpretations on the subject.

The Dageians, for example, considered the *agan* to be nothing more than an endless natural resource. They created channels to tap into Sheyor'r, draining what they could from whatever little pocket they could find. Sheyor'r, from what Dai could explain, was not a seamless land like ours. If our world was a boulder, Sheyor'r was about a hundred blankets of various weights and fabrics stitched together and wrapped around it. Some fabrics were thin, others were thick; some were riddled with holes, others impenetrable. Attempts to map Sheyor'r from our world had been met with abject failure. Even the flow of the *agan* was difficult to predict. What the Dageians called a "natural connection" was one that flowed on its own, requiring no mage or spell to draw it out.

The destruction of Rysaran's dragon created one of these natural connections. But instead of a small pocket of easily usable *agan*, the flow in the area was erratic and unstable. If fabrics were blankets, then the one here was woolen and full of ticks. Lahei told me about the contingent of mages Dageis had sent to take care of the problem. Dageis was concerned about the state of the *agan* fabric in those days, especially after reports came that the Dageian Empire's overdependence on mages was creating an abundance of holes that encouraged instability. As far as Dageis was concerned, they were just cleaning up.

No one knew exactly what happened. Somehow, the entire contingent was wiped out. When the reports stopped, a second group came looking for them and found creatures in place of the mages. They were still clad in the mages' robes, and some even attempted to initiate conversation with the second group, pretending to be the missing mages themselves.

The new mages, of course, knew exactly what they were dealing with—the idea that a soul from Sheyor'r could slip into someone's body was well-known. But it was always accepted that only those with natural connections to the *agan* themselves were vulnerable. When they discovered that the soldiers and servants that accompanied that first group of mages were *also* possessed, they panicked. They threw up more spells to try to fix the problem, but that was all they could do—bandages over a wound. And now the bandages were falling apart.

"Have you asked Dageis for help?" I found myself asking. We were around a campfire that same evening—one of the five that Dai's men had erected as soon as we got off the road. It was the most well-lit campsite I had ever seen in my life.

Dai shook his head. "They've fixed it, as far as they're concerned. Do you think Dageis cares what a handful of small towns and villages experience? An official inquiry might've worked better, but you can understand why we're not in a position to send out a request." He turned to me with a steely blue gaze.

I smiled at him. "I understand what you're implying, Master Dai, but do remember that this is an incident that happened years before I was born. Furthermore, it is not officially within Jin-Sayeng borders."

"Those mountains border Jin-Sayeng. You'd let brushstrokes dictate what you do or don't care for?"

"I have no jurisdiction—"

"It affects *your* people," Dai said.

"It's not that simple. Do you know what the warlords would've done if I had made an effort to reach Dageis *at all*, let alone on anything *agan*-related? No..." I paused to look at his face through the flickering flames. "I think you do know. That's why you never sent word."

"We *have* made requests to see you, Beloved Queen. Many times."

"You and others, on so many things. My council goes through them first. They picked what was most important for me to see." Saying this made me feel self-conscious. They had accused me of not caring. They weren't...wrong.

Our conversation was interrupted by the arrival of one of his men. "We've scouted the perimeter, Master Dai," he said. "Nothing's amiss."

I glanced at the burning torch in his hand. His sharp breathing and the colour of the skin on his face betrayed his fears. I also caught sight of an amulet around his neck. I didn't recognize it, but it looked like a piece of wood carved to resemble the branches of a tree. I remembered the god of the Kags in this area, Yohak, who was said to roam through the deepest parts of the Kag wilderness, where he battled beasts and spirits alike. While some people said that he took the form of an old, bearded man, others said he appeared as a walking tree. Bits and pieces of the legends I had read about over the years seemed to come together in my mind.

"They're actually out there in the woods, aren't they?" I asked.

Dai glanced at Lahei before nodding. "Is that too much to believe, Beloved Queen?"

"I'm bearing gifts from the last one I encountered." I glanced at my wounds. "More wouldn't be a stretch."

"Most of them seem to prefer living among us," Lahei said.

"You mean—as people?"

Dai smiled, eyes gleaming in the dark. "And why not? If you've been in darkness for so very long, wouldn't you want to see the light? Wouldn't you desire a whiff of fresh air? A taste of clean water?" He made a motion towards the fire. "If you have never known entrapment in your life, I can't imagine you could understand."

"I do know," I said in a low voice.

Dai looked at me curiously. "These souls… try to get along with their host for as long as they can, experiencing everything their host experiences—the joy of food, warmth, comfort, even the pleasures of lust. On the surface, it doesn't sound like the worst thing in the world, to share these things with another bereft of them."

I listened to the soft patter of his voice before nodding. "What I saw, however…"

"That is where the *corrupt* nature of these things comes into play," Dai continued. "For some reason, these souls want more. They are not *content* with living out someone's life. And so their hunger exceeds the limitations of the body and they attempt to sate the lust through flesh. They distort their host into these creatures whenever they can get away with it. They especially love to eat children—something about the purer nature of their experiences."

"When discovered, some of them just take over the host, like the one you just saw," Lahei added. "As you can imagine, this leaves little choice but to kill the creature, including the host. In a last-ditch attempt to save themselves and the body that had been so pliable to their demands, they flee into the woods."

I itched to stare into the darkness of the forest beyond us, but I stopped myself. "If this has been going on for the last few years, then these woods must be crawling with them."

They both nodded. "It's nothing these parts don't know how to deal with, you understand," Dai said. "Deeper into the Kag, the wilderness has been home to similar creatures. But they've kept there for centuries. These ones are right here, among us. If this spreads deeper into our cities…" He trailed off, letting me fill in the details.

I felt a shiver run through my skin. "Will they attack during the night?"

Dai got up and beckoned. I followed him to the edge of the camp, right where the light crossed into the shadows. They had fenced the area in with thin rope, about knee-high, threaded through bells. "That's it?" I asked. "You're protecting us with tripping hazards?"

"The simple things work best," Dai said. "Hopefully whoever's on watch calls an alarm if a bell rings, and it flees back into the woods. If we're lucky, we can kill them."

Agos looked like he wanted to laugh. "It won't just walk over it?"

"I dare you to try walking about in the dark without triggering a bell or two." I rubbed my wrist. "The thing back in the stables was *very* strong."

"They can be killed—you've seen it. You have to let their strength become their disadvantage. They lack finesse, and they're afraid of light." Dai swept his torch towards me before bringing his sword down with his other hand, stopping a hand's length from my neck.

Agos's own blade was out. "You—" he snarled.

"I was only showing the queen one of the many stances you take when you're facing these creatures," Dai said, stepping back. "I'm the last thing you should worry about here." He nodded at me. "You didn't flinch."

"I wasn't paying attention," I admitted.

"You were. It didn't bother you because the movement was too slow." He crossed his arms. "I was told you were a pampered brat."

The words amused me more than anything. "Are you saying your extensive spy network was wrong?"

"Information is different from firsthand knowledge. They train you Oren-yaro well. Maybe too well. Wolves, you call yourselves? Dogs, more like it." He glanced at Agos, who bristled.

"Watch your tongue."

"Why take offense? The queen doesn't. And well will that serve you, if you remember to think beyond what your clan *expects* you to."

"You said you tried to talk to my father about these," I commented. "He lost my brothers to Rysaran's dragon. Surely he would've believed you."

"Like I said," Dai murmured. And he left it at that.

CHAPTER NINE

THE BINDING DARKNESS

ᏫᎭᎳᎢᏅ

I didn't get much sleep that night. I did a good enough job of pretending that all of this newfound knowledge didn't make my skin crawl, but it made it difficult to close my eyes and not imagine a horde of creatures sneaking into camp and slaying everyone in sight. So I stayed up next to the fire, feeding it periodically to stop it from dying.

Khine joined me sometime before dawn. Without a word, he took my left arm and carefully flexed it. His eyes never left me—he was watching my face for a reaction. I flinched when he lifted my arm. He slowly placed it back down. "Just a pulled muscle," he murmured. "Didn't think you'd broken anything, but I didn't want to take chances. Do you hurt anywhere else? You were limping earlier."

"Just sore," I told him. "A couple of cuts, but nothing that won't heal."

"I don't really have anything for those," Khine said. He looked apologetic.

"If we can find some guava leaves, I can chew them up and spit on them. Old Jinsein remedy."

He shook his head grimly. I burst out laughing. "You have to start talking again," I said. "You shut yourself in your cabin for days. I know it was a big ship, but I shouldn't have asked Lahei to give you your own room—I didn't realize you'd gone and taken an Ikessar vow of silence."

"I needed time alone. I've been arguing with Cho."

"That out of the ordinary?"

"No," he admitted, and a shadow of a smile crossed his face—the first I had seen in weeks. He took a deep breath. "How does it feel? Being so close to home?"

"Confusing," I said. "I don't quite believe it, to be honest. As if I'll wake up any moment and I'll find myself back in Yuebek's dungeon. You do what you can to keep yourself sane, and back there, I must've made this journey a hundred times over in my mind. Even my dreams made it for me." I paused for a moment, taking in the faint outline of the mountains in the distance. "We're still very far, you know. Weeks away. To get to Oren-yaro, you have to follow the southern coastal cities until you hit the River Agos—"

Khine jerked his head back. "He was named after a river?"

"Let's not hold it against his mother. You take the road north, and you follow it all the way to where the terraced hills meet the river. And that's home." I breathed in the cool night air. "It's so far away, but the sky's right, at least. The stars don't look so strange anymore."

"I didn't know that's how it seemed to you. You took everything in stride back in the empire."

I had to laugh at that. "Was that what it looked like? It just seemed like everything went downhill since the first day. If I had known what was waiting there for me, I would have...I don't know. I'd have been restless if I'd stayed, I suppose." I turned my eyes back to the fire, where I nudged the unburnt side of a log with my foot. The flames crackled around it.

Khine made a soft sound in the back of his throat. "You do understand who you are, don't you? What you mean to people?"

I glanced back to meet his eyes. "My father never let me forget my responsibilities, not for a moment."

"There's that," he said with a small nod. "But there is also what people *think* you are and how the world bends itself around it. You turn your head and people follow your gaze. Who is she looking at? Why is she looking at them? And if you explain it, they will tear the words apart looking for a hidden meaning, and if you don't, they will dig into the silence for something that may not be there."

"It's silly."

"I didn't say it wasn't. But that is the tune the whole world dances to. Some are born with the power to turn the tide even before they realize what they are doing. Others...aren't. Some of us have to fight to make a difference from the moment we are born. We try to crest along calm waters because we are helpless against the tide, and even then, a single wave might be enough to sweep us away."

"Khine, if I could have stopped your mother's death..." I started to touch his face.

He wrapped his hand around my wrist to pull my fingers away. "I know that, Tali. It is the memory of my own helplessness that grates at me. This was a long time coming. A death years in the making, and I did nothing to stop it. My mother meant the world to me—why didn't I stop it?"

"I don't see what you could have done differently."

"None of these things would have happened if I had been able to bring my mother to Anzhao as I once dreamed. All I needed to do was get her out of there."

"If she had not done what she did, you would be dead by Yuebek's hand. And I'd be his prisoner again, or worse."

He pressed his lips together. "It's hard to consider it from that angle. Do not all lives have the same weight? It is one of the first things Tashi Reng Hzi taught me. One life cannot replace another. The loss...remains the same."

"I'm not a doctor, Khine. I'm a politician. I weigh things differently. Without you, Rai and I might both be dead, or in the hands of enemies who would use us—enemies who have slaughtered innocents without a second thought. Not that things have gotten better since." I lowered my voice. "Things are worse than I feared."

"Dai spoke to you alone back at the docks. What did he say?"

"He wants to extract Thanh from Oka Shto. But more than that...he wants his younger daughter betrothed to Prince Thanh."

Khine gave an amused snort. "Ambitious."

"Isn't it?"

"He's of common blood. Your people are royals. Don't you have forty or fifty rules governing every decision you make? What makes him think the rest of your nation will agree to it?"

"I told him as much. He thinks he has it under control, that I still have the power to make such an announcement *despite* everything. I cannot even trust the Oren-yaro. How many of the army are *my* men, and not my father's?" I kicked a branch into the fire. "He wants me to make this announcement and declare my husband a traitor, in turn. That anyone who supports him is a traitor and I should likewise declare Rayyel's accusations void in the face of his own infidelities."

Khine's face grew pale. "He's courting war. How does he plan to protect Thanh from the onslaught in the meantime?"

"Right now, Thanh stands as the only proof over my... my actions. His premature death will only cause more chaos, so I don't think they will kill him—not yet. Dai believes he can keep him safe."

"How do you do this?" he breathed. "Put up a brave face while you speak of your own child's fate?"

"A brave face is all it is," I murmured. "Inside, I feel like...like I'm falling and nothing will catch me. Like I'm already broken, but I can't even say a word about how much it hurts. I want it to stop, but it won't. It hasn't for months."

"Most would've given up by now."

"I am Yeshin's only daughter," I said. "I have never been allowed to be like *most*." I turned away from his gaze. "Right now, Dai is my only hope of ever seeing my son alive, but what he wants...it is almost too much. Of course it will result in war. My warlords will question why I would choose the support of peasants instead of my own. How am I supposed to explain to them that my father was likely a traitor, too? It doesn't matter who I side with—it will all end in bloodshed. You say I have the power to turn the tide, but where is it, Khine? I want it in my hands. I want it so I can take my son away from all of this."

He looked down apologetically. After a moment, he placed his hand over mine.

A sound in the distance interrupted us, something between a wail and a howl. I pulled away from him, my hands tightening around my sword hilt.

"Just like us to discuss philosophy when there's bloodthirsty monsters sneaking about," Khine said.

I forced myself to grin. "Why else did you think I brought you along?"

"I had theories, some of which involved my shockingly good looks."

"Spirits help you if you actually think that." I was about to remark at how much it meant to see him in a good mood, but when I turned to him, a shadow crossed his face. It wasn't fear. I was still trying to put a name to it when Nor strode up to us.

"There's things out there all right, but the fire's keeping them away," she informed me abruptly. "If you want to sleep now, Beloved Queen, I'll keep watch."

"You can't expect me to sleep after saying *that*," I sighed. "Sit with us, Nor."

"I'll stand, if that's all right with you."

"I need to ask—did my father not know of this? Dai said he tried to talk to him, too. Was he just as blind to his pride as the other warlords? I find that hard to believe. Oren-yaro suffered the worst from Rysaran's folly."

"I was just a young girl during the War of the Wolves," Nor said with some uncertainty. "Whatever went through Warlord Yeshin's mind was not something I was ever privy to."

"You weren't taught about these things in the army?"

She glanced at the woods. "Somewhat."

"Ah. Somewhat. Now I'm making some progress. Do you see how tiresome it is having everyone keep things from you?" I gave Khine a sideways glance.

"It isn't what you think, my queen," Nor quickly said. "The things Kaggawa told you are new to me, too. But in Oren-yaro, we've always had these stories. You know about the *anggali*?"

"Children's tales," I said. Hearing the words made me feel foolish. Of course they were more than that. I had *seen* one with my own eyes, hadn't I? I turned to Khine to explain. "The *anggali* is a creature from Oren-yaro legend, one that turns into a bat or dog at night to feed on unborn children. But if it's hungry enough, it'll go after anyone in the dark." I shivered at my own words.

"We would sometimes trade stories about how to keep ourselves safe from such creatures," Nor said. "They hate the sound of steel being sharpened, for instance, and the best weapon against them is a whip made from dried stingray tail. They're not mindless creatures... they say these things are open to bargaining. They hate the idea that they're found out, you see, so if you give them a chance to return to society, they might just take you up on it."

"Like how?" I asked.

"Offering to help them take over another body, for instance."

"Dai said these things were made with the destruction of Rysaran's dragon. And yet we've always had these stories in Oren-yaro."

"I don't know, Beloved Queen," Nor said.

"I would assume sources of the *agan*—natural or otherwise—have been tainted before," Khine said. "Small rips here and there, as in the empire."

"But nothing so big as this," I said. "Nothing that would spread like a disease among dragons and people alike. The things Rayyel and I missed, chasing after our foolishness." I pulled my sword close enough to rest it on my knee and stared into the blazing fire. Neither one of them said anything in response. I had, at the very least, honest enough companions.

The creatures did not attack during the night. We found gnaw marks on portions of the rope-fence, which told us they had ventured that far at least. But unlike Yuebek's creations, who had mindlessly gone after us at their master's bidding, these seemed intelligent enough to have considered our defenses with caution. I wondered if it would fool them a second time, if they would track us to our next camp. When I asked Lahei, all she said was, "There are other prey out there."

I tried not to think about what she meant by that. *Others* meant outlying hamlets in the mountains, lone hunters, and the occasional child. But reality outdid whatever horrors my imagination could come up with. On the road, we encountered limbs ripped from a missing torso and a head that once belonged to a young, black-haired woman. "It gets worse every year," Dai commented in the tired voice of a man who thought he had lived too long. I realized that they had been downplaying the urgency of the situation.

We buried the woman's head and whatever else we could find of her on the side of the road. Lahei marked the grave with a rock, where she used charcoal to scribble a brief description of the woman. We returned to our horses in a more sombre mood.

Sometime during the afternoon, we crossed the border to Jin-Sayeng. It was unguarded. The border at the southern road had the remnants of a stone wall, once erected in a vain attempt to keep the Kags to the west. But that was a long time ago—Jin-Sayeng had been open to the Kags since Dragonlord Reshiro's time. The northern road didn't even bear such markers—we reached a portion of the forest, and Lahei turned to me and said, "You're back in Jin-Sayeng, as I promised."

I felt my skin quiver, as if someone had poured cold water over me. But the feeling passed quickly enough. The road turned northward, away from home. I wondered how long before I could ever hold my son in my arms again.

We arrived in the next village by nightfall. They had been waiting for our arrival—a crowd of people gathered around us and dropped to their knees as I dismounted from my horse. "Beloved Queen," they uttered. "We are glad to see you safe from your journey. It is our honour to serve the crown." I felt embarrassed at the thought that I had never ventured this far west before. My council had deemed it unnecessary and dangerous. But the villagers were acting as if I, in all my dishevelled glory, was gracing them with my presence. What would they think of their queen if they knew I had been dragged here against my will?

I caught Dai watching me. I couldn't ask him what for—a village elder came up to take me by the arm and lead me to where the villagers had assembled a feast. My nose caught the whiff of roast pork—a whole entire pig, its skin crispy after hours of turning over hot coals, lay on a bed of rice in the middle of a long table, which was lined with banana leaves. There were also rows of sliced, salted egg, fried lake fish, sliced green mangoes, tomatoes, red onions, globs of pink fish paste, and eggplant mashed in vinegar. I soon found myself seated at the end of the table, with Dai to my right and Lahei beside him. The villagers came to join us.

The west, I quickly learned, was a world away from the east.

The concept of caste is something they never let you forget in the east. There are rules on how to mingle on an official basis, especially with someone of my rank—many of which had been borrowed from the Empire of Ziri-nar-Orxiaro back when the Zarojo and the Jinseins were on better terms. A meeting where an *aron dar* is seated for no reason beside an *aren dar* could be gossip fodder for years. I knew that the further away you travelled from the warlords' cities, the less people adhered to these traditions, but seeing it unfold in front of my eyes was a surprise. Everyone seemed to know their place without the need for someone to remind them, and it felt good not to be seated away from my companions.

We shed our exhaustion from the day's journey with the feast. The roast pork was seasoned with salt, lemongrass, and garlic. Eaten with a dab of rice and eggplant, it all but melted in my mouth in a sea of fat and crackling. Good Jinsein food was simpler than Zarojo, but just as hearty, and I had missed not feeling bad about eating with my fingers. I thought I saw Agos wipe away a tear.

Afterwards, the villagers came with bowls of water for us to wash our hands with, and then the elder came to pass around a jug of strong coconut wine. I took a long drink straight from the bottle, wiped my mouth with the back of my sleeve, and thanked him. The men laughed.

I turned to Dai, who was still looking at me. "Pampered brat, you said," I told him.

Dai smirked. "Anyone can drink, pampered or not." He was using the softer voice, the business-like tone. He passed the coconut wine back to me. "I entertained your husband here years ago, you know."

I paused, my hand on the handle.

"He left you and I was intrigued. I sent him an invitation—he accepted." I took a drink and passed the wine back to him. "A true Ikessar, that one."

"I could've told you that," I said with a smirk.

Dai didn't return the gesture. "This nation doesn't need another few centuries of Ikessar rule."

I watched the expression on his face before replying. "Perhaps I agree."

He wiped the rim of the bottle with his hand. "Do you know what their biggest problem is?"

"My vote is on the butterfly-keeping."

Dai chuckled, blue eyes deep in thought. "Among many things. The Ikessar clan has prided itself in valuing knowledge and education and scholarly pursuits. Progress can be found in an open mind, so an Ikessar or two have said. And yet...all these years, they remain a *royal clan*. Reshiro Ikessar fought for a merchant caste in order to facilitate trade all the way to the east. But why not abolish the castes altogether?"

"You know the warlords would never agree to it."

"And they were open to the idea of a *merchant* caste, you think? That people can keep their profit instead of passing it on to their lord?" Dai broke into a grin. "No, you see, the Ikessars talk well enough, but they're just like everyone else. They want to hold on to their power, too—they just want to look good while doing it. I proved that when your husband was here. I requested that he ride with me out here to show him these things, as I did with you. He refused me outright." His face tightened. "I need you to understand that you are not my prisoner."

I smiled. "And yet I feel like one, despite your best attempts. Perhaps you should've tried harder."

CHAPTER TEN

BARGAINING WITH DEMONS

ᘛ ᒑ ᖇ ᘖ

D ai returned my smile with practiced ease. "Is this too much to take in,
Beloved Queen?"

"Perhaps."

"Quarrelsome warlords. Monsters in the Sougen. Mad dragons. The
Zarojo." He pointed at the sky. "Your father left you quite a mess. I could've
told him it was a bad idea to entrust all of this to the hands of a young girl. I
would've never done the same in his position, not to our daughters. He was an
old man when he fathered you. Did he think he was going to live forever?"

Likely Yeshin did. I didn't know what had gone through my father's head
in those last few years of his life. To ask me to wade through the recesses of his
mind would be like asking me to dive into the blackest depths of the ocean. A
part of me wondered if his wits had grown feeble as he neared the end. I had
never questioned it. I was young and my father had ever been this strong, stal-
wart figure striding ahead of me. Never perfect—no, but for most of my life,
I had stumbled after him like a week-old puppy, blind and eager and without
question.

"Is it not yet clear to you?" Dai asked. "You've been forced into the jaws of
something you were ill-equipped to deal with from the beginning. Who would
you trust among your warlords? The very fact that you are here is proof enough
that you have no one willing to give their lives for you. Your own people, your

own *family*—has abandoned you. You cannot lead this nation in a war against the Zarojo, let alone fix the rest of this, alone. Did Yeshin think you could? *Just* because you came from his loins?"

I gave a thin smile. "It is ironic that I am hearing these things from a man who fought for the Ikessars."

He snorted. "I did not agree with everything my family did, nor to the extent they supported Princess Ryia. The Ikessars' methods bordered on hypocrisy: loudly denounce a warlord for his barbaric methods while asking us to dispose of his supporters in whatever way we saw fit. Poison, assassinations, blackmail—we did everything the Ikessars found too dirty and demeaning to do themselves.

"Years before Warlord Yeshin's civil war, during the rise of the merchant caste, my grandfather supported the Ikessars because he thought that Dragonlord Reshiro agreed with the common people, that he considered our plight. Yet when my merchant grandfather chose to marry a royal—not even an *aren dar*, but a minor noblewoman—for *love*, it was suddenly the worst thing in the world. I have proof that it was Reshiro Ikessar's doing that bankrupted my grandfather's business in Akki. There was a storm, and his ship sank—hired workers had sabotaged it to make it look like an accident. My grandmother's own family had requested it from the Dragonlord so that she would give up her husband and children, and come home. She hung herself from the ceiling instead."

"I have heard rumours of what Reshiro Ikessar did to the Kaggawa family in those years," I said. "I don't speak for the Ikessars, Master Dai, but I am deeply sorry for everything."

"Water under the bridge," Dai said. "You are here now."

"I don't know what you think that will do," I replied. "You've so much as pointed out how powerless I am. Do you think having my son here changes anything?"

"A beginning. Without these ancient rules that have given the Anyus free rein over this land, I will be able to bring in the mages that will help the Sougen. We can stop this godsforsaken plague, or whatever this is, from spreading throughout Jin-Sayeng."

"Have you ever tried just talking to them? Surely the Anyus would be open for negotiation. Both your lands are at risk here."

"Do you royals just *talk*?" Dai snorted. "I think you know the answer better than I do, Beloved Queen."

If I had heard him speak like this in the years before, his head would be rolling in the dust by now. Instead, I remained silent while Yuebek's insults rang inside my head. The land was more divided than I had feared. Was it a wonder why no law of worth ever came to pass, why progress was a dream foisted on the shoulders of the ruling clan? There once stood my father, clinging to the old ways even in death. And then you had my marriage to Rayyel, the counterweight of a land rearing to tear each other's heads off...my husband Rayyel who was royal by name only and then not even, not really. And now this man, Dai Kaggawa, watching me as the night fell around us, waiting for me to see this as an opportunity and then *seize* it for myself. Only he didn't know everything. He didn't know how tired I was of all of this. He didn't know I was done.

I reached for the wine now. Before my fingers could wrap itself around the jug, I heard someone scream. Dai bolted up just as a woman came tearing around the corner. "My son!" she cried, flinging herself at him. "He's missing!"

"Calm down, Mother," Dai said, taking the woman aside. "I'm sure he just wandered off." He gently set her aside and started for the edge of the village, where a group of men had begun to gather with torches. The grim expressions on their faces left little doubt as to what we were actually dealing with.

I pushed myself away from the table. The wine had left me unsteady, but it was nothing I couldn't shake off with a walk. "My queen," Nor said. "Perhaps we should refrain from helping. After all that we have seen so far..."

"Haven't you heard what the man thinks of us royals?" I asked in a low voice.

"Commoner talk. You shouldn't let it get to your head, Beloved Queen. I'm surprised Arro hadn't warned you about people like these: the man just wants to climb higher up the ranks. His family has always been ambitious. It's a well-known fact that his grandfather Goran Kaggawa only supported Dragonlord Reshiro to further his own interests as a merchant."

"And yet you agree with him, don't you? Rayyel and I have been so shortsighted that we've let our personal affairs get in the way of actually ruling."

"My queen," she murmured. "It happens all the time." But she allowed me to walk past her. I took a torch and lit it from the common fire before joining Agos by the village gate. He was strapping on his sword belt.

He met me with an amused grin. "You really can't sit these things out, can you?"

"I'm half-drunk and I want to stick my sword into as many of these creatures as possible if we're going to get run down anyway," I retorted. "Any sign of the child?"

"They said they last saw him walking into the forest with his uncle."

"So the child's uncle is one of these things. Wonderful. What else walks among us, I wonder?" I gave a sideways glance at the crowd in the distance, visible only by the light from their torches as they drifted into the woods. "Have you noticed Kaggawa's tics?"

"I don't know what you mean."

"Don't you? That one's pretty hard to miss. His daughter pretends it doesn't happen, which makes it more obvious. He slips in and out of voices, and his personality changes depending on what we're talking about. And his eyes. His eyes change colour."

Agos grunted.

I noticed a screeching in the distance, quick enough that for a moment, I almost thought I imagined it. But then I saw Agos's face. "You want to go to it, you said?" he asked. "Think I saw a path down there. I'll follow your lead."

It wasn't out of courage that I agreed. Sometimes, the best remedy for fear is movement. I held the torch as far out from my body as I could as I strode down the path, my heart in my throat. Having something come at you in surprise was one thing—knowing you were likely to meet it in the darkness was another. If I had known a safe place to flee, I would've scampered to it without question.

The light, of course, wasn't really helping. As comforting as it was to have the steady glow so close, I could barely see two steps ahead of me. The path opened up to a clearing. The moment we reached the edge, it began to rain.

"Shit," I heard Agos say behind me.

"I didn't even notice the clouds," I grumbled. I stared at the torch, hoping the fire would keep, but I had forgotten how heavy Jinsein rains could get. Each torrent felt like I was being pelted by rocks. Before I could draw another breath, the torch was reduced to a smouldering stick and I was drenched from head to toe.

"We should head back," Agos said with a measure of uncertainty.

I dropped the useless torch and walked to his voice. "What did the army tell you about the *anggali*?" I asked.

"To stay the hell away from them."

I tried to laugh the growing fear away and began to scrape my blade on the rock at my foot, hard enough for it to emit a high-pitched scratch. Not even a moment passed before I heard a resounding screech in the distance.

"There it goes," I said with a nervous laugh. The screech was getting louder. I looked up at the sky, automatically scanning the treetops.

Agos sighed. "First those walking dolls, and now this. Have I told you how much I hate these scrapes you get us into?"

"All the time."

"Well, I'm saying it again."

I paused for a moment before I repeated the motion with my blade. Nor had mentioned that the things hated the sound of steel being sharpened. It replied again, this time with the low wail of a caged animal being tormented. The fact that it could hear me meant it couldn't be too far away.

"Stay in the bushes, Agos. I'm going to draw it out."

"What?"

"I said—"

"I heard you. Are you mad?"

I didn't answer him and slowly made my way to the clearing.

"The boy's probably dead. Torn and eaten up. *Dinner*," Agos called after me. "What are you doing this for? To prove to Kaggawa that you're not like the other royals? We know you're not. You'd be dead now if you were."

I tapped my blade against the ground. It was hard, packed with gravel, and even in the rain I could still hear the scraping noise the creature hated. I made a wide circle around me. Before I could complete it, I caught the snuffling from the wet leaves.

I counted to three. The creature leaped from the bushes.

It was so dark that the only thing I could make out was the rain and the way it bent over the creature's skin. The fact that everything was shrouded in shadows helped—if I could see its face, the fear would've won. But I couldn't see any images beyond the darkness: black on black, deeper than the night. With the fear barely bubbling below the surface of my nerves, I struck without hesitation.

My sword sank into flesh. The creature's howl of pain was strangled short. I felt the hiss of air and blood and realized I had cut into its throat and chest. It dropped to the ground, and I could hear the clack of its teeth in its death throes.

I took a step back. "My queen!" someone called behind me. Nor's voice. I wiped rain from my mouth and turned up to see her appear with a lantern.

"Blessed Akaterru," Agos grunted as the light reached us. "It's the woman with the missing child."

I looked at the body on the ground and realized the truth in Agos's words. The creature had turned back to its human form, and I recognized the pattern on its skirt. "But she was the one who called for help," I said.

"The damned thing was trying to draw people into the woods," Agos replied. He grimaced. "If this problem is as urgent as they say it is..."

I turned to Nor. "Is Khine back in the village?"

Nor looked surprised. "I thought he was with you."

"I thought I saw him go off into the woods by himself," Agos said. "Right before I met you at the gate."

I stared at him. "And you didn't think to tell me this?"

"I didn't know we'd become his guardians," Agos snapped.

"We don't even know what Kaggawa has planned for us. The last thing we need is to be fighting amongst ourselves or, Akaterru forbid, stalking off into the woods alone."

"Don't tell *me*, tell him."

I sighed. "Maybe he went back to the village. Maybe—"

We heard another howl, deeper into the woods. It was the gut-wrenching sound of a dog who had lost its master, the sort that seemed like it was ripped from its throat into the wind.

Maybe it was my newfound confidence from the sight of the dead creature at my feet, combined with the energy from my still-frazzled nerves. Or maybe it was just the thought of Khine being in the woods alone. But I didn't stop to think about my next step. Even before the howl could finish, I tore into the bushes towards it, the rain blurring everything in my path. My guards lumbered after me.

I crossed a low ditch and reached the main path that led straight to the village gates. Here, I saw a figure standing very still. I recognized Khine immediately. Against the glow of the village lights, I also saw the dark, gangly shadow behind him, its shape a caricature of a wolf, stretched too far in every direction. One claw was touching Khine's shoulder.

"Khine!" I called.

"Stop," Khine said in an even voice. He pointed. I turned and saw a boy standing in the middle of the path. He didn't look any older than three, with threadbare clothes damp with mud. His face was red, but if he had been crying before, he wasn't now. He was staring quietly at Khine and the creature like his life depended on it.

I heard Nor and Agos panting behind me and turned my attention back to the creature. It lifted one finger up, pressing it over its lips.

"What are you doing to him?" I asked.

The creature grinned.

"He'll kill the boy if I fight," Khine said.

I pointed at the boy. "That? His mother was one of them. They were trying to fool us." I swung my sword through the air. "I killed her. Should I kill you, too?"

The creature threw its head back and answered. "He offered his life in exchange." Its voice was raspy, like dry sand and scorched earth. The sound made the hair on my arms stand on end. "A sweet life, a willing host. Unfortunate that my sister passed on, but we had to jump. The others were starting to suspect us."

"He's not willing," I replied. "We know it's a trick. The boy is one of you. You wouldn't hurt your own."

"He isn't," the creature said. It wrinkled its snout. "Or if he is . . . do you want that on your conscience?"

I laughed. "Dai says you live among us as if you were one of us. That means you were with us during the feast. You know who I am."

"Queen Talyien, Lady of Oren-yaro." The creature spoke as if reciting a memorized script.

I pretended that hearing my name uttered by such a foul voice didn't bother me. "Smart. Maybe you're smart enough to remember who my father was and the things he didn't care for."

It wasn't expecting that sort of response. It froze for half a second, which was all I needed. As my sword struck its exposed arm, Khine pushed back and stabbed it in the stomach with his own blade.

It howled and released Khine as it went for me. Khine left the sword inside the creature and made a mad dash towards the child. I forced my eyes back to the battle. Sword met fur, and I felt its claws creep up my neck as the corpse-stench of its hot breath blasted into my face.

Agos joined the fray. The creature flung me aside to face him. I slid across the mud. As I struggled to stand, slime in my mouth, Nor reached over to hook her elbow into mine. "It's over," she said as she pulled me up.

I blinked against the rain and saw Agos standing over the creature's body. Its head wriggled a few feet away, flopping about in the mud like a dying fish.

"Killing them isn't so bad when you know how," Agos commented.

I spat out blood from the inside of my cheek and walked up to Khine. He held his arm out, stopping me in my tracks.

I realized that he was standing very close to the boy. I thought *boy* automatically, but if you had met it alone in the dark, you would've been hard-pressed to call it that. *Imp* was a more appropriate description. Its face was twisted, creased with folds of dark skin. Its mouth was lined with rows of sharp teeth, and it regarded us with red, bulbous eyes full of tears and hate.

"The child, too?" I gasped. When I had accused the boy of being one of them, I was talking about family and blood. I hadn't meant *exactly* like they were. The thought had been too terrifying for me to consider, a blasphemy to the gods.

"Are you going to kill it?" Khine asked.

I found myself at a loss for words. The others were different. You don't stop to think about defending yourself against a beast. It is an entirely different thing when confronted with their hissing, spitting cub. Looking at the imp filled me with revulsion, but it wasn't attacking us—it just stood there, half shivering, drenched in the rain like a pathetic, mangy pup. It didn't help that I had seen it as nothing more than a normal child minutes ago.

"We can't just let it go," Agos broke in. "You've seen what they can do. The more of these things are out there, the more dangerous this trip becomes."

"Was it ever even a child?" I wondered out loud.

"It's not now, whatever it is," Nor said. "Kill it, Agos."

Agos took a step forward.

"Wait," I said.

He spat. "Don't tell me you want us to let the unholy creature free into the woods. These things have no place in this world."

I turned to Khine. "You were offering yourself as a host back there for *that*. Tell us what we should do."

Khine wiped water off his face before replying. "I thought I had no choice. It was threatening the boy, and…" He swallowed. "It told me about how this works. How it's just about having two souls in one body. Come into agreement with the thing and it won't fully take over. It told me that it would live with us peacefully if we let it—but the villagers kill their hosts if they find out what they are, so they're forced to fight back."

"You believed all of that?"

"I wasn't thinking," he mumbled. "The boy was crying."

It still was. But it was no longer the wail of a child, the sort that made you want to calm and soothe with promises of sweets and wooden toys. It was the grating sound of something unnatural, of something that needed to die. If you heard that sound rustling in the bushes you would stick your sword into it first and ask questions later.

"If it had spoken truthfully, the boy could still be saved."

"The creature lied to you, Khine. Remember the one in the stables? It saw an opportunity to feed and it attacked. They're controlled by their hunger. It lied to you so it could hide *inside* of you, because everyone already suspected its host was infected."

"I carried him earlier," Khine whispered. "He wasn't like that. He was just a child."

The imp continued to cry.

We would've stood there for hours, racked with indecision while we stared at this creature in the rain, if Dai and his men hadn't appeared from the mist. Without a word, he strode past us, grabbed the imp by its shirt, and slid a dagger into its breast.

My first thought was that its flesh was much, much softer than I imagined it to be. My second thought was shattered by its death-cry, louder than both its mother's and its uncle's. I smelled the sharp scent of blood and my eyes watered against my will.

Dai dropped the body and turned to us. "It was too far gone."

"What do you mean by that?" I asked.

"These creatures are tainted. Twisted, vile things. There is no reasoning with them, no bargaining with them, because even *they* can't control themselves. We've seen more than enough to know this to be true." He turned to me. "Much has happened in one day. You all need to rest—we'll be up early tomorrow."

"Is that all of them?" Agos broke in. "I can't see how we're supposed to rest if you have an entire village of these things walking around."

"You all smell of death to them, as far as they're concerned," Dai said. "You'll be safe for tonight."

"Not much of a consolation," Agos grunted.

They led us back to the village. I walked alongside Khine, unconsciously matching my steps to his. When the crowd had drifted ahead of us, I found myself giving voice to what was bothering me. "Were you that ready to die?" I asked.

Khine looked surprised at my tone of voice. "I told you already," he replied.

"Now that I think about it, death would've been vastly preferable to what you were offering that thing. A *willing host*, it said. And if I hadn't caught up to you when I did . . . would we have even known? Could we have saved you then?" I turned to grab his shoulders and angled my head up to stare at his face. "Am I still talking to Khine?"

"Don't be ridiculous," he said, pushing me aside.

I didn't let him. "You were making a deal with a demon, Khine. How do I know it didn't go through and that it's really you in there?"

"His eyes," Nor told us. "Your reflection in them will be upside down. At least, that's what they told us about *anggali*."

I tried to push his hair back from his face. "I can't see them. It's too dark."

"We can do it when he's sleeping," Nor suggested.

He frowned. "I'm still me."

"Are you sure?"

"Tali—"

I made a fist and punched him on the cheek.

He staggered back, wiping blood from the corner of his mouth. "The fuck, Tali! What was that for?"

"I wanted to make sure," I replied, flexing my wrist. "You didn't bite my head off for that, so I think you're safe."

He frowned before turning around to walk back to his hut.

"Khine," I called after him.

He stopped. "What?"

"Don't you think you continue to fail your mother if you've decided you're done with your life?"

He said nothing and continued on his way.

My dreams that night were long and confusing. Parts I don't fully recall anymore. But the most persistent scene was that of Khine with the demon at his shoulder. I saw it from every possible angle, saw the way the shadows bent around them as he came close to accepting its essence into his body. I don't know why the image bothered me as much as it did. I only knew that I reacted the same way with every transformation—straight at them, sword drawn, a strangled cry in my throat.

Around me, Mei's words repeated like a chant, a thin strand in the wind. I woke up screaming. It was still dark, and the rain had turned into a blanket that threatened to smother the world. I felt a hand on my shoulder as I forced myself up, and saw Agos's concerned face peering down at me.

"You care for Lamang, don't you," he said. Not a question. I looked up at him in confusion, and he shrugged. "You were saying his name in your sleep."

My heart was still racing from my dream. "He wants to die," I said. "And I'm dragging him into this mess, just like I'm dragging everyone else." Speaking my fears out loud tasted bitter in my mouth.

"He just lost his mother," Agos replied. "It's normal."

I took a deep breath and pressed my back on the bamboo wall, listening to the rain drip down from the thatched roof. The smell of the wet wind seeped through the bamboo wall.

My silence must've unnerved Agos. "Order him to go back home," he said.

"I remember people telling me the exact same thing about you."

Agos bristled. "Which people?"

"Just people."

"Maybe that's your problem. You don't know why you keep people around. You hold on when you should be letting go."

"Gods, we're not talking about Rayyel again, are we?"

He remained deathly serious. "We're talking about you."

"You and everyone from one kingdom to the next," I said. "I'm sick of it. Let's talk about something else. Let's...let's talk about horses. No—let's talk about *you*, Agos. What have you been doing all these years?"

I didn't think he knew whether I was sincere or not. I felt my cheeks burn, remembering we had walked down this road that same night. *The night I ruined everything.* I closed my eyes, hating myself for all my moments of weakness. I had to stop doing this. I had to stop trying to seek comfort if all it ever did was to make things worse. If the nation had a stronger queen, we wouldn't be on the verge of falling apart.

Agos gave a small huff, unaware of what was going on inside my head. "It's nothing important. Odd jobs here and there. Not the steady pay with the army or the guards, but nothing so dangerous, either. I peddled wares at one point, played at being a merchant. Wasn't very good with numbers and lost more money than I made. Good thing I learned that before I petitioned to have my name changed to *alon gar*." He chuckled.

"Probably a good thing—the officials would've given you too much trouble for a request like that. You were named *asor arak*, a soldier, for a reason. You were good at it, too." I swallowed. "Maybe I can find a way to put you back into service. I'll speak with Lord General Ozo on your behalf."

"Don't," Agos said. "I didn't find you to beg for my life back. You have enough on your plate already. I serve you—you never have to worry about me."

"Maybe Kaggawa is onto something," I murmured. "The castes were supposed to help Jin-Sayeng maintain order, to ensure everyone knows their duties, but what good is it when it becomes all about the name and nothing else?"

"And now you have an *anggali* invasion, to add to everything," Agos agreed. "A merchant's life sounds simpler, doesn't it?"

"An *anggali* invasion. Don't forget the Zarojo's meddling, too, on top of the squabbling warlords. And Kaggawa is bringing me to the Sougen, to show me *more*. Akaterru help us. I don't know if I can do this. Not without my father. Not alone." I shivered. "Tell me to run away with you again."

Agos paused. "Are you sure?"

"I'm going to answer *no*. But…" I hesitated. "But it makes me feel better that I still get a choice. I still get a choice, don't I?"

He gazed at me for a heartbeat. "I don't understand you," he finally said. "I never did. But damn if I don't keep coming back. I'm a moth to your flame, Princess." Agos took a deep breath. "Run away with me," he said, taking hold of my hand. "Even if I know you'd rather run off with Lamang."

His words jolted me out of the haze. I pulled away from him. "We've gone through this before."

"We have, and not in the way you think." Agos swallowed before gently stroking the side of my cheek with his thumb. "Go to sleep, Princess. Dream of whoever you'd like. I have to check the roof for monsters." He gave a crooked smile and left me alone.

I wrapped my arms around my knees, willing the rest of my thoughts away.

CHAPTER ELEVEN

THE RICE MERCHANT

Here is a topic of conversation my husband would've loved. The rice merchants of the Sougen made most of their fortunes before the *alon gar* caste ever became a reality. And while most of them supported Dragonlord Reshiro Ikessar's decree, a number of families actually went on a campaign *against* it, wanting the exclusivity and certainty offered by continuing to work under the warlords. It was all a very chaotic and confusing time. I have trouble keeping track of the various families, the factions, and their contributions in the chaos of those years, but I'm sure Rayyel would be more than happy to entertain any questions you may have. And then—if you're still awake by the end of his lectures—he'll probably quiz you to make sure you've been paying attention.

Seeing the Sougen Plains unfold in front of me did make me aware of how much I had taken Rayyel's endless trove of knowledge for granted. It was a strange region, one that didn't fit the Jin-Sayeng I knew. The vast grasslands rolled out like a sea of green, with long stretches unmarked by forest or hills. I've heard stories of people getting lost in the plains—without a landmark to guide them, they end up wandering in circles. The lucky ones stumble on a rice field or a road; the unlucky ones starve to death, their bodies lost in the midst of the bright, seemingly innocuous greenery.

According to many legends, we were all descended from tribes that used to roam the Sougen. They say that we first made contact with dragons in the mountains northwest of the plains, and that we learned to tame them in order to navigate the vast lands. They also say that the plains were as flat and unmarked as they were because of dragonfire, which burned down the trees and most of the shrubbery and made it so that only the tough, hardy grass could grow in its stead. It was a strange sort of grass, too—left on its own, it could grow tall enough to obscure a man standing on tiptoe, with sharp leaves that could cut skin.

The grass was one of the many challenges that plagued the region. A builder had explained it to me once: here, the grass plants grew almost everywhere, and could grow fast and strong enough to uproot building foundations. You had to be careful about where you wanted to settle. That meant that the Sougen was sparsely populated, despite what appeared to be vast amounts of flat and arable land. It had one city, Yu-yan, built on the eastern shore of the largest river that ran through the plains.

Well—perhaps all the years of following Rayyel around had their purpose after all. I didn't even have to struggle to remember these facts, and they sort of rolled around my head in his voice. Perhaps I was *forcing* myself to miss him. I did once; I thought, perhaps, that I could do it again.

"Did Lord Rayyel travel all the way out here just to meet with you?" I asked Dai, pushing my horse forward so I could ride abreast with him.

The mere mention of my husband's name made Dai grimace. "He did, though he came by riverboat."

I gaped at him. "We could have come by boat?"

"The letter I had sent to him asked him to go on horseback, that my men would meet him in Fuyyu and escort him the rest of the way. He didn't think the request was worth his time."

"We could have come by boat," I repeated, turning to Lahei.

She gave me a rueful smile. "We could've come on the *Aina's Breath*, actually, but..." She shrugged and pointed at her father.

"Would you have believed me about the beasts if you didn't see them with your own eyes?" Dai asked. "If I had welcomed you straight into my home and told you everything you have learned the past few days, you would have laughed in my face."

"I find it hard to believe that Rayyel laughed at you."

"*You* would have," Dai said, shaking his head. "Your husband has decorum,

I give him that. Polite. A true Ikessar. I didn't expect less. He asked me how I found him—I told him the truth, that there is nothing the Shadows cannot find. Nothing." He gave me the sort of look that could've meant anything, but I found myself fidgeting in discomfort. Eventually, he turned away. "He made a request, one we carried out with much discretion. Afterwards, we did discuss the state of Jin-Sayeng's castes, but he was tight-lipped about the situation with the Dragonthrone and with *you*."

"It *is* rather complicated," I said.

"Not to me. I am familiar with Ikessar pride and the thousands of ways such a thing can cause a problem. Your husband is an intelligent man, Queen Talyien, the likes of which hasn't been seen on the Dragonthrone for years. Not that he's ever actually sat on the damn thing, has he? Compared with the Ikessars before him, he has shown himself to be the most credible, the most learned. He had a good track record as Minister of Agriculture, and I'm sure anything he says would at least be considered by the warlords. I had high hopes for our meeting.

"And yet... even as an illegitimate son of Reshiro Ikessar's youngest daughter, he retained all the closed-minded stubbornness of his people. I was still trying to be diplomatic, and didn't think dragging him to the villages—"

"As you did with me?"

"—was the best idea. But I tried to broach the subject of the *agan* to him," he continued, without blinking an eye. "He refused to speak further as soon as I brought *that* up. It was nothing short of infuriating."

"You realize that talk of the *agan* in the east can get you killed," I said.

He pointed. "It doesn't seem to bother *you*."

"It would have in the past. You caught me at a good time. I'm open to a lot of things these days, apparently."

"That, and you actually saw the creatures," Lahei added.

"Was Rai alone when he came here?" I asked.

Dai nodded.

"And that request of his... did it have something to do with an innkeeper's family in a small town outside of Shirrokaru?"

Dai smiled. "You *are* Yeshin's daughter."

I bristled. "You lured Lord Rayyel out here with that information."

"Was it supposed to be a secret, Queen Talyien? That a certain innkeeper—dead after a fateful visit to Oren-yaro—would have family who had been spreading rumours about you in their small town? Well. We took care of it easy enough. Consider it a token of goodwill to show our loyalty to preserving Jin-Sayeng's peace. I told your husband as much."

"Why didn't you send word?"

"Why should I have?" Dai asked with a huff. "You already see what I have to deal with—the last thing I wanted was you knocking on my door demanding I turn your husband over."

I felt my face turning red. "What happened with the Baraji…"

"Like I said," Dai grumbled. "It's all nothing to me." He fell silent as we turned a corner, where the thick brush gave way to rice fields.

It was unnerving to learn that I was actually his second option. That instead of trying to send a message to Oren-yaro after his talk with Rayyel failed, he chose to wait for the right opportunity—one that involved having my back against the wall. I knew this was the sort of reputation I had tried to cultivate over the years, but to hear it with my own ears was disconcerting. To be told that despite years of absence, Rayyel's words carried more weight, that his stubbornness was vastly preferable to my own…

I did start missing Rayyel now, but for entirely different reasons.

My thoughts were drowned by thick, black smoke rising from one of the rice fields. I realized the whole thing was on fire. I turned to Dai immediately, but the man didn't seem alarmed. "A dragon must have come by," he said, as if he were observing nothing more than a blazing sunset. "Why do you look so surprised, Beloved Queen? You knew what was happening to your western fields all these years."

"You both did nothing about this," Nor broke in. She had been listening to our conversation in stony silence the whole time.

Unnerved, I turned from her to look at Dai. "Shouldn't we get water to put it out?"

"Rice paddies are wet already," he said. "For a dragon to set them ablaze, it would take fire that can't be easily quenched. No—there is nothing we can do. But watch, Beloved Queen. What you see burning out there can feed a whole village for a month. Think about it. Soon your nation will be overrun from the inside, and out."

We didn't see whatever dragon caused the fire, or any others, as we made our way to Dai's estate. It was set right up along the Sougen River, which we crossed from a timber-hewn bridge built along a narrow section. I could see the silhouette of the city of Yu-yan upriver, nestled perfectly between the visible chunk of mountain on the horizon and the shoreline. There were boats on the river, some of which were lazily towing logs downstream to sawmills along the banks. Because I couldn't spot any forests in the distance, I figured they came all the way from the mountains up north. Red-crested herons and spotted ducks milled around the water's edge in search for fish. As soon as our horses came within sight, they scattered to the sky.

We rode up to the gates, where about half a dozen servants ran out to take our horses. I tried to keep an eye out for any signs of Kaggawa's infamous sell-swords and couldn't spot any. He didn't even have guards—all his servants looked ordinary, slightly stooped and with the dark, suntanned skin common with farmers. The only weapons on them were the broad, single-edged grass-cutter blades that they carried unsheathed on their belts. I gazed past them across the road, where Kaggawa's rice fields lay. Narrow paths wove through the paddies, snaking around the aggressive patches of Sougen grass. I could imagine them going on forever.

More servants arrived to greet us. A portly old woman came out to take Lahei into her arms, half lifting her. Lahei laughed, a sound that caused a flicker of amusement on Dai's face. And then the old woman took my elbow with a gentleness that reminded me of Mei. "Is this the queen?" she asked, like I was a stray dog that had wandered into the yard.

"You're supposed to bow to her, *sang*," Lahei said.

"I'm supposed to feed her," the woman replied. She dabbed her jowls with a towel and gazed at the rest of my group. "I've set up a nice meal, if you'd all just wash your shoes by the pump before you head into my kitchen. Queen you might be, but I'll not have you tracking dirt across my floor."

A servant came to whisper something in Dai's ear. He frowned. "Let your men go ahead. I need to show you something, Beloved Queen."

"What are you talking about?"

"Huan and Eikaro Anyu have caught wind of your arrival and are on their way. I was hoping to have more time, but the bastards would just *love* to get their claws in you before I've had the chance to tell the rest of this story." He gestured. Biting back my inclination to argue, I followed him into his study.

It was larger than the one in Ni'in, with an entire wall of bookcases and several padded chairs. He leaned over the side of his desk to pull out a piece of paper from his drawer, which he then handed over to me. My eyes skipped over a list of names, followed by a description of what appeared to be fatal injuries: torn limbs, ripped throats, crushed hip bones, blood loss.

"I acquired that from the Yu-yan office," Dai said. "Those are people who died in these parts from the past month alone."

"Just the past month?" I flipped the page over. It was a very long list.

"The city officials conduct an investigation whenever a body is brought to the mortuaries."

"I know," I said. "They're supposed to send these lists over to the council at the Dragon Palace. I get a copy sent to Oka Shto later on."

"You ever read them?"

My cheeks coloured. "I've never seen the need before."

Dai made a dismissive wave. "No matter. You wouldn't have seen these, anyway. Warlord Ojika had them confiscated and sent false reports on. You don't seem surprised."

"It's common for the warlords to send false reports," I said, arms crossed. "Especially if it involves their crops, their treasury, or their army. The Dragon Palace has ways to spot them—they'll follow up with a line of inquiry and then alert me once they've started taking steps. Falsifying mortuary reports, though... I don't think I've ever seen that before."

"Are you reading those injuries?"

"Yes."

"What do you think?"

I realized he was indicating that I'd missed something. I read through them again. *Torn limbs, crushed bones...* "These are animal attack injuries," I murmured. "The dragons?" I ventured.

"Perfect," Dai said. "I should've asked for wine to celebrate dealing with an official who's not a complete idiot. Yes, they're dragons. It shouldn't be surprising."

"Warlord Ojika hid this from us." I flicked the next page, showing more of the same thing—name after name of people who'd died from a dragon one way or another. "Did he want to downplay the extent of your problem here?"

Dai snorted. "Worked, didn't it? I don't believe you've ever had an investigation on the situation here in all these years."

"The Dragon Palace sends an envoy to each province once a year to ensure things are running as they should. Every report we've received from Yu-yan has told us they have everything under control." Looking at the names and injuries suddenly made me ill, and I pushed the piece of paper away. "I still don't see what Warlord Ojika has to gain from pretending. A page from this report would be enough for me to send a whole retinue of soldiers to deal with it."

"The Anyus want the dragons," Dai said.

I closed my mouth. "The mad dragons."

"Sound familiar?"

Too much. The story of Rysaran's mad dragon was one I had heard straight from my father over and over again throughout the years. Having seen the destruction it wrought upon Old Oren-yaro with his own eyes, he was adamant that I understood the dangers of dabbling with the *agan*, as well as the price of misplaced ambition. It was also a tale of a father's grief, of lost sons and broken dreams. I had never imagined anyone would want to re-create such a catastrophe.

"The Anyus have been attempting to tame the creatures for years," Dai continued, noting my silence. "They are nowhere near the size or power of Rysaran's, of course. And the intent is entirely different. Rysaran had wanted a symbol, a way to hold on to his dying clan's claims. The Anyus want true, uncontested power. They believe if they can revive the dragonriders of old, they can eventually work their way up to the Dragonthrone."

"And yet these dragons are infested with these *corrupted souls*, just like the people we've seen."

"Indeed."

"So anyone who tries to *ride* them will be ripped apart, anyway."

Dai made a sound. "If that was my only concern, I'd be happy to just sit back and watch the show. To see fat Warlord Ojika heave his gouty self onto a dragon mad for his blood...I'd pay for such a sight. But he's gone and hired mages to help them out. Mages who don't seem to see the damage they have caused in this region, who are more than happy to help Ojika Anyu's bloated ego so that he continues to be the wall of thorns that stops me from doing anything to save Jin-Sayeng. *I* cannot bring in mages without causing you royals to want to put my head on a chopping block, but somehow the Anyus get away with it."

I took a moment to digest his words. But my mind skipped back from the gravity of what he was saying to a small detail. "Mages," I finally said. "The ones working with the Anyus. Dageis keeps a close watch on their own—I find it hard to believe the Anyus would've been resourceful enough to find a Dageian mage willing to work for them."

Dai smiled.

"Are they Zarojo?" I asked.

He nodded. My blood ran cold.

I suppose I had assumed that the nightmare would be over once I stepped back on Jin-Sayeng soil. I would be greeted by my council and doting servants, return to my throne, and order my army to find and end Yuebek's life once and for all. And then I could sit and wait for Rayyel to arrive and deal with that whole situation as best as I could. *We will forget that accursed meeting in Anzhao and resume our duties side by side.*

I had been so deep in my own thoughts that I didn't even notice Dai get up to look through the window. I blinked as I heard the sound of hooves outside. "What is it?" I asked.

"Let us not speak ill of the dead lest they rise and hurt you," Dai said with a wistful grin.

"That's a defilement of Kibouri. Shouldn't it be *Lest the words turn and hurt you?*"

Dai shook his head. "One of my father's sayings. He had a strange sense of humour. I never did get it. Thankfully, I never met him. He was named Oji, as it happened. After the same figure in history Ojika Anyu was named for. As if the gods weren't cruel enough." He nodded towards the window. "The Anyus have arrived. They are probably, as we speak—"

Three knocks sounded on the door. Dai grimaced. "Come in," he said with a sigh.

A woman poked her head through the crack. "Lord Eikaro and Lord Huan are at our gates. They seek audience with the Beloved Queen."

"Let me meet them," I said. "Seems to me like it's pointless to hide." All I had to do was *think* of going somewhere and people would be waiting for me. I didn't like it. I had never liked it.

"Keep in mind the things I have told you. If you should decide the Anyus are harmless..."

"I have known them since I was a girl, Master Dai."

"I'm aware. More than that—they're your friends, though I've seen how you've done your best not to claim so in front of me. I don't know if it's courtesy or deceit." He sniffed. "The brothers are not their father, but they do not move without the father's shadow hovering over them at every turn. This is not a drinking party, Queen Talyien. You will do well to remember that."

We made our way back to the yard. I got the impression that the Anyus were a frequent sight, and an unwelcome one at that. The servants had barred the gates and stood watching as the Anyu brothers' horses paced along the road.

"Let them in," Dai said as we arrived.

The servants pulled the gates open, but the brothers remained outside. Eikaro's and Huan's beaming, suntanned faces broke into grins at the sight of me. They visited court often in the past. *Friends*, Dai had called them, but I didn't know if I would extend the word that far. It was true that they never missed a festival or tournament, and I always sat by them because they were the closest in age to me. I spoke with them more than with many of my other officials, as a result, but I knew very little about them—not half of what a friend ought to.

"Queen Talyien," Huan greeted. I could tell him apart from his twin by the extravagant silver staghead around his neck, which he had worn since he was a boy. It marked him as his father's heir. "Your absence has driven the entire nation mad. We didn't think we'd ever be graced with your beautiful presence again."

"Spare me the flattery, Lord Huan," I said as I approached them. "You've hurt my feelings. I've been trapped in the Zarojo Empire for months and yet you didn't send soldiers after me. The honour of that belongs to Anong Kaggawa alone."

"And well may the Dragonthrone reward him for that," Huan said, glancing at Dai with a look of mock gratitude.

"We wanted to, Beloved Queen, believe us," Eikaro said. "But our father said we couldn't. There were orders. We couldn't even send word to inquire about your health—we were told we could be putting your life in danger if we did."

"Who made this declaration?" I asked. "Lord General Ozo?"

"I'd prefer not to speak ill of our Beloved Queen's own general—" Eikaro started.

"—but we're aware, of course, that the truth will come out sooner or later," Huan finished for him.

"Stop it," I said. "The concept of loyalty is a sore subject for me these days. Skirting around my questions makes me even more irritable."

Huan bowed. "My apologies."

"It is as you say," Eikaro added. "General Ozo would not tell us exactly what transpired. For the good of the realm, they will not confirm the queen's whereabouts or current condition. But he assured us of your safety and that he was working very hard to bring you back to Jin-Sayeng."

"The whole kingdom was in an uproar," Huan continued. "You should've seen the meeting. Plates thrown and everything."

"I'm almost sad I missed that," I said.

Huan shrugged. "I can give you a word-for-word report." He glanced at Dai. "That is, if your gracious host will let you. We can, of course, offer you to stay at Yu-yan instead, if you'd like. I'm sure we have better accommodations."

"What do you say, Master Dai?" Eikaro called out to him from across the gate. "Lend the queen to us for a spell? Although after the luxuries of Yu-yan, I can't guarantee she'll want to return to you. We've got a marvellous play going on in the theatre right now," he added in a lower voice. "The playwright is Yu-yan's own, and one of our finest. You're in it!"

"A flattering role, I hope."

"But of course, Beloved Queen," Eikaro said. "Nothing but the best for you.

You're played by the most magnificent actress the entire kingdom has ever seen. Her eyes—ah! You would love her eyes, not to mention her flawless skin."

I narrowed my eyes. "Now it's starting to sound like an insult."

"Also," Huan broke in. "You'll want to see our wives. I know we had other…arrangements, but seeing as you were missing and possibly dead…" He coughed, turning a slight shade of red.

Eikaro shrugged. "Life had to go on."

"So it did," I replied. "I'll forgive you for now."

Huan smiled. "You are too kind. And ah—perhaps you'll refrain from mentioning anything when you see them? It's not exactly a secret, but I'd rather avoid scandal if we can."

I gave a crooked smile. "You're wiser men than I've given you credit for. I look forward to meeting your women, but unfortunately, it's been a long day, and the thought of doing any more riding doesn't sit well with me. Will you extend your offer until tomorrow?"

"But of course, Beloved Queen," Huan said. "We'll meet you ourselves at this hour tomorrow if you wish. Yu-yan is only an hour's ride away."

I thanked them. They both bowed like perfect lordlings. You wouldn't think their father was a usurper.

CHAPTER TWELVE

THE SOUGEN ROYALS

*U*surper, of course, was a debatable word. Could one usurp a throne that didn't exist?

Yu-yan, the heart of the Sougen region, was traditionally run by rice merchants, not the royals. The merchant families sat on the council and functioned as city officials, voting amongst themselves and organizing their politics as they saw fit. The Dragonthrone didn't care—we allowed each province to function independently, making a fuss only with taxes and reports, and we certainly weren't going to interfere with a system that had worked for centuries.

That all changed during my father's war. Ojika Anyu, then a much younger and more physically capable version of himself, arrived with a few thousand soldiers to take control of the city. No one knew how this army had materialized without anyone catching wind of it—one of the many shortcomings of Rysaran as my predecessor. He had been so focused on his quest for a dragon that he had neglected his duties for years. It was said that even when Rysaran *was* in the Dragon Palace, he had allowed his regent to rule, choosing instead to bury his nose in books. Not that the nation should've expected anything less from an Ikessar, but...

Because of my father's war, everyone was too busy trying to stay alive or kill their enemies, and there was no one on the throne that could bring the Anyu clan to swift justice. By the time the war was over, the Anyus had been in Yu-yan for five years. Ojika Anyu appeared on the day of my birth to bow at my cradle and swear his fealty to the future queen. My father chose to pardon him as a sign of goodwill, that Jin-Sayeng's time of bloodshed was over.

Yesterday's news. Yesterday's failings. I spent the entire night thinking them over in bed after a hot bath and with a bellyful of beef, carrot, and potato stew, which resulted in wild dreams of the warlords screeching at the top of their lungs while hacking each other's heads off. It was oddly cathartic.

I woke up to the sound of screaming and clanging swords, and groggily reached for my own, thinking we were under attack. I heard the door open before I could hit the end of the mattress. "My queen," Nor said. "Breakfast is served."

My senses cleared. "What's happening outside?"

"Oh, that?" She grimaced. "The men decided they were going to do some sword practice."

"Men," I repeated. "What men?"

"Agos and Lamang," she said.

"You mean Cho?" I asked.

"Khine."

I tried to keep a straight face as I followed her to the dining hall. Dai wasn't there. A servant came by with a bowl of chicken and rice porridge and a note from her master, telling me he had gone visiting his farmers and would be back by lunch. I set the note aside and turned to my food. It felt good to wake up to a decent meal again, and the porridge was creamy, with enough bits of crunchy garlic, boiled chicken, and preserved egg to keep me busy.

I made my way to the yard after breakfast. The sound of metal on metal intensified, followed by the unmistakable *thwack!* of a fist hitting flesh. Khine stumbled back. Cho, who was sitting on top of the stone fence, chortled.

"How is that even fair?" I heard Khine call out. He was wearing his inner shirt, a thin piece of grey fabric that showed off the muscles of his bare arms.

"Nothing's fair in a fight," Agos spat out. *He* was shirtless, which was usually how he liked to practice. Sweat didn't so much drip out of his skin as gush from it. The size and shape of him left little question as to who was the seasoned fighter. "You had an opening. I took it. Keep that in your soft little Zarojo head, Lamang."

"Got bored waiting around, gentlemen?" I asked as I approached.

Agos wiped his jaw. "I got sick of watching Lamang whine his way through every scrape we've gotten ourselves into. If you insist on him tagging along, he's got to earn his keep."

"Well, I do have other ski—" Khine began.

Agos rushed at him. Khine had been hit that morning one too many times, because he jumped aside almost at once. His reflexes would've been impressive, except he wasn't holding his sword in a proper defensive position, and Agos simply reached back and clouted him over the head again.

Khine threw the sword aside and made a fist.

"You probably shouldn't—" I didn't have time to finish as his hand connected with Agos's jaw. Agos barely flinched. Khine doubled back in pain and started swearing like a sailor.

Agos flexed his neck and grinned. "If I had a coin for every time a recruit tried to punch me, I could buy Oka Shto from her."

"It's not for sale," I snorted. I turned to Khine. "I was going to warn you. He's got the hardest chin I know."

"No shit," Khine replied, face red. "I'm done."

"The hell you are, Lamang," Agos said. "Pick up your sword. You've stopped looking like a monkey dancing with a stick. That's progress, at least."

"High praise, coming from him," I assured Khine.

He gave me a look. "I'm not sure if your guardsman's praise is something I've ever wanted in my life."

Agos laughed. "You'll either get this guardsman's praise or his fist up your ass."

"I didn't know you liked me that way, Agos."

"Shut the fuck up and pick up your sword before I throw it at you!"

Khine gave a long sigh before ambling over to the sword on the ground. He fixed his stance as he faced Agos. There *was* a definite improvement, at least compared with how I'd seen him hold a sword before. I wondered how long they had been out here. Since before dawn, at least.

"Try to go easy on his head!" I called out. "I'm almost sure I need it."

"I'm almost sure you shouldn't be encouraging this," Khine said just as Agos charged him again.

"What's this?" I heard Lahei call behind me. She was coming up the garden path with Nor. "Some sort of pre-mating ritual?"

I turned red. "Wait a minute——"

"I meant with each other," Lahei said, one eyebrow raised. "You're really not familiar with army vernacular, are you?"

"I am," I retorted hotly. "I was just——distracted, that's all."

Nor shook her head.

"That distraction got anything to do with rippling muscles and heaving chests?" Lahei asked.

"I really shouldn't let you get away with such comments, Kaggawa," Nor said. "But——"

"No harm in looking," Lahei finished for her with a grin.

Nor's face remained expressionless.

"You're terrible," I said. "And Khine's getting his ass handed to him."

Lahei grinned. It was the first time I had seen her look so amused. "You've got to admit that it's a good-looking ass."

Nor crossed her arms and gave her a grunt of disapproval before turning back to me. "That's how they learn, Beloved Queen. You know what my opinion is about Agos, but his skill at making half-decent soldiers out of the most terrible recruits is well-known. They carry his name as a badge of honour, if they survive his training regimen." In the distance, we heard Khine grunt as he received yet another beating. "It's partly why Lord General Ozo loved him as much as he did."

I sighed. "I've always thought I could rely on General Ozo. But if it was indeed his doing that kept me in the Zarojo Empire, I'm not sure I can stay my hand. He'll have to die."

Nor's face tightened. "I don't know what to say, my queen. Before we had left for Anzhao, I would've been the first to assure you of Lord General Ozo's loyalty. Now…"

There was a loud clash. I looked up to see Agos holding up a bleeding thumb. "The fuck, Lamang!" he groaned.

Khine looked insufferably smug, the wind rustling through his shaggy hair. "You did say don't fight fair."

"No one uses a sword like that!"

"He's right," Nor called out. "Do that in a real battle and you'd be dead right about now."

"How the fuck can you protect the queen like that?" Agos thundered. "You'll make a fool of yourself and get her killed, all in the same breath!"

"Ah, lighten up, Agos," Khine said. "She can take care of herself just fine. She's strong enough."

Agos grabbed him by the collar, dragging him up to his chest. He whispered something in Khine's ear that seemed to knock the smile off his face. Eventually, Agos shoved him away, and he limped to me with a frown.

"And you said you wanted to be a soldier?" I asked Khine, speaking in Zirano.

He gave me a pained look before whistling at Cho. "I'm done," he said. "You go be his punching bag." He dropped the practice sword with a flourish.

Cho rushed forward eagerly, all knees and bone. Agos gestured at him. "Don't think that just because you're some weak-kneed snot-nosed kid, I'll go easy."

"He probably won't understand half your terrible insults, so I'd save my breath if I were you," Khine said.

"I do too!" Cho cried. Even with such simple words, his Jinan was terrible.

Khine strode up to me. He was a lot more hurt than I figured—there were bruises running up his face and arms, and there was a bleeding cut on his forehead, right above his brow. "What possessed you to agree to spar with him?" I asked. "You look like you went into a cage with a bull."

"Apt description," Khine said. He wiped his face and looked down at his fingers, as if amazed to see so much blood on them. "He dragged me out of bed this morning and told me he needed me to learn to be a little less useless. It didn't sound like a bad idea. Maybe I do need to learn to fight."

"Right. And now who's supposed to patch you up?"

"I'm sure I can talk you through it," he said. His voice was surprisingly sincere.

The cut on Khine's brow needed to be stitched. Khine flatly refused Lahei's offer of going all the way to Yu-yan, reasoning that he didn't want to wait hours for treatment and that a Jinsein healer was probably going to butcher his face into shreds. We went to the kitchen to clean him up, and while I was searching through the collection of bandages, he coughed and insisted I do it.

I blanched at his suggestion. "Agos must've rattled your brain loose."

"Cho's awful at following instructions, and I don't trust your guards with anything pointy that close to my eye," Khine said, crossing his arms. He waved the needle and thread in the air. "Just do it like I showed you. There's nothing to it."

"I'm a *queen*, you know. I shouldn't be taking orders from you." But I went to take the implements from him. He settled back against the bench, and after a moment's hesitation, I stuck the needle in. I had rubbed some sort of numbing salve over it, but Khine's face still twitched as the sharp end punctured his flesh. I bit back the sudden wave of nausea, cringing as I pulled the skin shut and hooked the sutures together.

I snipped the thread, wiped the blood off my fingers with a towel, and began the process all over again. "You're going to feel this tomorrow," I said with an exaggerated nod, as if this was something I did all the time.

He grew serious. "Physical pain is better than the alternative."

I paused over his wound. "There is that," I murmured. "Though I hardly think getting the sorrow pounded out of you is an appropriate cure."

"No," Khine replied. "Only time, and even then…" His shoulders heaved as he sighed.

I pulled back from the third stitch. "I think that'll do," I said. I reached down for more salve and applied it liberally over the cut. The entire process had taxed my nerves, and I was already starting to shake.

Khine grabbed hold of my bloodied hand and placed it over his heart.

I didn't pull away immediately. I stared at it, aware only of his heartbeat underneath my fingers and the warmth coming from his own. I felt like I wanted to hack my arm off so I could leave my hand there while the rest of me drifted away.

Outside, we heard Agos laughing.

The spell broke. The edges of his lips moved.

"What did he whisper to you back there?" I asked.

He shrugged. "It's nothing."

"Khine—"

"You're going to find it patronizing."

"Pretend I won't."

He hesitated. "Agos told me...when I said that you were strong enough to protect yourself. He said he knows. He grew up with you. He has no doubt you could take on anyone you wanted to. But even the strongest woman in the world is allowed to get tired once in a while. And he said when that happens, I have to be ready to bear the burden until you're ready to take it again."

He said it with gravity enough to make my cheeks burn. I turned away and lifted my hand under the pretence of getting more salve. "What do you think of backwards Jinsein medicine now?" I asked, trying to keep my voice light. "We know our way with herbs, at least."

He smirked. "In case you've forgotten, I'm really not qualified to have opinions about it."

"So that whole thing about a Jinsein doctor butchering your face..."

"Fact. Not opinion."

"Ah." I peered at my handiwork. "Well then, from one quack to another, I think you'll be fine. You'll get a scar. That's not usually a bad thing. Gives your face character."

"Maybe for you Jinseins. Zarojo women are particular about flawless skin."

"Maybe you should lay off from further activities that limit your options." I set the tray of bandages aside. "I'll ask Lahei to get someone up here to clean up. I believe I have to get ready for a trip to Yu-yan."

"If you give me an hour's sleep, I can join you."

"Are you sure? I was thinking of taking just Agos with me."

"From what I understand, you'll be walking into a lion's den. Having all of us with you is better. This is hardly the worst shape I've been in, and you've got a penchant for attracting trouble."

"Speak for yourself," I snorted.

Khine leaned back on the table. "I won't disagree with you there. I did find you."

I started to protest when I heard the door open. "Anong Kaggawa wishes to see you," the servant whispered, scuttling through the kitchen. She looked upset. My smile faded. Without a word, I patted Khine's knee and got up to follow her.

Dai was pacing in his office when I arrived. "You're back early," I said.

He rubbed his hands together before pulling himself into his chair. "You were entertaining Huan Anyu as a suitor?" he finally asked. His eyes, I noticed, were dark, so dark they were almost black.

"Ah. That's what this is about? I'm surprised *you* didn't know. I thought everyone did. And with your penchant for hunting down information, I figured you would've been in line."

"I don't pay attention to needless gossip. I've heard about rumours of suitors, and we had always known that Huan was one of these men. But it was brought to my attention this morning that you favoured him *in particular.*"

I leaned across the table to look him in the eye. "I don't see what the problem is. I had been without news of my husband for years. It was almost expected that I would start getting offers. I couldn't reject them outright. Needless gossip, like you said."

He looked the way I figured my own father might've, listening to me defend myself. "I didn't just *imagine* your friendliness with him yesterday."

"Of course I'd be friendly with him. Lord Huan was as eligible a prospect as any. He is a royal, his father is a warlord..." I knew as soon as I dropped the words that it was the wrong thing to say. Dai's eyes widened, and what started as irritation was turning into full-fledged anger.

"He stole this land from under our noses," Dai growled.

"Warlord Yeshin pardoned him."

"He had no right to!" Dai slammed his fists. "This was *our* land, Queen Talyien. We toiled in these fields, we took care of our own with blood and sweat and tears—the Anyus took things too far, claiming what wasn't theirs to claim. And you royals let them!"

"Kaggawa," I said, my voice growing cold. "Enough. Remember who stands in front of you."

"Yeshin's bitch pup," he said under his breath. He shook his head. "I thought you were different. I thought—"

"Because I was courteous to them?" I asked. "Perhaps it is *you* who disappoints me, Kaggawa. After all of your talk, you're no better than a Jinsein royal, taking offense at every perceived slight. I never gave Lord Huan anything more than the hope that I *may* start thinking about moving forward if I could prove Lord Rayyel's lack of interest in returning to me. Clearly, he grew tired of waiting—he married another while I was away. Or were you not paying attention?"

"If our daughters spoke to me like you do..."

"I am not your daughter, Kaggawa. I am your queen. You will let me speak to you however I want."

Dai curled his lip, dark eyes dancing. "Is this how you want to play it?"

"I wasn't aware we were in a game. You really didn't expect that I lived out in isolation in Oka Shto, did you?"

Judging from the look on his face, I realized that perhaps he thought I did. The reputation of the Bitch Queen was a hard one to shake off.

"I understand your concerns about them," I continued. "It's in our best interests to prevent the sort of disaster Rysaran's dragon visited on our land. But until I find evidence the Anyus have been involved in foul play, my hands are tied. The council won't entertain baseless accusations."

"They will try to speak ill of me when you are alone with them," Dai said in a low voice. "Warlord Ojika will do everything in his power for you to see me as the enemy."

"Perhaps he will, perhaps he won't."

"Yesterday, you were laughing with them like every other simpering royal I've met. But I suppose I'm as wrong about you as I was with your husband. As we were with your *father*. You are all alike—Ikessar hens and Oren-yaro dogs with your empty words and your empty smiles and your meaningless tenets, dragging this land down, bringing us *all* to ruin." He leaned across the table, breathing hard. "I am not your enemy, Queen Talyien, but you've left me no choice. I will not begrudge you for dallying with your fellow royals, but I need the assurance that you will return to us. That you will not scheme with the Anyus because you think I've let my guard down. When you ride to Yu-yan this afternoon, your men must stay behind."

I stared at him, speechless.

"I'm dealing with a queen who doesn't understand half of what's going on in her kingdom," Dai continued. "I think I'm being fair. Lenient, almost." He calmed himself with a quick breath and pulled away. "You can take the boy. The rest will stay. Remember that their lives are at stake, should you decide to do anything drastic." He walked to the door, where I heard him call for his men and order my people brought to his dungeons. I didn't stop him. Everything else told me I should—my father's teachings, my hand on my sword, the hard Oren-yaro values that I used to think ran through my blood—but the voices seemed to have lost all power over me. *Meaningless tenets.* Perhaps the merchant had it right, after all.

A commoner's tongue, a royal's temper, so the saying went. It hurt to see the look on my companions' faces as the hospitality was pulled from under their feet and they were dragged away like common prisoners. I had never felt the leaden weight of the queen's mask bear down on me as hard as that moment. I remember Khine telling me how much it angered him—how much *I* angered him whenever I fell back on that familiar pattern. You'd think that would've been enough.

The Anyus came to fetch me that afternoon. I greeted them with my head held high, as if nothing was amiss. Lord Huan's eyes twinkled as he bowed. He was a handsome man, almost near Rayyel's equal if the women's gossip was anything to go by, though it was his easygoing manner that briefly attracted me to him. I remembered that night—a drunken kiss during one of the loneliest times of my life, a quiet promise of consideration, and nothing more. Small moments that others could easily set aside. Not me, it seemed. Good intentions don't come cloaked with instructions. Seeing myself through the eyes of a man like Kaggawa, who was completely unimpressed with anything that had to do with the royal castes, was the final straw. I thought of the girl who wouldn't cry at her father's deathbed and could feel the last threads of his shadow slipping from me. *Have you discarded who you really are because you're not who you think you're supposed to be?* I must've. Trying to find yourself in a heap of broken shards shouldn't have to be this hard.

We rode north with only Cho and Lahei as my guard. Cho followed closely in silence, grumbling under his breath once in a while. When I found the opportunity, I rode next to him. "You're not in Shang Azi anymore, boy," I murmured, tapping the sword on my hip. "You Zarojo think the Jinsein uncouth, uncivilized. Keep your mouth shut and maybe you'll see the truth of that."

He was too shocked to speak back. It wasn't even that I was exaggerating. Back in the Zarojo Empire, murder was seen as an offense worth dragging someone to court over. In Jin-Sayeng, heads could roll and it would come down to the warlord's judgment. A necessary death could be reduced to an unfortunate circumstance. Even the idea of *blood money* was foreign to us. If Lo Bahn was Jinsein, the men who died under his watch would've been written off as casualties. The families would've been lucky to get an apology.

Yu-yan was a testament to how much the warlords get away with. Once a thriving city known for open trade and bustling markets, it was now a walled fortress against a mountain backdrop, with soldiers at the gates. Soldiers were a common sight at many checkpoints throughout Jin-Sayeng, so that by itself wasn't strange—even my own father once taxed visitors to Oren-yaro to help pay for the roads. It was the contrast between what Yu-yan had once been and what Warlord Ojika had turned it into that was remarkable. It made me understand Dai's animosity towards the Anyus, if not his methods of dealing with it. Perhaps I *should* have visited years ago.

The gates opened as we came within sight of the city. I heard Lahei give a small gasp, which told me this was out of the ordinary. I looked past the soldiers and noted a long line of people on the side of the road, waiting to get in. We stepped past the bridge, and the gates closed behind us.

"What is the security for?" I asked.

"Thieves, bandits, general riff-raff," Huan replied. "It's mostly a formality. We don't really require much in the way of paperwork—just a quick description of what a visitor means to do in the city and how long they're staying for."

I heard Lahei snort.

Huan smiled. "Do you disagree, Mistress Kaggawa?"

"You know I do," she said. "Not that my opinion means anything to you."

"The rice merchants think we're being too harsh, you see," Huan explained. "Quite unfortunate, really. All this resistance… if they would only work with us, we could bring the province into progress further than we already have. Look to your left, Beloved Queen."

I turned and saw a grand tower, the sort that wouldn't be out of place in Old Oren-yaro or Shirrokaru or Sutan. Only this one was newly built, not old and crumbling, and it rose taller than the surrounding walls, cresting up almost halfway to the mountain against which Yu-yan was built. A dragon-tower.

I turned back to Huan and Eikaro. They were beaming. "You're not even trying to hide it, are you?" I asked.

"Hide what, Beloved Queen?" Eikaro asked.

"You're trying to tame the dragons," I said. "This thing—why have I never received reports of it? It couldn't have cropped up overnight. You will explain this at once to me, Lord Huan, Lord Eikaro. I had been led to believe that our relationship was amicable all these years. Was I wrong?"

"Let me guess," Huan said. "Kaggawa's doing?"

Lahei's face twitched, but she refrained from commenting.

"I'm not blind, my lords. I don't need Kaggawa to tell me what I'm looking at," I pointed out. "If the Dragonthrone had known all about this, we would've put a stop to it. The land still carries scars from Rysaran's dragon. I can't gaze out of my balcony in Oka Shto without the bleak reminder staring back at me. You've both seen the ruins of Old Oren-yaro. We couldn't even rebuild on top of it after everything that had transpired."

"We knew you would react this way, Beloved Queen," Eikaro replied. "But remember—we invited you when Huan asked for your hand in marriage. We were only starting construction then—had you come, you would've received full reports on everything."

"And then you disappeared," Huan said.

Eikaro grinned. "Life…"

"Had to go on, right." I grunted. "So you've told me how, but not why."

"Kaggawa is only partly correct," Huan said, glancing at Lahei with a smile. "We're trying to tame the dragons…but only to help defend the city against the onslaught of wild dragons, which attack once in a blue moon. We built the dragon-tower as the first line of defense—if we succeed in taming our own, we can easily traverse to and from the city."

"I'm sorry," I said. "I'm lost. Are we talking about the same dragons? The *mad* dragons that have been plaguing these lands for years?"

Eikaro and Huan gave each other a quick look before turning to me. "The idea that these dragons are *mad* was perpetuated by Kaggawa," Huan said. "No offense to Mistress Lahei, of course."

"Don't even bother with the pleasantries," Lahei replied. "We all know what you really mean. And you're lying through your teeth. Don't think I can't tell when you royals are throwing your honeyed words about."

Eikaro grinned. "But maybe we should give you a tour while we talk, Beloved Queen. We hope what you will see will ease your mind."

"Very little does that these days," I said with a sigh. "But let's go." I dismounted from my horse and followed them down the street and up the wide stone steps that led to the tower, its shadowed form looming over the city like a rotting tooth.

CHAPTER THIRTEEN

THE DRAGON-TOWER

ᠠᡠᠥ

If you are ever lucky enough to find yourself in the library in the Dragon Palace in Shirrokaru, make your way to the end of the first aisle, where you will find an entire shelf dedicated to dragon-towers. Maps of old locations, sketches, renderings of towers that were never built... it is an endless trove, one that fascinated me back in the days when I was a student there. I can still remember curling up in bed with those thick tomes, poring over the fading illustrations while the monsoon rain beat a steady rhythm outside the glass windows.

Back when they first kept dragons, it was common to have landing towers made out of logs lashed together. The decks were often painted with the local ruling clan's symbol, which was visible from the air even in bad weather. As the years went on and the Jinsein clans started moving east, it became dangerous to keep the dragons in the rapidly growing cities. Some provinces solved this by banning dragons within city limits. Others, like Shirrokaru and Oren-yaro, began building the dragon-towers. The towers themselves kept the dragons away from the populace, but there remained the persistent problem of dragon-fire, which would build up inside a dragon's belly and needed to be released every so often.

The solution was large stone wells built right into the towers, into which dragons were encouraged to release their flames on a set schedule. These wells led to a system of tunnels under the dragon-towers. The buildup of dragon-fire was so strong that people began connecting the tunnels to their stoves and bathhouses to make use of it. The inevitable result was the rise and prosperity of cities with dragon-towers. Shirrokaru invested most of this back into their own infrastructure. Oren-yaro, in the meantime, focused on building its army.

I didn't mention to the Anyu brothers that I could tell it didn't take them mere months to build this tower from scratch. I strongly suspected that had I made this trip when I was first invited, half the tower would've been erected already. The base was enormous, easily twice the size of the throne room in Oka Shto, and made of heavy white stone with a dull sheen. There was what appeared to be a dragon-fire well in the middle of the hall, covered with an iron grate. I resisted the impulse to peer through it. It was big enough to look like a prison, and if creatures lurked underneath the tunnels below, I didn't want to know.

"This looks nothing like the old dragon-towers," I said, looking up. From where I was, the ceiling looked like an enormous grey sky, lined with shadows that danced with the flickering torches. The doors closed behind us.

"An entirely new design," Huan assured me. He gestured at the hall. "As mentioned, we built this partly for defense against the onslaught from the mountains. The old—and shall we say, diminutive—dragon-towers of the past were not equipped to deal with what we have now. This tower forms part of a wall that wraps around the mountain ridge beside Yu-yan. The dragons like to come from the northwest, using the ridge to drop right into the city."

"If this was such a problem for you, why have you never alerted the council?" I asked. "We would've sent men to help you."

"It's because they don't want to deal with it," Lahei said in a low voice.

Huan smiled at her. "So you people like to say. The truth is less interesting, I'm afraid. Our father is a proud man, and he knows the other clans' eyes are on him. We need to be able to stand on our own, to say that all of this was accomplished through hard work and resourcefulness—"

"—and thousands of lives..." Lahei droned.

Eikaro laughed. "I wouldn't say *thousands*. We *have* lost workers. Progress has its price. We must all be willing to lay down our lives for the good of this nation." He beckoned for me to continue walking.

"This stone..." I started. "I've never seen anything like it before."

"It was cheaper to import from Cael," Huan said. "If there was anything the Ikessars did right, it was to open trade with the Kags."

"Can it resist dragon-fire?"

"Our builders assure us it will."

"On pain of death, I suppose."

Huan gave me a soft smile before tugging at the thin moustache over his lip. "Do you think so poorly of us? May I remind you that one of your own laws prohibits the mistreatment of trades- and craftsmen. Your wish was that they be allowed to practice without fear of a warlord's wrath."

"Of course." It was one of Magister Arro's proposals, actually, which he drafted and left in my study after five builders lost their heads in Kyo-orashi. There had been an accident that wasn't entirely their fault—the design of a platform they built prohibited more than fifty people on it at one time. Warlord San, for some reason, decided that if he could squeeze twice that number onto it, it would still work. It didn't; ten festival-goers dropped into the gaping chasm of the sea below. Warlord San killed the builders in response.

I found myself wondering what Khine would've thought about all of this. You could find much truth in the idea that I relished Khine's company because it filled the void Arro left behind. I saw Cho scowling at the gleaming floor and made the split-second decision to hold on to that belief.

We came up to the end of the hall. Here, the ceiling shot straight up to the top of the tower, giving me a glimpse of every level. A set of stairs started from each side of us, long and wide. Two women came down to meet us as we arrived. "May I present our wives, Grana and Tori," Huan said.

The women bowed. They were quite unlike many of the royal wives I had met over the years, forgoing face paint and silk dresses in favour of trousers and short-sleeved tunics, better suited for the more humid weather in the west. They had daggers on their belts, and the one Huan had introduced as his wife, Grana, was holding a spear taller than she was. The one called Tori wasn't, but she was also heavy with child—I judged her close to being seven, maybe eight months' pregnant. How long had I been away?

"It's a pleasure to meet you, Queen Talyien," Grana said with a sweeping bow. Her skin had the complexion of sun-baked clay. "We've heard so much about you, but we've never met before, to our misfortune."

"You're twins, too, aren't you?" I asked.

Both women laughed. "Ah. You can see our fatal attraction to these brothers, then."

"We met these sisters on a trip to Kyo-orashi," Huan said. "Daughters of an *aren dar* Ishi, so I trust the marriage is to the Beloved Queen's approval."

"Ishi is an old, noble clan. Your ancestral home is in the southwest islands, isn't it?"

Grana nodded. "You flatter us with your knowledge, Beloved Queen. We are a simple folk who subsist on fishing and silk farms, nothing like the grace of you eastern royals."

"*We are but fingers in a hand*," I quoted from Kibouri, which made Lahei roll her eyes. I gave her a small grin before turning my attention back to the sisters. "Knowing these two, you met at Kyo-orashi for one of Warlord San's festivities?"

"For the opening of his arena, actually," Huan said, folding his arms.

"The last time I remember, that was still in the planning stage. Much has certainly happened while I was missing and possibly dead."

Grana laughed. "You have no idea, Beloved Queen. Shall we talk about it while we continue this tour?"

"Please do. I'd given up hope that someone would say that in the three or four days since I returned."

———

Neither Grana nor Tori gave me anything in the way of *news*. Gossip was the closest thing you could call it; for the next hour or so, I was treated to every marriage, birth, and scandal that happened from one end of the kingdom to another. For simple folk who subsisted on fishing and silk, they were well-informed. It was difficult to pay attention to everything they told me, though I tried to keep what seemed most important in the back of my mind.

They also showed me the rest of the dragon-tower. There wasn't much to it at the moment—each level was empty hall after empty hall. We reached the top, which opened up to a railed platform just like the old dragon-towers. The symbol of the Anyu clan was painted in bright red in the middle: a brace of oxen attached to a yoke. I stared at it for half a second before tucking my arms together against the sudden breeze.

"Enlighten me, my queen," I heard Grana say behind me.

I craned my head towards her. "I'm sorry?"

"You are the last direct Orenar, are you not?"

"I am."

"Your son carries the Ikessar name, yet Lord Rayyel is not a true direct Ikessar. Should your son not be an Orenar instead? It makes more sense to preserve that lineage."

"My father would have preferred that," I agreed. "As the old ways would, I'm sure. Lord Rayyel himself is an Ikessar when his father was not—his motherline, the *royal* line, takes precedence. But our royal traditions are too intertwined with Zarojo ways, and theirs prioritize the father's name. In a case where both are equal . . . I suppose we cede the battles we don't want to fight."

"How unfortunate. Your line dies with you, anyway."

I didn't answer. Inwardly, the conversation had made me aware of the fallacy of my situation—that my father would've never been content with the marriage arrangement if it meant his name would simply dissolve with the Ikessars. How could it have been anything but false? He wanted to win his war, not simply have the pretence of winning it only for the land to later return to Ikessar rule anyway. I stared down at the city and the flickering lights below.

"If it's not something you're comfortable discussing, my queen . . ."

"No," I agreed. "It isn't. You're aware of the unpredictable nature of my relationship with my husband, of course."

She bowed. "I will not ask further."

Huan drew close to us. "Is there a problem, Beloved Queen?"

I shook my head. "A simple misunderstanding."

"Did you bring up Prince Rayyel? Gods, please tell me you didn't bring up Prince Rayyel, she hates it when you do that," Huan said, which caused Grana to stick an elbow into his ribs.

"Nothing of that sort," I replied. "I shouldn't say this but—Lord Rayyel and I did find the opportunity to talk while I was away."

Huan's nostrils flared as he gazed at me. "What will happen now?"

"My understanding is that he wishes for us to set our priorities straight and rule together. You told me you've heard of no news about my son in Oren-yaro, but have you come across rumours? Anything that seems amiss?"

"No. My apologies, my queen."

"It just seems so strange," I said. "You knew I was here even before we could send word to you, yet my own people seem blissfully unaware. They should've sent an escort, at least."

Huan smiled. "It does take time to travel from Oren-yaro to the Sougen region, Beloved Queen, barring difficulties."

"I suppose." I nodded towards the chunk of mountain staring at us from the platform. "Tell me about this plan of yours to *tame* dragons. To hear you admit this with your own lips seem almost…foolhardy. You're aware of what the court will think of this."

"Indeed, Beloved Queen. You could even call it insanity, if you wish." He pointed. I strained my eyes to follow the direction of his finger and saw a faint movement in the mountains in the horizon, a quick flash of shadow that was soon gone into the trees. "These dragons are not the same as the dragons of old. We've tried to capture some over the years in an attempt to study them, so we know exactly what we're up against."

"If I call Lahei over to us right now, will she agree?"

Huan laughed. "Of course she won't. The Kaggawas are stubborn, I can give you that much. You should've seen Dai foaming at the mouth when we had that first dragon caged and chained. A tiny thing, no bigger than most dogs, yet you would think we had an army in our hands. Kaggawa's family has suffered much because of Rysaran's dragon."

"No less than others. My brothers were killed by that very beast," I reminded him.

"More apologies, Beloved Queen. I did not intend disrespect. The land will always remember your beloved brothers' sacrifice."

I brushed it off with a wave. "So what makes you think they're not as mad as Kaggawa believes they are?"

"The dragons are not afflicted with madness at all. Whatever it is that makes them difficult to tame can be…fixed. We think we have stumbled upon a procedure that will make this possible. Once that first dragon is tamed, others are sure to follow."

"This procedure," I said. "Does it have anything to do with mages and the *agan?*"

Huan didn't answer. He leaned over the rails, his eyes gazing back at the horizon, where the setting sun bathed the ridge in orange light. "Such accusations coming from the sort of man Dai Kaggawa is... I shouldn't be surprised. Forgive me, my queen—I know the east frowns on talk such as this, but the reality in this region is more complex than I think you're ready to deal with."

"Try me," I said.

"Now, my love, let's not scare the queen," Grana broke in.

"I'm not trying to scare her..." Huan began.

"Akaterru, if the both of you say something about my sensitive ears, I'll throw you over the rails. I said both *mage* and *agan* and didn't burst into flames. So." I fixed my eye on Huan. "What about Dai Kaggawa?"

"He's an abomination," Huan said in a low voice. "A foul thing that doesn't belong in this world."

"I wouldn't go that far, brother," Eikaro broke in. "I know we don't like him, and he's made our life difficult just like every other merchant in this accursed province, but—"

He stopped in mid-sentence, his mouth falling open. It had grown dark all of a sudden. It took a full second for me to grasp why. There was a dragon right above us. A dragon with its mouth wide open, close enough that I could count its teeth if I wanted to. *A dragon.*

"Run!" someone screamed. I couldn't tell who. But there was nowhere to run. The darkness continued to settle in as its enormous shadow covered the tower. The air grew cold and goosebumps prickled my skin. To see a dragon but feel nothing but winter's kiss was disconcerting. I watched it glide over us in silence, muscles rippling under its charcoal-black scales, wondering if it would simply pass us by. I held my breath, my fingers tightening around my sword hilt, and willed it to leave us alone.

It circled.

No, I found myself thinking. *No. Go away. Go—*

It roared, letting a blast of flame that tore through two scaffoldings at once. The sudden, searing heat felt as if I was wrapped in a burning blanket. I threw myself backwards, trying to avoid the sensation, even as I felt it enter my lungs and crawl up my eyeballs like a sharpened knife. I managed to wedge myself between two stacks of crates. Two soldiers behind me weren't so lucky. One burned to a crisp right in front of my eyes; the other jumped off the tower behind the dragon's snapping jaws to his death.

———

Through the sudden explosion of smoke and cinders, the creature landed on the edge of the tower platform.

I had never seen a full-grown dragon before. The one that had attacked me and Rayyel in our youth was about the size of a horse, and it had proven dangerous enough. This one was three times that, maybe more. Its scaly head was crested with spikes, and its mouth ended at a point, almost like a bird's beak. When it opened, I saw two rows of sharp teeth and a tongue that could easily knock a full-grown man to the ground.

That was as much observation as I allowed myself. The dragon pulled its head back. Cho was very close to it, and I screamed at him to duck. He dropped to his knees just in time. A smaller flame blasted through the air, setting a third scaffolding ablaze. I watched in horror as it toppled towards the hatch that would take us back into the tower.

Burning logs crashed above our only escape.

There was a moment of shocked silence, and then Lahei emerged from behind the debris to charge the beast. Stirred to action by her courage, I drew my sword and approached the dragon from the other side. It swung its head to face me, lips curled into a silent growl. The membrane around its throat vibrated as it regarded me with narrowed yellow eyes. I felt myself transported back to my childhood, facing that dragon in the woods in Oka Shto. The fear was the same, that odd sense of helplessness that nothing I was about to do in the next instance was going to matter very much. If it wanted to fling me off the cliff, it could.

I tried to take a deep breath, which I immediately realized was a mistake—the hot air scalded my lungs, almost as if I had breathed fire itself. As I struggled to catch a gulp of fresh air, I stepped aside in time to avoid its snapping jaws. I began to cough.

"Watch out!" Lahei screamed as the dragon's tail swung through the air.

It struck me in the belly, sending me backwards. I managed to land on my feet. I heard a rumble above and lifted my sword just as the dragon's jaws came down like a flurry of arrows. Teeth met steel. The dragon snapped its mouth shut, hot breath steaming through its nostrils; I refused to let go of the hilt even as the dragon renewed its assault, twisting the blade into the gap between its teeth.

Blood dripped down its jaw as I managed to cut into its gums. I screamed and twisted the sword again, my arms straining from the effort. The dragon flicked its tongue out in an attempt to wrench the steel loose. A bubble of fire appeared inside its mouth and I stepped to the side just in time to avoid another blast of fire. I realized that the dragon was losing breath—the flame wasn't as strong as before and the sac underneath its throat jerked up and down rapidly, like a drunk attempting to heave on an empty stomach.

It swung its head towards me and I kicked at the enormous snout, managing to pull the sword out in one swift motion. The dragon reeled back, spitting out slimy trails of blood—every exhale sent more drops spraying through the air. As it danced on the platform, I grabbed a protruding scale and heaved myself up its leg. I made a quick leap for the membrane under its neck, hoping I could end this with one quick stab.

It struck me with the damn tail again.

Black sparks shattered my vision. I flung my arms out to hold steady, but the force sent me flying halfway across the tower. I hit the far end of the rail, falling into a pile of hot ash and burning splinters.

Blood rushed into my head and down my nostrils, mingling with the dust and soot. I felt like I was breathing boiling mud. I wiped my mouth, fighting against the sudden urge to sleep. I couldn't even close my eyes. If I blacked out now, I knew I'd be dead. If I died, my son would die, too. I couldn't die. I wasn't allowed to die.

I grabbed the iron rail with one hand and pulled myself up. My insides felt like glass. I forced my eyes to focus.

In the distance, Lahei and Grana held the dragon at bay. It was still huffing from the cut in its mouth, distraction enough to have given the women time to gain the upper hand. Grana's spear was lodged between the scales behind its neck.

"Now, Kaggawa!" Grana called.

Lahei reached for the spear, clinging to the dragon like a monkey. It dawned on me what they were trying to do. I called for her to stop just as she reached up to swing herself onto the dragon's back. But before she landed, the dragon curled to one side and spread its wings, knocking her backwards. Lahei managed to hold on to the end of the wing and tried to drop back to the ground.

The dragon grabbed her leg. I thought I heard a bone snap.

She let out a scream as the dragon held her upside down, one that turned into a roar halfway through, as if the shock of pain had awakened her and transformed agony into rage. Somehow, she managed to pull the grass-cutter from her belt. Her arms were shaking as she tried to swing the blade, even as she was being kept alive by the strip of what remained of her leg—even as the blood streamed down her body, she was going for the dragon's eye.

I found myself racing back down towards them, but it was too late. The dragon chomped down before Lahei's blade could sink under its scales. Blood exploded in its mouth before it let go. There was a moment of silence, and then Lahei fell from the tower like a rock. I didn't even see her face before she disappeared into the mist below.

There was no time to look for her, no time to mourn. The dragon leaped towards Tori, who had been trying to keep away in vain, her arms wrapped around the delicate swell of her belly and the child that lay within it. Grana rushed in to protect her sister. She was slapped aside by the dragon's tail and tumbled through the soot, barely avoiding getting stabbed by her own spear. I bent down to pick her up and heard Cho scream from the other end of the tower.

"Choke on this, you ass!" Cho hurled a piece of lumber at the beast, sending it spinning past the dragon's brow. The distraction gave him time to reach Tori and draw his sword. He looked terrified, but that didn't seem to make him want to back down. The dragon pulled its head back, and I saw a flash of orange between its lips.

"Watch for the fire, Cho!" I called.

Cho snorted. The dragon flamed. He grabbed Tori's shoulder, pulling her down.

Eikaro chose that time to repeat Lahei's mistake. Or perhaps I shouldn't call it that—he managed to launch himself at the dragon fast enough, and then ducked when the dragon tried to pull the same trick on him. The dragon hissed and tried to bash him away with the other wing, but he managed to clamber up its back. Enraged, the creature began beating its wings in an attempt to throw him off. Eikaro reached down to yank the spear free and wrapped it under the dragon's throat like a collar to keep himself seated.

The dragon roared, sending another tendril of flame gasping into the wind. A moment later, it spread its wings and launched itself into the choking black smoke. Another second, and then it was gone. So was Eikaro.

I heard Huan's cry as he awakened from what seemed to be a stupor. He threw himself at the hatch, hands digging through the debris in an attempt to find the handle. The flames had died down, but the embers were still red-hot. I could see his face contorted with pain, the sweat pouring rivulets down his soot-stained cheeks, but he didn't stop. Cho rushed forward to help him. Eventually, there was a creaking sound as someone pushed the hatch open from below. The movement dislodged more of the debris, creating a gap big enough for a body to squeeze through. Huan dropped down, Cho right behind him. I gazed out at the railing where Lahei had gone over before rushing off to follow them.

The entire tower was in chaos. Huan screamed for horses, and when the soldiers arrived with them, I swung onto a saddle without a word. The fourth floor of the dragon-tower had gates that opened up to a bridge that crossed the chasm to the ridge. In no time at all, we were riding through the woods, swords drawn while we searched the skies for the dragon that took Huan's twin brother away.

Blood pounded in my head. I was so focused on the beast that my body wasn't even shaking yet, and I could feel no pain from my injuries. My mind did drift back to a single thought—that I had encountered dragons thrice now, and lived to tell the tale. I even fought it myself this time. Something about that called from the abyss. I survived. For all that my father had deemed me unworthy, I remained Dragonlord of this land.

I thought of my brothers. Had they even stood a chance? When I was a child, stories of my brothers were like fairy tales. My father didn't talk as much about them as I would've liked, so I subsisted on whatever the servants could offer behind his back. They were well-liked in the old keep—polite, brave, dutiful, true examples of the Oren-yaro spirit. But I didn't think the servants could've said anything less of them, especially not where I could hear it. Had they been caricatures, a false construct intended for me to model my own behaviour after? *Meaningless tenets.* My only true glimpse of how they might have been had been of that ghost in Yuebek's dungeon. Perhaps it was a trick of Yuebek's, but the phantom of my father had been accurate enough, so I could pretend the one I saw of Taraji—of the charming, bright-eyed young man—was also true. Rysaran's dragon had taken that man away from me.

These are the things you tell yourself, you understand, looking back. To make sense out of mistakes, the image behind spilled ink. In the haze of my confusion, my father's voice cut through like a whip. *Show me your worth. Let him die. You are queen of Jin-Sayeng—it is not your job to fix their foolishness. You've done your part. You already fought. Pretend to help, then turn back and ask for, theirs. Use their pain, their suffering, and twist it to serve your needs.* A dog, Kaggawa had called me, no better than the rest of them. A dog trained to the pantomime of a dead master.

My horse reared to a stop as we reached the end of the road. Dirt and gravel were piled everywhere, surrounded by wheelbarrows and shovels from where workmen had left them for the evening. After the confusion of the attack, the silence was deafening—like the moment after the last bell of a funeral, before the pyre is lit. Huan looked at the sky with dismay on his face. "No," he murmured under his breath. The anger exploded. "No! Why wasn't anyone keeping watch? You were supposed to—on the walls...!" He dismounted from his horse. One of his men followed him, and he turned and grabbed him by the collar.

"My lord," the man said. "It came out of nowhere. It must've seen you on the platform...there should've been guards there, bowmen, but it wasn't finished yet..."

He pushed the man away and caught my eye. "What should I do?" he gasped.

"You're asking me?"

His face was all white, a shell of the man who had been laughing and talking with me not even an hour before. "You're the queen," he murmured. "Tell me. Please."

I realized he wasn't asking about strategies or politics. The prelude to grief was in his eyes, like he was on the precipice and was looking for a push. But why me? Because I had lost brothers? I didn't even know their names until after they were dead. Raw grief was not something I was familiar with.

I sucked my breath in.

Use them. You have him. He will agree to anything you say. You can rid yourself of that commoner's blade at your back. Tell him to ride with you to Oren-yaro to save your son, and agree to reward him with anything he asks.

"We're not giving up on him," I said.

Huan stared in the distance, his eyes red.

"What do you know about these dragons? Where do they lair? Think, Lord Huan. Your brother's survival depends on it."

"Further up the mountains," Huan replied doubtfully. "If he even makes it all the way there, if the dragon doesn't pull him off like it did Kaggawa..."

"Just stop thinking." I glanced at Huan's man, who was waiting for us with a measure of uncertainty. "Have you seen this dragon before?"

"I think it's the same one that's been wandering the western wall the last few weeks," the man said. "A big male."

"Any idea where it could have taken Lord Eikaro?"

The man gave Huan a wary glance before answering. "There're caverns along the eastern side of the ridge where we think a few dragons have made dens. If it doesn't eat him mid-air, it might've taken him back for its brood to feed on. My lord," he continued, returning his gaze to his master. "He may still be alive. The dragon hatchlings might be asleep, or..."

"I dare not hope," Huan murmured. "Even after decades of living so close to them, we know too little about these creatures."

"He said the caverns are east." I reined the horse around and pointed at one of the men. "I need a spear. A few of us can make our way there. Too many may attract more."

"One is enough to attract the dragons," Huan said.

A man reached up to hand me his spear. I hefted it into my right hand, testing it.

"You're mad," Huan whispered.

"I'm angry," I said. "Weren't you just telling me about wanting to tame these things?"

"We were hoping to start them young...hatchlings..."

"Lord Huan, have you never ridden this far before?"

He swallowed. The truth was clear enough in his eyes. All his talk, and it was his men taking the brunt of these attacks. I tried to erase the image of the list Dai had showed me from my mind. "You'll come with me, then," I said. "Show your men how it's done."

He ran a hand over his lips. "My queen, it is extremely dangerous. The last scouting party we sent never returned."

"That was the middle of the mating season," Huan's man broke in. "They're more aggressive, then. It's the hatching season now—they'll want to stay close to their nests."

"Even better. Lord Huan..." I lifted the spear and pointed it at him. "You asked for my orders. I'm giving them now. We're heading to the dragon's den to find your brother."

To his credit, he didn't turn away. "As the queen wishes." He was starting to shake with fear, but fear was better than cowardice, as I knew all too well. I grunted in approval when he returned to his saddle, though he fumbled a bit with the stirrups and looked for a moment like he would fall off. A man came up to hand him a spear. He picked it up with the hesitation of someone who wasn't quite sure what to do with it.

"We'll take Cho and you," I said, nodding towards Huan's man. "What's your name and title?"

"Captain Seo, Beloved Queen."

"Pick two of your best men."

He nodded and gestured at them. They urged their horses forward while the rest fell back.

"It'll be dark soon," Huan commented.

My breath whistled through gritted teeth. "Then we don't have a moment to lose."

CHAPTER FOURTEEN
THE YU-YAN RIDGE

ゴイめ匕

We left the road, driving the horses deep into the forest, which switched among thick brush, steep slopes of loose dusty rocks, and white withered trees that grew close together in patches. Brown grasses sprouted knee-high in places, not quite as thick as the ones in the plains down below but substantial enough to slow us down. Captain Seo gazed up at the grey sky. "We'll get there by the time the moon comes up," he said. "Not sure if we should push through. The route gets rougher in places. Horses might slip in the dark."

I grimaced. "The sooner we find Eikaro, the better. If he's still alive, he may not be for very long."

"Breaking our necks won't help him if he's dead." Seo nodded off into the distance. "There's a waterfall not far from here. We can bed down there until dawn. Shouldn't be more than a few hours with a clear sky like this."

I turned to Huan, who was staring intently at his horse's mane. He gave me a look that said he was still deferring all judgment to me. "Very well," I murmured with a measure of reluctance. I hated waiting, but I could see the sense in Seo's words.

Seo whistled, guiding us up one last hill. When we reached the top, I heard the rush of water. We continued to ride on until the brush cleared and we stumbled upon a shallow basin, formed underneath a cascade of water tumbling over a staircase of flat rocks.

I dismounted, allowing Seo to take care of the horse, and approached Huan. He fidgeted when I drew close. "I shouldn't have let you get this far," he said. "This isn't... my father will not be pleased if you get hurt."

"I won't lie to you, Lord Huan. While your brother's safety is the first thing on my mind, I'm also curious to see how you are handling this entire situation. After all, a lord just admitted he had been sending me false reports."

"I never…"

"Kaggawa had a copy of the reports you were *not* sending to Shirrokaru. You said the Anyus wanted to deal with this problem yourselves. The council was never alerted to the high number of deaths occurring in your city."

He tightened his fists.

"You have to talk to me, Lord Huan. Your brother is possibly dead because of what *your* family has been hiding all these years. You see that?" I gestured at the sky, at the dazzling blue that was starting to spread through the blackness. "I know what it looks like when *agan* is spilling into the air. And there is *more* than that happening over those mountains, isn't there? Don't take me for a fool."

"I am not, my queen."

I placed my hand on his arm. "We were children together, Lord Huan. You knew me before I was queen, before these responsibilities were thrust on us. Of all the lords in the land, I always thought I could count on both of you—if not as friends, then at least as honest men. Was I wrong?"

Huan tilted his head to the side. "Beloved Queen," he said kindly. "It isn't that simple."

"We're rulers," I told him. "It's not supposed to be. But we're supposed to help each other out. We're supposed to put the land above ourselves, our clans, and our own interests."

He smirked. "Prince Rayyel always said you were an idealist, like your father."

"I—he said what?"

"An old conversation before you were wed. Eikaro…" His face flinched at the sound of his brother's name. "We were visiting the Dragon Palace at our father's urging. He was entertaining the idea of having us participate in the studies for the royal children, like you did." He gave a mirthless chuckle. "Of course, neither of us were keen on the idea. To be closeted with stuffy royals, most of whom looked down on us anyway for earning our position instead of having it handed over because of blood—we wanted nothing to do with it. But it is difficult to sway our father once he gets it into his head that a thing has to be done, and so we went."

"I don't ever recall seeing you there. This must have been before my time."

"It was, else we wouldn't have talked about you so freely. I asked Prince Rayyel how much he was looking forward to your rule together. Nothing but courtesy... I wasn't really expecting him to reply beyond courtesies himself."

"Rai's the sort of person who can't tell the difference," I murmured. "Tell me what he said."

"I probably shouldn't."

"I know my husband, Lord Huan. I won't hold it against you."

"He said you were a spirited child, and that you had more ideals than sense."

"Never mind that I could clobber him over the head with the exact same thing myself... he must've told me a version of that more than once during the time we knew each other," I said. "Is that it?"

"He was concerned about you following in your father's footsteps. That we had narrowly avoided Oren-yaro rule once and should take great care to guide you so that such a thing might never come to pass. He believed that hope for the land lay with Ikessar values, not the slaughter and bloodshed your father was known for."

I lifted my chin. "He thought I'd grow up to be like my father?"

"He was all but convinced of it," Huan said. "It gave him little hope that your wedding would ever yield peace and quiet for him. He thought the queen mother was... insane... to have agreed to this."

"She is not," I pointed out, "the queen mother. Who calls her that?"

"Some of the warlords do," Huan said. "In any case, Prince Rayyel thought she was misguided in allowing the betrothal to proceed in the first place. *Bed with wolves, do you not expect to get bit?* It was not a conversation we were prepared for, Beloved Queen, and we tried to remind him as best as we could that you were but a child. He agreed with that, but admitted he remained cautious over how that *child* would grow up."

He grew silent. Up in the distance, I heard the shrill call of a bird. "If you think you can distract me with talk of my husband..." I started.

"It used to work," he said listlessly. "I remember back in Oren-yaro, that ruckus you made in that restaurant after that cat-eyed wife of Warlord San's decided to ask you if you remained unaware of Rayyel's whereabouts, or were you even looking? You dropped about half a dozen threats within the blink of an eye. I had never seen Magister Arro so flustered in his life."

I smiled at the memory of those simpler times, even if I would have never admitted it back then, with the weight of Rayyel's departure still so fresh in my mind. "That won't work anymore. Not these days."

Huan gave an exaggerated sigh. "Well, I tried. The dragons, my queen, have two souls—their own and another, one that doesn't quite belong to the body." He hesitated. "This talk is . . . if the other warlords find out . . ."

"I don't see them anywhere," I said. "Go on."

"We believe if you can separate the other soul from them, then taming them becomes as easy as it ever was. You need the dragon whole and untainted, with only one pure soul inside of it."

"And you've been able to do this?"

"We've tried, in part, with no success. The *other* soul always kills the dragon before we can get close. We were hoping the hatchlings would work better, especially if we try it at the tower. That's why we built a tower larger than any in history. We wanted to start the process there."

"Dai said you have mages under your employ. Zarojo mages."

Huan grimaced. "It's not as bad as he makes it sound. I don't even know why he's so opposed, considering what he is."

"Which is what, exactly?"

"A man with two souls walking inside of him."

I woke to the same shrieking call I had heard last night. Seo was sitting right across me and looked up from the spear he was sharpening. "That's a dragon," he said casually.

"That doesn't sound like a dragon. I thought it was a bird."

"Well, when they're not trying to scare us shitless, that's what they sound like. Probably a mother trying to call her brood back to the nest. Some of them take them out at night, you know, teach them to hunt bats and civets to eat."

"I thought you didn't know that much about their habits."

"That's just Captain Seo's theory," one of the men broke in while he saddled the horses. "He makes them up himself. Who knows what they do out there?"

"We see bodies of the little creatures sometimes," Seo explained. "I figured they don't have enough meat for the grown-ups."

"Not for hatchlings, either," the man pointed out. "Regardless, we have to be cautious. You must have read about how the creatures used to be. They were always as powerful as you saw them, but they weren't so mindlessly aggressive, especially unprovoked. That one that attacked us at the tower wasn't even looking for a kill or it would have snatched the closest living thing and made off with it. That's not the worst we've seen. Sometimes, they…change."

Despite everything I knew and had seen, I felt myself shiver.

"Do not scare the queen, Seo," Huan said, striding up to me with a steaming tin cup. He thrust it into my hands. "I'm afraid it's only water with stewed herbs, not plum wine, but it'll put something in your belly."

"Did you mistake me for one of the gilded ladies at court? I thought you knew me better than that."

He gave a sharp bark of laughter. "I'm trying to be courteous. My own wife would bite my head clean off for forgetting to offer her a seat, and when it came to Eikaro, Tori would…" A shadow crossed his face.

"We'll find him," I said.

"Alive?" He made a sound in the back of his throat. "If he isn't…I will have to raise his child. I'm not looking forward to that. He was always better with children than I was."

"I used to think the same about Rai. He had more patience for the younger students…he'd sit with them long into the night to explain all sorts of obscure topics. Me? I would've thrown a book at them and told them to look for the answer themselves. And then when Thanh was born…" I paused. The memory of my son brought more pain than solace these days, worsened the closer—and further—I got to him. I held my breath. "Rai barely held him as an infant. I don't think he ever changed Thanh's nappies once. My Captain of the Guard did it more often." I paused, wondering how the rest of my companions were doing.

"A prince changing nappies…" Huan chuckled at the image.

I took a sip of the tea and immediately regretted it. It tasted like sour wine that a cockroach had died in. "It's not that hard. I did it myself all the time. I wasn't going to run down the hall in the middle of the night to rouse the servants and get them to do it for me."

"I thought Prince Thanh had nursemaids."

"I stole him from them as often as I could get away with. Rai didn't approve, of course—said I was spoiling him, but what did he know? Man like that, raised by monks…" I took another sip, because the tea did have a pleasant effect on my empty stomach.

"You *have* changed," Huan said. "We've been talking about Prince Rayyel the past few minutes and yet you haven't shown the slightest inclination of throwing hot tea at me. Have you truly come to an agreement with him? I find it hard to believe you would let it all go so easily after how you were the last few years."

"I thought I dealt with it all well enough."

"Well enough!" He laughed. "My queen, you were a dog bristling for a fight."

"I'd forgive you if it weren't for this tea. Now I feel like throwing you in prison," I said lightly.

"As long as I get to keep my head, I'll consider it an honour."

I pressed the cup against my belly. "What did I look like to you in those years?"

Huan scratched his ear. "Like a woman grieving," he finally replied.

For love. For love lost. For what it could have all been if we knew better. I stared at the green liquid in front of me, at the stalk bobbing on the surface. After a moment, I picked it up and flicked it away.

"And now…" I started.

"Now you look like someone who has buried the dead."

I swallowed, feeling the rustle of the wind around us.

"Why are you risking your life here?" Huan asked. "Back then, if someone had told you Prince Rayyel was in the other end of the city, you would've torn the door down and thrown yourself into his arms. And now—here you are, helping me chase after my brother in dragon-lands while your husband is alive somewhere… waiting for you?"

"He is in Zarojo land," I replied quickly. "Making his way to us as we speak. Why does it matter? I didn't know my personal life was under scrutiny."

"I made it my business to learn what I could when I courted you. You'll be surprised at how many books have been written about your relationship with Prince Rayyel. Your, er—obsession with him."

"Oh, wonderful," I groaned. "I need to go burn down some libraries after this."

"The price of being a public figure, Beloved Queen."

"So the reason you went and married someone else before I formally refused you..."

"I didn't want to get entangled in all of that," he said, gesturing at me. "My queen, I respect you, but I wanted a marriage where there was a fair chance of my wife falling in love with me, too. Your anger in those days told me you cared too much about Prince Rayyel, no matter what you said... or did." Huan coloured. "I found it fascinating, considering how mismatched you two were. Never mind that there have been no recorded marriages between an Ikessar and an Orenar in all of history—your temperaments seemed ill-suited for each other. Prince Rayyel is a sensible man, strict, traditional, and uncharismatic to all but librarians and accountants—"

"Priests seem to love him, too."

"And you," Huan said, with bow, "are out here with—as I've heard some people call us—the scourge of the west."

"Perhaps your assumption of me is correct, but you misjudge Rai. He isn't what you think he is."

"I never said there was anything wrong with what he was. But I do have one question, if it's all right with you to indulge the curiosity of a man trying not to think about how to arrange his brother's funeral pyre."

"Since you put it that way."

"Why does your voice no longer quiver when you say his name?"

I opened my mouth.

Seo arrived with our horses, sparing me from having to answer. "My lord, the men spotted a trail of smoke from the hill."

Huan's eyes lit up. "A campfire?"

"We don't know, my lord. We *are* in dragon territory. They set things on fire all the time."

"Then you would've reported a blaze." He swung into the saddle. "Which way?"

I mounted my horse and cantered after them. My mouth tasted acrid, but it was amazing how the state of my nerves was keeping my hunger at bay. I found myself riding beside Cho. His hair was ruffled from sleep. "Worn out?" I asked.

"Like you care," Cho retorted.

"I appreciate what you did for Tori back there," I said. "If you hadn't intervened, things wouldn't have gone this way."

"Are you blaming me that it took the lord instead?"

I stifled a sigh. "I'm trying to thank you, you little wretch."

He didn't reply. But he didn't need to—the conflict and irritation were plain enough on his face.

"If this is so difficult for you," I finally said, "why don't you head on back? The way to the tower is clear enough. Take the horse and tell them I'm sending you on. Go back to Kaggawa and report everything that's happening. He'll want to know about Lahei, if he doesn't already."

"Right," Cho said, giving a short bark of laughter. "Khine will kill me if I leave you behind."

"Do you at least have any expressions other than sulking?"

He nudged his horse forward without a word. I finally let out the sigh, wondering if I would've tolerated his behaviour if he wasn't related to Khine. Huan's words about my husband came back to me. *Why does your voice no longer quiver when you say his name?*

We rode up a shallow gorge, one that must've been a riverbed once. The trees were starting to crowd around us again, and the land rose sharply on both sides, the sharp cliffs fringed with moss-covered boulders. Such wildness was uncharacteristic of the Jin-Sayeng I knew. Back home, the hills rolled gently, and though the canopy was denser, the trees did not rise as tall as the ones around here did. And the shadows, instead of being sun-dappled like in the woods in Oka Shto, felt like an endless void into which you could walk and never be found again.

"If it was Lord Eikaro, how would he have started a fire?" one of the men said.

Huan grunted. "He's resourceful, and there's dragons everywhere."

"We're getting deeper into dragon territory," Seo broke in. "I suggest you all keep your spears ready. Never throw them—you need strength to pierce dragon scale, and a number of them have learned to catch the spears in their mouths and break them in half. That last scout didn't get much further than this—I believe their memorial is up at the next bend."

"Were you with them, Captain Seo?" I asked.

He shook his head. "I was with a party half a day away. You have to understand, Queen Talyien, that it took years for us to muster the courage to map the ridge this far. The dragons roamed closer to Yu-yan in the days when Warlord Ojika first took over, and we spent the first decade or so just trying to keep ourselves alive. Yu-yan was in ruins. They accuse Warlord Ojika of treachery, but all my lord ever did was try to save the city."

"All the more reason the Dragonthrone should've known about your predicament."

"There was, ahh—no Dragonthrone in those days," Huan reminded me. "There was only Warlord Yeshin."

"He wasn't regent. His authority never left Oren-yaro."

"My father remembers it differently. Warlord Yeshin was involved in all affairs concerning the Dragonthrone in those years. I'll let you imagine exactly what that entailed, Beloved Queen. Arguments and bloodshed come to mind."

"Arguments and bloodshed aside," Seo continued with the small smile of someone who knew how royals handled affairs, "when we were able to build the walls, we finally had a fighting chance. When it once took at least the deaths of two or three people to kill a dragon, now we could go for days without losing anyone. The dragons learned to keep away from Yu-yan. For a while, they went for the villages and fields."

"It's one of the reasons Kaggawa is so irritated with us," Huan said. "He believes we should have expended more effort to track stray dragons beyond our walls."

"You rule the Sougen now," I replied. "Isn't it your responsibility?"

"My queen, we don't have enough soldiers to spare. Most of the population of Sougen is clustered in Yu-yan, and we need all we can get on the walls. We explained this to the rice merchants. Unfortunate as the circumstances are, if their servants and livelihoods are being threatened, then perhaps they should shoulder the expense? Oh, but you see Kaggawa foam at the mouth if you ever bring up such a thing to him."

"What you told me about him having two souls…"

"Ah. Like the dragons, the *mad* dragons he likes to go on about. You can smell the hypocrisy from a mile away."

I didn't doubt what he was saying—Dai's tics had revealed themselves too often in my presence. But the events in the woods by the border were still fresh on my mind. Dai showed none of the same inclinations as those monsters did. I wondered if Huan was deliberately trying to mislead me, or if he really didn't know anything about the creatures that lurked so near his own lands. Not that I could blame him. Up until two weeks ago, I didn't know, either, and I was supposed to be queen.

The ravine continued to widen. I saw several rock cairns piled in a row near the rightmost cliff, marked with rusted swords that had been plunged into the dirt. Seo pulled off his helmet. "They were attacked right here, my lord," he said. He drew a line with his finger in the air, from one end of the ravine to the next. "We believe there were at least four different dragons."

"We barely survived the one," I breathed.

"And we are hoping my brother can survive against *more* of them while he's alone out there," Huan said grimly. He pulled out a coin from his pocket and flicked it onto the cairns. "With any luck, we'll all die out here and get to rest beside these bastards." He said the last part with a measure of affection. He must've known these men.

"Do you want to turn back now?" I asked.

"After seeing that smoke? No chance in hell. I almost wish Eikaro would've spared us the trouble and died where we could see him." He cleared his throat. "Beloved Queen, you were right to urge me to chase after him, but I think I have taken your offer too far. If anything happens to you under my watch, my father will never speak to me again."

"Then best we die together," I said. I dug my heels into my horse to ride ahead of the group. I should've known better than to let my guard down. I hadn't gone five paces from the closest rider when a dragon came hurtling from the trees, dividing me from the rest of the group.

CHAPTER FIFTEEN

DRAGON QUEEN

ʊȜ̂Ȝ̂ʏ̑ʎ

The dragon was different from the one that had attacked us at the tower—smaller and gaunter, though it was still larger than my mount, with a tail twice the length of its body. As soon as it landed on the riverbed, it flicked the whip-like appendage straight towards Cho's horse, wrapping itself around the panicked creature's torso and lifting it into the air.

Cho leaped from the saddle and rolled to the ground just as the dragon flung the horse aside. I watched in horror as the screaming animal slammed into the boulders above us. It fell silent immediately, its broken body sliding into the ravine.

"Get back, Lord Huan!" Seo cried. He came riding around the creature with three spears in his hand. The dragon turned half a circle right before Seo jabbed it under the chin. He left it hanging there as the dragon tried to claw it out. Seo drew back, and then pinned the dragon's tail into the ground with the other spear.

I almost didn't see the second dragon.

It drifted like a shadow from the corner of my eyes, smaller than the first, but stockier—a definite fire-breather. I yelled for Seo to get back. He turned in shock, managing to block the impending attack with a third spear. That was the best he could do—the dragon knocked him off his horse, which bolted straight into the first dragon's snapping jaws.

Huan and his guards dove into the fray.

The third dragon came for Cho.

By this point, my mind had gone blank. I rode towards him, the spear clenched tightly into the crook of my arm. The horse's movement caught the dragon's attention and it went for me. I tugged at the reins, stabbed it in the face, and let go. It struck the spear away easily enough, but the distraction was all I needed. I grabbed Cho by the arm and heaved him onto the saddle.

The horse protested at the added weight, dancing under me in a huff. As I tried to get her under control, the fourth dragon arrived, lumbering behind its brethren like a bull. I sucked in my breath, realizing we were trapped between the third and fourth dragons. Cho still had his spear, but I didn't know how well he could use it and I didn't have room to draw my sword.

Not that I had any room to think, either. Both dragons attacked at once. I didn't even have to direct the horse—she went straight for the embankment, dragging us up the boulders. As she dug her hooves into the sandy soil, Cho slipped from the saddle and landed on the ground. A dragon came snapping behind his haunches.

I held on to his shoulder as the horse struggled on the slope. The dragon hovered over him and opened its mouth. Cho twisted his body around, stabbing its tongue. It hissed. The back of its throat glowed. I expected it to flame. Instead, it began to change.

How do you turn an already monstrous creature into something more?

It starts with the eyes. We used the word *mad*, but it was wrong. *Mad* implied a creature that acted beyond sense—mindless, empty-brained, living only for the thrill of the kill. It was an apt description for the ones we had seen thus far.

But the change took it from *mad* into something else. It buckled against its form, fangs lengthening to the size of knives. Coarse hair appeared between its scales and along its forehead. And the eyes, which had always been golden orbs with a single black slit—empty eyes that existed only to direct the body to the next target—shifted. The black slits became pinpoints that spread, engulfing the yellow.

When it turned to me, I realized it was looking *at* me. It grinned.

I jumped from the horse in time to avoid the creature swiping me off its back. Freed from her burden, the horse lunged up the slope without us. I dragged Cho to the side while kicking the rocks from under me. Three more kicks set them loose, tumbling towards the creature's head in a spray of dust.

Cho tried to fumble with his spear. "No," I said, knocking him back. "Run."

"I'm done running!" he retorted.

"You want to fight that?" I pointed at the thing. The rockslide did little to faze it. It was climbing towards us, trying to squeeze its gigantic form through the narrow gap between the trees. *Just you wait*, its eyes said. *Just wait. When I'm done with you...*

I tore myself away from its gaze. "Cho—" I began, but he wasn't arguing now. We raced up the slope. When we reached flat ground, we saw the horse waiting for us, nostrils flared in anticipation.

I wanted to kiss her. I jumped into the saddle, reached down to help Cho up, and even before he could wrap his arms around me, we heard the dragon-beast breathing behind us. We took off into the forest.

———✦———

The ridge that had been so narrow when we first crossed the bridge from the dragon-tower now seemed like a wide, endless expanse of wilderness. Every time I expected to hit the edge of the cliffs, we burst into more open ground. Snowcapped mountains towered around us in shadowed layers.

Our added weight had worn the mare out and she soon slowed down, her head drifting sideways as if to beg me for mercy. I took a deep breath and dared to look behind. I could see nothing but the swaying trees, and the only sound I made out was the rustling leaves and birdsong. I forced myself to dismount and motioned for Cho to do the same. The horse grunted her gratitude into my shoulder, nose snuffling up my neck.

"I think we've lost it," Cho said.

"For now," I agreed, patting the mare's sweaty cheek. I looked around us. "But it seems like we've lost ourselves, too."

Cho swallowed. "What do we do now?"

"Find water before this one drops dead from exhaustion. One horse is bad enough. I'm not sure how long we'll survive on foot."

"I've heard about your track record with horses," Cho said. "I feel like we're doomed either way."

I couldn't exactly disagree with him. We continued walking, eventually stumbling on a small stream that seemed to bubble out of the ground itself. I allowed the mare to drink her fill, settling beside her to do the same. After I had quenched my thirst, I sat down on a rock to wipe the grime from my face. The mare returned to my shoulder with a sigh. I think she liked the spot.

I continued scratching her cheek, trying to drown my panicked thoughts. I was thankful that the Anyus had half-decent horses in their stables. I've known too many mounts that would've thrown us off at the first opportunity, straight into the dragon's snapping jaws. I heard Cho return from making water and watched as he bent over the stream to wash his hands. "It's getting dark soon. We might as well stay here for the night," he said. "I don't want to try to go back only to find out that whole stream's been turned into a feeding ground."

"You're painting a grim picture."

"Well, either they're dead or they're not. They're down at least one more horse, too. If that Seo was killed, they're doomed. The lordling can't fight his way out of a basket. Did you see how useless he was during the dragon attack?"

I had to smile at his assessment of Huan. The Anyu brothers had been trained well enough, but I highly doubted learning how to throw themselves at dragons was high on their father's list of priorities. It was a good thing the women they married were more than capable, or we might have all died there. "The guards will protect them."

"Useless snots," Cho grumbled.

"I didn't exactly see a grand display of dragon-slaying on your part, either."

"I don't come from people who like beating their chests in pride over their mastery of the damn things," he said. "If we go above the tree line tomorrow morning, do you think we'll be able to see the tower?"

"I'm sure we can, but my priority is in continuing on to the caverns. If Eikaro is alive..."

"You're kidding," Cho breathed.

I stared at him for a moment, allowing the mare to wander down the stream in search of something to eat. "I'm not, Cho. There was a clear sign of him being alive this morning. Unless we know for sure he's dead, I'm not returning to the tower empty-handed."

"You're *mad*!" Cho exclaimed. "Damn *queen*..."

"I *do* have a name if that's too hard for you to say."

"What do you even need to find him for? It's no skin off your back whether he lives or not. He's not your family. You're doing this because you're trying to run away from something."

"I'm not in the mood to argue with anyone, Cho."

"It's always about what *you* want, isn't it?"

I closed my eyes. "I don't think you're aware of what the word *queen* means."

"Maybe I'm not," Cho said with a laugh. "What the hell do I know? I'm just some poor kid trying to keep himself alive, and his fool brother, too, if possible. Hard to do it when some spoiled noblewoman decided she needed us to tag along. If I knew just how much shit you were going to drag us into..."

"How about you find food instead?" I asked. "Or would you rather send every unholy creature barrelling towards us with your yelling?"

He went off in a huff.

I took a few moments to gather my patience before joining him in the search. We found that the stream trickled straight into a small pool. Upon further inspection, I saw a school of finger-sized fish, near-translucent in that light. I returned to tie the horse to a nearby tree while Cho waded into the pool to catch the fish. He wasn't having much luck—the fish darted out of his reach even before he could get close.

I pulled out a blanket from the saddlebag and handed one end to him. He gave me a doubtful look, which didn't stray far from the usual expression on his face. I directed him to walk as far as the blanket would let him before allowing it to sink to the bottom of the pool. I held it down with rocks and motioned for him to stand perfectly still. In time, the fish began to swim back around us. Some even nibbled my toes. I waited until they were right above the blanket before signalling to Cho. We pulled the blanket up quickly. Water streamed down the sides, taking with it most of the fish, but we managed to catch a handful.

Cho's face brightened. "Maybe we can build a fire now," I said as I knotted the ends of the blanket together, draining the rest of the water away. The fish continued to flop around inside.

He cleared his throat. "I can do that."

I glanced at him. "Are we good, Cho?"

He didn't answer as he went off to gather sticks.

I didn't bother to clean or gut the fingerlings. They were too small, and we had to cook them flat over rocks near the fire. But food was food, and after over a day since our last real meal, the taste of spiny, bland fish was more than welcome. We washed it down with plain water, and when it was all gone, I found myself peering at Cho through the flames. Sated, he looked less irritable.

"It wasn't my intention for things to get this far," I told him.

He shrugged. "It's not really your fault, anyway. My brother was the one who threw himself at you since the beginning. And he didn't care that we'd get involved. He's kind of an asshole, if you haven't noticed."

I rubbed my hands together. They were starting to get cold. "*Threw* himself. I wouldn't phrase it that way."

"That's what it looked like. Don't flatter yourself—he'd have done it with anyone who so much as looked like they could use his help. Like how he is with those bandits, wasting all that time with them when he could be begging to be back in Tashi Reng Hzi's good graces..."

I nudged a burning ember closer to the fire. "I still don't understand what exactly happened there."

"Isn't it obvious? Khine blew his exams on purpose. He was angry with Tashi Hzi. For someone who preaches as much as he does, he's surprisingly good at sulking."

"He didn't have money to continue his studies because of you."

Cho looked embarrassed. "Well, yes, but that was my own shit. He didn't have to get involved, either. If he didn't fail in the first place, I'm sure Tashi Reng Hzi would've let him continue on in Kayingshe. Of course, they weren't on speaking terms by the time all of that happened. Don't think any amount of money in the world would've gotten Khine back in there. There's other places he could've studied, of course—there's a place in An Mozhi, too, but none as prestigious as Kayingshe."

"I thought he wanted to become a physician. Why would he fail on purpose?"

"He had a fight with the old man," Cho replied. "Something to do with that woman of his, Jia. She had a procedure done, with Tashi Reng Hzi as her physician. Khine didn't find out until it was too late."

"Did the procedure involve an unborn child?" I asked.

Cho gave a small shrug. "Rumours say. I wouldn't know. Never asked him about it. I'm just his brother."

I turned my eyes back to the flickering fire. I had a sudden image of the baker's daughter, young and pregnant, seeking refuge with her lover's mentor. Refuge away from Khine? From his anger? But I found it hard to believe he could've ever wanted to hurt her.

"Did you ever meet her?" I asked.

"Who? Jia?"

"I assume there was only ever the *one* her in Khine's life."

Cho snorted. "A few times. I was a kid back then, so I didn't really pay that much attention. I guess she was all right. Nice chest—" He stopped and for once looked almost embarrassed.

I narrowed my eyes. "Right."

"You're not my mother. You can't judge me."

"I didn't say anything. Do . . . do I seem that old to you?"

"I wouldn't know," Cho said.

"Do I *look* old?"

"You look like a queen."

"You said you don't know what the word means."

"*You* said it. I just agreed with you. Jia's younger. Maybe she was my age now when Khine met her. I think you were about to ask that next."

"I wasn't," I mumbled.

"It looked like it. She was young, but she acted a lot older—one of those women, you know? Khine doted on her. He'd make us wait in the market in the rain when she was off selling their bread to the vendors, for hours if we had to. So I don't know why he was the one to drive her away in the end. I don't think she wanted to leave him, and it's not like he stopped loving her. Maybe he was *too* much. Maybe that frightened her. Khine never did things that made sense to me. I've given up trying. I mean, apart from being Jinsein, you're *nothing* like Jia—you're loud and mean, you're part of the nobility, and you're married. I don't know what he sees in you." He stopped abruptly, as if he had said something he wasn't supposed to.

The fire crackled. "What are you talking about?" I found myself asking.

"Fuck," Cho grumbled. "Don't tell me you didn't know?"

I stared at him.

He ran his hands over his head. "After he followed you all this way, and with the way you were dangling yourself in front of him . . ."

"I didn't dangle anything. Your sister asked me to bring him."

"You don't think you would've been able to drag him against his will? *That* man? Honestly. Are all queens this clueless? Khine loves you."

Cho spoke as if out of a dream. "I'm afraid you're mistaken," I said. "He can't love me." Even my own voice sounded distant. I was watching the scene unfold in front of me, a mere observer who wasn't allowed to think or feel anything. *Remember*, I could hear my father's voice say. *You are a wolf of Oren-yaro. You do not bend to mere whimsy. We are swords first, servants first. Stand your ground, Talyien. Remember what happened the last time you got carried away?*

"I told him the exact same thing," Cho said. "But his damn head is harder than a brick. Nothing good will come out of it, I said. What was he expecting? You were busy searching for your husband, Lo Bahn was breathing down his neck, and—"

"He said this all the way back in Anzhao?"

"Not long before we left the city. Look, don't get me wrong. My brother isn't—he isn't trying to get into your pants or anything...I know how he is. Fuck, it's not like he has any trouble getting women to like him. Ask around. So don't think I'm getting you to mellow out on his behalf. He knows this isn't going to go anywhere. But the way you are, the way you think, he can't help himself. Some days it seems like you're all that goes through his mind." Cho gestured helplessly. "When you both start talking, it's like you're in your own little world, and I know maybe that kind of thing is normal for you but I don't see him get on with people that often. Not even with Lo Bahn and Inzali, and they can get into these long, boring discussions like you wouldn't believe." He took a deep breath. "You've seen my brother, Queen. You understand the sort of man he is."

"I consider him a good friend, Cho."

"Then you'll believe me when I say that he'll die for you."

Don't think. Don't feel. What lay inside my heart had no bearing over what needed to be done. I could listen to these words, but I wasn't allowed to take comfort in them. The world I lived in, with all its rules and blades flashing in the dark, left little room for anything else. My every breath had been determined before I even first drew it.

"Hey, Queen," Cho continued. "Still awake?"

I wiped my hand over my eyes. It was so dark that I didn't think he would notice. "Yes," I said. "Cho, I... I don't know why you're telling me these things. What do you expect me to do with this knowledge?"

"You're a queen," he replied. "People die for you all the time. At least that's what they say people do for queens. Just look at your guards. You're used to that kind of attention, aren't you? I think you almost take it for granted. But my brother... he isn't one of *yours*. What is he to you anyway? He's just another man, just another body you can throw between yourself and the enemy. It pisses me off every time I think about it, but I'm starting to think that maybe you just can't help yourself. You're born this way, and unlucky bastards like us just get trampled by people like you along the way."

"I'm..."

"Don't even bother. I don't want to hear your excuses. Just listen. All I want is to go back home with my brother. Every day I lose hope that we'll ever see Anzhao again. But do you think Khine will just drop it all and leave? Not a chance in hell. He's convinced you need him. *Until I'm sure she's in safe hands, Cho*, he tells me, the fucking ass. But I don't think that's going to happen. I think you're going to die here and our heads will be right in that grave with you."

I felt a chill run through me at his words. He paused from his speech to throw a fresh branch into the campfire. The leaves caught fire almost at once.

"What would you have me do?" I repeated.

"You really are some queen," Cho snorted. "Asking *me*, of all people. It's obvious. Order Khine to go home. I'm..." He swallowed, his voice rising higher. "I'm begging you. Don't use how he feels about you to your advantage. He's all sorts of fucked up but he's still my brother and I don't want him to die and I don't want to die with him. Maybe there's nothing you can do about all of this, but this is *your* life, not ours. And I know *you* don't love him, so please..."

Cho was suddenly in front of me, on his knees, his head bent so low it was touching the ground.

"Send us home," he whispered.

A restless night gave way to a morning of cold air and mist, cloaked by a light drizzle of rain. But the sun still managed to peek through as dawn broke, crested with black clouds that promised a storm later that day. I wondered whether dragons liked rain or not and hoped that they would stay in their dens today. The fire-breathers, at least, should find them uncomfortable. I had no desire to meet one again any time soon.

The mist was so thick that I couldn't see the smoke from the other campfire. I doubted that they had even been there at all. We broke camp and made our way to high ground, just off the stream. Here, I could see the sharp, jagged outlines of the northeastern ridge. The caverns lay somewhere in that area, and I thought I could make out the crevices if I squinted hard enough.

I ran my hands over my face before placing the horse's reins into Cho's hands. "You should head back now," I said. "With any luck, the dragons will be hiding. Ask them back at the tower to send more men if they can spare them. They may not be able to."

"What the hell are you yapping about, Queen?"

"*Tali*," I snapped. "If you're going to be rude, you might as well call me by my name. I'm saying that you should return to the city while you've got the chance. We won't be able to ride double for too long anyway, and I'm starting to get fond of that horse. I don't want to see either of you ripped apart by a dragon."

Cho frowned. "If I let you go alone, Khine will never let me hear the end of it."

"Then don't tell him," I said. "If I die, I'm sure Kaggawa will release him, and you can both make your way back to the empire."

"If you *die*—" He laughed. "You've seen how he was with our mother. You *can't* die."

"If Khine's mental state is what we're worried about, then neither can you. You see my dilemma here. I have no intention of dying at all if I can help it. But on the off chance it happens…well. Not your life, like you said. It'll be easy enough to forget me. He's already lost a mother. I won't take his brother from him, too." I nuzzled the horse for a moment before walking away.

"Mad bitch," Cho said under his breath. "You're as stubborn as he is."

I kept walking. He didn't follow me.

I was glad for it. I didn't like the silence that came with being alone, but I needed it to figure it out, all these things I was running away from, the things I was running towards, what my heart was afraid was waiting for me back home. The machinations my father had set in place before his death had overturned everything I knew about my life. My marriage was a sham. My son was of the enemy's blood to both our clans, and seemingly unwanted by both.

And I was Talyien of Oren-yaro, but I didn't really know what that meant anymore. Here I was, alone in dragon territory with no men to my name, no horse, and not even a spear, chasing after a lord who was probably both a traitor and a corpse. I imagined that if I died out here, the history books would find some glorious reason for my actions—she needed to bring peace to the land, she needed to stop the dragons, she needed to show the Anyus her worth as the true Dragonlord, make honest men and loyal servants out of them before negotiating peace with Kaggawa and the rice merchants. Good enough stories. Most aren't so lucky to get them. Most, like Mei, die heroes and are forgotten almost immediately.

But deep inside, I didn't know anymore. I knew my reasons for venturing out here, but I didn't know why I kept going. Are queens allowed to be confused? What about my father's daughter? I knew that my spirit was broken, but every step I took seemed to yield another, and then another, and then another, like the movement itself was enough of a guiding light for the next. I think even if I had willed every part of me to stop, I wouldn't have.

The storm never came. The clouds drifted into the distance, further out into the valley, and sunlight broke through with such frenzy that you could almost hear the plants shudder with joy. I pushed away the dread and foreboding long enough to find water. I didn't want to waste time fishing, but I found thorny bushes full of red, ripe berries that were safe to eat. They were sour and had too many seeds, but they kept me going all the way to the caverns.

The land here became solid rock underneath, sharp and slippery. The only paths that seemed safe were the furrows where water traversed when it rained. There, moss grew in grey and brown patches that allowed my feet a better grip. I still had to use my hands to grab roots and rocks to make my way up, but it wasn't an impossible task, and it kept my mind occupied. The mist was starting to blow in again when I reached another section of flat land. There were cliffs all around me now, and I made sure to walk as slowly as I could so I wouldn't slip off to the sides. I was almost glad for the cold, because it tempered my exhaustion. If it had been too hot and muggy, I wouldn't have gone very far.

I saw my first dragon of the day while I caught my breath on a ledge. I watched it soar through the sky, its feet kicking through the clouds with every stroke of its gigantic wings. Something about the ease with which it moved filled me with envy. I wanted to be that dragon. I wanted to fly without a care in the world and not be my own awkward self, fumbling through life and my responsibilities and the expectations handed down to me by people who never once asked if I could live up to them. But those thoughts drifted, taking me back to the moments I shared with Khine, and I recoiled from the memories like they were on fire. I turned to the cliff and spotted the trail of smoke from one of the ledges.

I continued the rest of the climb with renewed vigour. It didn't take long for me to reach the ledge. As soon as I pulled myself up, a figure lunged at me with a makeshift spear. I sidestepped the attack easily.

"Funny way to greet your queen," I said, gazing at Eikaro.

His tired eyes brightened. "Beloved Queen, you came after me." He tried to sketch a bow, but the rip in his pants showed a long gash running along his leg that prevented him from bending his knee. I grabbed his arm before he could exert himself any further and helped him return to his campfire.

"Are you alone?" Eikaro asked. His voice was strained.

"Huan and Captain Seo came with me, along with other men, but we were ... separated."

"Is my wife safe?"

"I believe so. We tried to chase after you as soon as the dragon left." I looked around the ledge. There was a small crack in the cliff behind us, big enough for a body to squeeze through. "What happened? How did you get here?"

"Damn bastard tried to rip me in half but I managed to get it to land here. Got away and hid there until it left me alone." He pointed at the crack. "I tried to get out yesterday, but the leg wouldn't let me. I made a fire to keep warm but I didn't really think anyone would send help. I thought for sure you'd give me up for dead."

"Have you got water? Food?"

"I sucked moisture out of the moss, but otherwise..."

I helped him sit down so I could take a good look at his leg. It was no longer bleeding, but the edges were swollen. I sniffed it and it smelled clean enough. I wondered if he had perhaps broken a bone somewhere. Khine would know what to do. Khine...

"Is everything all right, Beloved Queen?"

"I'll get you food," I said distractedly. I put his leg down. "There were berries down in the bushes below."

"I haven't seen the dragon the whole day," Eikaro called out. "Please be careful, my queen."

The berries here were wilted from the shade, but I gathered as many as I could, stuffing them into my pockets and sleeves before returning to the ledge. I spread them on the ground and picked at a few myself. Eikaro watched me with a sprinkling of unease.

"What's the matter?" I asked, wiping berry juice from my lips.

"You're very different from how you were back in Oka Shto," he said at last.

"I'm not sure if I should take that as a compliment or not."

He scratched his cheek. "You've risked your life for me. You're still risking it, with every moment you spend here."

"You didn't expect I spent all my spare time chopping heads off, did you?"

His face remained sombre; he had never been as quick to jump on my jokes as his brother. "I feel compelled to tell you the truth about all of this, but I'm not sure where to start."

"Huan has already given me a good idea," I said. "The dragons. The souls. The mages."

He nodded.

"Dai's information was correct, then? They're Zarojo?"

"Yes, my queen."

"How did you find them?"

He picked at the berries. "Beloved Queen..."

"There is no sense trying to hide anything from me now, Lord Eikaro. I'll find out sooner or later."

"They arrived some time ago, before we started building the dragon-tower. Three mages. They said they were sent by an official from the Empire of Ziri-nar-Orxiaro to assist our unique situation."

"They went straight to you," I repeated. "Not Dai?"

He looked shocked I would even suggest such a thing. "Dai Kaggawa is a rice merchant, Beloved Queen. We are lords of this land."

"Royals," I said. "Well-known to reject, sometimes outright kill, practitioners of the *agan*. Known mages have been held in the dungeons at Shirrokaru for decades. We cannot even talk about it in the east without igniting tempers. There must be a reason why they sought you in particular. They knew you weren't going to execute them."

"I don't know if I can explain with words," Eikaro said. "But perhaps I can show you."

He lifted his hands. I watched in disbelief as the fire grew larger. A lick of flame formed into a tendril that clambered from his fingers and into the palm of his right hand. There, it turned into a ball. He stared at me before tossing it up in the air, where it exploded into nothingness.

"You're a mage," I breathed.

CHAPTER SIXTEEN

THE BELLY OF THE BEAST

ง 8 8 จ

Not exactly," Eikaro said, giving me the pained expression of a man who had explained the technicalities one time too many. "Mages are what you would call those who have undergone formal studies. And I ... never have. I was born with a connection to the *agan*, something we discovered when I was a boy."

"How did you hide it?" I asked. "I was told untrained children were dangerous. Yet in all the time I knew you, I never even suspected."

"Why should you? We send children like me away, give us to the service of a deity with cloistered priests and priestesses, or kill us in secret." He smiled. "My father found witches in Fuyyu willing to teach me to control it. This is the west, Beloved Queen. Talk of the *agan* may be looked down upon in the east, but things are different here in the years since Dragonlord Reshiro opened trade with the Kags. Witches in Fuyyu are fairly common. They make potions or work as healers, and some can even scry for the future or get you to speak to someone who isn't there. But they are not as skilled as you think, not like the mages you find in Dageis or even Gaspar. The one my father hired couldn't teach me to do much beyond passing off as normal and simple tricks like the one I just showed you."

"Warlord Ojika made a wise decision," I said. "You would've been executed on the spot if you ever showed signs in front of the warlords."

"A wise decision? Perhaps. He wanted to kill me himself," Eikaro said with a wry smile. "Believe me, my queen, my father was not happy to sire a son with a defect. I slept three rooms away from my brother as a boy because he was afraid of me killing his heir in the dead of the night."

"This is why you're surprised we came."

He nodded. "If my father had been there to stop Huan from chasing after me, he would have. My life is not as valuable as his."

"You're both his sons."

"I am the broken spare," Eikaro said. "I don't disagree with it, either. Think how the warlords would react if they find out someone like me inherited these lands from my father. They would seize it from under our noses and put our entire family to the sword." He paused. "Please don't tell me you're alone because Huan was hurt."

"He was well and whole the last time I saw him."

"Why were you separated?"

"Dragon attack," I mumbled. "About four of them."

Eikaro gave a soft cry. "A warlord's heir and a queen in exchange for *my* life! Beloved Queen, I don't think I can live with the shame if either of you die because of me. And my child... my child will carry that taint..."

"Stop," I said. "We worked really hard to find you. If you devalue your own life, then you devalue our efforts."

"My queen..."

"Tell me about these mages. They knew you had the connection, so your father couldn't turn them away."

"Beloved Queen, you guessed correctly. My father did not enjoy entertaining them, but he was made to understand he had no choice, else word of me would get out."

"How did these mages act?"

He blinked. "They were very helpful. Friendly."

"That's hardly been my experience with Zarojo mages, but go on."

"They explained to us exactly why the dragons are as strange as they are and why we haven't had any luck taming them the past few years. They even walked the walls with us, showing us where to strengthen our defenses."

"Where are they now?"

"They left a few months ago for a personal errand. They assured us they would be back in time once we had captured that first dragon—a small hatchling, they instructed. We were to keep it in the third level of the tower, which they had laced with spells."

I wondered how deep the bastards had infiltrated my nation. How did they know of Eikaro's condition when none of us did? Arro would've brought up any suspicions. A thought occurred to me. "Did Warlord Yeshin ever visit the Sougen while you were a child?"

"Yes, my queen."

"He spoke to you."

Eikaro looked away.

"Lord Eikaro…"

"My queen," he said in a low voice. "I will not speak ill of your father."

I touched his arm. "I have heard everything there is to say about my father, Lord Eikaro. That he was a traitor to the crown and a murderer, that he would stop at nothing to fulfill his ambitions—even if it meant throwing his own people at the enemy. That he ripped my mother away from her own mother's arms and raped her repeatedly until I was conceived."

I was surprised that I could say these things as calmly as I did. Hearing them said by others always made me angry. Eikaro's jaw quivered. "I do not need your sympathy, Lord Eikaro," I continued. "I need your honesty. Please."

"It was a very long time ago," Eikaro replied. "While he was visiting, Warlord Yeshin caught me alone in the hall and saw me set the curtains on fire. It was an accident. I…I tried to run away, but he dragged me to a room and beat me bloody against the wall until I did it again."

It never even occurred to me not to believe him. My father had a heavy hand, and although he never struck me more than once or twice that I could remember, he could've easily done it to another child. I tried not to cringe at the image. The hardest part about hearing all the things my father had done was knowing they held more than a grain of truth. That I couldn't even defend him.

"When he was sure, he brought me to my father and promised to keep quiet so as long as the Sougen remained a *friend* to Oren-yaro. If he ever called for us, ever needed us, he expected full support. My father was very angry, but he kept to his word even after Warlord Yeshin's death. We may have hidden things from you, Beloved Queen, but we have always been loyal."

But loyal to whom?

I heard wingbeats and felt Eikaro stiffen. "The dragon," he murmured. "It nests not far from here."

I didn't want to wait around in the open to get roasted. I helped him get up to walk to the crack in the wall for shelter. He felt very light, and his body was too warm. "You've got a fever," I said, pressing the back of my hand on his neck. He drew away, looking uncomfortable at my touch. "You're not going to be able to walk all the way back, are you?"

"No," he replied with a grim chuckle. "Imagine me trying to outrun a dragon. I'm sure even the climb down will kill me."

I stared at the sky and caught a glimpse of a figure wrapping itself around the cliff in the distance. It was the same dragon that had attacked us at the tower, with its black scales and the same distinctive crest on its head. The crest glowed faintly under that light. So much we didn't know about these creatures, and yet they had always been there, right under our noses. We should have paid attention from the beginning.

"Our only chance is if Huan or the others survive," I whispered. But even the thought of that felt hollow. There weren't enough horses for all of us. We had to wait for someone to make it all the way back to the tower to alert them we were still alive, wait for them to find us, and try not to get eaten by dragons in the process. And without food and very little water, how long until we succumbed to weakness or lost our wits? My thoughts were still clear, but I didn't know how long I could last like this. Every passing day increased the odds for a fatal mistake.

In the distance, the dragon roared, expelling a wave of flame that knocked an entire tree to the ground.

"You should've never come after me," Eikaro whispered.

———◆———

Sacrifice. I don't believe there exists a royal who hasn't been taught this word, and we Oren-yaro believe we know it better than most. Sacrifice has maintained our legacies throughout the ages, and so we are taught to honour the captain who fights a losing battle so his general might escape, the minor lord who offers to end his life for his brother, or the woman who loses all five sons to a war. We hammer our own lives to serve whatever tenets our clans follow— servants to a greater cause, tools for a warlord's hands.

This is something that the common folk find hard to understand. Lahei alon gar Kaggawa spoke of the value of a life and why one man cannot equal another, but she failed to grasp the idea that a royal may not necessarily see things this way. Did the common fisherman carry an entire clan's expectations? Is the seamstress expected to bear an heir worthy of the name, a boy healthy and vibrant enough to stop the neighbouring clan from slaughtering your townspeople and seizing your lands? The individual itself is meaningless. The burden of blood goes beyond worth.

I know that others would disagree.

I suddenly understood that a life, every life, has value. "One life cannot replace another," Khine had told me. Khine, who had looked at a pox-ridden merchant and a prince the same way, and regarded me as if my head had never carried a crown. It used to be different. The Talyien of old wouldn't have let Cho go so easily, nor chased after Eikaro once the situation turned hopeless. She would've demanded both play their parts the way she tried to play hers: the same disregard for self, the same unyielding precision.

Or perhaps I was being too hard on myself that day on the ridge, sitting there with a man I didn't need to save, a man who was as good as dead. Perhaps it had simply been easier to carry the title of Yeshin's daughter and I never bothered to think about the kind of queen I wanted to be. "Kind," I found myself saying out loud, "And compassionate."

"My queen?" Eikaro asked. It was early morning. The past night had been sleepless; we did nothing except watch and wait for the dragon to leave. It never did. We were only able to snatch brief naps in between listening to the dragon bellow its lungs out. Now that the light was crawling over the mountaintops, I could still see it circling the sky.

"I could do it, couldn't I?" I asked. "A kind, just queen who listens to her people's concerns, not *just* the royals'. Forget tradition. Forget the path our elders have forged for us. Wasn't this how it was always supposed to be? The reason we chose a Dragonlord in the first place?"

Eikaro looked at me like I had lost my mind. "We've had rulers like that before," he said. "They tend not to last very long."

"Give me a name."

He hesitated for a moment. "Dragonlord Rysaran."

"Give me a better name."

"My queen, Dragonlord Rysaran carried his heart on his sleeve. I know what you Oren-yaro think of him, but there had never been a kinder or more compassionate king in all of Jin-Sayeng's history."

"The same king allowed a mad dragon to rampage through at least two of our cities. I think the kindness was a front."

"Isn't it always?"

I held my breath for a moment. "I am not my father."

"My queen…"

"I'm not," I repeated. "I know people have said things about me, and I've done things I'll own up to. I've killed people I thought I had to. Insolence. Betrayal. Treachery. My own guards would've done it themselves if I had chosen to look the other way." I swallowed. "But I would never near-smash a boy's brains out and then blackmail his father into submitting to me. I would never put an entire village to the torch under the misguided belief I was *saving* them."

"The Ikessars should hear you."

"The Ikessars like to talk, but they were just as bad. They pretended their hands were clean while letting others do the dirty work." I tore off a piece of moss from the stone wall, grinding it between my fingers. "A lot happened since I left for Anzhao City to speak with Rayyel. More than I know how to process. Jin-Sayeng is at the brink of disaster and war. I am tempted to just walk away and leave it in someone else's hands, only…who is more capable? Who wouldn't just use the whole situation to their advantage? I've spent my whole life keeping track of everyone at court and beyond, trying to read them, trying to learn how they think and what drives them. You'd think I could give you at least *one* name."

He stared silently.

"You don't think a queen should speak this way," I said.

Eikaro shook his head. "Perhaps I'm not the best person to advise you. I am tired. Hungry. Delirious."

"Magister Arro died in Zarojo lands. He was the only one I ever really trusted. Do you know what he used to tell me? He used to say that my father was the product of his circumstances. Some might use grief to tear the world apart. My father used it to try to piece the world together. It did not excuse what he did, but…" I swallowed. "Before I returned to Jin-Sayeng, someone I respected told me this: *A man has to make something out of this life or else it consumes him.* Another heard this with me. He, too, was grieving, yet it didn't stop him from trying to offer his life to save a little boy's.

"My father would've never sunk to such foolishness. He wasn't just feared for being ruthless. He was feared because he had a conniving mind, because he was always one step ahead of his enemy, defeating them with schemes they couldn't understand even after the fact, even *after* it was explained to them. It was better to be on his side than against it. He won the war—he really did. I am not saying this as his daughter. I am saying that if he had been young and healthy, without the limitations of old age and sickness and a single heir to his name, all the Ikessars would be dead and every corner of this land would be ruled by the Oren-yaro." *And I would be queen and married to Yuebek.* That last thought chilled me to my bones.

"And you, my queen?"

"I," I said, "am a product of peace. Arro never once made me forget that. No matter that I was raised by this same man, that he tried his hardest to hone me into a weapon he could wield even after his death, I have not yet suffered so much that my heart is empty."

Eikaro cracked a small smile. "Despite my misgivings about your father, my queen, you have to admit his methods were effective. You have warlords who will hear these words and think you weak."

"I have warlords whose heads need equal amounts of cuffing and caresses. I am Yeshin's daughter. But I am also the wife of an Ikessar. I still feel…responsible, somehow. Even though I don't want to be. All I want to do is run away, but the world won't let me. *I* won't let me."

"Beloved Queen," Eikaro said. "It grieves me to hear these things from you. Not because I disagree, but…"

"Because we're about to die?"

He smiled.

I snorted. "It's just a dragon. Two of us against one—we should be able to outsmart it. Isn't this our land's legacy? Jin-Sayeng, land of dragons. We Dragonlords shouldn't be sitting on our haunches, quivering in fear."

We watched the creature do yet another sweep through the clouds.

"I think it's taunting us," I said. "It knows we're here."

"I suspected that," he murmured.

I slowly made my way to the edge of the crack. "I'm done waiting. I'm going to kill it."

"What?"

"I'm going to—"

"I heard you, my queen. But I'm not sure you heard yourself."

I smiled. "I'll explain my idea to you. It's not as insane as it seems."

Two things were on my mind: hunger and a scree, gathered right outside the ledge where we could see it.

The hunger was the primary thing. The longer we stayed there, the weaker I was going to get, the more scattered my judgment. If the dragon decided to attack us in a day or so, I didn't think we would be able to survive the onslaught, let alone find a way to defend ourselves.

The scree consisted of large boulders that spilled out from one side of the mountain above us. I had noticed the whole entire evening, and for much of the morning, that the dragon avoided it. When it flew past us with a roar, one of the boulders tumbled from the top, causing a small rockslide to occur.

There was another ledge at the bottom of all of this, a large lip of overhanging rock. I thought that I could attract the dragon's attention, enraging it to the same sort of frenzy it had attacked us at the tower with. Another roar or two would cause a rockslide. If I could time it correctly, I could slide down and hide there while the boulders tumbled over the dragon. The path from where I was to the overhang seemed clear enough, and well-protected from the worst once the rocks came tumbling. I didn't need the rockslide to kill the dragon—if I could just knock it back enough, if I could weaken it somehow, then I could get in and finish it with my sword.

It was as good a plan as any. I had nothing else.

I could hear my father screaming in my head as I crossed the ledge towards the rock field, grabbing on tree roots to maintain my balance as I dug my toes as deep as I could get them into the small footholds. Sword re-strapped to my back, hands shaking, wind on my hair while the shadow of the dragon crossed over me—I felt like a fool. *Forget this,* my father's voice said. *Return to the city, to Oren-yaro. I have everything under control. Did you not hear what Lord Anyu said about the mages, how easily I took care of the west? Taming the dragons, the tower, the Anyus' loyalty... it was all me. They will bend their knees to you and your prince—your* actual *prince, not the ragged Ikessar. Return and it will all be forgiven. You don't have to die like this.*

"Fuck you, old man," I grumbled. Maybe I *had* spent too much time in Shang Azi. But the words made me feel better. I found even footing at last and made my way across the boulders. I heard a roar and felt the air dry up as a lick of fire streamed past my shoulder. The dragon had seen me.

Heart pounding, I kept my eye on the ledge and drew my sword. There was no time for hesitation. When I reached the steepest part of the scree, I turned to stand my ground. The dragon was right behind me. It opened its mouth.

The Oren-yaro do not lack for courage, it is true. We know how to face battles when the odds are stacked against us. We know how to give our lives for our lords and believe we know sacrifice like no other. But I did not face that dragon as an Oren-yaro. Our tenets may run deep, but they do not make us. I decided that if I ever got out of this alive, I would tell Rayyel that. We are flesh and blood, not words; we bend, we break, but our failings need not be etched in stone. I faced the dragon as someone willing to give her life for another not because of some deep-seated arrogance that I was better but because it was the right thing to do.

The dragon reached me, its tail sweeping over the boulders behind it. The rockslide began. I struck the outreached muzzle with my sword before making a run for it.

One step in, I slipped.

It was the dragon's bulk that saved me from the onslaught of rocks in the end. The hollow between its body and its left wing provided a refuge, covering me in darkness.

The rocks soon stopped falling, but I kept still for a very long time, my breath coming out in ragged gasps. The thought that my plan had actually worked both frightened and exhilarated me. Eventually, I got my wits together. Wiping the sweat from my eyes, I tried to push the dragon's wing out of the way so I could squeeze past the rocks. I was almost out when I spotted the dragon's head twisted at an unnatural angle. For a moment, I was certain it was dead.

Its eyes snapped open.

I threw myself back, sword flashing in front of me. The boulders streamed past the dragon's body as it pushed itself up. No rockslide this time—the first one had flattened the base of the scree and I had missed my one chance to deal a death blow. My thoughts turned towards escape. The ledge was completely covered. If I could make it to the valley below, I could use the trees to my advantage, but it was a steep tumble down. I wouldn't have time.

The dragon charged while I was thinking.

Its wings came up first as it tried to knock me aside. My blade came down hard along its elbow, cutting through the scales. I felt bone and drew a slight spray of blood, but the dragon didn't even look like it felt it. It spread both its wings and tried to breathe fire into my face.

A spear came flying through the air, pinning the dragon's right wing to the ground. It hissed, fire curdling through its teeth. It seemed trapped for the moment. I backed away, wondering if that was it. Could I outrun it now? But I didn't want to turn my back to a thing that wanted to kill me.

I saw Eikaro limping over the rocks, dragging a leg that looked useless. It was bent at such an angle that it was clear he had fallen and torn the wound further. His entire left side was drenched in mud.

"What are you doing here?" I asked, running to him.

"I can't let you die for me," he croaked out.

"So now we *both* die," I snapped. "If we get out of this alive, I'm going to make you into an adviser. We'd be the life of the council. Stand down, my lord."

"No, my queen." He swallowed and held his hand out. "Give me your sword. If you run now—"

The dragon roared as it tried to dislodge the spear.

I grabbed his arm. "Eikaro, you must be delirious if you think I'm going to let a half-dead man defend me."

"Please consider that it doesn't look that much better from my end."

"I disagree. I can stand on two feet and didn't just throw my only weapon at the damn thing. Stand down, Eikaro!"

The dragon recovered, ripping its wing off the spear. As thick rivulets of blood cloaked the ragged gash, it flung its entire body into an arc, swiping at both of us with its free wing. I smashed into a rock. Blackness set in.

CHAPTER SEVENTEEN

THE PREVAILING SYMPHONY

TIM

I grappled with the darkness, dirt in my mouth, blood on my tongue.

Laughter. My father's.

I don't remember if it was a dream or a memory that next flared in my mind. I was throwing sticks for the dogs into the river while Yeshin stood nearby, arms crossed. He didn't like the dogs licking him, didn't even seem to like them in general, but he tolerated them for my sake. Occasionally, he even found them amusing.

"Your brothers loved dogs," he commented as I threw yet another stick and the dogs plunged into the grey water, racing to be the first to reach it.

I turned to him, unsure of what he was trying to say.

His face was blank, unnaturally so. He took one step before cringing. His joints had become more painful as of late, and some days he found it hard to get out of bed. That he had decided to take me to the riverbank at all had struck me as strange, although I never questioned it. I never questioned anything Yeshin did in those days. "Get your dogs and come take a walk with me" had been enough to send me running from my room and down to the kennels, where I nearly tripped over the door in my haste. For all that his anger could frighten the wits out of me, time spent with my father was still a rare, precious thing.

"The dragon that killed them," I found myself saying. "Was it really impossible to tame? Everyone says it was mad."

His lips twitched. "Mad. Tainted. An unholy thing."

"If we could find dragons that aren't tainted..." I began.

"That talk is what ruined Rysaran," Yeshin said. "He grew obsessed with what could have been instead of trying to fix what *is*. Our land has more problems than our lack of dragons. Economy. The balance of power. The zealous religions of every province, all of which say completely different things."

"The dragons once united us."

He grabbed my jaw, craning my head up towards him. He didn't hurt me, but he kept a firm hold. "Never speak of this again, Tali."

"Father—"

"It killed your brothers, do you understand? It killed your brothers. My sons..."

Yeshin dropped my chin and turned away. I watched him hobble off, shaking, before whistling to the dogs so we would follow him. I came up to hold his arm and help him walk. He looked down. Except for his completely white hair and beard, sometimes he didn't look all that old. It was his eyes. You could still see the wildness of his youth in them, the ambition, the strength of the dreams that were denied him. *But they aren't mine, Father.*

I started coughing. I opened my eyes to a clear sky and realized, as pain struck me, that I was still alive.

I struggled to stand and saw that the dragon was pinned to the ground, roaring as it tried to give out a few short bursts of dragon-fire. Eikaro stood a few paces away, eyes closed. I didn't know what he was trying to do, but there was blue light around his hands.

I called to him. "Stay back, Queen Talyien," he said in a low voice.

"You idiot," I hissed. "It's breaking loose!"

"Then perhaps it's best if you—"

The spear broke. The dragon pounced on Eikaro, knocking him flat to the ground. Whatever he had tried to do in the short amount of time I was unconscious, it had made the dragon very angry.

Another spear whistled through the air.

It was thrown so swiftly that I almost didn't see it. It struck clean into the dragon's nose. The dragon roared and slid back against the boulders, knocking a few more loose. I rushed to Eikaro's side before turning around.

Cho appeared, looking all smug.

"Another fucking idiot," I said. "I'm surrounded by them."

"You really should stop hanging around people like me," he replied, almost brightly. "And why the long face, Queen? It was a great throw."

"You were supposed to get help!"

"Who says I didn't? Lord Huan sends his regards."

The dragon roared. "I don't think we're going to have time to talk," Cho said, drawing his sword. "I've been itching to use this."

"Akaterru help us all," I groaned. "I suppose we have no choice but to kill it now."

"Hold its attention," Eikaro told us.

"What are you going to do?"

"The more I try to explain to you, the less time I'll have to actually do it."

"Dragon!" Cho thundered, waving his arms at the beast. It turned in a circle, snarling as blood dripped from its nose.

"Watch its tail!" I called out.

Almost as if it heard me, the dragon whipped its tail from under its legs. Cho leaped back, avoiding it, before striking the dragon on the mouth. The dragon roared, spitting out another spurt of fire that fizzled out as soon as it hit the air.

"What's wrong with it?" Cho asked.

I held my sword out, approaching it from the other end. "I think it needs enough air for a good flame. But it's stuck down here with us, so..."

The dragon snapped its head towards me. I struck back with my sword with such force that it knocked the spear out of its nose. It clattered to the ground, and I quickly sheathed my sword to grab it. The dragon reached out for me just as fast, teeth bared.

I spun on my heel, managing to lunge at the dragon with one end. It dropped back warily.

"It's scared," I heard Cho call out.

"No thanks to you," I grinned.

"That a compliment, Queen?"

"The best you'll ever get from me," I said before steeling myself for the next attack. I threw myself off to the side as it barrelled forward. Behind, I heard Cho's sword clatter uselessly on the dragon's hind leg.

"Fucking bastard, why aren't you flying off?" Cho asked. "Get the hell out of here! Shoo!"

The beast drew itself up.

"Get back, Cho!"

I had forgotten about the change. The beast had shown no hint of it during its attack on the tower nor the entire time we had spent on the scree. Now its body contorted, growing straighter, taller, more human. Its hands reached out to grab Cho and it opened its mouth, as if to swallow him whole.

I wasn't going to let that happen. I screamed at it, and as it turned, I grabbed it by the horn and stabbed it in the gums with the spear. It rolled its tongue and lifted its head. My boots dug into its scales as it dropped Cho and tried to swipe me off.

It started to flap its wings.

"Jump, Tali! Jump now!" Cho cried.

I squinted. The creature had grown so big that I couldn't see below me now, and I didn't want to break my body between boulders. I realized, too late, that we were airborne. I swung up to a more stable position above its neck and saw Eikaro clinging for dear life on its other wing. The dragon-beast shot straight up into the clouds, trying to shake us off.

My head spun, and I felt like my brain was being squeezed through my eye sockets. Somehow, I managed to make my way across the creature's back and grab Eikaro by the arm, pulling him to me. Before I could draw another breath, the creature dove. I imagined losing our grip and plunging into the mountains below.

In the split second that this happened, I found myself oddly at peace. Impending death was a curious thing. I didn't stop to think about whether it was going to hurt or what was going to happen to me once it was all over. Instead, I watched the scenery unfolding around me like an observer drifting from empty space, my fears stretching so far behind me that they became unrecognizable. The blood pounding through my body and the breath that tore out of me felt weightless. I felt as if I *was* the sunlight, the sky, the clouds, the fields stretching out like a sea of green below.

"Hold tight, Queen Talyien," I heard Eikaro say, pulling me back from my thoughts. His hands were still glowing.

I looked at him, blinking.

"If this works, tell my brother—"

His eyes turned black.

The dragon-beast stopped in mid-air, its wings holding us aloft. I realized that it was shrinking, returning to its true dragon form. The light around Eikaro's hands faded as whatever was causing the dragon to change in the first place disappeared.

My first thought was to congratulate him. He had managed some sort of spell, unskilled as he claimed to be, and now if we could only figure out how to make the dragon land without killing us in the process, we might actually be able to survive this.

My second thought was that his eyes were still black.

The thought died quickly. Eikaro's jaw unhinged, revealing a mouth full of the same sharp teeth as the beasts we had encountered in the village weeks ago. I managed to throw my arm out as he lunged, sharp fangs ripping into my skin.

I kept my hand on the dragon's scales—I wasn't sure why I hadn't fallen yet, but the dragon seemed to be gliding steadily, smoothly, across the sky. I tried not to worry too much about that as I turned to more pressing concerns. My free hand grabbed Eikaro's throat. I was loath to squeeze tight, but he was starting to gnaw at me, trying to *eat* me alive. I sank my foot into his groin and tore my arm away from him, knocking him back with a closed fist.

He hissed, mouth open and tongue curling out. I recognized the motion of a dragon trying to flame.

"Lord Eikaro!" I cried. "Get ahold of yourself!"

The dragon flapped its wings, as if to warn me, and began another climb. I managed to hold on to its shoulder, my boots digging into its scales.

"Lord Eikaro!" I repeated. I could barely hear my own voice against the wind.

Eikaro began to crawl forward.

My insides knotted. His head jerked left and right while blood pulsed freely from his torn leg. His face had changed completely—dark hollows under his eyes, his ears flattened back, his tongue drooping down to his hands. There was fur around his elongated mouth.

He attacked again. I braced myself.

Beneath us, the dragon finally turned, its wings pulling its body into a graceful loop through the wind. I tried to wrap my fingers tighter around its scales, but the hold wasn't strong enough to take my whole weight and I felt myself falling.

The sensation lasted no more than a moment. I bounced back behind the dragon's shoulders, landing on my hip. I heard a guttural snarl and saw Eikaro clinging to the dragon's tail, face contorted in rage. I reached back down to grab him.

"*Leave it!*" I heard someone call. The timbre of it was familiar.

I opened my mouth in confusion. "Eikaro?"

"*It is broken! Let it fall!*"

The dragon roared and whipped its tail, sending Eikaro's body flying into the air. I watched it howl like a beast before it went crashing to the ground below.

A sob tore itself out of me.

"*Are you crying? Why are you crying? For me? I am honoured, but . . . that body wouldn't have made it back home, my queen.*"

I turned to the dragon in shock.

"Eikaro?" I repeated.

The dragon roared.

———◆———

The dragon took me all the way past the clouds and up to the mountains, where we landed on the shore of a bright-blue lake, surrounded on all sides by stone slopes, ringed with step-like ledges. Large boulders lay scattered everywhere. Although the weather wasn't terribly cold, a thick sheet of ice floated at the end of the lake, where it seemed to have poured down from the snowcapped mountains above. Blue veins marked the ice where water still pulsed beneath it. I could also hear the sound of a roaring waterfall from somewhere, though I couldn't see it.

Sandy-brown logs, streaked with black and red pebbles, drifted in piles along the shore. I jumped on them as the dragon dropped to his knees, allowing me to clamber down. I tore a piece of my sleeve to wrap around the throbbing wound on my arm before I allowed myself to face him.

The madness in the dragon's eyes was gone. The yellow light was replaced by a deep, warm brown that seemed almost human. He craned his head back as I continued to stare at him, his lips curling into a half grin.

"I wasn't dreaming when I heard you talk," I said.

"No, my queen."

"I did bash my head back there. You could be an illusion created by my addled brain. It's done it before."

"This is real."

I finished tying the bandage. "You're Eikaro, then. Not that thing back there."

He gave the slightest indication of a nod.

"You're going to have to explain it a bit better than that."

"You said my brother told you about how we planned to tame the dragons."

"He did. He said the dragons were mad because of another soul, one the Kaggawas called *corrupted*. He also said that when you tried to separate the souls in the past, the corrupted soul attempted to kill its host."

"Yes."

"So what happened?"

"I offered a trade. My body for this one."

"And it agreed?"

A full grin, now. *"I told it I was a lord with a pregnant wife, and a brother who looked exactly like me. It couldn't resist. But when I offered the bridge, I pulled the dragon's soul along with it and locked both of them into that body. You would never be able to live with a corrupted soul, my queen. They take over. Your life will never be yours again."*

"What about Dai? Huan said he has two souls inside of him. He seems fine."

"You will have to ask him about that, Beloved Queen. But it is why we have never trusted him."

A cold breeze fluttered over us. I found my eyes drawn to the lake. I carefully limped to the edge of the water and dipped my injured arm into it. The shock from the cold passed quickly, and I felt the flesh become pleasantly numbed. I stared at the brilliant blue. The sunlight reflected so strongly on the surface that I couldn't see if anything lurked beneath. But despite my inclination to be suspicious these days, I allowed myself to let my guard down. The scenery was too peaceful, and after everything that had happened, I felt like the fates owed me a moment to breathe.

I heard the dragon lumbering behind me.

"What now?" I asked.

"What do you mean?"

"Your body is gone. They will think you're dead. I mean—you are...in a way. Are you?" I looked at him dubiously.

"I meant what I said. I would have never made it back home in one piece. That body had lost too much blood and would have attracted every slithering beast along the way. You would've died, too."

"Will you always be able to talk like this? Or will you succumb to the nature of the beast?"

"I don't know, my queen. This was...unexpected." He spread his wings to look at them. *"I can take you back to the ridge, as close to the tower as possible."*

"You will not come back with me?"

His throat rumbled. *"My own people will kill me at first sight."*

"You can speak with them."

"My queen, I cannot."

"But you're doing it to me right now."

He showed me a tooth, another attempt at a smile. *"You were with me when the trade happened. I believe a part of your essence skipped towards me, allowing me to show you my thoughts. You are blind to the agan—I don't think you can see the connection or do much else with it. But it's there."*

"But this is what your people have been trying to do, isn't it? Trying to drive the *other* soul back, leaving only one inside the beast."

"I'm not sure this was what we had in mind. We were counting on the dragons to remain dragons, and nothing more."

"If I tell them this happened..."

"They will think you're mad."

I pulled my arm from the water and turned to him. "I may already be, anyway," I murmured. "Let's go."

He allowed me to climb on him again. It occurred to me, as we returned to the air, that I was the first Dragonlord to have ever ridden a dragon—at least, one that wasn't trying to kill its rider—in centuries. The irony of that was not lost on me.

Eikaro didn't take me back to the ridge immediately. Child-like, he took me through the clouds, relishing in the feel of the wind with every beat of his wings as we soared through the air. Without the fear of trying to keep myself alive, the experience was exhilarating. It was twilight when we finally returned to the end of the road leading from the dragon-tower. I felt a pang of regret as he tucked his wings under him, allowing me to climb down one last time.

"I can get Huan out here," I whispered, cupping his muzzle with my hands so I could look into his eyes. "He'll believe me. He loves you. He'll have to."

He snorted a blast of hot breath. *"Please do not tell him. Until I am sure of what this means, of what will happen to me in this body, I would rather not give them hope."*

"Your family will mourn you."

He was silent for a moment. I pressed my forehead on his blood-caked nose, wrapping myself up in the feel of his presence. Funny how quickly I had switched to thinking that *this* was Lord Eikaro all along, and not the shattered body lying somewhere in the fields. I felt him nuzzle my cheek.

"They'll live through it," he murmured. He stepped away from me and took flight.

———————

I limped down the road. Cho was waiting for me within sight of the dragon-tower gates. He broke into a grin, but I didn't return it.

"The lordling..." he said, reading the look on my face.

I didn't reply. We strode back into the city to revelry and cheers, and proclaimed to the hopeful faces that Lord Eikaro was dead.

Lord Huan, who had survived the dragon attacks with Captain Seo and one other man, heir to Yu-yan and Warlord Ojika's legacy, broke down like a little boy. After everything that had happened, it felt odd to look at his face, the replica of his brother's. I had barely gotten my head around this when I heard a guard proclaim Warlord Ojika's arrival. I stepped back, feeling nauseous all of a sudden.

To the best of my knowledge, Warlord Ojika was a morose, reclusive man who had refused to ride out east over the last few years. In the few times I had demanded the warlords' presence in my court, he had sent either a proxy or his sons. He had missed even Warlord Yeshin's funeral, citing a bad leg from a horse injury and ordering a cousin to attend in his stead.

I supposed that there were worse circumstances to meet someone for the first time other than the morning after his son's supposed death, but none came to mind immediately. Ojika's expression bordered on revulsion. The wrinkles under his eyes were swollen, the after-effect of a sleepless night. He was a shorter man than both of his sons, with a balding head, small eyes, and a brow that seemed permanently furrowed.

"You," he said.

"I'm getting very tired of being greeted that way," I replied. "Warlord Ojika, I am sorry for your loss, but I did the best I could." I would have been less irritable if Eikaro *had* died, but considering the circumstances, I found it hard to feel sympathy for his father.

"As I told you, Father," Huan said from behind him, voice cracked. "She did more than most would—"

"Be silent!" Ojika roared, flinging his arm out. Huan dropped his head quickly. A true son, showing proper respect to his elder—a Jinsein, through and through. Ojika ought to be proud.

"Your son Eikaro died a hero," I said, the lie whistling easily through my teeth. It was the truth, as far as I was concerned. I had no other words for what he did. "I would not be here if not for his sacrifice."

"For what did my son give his life?" Ojika hissed. "You're not even queen anymore."

"What do you mean?"

He waved a letter in his hand. "This came from an official courier hours ago. Perhaps you could explain to us what it means."

I picked it up and felt the blood drain from my face. The wax was black, imbedded with the official Ikessar seal. I didn't even have to see the falcon on it—I'd know the feel of the damn thing in my sleep.

"Please read it out loud for us all," Ojika said through gritted teeth.

I frowned as I indulged him. "*I, Rayyel aren dar Ikessar, heir to the*

Dragonthrone, hereby declare my wife, Talyien aren dar Orenar, a traitor to the throne. She has transgressed and planted a false heir, the boy Thanh." I paused, swallowing back the rage. "*Until she is proven innocent and Prince Thanh is determined to be my own trueborn son, her title as queen of Jin-Sayeng will not be recognized. She is to be detained and sent back to Shirrokaru by order of the council.*" The letter was signed at the bottom.

My first thought was that Yuebek must have forged it, as he had done before. But then why? Why remove the one thing that would bring *him* closer to what he wanted? He wanted to be king of Jin-Sayeng; if I didn't hold the title of queen, he couldn't get it through our union. Was he trying to get Thanh killed? It seemed too indirect for Yuebek. The letter came from a messenger that Warlord Ojika believed was official, so was he lying to me? Did it really come from the council, penned by my husband's actual hand? Only Rai would've known the channels through which he could send such things *directly* to the people that mattered. But...

Ojika spat. "The explanation," he said. The man wasn't going to give me time to think things through.

"Rayyel is a bloody idiot," I said, gritting my teeth. It was all I had.

"You really have made a mess of things."

"Father—" Huan said.

Ojika shook his head. "I lose my son and this nation is in shambles," he hissed. "A fine day, indeed." He glanced up to see a guard walk in, another letter in hand. "What now?" he barked.

"Dai Kaggawa," the guard murmured.

"What about that bastard?"

"He blames us for his daughter and demands that we return the queen to him."

Ojika glanced at me. "Some ally you've got there."

"He has my people," I said. "He wouldn't dare speak that way otherwise. Are you a wise man, Warlord Ojika? Or has the gout eaten away what's left of your brain?"

Ojika's eyebrows shot up. "Spit it out, bitch."

"Do you want my cooperation?"

"You are disgraced," Ojika hissed. "Your cooperation means nothing. You read the note—you have to be sent to Shirrokaru, in chains if I need to. I don't want the Ikessars on my back."

"Father—" Huan repeated.

He turned to his son. "What?"

"A reminder of our loyalties," Huan said in a low voice.

Ojika laughed. "Eikaro is *dead*. What can they do to us that they haven't already done?" But a moment later, he frowned and turned back to me. "Kaggawa has your men. What else are you keeping from me? Why were you even *with* him in the first place?"

"He promised to save my son."

"Because you knew this scandal was coming?"

"Because a Zarojo prince is on his way," I said, "and the man intends to sit his rump on the Dragonthrone, consequences be damned."

His eyes widened. I had expected him to ask me to explain myself, but instead he called for Captain Seo.

"When I return to court, I intend to contest my husband's misgivings," I continued. "There is no truth to the claim. The boy is Rayyel's."

Ojika stared back with a measure of scrutiny. "Prince Rayyel seems pretty convinced. To have roused the council within the span of a few days..."

"The council comprises mostly Ikessars. They hold no love for me."

"And so the mystery of the missing Dragonlords has been solved at last," Ojika murmured. He was silent for a moment before turning to Captain Seo as he arrived. "Rally our soldiers. If Kaggawa thinks he can make such demands, then he needs to be kicked down a notch. We attack at dawn."

CHAPTER EIGHTEEN
THE DRUMS OF WAR

Despair is a cliff in front of you while an army marches at your back. A broken sword in battle, a quiver with no arrows, a hangman's noose. It is water in your lungs when all you want to do is breathe.

That morning felt like water in my lungs, dragging me into darkness even as I kicked and struggled against the choking sensation. As far as the Anyus were concerned, Rayyel's proclamation—if indeed it was his—was true. How many warlords had received the same letter? Who would seize the chance to *believe* it in order to cause chaos? I didn't have the support of my father's army anymore, so it didn't matter if it was the largest in the land; almost anyone could use this as a blade to sink into my throat.

With no title to my name, what did that make me?

What did that make my son?

I stared at the ceiling, where the wooden beams blocked the clear sunlight streaming through the curtains over the windows. The barred windows. They had given me the most lavish prison-room in the castle, but it was prison nonetheless. I had to escape. Taking me to Shirrokaru meant handing me over to the Ikessars, which would bring me a step further from where I needed to be. A step too far from my son. I didn't know if I had that much time.

There were two knocks at the door. I held my breath. "Come in," I said, after a moment.

Huan stepped through the doorway like a man who wasn't quite sure he was supposed to be there. His hair looked slept in. He was also unshaven, and reeked slightly of drink.

"How are you doing?" he asked, scratching his neck.

"Wondering if I'm torn between wanting to shake Rayyel and demand why he would do this, or shaking him harder and watching his head fall off?"

"You said it, not I," he replied.

I grew serious. "They tricked me in the empire, over and over again. So that I would hate my husband more than I already did, and set him aside to marry the Zarojo prince. I don't know if this is another ploy. Do you believe me?"

Huan slumped down on the floor next to the window. "I don't know what to believe," he said at last. "The last few days have taken everything from me, Beloved Queen. My mind is clouded. I am angry. I want to throw that anger somewhere. I know this isn't Kaggawa's fault, and yet I want to crush his neck between my fingers. And my father—my father is more obsessed with seizing control than mourning his son."

"I take it he hasn't changed his mind."

"We are to attack Dai Kaggawa in an hour."

I wrinkled my nose. "You smell like you've been drinking. War, at your state, seems ill-advised."

"I'm aware of what it looks like," he grumbled. He rubbed his nose. "But give this to me, my lady. My brother just died."

I thought of Eikaro, tearing through the sky with his dragon-wings, and longed to tell Huan what had really transpired back there. But I had to respect Eikaro's wishes, and given the state that Huan was in, it felt like too much anyway. I might very well push him to the brink of insanity.

"Let me ride with you," I said. "You're not in the right state of mind to do this alone."

"Have *you* ever led a battle?"

"I've been in a few."

Huan shook his head. "You've been accosted by bandits several times, I've been told. It's not the same thing."

"Reassure me, then, that you'll prioritize getting my people out. That this isn't just Warlord Ojika's ego reacting to Kaggawa's arrogance."

I was starting to learn that Huan was a bad liar. He stared at the ceiling, grumbling slightly to himself.

"Lord Anyu—" I growled.

"These people of yours . . . they're just your guards, aren't they? Servants?"

"My cousin, Nor—"

"An *aron dar*. Yes, I'm acquainted with her. None of them are worth risking your life over. Queen or not, your importance to this nation can't be overstated. Even what you did for my brother was already a touch too far." His face twitched as he spoke.

I came up to him. "Do you really believe it when you say these things?"

He swallowed and didn't answer. He didn't know how to.

"You kept saying that I *ought* to have stayed behind and yet you never really did stop me. Your brother means something to you, Lord Huan—that much is clear. Outside of all these structures, our clans, our regions, we exist as people, don't we? Forget these wolves, these falcons, civets, anchors, oxen . . . whatever images and words we use to give ourselves worth. Who we are, who we care for, that's enough, isn't it? Even if it doesn't serve the nation?"

Huan ran a hand through his hair. "I don't know what you're saying, Lady Talyien. As royals, it is our duty to uphold the safety of Jin-Sayeng. Look at this man, Kaggawa. His actions the past few decades—his ambitions—they have been threatening this land for ages. Without that *oxen strength* of the Sougen royals, we would've cut him down from the very beginning. But your father told us to hold the peace. Let him insult you, he ordered. Do nothing."

I looked up in surprise. "My father said that? *Yeshin?*"

"He said it would throw the land in disarray if we punished Kaggawa. By himself, he isn't important, you understand. He is an *alon gar*, sure, but he isn't exactly descended from the rice merchant families. *Kaggawa* is a name from Akki, a poor family, with nothing to call their own. But his half-brother through his mother, Goen alon gar Shoho, is heir to one of the oldest rice merchant families, and anything we do to Kaggawa would stir their ire."

"So why attack now?" He drew away, and I reached out to grab his wrist. "Why attack *now*, Lord Huan, if my father told you not to? All I did was mention the Zarojo prince. What do you know that I don't?"

"Nothing," Huan said. "That's not a lie, Lady Talyien."

I tightened my fingers around him. "It is. I know about Eikaro, Lord Huan. I know your obedience to my father was because he threatened to expose what Eikaro was to the land if you didn't. So. The Zarojo prince. Were you in on that, too? Did you know my father sold me to him before my betrothal to Rayyel?"

Huan shook his head. "I didn't—I didn't know that part. Believe me, Lady Talyien—I wouldn't have asked to marry you otherwise."

"A proposal you quickly dropped. As soon as your father caught wind of it, perhaps?"

"I know nothing," he repeated, painfully.

I relaxed my fingers, allowing him to slip away. He staggered back and then, without another word, opened the door and left. I considered running after him, but quickly realized that force would get me nowhere. I just hoped he wouldn't get his fool head lopped off.

I sat back at the edge of the bed and stared at the wall. No more than a few minutes must've passed when I heard footsteps again. "Listen here, Anyu—" I began.

A woman stepped in. Tori, Eikaro's wife. "Beloved Queen," she said.

I grimaced. "Didn't you hear? I'm not allowed to go outside."

She wrung her hands over her swollen belly. "I heard what you did out there for my husband. How you tried to save him."

"*Tried*," I murmured. "I'm sorry I couldn't do more."

"Lord Huan just left for the Kaggawa estate. You understand that he cannot go against his father's wishes."

"The dilemma of the ages," I said wryly.

She smiled. "But Warlord Ojika is not *my* father. Come." Before I could recover from my surprise, she handed me a sword.

I followed her out of the keep, flanked by guards marked with the Meiokara crest, in colours I wasn't familiar with. I stared at them apprehensively. Tori noticed my gaze.

"We're Lady Rag-ayaon's daughters," she explained.

"I'm not familiar with Meiokara's politics."

"Maybe you should be."

"Did you fight at my father's side during the war? Or the Ikessars'?"

"Neither. We were some of the cowards who sat it out."

"I wouldn't call that cowardice. *Prudence* is a better word."

She paused. "When it comes down to it, you really don't talk like I'd expect from an Oren-yaro. My husband and his brother told us you were friends. I wondered about that. I always thought they were joking. The Bitch Queen, calling *anyone* friend?"

"I have to admit, I didn't think they regarded me that way."

"Not everything has to be about politics all the time," she said. "Especially given that some of us are born to this. So many of us don't have a choice." She placed a hand over her belly. A twitch on her cheek told me the child had turned. I thought I felt it, too; a remnant from when I carried my son.

We left through a small gate that led to a narrow walkway outside the palace. Guards blocked the entrance.

"Step aside," Tori told them.

"You don't have the authority, Lady Tori," the guards said. But they eyed the Meiokara soldiers—with their golden earrings, their bare, tattoo-covered arms, and the wave-patterned, double-edged swords on their belts—warily.

"I'm the mother-to-be to your warlord's heir."

"Third in line," a guard said. "Tell your island savages to walk away."

Those were the last words he ever uttered. One of Tori's soldiers drew his blade and cut his neck, as deftly as a butcher bleeding a pig. The soldier desperately tried to cover the wound with his fingers in horror before falling to the ground, blood spurting from the ragged cut. "Grassland scum," the Meiokaran hissed, spitting on the body.

The other soldiers charged. Tori threw her arm in front of me, urging me back before I could get involved. "This isn't your battle," she said.

"Your father will punish you."

"A woman pregnant with his son's child? I don't think so. My soldiers will make it seem like a drunken fight. Don't worry about me." She led me past the clash of swords, past the grove of bamboo fences, and towards another gate. She pulled out a key and quickly unlocked it, revealing a bare field overlooking several rice paddies. Cho stood waiting with two horses.

"Thank you," I said, turning to Tori.

"My husband..." she began, placing one hand on her belly, where Eikaro's unborn child slumbered.

I held my breath. Huan was easy enough. But I recognized that look of loss and terror in her eyes and realized that if she asked me outright, I would've found it difficult to maintain the lie.

She shook her head instead. "It doesn't matter anymore. Go, Beloved Queen, with all the gods' blessings."

———

We rode between the rice fields, just as the sound of impending battle filled the horizon. Soldiers and horses, swords and spears, warhorns, wardrums. How much of a threat did Kaggawa pose to Warlord Ojika that he felt the need for such a show of force? Was he planning to arrest the farmers and march them all the way back to Yu-yan in chains?

A dragon appeared in the distance, so far away it seemed like a speck of dust. The horse panicked, but I kept it steady, wondering if it was Eikaro. It wasn't. This one was covered in scales of yellow and green. It dove on the far side of the soldiers, setting yet another field ablaze. The soldiers parted, giving room for archers to step in. A wave of arrows sailed through the air, some imbedding straight into the dragon's belly.

The dragon roared before flying off, seemingly unhurt, white shafts stuck between its scales.

Just as unfazed, the soldiers returned to their formations. The drums began to sound again, pounding like a thousand heartbeats.

"Why do you even stay in this godsforsaken land?" Cho asked.

"It's our home, Cho," I said.

"Your people are crazy," he replied. "You've got dragons and monsters tearing your kingdom apart, and instead you're going to fight *each other*?"

I didn't know how to answer. He was right. It was ever Jin-Sayeng's disease, and I knew it was going to bring her to her knees.

CHAPTER NINETEEN

CAUGHT BETWEEN TIDES

ᴛᴜᴍ

No rest, no respite.

The clouds swirled above us as we rode towards Dai's estate. We took the side roads between the rice fields, not the main road where the Anyu army was marching through. It soon opened up to the riverbank, where I could soon see the dock behind Dai's house.

"What's the plan?" Cho asked.

"I don't know," I said. "Sneak around the back, try to break everyone free while they're distracted?"

"Doesn't sound like a very good plan."

"You got anything better?"

He laughed, urging his horse faster. He enjoyed this sort of thing, the complete opposite of his brother—not a worrier, but someone who grew bolder the more you threw at him. You needed that sometimes, when you had nothing else. Cho's face grew serious and turned my head from him to the single figure standing at the edge of the bank, seemingly waiting for us. The weight of the last few days fell away, replaced by relief that exploded like a warm hearth from deep inside.

I found myself dismounting from my horse. Khine walked up to me without a word, and I didn't stop him as he held me with the strength of a man who thought he had lost me for good. As much of a betrayal as it seemed, it felt right to wrap myself up in his presence, to feel his lips on my head and the beat of his heart against my ear. Like I needed nothing beyond this, and the whole world could fall apart in a sea of arrows and dragon-fire around us.

I allowed the illusion to continue a moment longer before I pulled away.

"Tali," he managed. He turned to his brother. "Cho. I'm glad you're both well."

"Are the Anyus at the gate?"

He nodded.

"My guards?"

"Still imprisoned," Khine said.

Cho snorted. "Why aren't you?"

"He set me free a few days ago to work on his daughter's injuries."

"Akaterru—she survived all of that?"

"Barely. I believe she got caught on one of the buttresses. The dragon had twisted her leg beyond recognition—I had no choice but to amputate it. They said you rode north. We weren't sure you'd survived." He took a deep breath. "You escaped the Anyus?"

"I want nothing to do with either of them," I said in a low voice. "Sharks, the both of them. Kaggawa. Anyu. Cut from the same cloth, no matter what they say. I am done with it. I will save my son myself."

He smiled grimly. "Daring words, but how do we start?"

"Get me to my guards first."

We walked all the way through the courtyard and strode down the staircase in the alcove behind the kitchen. There was a single guard on the door to the basement, a tense-looking servant who immediately stood up straight at the sight of us. "What are you doing here?" Khine asked, drawing close to the man. "Sir?"

"The Anyus are attacking, didn't you hear? They need every man out there!"

"I was told to stay here in case—"

"You'd rather wait for them to come and hack you to pieces? Those are royals out there. We're commoners. You know what that means, don't you?"

The man's eyes widened before he stumbled off in haste.

"What *does* it mean?" I asked Khine, as soon as the guard was out of earshot.

"I'm not sure myself," Khine said. "Would've had a hard time following that train of conversation. But we got what we wanted, see?" He held out the key, which he had pilfered from the guard.

"You're going to have to teach me that one of these days." I watched as he unlocked the door. "You've heard about everything, I suppose."

"Ah, yes. It was all everyone could talk about." We went down the steps, leaving Cho to keep watch outside. Khine cleared his throat. "You are *still* queen," he reminded me. "You may not have to do this alone. Is there anyone else in Jin-Sayeng you can turn to? Did you think the weight of who you are disappears overnight?"

"The entire council would disagree with you there."

"The title—they can take that away. But it doesn't change how you were raised."

"You know little about how I was raised."

He cleared his throat. "Perhaps I don't. Enlighten me."

"It is more than about blood and pushing your weight around. There are tenets we follow, values carried down by every family or clan. We give ourselves names, too. A falcon of the Ikessar values pacifism, knowledge, and diplomacy. A Baraji civet implies someone with wit who uses cunning to shift the winds to their favour."

"A Baraji *civet*? That doesn't exactly roll off the tongue."

I smiled. "Kyo-orashi's crest is the giant mud crab."

"That—all right, that's worse."

"Then you have the Jeinza, who use the image of a ship's anchor on their banners. They value tradition, goodwill, and harmony, and have been strong supporters of the Orenar clan—so as long as we remember to put the good of Jin-Sayeng over ourselves. Which has never been a problem, though the rest of them think otherwise."

"Because the Orenar, as head of the Oren-yaro, are honourable beyond question."

I grimaced. "It isn't honour."

"What is it, then?"

"It is hard to explain in simple words if you aren't born an Oren-yaro yourself. Only within the Oren-yaro have our tenets managed to transcend into an ideal that has shaped an entire region. It wasn't easy to get that far. Our warlords have created a reputation over the years as harsh and unrelenting, but such behaviour would've reduced us to tyrants if not for one thing: we strive to be the very personification of these tenets ourselves. And so you have these values that the royal clans share with the common people, which gives them pride, which is dangerous."

He halted in his steps. "I don't understand."

I shrugged. "It's simple. I have no power if I am not supported by my clan. After all of this, *especially* after Rayyel's announcement, it would be all too easy to accuse me of putting too much importance on my own needs. On frivolities."

Khine's face flickered. "Your son's life is a frivolity?"

"You see my fear, Khine?" I paused to stare at him. "I am not here as queen, not anymore. They've made that easy for me, at the very least. I am here as Thanh's mother, because I need help to save my boy, politics be damned."

"What about Rayyel?"

I stared at him, knowing what I knew. His expression betrayed nothing. Even the question came off nonchalant, uttered by a concerned friend. Too good of an actor, Khine—if Cho had kept his silence, I would've missed it. I hoped I was just as good.

"Sorry," he quickly said, before I could reply. "I suppose it's a foolish question."

"I will always..." I began.

He drew a sharp breath.

I turned away. "I loved my father, too. I still do. And yet I knew what he was, and the more I find out about him, the more distasteful the idea of being his daughter becomes." I paused, lowering my voice to a faint whisper. "It is painful, Khine. Painful to have all this love I cannot fully throw myself in, to have it exist within a sphere that belongs only to me. I cannot take comfort from it, cannot hope to be understood. The only time I've ever known love that I could wrap myself in, that I could get lost in, was with my son, and even then..." I trailed off, finding that we had reached the end of the hall.

There was a single cell at the furthest corner. Agos was leaning on the bars, hands hooked through the metal, long shadows dancing on his face. "You're safe," he breathed at the sight of me. "We heard all sorts of things from the guards, but they wouldn't confirm either way, the fucking bastards."

Nor got up from her seat to draw close to him. "They said you are no longer queen. Lord Rayyel claims Prince Thanh isn't his." Her face was like hard steel.

"After everything that has happened, Nor, you really don't think—"

"Talyien," she said evenly. "Is there truth to this claim?"

"Leave her alone," Agos broke in. "She's had enough to deal with. This isn't the time."

"It never is," Nor continued, striking him on the chest to push him back and give her space. She reached through the bars to grab my arm. "Talyien."

"He has reason to doubt it," I said at last.

"Damn you," she said.

"Captain Nor—"

"My daughter is in Oren-yaro, too, Talyien! If they kill your son, you don't think they'll slaughter the rest of the Orenars?"

"You can't save anyone if you're stuck arguing here," Khine said, his voice jerking me back to reality. Nor roared in frustration, finally letting me loose. I stepped back as Khine unlocked the cell. We strode up the steps leading out of the dungeons in silence, one that broke at the sight of Cho grappling with two men right outside. I started to draw my sword when I heard someone sigh.

"What did I tell you?" Dai asked, appearing at the yard. "A royal, through and through." He drew his sword and went for me.

—————◆—————

A lesser man would've been down on the ground with a slit throat in an instant.

But I had seen Dai fight. I knew his reputation, and didn't want to stake my life against it. Instead of going for my dagger, I turned to flee. I was hoping either of my guards would engage him first, which would give me a chance to strike in my own time. Dai was way too big for me to face directly.

I saw Yu-yan soldiers in the distance, headed by Huan, who had blood pouring from inside his helmet down both cheeks. He cut a terrible figure against the sunlight, no different from any of the blood-drenched warlords from our sordid history, and I thought he would simply rush in and finish all of us without thought. But he paused at the sight of me.

"Lady Talyien!" Huan roared. "You're supposed to be back in the city!"

"This is a surprise," Dai said with a shadow of a smirk. "What's the plan, then? You take on the whole nation by yourself?"

"If I have to," I replied evenly.

"I thought you were simply allying yourself with your own kind," Dai continued in a low voice. "I had no idea you were a fool, too. I never did understand you royals." He craned his head towards Huan. "Your chosen queen, the decision sealed with a blood pact between the warlords—your own father included. Yet the instant her missing husband decides to show his face and announce her a *traitor*, you stumble over yourselves to be the first to claim the prize."

"Don't pretend like you're not an ambitious dog yourself, Kaggawa," Huan said, his voice seething.

"I have never denied what I truly want," Dai said. "*Someone* has to keep an eye out for this land while you royals are busy tearing each other apart for the smallest scrap of meat."

"Is this why you're playing hero? Commoner rabble like you?"

"You've got a head wound, Anyu," Dai called. "My commoner rabble caused it, I'm sure. Better get it checked before your brains leak through your eye sockets."

He glanced at his men. They lunged—not for me, not for Huan, but for Khine. I froze, too stunned to react. Khine's neck was between two naked blades.

"Stop!" I bellowed, just as Huan lifted his hand to order his soldiers to attack.

"With me now, Beloved Queen," Dai said, drifting close to squeeze my shoulder. I resisted the urge to strike him. "And you, Anyu brat—I'm sure the last thing you want is to report that you got Talyien Orenar killed because of some hasty decisions." He whistled. I saw more of Dai's men appear at the fringes around Huan.

"You won't deny me my guards, I hope," I told Dai. "You *do* want my cooperation."

He nodded. His men dragged Khine down to the riverbank just as the rest attacked the Yu-yan soldiers. Agos and Cho strode through the sound of clashing swords and screaming men. I noticed Nor hanging back.

"Captain," I said.

She gave me a look, one sharp enough to carve a hole in the pit of my stomach.

No, I thought. *I'm down to four people, Nor—please.*

"Captain," I repeated. "Nor."

"I don't think I can do this anymore, Talyien," she said. "If you're not queen…"

"We're still family. I will find a way to save my son, and no harm will come to your daughter."

"You can't promise that. You don't know what's happening to your own nation. You don't even know yourself."

"Nor, please."

She didn't move. Watching her make that decision felt like forever. I wanted to drop to my knees to beg her not to turn on me, too. The feeling was followed by a twinge of shame. Was this how far I had fallen?

Yeshin's voice flared inside my head, that crack of lightning.

If you had stuck to your path, girl…!

"Cousin!" I could hear the anguish in my own voice.

She turned away like I didn't exist, drew her blade, and sank it into the nearest man. Dai's. She was throwing her hat in with the Anyus. I was nothing to her now. I had done this. My own inabilities, my failures…

It must've all happened in a flash, because I felt Dai squeeze my shoulder again. "*Now*, Talyien, before I change my mind and your lover stands a head shorter," he growled.

I didn't have time to respond to his choice of words. I followed him down the steps to the riverbank, silently counting the number of men he had. There were six—too many for us to take at once, not when Agos was my only reliable swordsman left.

The path led to the entrance of a tunnel, held up with half-rotten beams and pillars. It looked like it had been there for some time.

"I don't see why you're so worried, Queen Talyien," Dai said as we stepped into the shadows, where it smelled of damp and moss. "My agents are on their way to Oren-yaro as we speak. Your treachery aside, I will stick with my agreement—your son will be rescued, and not a moment too soon. After what your husband just did? His life hangs on the balance." He retrieved a lantern hanging from a pillar and held it out.

I blinked as warm orange light flooded the cave. I could now see that the tunnel led straight to a rocky overhang, overlooking what appeared to be part of the river. I caught sight of a boat bobbing along a small dock below, where a silent figure sat. A woman. I recognized Lahei, and tried to hide my surprise at seeing her alive.

"Beloved Queen," Lahei said. "The preparations are ready. This can take us to the underground river systems, deeper into the heart of the Sougen."

I swallowed. My eyes skipped towards her right leg, which ended in a bandage-wrapped stump. She stared at nothing, blood seeping through the cloth. There were dark hollows under her eyes.

"You left my daughter for dead," Dai said grimly.

"So I did," I whispered. I turned back to him. "Is this what you want, then? An eye for an eye?"

He glanced at Khine, who looked almost calm for someone with swords a hair's breadth away from slitting his throat.

"You know what I want," Dai said in a low voice.

"My son and I as hostages. Yes. You can see why I didn't exactly warm up to the idea." I swallowed. "Should I offer my own bargain, Kaggawa? Point out a chink in your armour? I have no desire to explore this region any more than I already have. I want to go back home, to Oren-yaro."

There was hardly a flicker of concern on his face. "I'm not sure what else you've got that I'd be interested in."

"I know about you, Dai Kaggawa. I know you've got two souls in that body. You know I've heard it, too—that change in your voice, the way you swing from irritable to complacent. *Our* daughter, you said once. Did you think I'd miss it?"

I had been expecting a bigger reaction and was sorely disappointed that he didn't even seem concerned. He leaned back, crossing his arms in front of him. A shadowy expression flashed across his face for a moment. "Irritable," he said at last, in that softer voice. "I love that. You do have a way with words, Queen Talyien."

I swallowed.

It was his turn to grin. "Were you expecting me to change? Ah, but I think we've had enough excitement for today."

"After all the trouble you went through to convince me of the sort of situation we're dealing with…"

Dai walked over to Lahei, a thoughtful look on his face. The expression accentuated the dimples in his cheeks. He paused to press her arm. "I do love it here. There is so much to get attached to."

"Oh, Da," Lahei murmured.

A moment of silence followed. "This *other you*—you," Khine broke in. "You're not born here."

Dai nodded towards his guards, who took a step back, giving him room to breathe.

Khine rubbed his hand on his neck. "I figured it from the way you talked. You lapse into a non-native accent when you carry that voice."

I blinked. "I didn't even catch that."

Khine shrugged. "It's something you pick up when you've had to learn to speak Jinan like I did."

"I was from the Kag, in fact," Dai—or at least, what appeared to be the *other* Dai—replied. "From Hafod. I was born there a long time ago, and I died there a long time ago, too. So no—I am not exactly like these corrupt creatures. I am well aware of what I am, and what Dai gave me." He paused for a moment, drifting into thought, before laughing. "Well. He wants a quick correction. I forced myself in, but Dai was gracious enough to let me stay."

"I still don't understand the difference," I said.

"This happened a long time ago," he continued. "Well before the destruction of Rysaran's dragon. I am not part of whatever foulness resulted from that. The reason I was drawn to Dai was... personal. My soul remains intact."

"I believe him," Khine said. "The other thing, the one that spoke to me in the village, felt different."

"You'd leave this up to *feeling*?" I asked, trying to keep the horror from my voice.

Khine sighed. "Like you, I've suspected as much with Dai. It couldn't be a coincidence that he was acting so strangely, especially in a world where these incidents seem commonplace."

"You must have such a poor impression of our nation."

"Don't I? There's time to play tourist later." He grew serious. "That other thing back in the village was... sinister. *Foul* is a good word for it. The way it spoke sent shivers up my spine. You know that feeling, don't you? When you're around someone and everything they say rings empty—you're just listening to how they string words together, words that don't even fit. Like a coward babbling on at sword-point. This one..." He glanced back at Dai.

"Myar," the old man replied. "Since we're on the subject, my name is Myar." His eyes were sparkling blue now, iridescent.

Khine nodded in acknowledgment. "Myar, you speak with the intent and grace of someone who not only lives in this body, but belongs to its world. You aren't occupying it simply to further your life or drink in its experiences. The cares of Dai are your own. His daughters know about you, and love you as an entity separate from Dai. No—they are *your* daughters, too. They consider you a second father."

The old man broke into a grin. "I appreciate the observations, Khine Lamang. But you are wrong. I *am* here for all those reasons, and more. I lost my life far too young, and Dai's was...so tempting. It's why I've never left all these years."

CHAPTER TWENTY

THE MAN WITH TWO SOULS

ℐℐℚℐ

Despite Khine's words, I did feel a chill descending on me then. I wondered if it was from the wind whistling through the tunnel. Whatever light there was seemed to focus solely on Myar's face, the flames playing with the shadows as they danced against that unsettling blue gaze.

My expression must have betrayed my thoughts, because Myar held a hand out in a gesture of peace. "Dai knows this, of course. And for his part, for a while he was tempted to drift away from this body and leave it to me, returning to the *agan*. Both desires go against nature. A soul belongs to the body it was born to, and it must stay until the body dies. An intruder, over time, will find itself at odds with its host. A soul ripped unnaturally from its body, without the proper mechanisms of death, will become *corrupt*. They lose all sense of where they belong and instead of following the natural process of wherever it is souls go off to—another realm in the *agan*, maybe, or back here into a new life— they turn into predators, eager to jump into places, lives, where they ought not to be. If anything, our arrangement is a compromise. It keeps our natures locked in place while allowing us to indulge a little in our desires."

"So you do not stay for very long?" I asked.

Myar shook his head. "I come but once in a while. I dare not even stay an hour, else I risk tainting this body."

I thought about Eikaro. How long had it been since he had taken over the dragon? "What happens if the other soul isn't there?" I found myself asking. "If you had thrown Dai back into the abyss, then you wouldn't be at odds with him, would you? There would be no *other* soul to take over, no one else to hold at bay and cause these changes. This body would be your own."

"I, ah, don't think you should be giving him ideas," Khine whispered.

"Believe me when I say it's crossed my mind once or twice," Myar said. "But I wouldn't dare. For one thing, in such a case, the possessed become mindless monsters. And I wouldn't do that to Dai. Believe it or not, I do like the surly bastard." He laughed after a moment, as if responding to an unheard statement.

"So you wouldn't know what would happen in that sort of situation."

"No," he replied. "I think you'd need to have some sort of attunement to the *agan* to accomplish such in the first place, a thing neither of us have. The circumstances of my attachment to Dai are...unprecedented." He pushed himself away from the rails. "Does this answer your questions for me, Queen Talyien? Or do you have others?"

"For *you*," I said. "Not Dai?"

He smiled thinly. "The entire realm knows how you are, Beloved Queen. Bold. Rash. Lovely qualities for a leader, mind, particularly if combined with wise counsel—"

"Yours again, I'm assuming. Not Dai."

"If it was up to Dai alone, he would be content with setting the Sougen free of these creatures. But I believe the problem cannot be solved so simply. The concerns of Jin-Sayeng start from within, and until we fix it from the inside, we cannot hope to fix it from the outside. Marrying your son to our daughter will usher in a new era, the sort your ancestors have all been dreaming of. Consider how you and your people have botched your rule. If everything continues down this road, you will be faced with more trouble than you know how to deal with. I told you I loved it here. These lands, this nation, this people. The last thing I want is to see it go up in flames."

"Then help me," I said. "If you truly desire to serve the land, you will not look at me as an enemy."

"We do not, Beloved Queen. We still acknowledge your title."

"My son and I—are we to be mere puppets in this new regime? One noose in place of another?"

"You are being overly dramatic. I don't see a noose around your neck. Did you not have a warm bed in our home? Good food? This man, your lover—" He nodded towards Khine.

"He isn't," I bristled.

"Is that right?" Dai asked. "Why hide it now, after your husband's announcement? The way you look at each other..."

"I met him in the empire. In any case, if I support you, if I dare proclaim my son's betrothal to your daughter, we are *all* as good as dead."

Myar's eyes turned back to me. "We will protect the both of you. You have my word on that."

"And therein lies my noose," I snarled. "I will not be able to walk two steps in any direction without one of your men shadowing me. You told me once that you needed to show me what was happening in the Sougen. That you would risk war to save us from *that*. Well, there is no need for war. I've seen it with my own eyes—let me return home. Once I have cleared this mess with my husband, I will send people to you."

"Don't you understand yet, Queen Talyien? You have nothing to bargain with. Change cannot happen without sacrifice."

"My father would say such things," I whispered. "How are you planning to stand against the entire realm? Your sellswords? Do you even have enough? You'd dare talk of war as if it were a game...that's more arrogance than a mere rice merchant ought to have."

"Ah, but see, *Dai* is the rice merchant," Myar said.

"And you?" I asked, realizing the source of my trepidation. I had been looking from Dai's point of view. I never once considered the ambition of the *other*.

"Well," Myar replied. "You could say I was once a king's son. My father was Agartes Allaicras, hero of the Kags."

I frowned at the name. A part of me couldn't blame people for wanting the Dragonthrone. It was, after all, a tasty prize, one that others had died and killed for. My own father had given up so much for the chance to sit on it. I suppose I don't need to go through a history lesson to convince you. Power is power. Everyone thinks they want it. I knew Dai did, but it caught me off guard to what extent. What began as an innocent suggestion to undermine Jin-Sayeng's ruling class was now a full-fledged intention to turn everything upside down.

I should've seen it coming.

As queen, such things were my responsibility to ward against, were they not? To maintain the balance of power, break the legs of whoever dared rise beyond their expected position. But embroiled in my own personal affairs, I had neglected to look beyond the obvious. Dai Kaggawa's *friend*, a certain Myar Allaicras. I recalled reading about him once in a half-hearted translation of prominent Kag figures in Jinan. Myar Allaicras was a footnote in it. Son of an old hero, an important general and would-be king. The boy was cut down before his twelfth year, along with his entire family—slaughtered by Dageians, as the story goes.

I watched Dai—Myar—whoever he really was. He had his back against a rock column, not an ideal place to attack him from—I wouldn't have room to draw my sword. I glanced at the three men with me; we weren't in a good spot to charge him, either. It was too dark, and Agos was too far away to take signals from me. I couldn't expect Cho and Khine to do much more than keep themselves alive. Anyway, Kaggawa had six guards, all of whom were blocking the entrance to the tunnel. The only clear path was down the slope to the underground riverbank, down to the dock where the boat was.

I turned my gaze to the side, towards Lahei, and my mind started to form a plan. Her form was clear under the streaks of golden sunlight pouring from the cracks of the cave, the shadows of the current dancing on her face. She could barely sit straight. By all rights she should be recovering on a bed somewhere. They had all forgotten she was now an invalid.

I held my breath for a moment, wondering if Dai's reflexes were faster than mine. Did a second soul lend a touch of strength to him, just as it did with the dragons? I had to make a decision. I made one step towards Lahei before dashing down the slope.

"Myar, you careless fool!" he thundered. Dai's voice. He tore after me, but it was too late. In the blink of an eye, I had my dagger at their daughter's throat.

"Queen Talyien," Lahei croaked. "This is a mistake."

"Everything is," I murmured.

"You hate not having power," she whispered. "I understand. But hating it won't change the truth. We're offering you a chance to regain it, Beloved Queen. You speak of a noose. You're looking at the wrong place. It's in the east, with your royals, waiting for you to stick your head in."

"Into the boat," I told my men, ignoring her.

It was Khine who moved first, shrugging his way out of the guards holding him. Cho quickly followed. They started down the path leading to the dock.

"Princess, maybe we should—" Agos began.

I turned to him. "What?"

"I think he is remarking on the foolishness of this," Dai said. "How far do you think you'll get before one of your enemies catches up? The whole world is against you. We've offered you something valuable here, Beloved Queen. All you have to do is open your mind a little."

I smirked, holding the dagger at Lahei's throat as I directed my men to board the boat. Khine clambered in, followed by Cho, who began to untie the rope.

"Agos," I said. "Get in."

He conceded with a small grumble. The boat creaked with his weight. Cho finished untying and held the rope with one hand, keeping the boat from drifting away. I pushed Lahei towards her father before jumping in. Cho let go just as the guards attempted to chase after us. The boat was at least two arm's lengths away by the time they reached the riverbank; one tried to wade into the river, stopping only when he realized the current was too strong.

Dai didn't move a muscle. He remained watching from the shore, arms folded. We drifted down the river, deeper into the cave, into the shadows.

"You should know," he called out, when we were halfway down the channel, "that Zarojo landed in Kyo-orashi several days ago."

I folded my hands across my knees.

"From one trap to another, Queen Talyien. When will you learn?" His voice faded into the darkness.

We sat in silence for several moments before Agos and Khine began to work the oars, shifting the boat steadily downstream. "This should just lead back to the Yu-yan River," Agos remarked. He coughed. "You realize we're not going to make it all the way to Fuyyu on this dinky little thing, right?"

"He said Zarojo," I said. "Does he mean Yuebek?"

"Anything is possible at this point." Agos sniffed.

"He wasn't wrong. *The whole world against me* sounds about right."

"It's not *you*," Agos said. "You just happened to be right in the thick of it."

"Me and my son," I replied bitterly.

"They want the Dragonthrone. Maybe you should let them have it. The world is bigger than Jin-Sayeng." He craned his neck to the side. "I can turn this boat back, if you want."

"Don't joke around, Agos."

"You *realize*," he repeated, "that there is no way we're getting Thanh out of Oka Shto by ourselves. Kaggawa has given you the most sensible option."

"Marrying Thanh to his daughter is far from sensible. It's just another pathway to war."

"Gods, Princess, after all this time, you still don't get it? You don't have to stick to your word. Just agree to it long enough to get Thanh out, and then ditch the bastards. Easy enough to do."

"You've seen what he is. I wouldn't trust the man with a dog, let alone my *son*."

Agos grimaced. "He's already sent people after Thanh. How do you expect to get there before them? *Or* the Zarojo? *How*, Tali?"

I couldn't muster up a reply. Exhaustion had rendered my mind blank. With the chaos erupting around us and the sting of Nor's betrayal still fresh in my mind, all I wanted to do was see my son again. The details didn't matter.

The tunnel ended. We found ourselves floating down a narrow section of the river, into a sea of fog.

Sometime before sundown, we took a fork in the river that opened up to roaring currents, transforming tranquil waters into a sheet of raging foam that went as far as the eye could see. We pushed ourselves to the bank while we still could and landed on soft, silty ground that went up to my knees as soon as I stepped in.

"We'll walk the rest of the way to Fuyyu," I said as I emptied mud and water from my boots. "Take a boat up River Agos."

"If there's even any running this time of the year," Agos said. "I'm worried about Anyu's soldiers. They catch up to us, they'll take you back to Shirrokaru. *Then* we'll be really hopeless."

I didn't like the tone of his voice, and turned away from it with a frown.

"We'll follow the river and then crest along the coast. It'll be slow walking, though."

"Not a problem unless you have basilisks," Khine replied brightly.

"I'd pay to see them all ripped apart by basilisks," I huffed. We gathered our things and began to walk downstream. The fog had lifted, but the wind still carried wisps of rain with it, light enough not to soak.

It was evening when we finally stumbled on a small village on the eastern side of the Yu-yan River, the sort that didn't have inns or other facilities for lodging. Khine managed to convince a fisherman to offer us use of his hut in exchange for a few coins. We were all exhausted, but Agos went off to do a quick patrol and keep an eye out for anyone who might be sniffing around for us, leaving me alone with the Lamangs.

I sat cross-legged on the small porch overlooking the dark river, watching as the window shutters shivered slightly in the breeze. Khine was standing beside me, arms crossed, his attention captured by the wind chimes on the beams. Eventually, he scratched the side of his face and said, "We need food, Cho."

From inside the house, Cho started to grumble. He fell silent when Khine peered through the door and flipped him a coin.

"Tell me how this all works," Khine said as soon as Cho disappeared. "You're queen, and then suddenly you're not. What've you left to work with?"

I sighed. "Even as queen, I can only really lay claim to the Orenar lands. The throne and I are two separate entities."

"What about this city we're travelling to? You've got no allies there?"

"Back in the days of the Merchants' War, Fuyyu was designated as the official port. It's nearly a Kag city. I'd say about half the population are immigrants. We're not exactly closed to foreigners, but many of the warlords make their lives difficult and you'd be hard-pressed to find an immigrants' quarter as expansive as Dar Aso in many of our cities. So instead, many of them prefer to settle in Fuyyu. Our soldiers are supposed to leave the foreigners alone, too—despite my father's efforts, many of Reshiro Ikessar's policies remain in place." I took a deep breath at the tired old answers, the ones that seemed to just fall out of my mouth without bidding. "To answer your question, no. I have no allies. Fuyyu has no warlord. The guards all answer directly to the Dragonthrone, which really means they're the Ikessars'."

He watched with that same expression he always regarded me with. I suddenly had the distinct impression that he didn't listen much to what I said; it was *how* I spoke that he paid attention to. I remembered we were alone.

"It's Rayyel's influence," I murmured. "And my father's. I'm still not entirely sure how to talk like—like real people do."

"You don't always have that problem," Khine said softly.

"What do you mean?"

"Back in the Ruby Grove…"

I felt my cheeks burn at the memories. "Ah. Yes. A world away."

"Now we're back in the world you left behind."

"When all I want is to be elsewhere, away from all of this." I smiled. "Yet why does it matter? My very existence attracts the power-hungry like vultures to a slaughter. What Rayyel did ought to have come as a relief. My own Captain of the Guard abandoned me. My own *cousin*. Nor—"

Khine ventured closer and placed a shawl around my shoulders. Only then did I realize that I was shivering. I wrapped my fingers around the moth-eaten cloth, feeling both the discomfort and ease that I had come to expect from his presence.

"What happened to you out there?" he asked.

I mulled over my answer. "I saw myself against the backdrop of everything else," I murmured. "For once in my life, I felt…real. Not a construct, not Yeshin's daughter or Rayyel's wife, not a wolf of Oren-yaro. Just me, making my own decisions. But I suppose when you're down to it, that sort of thing doesn't matter. Not to these people."

He didn't understand.

"Eikaro…isn't dead, you know," I said.

The confusion in his eyes deepened. But even before I could say anything to chase it away, I felt his hand on mine. I allowed him to wrap his fingers through my own before he turned my hand over, squeezing it. Warmth. Comfort. Acceptance. I wanted to pull away, but my body was starting to betray me. My skin prickled at his nearness.

"Explain," Khine said, blatantly ignoring what was going on, this unsaid thing between us.

The words tumbled out of my mouth as I told him everything, about the mad dragons, and how Eikaro had sacrificed himself to save me, dragging the dragon and the corrupted soul into his own body and becoming the dragon himself. He listened without interrupting. I tried to focus on my narrative, but as I spoke, I considered his half-open mouth and my eyes traced a line from his neck down to his collarbone. For an instant, I became aware of nothing else.

My other hand came up his arm, drifting towards his chest.

The wind started to rattle the windows. He turned away from me. "Tali."

I stopped.

"You're tired, I think," he whispered. "You should go to sleep."

"Not that tired," I murmured, playing with the hem of his shirt instead.

He swallowed. "Has Cho been talking?"

I felt myself flush. "He may have said something."

"It wasn't his place."

"Khine…"

"Queen Talyien," he said. "Let's not complicate things any more than they already are." It was as if he was speaking for his own benefit, reminding me who I was. Reminding *himself.* But the coldness of his voice felt like a blow. It carried echoes of how Rayyel used to treat me—the guesswork, that distant uncertainty, when all I ever really wanted was to rush head first into fire. That was why I'd slept with Agos, after all—a thing I had done out of weakness, trying to catch a glimpse of whatever it was Rayyel found in Chiha, a wave of emotion worth risking a kingdom for. If you believed yourself to be numb, you stuck your hand in the fire. That was what it was—a burning expression of rage I wasn't allowed to feel, of passion that seemed to exist in everyone else's world but mine.

Why *couldn't* it exist in mine?

"What you're feeling right now…" Khine continued. "You don't have to feel indebted to me."

"That's what you think this is?" Outrage crawled into my voice.

"My own feelings are mine to bear," Khine whispered. "You figure yours out."

I stared at the river. "I don't think I'm allowed to," I found myself saying. "I never was." I closed my eyes, the blood pounding in my head.

And I remembered something I had first learned when I was young and all I had was a father with the blood of thousands on his hands. People speak of love and all these things it ought to be, but the truth is that love is not always this wondrous thing to be carried with pride or celebrated. I can imagine, of course, that there is no comparison to joyous love, the kind that comes with no baggage or expectations attached. But I can only imagine. We cling to what is broken when we have no choice. Even love that tastes like poison, that presses like a blade on your throat, is better than gaping emptiness.

Khine placed his hand on my shoulder. I found myself turning around to gaze into his eyes. And I thought that if I could do this, if my heart was mine to give away and *tomorrow* was not a word fraught with burden…

He was reading my expression now. I wondered if he knew something I didn't. Eventually, he ran his thumb over my cheek. "Go to sleep," he repeated. "I will wake you when they return."

I didn't have it in me to argue. What else could I say that wouldn't make me sound like a desperate woman longing for something she couldn't have? I removed the shawl and stepped back inside the hut, willing my thoughts to leave me be. If only we could drift through life unfettered, and not feel. If only.

CHAPTER TWENTY-ONE

THE STREETS OF FUYYU

ʋɔ̃ʈʕ

That night, I dreamed of Thanh walking towards me with blood pouring like rivers down his face, his skin as white as snow. I woke up before I could reach him, grappling in the dark with a mouth that tasted like cotton. I spat to the side and tried to drown out the image with the thought that my son was still alive. He had to be. If anything had happened to him, they would've trumpeted the news from every corner of the nation.

Why did I think I could save him by myself? The terror was a cold hand around my throat, choking me senseless. Alone with my thoughts, I could almost admit that I wasn't sure what I would do once I returned to Oren-yaro. The survival of Thanh the *boy* seemed all but impossible between my husband and my own people's treachery. My eyes wandered over to the dagger beside the mattress and briefly considered if my own death would solve anything. Without *me* as the prize, Yuebek's claims would fall on deaf ears. Without *me* to blame, wouldn't Rayyel show mercy to the boy? He would be free to marry anyone, Chiha even. Perhaps he might even be generous enough to let Agos take Thanh away from court.

The temptation was strong. I picked the dagger up, running my hand over the length of it before I slid it out of its sheath. The sharp edge glinted in the dark with a sort of predatory smile.

I was Yeshin's daughter. The thought of death didn't scare me. My father had threatened suicide in front of his lords and officials before, the few times he didn't get exactly what he wanted out of them. I had already given birth—I figured the pain would be similar, though probably not as far-reaching. It certainly wouldn't hurt half as much as losing my son.

There were two gentle knocks at the door. I froze, dropping the dagger with a flush of shame. "We're ready to go, Tali," Khine called out.

I glanced at the window, noticed that the sky was grey. Dawn. "Yes," I managed to croak out. "I'll join you shortly." Shaking my head, I got up and returned the dagger to its sheath. The promise of sunlight brought a glimmer of hope. I didn't really want to kill myself. I wanted to see my son grow up—I wanted to hear his laughter again so badly that it hurt just to think about it.

But to have slipped so far that every step I took felt like a mistake, like I was sinking deeper into the mud, was not a good feeling. That the thought of rejecting my father's upbringing came with the rejection of the nation itself didn't seem like a coincidence. I was a dead woman walking. Was a dead woman worth risking my son's life for? It wasn't even much of a question.

I got dressed and followed the path out of the riverside hut. The fog had lifted, revealing much of the village that I hadn't seen the day before. It wasn't much more than a handful of small houses, separated by bamboo fences. The smell of chicken and pig droppings pervaded the air. Off in the distance, I spotted a log mill, the only structure of noticeable size in the vicinity.

I strode up to the mill and watched as the men pulled logs from a barge with a pulley and dropped them into a chute that led straight to a rusty circular saw. A man with a towel around his neck stepped out of the mill to wipe his face. He was shirtless, with a rotund belly that spilled over his trousers.

"Where do you deliver these?" I asked, pointing at the wrapped piles of sawed logs gathered on a platform a few paces away.

He turned to me and gruffly said, "*Those* in particular?"

I gave a small shrug.

"They're going to a builder outside of Fuyyu. Special order by his client—man wanted *narra* wood all throughout his house. Rich folks." He rubbed his moustache and sniffed to show exactly what he thought about such extravagance. I felt a pang of embarrassment—Oka Shto was decked with the beautiful red wood from top to bottom.

"May I ask about your delivery schedule?" I gave him the sweetest smile I possibly could.

He glanced back at his men for a moment before nodding curtly.

"We're travellers," I continued. "If you can bring us all the way to Fuyyu, I'll make it worth your while. There's three others with me."

He stared for a second. "You a royal?"

"No," I said quickly.

"You sound like a royal."

"How does one sound like a royal?"

"Like that." He sniffed. "And royals ask things like that all the time. Don't stop to think about what my boss will think."

"What *will* he think?" I asked.

The man paused for a second, scratching his belly while he thought. "Well, I don't know. He ain't here, so..."

"I've found us a ride," I told the others as soon as we met back in the village square. "They've got a delivery of lumber ready to go. It'll only cost us—oh, about a couple hundred *aekich.*"

"We don't even have ten left." Khine patted his pockets to emphasize his words. "Maybe if you gave me a bit of time to find someone to pilfer from..."

"Begging for transportation. Stealing. How far have we sunk?" Agos grumbled, a basket of rice cakes in his arms. I took one from him. Unwrapping the banana leaf covering revealed a flat, purple cake frosted with dried coconut and brown sugar. I hadn't eaten one of those in so long and I had to stop myself from cramming all of it into my mouth.

"And it's not like we can leave someone behind to work it all off," Khine said as we walked back to the mill. "Although if we *have* to, if we really have to, I think Agos would be happy to volunteer."

"I was about to say the same thing about you, Lamang," Agos growled. "They'd prefer you. You're fresh. Exotic."

"No, no, I do think they'd probably like someone more *seasoned.*"

"Did you just call me old?"

"I did no such thing."

"Maybe you'd like me to even out that cut on your head. Give you another."

"I was praising you, you big lump," Khine said in exasperation. We reached the mill, and he came up to the foreman with a big grin. "My dear man," he continued, patting him on the shoulder as if they had been friends forever. "I want to give you my most heartfelt thanks in allowing us to secure your carriage for transportation."

The foreman grinned. "Er, it was my...pleasure?"

Khine squeezed his arm. "If you must know," he said, lowering his voice to barely a whisper, "my lady here is on a secret errand. For her to ask your help at all is a great honour."

"Are you a foreigner?"

"We both are," he said. "Officials from the Empire of Ziri-nar-Orxiaro, sent by the Esteemed Emperor's Fifth Son, Prince Yuebek, himself."

It took a great deal of restraint for me not to choke on the rice cake. "Indeed," I said, after I swallowed the last of it down. "I wasn't truthful earlier because— well, you can understand why. Your assistance, you know, will be seen as a great thing by the Zarojo Empire." I dropped a few Zirano words into my speech.

The man narrowed his eyes. "So you mean I'm not getting paid now," he said.

I smiled. "Not immediately."

"So *no.*"

"My good man—" I reached for his other arm. Both Khine and I were clinging to him now. "Let's not make hasty judgments. It's not every day that an opportunity like this presents itself."

"Aren't we at war with your empire?"

"We are most certainly *not* at war with Jin-Sayeng," I said firmly. "If you must know, it is more than that."

"Indeed. Do you know that Queen Talyien will be marrying Prince Yuebek soon?"

I wanted to punch Khine in the face. Instead, I smiled even more, so much that my lips felt stretched out. "It's a big secret. You know how the queen has been having problems with her husband, Lord what's-his-face..."

"Lord Raiju," Agos said.

"Raikar," Khine corrected.

"Raijel," Cho chimed in, catching on to the joke.

The man cleared his throat. "Prince Yuebek," he repeated. "I think I've heard that name before. Funny I'm hearing it again."

The smile fell from my face. "You have?"

"Years and years back, when I was still a young man, some foreigners hitched a ride on the barge up to Yu-yan. Didn't mention anything about him marrying the queen, but one did brag about preparing Yuebek's kingdom for him. Laughed about it, too, like he wasn't even taking it seriously." He sniffed. "Just get in the wagon and try not to get into trouble." He stepped away from us quickly, looking like someone who had been badgered into something against his will. He returned to the building, grumbling under his breath.

"Must be those Zarojo mages," Khine said as soon as he was out of earshot.

"Not a stretch that Yuebek is behind them. But what would they mean by preparing Yuebek's kingdom? They came out here to assist the Anyus with the dragons. Not that the Warlord Ojika even wanted their help in the first place. Eikaro told me that his father's hand was forced under threat of..." I trailed off as a thought clicked solidly into place. *Yeshin knew Eikaro's secret. Did he hand that knowledge over to Yuebek? What for?*

I took a deep breath. No—I couldn't kill myself, not now. I needed to see my son safe, and my death would do nothing to protect him from my dead father, my husband, and Yuebek combined. Their plans had permeated the land, right down into its very crevices, and if I wanted to discover them, I needed to return to where it all began: back home to Oren-yaro, where my betrayers waited for me with open arms.

The transport wagon was drawn by four water buffalo—large, hefty creatures with enough strength to carry lumber down the rough southern road. One pressed its wet nose on my arm as we passed by, and I obliged by tickling it under the muzzle. As it stretched under my fingers, Khine laughed. "Do you remember the *rok haize* figurine you bought from that first shopkeeper we tricked?" he asked.

"Yes. I have it in my pack somewhere."

"It feels so long ago," Khine mused. We followed Agos onto the lumber pile, seating ourselves on the top of the sawn logs. It was the sort of dangerous arrangement that would've had Arro frothing at the mouth. I could hear his voice now, begging me to use my head, to *please* consider the consequences of my actions.

Ah, but Arro, I thought. *Did you know you would be killed in a private dining room half a world away?* I gazed out at the horizon as the drivers yelled at the beasts and we began to inch slowly along the road.

It was late at night when the workmen finally let us off at the main road about an hour's walk from Fuyyu. The stars and the moon had appeared, a blue haze over them. Tiny bats flitted over the trees.

Khine took a deep breath. "I can already smell the city."

I sniffed. There was a slight acrid tinge in the air. "They've got tanning factories at the outskirts," I explained. "The Kags prefer leather over woolen cloaks in the winter."

"How harsh are your winters here?"

"More rain than snow around these parts. In Oren-yaro, we get a few days of snow every year—still not as much compared with the regions near the mountains—the Ikessar lands, in particular. That's why they say the Ikessars took to studying and reading so much. Long winters, nothing else to do."

"How did the Ikessars come to power, anyway? You've painted them as a people entirely different from the rest of you. Without a sizeable army like the rest, what got them to where they are now?"

"Ah, a history lesson," I said brightly. "Agos, cover your ears."

Agos made a choking sound.

"You've seen what Rai was able to do in a matter of days," I continued.

"I find it hard to believe it had anything to do with his charm or...anything to do with him, really. Not that I don't like the guy, mind you—"

"Wait," I said. "You *like* Rayyel?"

"He's interesting. I've met worse fellows."

"You're an idiot, Lamang."

"And you were telling me a story. Let's not veer off course here."

I sighed. "Rai is reaping the benefit of hundreds of years of work by his ancestors. Back in the day, the Ikessar clan was just one of many, living in the mountains among Kibouri priests and monks and whatever else they had up there. Like all the major clans, they became well-known because of their connection with dragons. There were a number of famous dragonriders from the clan, most of whom served the warlord of the city of Darusu, which lay right at the base of the mountains in that region.

"The Ikessars also made a name in capturing and training dragons. For a time, the majority of dragons came from the eastern mountains—small, hardy creatures who were easily tamed, or so the texts say. There's still dragon-towers scattered among the villages in those mountains. So the lords from all across the land would come to take their pick of the creatures, and somewhere along the way a friendship between the warlord of Bara and the head of the Ikessar clan was formed. Warlord Luban, I think was his name; he brought the Ikessar clan chief to his palace.

"Now, I've got to confess that I don't quite remember the entire chronology of events. I know that this man, Chief…"

"R—?" Khine ventured.

"Ryar," I said with a grimace.

"Spirits, how do they keep track of everyone? At least without sounding like a spirits-be-damned pirate?"

"It's why I named my son *Thanh*," I replied. "I wasn't going to follow along with that madness."

"So instead you started your own? Talyien. Thanh."

I frowned at him. "Maybe you don't want to hear this story."

"*I* don't," Agos sighed.

"Please go on," Khine said with a grin.

"Chief Ryar quickly gained the reputation as a levelheaded, intelligent man. He was also a devout follower of the Nameless Maker and the prophet Kibouri. The land, which was suffering from all sorts of skirmishes among the warlords, greatly admired him. In the following years, an idea for peace was born: why not have *one* ruler? Someone wise and powerful, and more important—someone who posed no threat to the warlords who could put him in such a place."

"Let me guess," Khine said. "The Baraji warlord suggested this."

I was surprised. "You've been paying attention."

He bowed with false modesty.

"They did not want to use the word *king*, not directly. Such a word implied power and dominion over all. No, instead they chose to bestow the title *Dragonlord*, peacekeeper and uniter of the royal clans. *Dragon*, you see, because they chose Chief Ryar for this and he came from the dragon-lands of Darusu."

"There's people who will disagree with that explanation," Agos broke in. "Dragonlord. King. It was always the same thing."

"I don't see them around anywhere, so I'm telling this story the way I understand it," I snapped. "So. Not all the warlords agreed; I believe only half even attended the coronation of this so-called uniter. But the important part is that suddenly, *some* of the warlords were cooperating, which was something that the land had never seen before. They contributed coin from their own treasuries to fund the Dragon Palace in Shirrokaru, a small town on the shores of Lake Watu. Of course, most did it to further their own interests—to increase their influences and grow closer to Dragonlord Ryar.

"Except Dragonlord Ryar...wasn't that kind of man. It's funny to admit it, but it was clear why people found him endearing. He was kind to all but himself, and clearly more interested in working with the warlords to better the land than to seize power for his family. *Incorruptible*, the texts say. Warlord Tal of Oren-yaro, of course, didn't agree."

"Warlord *Tal*," Khine breathed. "I just realized. Gods, you people."

"*He* had clashed with Ryar from the moment he appeared in the Bara court," I continued, ignoring him. "Warlord Tal was always one step behind him, breathing down his neck. Nothing Ryar did was ever good enough."

"This story sounds oddly familiar."

I smiled. "Warlord Tal was one of those who refused to attend the coronation, finding the whole thing ridiculous, a sham orchestrated by the other warlords to seize more power for themselves. Nevertheless, the palace in Shirrokaru was built.

"Some of the warlords who opposed the Dragonlord banded together. Kyoorashi, Osahindo, and Natu gathered over three thousand soldiers and marched for Shirrokaru and the Dragon Palace. Dragonlord Ryar didn't have enough men to defend the palace and was forced to flee. He thought this was enough to dissuade the rebels.

"But the soldiers came anyway, and they ransacked the city. The Slaughter of Shirrokaru, the textbooks call it. What the soldiers did to the civilians was atrocious. Rape and murder, and even children weren't spared. You know how it was in Dar Aso? It was worse than that, and for what? Just to send a message to the others that they didn't agree with the idea of *peace*? Oren-yaro, the closest city, could no longer stand to listen to the stories of refugees as they rushed through our gates. Warlord Tal gathered what men he could and rode to liberate Shirrokaru. They caught the rebels unaware, entering the city through the sewers. And then they fought their way out, down to the last man."

"Five hundred against three thousand," Agos said. "The Oren-yaro legacy."

I couldn't tell if it was pride or scorn in his voice, and berated the interruption with a sigh. "Mind you, it was three thousand mostly *drunk* and unarmed men, caught unaware. A good number were enjoying themselves in brothels. I believe Warlord Tal released several dragons from the pits to spread chaos through the streets."

"I think you've told me part of this story before," Khine said. "This Warlord Tal was the last one standing when Dragonlord Ryar returned with reinforcements."

I nodded. "He finally conceded to the Dragonlord when he died. He wanted peace himself. Who doesn't? He wanted his son to inherit a land that wasn't drenched in blood." I fell silent as we approached the gates. There were guards checking the horde of newcomers. I tugged at Agos's arm. "Those don't look like Shirrokaru soldiers," I whispered.

"They don't," Agos said. His eyes focused in the darkness. "They're Kyo-orashi."

"They're not supposed to be there. Kyo-orashi has no authority in these lands."

"Well, they're there," Agos hissed. "Let's turn back before—"

"You!" they called out. "To the front of the line, now!"

I took a step back and glanced at my companions. If I could make a dash for the bushes, perhaps...

"There's archers on the towers," Agos hissed. "Don't do anything hasty."

"It's too dark," Khine replied. "Will they even hit us?"

"Oh, they'll hit you," Agos said through gritted teeth. "The Kyo clan have mastered the bow and arrow. You'll be riddled with arrows before you can take two breaths."

"What's this?" I said out loud as the soldiers approached us. "Mere travellers like us getting accosted by guards at night. Except—" I pretended to peer closely at the soldier's helmet. "You're not a guard. You're a warlord's soldier!"

"Smart woman," the soldier said, reaching for my arm.

I jerked back. "What happened to the city guards?"

"Quit your yelling, woman," the soldier snapped. "Haven't you heard? The Dragonthrone's in disarray. Nobody's sitting on it right now. The council has removed Queen Talyien from her position, but since Lord Rayyel has never been crowned—"

"We won't get very far if we explain the details to everyone," another soldier broke in. He looked like the other's superior.

The first soldier frowned before turning back to me. "You are *cordially* invited to Warlord San's palace, along with every woman travelling into the city. Don't worry. Warlord San merely wishes to ask you a few questions, and if he's satisfied, you'll be returned to Fuyyu on the next ship."

"And if I don't go?" I snapped.

The soldier gave an ear-splitting whistle.

I drew my sword just as more soldiers came around the corner, enough time to pin the first soldier against the gate with my left elbow. With my right hand, I slammed the hilt of my sword against his jaw. Before he could counter, I pulled his helmet off and struck him with it, hard enough to draw blood. He sank to his knees. In the meantime, Agos charged the officer—both men crashed to the ground.

"Into the city!" I ordered Khine and Cho. "We'll find each other later!"

Cho hesitated; Khine punched him on the shoulder to get him to move. They disappeared around the alley.

Agos got up before his opponent, and stabbed the officer through the throat. In the meantime, my soldier was still reeling from the head wound I had given him. I pulled out his sword and flung it straight into the path of the incoming soldiers before dragging the man to his feet, using him as a shield. I pressed my sword against his throat and whispered something into his ear.

"Stop!" he screamed.

To their credit, his friends listened.

"It's the queen, isn't it?" he asked me, his breath whistling through his teeth. "It has to be."

"How perceptive of you," I replied. I continued dragging him into the alley with Agos at my flank. An open sewer gurgled to my left, with a stench so thick it made me dizzy.

"Except they all say you're not queen anymore," the soldier said. "They say you—"

"Shut up."

"—can't keep your legs closed so—"

I struck his mouth with my sword handle.

"You can't kill me," he hissed. "You'll lose your hostage."

"You've got a bloated sense of your own importance here, soldier."

"So do you, Lady Oren-yaro."

"Why are you even here? Has the Kyo clan decided they're done sitting things out? Warlord San must have run out of entertainment in his fine castle."

We heard footsteps behind us.

"We don't have time for this," Agos snarled. "We have to run!"

I twisted the soldier's arm before shoving him into the ditch. He stumbled, falling face first into the dirty water. "My bloated sense of importance showed you mercy," I said. "Remember that, soldier."

He spat.

I turned to follow Agos around the next bend. "They'll be waiting for us when the street opens," he ventured. "Can we go up the rooftops?"

I glanced up. The walls were very high up here, with moss-covered stone. I tested the edge with the tip of my boot and swore as it slipped. "We're out of luck," I grumbled.

"Shit."

The soldiers were gaining on us. I swore again, turning around to meet them. There were two that I could see, though there might be more down the narrow alleyway behind them. "More coming down that end, too," Agos said, his back against mine. "Has your time in dragon country whipped you back into shape?"

"You talk like *you* haven't gained weight. Can you even see the ground from where you're standing?"

"Hey, now hold on, I didn't say you were—"

The soldiers charged.

I shouldn't enjoy fighting as much as I did, but it was easier to admit now. Fighting with Agos felt like a dance, a dance I was *good* at, and it felt like fire through my veins. It isn't that I don't feel fear during the process—that I don't worry about taking the wrong step, or neglecting to see a strike that would end it for me then and there. If anything, it was like wading into an ocean of uncertainty, a sensation that felt like I was hanging off the edge, with nothing to catch me below.

But every blow I dealt my enemies was a blow against those fears; here, with my oldest guard at my side, I wasn't striking at nothing. I wasn't helpless. I struck the sword out of one soldier's hand before I met the incoming attack of another. My blade grazed his side and I stepped away, letting him run straight into Agos's blade. He cleaved him from the neck down across his chest, almost splitting his torso in half from the strength of the blow as easily as a butcher's knife cracking a chicken. Kyo-orashi soldiers didn't wear much armour; maybe Warlord San would start seriously rethinking that after this.

Maybe.

An arrow struck my leg, lodging itself partway into the meaty part of my thigh. My breath turned into a scream. I doubled forward, heading for the archer, who was hiding behind a shrub, desperately trying to load another arrow into his bow.

The blow took me from behind.

When my senses returned, I was lying on the ground, drenched in blood. "Princess," I heard Agos whisper over my ear. I gazed up. We were in an abandoned house. Piles of stone and debris littered the ground.

I stirred, lifting my fingers, which were soaked in red.

"Not yours," Agos croaked. "I killed them all." His eyes were red, as if he had been crying.

I tried to get to my feet. He held me down, before pointing at my leg. The arrow was gone. "Wasn't a bad wound," he said. "But maybe you should rest it a little longer."

I tested the muscle. "It's nothing," I said.

"Still…"

"Agos. I'm fine."

He rubbed his forehead. "I know you're fine." But his face remained shadowed.

"Out with it," I sighed.

"It's nothing."

"Talk, Agos."

He looked like I was twisting his arm. "It's just that...how much *longer* are you going to be fine? Look at us. This is...this is pathetic. I can't protect you like this. No guards and four rusty swords between us, with two idiots who can't even hold a blade or throw a punch properly. I thought you were dead. That asshole—the one you spared—cracked a log over your head. Don't know how he got the jump on us. I cracked *his* head open but it was too late. Fuck, Princess. I try, but I don't know how much more of this I can take. I don't know how to keep you alive long enough to get to Oren-yaro."

"What are you saying?"

"Kaggawa's offer isn't too bad, is it?" he asked. "We just have to swallow our pride."

"I can't play politics while my son's life is in danger. That letter from the council—"

"It could be fake."

"Even if it is, the damage is done. Kaggawa will want me dancing to his tune all so he and that soul inside of him can quench their thirst for power. I won't entertain him further." I took a deep breath and tried to stand again. The cut on my leg didn't hurt much, and I could still put weight on it. I turned around to find my sword.

Agos handed it to me. "I can't protect you all the time, Princess," he said in a low voice.

"I don't need you to. It's not your job anymore." I paused for a moment, gazing at the pained expression on his face. "You're here as my friend. Can you do that for me, Agos?"

He looked confused. His eyes flicked downward. "I don't know how to be your friend anymore," he said at last. "It was different when we were children. Easier. Simpler. Your life wasn't in danger, then. Now it is—all the fucking time. And it's my fault, isn't it?"

"It's—"

"Before your wedding. I should have said no. Fuck. I should have refused. You gave me a choice. But the fucking idiot I was didn't know..." Agos shook his head slowly, his face flooded with discomfort. "Lamang, now, *he's* your friend. I know you've got with him what we used to—that you can be in his company and not be reminded of every chain and every lock of our damn lives. That's why he's here, even when he's barely keeping himself together. I didn't appreciate that before. Me, I'm just your guard now. I don't know what I am if I'm not. I told you. I'm no good at anything else, and even this I'm failing miserably at. I just...I don't know what I'll do if anything happens to you, Princess." With a sigh, he turned away and stepped through the cracked doorway.

I followed him wordlessly, both of us stumbling through the alleys like drunkards.

We had barely gone two streets down when we encountered more soldiers on the path. Agos fiddled with his sword; I touched his arm, imploring him to back down. There were too many, and I didn't have it in me to fight again so soon. He held his breath, his jaw tight.

"You're that troublemaker," an officer said, pointing.

"Spare my companion, and I won't resist," I replied.

The officer hesitated. But it was too easy of a catch, and I could tell he didn't really want Agos. He nodded. His soldiers stepped aside, giving Agos room to walk past them.

"I can't do this," Agos said. "I won't."

"You will. Go and find Lamang."

He conceded, though it seemed to take forever for him to turn around and walk away.

"Don't worry," the soldier said as they strapped chains around my wrists. "We're not barbarians. If anything, this is the most fun you'll have all week." I found myself being dragged down the streets.

CHAPTER TWENTY-TWO

THE WARLORD OF KYO-ORASHI

ༀ ༄ ༅ ༆

Kyo-orashi City lay at the tip of a peninsula somewhere in the middle of the coastline of Jin-Sayeng. It was a good few days' travel from Fuyyu, if the weather was fair. Not that I would know anything about the state of the wind or waves during that time. I was separated from the men and stuffed unceremoniously belowdeck with about thirty other women chained to each other, with only a single chamberpot shared among a number of us. I quickly lost track of time.

Most of it I spent in a trance, half-asleep, half-awake. It was difficult whenever the ship rolled and the women would strain at their chains or wail out loud, wanting to know the reason for their capture and why they were being treated this way. I was the only one keenly aware of our predicament. I was the reason for all of this, after all.

Not that I knew exactly why, but I could tell enough from the snippets of conversation I was able to gather from the guards. Warlord San, not liking the uncertainty surrounding the Dragonthrone during that time, had taken matters into his own hands. He had seized control of Fuyyu in order to find the queen himself.

Or so it seemed, anyway. After everything that had happened in the Sougen, I was no longer as sure of myself as I once was. Warlord San had always seemed harmless. A tall man, muscular, younger than most of the warlords—though he had at least two grown sons already—and with a booming laugh that could travel from one end of the courtyard to the other. He never took anything seriously, didn't attend meetings unless he had to, and went as far as to relinquish his offered seat in the council to his cousin Lady Esh. "I've got no head for ruling," he liked to brag. "If my father had given me a choice, I wouldn't have inherited Kyo-orashi. I'd have gone sailing."

Sometime during the first day of my imprisonment in the ship's hold, I pulled out Rayyel's letter to the Anyus, the same one he had sent out to every corner of Jin-Sayeng. I had kept it tucked in my pocket the whole time. I held it up to the porthole, under the shaft of sunlight, wondering why my husband would do something so drastic so quickly. As embarrassing as it was to admit it, such an impetuous decision was something I would've done.

I stuffed it back in my shirt and let out a sigh.

"From your lover?" the woman beside me asked.

I smiled at her, choosing not to answer. Not that she would've heard my response—from across the other end of the room, we heard a piercing scream as one of the women was unclipped from her chains. Two sailors tried to drag her up the ladder.

The other women grabbed her before they could get her up the first rung and reached out to attack the men. The sailors fought back with clubs and chains, but soon retreated to the deck without their prize. I didn't realize I'd been holding my breath until I felt myself sigh with relief.

"That's just going to keep happening until we get there," the woman beside me whispered. "Do they think they're going to get away with this?"

Yes, I thought. But I kept my mouth shut and my eyes downward. The woman found my silence uneasy, and shuffled close, her chains clinking against mine. "You're a strange one. You don't like it when people talk to you or something?"

"Oh, leave her alone," someone behind us piped up.

"I'm just trying to make our situation less miserable," the woman snapped. She turned her gaze back to me. "Look. Maybe you just don't like to talk to strangers."

I cleared my throat. "It's not that," I said.

"Well, there you go," she replied, her eyes brightening. "Not so bad, is it? How did these bastards get you, anyway?"

"Came in from the Sougen." I tried to keep the rough, rural slang in my voice. It was harder than I thought.

"I came to visit my mother-in-law, who works at the docks. If I knew this was going on, I would've just been a bad daughter and stayed home. You think they're serious about sending us home after Warlord San questions us? What would he want to ask us about, anyhow?"

"I think they're looking for the queen," another woman replied. There was a general buzz of assent.

"Whatever for?" the woman talking to me asked.

"Haven't you heard? She fucked around."

I had to let the rush of anger go right through me.

"We've been hearing that for years," someone else added. "Her guardsman, or something like?"

"Guards*men* is what I heard."

"And her husband got tired of it and complained to the council."

"Wait a moment," she said. "This the husband who's been missing for years?"

"I guess so," the other woman replied.

"So he's finally gone and shown himself. And the queen—she's still missing?"

A confused murmur.

"That doesn't sound right," the woman beside me continued. "You all know what this sounds like to me? Those damn royals are getting into a pissing match all over again, and we're caught up in it."

"Nothing new," someone agreed. "Not surprised. It's not like the queen's done any good this whole time. Having her as ruler was supposed to mean progress, but look. We're just as poor as ever, and the royals are still having their way with us. And I thought moving to Fuyyu meant I could put all of that behind me."

She shook her head. "It's gone too far. It's a fucking royal who's gone and taken us against our will. Like we'd know anything about the queen."

"Maybe Warlord San thinks the queen's among us."

She laughed. "Then he's deluded. Look at us! Any of you look like a queen?"

They began to laugh with her. I adjusted my chains and closed my eyes. I told myself there was no sense in getting angry. The women didn't know what they were talking about, and trying to correct them wouldn't do any good. If I couldn't even convince my own husband, what more strangers?

Numb it, I thought. *Numb the pain. Why are you so upset?* I must've known what being queen meant. My father had tried to prepare me. "*They will bring blades, Tali. And they will strike you everywhere it hurts. Don't let them.*" He used to say these things when I was going through my sword practice, so I thought he meant physically. It was only lately that I was starting to understand the layers in both Yeshin's words and actions, the tangled depths of his mind. They had all feared my father for a reason.

But the pain was still there, a drop of blood spreading like a cloud in a vat of water. If I was Yeshin's sword beyond the grave, what had I done wrong? Had it been up to me to decipher his cryptic plans even before I married Rayyel? Perhaps if I had been smart enough to learn of them in time, I could've avoided the whole thing. I wouldn't have married Rai at all. That my people still followed my father meant one thing, at least: they didn't see me as a capable leader. Everything I had done up to that point was not enough, not when you are one person struggling against the tide of thousands of others whose interests did not always align with yours. Even if you *are* a queen.

I mulled over these in the next few hours, the thoughts digging deeper than I expected them to. I kept thinking back to the courage I thought I'd found when I faced that dragon while trying to save Eikaro, and what had gone wrong. If I made the decision to be a queen on my own terms and not how my father and my husband wanted me to be, how would I go about it? *You'd first need an army*, I found myself thinking, falling back on the same old patterns my father had instilled in me. There was power in strength, in fear.

Except the Ikessars never needed either. Not the feeble regime that gave birth to the Shadows, but the old Ikessars, the ones who made Warlord Tal concede. *He wanted his son to inherit a land that wasn't drenched in blood.* My own words to Khine, coming back to haunt me.

The sailors tried to come back the next night. There were more of them now, blades instead of clubs in their hands. They pointed at the women who had fought back in the previous assault. As they came for them, I stood up. Amongst the throng of women who were now frightened into stupor, the clang of my chains was almost deafening.

"What do you want?" a sailor asked.

"I would like to speak to your captain," I replied. I felt a woman's hand on my leg.

"Sit down," she whispered. "What are you doing?"

"Let's end this," I continued as the sailor came up, his face twisted in disbelief.

"Think this one is volunteering," he sneered. He tried to grab me.

I struck him in the crotch with my chain. He jumped back, howling in pain. Another sailor came rushing to his aid and tried to frighten me by brandishing his sword. I looped the chain around the blade before he could bring it down and wrenched it off his hand. I tugged, and the blade fell to the deck, where I quickly grabbed it. I was still bound, but now armed. I grinned at them.

"Get her," the one on the ground groaned.

I now had their full attention. "Warlord San sent you on an errand that came with explicit instructions to *return* these women to their homes after his questioning. How do you think he'll react if he finds out you've been sampling them behind his back?"

"What's it to him?" one of the sailors spat.

"Everything, I would imagine," I said. "I know Warlord San doesn't like it when his men are presumptuous. You must be new to his employ. Where are the soldiers?"

"Soldiers promised to keep quiet," the sailor grinned. "We're not getting paid enough for this shit. Maybe if you bend over now—"

I shook my head. "You're still not getting it. Maybe the soldiers will keep quiet, but you don't think these women will talk? Do you even *know* how Warlord San will react if he learns you've tainted his *invitation*?" The women lifted their heads, and I turned to them briefly. "You all heard what the soldiers said when they took us in. Warlord San *does* intend to offer his full hospitality if we cooperate."

"This doesn't look like hospitality," the woman said, glancing around the hold.

"Of course it doesn't," I snarled. "I would assume he gave orders and these men didn't see them for what they are. Maybe you should go ask your captain. Go on."

The sailor lifted his fist. "Fucking bitch..."

"Fucking bitch has a sword and knows how to use it," I reminded him. "Maybe I'll ask him myself. You all went through this trouble to find a certain *someone*. I'll make this really easy for you. Take me to your captain now. Tell him you've found *her*."

——◆——

I wasn't sure if they believed me or thought I was just mad, a woman spouting nonsense to save her life. But they removed me from the hold—still in chains— and took me up to the captain's cabin. I had to give up the sword for them to agree to this, though it wasn't much of a loss, anyway. I didn't think the rusty thing would take two blows without shattering.

I ducked my head as they pushed me through the narrow doorway and slammed the door shut, leaving me alone with who I thought was the captain. The man turned at the sound of my arrival, and I realized my mistake at once.

It was Ino Qun.

"Ah," he said, holding out his hands. "The Bitch Queen comes home at last." He was seated near the desk, legs folded over each other. He smiled. "Although, forgive me if I'm getting it wrong, but aren't you lacking a title at this point in time? Your husband made an announcement regarding your infidelities, I believe. A grave accusation. Such a shame. And you were trying *so* hard."

I took one step towards him. "Don't test me."

"Test you? I'm not testing you, my lady. Although you're not a lady anymore, either, are you? No, the accusations were too harsh, and Warlord Ozo had no choice but to salvage your city, your lands, and your people for the good of the realm." His eyes twinkled.

I reeled back at his words. *Warlord* Ozo?

"Oh," Qun said. "You didn't know? How awful! Your own general, and a man your father trusted! And it wouldn't have been possible if the rest of your lords didn't agree! Well, no shame in being the last to hear the news. The report came right around the time we left for Fuyyu, at the heels of the council's stripping down of your title. Your nation has *very* interesting ways to do things. I'm sure you're dying to know what I'm doing in a Kyo-orashi-sanctioned ship, surrounded by Kyo-orashi guards."

"Not as much as I'm dying to strangle you to death with these chains."

"Such language." Qun shook his head. "You should learn by now I am not as easy to get rid of as so many others who had the misfortune of crossing your path. Did you think, for instance, that your little trick in An Mozhi would've worked for long? It was almost brilliant—using Lo Bahn to incriminate himself and drag *me* with him."

"It worked."

"So it did," Qun said with a grin. "But I think you were hoping for more, else you wouldn't be surprised. Ah, but what can you do? The word of a common thug, against the word of a prince..." His smile deepened, gleamed.

I knew there was no sense pretending as if none of this was happening. I kicked one of the spare chairs close to me and sat down on it, my chained hands on my knees. "How's Yuebek doing these days? His nose fall off yet?"

"He's at An Mozhi cleaning up after the mess *you* made. He entrusted me with preparing Jin-Sayeng for his arrival."

I crossed my legs, mirroring his posture. "And, er, how are you supposed to do that, exactly?"

"My, but aren't you chatty? It's nothing you need to concern yourself over. You're exactly where I need you to be."

"Let's imagine that I'm willing to entertain Yuebek's proposals," I said. "What's the point? You already know what's happening out here. No longer queen, and as you said yourself—no longer lady of Oren-yaro." I smiled, now. "An impasse, Qun. Your prince wants a pauper for his wife."

He cleared his throat. "Don't you think we know that?"

I stared back at him.

He turned around to flick the shutters open, letting a spray of sunlight into the small cabin. "Prince Yuebek's arrival, the ships we've chartered—these are, unfortunately, things not easily hidden, and smoothing things with Hizao was about all An Mozhi could talk about for weeks. Your husband Rayyel must've caught wind of everything and boarded a vessel ahead of me. His risky accusation was my welcome to these shores. To think that he would cut through you to get to us—"

"That's not what he did," I said.

"Isn't it?" Qun asked. "I was under the impression your husband was a careful man. Did this sound like something he would do?"

He was right about it, of course. I had thought as much back in the hold. The husband I knew would've waited until he reached the capital first. The letter also claimed council approval. But there was no way the council would've had time to approve such a thing unless . . .

Rai had lied through his teeth.

It sounded even more ridiculous now that I thought of it that way. In time, the council would catch wind of what he had done and punish him accordingly. Either he was counting on the fact that the majority of the council were Ikessar supporters and would allow such audacities to slip through, or he only cared what would happen *in the meantime.* If I was disgraced, Yuebek's claim was worthless. "Marry her then," they'd say while they squabbled over everything else. "What kingdom could you claim?"

I turned to Qun. It almost sounded like an excellent plan. Almost. Except Qun wasn't worried. He had the look of someone who was *daring* you to do better than your best just so he could show you what he had planned.

"You were telling me about Kyo-orashi," I said, trying not to let the panic creep into my voice.

"Ah, Kyo-orashi," Qun replied, settling into his seat with a satisfied smile. "Warlord San, for all his reputation, is a shrewd, reasonable man. We had him noted as a potential supporter, and we were right—and lucky enough that he was in Fuyyu the week we arrived. During our brief correspondence, we were able to formulate a way to not only flush you out of hiding—there were rumours that you were at the Sougen, and Fuyyu was naturally the easiest way to get back home for you—but begin the path to restoring your name just in time for the prince's arrival. What! You look surprised. Did you think we would wait for all of this to blow over?"

He clapped his hands. The door opened, and a soldier stepped in, bowing. "Unchain her," Qun commanded in deeply accented Jinan.

The soldier hesitated. "Are you sure, sir?"

"She's not going to try anything," he said with the confidence of someone who had never faced me with a sword.

I held out my manacles helpfully. The soldier held out a key and undid the locks as if he had been asked to pet a rabid dog. "You do understand what your cooperation means, don't you?" Qun asked as soon as the chains fell off.

Rubbing my wrists, I turned to him. "We've had this conversation before."

"So we have. I'm glad you remember." Qun crossed his arms. "You will be treated as befitting who you are, Talyien Orenar. Not that I would mind if you acted like a common criminal." He showed me his teeth to show exactly how much he would enjoy putting me in my place, just as he'd tried to do back in Anzhao.

———

The rest of the women were unloaded in the city of Natu and I was locked up in a tiny room in the upper deck, staring at the sea. My thoughts carried with them a potency that would've been dangerous if they had let me keep my sword. I wondered at how much easier the whole situation would've been if I had a loyal handmaid. If I still had Nor, even. She could've pretended to be me while I slipped away to rescue her later. The queens and princesses of old seemed to have no problem finding servants and dashing, charming princes who would stop at nothing to save them. Even someone like me, who had learned from an early age that life was not a fairy tale, had been swept away by such fancies. Most of us have. We want to believe that problems, once solved, pave the way for happily-ever-afters. We don't want to know that life is always going to be a stormy sea and that you're supposed to weather every wave until the waters consume you. Yeshin had been an old man, happily married with four grown sons. It should've ended there. Instead, he outlived them all. And someone who had been queen should've had more, shouldn't have felt so powerless, shouldn't have been alone.

But I was used to being alone.

I was used to staring at my reflection, my own dark eyes gazing back in silence. To the company of my thoughts, to conversation followed only by the echo of silence. It was no worse than what I had lived through during my childhood, when the palace staff and my father were too busy and I was ordered to stay in my room for days on end. I had learned later that my father intended it to teach me how to survive prison torture, that he had wanted to do more but Magister Arro somehow found ways to dissuade him. Well; it had worked for me back in Yuebek's dungeon, and this was luxurious compared with that.

Qun knew it wouldn't be enough to break me.

On the second night after we left the port at Natu, I woke up to knocking, and nearly bumped my head on the windowsill as I scrambled out of bed. And then I heard Qun. "I hope you're sleeping well, Beloved Queen," he said in a voice that indicated the complete opposite.

"What the hell do you want?" I asked.

"The captain said we should be at the next port in three days, if the weather remains fair."

I sucked in my breath, waiting.

He cleared his throat. "I do hope you continue to be on your best behaviour. I hate to think of what I'll have to do otherwise—like what will happen, say, to little Thani if you don't remain in perfect compliance. Tan? Your infernal names make me dizzy. Thanh! There you go."

"Qun, lay a hand on him and I swear to all the gods of this land you will not live to see the day."

I heard a muffled laugh from behind the door. "You threaten me as if you have a sword at my throat and not, proverbially speaking, the other way around. It's oddly amusing. I think it's because you know there's not much I can do to you while we're on this ship. If I said I could have the men take turns raping you, you'll probably just laugh and threaten to break their cocks off."

"How perceptive of you."

"And of course, my prince wouldn't appreciate that. He still wants to preserve whatever little…dignity…you have left." He chuckled once more. "Having said that, have I mentioned that some of my men have a fondness for little boys?"

I felt the blood drain from my face.

"Yes," Qun continued. "*That* would do it. He'd squirm, probably. I'm told they do that. So they'll have to break his arms and legs first, make it easier to stick it up his little bunghole. But no, you're thinking. They would never dare do such a thing to the heir of Jin-Sayeng! No. Have you forgotten that in the eyes of your whole kingdom, your boy is a worthless bastard? Nothing but a sack of meat, and by the time my men are done he'll have less value than the most disease-ridden whore in Shang Azi. It'll be a mercy to chop him up and feed him to the dogs, which I'm told you have more than enough of in Oren-yaro. Remember this on the off chance you're tempted to forget your manners, Beloved Queen. Do everything I ask and maybe you'll find the chance to redeem your boy from your debaucheries."

I heard him walk away, my eyes on the foaming waves as I imagined the things I would do to Qun in return for the things he had said. When we have nothing else, even despair can be a weapon.

The days passed. I woke up early enough to see the faint outline of the Orashi Peninsula on the horizon, marked by the tall cliffs that bordered the shoreline. The city of Kyo-orashi itself lay on top of a hill. With only three dragon-towers around the base of the tall, imposing palace, it looked like a lighthouse. Rai told me once that a lighthouse, indeed, was the inspiration for its design, and that in the days of the dragons their fire could light up the city so that you could see it halfway across the Zarojo Sea.

We docked at the harbour, about an hour's walk from the city gates. There were guards gathered at the far end of the platform when we arrived. They all stepped aside as we walked through, me one step behind Qun. As soon as we reached the sandy bar along the docks, we came face-to-face with the tall, imposing figure of Warlord San aren dar Kyo.

Boyish is perhaps the first word that comes to mind when you look at Warlord San. Though he was dressed every bit as a warlord, in full armour and helmet, the attire didn't seem to fit him. He smiled often, with wrinkles around his eyes to show exactly how such an expression had served him all his life. Despite his age, most of his hair was still black, though I had heard it uttered more than once that his women dyed it for him.

"We meet again, Warlord—" Qun began.

San walked right past him.

"Warlord San," I said, allowing him to take my hand. He pressed his lips over it. "You've been expecting me, then."

He laughed, pulling away to spread his arms in a warm gesture of welcome. "I did send a ship after you, didn't I?"

"And an entire hold of other women you were hoping might be me," I said. "Is one Lady Talyien truly not enough for you?"

"You know full well it's not," he said, using his most flattering tone. *Now* he turned to Qun, who didn't look too happy at being ignored. "Deputy," he began.

"Governor," Qun corrected.

"Ah. Indeed. Forgive my oversight."

My eyes flicked between their faces. Qun had his politician's smile on. San's seemed more genuine, but his eyes were distant, like he didn't really want to look directly at Qun at all. Blackmail? Yuebek's information on Jin-Sayeng must've been extensive. Did they unearth skeletons from Warlord San's closets and were now using this against him? Potential ally, indeed.

San made a sweeping gesture before leading us down the road to a restaurant overlooking the wharf, one that his ancestors had built long before they were ever recognized as a royal clan. His family had been running it for years. Their specialty was crab, which was hardly surprising. I had the satisfaction of watching Qun hesitate at the sight of the tray heaped high with cooked crabs, glistening orange and yellow—his fastidious native Zarojo ways didn't know where to start. In the meantime, I cracked a crab in half without missing a beat and drew out a piece of white meat, covered in the rich, yellow fat that lined the inside of the shell. A fat, happy crab—Kyo-orashi must've been blessed with a good season. I popped the meat into my mouth, followed by a pinch of rice and squash. It was heavy with the taste of the coconut cream they had boiled them in.

San smiled. "It's all delicious, isn't it?"

"Delectable," I said with a drawl.

"They're coconut crabs, fresh from one of the islands."

"Warlord San—"

He glanced at Qun before switching to Zirano. "You seem to think you're here against your will."

"I really wasn't given much of a choice," I said. "Isn't that right, Governor?"

"You wouldn't have come if we'd asked nicely," Qun scoffed. "You *do* have a reputation."

"And leaving you to be picked up by just about anyone, to be sent off to the

Ikessars, seemed a bit...unreasonable." San spat out a piece of orange shell and wiped his mouth. "It was *their* missing brat that you went to meet in the empire, wasn't it?"

"Brat—" I started.

"We're in Kyo-orashi, Lady Talyien," San said with a grin. "We can speak frankly, can we not? You *are* among friends."

"Am I?" I asked. "I seem to recall being trapped in the empire and not having a single soul come to save me. *You* certainly didn't."

He waved a crab leg at me. "While you were in the Zarojo Empire, I waited to see what the Oren-yaro would do—I didn't want to be blamed for *imposing*. You can hardly fault me for not having the sort of resources the rest of them have. Well, forget all of that. You're here now, aren't you?"

"You undermined Fuyyu authority."

"I did! Not that the Fuyyu guards had any sort of authority without a Dragonlord on the throne. I told my men to point out this little fact when I ordered them to march for Fuyyu, and considering there was no reported bloodshed, I'm sure the city guards were more than happy to step aside. You can punish me for it later." His eyes twinkled. "This meeting with Prince Rayyel—I suppose he didn't get what he wanted, else he wouldn't have started accusing you like he did."

"You could say that." I gathered rice and squash between my fingers and took another bite. From the corner of my eyes, I observed Warlord San's expression. He had turned away from his food to look out at the shore.

I wiped my fingers on the wet cloth beside me. "Let's not mince words, Warlord San," I said. "Why am I here?"

San smirked underneath his thin black beard. His small eyes seemed to smile with the rest of him. "I signed the pact to put you on that throne." He bared his arm, revealing a long scar from his wrist down to his inner elbow. "You could see I was rather enthusiastic with the blade."

"So it looks like."

"The point—" Qun said.

San snarled at him. "I was getting to that. Look, Lady Talyien. I'm not in any sort of hurry to throw the land back into the days of the Ikessars. I'm a traditionalist, and the Ikessars entertain too many strange ways—ways that have been curbed ever since your father's little war."

"I see." I glanced at Qun. "And what was the dear governor's idea?"

By now, the crab on his plate was nothing but a pile of orange shells, piled higher than the candles around us. San flicked his fingers and grinned. "A chance to gain some respect back, to remind the land who you *truly* are. Not Prince Rayyel's forlorn wife, brooding with her infidelities, but Yeshin's bitch pup, all grown up."

CHAPTER TWENTY-THREE

THE KYO-ORASHI
ARENA

ᴛ ɪ ໑

The expression on my face, more than making San think that he had crossed a line, only seemed to amuse him further.

"Are you suggesting war?" I asked. "The Zarojo and Kyo-orashi..."

"And Oren-yaro," Qun said, uncrossing his arms.

My nostrils flared. "And you really think I'd *agree* to this?"

"Prince Rayyel has forced our hand, Lady Talyien," Qun replied with a smirk. "Believe me, it wouldn't have come to this if you had only abandoned him *then*. Look where it got you."

I bristled, turning to San. "You'd agree to this. You'd let us ally ourselves with the Zarojo—"

"As we *once* did," San said with a snarl. "Do you remember, Lady Talyien, how we *used* to be allies? And how prosperous Jin-Sayeng was in those days? The Ikessars meddled, and look what it got us."

"Rest assured," Qun added. "We are not riding off to war. Not yet. First you need to show your nation that you are in fact alive and very much worthy of the throne, and not crawling around *begging* for help, as it were." He gave another smug smile. Gods, but I wanted to wipe it off him, with my bare fists if I had to.

"Don't presume to tell me what my nation needs," I said in a low voice.

"Temper, my lady," Qun crooned. "I thought we had an understanding."

"You've heard of my arena," San continued with a cough. "I believe I showed you the plans a few years ago. You even praised the design and my architect's ingenuity." He cleared out part of the table and began making a reconstruction using crab shells.

"I remember," I murmured, forcing my attention away from Qun towards him. "For horsefights and *Karo-ras* tournaments, you said. What of it?"

San rubbed his jaw thoughtfully. "I may have expanded on that. You see the sides here? Seats for over three times what I wanted before. We built it right across the palace where the barracks used to be. Didn't think the guards needed all that view, anyway. We hold more than horsefights here, my lady."

"What Warlord San is trying to so eloquently say," Qun said, "is that you need a glorious return to Jin-Sayeng's public eye. War is *not* just about who has the most powerful forces. If we don't sway the public, how much support would we get from the rest? You need to convince them that you are worth the trouble—that your defiance of the Ikessars comes from within."

"And so what—you want me to put on a show?" I nearly laughed in outrage. "Hack my way through—what? A select force of your fighters, hand-picked? Do you want me to wear a blindfold and wave a wooden sword around?"

"Not quite," San said. "Though the picture you painted *would* be amusing."

"In case the expression on my face isn't clear enough, my lords, I am far from amused."

San smiled. "If we announce an alliance with the Zarojo, we are making a pact to return to tradition, to the roots that gave this nation strength. *Traditionally*, warlords got their titles by proving their worth in battle, or at least a worthy pursuit of some sort. Back in the day, most of this involved dragons. Chief Ryar won the hearts of the people not only by being part of a clan well-known for raising and training dragons, but also by being a renowned dragonrider, one who tamed his dragon himself. A worthy feat in all of Jin-Sayeng's eyes."

"Your clan was one of those who rebelled against Chief Ryar's position as Dragonlord."

"Of course we did," he replied brightly. "The Kyo clan didn't worship dragons like the rest of you did. They had their uses, of course, but we saw them for what they were: beasts of burden, nothing more. Do you not see how

Kyo-orashi soldiered on while everyone else in the east crumbled? We didn't pin our hopes and dreams on the existence of dragons.

"But still, we understood the significance. After your own glorious ancestor chastised mine severely, our clan came to realize how dragons can symbolize power, and why someone like Rysaran the Uncrowned could become so convinced that simply owning one would mean the difference between life and death for the nation."

"Not that I don't agree with you, Warlord San," I said. "On any other day, I'd even drink with you on it. But today, I just feel like you're making a joke at my expense. If your soldiers hadn't confiscated my sword, you'd both be dead on top of those shells."

San whistled for a servant. "The lady requires her blade," he said.

I struggled to keep my mouth shut as the servant rushed out. She was back before I could form any coherent thoughts, all but tripping on a chair in her haste to deliver me the proffered item. It was the Zarojo sword Agos had stolen from the temple and gifted me for my nameday.

Expecting a trick, I took it with shaky fingers. I drew it from the scabbard and observed that it had been cleaned and sharpened. There was also a fresh coat of oil on the leather hilt, likely applied while we were having our meal. I wiped my hands on my trousers and glanced back at San, who was still grinning. "Well," he said. "You were just speaking about running me through."

I flushed as my bluff was called out. "You've got my attention. What do you want?"

"Since you're so kind to ask, about two or three women with alabaster skin and luscious red lips—"

I sheathed the sword. "Don't be ridiculous."

"You're right. At my age, maybe just two—"

"Let's start with the dragons," I said. "Do you want me to tame one?"

"Don't be absurd," Qun drawled.

San grinned. "Tame? Ah—you've just come from the Sougen. You've been talking to the Anyus." He waved his hand. "Nothing so drastic, I assure you. We caught a dragon wandering out along the plains some time ago. Not a huge thing—small, but vicious enough. Rysaran would've gone into convulsions if he had seen the thing. I simply want you to slay it."

A few ready responses flittered through me. I settled on the most diplomatic one. "You buffoon."

"Careful there," San said, lifting one brow. "People may think you're being unreasonable."

"You're the one who just asked me to slay a dragon for entertainment!"

"And you're the one in my lands," he reminded me coolly. "Let's not split hairs over this. It's not a big creature. It could maybe fit in—oh, that kitchen over there. With the kind of training you Oren-yaro go through, I'm sure it won't be a problem. We'll provide you with all the weaponry you need."

"How about twenty archers equipped with the largest bows you can find?"

He smiled. "One-on-one combat."

"I'm sorry—*buffoon* was too kind. You're both madmen."

San chuckled. "I've been called worse things. Look, Lady Talyien. I'll be honest with you. I have no desire to keep you here any longer than I have to. Once the word gets out, sooner or later one of the other warlords or even your own vassals from Oren-yaro will come riding in to rescue you. Dying in a sea of blood is on the bottom of my priorities."

"It won't come to that if we play our cards right," Qun said. "Kill this dragon. And then declare war on the Ikessars."

"And you've got enough men to hold against every warlord who desires to contest us?" I replied.

"With Kyo-orashi and Oren-yaro forces backed by Prince Yuebek, the land will fold in a matter of time."

"I see," I said, glancing at Warlord San. He was chewing his moustache as Qun spoke. "You're prepared for this, I suppose. These reinforcements won't come overnight. Or have you grown fat and senile over the years?"

San didn't even flinch at the insult. "I like you, Lady Talyien. Always have. Have I ever shown you anything but honour and respect in the past? When Prince Rayyel abandoned you for reasons unknown, I kept my mouth shut, choosing to let you prove yourself as a capable ruler in your own time. Oh, they all had their misgivings, and I wouldn't be lying if I told you more than half of your lords have been sitting on the sidelines, waiting to see you fail. But while others may disagree, your rule has been good for me. Profitable, even. Our apiaries have been yielding good honey, and our fishing boats have returned full every season. Clearly, the gods favour you. Yes—we will throw our swords behind *you*." He said this looking straight at me, with nary a glance at Qun.

I very nearly laughed. "*Me*. Are you sure, Warlord San?"

He gestured at my sword. "But first you must prove your worth. Slay the dragon."

I shook my head. "Madman," I repeated.

"In this land, we are all mad," he replied. "You want to know how your father nearly won his war? He was madder than the rest of us put together."

"A dragon." I smiled. "All right," I finally said. "But you better hope I die quickly, because if I live to sit on that throne again, I may just have your head for this insolence."

His reply was a booming laugh, one that could've been heard across the sea.

——◆——

The prospect of facing a dragon shouldn't have scared me as much as it did. I had faced too many in the last year alone, and managed to survive every encounter with all my limbs and my sanity intact. But you don't live through dragon attacks only to throw yourself at yet another. I would have been perfectly happy never meeting the damn creatures again in my life.

My unease was multiplied by Qun's presence and because there was no one I could turn to who didn't seem to have his own hand in the rice pot. Warlord San might have claimed I was a guest, but he had certainly done his part to make sure his servants kept quiet about my arrival in the region. No fanfare greeted me in Kyo-orashi. In fact, we waited until it was late at night to stride through the gates, and the guards who met us seemed to avoid looking at me altogether. Rumours of where I really *could* be still permeated the palace gossip. The very servants who led me to my room were talking about how there had been sightings of me in Kai to the northeast, or even up in the islands of Meiokara.

But at least I had a room, where clean clothes were laid out for me. Another servant arrived to take me to the baths. I had not had luxury of that sort for months—Dai Kaggawa's people, perhaps surprisingly for someone as prosperous as him, washed themselves with cold water straight from the pump—and I allowed the servant to strip me down and scrub me from head to toe. Under orders by Warlord San, no doubt. She didn't refer to me by name, but I suppose it was enough that I was a royal.

I returned to the room, where the servant left me to dress myself. I recognized the view from the window—a small outcrop of islands in the distance—and realized that this was the same room I had stayed in the last time I was here. Back then, there had been a feast—one of the warlords had casually mentioned Rai and harsh words were exchanged. I remember leaving Arro behind and storming up here while my handmaids walked on eggshells around me. "Will you be returning to the party, my queen? Will you require a change of jewellery?"

I had sent them out with a roar before locking the door, which did little to dampen the music below. Later, Arro came by, announcing his presence with three knocks. "Are you well, my queen?" I never thought about it then, but he always said *queen* differently. Most people said it with respect; Arro said it with love.

"No," I remember replying.

He opened the door, shuffling inside with small steps. "Well," he continued after gazing at me for a moment. "You *look* well. I suppose that's all that matters tomorrow morning, when you have to face them again. You *are* aware that Warlord Graiyo enjoys irritating you. Try not to give him more ammunition."

"How am I supposed to do a good job of this when people don't even start by giving me a chance?"

Arro was silent for a few moments. "The problem," he finally replied, "is in thinking that you are entitled to chances. You do or you don't, my queen."

"And if I don't?"

"If you don't," he said, "you die trying." He was a true Oren-yaro, Arro, even though he was half a foreigner and his mother was a Kaitan. I should have never let him die.

But did you ever consider that I would die trying by dragon-fire, Arro?

I went to bed, wrapped up in silken sheets while the sound of the waves crashed on the cliffs underneath me.

A servant came by the next morning. I washed my face in a basin, changed out of my sleeping clothes, and was led out of the hall, where another servant appeared to ask how I would like my breakfast. I asked for a drink of water and nothing more. The last thing I wanted was to be heaving my guts out in front of an entire arena.

They gave me herbal tea instead, to calm me. Maybe Warlord San was being presumptuous—I didn't think I *looked* nervous. Afterwards, they brought me to the armoury, where I spent the better part of the hour looking through various pieces. The image of a dragon crunching through a thick piece of scale armour and then leaving me to bleed inside a cage of sharp, twisted metal made me recoil towards the leather. I needed maneuverability, anyway. There was no sense trying to meet a dragon's attack head-on—avoidance was my best defense.

For my weapon, I picked a spear and kept my sword. I lingered at the selection of bows, the craftsmanship of which was one of the things the Kyo clan prided themselves with. Dropping a dragon before it got close to me would be nice, but I had never been a good shot. Making a fool of myself by fumbling around with a bow and arrow—especially in front of this crowd—was probably not what San had in mind.

No, I told myself. *You have to face the damn thing.* Not that I put much thought on Warlord San's rationale—a leader should be able to command respect, dragon or no. How often had my father preached against the sort of madness that consumed Rysaran? Still, San had promised a small dragon, one that would've been weakened by its time in captivity. Certainly nothing compared with the wild dragons I had faced in the Sougen. I just needed to use my wits, control my nerves, and use my surroundings to my advantage. Perhaps I could trap it somewhere. I knew now that it needed momentum while in the air to stoke the flames inside its belly, so if I could keep it grounded, pin it down the way I did last time, I might have a chance.

I reconsidered my equipment and took an extra spear.

Warlord San's people had been thoroughly informed of the whole situation. Every step seemed rehearsed. No one made small talk around me or even questioned what was happening. From the palace, they led me down a long, narrow hallway, which opened up into a stone tunnel. The far end was lit with torches. A guard came up to check my equipment and to ensure that my armour was strapped on properly. From behind the giant wooden door, I heard the thunder of what sounded like thousands of people cheering.

"Warm-up sessions," the guard said to my confused expression. "Don't worry—you're the main attraction. Shifted in at the last moment. We didn't think anyone would actually take it. I know the prize money is big and all, but a dragon! You're a braver woman than most."

I gave him what I thought was my most foolhardy smile. "Maybe I just don't know enough to be scared. Have you seen it?"

He patted my shoulders. "I saw the first. Bony little thing—not much fit for a battle. It's been sick the last few days. Good thing we found a new one before Warlord San found out, especially now that we've learned he actually got someone to take the offer—"

"Wait." I grabbed his arm. "What do you mean a *new* one?"

The guard clinked his helmet. "The first dragon wouldn't eat. Wolves and wildcats have no problems feeding on carrion, but I think it wanted clean prey. It's been listlessly lying at the end of its chain—can barely move—and we didn't want to tell Warlord San until we found a replacement. As luck would have it, they found this new one wandering around the foothills near Natu. They brought it in just this morning."

"And you haven't exactly seen this other dragon?"

"No. But I wouldn't worry—the men said it was big and vicious enough. You'll have plenty enough beast to sate your lust."

"That's not really what I was worried about."

A gong sounded from the arena. "That's your signal," the guard said, stepping to the side to lift the bar. "May the gods keep your sword sharp and your aim steady." Before I could say anything else, they pushed me through. I heard the doors slam shut behind me.

The sun was in my eye. I lifted my hand to shade my sight and realized I was now standing on one end of a rectangular pit, covered with a near-transparent roof membrane of some sort. The crowd was seated above me from every corner. At the far end was a closed platform, where I could make out the figure of Warlord San as he stood on the edge of the railing, arms outstretched.

"And now, to grace our arena and attempt to slay a dragon to prove her worth," he said, his voice booming, "may I present Lady Talyien aren dar

Orenar, rightful ruler of Oren-yaro and claimant to the Dragonthrone, *council be damned*." He turned to me with a grin.

The crowd fell silent.

It was the absurdity of the situation that caused it. Under any other circumstances, I could tell that they would've been inclined to disbelieve it. Right behind Warlord San, Qun was sitting as an honoured guest in a semi-closed platform with his soldiers. I also spotted a few robed lords among the crowd, most of them very close to the front. Only the banners of Natu and Meiokara, Kyo-orashi's neighbouring cities, floated above the seats, which meant that Warlord San hadn't planned this more than a few days in advance.

The certainty, even amusement, in his voice said it all: it was his plan to reveal me as a surprise all along. The queen of Jin-Sayeng's triumphant return after slaying a dragon—and who else was responsible for her rise to glory but the Warlord of Kyo-orashi himself? Absurd *and* brilliant. I was starting to think that madness was a necessary component for a successful ruler. It certainly seemed to work for Yuebek. I wonder if Qun was aware of all of this. I doubted it—he wasn't Jinsein. San's subtle manipulations would've flown over his head completely. No—Qun wasn't as much in control as he thought he was. San was playing him somehow.

The thought gave me renewed energy. I hefted the spears in my hand and made my way to where the royals could see me better. I wasn't wearing a helmet, and the royals among the crowd recognized me. The silence turned to cries of outrage. The royals began to demand San remove me from the arena at once.

"My lords and ladies of Kyo-orashi!" I called out. "Why the pandemonium? Do you not want to see me crushed between the teeth of a dragon this fine morning?"

I clambered up the stone platform nearby, one of the many scattered among the pit. The steps were already slick with blood from the earlier fights. "My lords and ladies of Jin-Sayeng," I continued, the words bubbling through my throat as if they had a life of their own. "Is this the best greeting you could give the queen *you* chose? I spent months trapped in the Empire of Ziri-nar-Orxiaro with no assistance from any of the royal clans. Yet here I am now, ready to kill a dragon to prove to you that I am more than what you say I am. More than Lord Rayyel's unfaithful wife, more than Warlord Yeshin's bitch whelp! At least stay and watch the show! Warlord Graiyo!" I lifted my spear and pointed it at the audience.

The pale-faced warlord of Natu turned on his heels. His wife, whom I recognized by the atrocious amount of paint she loved to apply, gawked at me.

"You would turn your back on me?" I asked, feigning shock.

"Enough of this farce, this play, *whatever this is*. You are *not* queen," Graiyo replied. "I don't know why Warlord San would go to such lengths, but it's no matter to me. The council wants you. I intend to send a message to inform them of your presence in this city at once."

"And here I thought you'd be the first to want to see me fed to a dragon," I said. "I'll be gone by the time the council gets here, one way or another. Unless—" I stabbed the spear in the air. "Perhaps you'd rather fight me yourself?"

"Don't be ridiculous," Graiyo snorted. "We all know the *Lady* Oren-yaro is an unrefined, uncouth woman who would be more at home on a battlefield with her *soldiers*." He laughed. A handful of his lords and ladies followed suit.

"Warlord San himself reminded me recently that in the old days, a warlord achieved his position by proving his worth in battle," I said. "Of course, Warlord Yeshin's treaty with the Ikessars was too effective. It seems as if most of you have gone fat and soft."

This time, it was San's booming laugh that echoed through the arena. "Oh," San managed, after regaining his composure. "Do take the challenge, Warlord Graiyo. A duel would be most welcome on this fine day."

"I've been wanting to beat that golden helmet into your skull for years," I added.

"I refuse to entertain this nonsense," Graiyo hissed. He started to walk away again.

"If I'm at home on the battlefield, then let it be said that Warlord Graiyo belongs in a dress shop!" I called to his retreating back. "And Akaterru knows, it would still be an insult to the seamstresses!"

The crowd parted as Graiyo and his retinue disappeared through the doors. I turned back to the remaining royals. "One down," I said. "Any of you want to try your luck here with me?"

They stared in silence. If *madness* was the route I was going for, I was doing a damn good job. The fear in their eyes had a touch more panic than usual.

"If we're done talking...," Warlord San broke in.

"I'm bored. Bring the bastard out," I droned.

San nodded towards his guards. The gong sounded a second time. I checked my spears and my sword, noting that somewhere during the entire process of addressing Warlord Graiyo and the rest of the crowd, my fear had all but dissipated. My every movement was smooth, unhampered by nerves, and I was almost excited to see the dragon.

I heard gates creak open from the far end. The dragon came barrelling like a bull and my heart sank.

It was Lord Eikaro.

The black dragon was gaunter than the last time I had seen him, as if he hadn't eaten since. I felt my whole body grow limp. The spear I had been holding with confidence this whole time suddenly felt like a red-hot poker. I wanted to drop it—I had no desire to kill Lord Eikaro, not after what he had done for me. Not for a mere throne.

I made my way down the steps to meet him. "My lord—" I began.

The dragon continued running towards me with an open mouth. I swung my spear out, dodging just in time. He crashed into the platform, sending loose rocks spraying. He turned.

"Lord Eikaro!" I called out again. I could barely hear myself above the sound of the cheering crowd. The dragon snapped his teeth, black scales quivering. I knew I wasn't mistaken—it was the same dragon, that very same head. Only...

His eyes were black.

They had been yellow with black slits when this body contained the original dragon and the corrupted soul, and then brown and human-like when it was Lord Eikaro speaking to me. Now they were just black, and I gained the impression that he wasn't seeing me so much as he was reacting to my presence.

I made an arc with my spear and began to walk around him. He watched me like a wild animal, a creature wary of a hunter who had dared step too close, before he spread his wings and flamed. It was a weak fire, no bigger than a torchlight; I rolled out of the way and half-heartedly jabbed at his exposed belly with the tip of the spear. He smacked the weapon with such force that it broke.

The crowd cheered louder.

I was down one spear now, and I still had no plan. I managed to avoid the dragon's tail and found myself standing close—too close. His jaws came snapping again and I hurled myself onto the familiar shape of his back.

He flapped his wings and tried to make his way to the ceiling. My body swayed with the motion and I felt as if a club had come swinging down on my skull. I tried to gather my senses, grabbing onto the scales of his neck for dear life just as he reached the end of his chain.

"Eikaro," I tried again, getting close to his head. I thought that if he heard my voice, it would be enough. "Eikaro, it's me, Talyien. Snap out of it, Eikaro. Remember? You said you were going to fight it. Lord—"

The dragon turned his head and grabbed me by the shoulder, his teeth catching on the cloth of my sleeve. He flung me halfway across the arena. I crashed into the ground. If he had been flying any higher, I would've smashed into a thousand pieces. Not that it didn't feel like it. I struggled to get up, but my body wouldn't cooperate. I glanced down and realized the dragon's teeth had punctured my flesh. The jolting pain was spreading throughout my arms and down my fingers.

But there was no time to think about the damage it had caused. The dragon had returned to the ground and was lumbering towards me once more. I forced myself to draw my sword. Even just wrapping my fingers around the slippery hilt felt difficult—I could feel the blood pulsing around the swollen flesh on my shoulder, and my fingers were tingling. I faced the realization that there was no way on earth I could fend off another attack. My mind began to run through my decisions. Couldn't I have tried something else? Had I really come out here just to die?

The crowd's roar had become deafening.

I took a step back, keeping my eye on the dragon's jaws. My head was spinning. I felt like if he didn't kill me in the next instant, I was going to black out, anyway.

The gong sounded a third time. The ground began to shake. Before I realized what was happening, bars shot up from the floor just as the dragon lunged at me. His body battered on the iron barrier.

Although I had been trained never to turn my back on an opponent, I found myself gazing up to Warlord San for an explanation.

CHAPTER TWENTY-FOUR

THE PRICE OF LOYALTY

The Lady Talyien fought bravely!" San called out. "I think none here will dare contest that. She faced an attack head-on, bearing the dragon's savagery on her body, and yet she still stands."

The crowd cheered. Behind me, the dragon hissed as it tried to claw its way through the bars.

"But shall we let her fight on?" he continued. "She is tired, she is injured, and she is more than horribly outmatched. Is a warlord ever expected to fight alone? Is he not supposed to have blades at his side—guards to protect him, soldiers to die with him?" Now he faced the audience, holding his hands up in the air. "Is there anyone willing to face the dragon as the lady of Oren-yaro's champion?"

The crowd began to clap—not the torrent of applause, but a low, steady clap, like the pounding of battle drums. Someone was walking towards the royals' platform. San dropped one hand, holding the other out, and the crowd fell silent.

"I'll do it," the figure said.

A wave of anguish tore through me as I recognized Khine's voice.

"A brave, loyal servant." San didn't even sound surprised. "You'll fight for this woman? You could die out there."

Khine turned his head. I almost caught sight of his smug smirk. "No better death than to die for her."

Qun looked outraged as the crowd began to cheer, though he remained glued to his seat. I realized what Warlord San had done—what he and Khine were *both* doing. Throwing me at the dragon had never been the plan. It was a trap—they only wanted it to look like I meant to fight it before stopping me at the last moment. And then...

"You fucking idiot!" I yelled in Zirano. I didn't know if he heard me. I started to walk back towards the platform, but more bars appeared around me, caging me like a rat in the middle of the arena.

Khine clambered down from the platform and marched across the field. There was a spear in his hand—a glaive, really, heavier than the ones I had picked—and a look of grim determination on his face. "You're struggling to hold that weapon properly. Stop flattering yourself," I snarled as he walked past me. "You can't even face Agos without splitting your head open!"

"Exactly why I think I'll survive this," Khine replied. "Agos, dragon, what's the difference?"

"Go back there *now*. Of the two of us, I'm the one more likely to get out of this alive."

"Considering you're all chewed up—"

"You're going to get chewed up a *lot* faster."

"I'm touched by your concern, my queen. I'll cherish it to the grave."

"This isn't a joke!" I reached through the bars to grab his elbow.

Khine's expression softened. "I am a starving con artist from Shang Azi. What value does my life have compared with yours? What you are, what you can accomplish—"

"Don't talk like everyone else," I hissed. "You're the one who's been lecturing me about lives having the same weight this whole time. You—"

"We assign value to lives whichever way we want. To a mother, her own child's life is easily worth hundreds. My own life, to yours?" He placed a hand over mine. "Consider me a soldier willing to give it all up for his liege lord. They certainly will." He jerked his head over to the crowd.

I refused to let go of his arm. "It's not like that. You know it's not like that. But if you want it that way, then we'll do it that way—I *order* you to go back."

His eyes crinkled. "Like you said." And then, taking my hand in his, he lifted it up and kissed it.

Even knowing it was all an elaborate act, that he was mimicking the highest Jinsein gesture of respect, I felt the heat creep up my cheeks. It was only slightly less distracting than that gnawing irritation over what he had done. He pulled away from me and held his spear aloft, signalling to Warlord San. An idiot, through and through. If his sisters were here, they would've gone into hysterics.

The gong sounded. A portion of the bars separating us from the dragon dropped. I was still caged, but Khine was now free to approach it.

The irritation turned to fear. Real, tangible fear, the sort I didn't realize I could experience in my life. Even fighting our way through Yuebek's dolls had been straightforward next to this. Here, I was suddenly a helpless spectator, watching a man I had come to care for—a man who loved me, for all the uncertainty that knowledge created—about to face a dragon on my behalf. I had known girls who longed for such things, who would swoon over such a passionate act. I might have once been one of them. But the selfishness of the notion struck me now. This was not the rose-tinted atmosphere of a dream. Everything about this—the smell of blood in the air, my racing heart, the feel of the ground disappearing from under my feet—came straight out of a nightmare.

The dragon charged.

Khine moved faster than I had given him credit for. Everything that had led up to this moment may have been fabricated, but the look of concentration on his face now seemed real enough. He stepped to the side, keeping the dragon's jaws away from him with the tip of his glaive. The dragon stared back at him, throat membranes quivering.

They circled each other until Khine found himself with his back to the wall. With a sudden spark of intelligence, the dragon chose this moment to lunge a second time. Khine managed to avoid him again—the dragon smashed into the wall, cracking it slightly. The dragon recovered quickly, pushing up against the stone to chase after Khine.

It turned not into a battle, but a game. The prospect of attack never even seemed to enter Khine's mind. He fell into trying to avoid getting ripped apart in the first place—the dragon gave no quarter, and was now almost relentless in his pursuit compared with how he had been with me. It was small comfort. I didn't want to see Eikaro killed, but neither did I want him spared in exchange for Khine's life.

They reached the far corner of the arena, where I could hardly see what was happening. But then I heard the crowd give out a cry. I dashed to the edge of my cage and caught a glimpse of the dragon's jaws around Khine's weapon. The thicker, stronger shaft of the glaive seemed like it was holding up to the dragon's assault.

The dragon's tail curled back. A memory of the attacks on the Yu-yan ridge returned to me. I called out in warning, but Khine was too far away to hear.

It caught him by the ankles. Khine dropped his weapon. The dragon flung the glaive away and pounced on him. There was a crunching sound as he attempted to tear Khine's arm off. The blood drained from my face.

Khine reached down to his belt and pulled out a dagger, striking the dragon's nose. The dragon reared back, sending a short blast of flame into the air. Khine rolled away, a ragged line of flesh and torn clothing along his left arm. He dropped the dagger and drew his sword. He was having trouble keeping it steady.

The injury hardly seemed to faze the dragon. He advanced on Khine once more, huffing as the blood bubbled around his nostrils. The crowd was beginning another rhythmic chanting. To them, Khine was nothing but a sacrificial lamb, a pawn for their entertainment. Warlord Graiyo had been right, after all—it was just a show. A man dies for his queen and Warlord San gets to parade the gods-ordained Dragonlord for all to see. Khine would have known all of this, yet that didn't stop him. And now, standing there in front of the dragon while bleeding half to death, he had yet to turn tail and run.

"Warlord San!" I called out, turning back to the platform. "Enough of this! This was my battle from the beginning!"

"The man volunteered, Lady Talyien," San replied. He never even looked at me—he remained addressing the crowd.

I roared and smashed my sword against the bars. The sound of steel on iron clattered inside my ears.

"If he dies and I live to return to my throne," I thundered, "I will see to it your head decorates the garden fountain in Oka Shto. You have my word."

"Your father had no taste. It's a despicable fountain. My head would be an improvement."

I struck the bars again with such force that they sparked.

The crowd fell silent. Up ahead, Khine was hiding along a stone platform while the dragon tried to smash its way towards him. The fear became a gaping well in my stomach. I renewed my attack on the bars.

What people liked to call *battle lust* my father had a different term for. He called it desperation.

He liked to say that people who went into battle looking to win never really stay too long. Perhaps you cut down one or two easy opponents, but sooner or later you are confronted with someone bigger, someone with a larger sword or axe that could cleave you in half with one blow. You'd be a fool not to see your own mortality then. "Mind you," he'd add, chuckling, "these fools do exist. You can spot them from across the field, hesitating, as if the wave of the battle is up to them and if they decided not to join after all everything would just go away. Walking dead men—they're the easiest to kill."

You had to pull yourself back, Yeshin told me, and fight to live for the next moment. You didn't swing your sword to win a war. You cleaved your way into a seemingly impenetrable barrier of bodies because if you didn't, *you'd* be the one killed. So you see these brave warriors rushing off into a battle like they ate iron for breakfast and shat steel in the night, but most of them, Yeshin believed, did it out of fear. They did it to survive, because they had no choice. There were the rare one or two exceptions—madmen who killed for the thrill of it, who enjoyed the rush of bodies breaking underneath them—but my father liked to simplify things for my sake.

"Feed on your own desperation, if you must," he said. "The Oren-yaro understand this more than most. Some fight for glory, others fight for honour and justice, but we fight for the sake of the fight. We do not fight for duty—the fight *is* our duty. It is how we seem to win these *impossible* battles. Every armour has a chink. Beat at it long enough, it'll break."

My fingers were bleeding from the spray of metal and my sword was starting to chip, but I continued battering at the bars. They were starting to rattle.

Behind me, I heard the dragon strike the platform. The ground trembled.

One of the bars broke loose. I shoved my body into the gap, ignoring the pain of my mangled shoulder as I squeezed through.

The blasted gong, and then a trumpet.

From the far end of the arena, the doors opened. Two men, both armed with spears and shields, strode in. I immediately recognized Agos's burly form. The other was unfamiliar at first, until I saw his eyes from underneath his helmet. It was Lord Huan aren dar Anyu.

They rushed the dragon almost immediately.

They must've discussed some sort of strategy beforehand, because their movement was precise, calculated—the advantage of men trained in the army. Agos reached Khine first, blocking the dragon's next assault with his shield before jabbing him in the jaw. When the dragon tried to strike him with his tail, Huan stabbed him through the scales near his leg.

Blood spurted from the wound. The dragon swung his head to strike. His teeth snapped a hair's breadth from Huan's face. The dragon opened his eyes.

The blackness receded.

I wasn't sure what happened next, exactly. Myar had spoken of becoming a mindless monster if a soul that did not belong to a body tried to steal it for its own. But there was clearly more to it than that. Whatever the reason, I felt Eikaro's presence flare up like a lit torch.

Brother, he called out.

Huan tried to stab him a second time. He lumbered backwards, blood pouring from his wounds. I remembered that I was the only one who could hear him.

My mind began to race through my options. There was no time to tell Huan about his brother, and even if I did, it wasn't a guarantee that Eikaro would remain in control of himself. I spotted the chain that kept the dragon tethered to the arena and followed it all the way down to an anchor in the floor.

As Huan continued his assault, I dove for the anchor. The lock holding the chain in place was already bent from the dragon's attempt to escape earlier. I jabbed my sword into the mechanism and kicked. It shattered.

"Fly, my lord!" I screamed as Huan's sword flashed through the air.

Eikaro listened. He reared, his wings knocking Huan back a step, and then he shot straight into the ceiling. One sharp intake of air, one quick blast of fire, and he tore a hole through the roof and ruptured his way to freedom.

I didn't pay attention to how the crowd reacted to all of this. My first and only thought was Khine. I rushed to his side. He was gasping for breath and didn't respond when I spoke his name. "Just like the fucker to try to get himself killed behind my back," Agos fumed. "Didn't even think to tell me. Serves you right, you son of a bitch."

I ignored him, tearing the sleeve from my shirt to hold the flesh in Khine's arm in place to stop the bleeding. "Are we done here?" I said, turning to Huan.

Huan was staring at the distance, where Warlord San still stood. I don't even think the battle had gone on long enough for him to return to his seat. "You heard Lady Talyien," Huan called out. "Have we won her freedom?"

"The dragon isn't dead," Warlord San replied.

"You want to go get it?" I cried. "Be my guest!"

San visibly hesitated. He hadn't thought things through, not this far. His silence turned the anger red-hot inside of me, lending it a life of its own. I found myself walking towards the gates where Eikaro had come from. "Open them!" I screamed at the guards.

They didn't move. They looked confused.

"I am the lady of Oren-yaro," I reminded them with a snarl. "I order you to open them *now.*"

That did the trick. They scrambled to turn the winch and lift the gate. I ducked under before it was even fully raised, making my way down a hall with a stench that stung my nose—animal urine and droppings, old and new. Further down, I encountered cages, where gaunt wolves snarled and wild boar shrieked loud enough to wake the dead.

I found the other dragon chained inside a room at the far end. It held the expression of a creature begging for its death. For a moment, I wondered if there was even a corrupt soul in this one, or if its horrendous circumstances had forced the creature to flee. One way or another, it was too far gone.

I remembered that I had ruined my sword and reached out to grab the closest guard by the collar in order to draw his. I pushed him away, turned back to the dragon, and killed it in one stroke. Its body was so weak that it didn't even resist. Once it lay limp on the sparse bed of hay, I hacked its limbs loose from the chains and dragged it out to the arena, leaving behind a thick trail of blood with every step.

I emerged from the darkness with the dragon's body. "I promised you *one* dead dragon," I snarled, flinging the carcass before them.

I saw Qun get up to walk away from his seat just as the crowd erupted with applause.

I was removed from the arena and taken straight to the guest quarters, where I learned that my injuries were a lot worse than I thought they were. A healer appeared to bleed the puncture wounds while Huan explained that dragons' teeth—while not venomous—were dirty and bite wounds could cause a nasty infection if left uncleaned.

His words were all garbled, but I didn't care about all of that. "Where did you take Lamang?" I asked.

The healer turned to Huan for confirmation.

"He's with the chief surgeon," Huan answered for him. "They're going to try their best. Apparently, he lost too much blood."

"They're going to *try* their best?" I repeated, growling as the healer stabbed me with a needle. "Maybe there's a reason he doesn't trust Jinsein healers."

"With all due respect, Lady Talyien," the healer said. "We're Zarojo-trained."

"The sparse fuzz on your lip tells me your knowledge was acquired secondhand."

The healer coloured. "The surgeon trained me himself, and he had the honour of travelling to Anzhao City in his youth for his education. He's a member of the Zarojo Physicians' Guild. Your guardsman is in capable hands."

"Old, rheumy hands from the sound of it," I grumbled. "And he's not my guardsman. You people have to stop it with the bloody guardsmen. It stopped being funny years ago."

"Your temper is getting ahead of you, my lady," San broke in. He appeared at the door, a wide grin on his face. "What a spectacular scene. I couldn't have orchestrated a better show myself."

I fixed him with a glare. "You *bastard*. Our lives for your little show—"

"You knew full well what you were walking into."

"Me. *Alone*."

"We made the decision to fight for you," Agos said. He had been standing in the corner with his arms crossed. "Bit too late, honestly, since Lamang tried to steal the honour himself, the rat bastard."

"Explain yourselves a bit better. I can't hear you very well above the sound of this man butchering my arm." I glared at the healer.

Agos jerked a thumb towards Warlord San. "After his guards took you, Lamang and I learned you were being taken straight to Kyo-orashi. We ran into Lord Huan at Fuyyu and told him everything. Lord Huan found us a fast boat, and we got here two days before your ship did."

"I had figured Fuyyu would be your next stop after the events at the Sougen," Huan added. "I didn't know Warlord San was... doing what he was." He gave San a wary glance.

The warlord gave a quick bark of laughter. "Snatched her from right under your nose, did I? Poor Anyu whelp! No hard feelings, eh, Little Huan! But you did your part for her as well. I can't fault you for that. I knew you and your brother were fond of her."

"I'm sure you had your reasons," Huan said with a grim smile. He turned back to me. "When we arrived here in Kyo-orashi, we decided that the best way was to approach Warlord San directly."

"I told them what I told you," San continued for him. "About the dragon, and how the title of *warlord* needed to have weight behind it. You were a young, untested warrior, as far as the land was concerned. Now you will bear dragon scars for the rest of your life—"

"I'm not sure I share the same sentiment about scars..."

"—a feat you accomplished with an entire city's eyes on you. You should thank me, Lady Talyien!"

"For making me look more horrible in a dress?" I sighed. "Let me guess. The rest of this plan was Khine's, and he did it behind your back."

"The fuckface forgot his place," Agos snorted.

"I had thought that I was still in the process of... discussing... a more reasonable solution with Warlord San," Huan said, still the very picture of diplomacy. "Until I heard this morning that *you* were here, and that you were already in the fighting pits."

"Her decision," San said.

Huan smiled politely. "Your man Agos and I rushed to the arena as fast as we could. By the time we got there, we heard that Lamang had already gone in after you."

San nodded. "He made a good argument—if the goal is to draw attention to your return to Jin-Sayeng, to show the land your true value, then the prospect of someone giving his life for you after you had put up a good fight would have more impact. And the fact that we had a bigger, fiercer dragon than I anticipated—well, even you must admit that you took the crowd's breath away."

"You sent him there to die."

"His words, not mine. Mind you, we spoke about this long before I came to fetch you from the docks. We didn't know it was going to be this big of a dragon. It was all a show. I highly doubt he *meant* to die."

But that look on Khine's face…

My own life, to yours? It was a startlingly simple choice for him.

"And all of this," I said at last. "Qun had no idea."

"Not a damn thing," San replied with a laugh. "He thought you were going in there alone. He didn't know your men were here."

"What did *he* want to happen?"

"Everything you saw," San said, "except *he* goes in there to save you instead of your people—to show the land Zarojo supremacy, that even such a powerful woman would be feeding off their hand."

"He thought you were working with him. Allies."

"Shows what he knows about Jinseins," San sniffed. "We take care of our own first. I would've had him killed the moment he approached me in Fuyyu, only…well, he had my balls in a vise. A family thing. I'll spare you the details."

"I figured as much. Aren't you afraid of him now?"

"*You* interrupted our plans, not I," he said with a grin. "I'll pretend I thought Lamang was his. A Zarojo—why would I question it? As far as I knew, I was still doing what he asked. You're both gravely injured right now—the physicians will confirm it and my guards will see to it that no visitors make their way to this wing. When you're both better..." His eyes flashed. "You're going to escape in the dead of the night."

"Yet again," I murmured. "And then what?"

"I don't know, Lady Talyien," San replied. "This is your mess to fix, isn't it?" He bowed before walking away.

Lord Huan started to follow him, but he lingered at the doorway. "My lady," he said quietly. "Before the dragon flew off, you called it *my lord*."

"I did," I replied without looking at him.

I heard him clear his throat. "Why?"

I didn't answer.

"My lady," Huan continued. "That dragon..." He paused. "It's the one that attacked the tower."

"Yes."

"The same one that killed my brother?"

"My lord," I told him. "We will speak of this later. I am tired and would like to sleep."

"As you command." The door creaked shut.

The healer finished stitching my wounds, bandaged my arm, warned me not to accept any more visitors and to eat when the servants come by with my meal, and then left with what appeared to be a breath of relief. I stared up at the ceiling as Agos pulled up a chair to sit beside me.

"You're the craziest bitch I know," he said with a sigh.

"I should have your head for that," I murmured.

"You won't." It was probably our oldest joke.

"I broke your gift," I said, remembering the sword.

"I saw. Don't worry, I'll get you another. A better one."

"It worked though, didn't it?"

He cracked a smile. "All that for Lamang, huh?"

"Agos—"

"You don't owe me an explanation. I was just going to say that maybe if I was the one getting chewed up you'd have ripped the bars apart with your bare hands. A man can dream."

"No offense, Agos, but that is an awful dream. You could do better."

He snorted. "Maybe." He got up. "I'll go check on the bastard, see if he's still breathing. Least I can do right now. Don't know what got into his head. I'm surprised he lived as long as he did, to be honest. Man's got two left feet when he fights."

"He said he didn't see the difference between the dragon and you."

"Didn't he? Fucking idiot. I hope he doesn't croak before I can throw him around some more." He squeezed my shoulder and left me on my own. The herbs took effect not long after, pulling me down into a dreamless sleep.

CHAPTER TWENTY-FIVE

THE PRICE OF LOVE

Khine almost died.

I only learned about this the next morning, when Cho came bursting into my room, startling the servants and the healer, who had come to check my wounds. "You promised you'd let us go home!" Cho screamed. The guards rushed forward to detain him.

I stopped them with one hand before turning back to Cho. "I made no such promise," I said. "I told you I would consider it if it was safe. You know how it's been since we left Kaggawa's estate."

I might as well have been talking to a deaf man. "I warned you," Cho snarled. "I warned you about what he could do."

"I didn't ask him to."

"But you *knew*! You knew the risk of having him beside you! And now he's lying back there dying because you were too busy with your own shit to realize what other people are willing to sacrifice for you!"

"What does he mean?" I asked, turning to the healer.

"I'm sorry?"

"His brother, the one your chief surgeon was taking care of. How is he?"

A shadow crossed the healer's face. "He may not make it."

I pulled myself up, nearly ripping the bandages off my arm. "What are you talking about?"

"Please calm down, Lady Talyien," the healer replied. "It isn't as bad as it sounds. At least—not yet. We just haven't gone into his treatment long enough to make an assumption one way or another. He did lose much blood, and I believe he has a long road of recovery ahead of him in order to use that arm again."

"Cho—" I began in an attempt to explain.

He tightened his face. "What's he to you, anyway? You're a queen. He's a con man, scum from Shang Azi who can't even hold a job longer than a few months at best. Yet you're clinging to him like he's some gallant knight. You're just using him, aren't you? He's going to die here like some dog because he's too stubborn to listen and you're too stubborn to care!" He pounded his fists on the side of the mattress. The guards came for him now, cuffing him as he turned his anger on them. They dragged him through the door.

"Zarojo pests," the healer said as soon as they were gone. "They're crawling through the whole castle, now." But the impact of Cho's words remained. Perhaps I might have known how to ignore them before—I have been accused of worse, have weathered critics that didn't know where to draw the line. Now his words only reopened those feelings from yesterday, reflected back by the state of my bruised and bloody hands.

I had always known, of course, that men were expected to die for me. Warlord San's little show hinged around reminding people of that fact. A warlord for whom no one would die was as useless as a rotten tooth. Khine had given me a gift, one my own father wouldn't have squandered. Even now, I could hear him whispering in my ear. *Proclaim him a hero. Appoint him as your personal guard. And if he should be close to death, grant him land, maybe even a village to call his own. Make his funeral into a national ceremony and dare your warlords to defy what people have seen with their own eyes.*

Mere thoughts stirred by a lifetime of drilling by a man who saw opportunity everywhere he looked. Sometimes one needed to make ruthless decisions for the greater good. If my goals were the only things that mattered to me, then Khine's circumstance—while unfortunate—was necessary.

It was the anguish in Cho's voice that bore down on me, that cut deep enough to hurt. A commander out on the battlefield, seeing his captain arrive with reinforcements, might've been filled with warmth and relief. Not dread. Raging against iron bars because I couldn't save him—and if Agos and Huan hadn't come in time, they would still be sweeping parts of him from the arena grounds this morning—these were not feelings someone like me should have.

I was starting to understand, perhaps for the first time in my life, that the path between my mind and my heart was not as clear as I had once believed. Khine's death might suit my purposes very well, but I couldn't even think about it without a surge of panic. They were feelings unbecoming for someone in my position. Cho was right. If Khine lived, he had to go.

The healer wouldn't allow me to leave my bed, so I spent the next two days shifting between herb-induced sleep and staring up at the ceiling, trying to find the words I could use to get Khine to listen to me. Sometime during the third morning, they stopped forcing tea infusions down my throat and told me I could exercise my legs—at least as far as to the window and then back. Against the servants' protest, I immediately hobbled out of the door to the next room.

A greying, wrinkled man met me at once. "I thought you'd be here once they let you," he said. He glanced at the figure on the bed. "The worst is over. He'll live."

"And the arm?"

"That's up to him. If he tries to exercise and move it, and not let it wither . . ."

"I would like to speak with him alone."

For a moment, I was afraid he would say that Khine's health did not allow for that. But the chief surgeon bowed and stepped outside, closing the door behind him. I locked it.

Khine was awake and staring right at me. There was a sickly tinge to his skin, its usual glow replaced by an unnatural paleness—proof enough of his brush with death. There were black hollows under his eyes and dark bruises along his torso and down the side of his face. His injured arm was in a sling, streaked with blood.

I pretended that the sight of his injuries didn't make me want to weep and sat on the edge of the bed. He scooted over to make room for me. "You look well," he said, cracked lips breaking into a grin.

I looked away. "Well, you know, I nearly *died*."

"I hear that can be painful."

"Tell me about it. Speaking of which, how was it having a dragon for a dance partner?"

"It was lovely. We had a wonderful time. You should've been there. They had snacks."

".It's good to know you seem like the sort who doesn't get killed by dragons easily."

"No, fortunately enough it seems. Women are a different story altogether."

The smile on my face faded. I took in the shadows on his, his ghost-like complexion. I didn't even want to touch him. I was afraid his skin would be as cold as my father's the day he died, a thought so repulsive I physically recoiled from it.

"You shouldn't have done that," I said, the anger suddenly thick in my voice. "It was unnecessary."

"I wanted to do it," Khine grumbled.

"You wanted to *die*? Just like back in the Sougen?"

He was quiet, staring at the ceiling.

"Damn you, Lamang. I thought you were stronger than that."

"I thought *you* were, too."

I felt my skin crawl. "What the hell are you saying?"

"I'm..."

"What are you saying, Lamang?"

He took a deep breath. "I've seen you change the last few months. Slipping slowly, staring too long at nothing—and you don't even see it, I don't think. You've given up, haven't you? Deep inside? Why are you worried about *me*? You're the one with a son to live for."

"Don't start," I said in a low voice. "You don't know anything."

"I know enough," he whispered. "I once thought that if you could peer out from behind that queen's mask, the weight would fall off your shoulders just like that. I even thought that if I got you to see what was happening around you, things would change for the better. An arrogant fool, pretending I knew of the world when I didn't have a fucking clue. I thought that if I could give this back to you, give you back who you *are*—"

"You're right. You don't know *anything*," I repeated, my voice rising. "You don't know the decisions I'm faced with every day, and you're certainly not in the position to make them for me. Your feelings are going to get you killed."

Khine pulled away. "So they will," he conceded. I think he found the idea amusing. "There are worse things in the world to die for."

"This isn't a joke," I hissed. "Cho wants you to come home with him. He's been asking me to let you go since the Sougen. If I knew it would come to this—"

"I have no intention of leaving. If Cho is harassing you about it, tell him to stop. *He* can go home if he wants. Let me get better and I'll send him back myself."

"I don't want your service, damn you."

"I thought you did. I thought that's why I was here."

"Not like this!" I hissed. "If this is the road you'll take, then I have to forbid it."

Khine pressed his lips together as the humour left him. "I don't need your permission."

"You..." I held my breath. "What do you think will happen over time? That all you have to do is stay a little longer and then maybe someday I'd love you back?"

His face contorted. I knew it wasn't fair for me to use something I knew would hurt. But I was never the sort of person who pulled punches. If it got him to see sense a lot faster, I was willing to strike deeper. If it saved his life, I was willing to make him bleed. I had taken worse upon myself.

"I thought I made it all clear back in the Sougen," Khine whispered. "I know the troubles that ail you, Tali. It was never my intention to add to them."

"Yet you are," I snapped. "You just did. Did you do this to impress me, Lamang? Because I am very much impressed—*by your foolishness*. I expected more from a man as intelligent as you."

"I thought queens are used to that sort of thing."

"That's what I've been telling myself the past few days. But I can't do it, Khine. I can't watch you do this to yourself anymore."

"Tali—"

"I will not give you hope," I murmured. "Whatever we are, whatever you think we have..."

Khine's eyes softened. "I know you aren't free to love. I've known that from the beginning." His voice dropped an octave. "When I fell for you, I fought it, believe me. I realized it not long after you last saw your husband in Shang Azi, and I threw myself at my work with Lo Bahn to distract myself. I thought I could still be that man you first met—the one who couldn't care less who you were or what you did with your life. But the more I struggled to keep away from you, the more I convinced myself you are not the kind of woman who should ever cross my mind twice, the worse it got. You are everything I hate about this world, Queen Talyien. You remind me of how helpless I am, how infuriatingly pointless my life is in all of this, how much I detest people with as much power as you have. And yet none of it mattered. I felt like I would drown if I couldn't be near you."

His words left my ears ringing. "You're looking for Jia. You visited Dar Aso as often as you did because you wanted a glimpse of her and you found that with me."

"Don't bring her into this. You don't know her. This is..."

"Different? Lamang...you're in love with an idea, a shadow."

"So what if I am? I have no desire to possess you, Tali. I would not dream of stepping between you and your husband."

I started to laugh. "Gods. If we're going down that route, then let me tell you in turn: you don't know anything about me and Rayyel, either."

"You loved him. You still do."

"You think you know me better than I know myself? I can love again. You know this." I spoke without meeting his eyes, because I didn't think I could bear to see a spark of—of anything in them. "You may deny it, but a part of you is watching, waiting, to see how this unfolds. My father raised me to read people. To look at them and judge them, to see what they want, what they hope to get out of me. You think I don't see how you look at me? Do you think I'm foolish enough to believe that you're some saint, completely void of desire? Lo Bahn, at least, didn't hide it. Agos doesn't. You—I still don't know what con you're trying to pull. Are you just waiting for a reward? Is that it?"

"That's—" His face contorted. "That's a low blow, Tali."

"It's only a blow if it's the truth," I said. "My father would have me *use* it, use you, to accomplish my goals. Maybe this is what makes me a weak queen, but I won't. I do care about you, Lamang—enough not to want your head on a spike for me. I will not pave the way to my throne on a sea of corpses." I began to walk away.

I heard him sit up in alarm. "What are you going to do?" he gasped.

"I intend to leave without you. By the time you can stand up and walk through these doors, I'll be long gone."

Khine laughed. "I'm just going to find you again. You should know to give up by now."

"But first," I continued, ignoring him, "I'm going to pay Agos a visit. Don't be a martyr, Lamang. You're not the only one who got hurt trying to play hero."

"Tali," he growled. It was a warning.

I hesitated at the lock.

There are worse things…

"Tali—!"

I undid it and walked out, slamming the door behind me.

My entire body was screaming at me, telling me I was making a mistake, that I had to turn back *now* before I lost Khine forever.

But to lose him was exactly what I needed. I had seen what chasing after a man did to my life, and I had no desire to repeat my mistakes. More than that, though— what I felt that day in San's arena, seeing Khine walk straight to what would've been his death, terrified me more than I could explain. Nothing in all the years of me pining for Rayyel could rival the gaping hole that moment left in me. One thing was achingly clear: Khine didn't belong in my world. In my world, love was a drawn sword. You could use it to cut others or you could use it to cut yourself.

I supposed I was doing both when I found myself in Agos's room that night. He was sitting on the edge of his bed, wrapping a bandage around his knee. "Princess," he greeted me easily. "Lamang is still alive? Damn kid's harder to kill than he looks. What are you—"

I locked the door, trembling, heart and soul begging me to reconsider. I shouldn't be here. I should be in that *other* room, to hell with mistakes and opening my heart again. But then what would that do? A dead woman—I reminded myself that I had so very little left. I wouldn't risk Khine, either, not for a moment's reprieve.

I heard Agos draw a sharp breath.

"Princess…" he began again.

I walked towards him and pressed my lips over his.

Silence filled the room as our lips locked. It was brief—so brief it felt like a butterfly's touch. His hands came up to stroke my back before he flipped me onto the bed, a smile tugging at the corners of his mouth. "Look," he said. "If you're just doing this to get someone out of your system…"

"Just shut up, Agos."

He grew serious. "You're a married woman."

"*Now* you notice?"

He grazed my cheek with his hand. I could hear his heart beating. "We've made this mistake before."

"I can't turn back time."

"We both know the man you really want is in the other room. It's not too late. Princess—"

"If I can use my power for one good thing, for *once*, then I will." I stared into his eyes. "Kiss me," I ordered. I wasn't giving him room to back out.

He knew that, too. He didn't even flinch as he obeyed. "Is that all?" he asked, after he pulled away.

"You know very well that's not all."

He tugged his shirt loose. I reached up to help him take it off.

A memory from that first night returned, unbidden. I pushed it away. I was a woman now, too old to really be confused about why I did the things I did. Too old to start on something and then just let it fall through. Things were different from what I remembered—the tension, the uncertainty, was gone. I knew what I wanted out of it this time around, knew that I wanted to cross a bridge from which there was no turning back. I allowed myself to explore his body with my fingers while his tongue did the same. There is not a lot of room for thought when you haven't been with a man in over five years, and even less so when that man was someone as restrained as Rayyel. I found myself responding easily to Agos's touch, which made the entire thing less difficult than I thought it would be.

And it helped that *restraint* was not a word Agos was familiar with. He grabbed my hips and pulled himself up to undress me, hands tearing at my robe so he could nip at my bare shoulder. He traced a line from it and down my chest before drawing his attention to my bandages.

Between the haze and the heat of our bodies, I was almost afraid he would hesitate. Instead, his lips quirked into a smile.

"What's so amusing?" I asked.

"Nothing." He pushed my robes aside and began to run his hands down my belly. He paused at the scarred flesh there. I wondered if he was comparing me with the girl he'd had a long, long time ago, the one with the smoother skin and a heart that had only once been broken. But before I could ever really start to doubt myself, he grazed his teeth along my belly button and down, his fingers working their way into my inner thighs. I reached down to clasp his shoulders, stopping him before he could get any further.

"Now?" he asked.

I nodded.

"But—"

"Now," I said, through gritted teeth.

He stroked himself to stiffness and went in. No pain, no resistance—only a fullness, a burning need to be lost in…something. I didn't love Agos, not that way, but it was enough that he wanted me. Enough that I found warmth in his arms, that I knew exactly what we were in each other's lives. I gasped as he pushed deeper and found a rhythm. Against the candlelight, sweat gathered over the muscles of his arms and his chest.

No room for thought, now. Not anymore. I was lost in the moment and the heat of his mouth. As he climaxed, I felt my own insides shudder around him. It was an unexpected response, and he saw it, too. Before he could say anything about it, I pulled him into my arms and hid my face in the crook of his shoulder. If there was anything on my expression there—an absence, or longing for another—I didn't want him to see.

He fell into the bed beside me. "And now," I murmured against his racing chest, "everything they say about me is true."

"Princess…"

"Don't start," I said. "I don't want to hear it." I turned my head away from him and stared at the wall. "Tomorrow. We head out tomorrow night before Qun catches on to what Warlord San has done."

"I suppose that means we won't be getting any soldiers."

I shook my head. "If I manage to fix things back at court, *then* I get Kyoorashi's full support."

"And how do you plan to deal with him?" he whispered into my ear. "Your husband."

"Kill him between horses? I don't know." I turned to look at him. "You're talkative all of a sudden."

"Let me have a drink and a few minutes. I'll be less talkative again."

"Agos—"

He cleared his throat. "Is Lamang even allowed to leave? Last I heard, he was at death's door. I'm not looking forward to dragging a corpse around, just so you know."

"It's just going to be the two of us."

"Really? He agreed to that?"

I didn't reply. The smile on his face faded.

"I see," Agos grumbled, realizing what I had just done. What I was still doing. "You argued with him. You're not just trying to get him out of your system—you want him out of your life."

"I can't fall in love again, Agos," I whispered. "Not after everything. Look at how it is. Look what almost happened to him. He can still...live a good life, away from all of this. Away from me. It's too late for us, but I can still save him."

"And falling in love with this man scares you enough that it's worth making this mistake all over again?"

I didn't reply. Eventually, I mumbled an apology.

"You said that the last time. I should really work on my performance." Agos pressed his lips against my shoulder. I turned to glance back at him. After a moment's hesitation, he kissed me again—softly.

I was wrong, at least, about something. There could be comfort in need, between rustling sheets and flickering shadows. We measured time with each ragged breath, rising higher and higher until the blessed darkness came, leaving only the bittersweet tinge of my sins in my mouth.

But long into the night, I stayed awake and thought of my father and the things he had done, the things he felt like he had to do, and wondered how he coped. You built walls around your heart or you drowned in the harsh truths. I didn't know if Khine would ever forgive me, and I supposed it didn't matter. It was enough to know that I could never forgive myself.

ACT THREE

THE PRICE OF
A CROWN

CHAPTER ONE

PICKING UP THE PIECES

ᒍᐟᕿᐤ

I write this now without skipping a beat, because it is the dead of the night and I am afraid Sayu will awaken if one of her boys stirs from a nightmare. I don't want her to see these pages, and I know I will lose my courage and stop writing if she does. Some things you can only begin, and you count on happenstance to carry you the rest of the way. Such as it is with the memory of that night. I wasn't even sure I could recount it, or that I would want to, given what unfolded after.

I don't know what else I can say. That I regret it? Even if I did, I cannot take it back. Agos was safety, Agos was security, he was the world I had known before everything had gone awry. It stung that I couldn't love him. After that night, I wanted to. I wanted to forget Rayyel, and Khine, I wanted to pretend there was still a way even a woman like me could be happy again.

That last part, right there, is the part of me that was raised by Yeshin. It is the *princess* that Agos so loved to continue to call me, the queen of Jin-Sayeng even when they say she can't be anymore. She still doesn't understand. She cannot grasp that you cannot build a foundation on sand, that this is the price she continues to pay for her father's decision to offer her whole life in servitude to the land. What else should I have done? Should I have sought comfort in Khine's arms instead, damn all the consequences? Then you'd say I was a woman who took advantage of a grieving son, who risked a man's life because she felt sorry for him. Maybe I should have gone to bed alone...to continue making both men hope, when the truth—the *actual* truth—was there was nothing to hope for. Everything I had to give had gone to my husband, who had done his part to waste it all. Whatever was left inside of me wasn't worth the trouble. All the ache, the burdens I continued to carry…what kind of a woman would I be if I shared them with anyone?

I slept with Agos. What else is there to say? I woke up after what felt like less than an hour of sleep to the sun's rays spilling through the curtains and the knowledge that I couldn't have done a better job ruining my life if I'd tried. I was in a bed that wasn't mine with dried semen on my thighs, sore after a night spent with a man I had ordered to fuck me so that I wouldn't have to face the man I didn't want to love. It doesn't get lower than that. There are women born with so much less than I have who never had to resort to such measures.

But I can't say that I regret it. I regret the circumstances that brought me to it, that it had to happen at all, that I hurt more people than I intended to. But without that night, a thousand other possibilities would have opened up, caving in like that sand that was my father's foundation for my rule. What other choices would have landed on my lap, who else could I have gotten killed, how much more complicated would that have made the chaos I have yet to fix? I didn't know it then, but it made all the difference.

I didn't visit Khine again the next day. There was nothing left between us and nothing more to say. Last night's memories still throbbed like an open wound, and the very thought of facing him again after what I had done left me feeling light-headed. I asked a servant to check up on him and was told he was sleeping. The chief surgeon promised he would take care of him—his antics at the arena had won him friends, at least. He wasn't back-alley scum to these people. Sometimes a single moment is enough to define a man's worth.

Lord Huan met us at the gates. Even in the dark, unshaved and dressed in loose robes, he still looked as lordly as a man ever could. The effect of having faced a dragon. I wondered how I looked to him. "By now people will have heard of what happened," he said. "The other lords will send their men, my own father included, to intercept you. Be careful. Warlord San says he will sound the alarms the moment the sun rises."

"That's not much time," I grumbled.

Huan looked apologetic. "It's the best he could do. He and Governor Qun had been at odds. This would be the final straw in this *alliance* of theirs."

"Have you any idea what dirt Qun has on him?"

Huan scratched the back of his head. "The thing with Eikaro…"

"His connection to the *agan*?"

He glanced around warily before dropping his voice down. "It's the same with Warlord San. One of his daughters. She's being kept in a temple of Sakku on an island off the coast."

I took a deep breath. "Akaterru. And let me guess—*Yeshin* found out and fed the Zarojo this information. What's he been doing, keeping tabs on all the royal children from the start? And then he *gives* this all to the Zarojo so that it would be easier to manipulate the warlords into doing their bidding?"

"Your guess is as good as mine."

"That old man—" I shook my head. "I don't know whether to be revolted or in awe of him."

"Most of us think the same way, my lady. Your father was a force to be reckoned with. Somehow, he still is."

"He gave them too much," I said. "Too many tools to use against us. Does Warlord San know of how much Yeshin's hand was in all of this?"

"I don't believe so."

"Can you keep it from him? At least until I get to Oren-yaro?"

Huan looked surprised that I would say such a thing. "The thought never even crossed my mind." He bowed. "Someday, we will speak of the dragon and my brother. Someday. I'm not ready now. But know that when the time comes, Yu-yan will raise her banners for you and I will ride with you to hell and back. *You* are the true Dragonlord, the Ikessars be damned."

I felt a chill run through me. "Lord Huan," I murmured. "I am honoured."

"Just give me time," he added with a grin. "Perhaps not until Tori gives birth. She's not too far along. And my own wife may be pregnant, too—I need to learn the stakes before I make a move." He nodded towards Agos, who was walking up to us with our horses. "Take care of her," he said.

Agos snorted. "When have I not?"

"Actually—" I started.

He gave me a look.

"You know what," I said, "I'll let you have this one. Until we meet again, Lord Huan."

Huan reached out to take my hand, pressing it on his forehead before placing his lips over it. "Safe travels, Beloved Queen."

We started down the road. Agos began to whistle.

"You're in a good mood," I commented.

His eyes gleamed. "Don't tell me I need to explain to you."

I ignored his implication. "We're going back to Oren-yaro. As lovely as those words sound, we know the entire castle is going to be crawling with council representatives and Ikessars from top to bottom."

"So what's your brilliant plan for when we get there? I assume you want to give Lord General Ozo a tongue-lashing. I'd love to be there for that. I doubt they'll just let you waltz in there and call Rayyel a liar to his face."

"I have no intention of *waltzing* in."

"That's what you royals do, don't you? Waltz." He gave me the goofiest smile.

"I'm glad this is all very amusing to you."

"Master Dai's proposition seems less drastic, if you think about it." Agos crossed his arms. "He's a lot of things, that Dai, but I feel like he wants to do right by you. I told you that maybe you should've considered his offer. Royal with a commoner—you see anything wrong with that?" He gave me a knowing look.

I glanced away, hoping the darkness hid my expression. "Don't jest about such things, Agos."

"It's not a jest."

"What happened between us was . . ."

He grunted under his breath as I trailed off, forging ahead into the darkness. We were silent for a while as I tried to push away last night's decision into the furthest reaches of my mind. I needed to stop letting Agos take the fall for my incapacities.

"You *do* have a plan, I hope," Agos said some time later. "Else you wouldn't have dared to get us this far."

"I didn't want to say it out loud while we were in the Sougen, with Dai's spies everywhere," I murmured. "But I think there's tunnels under Oka Shto. I'm not sure where they are. But I know they exist. I used to hear my father and Arro talking. There's more to the castle than what meets the eye."

His horse suddenly surged forward, blood pouring out of its mouth as it crumpled to the ground. Agos managed to jump off in time to avoid getting crushed under its weight. As I yanked the reins up in an effort to get my own mount under control, I saw the arrows sticking out of the dead horse's neck just as more came flying out of the shadows, imbedding themselves underneath my saddle.

My own horse dropped to his knees and fell to the side. I leaped from the saddle and landed on my shoulder. I rolled to the ditch, where I drew my sword. Agos was already making a headlong rush into the darkness. He threw the lantern and heard someone cry out as it smashed into what I hoped was their face.

"You really don't learn, do you, *Beloved Queen*?"

I turned and saw Qun standing on top of the hill overlooking the road.

"Come down here, you bastard," I said. "Let's end this."

"Why would I want to do that?" Qun asked. "I don't know why you believe this little outburst would be enough to win you your freedom. You know what you are, don't you? A gift mare for my prince. You can try to escape as much as you want, but you will always be roped back. *Always*. He'll break you yet."

"Like I'd let him," I snarled.

He smiled. In the darkness, it looked pasted on, the shadows adding extra angles to each corner of his lips. "Do you understand how patient I've been with you?"

"I didn't realize. I apologize for being *such* an inconvenience," I said smoothly.

"You were not, as I recall, as patient with my wife."

I tightened my grip on the sword. "Then come," I said. "Take your vengeance. That's what you really want, isn't it? You don't care about Prince Yuebek at all—this is all for *you*. Come down, Qun. I'll let you have the first strike."

He chuckled. "You once accused me of not knowing the stakes in this game. Oh, but I do know, Beloved Queen. Why do you think I got this far? I do care. I care about my prince claiming his kingdom at last, and the power I stand to inherit paving the way for him. But I was *also* fond of my wife. And if my vengeance comes in watching you suffer, in seeing you wriggling in my prince's grasp while we take care of your boy—"

I heard another cry. Agos appeared beside me, soaked in blood. From the way he was still standing, it didn't look like his.

"No horses," Qun said, giving a mock shake of his head. "And down to one man. How *ever* will you get to Oka Shto before me?"

"We can finish this now, Qun!" I roared.

"You never did answer my question about your son. I guess I'll find out soon enough. Until we meet again, Beloved Queen!"

"Qun!" I thundered.

But he drew away, disappearing with the sound of hooves.

———

My father had taught me about winning—how to overcome one's opponents by planning ahead, and being gracious in victory, and knowing how to deal with the aftermath and the spoils. He never taught me how to lose.

I didn't know, for instance, that you could be down on the ground already and *still* fall. That the pain of abandonment and humiliation could stretch out like stars before you, every flicker a reminder of the things you should have done, the things you have failed to do. You begin to lose sight of the end and you start to second-guess your actions. Everything becomes an exercise in frustration, as if the act of catching your thumb in your scabbard, or getting a stone in your boot, is a clear sign that the gods do not favour you.

I still don't know how I made it out of that road, let alone through that night—limping, horseless, with barely any provisions and Qun's words still fresh in my mind. If you ask me now, I can only remember wanting to curl up in the ditches to die. Why was I being kept alive? Just to serve as Yuebek's *gift mare*? Others seem to taste the sweet release of death long before they know their place in time. I, on the other hand, couldn't seem to turn my head without getting hammered by someone's grandiose idea of what I *had* to be.

But I walked, and kept my thoughts on my son. I made myself remember the sound of his laughter, how he seemed to pour his whole soul into it whenever he found something amusing. He wasn't the sort of rebellious spirit I was as a child—rather, he had a way of just taking everything in, as if he was content swimming with the water instead of against it. I had often wondered, idly, how this boy who looked like Yeshin could be so, so unlike him.

I thought of his sixth nameday, how I had taken him aside in the midst of the preparations. "Let's go down to the river and skip stones," I said.

He immediately dropped the book he was reading. I had heard of children who detested time spent with their parents, who would resist such a request. Never my son; he tore through the study with the eagerness of a small pup, which was immediately hampered by one of his guardians, who blocked the way between us.

"The prince needs to finish his lessons," the woman said in a flat tone. She wasn't looking directly *at* me. Experience had told her I didn't like getting stared down.

"It's his nameday, woman. I think we can make an exception."

"As heir to the Dragonthrone of Jin-Sayeng, he needs—"

"A break," I finished for her, walking past her to grab my waiting son's hand. "You can come," I added, inclining my head, "if you want. We'll find you a good rock to throw."

She glowered. Thanh only giggled.

I led him down to the hall, ignoring the woman—and eventually the parade of guards and guardians—behind us. As far as I was concerned, it was just me and him, as it had always been since his father left. On the steps leading down to the city, I paused, not for anything but because I liked seeing my son's retinue pile up uncomfortably on the narrow trail along the mountainside. The Ikessars hated Oka Shto, and I made sure to remind them why every chance I got.

"How do you feel about sweet tea, before we go?" I asked. "There's a shop just by the riverbank. I have enough coin for the both of us."

"The prince—" one of the guardians intervened.

"Yes!" Thanh exclaimed. And then he paused, glancing at the man who had spoken. "Can we?"

"You don't have to ask him, my love," I said. "You're the crown prince."

"They told me just because I'm the crown prince doesn't mean I get to do what I want," he said gravely.

I felt like I'd been slapped. It was true enough, but to hear it uttered from my son's mouth was something else. I watched as he turned back to his guardian and bowed. "*Can* the queen mother and I have sweet tea?" he asked.

The man opened his mouth, half stammering. He hadn't expected that. I think he only wanted to refuse my request on the grounds that it would irritate *me*.

"I'm sure we can ask them to give a cup for everyone," Thanh continued, glancing at the rest of them.

The man conceded. My son laughed, reaching up to grab my hand again, and I let him lead us down those steps. And as proud as I was of him for that moment, as much as it filled me with warmth, I remember wondering if my son was the sort of boy who could ever survive a war. My son was neither wolf nor falcon; he was sunlight, the kind that couldn't exist in darkness. I had to protect him, I had to be by his side.

Somehow, we made it to the next village, where we spent the next few hours trying to find transportation. There were no horses for sale—the village only had one sick-looking buffalo, and the wagons weren't due to pass for another few hours, at least. I came to the acceptance that there was no way in hell I would ever overtake Qun. If we could walk to the coast, perhaps, and find a boat…

"There'll be soldiers on the road and soldiers on every dock from here to Osahindo, and beyond," Agos told me. "Qun's the least of your worries."

"So what would you have me *do*?" I snapped at him.

"I'm just saying that out of all the options you've got left, the most sensible one remains."

"You want me to march back and beg Kaggawa for forgiveness?"

"If it makes you feel any better, his men must've been in Oren-yaro for weeks."

"That *doesn't* make me feel any better," I hissed.

"They won't let anything happen to Thanh."

"The fact that they've been there for weeks and we haven't heard anything must mean they've got no idea how to get him out," I said. "So much for Kaggawa's spies."

"Let them know about the tunnels. If they know they're there, they'll know how to look."

I turned to him. "How the hell am I supposed to do that?"

He looked away, grumbling. "It's just a thought. No need to be snippy with me."

I turned away from him as a figure on horseback caught my attention.

Agos squinted. "I'll be damned," he growled. "That's—*Lamang*!"

Khine turned at the sound of Agos's voice. He looked even more sickly under the sun, his skin all the paler under the bright light. He sat loosely on his saddle, struggling to stay upright. I hung back as Agos strode towards him.

"Are you really trying to get yourself killed?" Agos roared. "How about I save you the trouble and smash your head on the road myself?"

Khine ignored him. He clambered down from the saddle and pushed the reins into Agos's hands, but he never once looked at him. He slowly made his way to me. His eyes were hard, his face a stone wall.

"I told you I'd find you," Khine said. All the playfulness, the smooth tones I had come to expect from him, were gone from his voice. He was angry with what I had done, angry that I had chosen to use his feelings to cut him loose from my life. I didn't regret it, either. I'd do it all over again if I had to.

"There's nothing for you here. Go home, Khine. With the embargo gone, there'll be fishing boats heading to Ziri-nar-Orxiaro from Kyo-orashi again."

"I know. I sent Cho on one."

"Let me guess—he didn't know you weren't planning to come."

"Of course not," Khine said. "He thinks I'm being foolish."

"We all do."

"And you think," he continued in a lower voice, "that I'm the sort of man you could drive away that easily. I thought you were a better judge of character than that, Queen Talyien. Do you think I care what you do or who you take into your bed?"

"You care," I hissed. "You wouldn't be so angry otherwise."

"Consider, perhaps, that what you think are my feelings, and what I actually feel, may not resemble each other."

"You should tell yourself the same thing about me, Lamang."

He gritted his teeth. "I agree that it seems to be a flaw in both our personalities."

"I'm glad we've come to *some* agreement. Now, if you'll excuse me, I have a son I need to save, and I am *not* going to worry about your soft, foolish skull while I'm at it. Go home, Lamang."

I started to walk down the road without looking back. Agos returned the horse to Khine and raced back to join me. Ten, twenty paces in, I heard Agos give a soft sigh. "Fucking idiot is still following us."

"Of course he is," I murmured. I could hear Khine's horse clopping on the road.

"I'm not even sure he can see straight. The idiot is swaying from side to side. What the fuck does he think he's doing? I'm not going to play nursemaid if he bleeds out here."

"Neither am I," I replied. "Let's see what happens. I really doubt he can keep up with us the way he is." I bit my lip and focused on marching north for the rest of the day.

—————— ✦ ——————

The Jinsein people know persistence better than most. Persistence wins battles. Persistence bleeds the enemy. Persistence keeps you planting rice on fields ruined by hurricanes, year in and year out, each forward motion defined like the beating of a drum. But my people did these things to get something in return, little as those chances might be. If you managed to kill the enemy, you lived. If you planted rice, you ate.

I didn't know what Khine thought he would gain by pushing his body beyond its limits. And I wasn't heartless, although I tried to be. When I saw that he was still riding behind us at the next village, I decided to call it a night, to Agos's disappointment. I all but dragged Khine off his horse, found a room to stuff him in, and then went off in search of a healer. I found someone who agreed to look at him—a wrinkled old man with toothless gums and the smell of herbs clinging to him like a second layer of skin. He wasn't as conservative as Warlord San's chief surgeon and thought all that Khine needed was a good night's sleep, hot soup, and copious amounts of *sambong* tea.

"Please don't insult me any further," Khine murmured as soon as the man was gone. "I think I know what I'm capable of surviving or not. You could've saved your money."

"Good to know," I snapped. "I don't need the baggage."

Agos called for me from down the hall. I started for the door.

"Tali," Khine breathed in a voice that was almost pleading.

"What?"

"I'm not—I'm not asking you to reconsider anything," he said at last. "Just talk to me again. Like you used to. Don't drive me away. Please."

His words felt like shards of steel. I slammed the door shut. I didn't want to be caught alone with him ever again.

Easier said than done. I had made decisions that were harder, it seemed, to follow through than I imagined. Agos was sitting on the floor as I walked in. "We could leave before dawn, see if we can outrun him," Agos said. "At the state he's in, he won't get very far."

I didn't say anything as I slumped down on the other end of the room and unlaced my boots.

"I can talk to him, Princess."

"Don't. It will only complicate things."

"You can't lie to him, but I can."

I said nothing as I picked up the single blanket and dropped down on the edge of the mat. I felt Agos settle down beside me before tentatively touching my shoulder.

"Go to sleep," I said. "I'll decide what to do with him tomorrow."

"And you?"

"What about me?"

"If you can't sleep, then—"

"Agos."

He pulled away with a cough, turning his back to me. I closed my eyes. That night, at least, the size of Warlord San's quarters and the stone walls had given the impression of my decisions being made inside a bubble. But we were in a small hut, vacated hurriedly by a family for a paltry amount of coin; I could, if I tried hard enough, hear Khine's breathing through the gaps of the bamboo wall. I was sure he was awake, too. The minutes crawled on like that, and I felt like I was still walking on the long, dusty road. It was a relief when exhaustion finally claimed me.

I woke up very early the next morning while Agos was still snoring to pay the healer another visit.

He had the herbs I needed and didn't even ask for too much for them. I paid him and went up the path, and Khine was there, waiting. He must have followed me straight from the hut. He should've forgotten trying to be a con man or a doctor—life as an assassin would suit him better. I glanced away from him irritably.

Khine cleared his throat as I walked past him. "I overheard something from the castle yesterday. You probably know about it already, but...I didn't want to take the chance that you didn't."

"And you're going to say *this* is why you followed me."

"One of many reasons."

"Out with it, then."

"They said that a small pocket of Kibouri worshippers are rallying in your city, led by the priests. They're protesting your general laying claim to the city."

"Those people hate me. I'm a little relieved to know they hate Ozo even more. Still, I don't know what good that information will do for me."

"Your husband is a priest of Kibouri, so by extension, your son should be of some importance to them. If you go to them for help, they'll have to give you some form of assistance. His very name is a reflection of their religion, isn't it?"

"They won't help me. I've done nothing but tolerate their presence in my city all these years."

"It is never too late to begin reparations," he said. "You *are* trying to learn diplomacy, aren't you?"

"I know how to fight, Khine. I know how to make men bleed. But if what happened in Sougen is any indication, I don't know much beyond that. Every diplomatic attempt I've made has ended in disaster."

"I can help you with that," he said. "I can pretend to be a Zarojo priest, from perhaps the sect that sprouted the Kibouri religion in Jin-Sayeng in the first place. We'll make something up."

"You're going to lie to priests for me?"

"I'm already going to hell, anyway."

I sighed.

He pointed at the packet in my hands. "And could you at least let me take a look at those? To make sure they don't tear a hole through you?"

"Quacks shouldn't be judging other quacks," I snapped.

He held his hand out.

"You're unbelievable."

"No," he replied. "I remain reasonable, considering what you're doing." Now he reached out to take the packet without my permission. I frowned, watching as he ripped it open. He sniffed the contents.

"Well?" I growled.

"Badly dried," he replied. "It's not moldy, and it's at least the right kind, but... what is this, Tali? Is this all just to make a point?"

"I was wondering when the lecture would start."

"You don't even know what I was going to say."

I clenched my fists together. "Whatever it is, I don't want to hear it."

He spoke, anyway. "I want to talk about Agos."

"That's none of your business."

He took a deep breath. "I know it's not."

"Then leave it be."

He was silent for a moment. "Tali," he finally said in a low voice. "Are you aware that Agos has a family?"

CHAPTER TWO

THE BOWELS OF OSAHINDO

ʊɔɾɛɾ

I felt my senses swirl.

Khine took my silence as a signal to continue. "He has a wife and two sons. I believe he brought them to Oren-yaro before he went across the sea after you."

My heart tightened, as if an unseen hand had reached out to crush it. "No," I murmured, not because I didn't believe the truth of it. I knew. He was gone for five years, too—time long enough to fill with things that had nothing to do with Oka Shto or the Oren-yaro. Why didn't Agos tell me? *Did you really expect him to?*

"He knows it is dishonourable, but he would leave them for you. He said he promised he would take you away from all of this, that he would build a life together with you and your son. I thought you'd want to know what he is giving up...what you *are* to him, that this isn't just some game he's decided to play with you."

"He told you all of this?" I asked.

Khine hesitated before nodding. "Back in the castle. He...apologized to me. Said things have changed, but he didn't want me to think less of him for it. He wished me safe travels. Tali...I didn't follow you to judge. I came because I know I can still be useful to you, even if you've decided you're done with me."

I didn't want to hear the rest of whatever heartfelt thing he had planned and started back for the hut. I heard him take another deep breath before he began to walk, one hand on his stick. Every step seemed painful. The guilt began again. I moved to contain it.

Agos was sitting on a bench outside when we arrived. A small table with breakfast had been set out—dried squid, garlic rice, salted egg, raw tomatoes and onions, and hot coffee. "I was wondering where you got off to," he said, draping an arm over my shoulder. I patted his hand before taking it off. I couldn't really look at his face. I was thinking of Khine's words—of Agos's wife and children, and then the last five years I had spent waiting for my own husband with my son. I had often wondered if he had found happiness elsewhere. Now here I was, causing the same troubles for another woman—a woman I didn't know, with sons younger than mine.

"We just visited the healer," I said, trying to keep my voice steady. I sat down and helped myself to the food.

"At least Lamang is getting his exercise," Agos said, unaware of my discomfort. He pulled a stool closer to the table. "Well, come and sit, you fucking idiot. You won't do us any favours keeling over in hunger, either. Just don't expect me to spoon-feed you or anything."

Khine heaved himself into the seat. "Thank you, Agos. You're a good man." He looked at the dried squid and then, as if making a decision, reached out with his bad hand. His fingers twitched as he forced himself to grab the food.

Agos looked almost embarrassed. "Well..."

"I'll try my best not to be a burden," Khine said. "I know the queen is concerned for my safety. She is right about the dangers she faces, at least. It's why I made the decision to send my brother home." He took a bite and set the squid down on the table with some effort. After a moment, he started to do the same with the rice.

"Akaterru be damned," I sighed. "Stop it, Khine. That sort of courtesy sounds odd coming from you."

"Would you rather I be savage and uncouth?"

He said it very softly, but I wondered if it was a jab. It was difficult to tell with Khine sometimes. Agos, thankfully, didn't catch on. "Cho's going to be pissed by what you did," Agos said with a snort. "That boy's got fire in him. A hundred of him in an army—ah! You just have to drill some discipline into him, that's all."

"I wouldn't be surprised if he tries to jump on the next boat back," Khine said.

"Still, he may not. The boat goes straight to Anzhao. With any luck, he'll just spend the next few weeks drowning out his complaints about me in wine amongst friends."

"He'll be all right. Young man like that—" Agos paused, a handful of rice halfway into his mouth. A villager, a beggar, was walking straight towards us. "Hey, you," Agos said. "Not another step. Stop right there!"

The beggar was deaf to his words and continued walking.

I wasn't sure who reacted first. Me, I think—I drew my sword just as the man pulled out his knives. A sharp tang in the air warned me they might've been laced with something. I jumped back just as he came rushing for me, striking his legs in the process. The assassin sidestepped before lunging, knives flashing in the morning light. His eyes were sharp, clear, staring only at me, as if they were trying to bore holes into my skull.

I had one, distinct thought: *This man wants to kill me.*

The knives struck the bamboo hut, missing me by a hair's breadth.

Agos flipped the table, food and all. The bamboo snapped against his body. "Get back!" he screamed, holding the bench with one hand. I rolled to the side just as he flung it at the assassin. The man pulled himself up from the debris, but instead of trying to attack again, he sprinted for the tall grass behind us, disappearing into the brush.

The attack had happened so fast that the spilled coffee on the ground was still steaming. The villagers were starting to cluster around us. "We have to get out of here," I whispered.

"My thoughts exactly," Agos said.

"I'll get our things ready," Khine broke in. "Pay them to keep quiet."

"They'll be gabbing the first chance they get," I whispered.

"Tell them you'll come back with a bigger reward next time," he said. "Some will talk. Others won't. You want them fighting amongst themselves. Quickly, now."

I wrapped my fingers around my purse and stepped towards the crowd.

———◆———

An assassin behind me, Qun ahead, and warlords rearing all around. Too much, too fast. I thought it would be enough for me to cave. That somehow my mind would snap under the weight.

It didn't, not yet. Something strange happened after that assassin attacked. I felt like I was soaring. As if—now that almost everything that could go wrong *had* gone wrong, it suddenly seemed easier to throw caution to the wind. The days rolled on top of each other, the deafening silence irritating enough that I almost wished they'd just get it all over with. What the hell were they waiting for?

The idea of easy travelling, even with Khine's injuries, was forgotten. With one single horse to carry our supplies, we kept away from the villages and stayed in the forests as often as possible. Some days we went without food, and we would huddle in makeshift tents under the beating rain with growling bellies. Summer had ended and we were in the midst of the monsoon yet again.

We also travelled on the inland roads, which were rough and wound around like a maze through the foothills. The riverside road leading straight to Osahindo would've been too dangerous. Or so we figured—the days passed, and other than that lone assassin from the second village, we encountered no one else. I turned to other worries. Where were the warlords' soldiers? I had imagined that after word from Kyo-orashi got out, hordes of them would be scouring the roads for me, as Lord Huan had warned.

Yet there were none, and we were travelling so slowly along those hill roads that it was impossible to have missed them. We passed by other travellers or the occasional farmer transporting animals or crops, but no soldiers, and no word about what was happening at court or how the council was dealing with Warlord San's antics. The silence grated my bones.

Days later—I had lost count exactly how many by then, and knew only that my own injuries had faded into the realm of scabs and bad memories—we came up to the silhouette of the riverside city from where the smaller paths and the main road converged on top of a rocky plateau. I patted the slick rain off the packhorse's neck and stared at the River Agos from the distance. I recognized the area. Upriver and into the left fork on a boat would lead me straight into Oren-yaro. I took a deep breath, taking in the familiar scents and sounds. So close to home, and yet…

"I know what you're thinking," Agos said. "It isn't safe."

"We haven't met any soldiers yet," I said, wiping moisture off my face. "Maybe they're not looking for me at all."

"Let's see, the chances of the warlords deciding you're not worth the trouble... what do you think, Lamang? I've heard you're a gambling man. You want to make a bet?"

Khine cleared his throat. "I think, perhaps, that the wisest choice would be to stay away from the cities."

Agos laughed. "I thought so, too."

"But—" Khine continued, turning back to me. "You have every intention of going straight to the heart of Oren-yaro anyway, don't you? You know too little to be walking into this blind. Let me go into the city to learn what I can. If there's talk about you, I'm sure it wouldn't take more than a visit to a tavern or two." He turned around.

I watched him trot down the bend before following him. "We'll all go together," I said.

"I'm not as weak as I was," Khine reminded me. "It's too dangerous for you to show your face."

"It's dangerous for me to stay waiting for you in the open road, too." I glanced at Agos. "We'll just have to keep our eyes peeled."

"Don't think we haven't been doing that this whole time," Agos grumbled. "Bastards still manage to sneak up on us."

"We've lived this long."

"Luck don't mean you're blessed by the gods, Princess."

But as luck would have it, there were no guards at the gate. Lady Bracha of Osahindo's influence was weak compared with that of other warlords in their regions. A big reason for this was the structure of the river lands—too many minor lords of major clans who believed they should've been awarded the city refused to bow to her claim. Politics within politics. We heard no talk about me, and noticed no posters hanging on the walls with Rayyel's proclamation and promises of a reward. Odd, unless Lady Bracha was making a statement— she would not support a possible ploy of an Ikessar to dethrone me. We decided to get an inn to stay until nightfall. By boat would mean docking right in the heart of the city, where I could easily be recognized, but if we arrived while it was still dark, I might be able to slip through undetected.

We sold the horse at the nearest stables. I let Agos do most of the transactions, choosing to keep as far away from people as I could. Not that it would've helped. Either they recognized me or they didn't. I was as close to home as I had ever been, and my appearance and manner of speaking no longer stood out. It was Khine who had to keep quiet this time, a thing he didn't seem to have any difficulties with these days. Or at least, he was quiet most of the time around me.

He spoke more often with Agos. I had assumed the awkwardness would persist, but if anything, they seemed to get along better now that Agos no longer considered Khine a threat for my affections. I had woken up at least a few times to the sound of them sparring, trading blows with their swords in the falling rain with Khine's arm still wrapped in bandages. I expressed my disapproval to Agos that first time, reasoning that Khine wasn't well enough for such exertions.

"He needs to use that arm," Agos had thundered. "It'll wilt if he doesn't. I've seen it happen before. And anyway, it was his idea. Said he didn't want to be useless. Meant what he said about not wanting to be a burden. Footwork's getting better. Think I'll make a fighter out of him yet. Hell, made one out of you, didn't I?"

"Wonder what old Sharkhead will say about you taking the credit for that."

"He *taught* you, but I sparred with you the most."

"I always thought you were warned to take it easy on me."

"Believe it or not, Tali, I never did," he said, growing serious. "I was as hard on you as I was with anyone. Probably made you a bit foolish, if I can be honest. Now you probably think you can fight a bear bare-handed and win."

"Did it already."

"That was a dragon, not a bear."

"Dragons are bigger than bears."

"Still cheating. You had a sword." He was warmer towards me now than before, hardly noticing how I kept myself away from him whenever I could. I couldn't bring up his family when our lives were still in danger, but the knowledge felt like a ghost drifting between us. *Remember when it was you? Remember all your anger? Where is all that now, you coward, you fool?*

I shook my head, tearing my attention back to the present. Agos was still talking to the stable manager. Khine was staring at the river, where houses were stacked on top of each other like boxes. Wooden docks sprawled out into the water. They were empty at that time of the day—even though it was still early enough in the morning, most of the fishermen would've ventured out to try their luck further into the river. Some might even make it all the way to the southern wetlands for mudfish, and eel, which was a delicacy in those parts.

"It doesn't get much better than this, in case you're wondering," I said. "Oren-yaro is not that much different. It's all so provincial compared to Anzhao City."

"I was actually thinking about how peaceful it is," Khine replied.

"Ah. It's only because you've stumbled upon a rare instance in Jin-Sayeng history when the warlords aren't living up to their titles."

"Is this the longest you haven't had war?"

I counted back the years to my birth. "I suppose," I found myself saying. "I've never thought of it that way. Reshiro Ikessar's reign had its rough spots. Yes... I think this is the longest we've gone without us trying to kill each other." I gave a grim smile. "If Rayyel could only see it this way... if my father wasn't a conniving bastard... if, so many ifs, Khine." I stared at the grey water, my eyes blurring.

Khine suddenly grabbed my arm. "Don't say anything," he said in a low voice. "Just walk and laugh."

I glanced behind us for a moment. A man with a rice hat appeared in the corner of my eyes and then disappeared. I hooked my arm through Khine's and made a chortling sound, pretending to laugh over some joke or another.

We headed straight for the alley. "He'll strike where it's dark," I murmured, reaching for my sword—an elaborate piece of weaponry gifted by Warlord San before I left Kyo-orashi. "Let him. I want the bastard dead."

"If you kill him, you'll alert the guards," Khine whispered back.

"Then we'll have to hide the body."

"No. Too risky. Too many people."

We turned into a corner. The buildings here were pressed close together, towering over us like trees. Grey brick and stone everywhere, remnants of a Kag-fashion building craze from decades ago.

Khine swore under his breath. "Tali, I think there's two of them."

"What?"

He pointed at the other end of the alley. "Over there, I saw—"

The first assassin attacked.

He moved so fast that he almost nicked my shoulder with his blade. I tried to strike back, but he had sprinted for the shadows. I felt my heart begin to race. This was almost not fair. Yuebek's assassins had been slow and lumbering, easy enough to fight once flushed out. These knew what they were doing.

Khine grabbed my arm and dragged me into one of the buildings. He slammed the door shut behind us, dropping the bar over it.

Sweat dripped from my forehead to my neck. Hands shaking, I turned around and saw that we were inside a warehouse. The only source of light came from a few barred windows along the ceiling, too small for a person to fit through.

"There were more than two," Khine breathed. "They would've seen us go in." He tapped the door, testing it.

"Let's find another exit."

"I'm hoping we get to it before they do. Three assassins, maybe more. Agos—"

"He can take care of himself," I said. I didn't even want to think about the idea of *more* of those bastards skulking about. If Agos remained around other people, he was safe.

The warehouse was packed with shelves, full of dusty crates and barrels. There were no workers from what I could see. All the lanterns were cold, the oil wells unfilled. The strangeness of this left me with an uneasy feeling, but I dared not say it out loud.

We found a door at the far end. It was covered with cobwebs, which did little to reassure me. It creaked inwards when I touched it, pivoting around rusty hinges. I stepped through the doorway and into a strange, narrow corridor hall. I waited for my eyes to adjust to the darkness before I proceeded forward, finding the way by touching the walls like a blind woman. I could hear Khine behind me.

The knob to the next door took a few tries for it to turn. I finally got it to swing open, stepping into a swirl of sunlight and dust and moldy air, thick enough that I shielded my eyes for a moment. When I finally opened them again, I saw the dummies inside the room, and nearly screamed.

There were dozens of them lined up in a row, faceless, nothing more than stuffed sacks with heads and bodies held up on poles. Light streamed down from the railed windows around the room, casting an unearthly glow on the figures. I tried to steady my racing heart as Khine walked past me to touch one. "They're props," he said.

"I'm sorry?"

He pointed at a pile of clothes in the corner. They were strange clothing, extravagant almost, except for the thick layer of dust and moth-eaten edges. "Costumes. Props. We must be in an abandoned theatre. Look." Next to the clothes was a barrel full of wooden swords and shields. There were also helmets, brightly painted and decorated in a mocking attempt to mimic those of well-known clans. At least one had the soaring Ikessar falcon on it, though it looked more like a chicken. It was clearly done on purpose.

I swallowed. "I thought—"

"I know," Khine said. "I thought so, too. Fucking Yuebek." He looked at one of the dummies and gingerly touched it. When it didn't move, he drew his sword and knocked its head clean off its body. It landed on the ground, spraying moldy sawdust into the air.

I held my breath. "I still don't like this. Can we go now, please?"

Khine nodded. We drew back into the dark hall, leaving the door open to let light in, and continued to walk.

"Are you all right?" he asked.

I turned to him. "Why do you ask?"

He pointed at my hands. They were shaking.

I frowned. "I've got to see a healer for this one of these days. It doesn't suit a warlord's daughter, let alone a queen. I—"

"Tali," he said softly. "You should know by now that you can't fool me."

"I don't know what you mean," I said, walking past him.

Khine reached out to touch my arm before stopping himself. He dropped his hands to his sides. "Something's bothering you, and it's *not* just the assassins or the dummies. Tell me."

I wilted under his gaze. "Back in Zorheng," I whispered. "You remember I was in Yuebek's dungeons."

"You said he allowed you to escape, only to send assassins after you." His eyes narrowed. "Did the bastard touch you?"

"Not that I know," I murmured. "I was in a prison cell the whole time. He was trying to wear me down and left me alone. But then...they drugged me and I woke up in a strange, abandoned place, just like this one."

As soon as I spoke these words, I thought I heard the music, the piece my brother had been playing in that place. I held my breath, trying to form words for something I never imagined I would ever tell someone. "Back there, I thought I saw...ghosts."

"Ghosts," he repeated.

"Spirits. Of my family. My father and my brother, to be precise." I let my voice carry the weight of this. I didn't think I could take it if he thought I was trying to make a joke.

But his expression remained sombre. "Yuebek's mage tricks?" he asked.

"I was convinced it was," I replied. "Now I'm not so sure."

Khine stopped in his tracks to face me. "Why have you never told me before, Tali? What did these ghosts do?"

"They...confronted me," I murmured. "Or at least, the ghost of my father did. About the things I had done wrong, with my rule, with Rayyel. Do you know why I was never sure it was Yuebek's doing all along? If he had used something in that room to make me see things from my memories, then it would all make sense. But I've never met my brother, Khine. I wouldn't know what he looked like, and my father never spoke enough about him or my other brothers to know how their relationship was." I held my breath. "After everything that had happened, the weight of what I've had to deal with...I'm afraid I may be going mad, Khine."

"That's ridiculous."

"Is it? Yuebek was proud of his tricks. Yet why had he never thought to mention this one? For me to wake up in a room with the ghost of my brother playing the piano, and then later, to stumble on my father in one of the cells..."

"He wanted to wear you down."

"Maybe he didn't have to. Maybe all he did was show me the edge of the cliff, and then wait for me to do the rest."

We walked in silence for some time.

"In my opinion as a well-educated quack," Khine said, "if there's anyone who's mad, it's Yuebek. He's straight out of a textbook."

"Maybe the very idea of *ruling* brings one close to madness. My father went mad, once. Not the way they used the word—not like when Warlord San called him *madder than the rest* because he was foolhardy and did drastic things. No…he lost his mind after my brothers died. They said he just snapped. He would say strange things, hide inside closets, and talk to himself all night long. And although he put up a good show afterwards, people remain convinced he never recovered." I swallowed. "I've been so exhausted lately, Khine. And I've been taught to keep a brave face, so I press forward, but I feel like a leaf on a branch spinning in the wind. Just one more gust and I'll be swept away."

A darkness set in, one that had nothing to do whatsoever with the shadows that seemed to breathe around us. I felt my hand grip the handle of my sword tight. Was this what the warlords wanted—was this why they drove me to the edge? Had they been waiting for me to follow my father's footsteps, to bring out that streak of madness before turning against me? Would that they were all in front of me now. Then I could cut them down, or die trying.

I didn't even know I was crying until I felt Khine's hand on top of mine. As he peeled my fingers from the sword, I saw the gleam of tears on my palm. *When did I wipe my eyes?* "I told you," I murmured. "You're in love with an illusion. The Queen Talyien you know…"

"But I don't really know her," Khine said. "Only Tali. Only the woman I met in Shang Azi, trying to survive. Only you." His fingers reached up to caress my cheek and wipe the tears from my eyes.

I regained my composure, the years of training attempting to override the flood of emotions within me. "We should keep going," I said, pushing his hand away. "Those bastards are still after us."

"Tali, wait."

"No, Khine."

He lifted his fingers. "Tali, if you need someone to take you away from this, all you have to do is ask. You know that I can…"

"There is no room in my life for you, Khine. I thought I made that clear."

"It's not about that. Do you still not understand a damn thing?"

"No, Khine. No, I don't. I especially don't understand you, of all people. Back in the Sougen, you said you didn't want to complicate things. And you know what? You were right. You are foolish and staying with me will only get you killed and I don't want you to die, I don't want to see you get hurt. When you were out there with that dragon I felt like..."

I swallowed as the words began to crawl over each other. "*There is no room in my life for you*, but you won't listen. And now..." I laughed. "Now you're telling me you'd take me away, like I could even consider that. Leave now, and let the whole land burn to the ground? You say I have power, but not enough that I can just walk away from this, even if I wanted to. No," I repeated. "I don't understand you. I don't understand why you're still here. I've done everything I could to make you leave and *you're still here.*"

He gazed back in silence, as if he knew I was falling apart and wasn't going to give me a chance to be swept away. Inside, I felt myself struggling with the waves, beating my head against the barriers my father had built up. Everything I ever was, everything I *thought* I had to be, shattered upon this man whose own mother had thrown herself off a bridge to save him, a man who would do the same for me without a second thought.

"Love," he murmured, mirroring my thoughts, "doesn't have to be returned. Nothing you do will drive me away from your side. *Nothing*, Tali. These silences the past few days, what you do with Agos, even if you decide to sleep with your entire guard—"

I slapped him. My fingers stung from the blow. He didn't understand, either.

"*I cannot love you*," I whispered.

"I'm not asking you to."

"I *can't.*"

But the gods knew I already did.

And there, because he was also the sort of man who was convinced he could read me like a book, he bent down and pressed his lips over mine.

Time crawled to a standstill. I had every intention of pushing him away, but I didn't. I knew what desire felt like, but I didn't realize it was possible to go beyond that, that the mere act could carry a force that threatened to unhinge my thoughts. I could taste the salt of my own tears in his mouth as he pulled me into his arms and dared to deepen the kiss. For a moment, maybe more, I was lost in the feel of him, his cracked lips, his stubbled chin, his every breath a reminder of how he had plagued my thoughts since the moment I met him. I never wanted to be found again.

But then, as quickly as it happened, he stopped. Khine took an indrawn breath and slowly removed his hands from me, like it was the hardest thing he'd ever had to do. "I'm sorry," he said. "It won't happen again."

I stepped away from him. "Khine, we—"

I heard something creak.

My reflexes kicked in before I could gather my thoughts. There was a staircase right beside us, wooden floors above. The assassin must've heard us talking and thought he had the advantage. I raced up the steps, drawing my dagger as I went. I caught him crouching on the floor. He turned in surprise.

I stabbed him right in the throat.

My senses returned amidst my pounding heartbeat. I noticed my fingers were coated with the assassin's blood and bent down to wipe it on my trousers. I turned back to the body to drag it where the light shone.

His pockets were empty. I wrenched his headscarf loose just as Khine arrived. "He look Zarojo or Jinsein to you?" I asked.

"I don't know," Khine replied.

"Doesn't matter, I guess," I murmured. I looked down at my fingers again. Surprisingly enough, they weren't shaking this time around. I wondered if my nerves had somehow fixed themselves. Or was everything so frayed that I was now on the verge of snapping, and nothing worked the way it was supposed to anymore?

The room was covered in shadow for a moment. Only a moment, but it told me someone had crossed the window while we were speaking. "They're getting careless," I said. "They're on the rooftop."

"I wonder if they know their friend is dead," Khine said.

I pushed the body into a shadowy corner. "They will soon enough. They know where we are, in any case. There's no sense trying to meet them on the roof. Your sword arm isn't of much use, and I don't think I can fight them all at once."

He looked embarrassed at my assessment but didn't deny it. "I saw the doors to the auditorium. There must be gates leading out. But the roof is open."

"Worth a try, anyway."

We went back down the stairs. The doors were at the far end of the hall. The hinges were so rusted that Khine had to brace himself to push one open. I stepped through the archway into an amphitheatre. Sunlight streamed from the sky, revealing rotting, broken benches lined row by row. Even the stage was rotting, with enough holes on the floorboards to look like the bottom of a wasp's nest. The building must've been built a long time ago, back when our relations with the Zarojo were at their peak. The Zarojo influence was plain on the architecture of the rooftops. There was even a statue of Saint Fei Rong on the gates inside an alcove on one of the stone posts. It was so old that moss had grown around it, rendering the statue's features unrecognizable.

My suspicions returned to Yuebek. Yes, he sent Qun, but who knew what lay within the recesses of that twisted mind of his? The mages in the Sougen had been his doing, and sending assassins after me again wasn't unlikely. Surely the man didn't have an *endless* bag of tricks. I wouldn't put it past him to start repeating them.

There was one person who never seemed to run out of tricks, though. As I stepped further into the grounds, I realized Khine wasn't with me. I turned, too late, to him closing the door between us. It slammed shut just as I returned to the doorway.

"This isn't funny, Khine," I hissed as I tried to force the door open. He had locked it from the other side.

"I'm sorry, Tali," he said. "I'll try to draw their attention. You get out through the main gates while they're distracted."

"Don't do this to me, you bastard. Not now. I promised myself I wouldn't let you do this *again*."

"I've got no intention of dying."

"What makes you think they intend to let you live? Don't be an idiot, Khine. Khine!"

Silence. He was gone.

I cursed him even as I dashed out to follow his instructions. He might be a softheaded fool, but I wasn't going to waste the advantage he had offered me. The gates were rusted shut, but the wrought iron provided so many footholds that it wasn't a problem for me to climb up and heave myself back on the street.

I had been hoping for people on the other side. But I found myself on a wide, empty street of cobblestone, with arches and streetlamps every few paces. I realized that I must be in one of the old neighbourhoods once occupied by wealthy Zarojo merchants and their families. There had been so many that were displaced during Reshiro Ikessar's time—most had to pack up and return to the Empire of Ziri-nar-Orxiaro, even the ones with Jinsein wives and children. Some had lived in Jin-Sayeng their whole lives.

The price of war, I found myself thinking as I strode up to the carved doors to what appeared to be a restaurant of some sort. It looked like a quiet establishment, but there were flickering lights, and if I could find the right sort of excuse I might be able to find someone to help me get Khine. I tugged at the smooth handles, then walked past a fish tank and into a dimly lit room, decorated with embroidered wall tapestries and a red velvet rug. The manager came up to greet me.

"I need help," I said. "My friend is—"

"Queen Talyien?" the man asked.

The restaurant fell silent.

CHAPTER THREE

THE JIN-SAYENG DRAGONLORDS

✓✓✓✓

The old man wasn't familiar—plain-faced and clean-shaven, he looked like any of the number of faces I had seen on the street just that day—but suddenly the inside of that restaurant was. I'd been there before in some meeting or another, probably one that went on for hours with everyone half nodding their heads over cups of tea, staring at the lanterns while chasing stray flies with their paper fans. I thought I could even recognize the fish, with their ghost-like grey fins and bulbous heads. I couldn't recall what the occasion was—Arro would have, but then...

"It *is* you, isn't it?" the manager said in a lower voice.

I had been travelling in secret for almost a year, and the prospect of being confronted by my own people at last had seemed like it would never come again. But I was in the river lands, so close to home. I carefully shuffled my feet before drawing the manager aside. "Can you tell them it was a mistake?" I whispered.

He seemed to recoil at the idea of having to lie, but I placed a hand on his wrist, firmly squeezing it. He finally nodded, turning to his patrons. "It's just the delivery girl," he laughed. "At my age, my eyes are playing tricks on me." He laughed again, a little too much. I dragged him out on the street, where he quickly dropped to the ground in a bow.

I pulled him up. "My friend is locked up in the building down the street."

"The abandoned theatre?"

"There's... there's thieves chasing after him. From the market. I'm afraid he might get hurt."

He looked confused.

"Can you call the guards?" I asked. "I can't. I'm not supposed to be here."

He closed his mouth before slowly nodding. "You can wait in the kitchen."

"No one can know I'm here, Anong."

He took me through the back door, where he screamed at one of his daughters to fetch me cold tea and snacks. The prospect of eating anything while Khine was possibly getting hacked to pieces didn't sit well with me, but I pretended to accept his hospitality with a bow. The daughter left just as quickly as her father did, and I found myself sitting on a ragged-looking chair in front of an even more dilapidated table, surrounded by bulbs of garlic hanging from the ceiling.

I took a sip of tea, wondering if I could remember where the closest guardhouse was from here. Down at the river, where we left the horses? That was only a few streets away. Supposing they entertained the manager immediately, I only had a few minutes before someone came back here for me. I placed the tea back on the table and realized my hands felt tingly. The edges of my vision were starting to blur.

I thought I simply needed fresh air and rushed out to the back alley. I had barely taken two steps before I fell to the ground, shaking. My mouth suddenly tasted acrid. I quickly jabbed two fingers into the back of my throat, vomiting bile and something else that tasted much fouler right into the sewage ditch. After my stomach heaved itself empty, I got up, wiping my mouth. Poison? But I hadn't been there for more than a few minutes at best; the chances of an assassin slipping through the kitchen *just* as the manager told me to stay there felt too much of a coincidence. The daughter had grabbed the tea from a fresh batch she'd just made... was it possible the poison wasn't intended for me?

Who else did they want to kill?

I reentered the kitchen, where I found the tea jug and spilled the rest of it on the ground. Afterwards, I slowly made my way through the narrow hallway leading to the main restaurant. The other servers were busy at work and mostly ignored me; one glided past me with a tray, where I spotted a simple meal of rice, a hard-boiled egg, and roasted fish. It was one of the few meals

I remembered Rayyel actually liking—he otherwise didn't seem to notice the taste of food at all. I spotted a glass of the same cold tea with grass jelly I'd just had.

Without thinking about it, I knocked the tray from her hands.

Food and plates crashed to the ground. The server began to swear, pulling me aside so she could scream at my face. But I wasn't looking at her.

I was staring at my husband, who was sitting at the table across from us.

He stared back in silence. Always so calm, Rayyel. The whole world was burning, and he remained unaffected, as if he had nothing to do with any of it. It made me envious, thinking about it now.

I tore myself from the server's grasp and marched towards him. Before I could open my mouth, Rai reached across the table to grab my wrist. I tried to draw my sword, and he twisted my arm.

"You son of a—"

"*Not here*," he whispered. He flicked his eyes behind him. Off-duty guards chatted around a table, tearing through enough food to last a week in some households. It appeared to be a celebration of some sort—I caught sight of a roasted suckling pig, sitting on banana leaves with golden skin. I could smell the meat from where I was standing.

"Upstairs," he said.

I started to laugh. "If you think I'm going to fall for that again…"

"It wasn't me that first time, if you recall."

"Is everything all right?" another server asked, intervening on behalf of the first, who was seething in the corner, looking like she wanted to skin me alive. "Will she be joining you?"

"She most sincerely won't be," I hissed.

"We need to talk in my room," Rai said in a low voice. I always hated how he made me sound hysterical. He nodded at the server. "I'm sorry about the accident. Could you just bring the replacement up?"

"Of course." She smiled sweetly, unaware of what was going on beyond the appearance of two lovers having a spat. Her presence saved me from embarrassing myself. Rai crossed his arms and shuffled forward, and the servant gave me such a sheepish smile that I was stunned into silence. She gestured down the hall with a bow, and I found myself turning to follow Rayyel.

He led me up a short flight of stairs and down to a long hall lined with doors. Rai made a small noise to himself when he touched the handle to the wrong room, and started to apologize while he fumbled with the key. He apologized a second time as the door opened and he directed me inside. "The state of disarray..." he began.

"You should start by explaining what you did," I asked with all the anger I could squeeze into a small voice. "The letters to the warlords."

He blinked, closing the door gently behind him. "I don't understand."

"Do I have to spell everything out for you, you irritating bastard? I thought we had an *agreement*. But as soon as we were separated, you went behind my back!"

"Ah," Rai said. "That." He rubbed his beard.

"*That?*" I exclaimed. I finally wrenched my sword loose from my belt. One step and I had the blade against his throat.

His face remained impassive. "I thought you would've learned to control that anger over these years."

I tightened my grip. After a moment, I drew back slightly, only enough that he could breathe without nicking himself. "Talk fast."

"I wrote that letter from An Mozhi while I was still recovering. It had to be done. Governor Qun was heading this way. I didn't know how else to stop him. I had to render you powerless—I was hoping it would dissuade him. Dissuade Yuebek."

Qun himself had alluded to it. I stared at him for a heartbeat.

He managed a long, ragged breath. "Will you sheathe your sword now, my lady?"

I sighed and pulled the sword away from him, letting him stand straight. "I did meet the bastard," I said. "I suppose I'll have to take your word for it. Did you come up with all of it yourself?" It was hard to believe, even after he had explained everything. Such forward thinking wasn't Rayyel's way.

"It was Inzali's idea," he replied. He seemed embarrassed to admit it. "I thought it was too drastic at first, but Namra assured me it was sound. In any case, we were running out of time. We had to make a decision."

"I thought she and the others were taking you east," I murmured as I tried to piece the last few weeks' events together.

He pursed his lips. "They were. I awoke two days after we parted and insisted we follow you. We didn't have a ship and it was slow going on the road. You were gone by the time we arrived."

"With that snake Qun right behind us." I sheathed the sword so I could sit down. "Namra and the others—where are they now?"

"I took care of the letters from here. They went straight to Shirrokaru to ask the council for assistance. The Dragonthrone should still care about the queen and her son's safety, no matter what the rest of the land thinks."

"Your council is overrun with Ikessars."

"I asked them to be discreet, to find a group of soldiers loyal to the Dragon-throne only."

"Easier said than done. If only that bastard Kaggawa hadn't insisted on taking me all the way out west, perhaps I would've had time to…" I stared at my hands. "No," I murmured. "None of that matters. I came here for help. There were assassins. Khine's in trouble. Rayyel—you didn't send them, did you?"

"I have never, in my life, wished you dead," Rai whispered.

My insides knotted. Not for what he said, but at the memory of what had happened mere moments—it must've only been moments—ago in the theatre. *This* was my husband, the one standing right next to me. Why were my thoughts full of another man? "Khine's in trouble," I numbly repeated.

Rai continued speaking, breaking my thoughts. "I wrestled with an assassin myself just yesterday. I managed to give her the slip and let the guards take care of it."

"Ah," I said. "The poison. That was for you."

"Poison?"

"The tea, on the tray. I had a sip earlier. Another, and I'd be dead."

His face grew white. "Somebody wants, at the very least, the both of us out of the picture. Maybe we should—"

I heard a creak right outside the window, so faint that in any other circumstance, I would've dismissed it. But Rai heard it, too. He glanced at it, at the shutters that were swaying slightly with the breeze. "We should what?" I said as I hefted my sword and started walking towards the window. "Out with it, Rai.

You know, you've always had a problem with talking. Don't you understand how a marriage works? We're supposed to communicate. This is why everything's gone belly-up, and I can't even tell if the problem is with you or me or Jin-Sayeng or this fucking bastard!"

I jammed the sword straight through the small crack between the shutters before kicking it open. The assassin was still clinging to the side of the window, my sword in his throat. He was trying unsuccessfully to pull it out. Without blinking, I yanked the blade out and slit his throat sideways, leaving his vocal cords hanging. Before his body slipped to the yard below, I hauled it by the shoulders, dragging it into the room. It flopped like a dead fish, leaving a pool of blood on the floor.

"Nameless Maker," Rai gasped.

"I think we've found our poisoner," I said.

He regained his composure. "And there's others with Lamang, you said?"

"Three, as far as I know. I killed one. He's trapped with the rest in the abandoned theatre down the street. I had the manager call the guards for me. But he knows who I am. We can't stay here."

He nodded. I watched him walk the length of the room to retrieve his sword from under the bed. His movements had the same mechanical precision as always. I followed him down the stairs and through another door leading to the street. For a moment, you would have been able to fool me into thinking we were back to the way things used to be: a couple on their way to a meeting, to delegations and politics and a marriage as empty as my bed the last six years.

———◄———

A handful of guards were standing at the entrance to the theatre by the time we came around the corner. I caught sight of the manager bowing profusely in front of them. "There's thieves you say, eh?" a guard was saying, prodding his shoulder with a spear. "There's thieves everywhere. Why are you so concerned now?"

"It's right by my restaurant," the man stammered.

"Rats bedding down for the night," the guard said. "Go home, Anong. We've got this covered." He gave his companions a knowing look, and they began to pace the length of the street outside. None looked like they wanted to enter.

"Something's wrong," I mumbled over to Rai. "They're just pretending to check it."

"You believe they're working for the assassins?"

I said nothing as I scanned the windows for any sign of movement. The irony of being in the exact same situation as I was a year ago, except it was now Rai at my side instead of Khine, wasn't lost on me. I'd gotten out—wasn't that the important thing? I was still alive and Rai was right there with me and we still weren't trying to kill each other.

"I don't see your guards," Rai commented, breaking into my thoughts.

"Captain Nor abandoned me after your announcement," I said in a low voice. "She thought it was a step too far. It didn't just threaten my son—it threatened her daughter, too. I suppose she's trying to find a way back to Oren-yaro on her own. I wish her all the best."

"An Oren-yaro breaking her vows..."

"I already broke mine, as far as she was concerned." I shrugged. "Lord General Ozo has turned on me, too. It was only a matter of time." I caught a look of surprise on his face, that I could say these things calmly. But there was no sense denying them. When you name your fears, when you name your enemies, suddenly it's easy enough to accept.

I cleared my throat as the guards returned to the manager, who was still standing there with his mouth half-open. "Who sent you?" one asked, pushing him to the ground.

"It's—it's Queen Talyien," the manager stammered.

I wrapped my fingers around the hilt of my sword. Rai hesitated for a moment, and then pressed his hand over them. "Give it a moment," he said.

"I don't think we have a moment. If they attack now—"

The guards began laughing.

I watched as they slapped the manager on the back, tears rolling down the sides of their faces. "Come on, Anong, I'll walk you home," one eventually said, taking the manager by the arm. "The queen, indeed. Don't guzzle wine before lunch, old man!"

They walked away, and I watched in horror as the guards returned to their posts.

Wordlessly, I darted down the steps that led to the river docks, where we'd left Agos. There were boats tied along the piers, some with fishermen selling their wares straight from the nets. I crossed to the other end of the boardwalk and then up to the stables. Agos was gone, predictably. He wouldn't have stood around and waited for us when he noticed we had disappeared. How long ago was that? An hour? Two?

Heart pounding, I turned around when I heard someone whistle from one of the passenger boats heading upriver. "Got two seats left!" the conductor, a short, fat man holding out a bucket of coins, called out. He jiggled them, as if the sound alone would be enough to send more coming his way.

A skeletal-looking woman jostled her way through the crowd, squeezing between people waiting in line. "Let me on this one!" she screeched, waving her basket in the air. "Some idiot took my seat from the last boat!"

"You're not talking about the priests, are you, lady?" the conductor laughed. "You know that's blasphemy."

"Kibouri priests don't belong in the river lands," she said, heaving herself onto the deck. "Don't know why a group would feel the need to travel to Orenyaro, unless it's to join their friends in causing trouble. This damn nation's falling apart at the seams."

My ears prickled. I remembered Khine talking about the protests through the city. Was it possible he had escaped the theatre?

"Hey!" I called to the woman just as the conductor began yelling for a final passenger. "What did this man look like? The one who stole your seat?"

"Didn't get a good look at the asshole," she replied. "Why, are you reporting him to the guards for me? Tell them he pushed me. I almost *fell* into the river."

"Stealing a seat isn't a crime."

"The hell it's not. He looked Akkian. Those bastards are the rudest, most irritating people I've ever met."

"Was he tall? With a blue shirt?"

"So you know the bastard! Well, if I miss my appointment, I'm going to—"

The last passenger clambered in, and she began screaming as the boat left the dock.

"It sounds to me like he escaped," Rai said.

"He would have seen the Kibouri priests. He told me he thinks we should ask them to help."

Rai shook his head. "They won't. They're traditionally associated with the Ikessars, but it's a one-way street. We embraced the religion—they didn't exactly embrace *us*. The sect itself refuses to be politically aligned."

"But the protests..."

"They're for Jin-Sayeng. They think the royals have gone too far. They are urging people to do something about it."

"You mean the commoners? They should talk to Kaggawa, then." I turned around and clambered back up the steps to the street.

"Where are you going?" Rai asked.

"Back to the theatre," I breathed. "I want to make sure. The assassins might still be there."

CHAPTER FOUR

THE COMMONER'S HAND

ⲦⲒⲘ

We ran into Agos on the street. His eyes lit up at the sight of us before his face twisted into a snarl. Without a word of warning, he roared and grabbed Rai by the neck. I jabbed him in the gut with the hilt of my sword.

"Stop it," I said. "We're not fighting right now."

Rai attempted to dislodge him.

"I'm supposed to just take this?" Agos asked. "This man has been a thorn in your side for the longest time. Let me get rid of him for you."

"I order you to let him go. Don't make me repeat myself."

Agos obeyed, though not eagerly. Rai stood still, hands at his sides. "If I may continue walking without being accosted..." he began. If I didn't know better, I would think he was being polite. I knew now, of course, that this was far from the truth.

Agos spat to the side. "Don't act all high and mighty in front of me. You aren't Dragonlord."

"At the moment, neither is she."

"No thanks to you, you bloated piece of shit." He turned to me. "Really, Tali, you don't think—"

"Not *now*." I strode forward, my head aching. I had owned more reasonable dogs. We reached the theatre, and I turned my thoughts away from them to stare up at the rooftop from the street, waiting for a sound, or a glimpse of shadow, anything that told me there were still people up there.

"What are you looking for?" Agos asked.

"Assassins," I said.

It took a moment for him to reply. "Shit. They got Lamang?"

"We led them there to lose them, but he got trapped there with them. But I think he got out. Someone said they saw him take a boat to Oren-yaro."

Agos huffed. "Lamang wouldn't have engaged them. He's too smart for that. I'll take a look around. Stay here—" His eyes fell on Rayyel. "And guard yourself. If he tries to do anything, stab him first and ask questions later."

I gave a small, resigned nod.

"You let him give you orders now?" Rai asked as soon as he was out of earshot.

I sniffed. "Not really your concern after everything that has happened, is it?"

"I told you..."

"Yes, I know," I said. "I understand why you did what you did. I do pay attention, despite what you've said in the past." I bit back the anger. "But it doesn't...couldn't you have tried to send word to me? To warn me?"

"I didn't know where you were," Rai replied.

"You've as good as put a bounty on my head. I've become a prized deer in the other warlords' eyes. Getting here was hard enough without all of that to deal with. What would you do if I *had* been dragged to Oren-yaro in chains, as you asked?"

He shrugged. "Putting a stop to the Zarojo was my concern. Besides, I was counting on your resourcefulness, and you've proven me correct so far."

"If you think flattering me is going to make me forget that I had to face down a dragon in Kyo-orashi..."

Rai nodded. "I heard of that, and that you declined Warlord San's hospitality to make your own way to Oren-yaro."

"Is that what they're saying?"

"I had hoped to come across you along the way. I *would* have warned you, Talyien, if I had known how to reach you. But you know we have enemies everywhere now."

His logic was difficult to deny. It was ever my dilemma with him. To him, emotions held little meaning. I shrugged. "And Qun? Have you heard news?"

"They arrived in Oren-yaro a few days ago."

"A few days too many," I repeated. "The bastard. If he hadn't killed our horses, we'd be right behind him, at least."

"An official Zarojo delegate, according to reports, come to see Queen Talyien. Sent by the Esteemed Prince Yuebek, Fifth Son of the Esteemed Emperor Yunan."

"Right," I said. "So he's not even trying to hide anymore. Years of scheming in secret, and then he goes and blows it out in the open."

"I would assume…" He paused, because I had thrown him an angry glance. He looked oddly uncomfortable.

"Go on," I said.

"He is aware that recent events have pulled you further and further away from power. This is his last, desperate move to salvage what he can. If he had waited a little longer, his claim might have no meaning." His face tightened. "I did what I had to."

I closed my eyes for a moment. When I finally opened them again, the expression on his face looked even more exhausted than mine. And it occurred to me that in another time and place, we would have been the perfect Dragonlords, a match made in heaven. We both bore the weight of the nation, and even with every reason to resent what was thrust into our arms, we would have given our lives for our people without asking for anything in return. We were shaped to rule from the very beginning—the nation couldn't have found better candidates for the throne. Had we not been human…

But we were. The concerns of our lives took precedence. Even when I had loved him and he had loved me, we couldn't erase the wrongs our families had done to each other or the wrongs we had done to ourselves. And time carried these things forward with a resounding echo; I was sitting beside Rayyel now with another in my thoughts, and I realized what it was that I had felt for this man all these years. He was just like me. Maybe not *exactly*, but no one else in the world knew my burdens the way he did. Once upon a time, this should've been enough. It wasn't anymore.

Agos returned with a grim look on his face. "I don't think there's anyone in there."

I swore under my breath.

"Those assassins," Agos continued, "will be looking for you. Maybe it's best we don't lead you straight back to their clutches. If Lamang truly has escaped, we can find him later."

"No," I said. "I have to be sure."

"Princess, he's either one step ahead of everyone or he's dead. There's nothing you can do." He tried to reach for my shoulder.

I tore away from him and raced down the street. The building took up an entire block. I heard someone behind me and was surprised to see that it was Rai following closely. "Would he be hiding?" Rai asked. "It seems likely that if Lamang would not engage in a fight—"

His voice faltered. An assassin broke through the window, landing right in front of us. In the space it took for me to get over my panic, he went straight for Rai.

A flash of a dagger, followed by the glint of its edge. Rai dropped to the ground, bleeding. A blink of an eye.

I attacked, my own movements slow and cumbersome against the assassin's gracefulness. He abandoned Rai to lunge at me. There was nothing orchestrated about this. He drew his sword. I pulled my own blade up to block it. Metal against metal; I wasn't in a good spot to sidestep, so I tried to overpower him, pushing my sword up to strike him between the eyes. His blade slipped down, grazing my belly as I jumped back. His dagger lashed out and caught me on the arm once, and then twice, before slipping down to catch me a third time on the leg.

Blood poured down from my cuts, down to my fingers. I knew that if his blade was poisoned I would be dead soon. It was the sort of useless thinking you engaged in when you felt you were in a losing battle, when the only other alternative was to meet every strike with your own, parry, step back...

The assassin tumbled forward as Rai cut him from behind. He turned out of reflex, a moment's mistake. He died before he could rectify it.

"Should've asked him about Khine," I mumbled. I heard Agos running up to meet us and realized the attack must've lasted no more than a few seconds. I reached down to wipe my sword on the assassin's shirt before pushing him over with my foot. Rai watched as I rifled through his pockets.

"The one from earlier dropped a locket," Rai suddenly said, as if he just remembered. He reached into his purse and pulled it out.

I stepped over the dead body to take a closer look. It was heart-shaped, with a golden chain wound through. "It's Kag, isn't it?"

"Possibly," Rai said. "Not that it means anything."

"Would a Zarojo assassin carry items from the Kag?" I asked. "They look down on them."

Rai put the chain away, his face in deep thought.

I turned to Agos. "No sign of the other one?"

Agos shook his head.

I stepped towards Rai. "Let me see your wound," I said.

"A scratch," Rai replied, tucking his hand away from sight. "You've got more."

I noticed I had three cuts—one along my right arm, another on my shoulder where the dragon bites were still healing, and a nick on my leg. I wondered, not for the first time, how I looked to him—a scarred, aging warrior instead of the woman he wanted to love. Perhaps. I had been so sure of the world once, convinced that I knew my way around the cracks and that the answers to my questions would appear somewhere along the line.

I gazed up at the sun, shielding my eyes from the bright light for an instant. And then, without another word, I slowly climbed the side of the wall where the assassin had come from. It was not a steep drop—only a floor up—and I made my way to the window easily enough. I kicked the shutters in, stepped through the wreckage, and found myself inside a hall.

I went down the staircase and found a door that opened to the alley. "We shouldn't be here," Agos said. "Let's leave now, Princess. Lamang clearly isn't here. If you think he's on a boat to Oren-yaro, then he is. He knows that's where we're headed."

"They led us here," I said, ignoring him. "On purpose." I turned to Rai. "Do you know who owned this building?"

"I would assume one of the businessmen who fled for the Zarojo Empire after the attacks," Rai replied. "This type of theatre is not the traditional Jinsein. You can see the Zarojo architecture from—"

"Yes, yes, I figured that much. Who would've bought it?"

"I assume no one. If someone had spent the money, then they would've made improvements to it already. Yet it appears as if this has been abandoned for years."

I turned to Agos. "Drag that body where the guards can't see it. I'm going to find the other one."

"Princess, I don't think you should be with him alone," Agos huffed.

"Agos. *Not now*." I found it difficult to remain patient with him after everything I had heard.

He gave a resigned look and drew away slowly.

I gestured to Rai, who shuffled after me without a single comment or change of expression. Knowing Rai, he was probably already deep in thought. I turned to ripping my sleeve off in order to wrap it around the cut on my arm, which bothered me the most. The others had stopped bleeding and likely wouldn't need stitches.

The hall where I had killed the first assassin was empty. Someone had taken the body. It wouldn't have been Khine—he would've been too busy trying to escape, or at least keep himself alive. I felt the panic begin to bubble again.

"A theatre like this would have an office," Rai said. "Perhaps we can find out more about this place and what we're up against." For the first time, his monotone voice felt like a balm. I nodded, allowing him to lead the way. He followed the signs and found it on the first try—a large room with a single marked door.

A large desk at the far end engulfed the room. I pointed down the hall. "You keep watch."

Rai suddenly looked uncomfortable. "Perhaps it's best if you do it."

"By all the gods, Rai, you've had sword training. Stop shaming your ancestors and have a little confidence."

I heard him give a small grumble before he drew his sword and stood halfway across the doorway, like he wasn't entirely sure he agreed with me. I tugged the drawers open, coughing at the spray of dust.

"A light would help," he said.

"Eyes on the hallway, Rai," I snapped. Frowning, I wiped my nose and turned around to push the shutters open. Sunlight flooded the room. I pulled out papers from the desk, blowing more dust from them as I read. Most were pamphlets—a list of actors and musicians. It was dated decades ago, from before I was born.

I found the deed of sale for the building at the very bottom of the drawers. "Here's something," I said, and Rai immediately came up to me, his post forgotten. I sighed and pushed the papers towards him. "This place was sold a few years ago to a certain Tar'elian. That name mean anything to you?"

Rai's brows were furrowed. "It doesn't sound Kag."

"Are you sure?"

"Kag names have—"

"Forget I asked. What is it, then?"

"My guess is Gorenten."

I blinked. "That's—are they even allowed to own property in Jin-Sayeng? I thought we only let Kags do that?"

Rai pursed his lips together. "Shouldn't you know a bit more about your own laws?"

"I really don't."

He sighed. "Dragonlord Reshiro opened the doors to all, even the Zarojo after the initial trade embargo with them—though of course *they* in particular got heavy restrictions. The economic repercussions resulted in many businessmen abandoning Jin-Sayeng for better waters, but we couldn't have let the Zarojo go unpunished for what they did to our cities. The Kags are a mixed people, and although most of what we refer to as *Kags* come from Baidh and Hafod, it doesn't mean that..."

"Oh," I said, remembering something. "Kaggawa...the Kaggawas were involved with the Gorenten. One of my father's old soldiers mentioned a Gorenten accompanying Sume Kaggawa once in Oren-yaro. My father met him."

"I've not heard of this."

"Something I know that you don't? That's new."

He ignored my taunting and pulled the document closer to him. "It's a strange bit of coincidence, either way. Why would the Kaggawas be involved?"

"About that..." I began. "I met Dai Kaggawa in the Sougen. It's a long story, but I believe you were down there once yourself."

"I was," Rai conceded. "Kaggawa was treading upon dangerous thoughts, things I had no wish to discuss with the likes of him. I chose to remove myself from there as quickly as I could."

"But not before availing yourself of the Shadows' services."

He looked at me blankly.

"Don't bother to deny it, Rai. You used the Shadows to take care of that innkeeper's family."

"Kaggawa made me understand that we had little choice in the matter. He..." He swallowed. "He also suggested we send someone to keep an eye out on you. To make sure you remained safe from harm—"

"And true to my duties. Akaterru be damned, they supplied Kora to you!" It explained why Kaggawa and his people knew so much, right down to my interactions with Huan Anyu. Kora had been my handmaiden during most of those nights. Somewhere out in the Sougen were people with pages of information about me. I struggled not to lash out at Rai. "Do you know he believes that the best way to solve all our problems is if I betroth Thanh to his daughter?"

"His commoner daughter," Rai said. "This is news to me."

"I was just as surprised."

"Isn't she too old for him?"

"What? Oh, no—he presented me the younger one."

"I see." He flexed his jaw. "A daring proposal, but one that is ultimately flawed. I hope you didn't agree to it. Not that you have the authority for such an arrangement right now, of course, but it would be very awkward for all parties involved."

"Right, awkward. The *least* of our concerns at this moment." I smiled at him. "I may have left on bad terms."

"I don't understand."

"Let's just say Kaggawa's rebels and Yu-yan are now at war. I had no desire to offer myself as hostage, even to someone as seemingly honourable as Kaggawa." I stared at the document. "Though perhaps he isn't entirely as honourable as I've expected. I think he sent the assassins. He must have. They're well-trained, better than anything Yuebek ever sent after us. The Shadows...and this here, this connection, is good enough to convince me." I jabbed at the owner's name.

"What would our deaths accomplish? It would simply put Thanh further from his reach."

"Too many fingers in the rice pot, Rai."

"I don't—"

"Thanh. All he wants is Thanh. Why does it matter what his rationale is? We need to get to our son."

"*Our* son...?"

I pushed the paper away and looked at him. "Let's not start this again. We have to work together from here on out, Rai. Do you understand? We can't afford to fight anymore."

He licked his lips. He was thinking it through. As much sense as I thought I was making, he still *had* to think things through. I realized he probably wouldn't have believed me without this proof of Kaggawa's connection to the assassins.

Agos chose that moment to appear. He was wiping his hands on his trousers, a revolted look on his face. "In this heat, that body's going to start stinking by late afternoon," he said. "Wouldn't be surprised if it attracts the attention of every cat, guard, and washerwoman out on the streets. What's the matter with you both?"

"Dai sent the assassins," I told him.

He rubbed the back of his head. "So?"

"So we know he's getting desperate. We know he wants Thanh—he must've already sent men after him, too. We need to get to Oren-yaro as quickly as we can."

"It is inadvisable to head for Oren-yaro," Rai broke in.

"Nobody asked you," Agos snarled.

Rai turned to me with the expression of someone who knew he wasn't going to win the argument even if he tried. "Do you think the Zarojo wouldn't have spies throughout the city? You'd be discovered the moment you walked through the gates. We need to wait for Namra and Inzali, to hear back from the Ikessars. If we make it clear the Zarojo are a threat, they'll get rid of them for us along the way."

"Do you really think we have the time to *wait*? Thanh's life is at stake here."

"What forces do we have against our enemies, should they decide to strike? You cannot trust the Oren-yaro, and even my own standing with the Ikessars is...shoddy, at best."

"Shoddy," I repeated. I didn't think I'd ever encounter Rayyel with as much self-awareness as I did at that moment. "I'm surprised you'd admit it now."

His eyes darted from me, as if he didn't want to face me while he talked. "It has always been shoddy. I'm a bastard, as has been so eloquently brought up not that long ago. If I am careful, my words at least have weight with the council. If I am not...the Ikessar clan can remove what little power I have as quickly as the weather might turn."

"Your mother wouldn't do that. She is still head of your clan, isn't she? Why would she disinherit her own son?"

"You don't know my mother."

"Not really something you can blame me for. She's refused to see me all this time."

"You know why that is," Rai said.

I sighed. "Her hatred for my father..."

"Waiting won't save Prince Thanh," Agos spoke up. "I'm guessing your priestess can't do a damn thing for him if worse comes to worst. Maybe you don't care. I know you wanted him killed—"

"I never said such a thing," Rai said.

"Don't shit me, princeling. You wanted the boy dead from the beginning."

"You distort my words," Rai replied. "If he is found not to be of my blood, he will have to be killed. Do you think the warlords will accept two successions of bastards on the throne?"

Agos threw his hands up. "Are you hearing this, Princess? Can you believe this ass? Why the fuck do you want him alive again?"

Rai drew his sword and stepped towards him.

"Rai..." I warned.

Agos stretched his arms out and laughed. "About time you grew some balls. Come on, princeling! Strike me! I know you've been wanting to for years!"

Rai's eyes flashed, but he didn't move, allowing me time to reach him. I yanked his arm away, knocking the sword from his grasp. It clattered uselessly on the floor.

He continued to stare at Agos. "It is what it is," he said in a low voice. "In any case, that is not the issue right now, and will not be until this investigation is resolved—a thing I have no intention of carrying out until we've gotten rid of the Zarojo. How are we supposed to save him with no men, no army, behind us? They will not just let you take him away because you asked."

"You forget I was Captain of the Oren-yaro Guard," Agos said.

Rai fixed him with a glare. "I haven't."

Agos laughed. "Don't give me attitude, princeling. I can snap your spine in half if I wanted to."

"What are you thinking, Agos?" I said.

"We can bypass the gates and get into Oren-yaro through the sewers. They're not protected, and I know a way to open them from the outside. Ozo taught me how."

Rai cleared his throat. "Ozo trusted a cook's son with knowledge of how to infiltrate Oren-yaro single-handedly?"

"He trusted me to protect her," Agos snapped.

"Protect," Rai repeated. Even for Rai, the word was swathed in seething tones.

"Yes," Agos said. "You know, that thing *you* haven't done for her at all. Not that she'd need it, mind. Not from you."

"This is ridiculous," I broke in. "If we're going to make it all the way to Oren-yaro in one piece, we need to stop arguing amongst ourselves."

"You really intend on bringing him along?" Agos countered. "What for?"

"He's an Ikessar. I imagine he'll be of some use. Khine's plan is to ask the Kibouri priests for help."

Agos snorted. "And what makes you think he's even willing to do that much for you? Remember, it was his actions that got you here in the first place."

I turned to Rai.

"He is right, as much as I hate to admit it," he replied. "I cannot condone this. I told you—the sect will not take a political stance."

"My son isn't a political stance. He's just a boy."

"Believe it or not, Tali, you're the only one who sees him that way." He pulled away from me and walked towards where his sword lay. He bent over to pick it up.

Agos grinned triumphantly. "Looks like it's just going to be you and me again, Princess."

"A hasty decision," Rai said. "Not that I have ever been able to prevent you from making them. I am aware that you do not care for my opinions, but I shall give them to you anyway in the hopes you will someday learn: you let your heart sway you too easily."

I took a deep breath. "It is still better than doing nothing, my lord. Better than letting myself be defeated in silence. Do you think the world stops because you want it to, Rayyel? That it slinks back to wait just because you're not ready? This isn't a situation you can just *meditate* away. No," I continued, because he had started for the doorway. "Do that. Leave, just like you always do. We can't even decide on a single thing without barking our heads off. No wonder the whole damn nation is falling apart."

Rai paused long enough to make me wonder if he had at last come to his senses. I felt him scrabbling for an answer. Here we were, two pieces of a puzzle that no longer fit together—not that they ever did in the first place. The winds were changing in a way that had nothing to do with the monsoon. Eventually, he turned away. The promise of peace our marriage was to bring Jin-Sayeng was not just over—I knew now that it had never really existed at all.

CHAPTER FIVE

RIVER AGOS

A part of me hoped Khine would be waiting for us when we returned to the inn to grab our things. One less thing to worry about, one less distraction. He could have taken the boat, jumped into the water, and swum back to me. *To you?* I pushed the thought away.

He wasn't there. I approached the innkeeper, hoping for news of him—for anything. I would have even welcomed an assassin or two, if it meant a chance to confirm he was still alive. But the innkeeper had seen nothing, and we were greeted with empty rooms. I lingered at the doorway to Khine's, staring at his things. The memory of that kiss, mixed with yet another tense meeting with Rayyel, had created a fog over my head that I didn't need.

I felt Agos's hand on my shoulder. "We'll save Thanh," he murmured.

I pushed his fingers away. "Easier said than done."

"I've secured passage on the river. Don't think they'll be everywhere at once. Dirty fishermen, screaming children, we'll blend right in. Hey, look here…" He tried to draw my chin towards him.

I drew away in discomfort. "No, Agos," I said. "I told you back in Kyoorashi, didn't I? What happened there with us—it's not what you think it is."

His eyes hardened. "It's Rayyel, isn't it? That damn worm's slid his way back under your skin."

"It's not. But even if it is, I don't want to talk about it."

"Maybe you should. Hell, Tali, six years isn't enough? Are you going to give him more? Ten? Twenty? You'll die a lonely old woman pining for your prince, when..."

"When you're right there, is that what you're going to say?"

He fell silent, his eyes searching.

"I'm sorry if I made you think otherwise, Agos," I said. "I thought you understood the situation."

"What's there to understand?" Agos snorted. "Your lord rejects you, so you find some poor sop to make you feel better. Why else were you hanging around Lamang in the first place? But I'm easier, hey? I'm the safe bet. I don't mind. Hell, the only reason I knew half of what you went through with your damn lord is because I have to go through it myself every time I look at you."

"Agos..."

He saw the look on my face and what it meant. He scowled, turning his head to the side. "No, don't worry. I'll let you brood over it. Would rather you cried it out in my arms, but we all can't have what we want now, can we?" He left the room to continue packing our things.

We returned to the riverside docks just before twilight. A part of me was still hoping we would run into Khine, bearing a happy smile and a ready tale of how he led the assassin on a merry chase around Osahindo. But when we reached the main path, it was not his figure that emerged, wraith-like, from the evening fog to stare at us in silence.

"Rai," I said. I think he had been waiting for us since we'd separated.

Agos moved to draw his sword. I reached out to stop him.

"You are right," Rai said, pressing his fingers over the bridge of his nose. "We have too many enemies. You, at least, are the one thing I'm sure of, despite... everything." His eyes fell briefly on Agos.

I pulled my chin up. "You're going to have to keep up with us."

"No servants for your pampered ass here," Agos added.

Rai ignored him. "Once, I might have said the same about you, Beloved Queen."

Agos laughed. "Call her a pampered ass? I dare you to try."

"But I believe we are long past such labels," Rai continued. "I may not approve of your methods, but I believe that perhaps, with the right counsel..."

We started walking past him. I heard him draw a long sigh before shuffling his feet after us.

Even though the sun had set, there was still a flurry of activity on the docks. Instabilities within the government did little to hamper the beat of everyday living. I heard snippets here and there while we waited for our fisherman, a man Agos once knew who was supposed to give us a ride. A turnip vendor and a waste collector traded rumours that Lord General Ozo—*Warlord* Ozo, they all called him now—had moved his entire household to Oka Shto. They said the streets in many other cities were swarming with soldiers looking for me. I felt a chill descend on me; I hoped fervently that in the shadows, I looked indistinguishable from any other commoner, no more than a woman with her husband under the moonlight.

Rai seemed strangely attracted to all this talk, listening in with silent observation. As the vendors wandered away, pushing their creaky carts along the narrow street, I sat next to him. The bench was set up along the wall of a dock-side corner store and was so low I had to stretch my legs. "Look at us," I murmured, using my finger to draw a streak of dust from my arm. "Some Dragonlords." I fought against the urge to wipe it on his face. Khine might've laughed, but Rai found such antics far from amusing.

Rai grunted. "This is normal for me. You were the one who grew up in your palace. *Princess*, he still calls you, when you haven't been for years." He inclined his head towards where Agos was chatting with the fishermen by the water's edge.

"Have you always thought I was spoiled?"

"I wouldn't have said it like that." But he glanced away, betraying his true thoughts.

"I'm not surprised," I said. "I guess it looked like that to you from the beginning. Warlord Yeshin's precious daughter, running around her pretty garden with servants and soldiers at her beck and call. You were a prince—I thought it was the same for you."

"No. It wasn't."

"I know that now, too." I exhaled. "These assumptions we've made about each other haven't helped us at all."

Rai didn't reply. I wondered if it took a lot of effort for him to appear so expressionless. I knew now that he wasn't as dead inside as he made himself seem.

"When we get to Thanh," I ventured, "will you really let us just walk away? That's not what you said before. "

He paused, crossing his arms in front of him. "It pains me to admit that my judgment was clouded up until we had a chance to talk to each other on our way to that temple in Phurywa. I had time to think about things while I was ill. I have disagreed with much of the way you have acted over the years, but I realized we do have bigger concerns, and I have allowed my emotions to sway me."

I stared at him. Emotions, indeed.

Rai cleared his throat and continued. "It is why I did not entirely support Inzali when she presented this idea of declaring your infidelity in front of the entire nation. Ironic, considering it was what I'd set out to do in the first place, but it was never my intention to hurt you." He faltered, staring at the distance.

"Ironic," I murmured. "I suppose the next time I need you to see sense, I should just try to drain half your blood first."

"You love your son. I cannot fault that. It may not look like it, but I admire it, really. Would that my own mother cared half as much." His jaw quivered slightly, a shift so subtle I would've missed it if I wasn't paying attention.

"But you still don't think he's yours."

Rai's face tightened.

"We have to let this go, Rayyel."

He said nothing. I caught him looking at Agos. "How much do you trust that man with what we are about to do? I feel as if his loyalty is questionable."

"He has always been loyal to me, Rai."

"Let me clarify. His loyalty to the *nation* is questionable."

"Maybe that doesn't matter."

"It matters," Rai said. "A true, loyal servant to the Dragonthrone would've refused to sleep with you, even if you had ordered him to. A girl's whimsy may be understandable, but he was a grown man when it happened. He shouldn't have allowed it."

"A girl's…" I resisted the urge to hit him. We needed to learn to talk to each other without screaming our fool heads off. "It is remarkably naive to think you can find anyone in this nation who will put loyalty to the Dragonthrone over loyalty to their warlord or their clan."

"Consider, then, how a moment's decision has impacted Jin-Sayeng's future."

I wanted to tell him that life, no matter how much you tried, was impacted by moment's decisions. He had done the same thing. But I couldn't find the right sort of words he would've understood. I had tried to, our whole marriage through. Had been convinced I could, on my own, find the pieces to make it all work the way I wanted to. I fell silent as Agos returned to us. He looked conflicted. A man in a straw hat followed behind, nervously chewing on a piece of sugarcane.

"We're fucked," Agos proclaimed.

Rai got up. "What's the problem?"

"The problem," Agos whistled. "Where to start?" He nudged the man. "You explain to them, Juresh."

Juresh scowled as he took a bite of sugarcane. He was thin and dark, with white stubble peppered all over his face, including his chin. "Agos said you want to go straight to Oren-yaro. The entire city's locked down, though. Word came this morning. No one gets in or out without a thorough inspection. They say it'll take about a day for them to be finished, maybe more. I can't do that—I've got fish to sell. They won't last a day in this heat." He wiped sugarcane juice from his mouth before spitting a whole wad out.

"Why is the city locked down?" I asked.

"Orders from Warlord Ozo."

"He's really enjoying his cushy new job now, isn't he?" I grumbled.

"You talk funny," Juresh said. "What did you say your business was in there, Agos?"

"They're wannabe merchants," Agos snorted. "Wouldn't pay much attention to them if I were you. Bound for ruin, but they don't pay me for my opinion, now. Tell them the rest, Juresh."

"There's Xiarans up in the city," Juresh continued. He tapped the sugarcane on his forehead, leaving streaks of sap where it touched his skin. "They brought news of Lady Talyien. Said she fell into a trap set by Lord Rayyel, and that it was only with the grace of the Esteemed Prince Yuebek that she was able to escape. She's on her way to Oren-yaro, they said, quite probably in disguise to prevent Lord Rayyel from capturing her. The lockdown is to make sure she is safely taken home before the other warlords get her."

"Bastards, all of them, eh?" Agos said, drawing Juresh away. "Let's talk about your payment." They disappeared around the corner.

I felt my knees grow weak. "That Qun..." I said.

Rai swallowed. "Putting the blame on me to take wind out of my announcement. I'm curious to see how the council will respond to this."

"You're *curious*?" I asked. "Surely you can muster a more suitable reaction than that. Outrage? Indignation?"

"It is a remarkably foolhardy move, unless they have the numbers to back it up."

"Yuebek claims to have thousands of men at his disposal. If he doesn't get what he wants..."

"We've not heard of these soldiers landing on our shores yet."

"I suppose. We still have Qun to contend with." Inwardly, I wondered why I hadn't killed the man when I had the chance. I should've gouged his eyes out the same day I killed his despicable wife.

Agos reappeared alone. "What do you make from all that?" he said. He glanced at Rai. "This is all your doing, you royal ass."

"It is not *mine*," Rai said, refusing to take his bait. "Warlord Yeshin planned this long before Lady Talyien was born. I wouldn't be surprised if Lord General Ozo was involved from the beginning."

"*Warlord* Ozo," I breathed. "The Oren-yaro recognize him. I can't believe they would set me aside that quickly."

"You've been gone over a year," Agos reminded me. "Not *that* quickly, if you ask me. And he was the next in line, if you don't count Thanh, which your lords wouldn't at a time like this. Too young. If there's anyone to blame, it's this slimy fuck in front of us."

"You know how I feel about this whole thing, Agos, but even you have to admit you can't put all of this on him," I said. "And I know you favour Lord Ozo—"

"I don't favour the man. But he's not the kind of ambitious snake you're implying he is. If anything, his only fault lies in believing whatever the hell the Zarojo are saying. Why shouldn't he? The things *he's* done—" He jerked a finger towards Rai. "Underhanded as fuck."

"Let's not do this," I murmured. "We'll attract attention."

Agos took a deep breath. "There's at least one thing we can do. I get Thanh out. You *don't* show yourself at all. You'll be falling into yet another one of Yuebek's traps if you do."

"I see. He wants to play hero, too, doesn't he?" Rai broke in.

"He doesn't," I bristled. "I can't risk my son's life on a single man, no matter how much I trust him."

"You're doing exactly what that Qun wants. Think about it. They can't do a damn thing if you're not around for Yuebek to marry now, can they?" Agos countered. "Let your prince here worry about the rest of it, for once. Hey now, Lord Rayyel. Didn't you always want to be king? Go, damn you! Proclaim yourself the one and only Dragonlord...it's all yours for the taking! Maybe Yuebek will want to marry *you* for the throne then. Just leave her and Thanh out of this, all right?"

Agos's sudden declaration left him panting. I reached out to wrap my hands around his arm.

"Leave it, Agos," I murmured, trying to soften my voice.

"Don't want to," he grumbled. "He should know."

"Know what?" Rayyel asked in a low voice. "That you're as convinced her son is yours as I am that he is not mine?"

"It's not like you want him," Agos said. "Hell, it's not like you wanted *her*, either."

"We're not dogs," I replied. "Nobody gets to decide who we belong to."

"But *I* am, right?" Agos fumed. "*I'm* the bloody dog, curled up over your legs, keeping you warm, licking your damn boots every time you so much as look at me. And fuck me if I don't fall for it every time." His hands were curled into fists. Before I could say a word, he tore himself away from me and thundered back down to the boats.

I sucked in a quick breath of exasperation.

"He's unhinged," Rai observed.

"We all are," I sighed.

"He adored your son," Rai suddenly said, as if drawing from memory.

"When Thanh was born, he doted on him. Worshipped him, almost. When the boy was learning to walk, he would take him down to the garden with Thanh's hands around his fingers."

The same memory flashed in my mind. I recalled Rai looking oddly discomfited whenever Agos would request to take Thanh for a stroll through the gardens, or to switch shifts with Thanh's personal guard whenever he was off duty. He was a trusted soldier, and Rai had not seen a reason to deny him. I hadn't, either. We were a family in Oka Shto—a strange little one, now that I looked back. And I think, for a while, we were happy.

"I admired what I thought was his utter devotion to the throne," Rai said.

"Rai..."

He shook his head. "It's nothing. Mere details... it only makes me wonder what more I missed. A king, he says. I never wanted to be king. The word *Dragonlord* makes me feel ill. Does it even seem like I'm a good fit?"

He left it at that.

Juresh agreed to take us all the way to Oren-yaro for a hefty price, one that depleted the last of the coin Warlord San had given us. The good thing about it was that we didn't have to share quarters with his fish. We pulled away from the docks and drifted down the river by midnight. With those currents, Juresh guessed we were two days away from Oren-yaro, if we went at a leisurely pace that allowed us to rest in inns along the way.

Or we could be there in a matter of hours if he paddled up the river all night long. But as much as it grated on me to choose the slower route, I didn't want to arouse suspicion. Merchants we were supposed to be, and so we acted like merchants in a way that would've made Khine proud.

Still, it was the longest two days of my life. I could have never imagined that I would find myself stuck between Rai's usual silence and Agos's brooding temper. Not that I had never journeyed with both before—we frequently travelled together in the past, from Sutan to Darusu and even once to the island of Meiokara. But back then, Agos had been preoccupied with his soldiers, while Rayyel was preoccupied... with being himself.

Things were different now. My intimacy with Agos had created a well I was helplessly trying to scrabble out of. He didn't want Rai around, that much was clear. He was convinced we could save Thanh without him, that Rai's presence was an affectation I needed to wean myself off. More than that, however, he regarded Rai as a threat—as if by some stroke of fate I could somehow undo the past six years and I would find myself back in my husband's arms.

To say that Rai disliked Agos would be a gross simplification. But I didn't know how to delve deeper than that, and I wasn't sure I wanted to. What I saw back in Anzhao City, the last time we had talked there, was one crack too many. My husband claimed to have loved me. Did he love me still? Did I want him to? If we could somehow get past all of this—save Thanh, thwart the Zarojo invasion, reprimand Lord Ozo, and convince the council we yet belonged to the throne—could we still be together?

That left Khine. The wisest thing would be to bury all of that in the dust like I had intended to from the very beginning. Let those fifteen, twenty seconds I was in his arms be all there ever was, memories enough to last a lifetime. It was already more than I deserved.

There was still no word on him, but I had to believe he was all right, that he *was* on his way to Oren-yaro mere hours ahead of us. A man who lived as loudly as Khine Lamang did could not possibly die in silence. For the two nights we spent in those riverside inns, I kept a lantern burning outside the window of my room. I reasoned that I didn't want to sleep in darkness in case the assassins returned, but the truth was that I was keeping an eye out for him, half longing to see him on a raft or a boat somewhere in the distance. Beyond foolish, my heart. The other half longed for me to learn from my mistakes and cover everything up in a layer of cold, hard steel.

And so the next two days went. The journey itself was pleasant—calm winds, a touch of rain in them. I had expected torrents, but the monsoon storms were late. "Better they don't come at all," Juresh added. "Just got my house fixed, too. Roof shingles are expensive."

We saw Oren-yaro in the distance the morning of the third day.

The city...how do I describe it to you in such a way that you will see beyond the ruins of the dragon-towers and the buildings spilling from the rice terraces down to the riverbank? No one can see my city the way I can—the cracks between the patches of sunlight, hopes and dreams stretched out over the expanse of years and reflected on every flooded street, every failed project, every empty house. It is a reminder of both my father's bloody legacy and the grief that has taken us through the years—all the way from Oka Shto on the mountain in the distance, and down to the shadows of Old Oren-yaro on the southern end of the river, where the buildings are dark, and grey, and crumbling. Pride, mixed with sorrow; fondness, with pain. Nothing is ever simple. I wanted to be back in its soft embrace, to feel the mountain breeze while I gazed down at those old, broken buildings, wondering if I could finally find the means to fix it all, to restore life where there had been too much death.

But I also knew that if anything happened to my son, I would want it all burned to the ground.

Agos was already awake, though the sun had yet to rise. "I know you've been away longer than I have," he said, standing at the edge of the boat with his arms crossed. The city was unfolding on the horizon in front of our very eyes. "And I used to see this all the time, back when I had to travel in the army. But still, the sight never ceases to amaze me. *Home*, it says. Home. You remember..." His face fell, as if whatever memory he wanted to share with me was suddenly too painful to recall. He shook his head. "It'll pass, don't worry. I haven't turned into a sentimental old fool."

I stared at his solemn face for a moment. "Khine told me you have a family here," I said.

He frowned. "I told him to keep his mouth shut."

"You didn't think I'd want to know?"

Agos scratched his head. "It's not a thing you stop to think about, all right? You were gone from my life as far as I knew. *Go. Never come back.* So I went, damn fool that I was. Didn't think it would affect me as much as it did, but there you are. I tried to forget you. Tried my best. Found someone in one of the riverside towns, north of Oren-yaro. But it doesn't matter. Say the word and she's nothing."

His dismissal of her stung. I felt a wave of disgust over what I had done to this woman I had never met. "She's your *wife*, Agos."

"And I appreciate that. I tried my best, I said, but I was a damn rotten husband. I'd hear some news about you or Oka Shto and I'd find myself gambling or drinking the hours away. I couldn't help it." He looked down at my hands. "You *were* my life, you know. You and the whole damn Oren-yaro, the castle, the army, but mostly you. What the hell else did I know? I burned the rice every time I tried to make it. Some cook's son...pah! I wore her patience thin."

Agos rubbed his jaw. He had been keeping it shaved clean since An Mozhi. "My wife's a good woman," he continued. "Deserves better than what she got, Akaterru knows. Better than me. I dragged them all the way to Oren-yaro when I found out you were missing. Didn't even tell them why. Made up some bullshit excuse about some business with my mother, not that she's ever met her, not that they know about each other. Found a job within the first week doing scribe work for one of your minor royals. She'll be fine. She's smart, you know. Tough. She'll find someone who can give her more, I know she will. The boys…" He grimaced.

"I can't ask a father to leave his sons," I murmured. "Agos. I know exactly what that feels like. To be abandoned by the man you love…"

Agos shook his head. "I don't love her. Not the way I—"

"No," I said, my voice rising. "Stop it. Right there. I can't knowingly let you leave a woman the way Rayyel left me. If I had known what I was doing I would have never—"

"You're a royal," he snarled. "You people never think about what your actions mean to the rest of us." He glanced away, his face red. "I mean, it's either that or I leave you and Thanh with him." Agos jerked his head back to where Rai was still sleeping on the other end of the boat.

"You don't have to do this. This is not your duty anymore."

"I know what you're thinking. Truth be told, Tali, I don't care. Whether I'm the boy's father or not doesn't change a damn thing—what I am, what I feel about you. I *know*," he quickly added, before I could open my mouth, "that you don't love me. I've had years to deal with that. If I'm just your dog, then I'll happily be your dog so long as you don't send me away again. I can't take that a second time, Tali. Burn me, drive a stake through my heart, just let me be with you."

"This is ridiculous. You're being an idiot."

He flushed at the anger in my tone. "My boys…they'll be all right, too. They take after their mother. So young, still. Five and three. Happy children, not a care in the world. They'll forget about me soon enough."

CHAPTER SIX

THE WOLVES OF
OREN-YARO

ᛏᚢᛗ

A curious thing happens when you return to your childhood home. No matter how long you've been away, the wave of nostalgia becomes inescapable. You get glimpses of a life you thought you had left behind. *A long time ago* becomes yesterday and you find yourself automatically searching for other familiar sights and voices, even those who had long since left the world. I remembered riding in a boat much like this with my father, the same muggy sky hovering over us. He had pointed to Oka Shto on the mountain in the distance, his hand on my shoulder.

Almost out of reflex, I found myself reaching up to touch it. It was the same shoulder the dragon had bitten; I cringed at the dull pain. My father could be affectionate, given the chance, but there was always a layer over it—an almost orchestrated warmth that didn't run any deeper than *You are mine.* But you hold on to what little you get when you don't know any better. Knowledge of Yeshin's betrayals did little to sway the fact that once in a while, I still missed him.

Even now, I don't like to admit this. I always knew what my father was. I must've been only five or six years old when I first heard them call him *murderer.* A quick word, uttered by one of the kitchen staff. She was hushed as soon as it left her lips. Two days later, she failed to show up for her shift, and it was assumed she had gone off with a lover on a riverboat. But even at that age, I knew what had really happened. There was a layer over my affections towards him, too. I loved and respected him, and I believed he could have led a better nation given half the chance, but a part of me still wanted a father I didn't have to defend.

I set these thoughts aside. I was not as emotional as Rayyel liked to believe. Warlord Yeshin was sixteen years dead. Whatever had happened, whatever motions he had set into place, this world was my creation, too. If I was to escape the shadow my father's actions had cast over my whole life, I needed to understand the part I had played in everything. My doing, my mistakes.

We reached Agrayo Bridge before dawn. As the boat crossed the shadow of the enormous stone structure—a project that had nearly bankrupted the Orenar clan, I was told—we jumped. I was not a very strong swimmer, Rai even less so, and so we drifted along the bank on wooden boards, all the way to a storm tunnel that fed right into River Agos.

The tunnel itself held nothing more than a trickle, a by-product of the drier-than-usual season. We plunged into the darkness. Agos knew these tunnels by heart—had to learn them, he explained, in case he ever needed to take me out of the city in a heartbeat. I wondered if Nor knew these things. I had always imagined that all my guards ever had to do was stand nearby and stab people who looked at me the wrong way.

Spoiled, Rai had said. Perhaps the reason it stung so much was because I was starting to suspect it was closer to the truth than I would have dared to confess. Not in the way I would've put it, of course. I was knee-deep in sewage and apart from the initial shock from the stench, which threatened to bring my last meal back up my throat, I was dealing with it remarkably well. But I knew so little about the people around me, and even less so of the machinations that had been put in place to preserve my existence and position in the world. Somehow, this needed to change.

We emerged from the tunnels into a narrow maze of alleys, populated by a single beggar who snored in a dirty gutter while cats slept beside him. I dropped a coin into the dirty tin cup in his hand. I noticed Rai staring at me.

"What?" I asked. "I've always been charitable. You'd think you would know your wife a little better."

"Perhaps." Rai shrugged at his wet clothes. "We've never been in a situation where it's come to light before."

We heard bells in the distance, straight from the Kibouri temples, marking the beginning of morning prayers. "Khine might be there," I said. "I'm going."

"Princess—" Agos began.

"We look like beggars. They won't look twice." I pulled my wet hair over my shoulders. "See? I don't look like me."

"You always look like you," Agos grumbled.

"Keep an eye out for guards and wait for us here," I said. "Rai, come with me. I need you to guide me through the prayers."

"They'll know me."

I reached over to yank his hair tie loose. As he glowered, I flipped his hair forward until he looked like something that had stepped out of a nightmare. "Now they won't."

He scowled. "And you really think this will—"

"Move along, Rai."

"Princess," Agos repeated. "You can't be alone with him."

I didn't reply. I strode up to the temple, where the acolytes were just beginning to open the gates. Rai eventually followed, shuffling his feet one after the other. The acolytes didn't comment on our appearance, but directed us to take our shoes off and wipe our feet on the rugs by the entrance.

Marble slabs adorned the surface of the floor. "This stone is imported from the Kag," I commented.

"Occasionally, warlords try to curry favour with the Ikessars by donating to the temples," Rai said. "It never really works, but we're happy to accept the help."

I glanced at the pews. Most of the early worshippers were people who must've been sleeping out in the streets. No wonder we weren't out of place. An acolyte was going through the crowd, offering bowls of steaming hot soup. He passed us with a quizzical look, and I turned my head and refused the bowl. "It's freshly made," the boy said.

"Thank you," Rai replied. "We've eaten already."

The boy stared at him. "Prince Rayyel?" he stammered.

Rai squeezed the boy's shoulder before placing a finger on his lips.

"Oh," the boy murmured. "But..."

We took him aside. The boy now couldn't stop staring at me. I had never been inside the temples here, but we'd called on the Kibouri priests a number of times during celebrations up at Oka Shto, and he must have been up there to assist. "I've heard there's been disturbances around here," Rai said, drawing the boy's attention back to him once more.

"The high priestess is demanding Lord General...Warlord Ozo step down until everything is straightened out," the boy replied. "She wants Oren-yaro to turn over the Zarojo to the council. Warlord Ozo deemed her hostile and wants her arrested. It's...it's a mess, Prince Rayyel. I'm glad you're here."

"Will the high priestess be leading the ceremony this morning?"

"No. She's at the square, with the others. We're not having morning prayers at all. I told you. People think there's going to be a war soon and..."

Rai cleared his throat. "With the Nameless Maker's help, there might not be. Have...have you heard about the condition of the crown prince?" Not *my boy.* Not *my son.* I knew he was right that to everybody else, Thanh was a political tool, but I still couldn't accept it.

The boy stared, and hesitated for a second. My chest tightened. "He's still up in the castle, last I heard."

"So he's not dead," I broke in, stopping before I could say *yet.* How much longer did I have? The Zarojo were already *here.* "Do you know exactly who Warlord Ozo is entertaining in the castle? Say, a man going by the name of Ino Qun?"

"There's a governor going by that name," the boy said. "He likes to taunt the high priestess during protests."

I walked out of the temple. Rai turned to run after me. "Don't be hasty," he said.

"I'm going to kill him. I'm going to kill that son of a bitch. He's Yuebek's right hand. I kill him, I buy my boy some time." We reached the temple gates. Agos wasn't on the street. I swore. For a moment, I contemplated waiting for him, before deciding I was *too* close. If Qun was in the square right now, I could end it here.

Around us, the wind grew colder, bringing with it the first, biting turn of the season.

———◆———

We kept to the corners of the street as we arrived at the fringes of the square, at the base of the mountain. Mount Oka Shto towered over us—not the benevolent guardian it had always been, but something darker, more foreboding. And the reason had nothing to do with the mountain itself, or the weather, which had turned gloomy.

No—it was the guards. There were guards everywhere, all Oren-yaro, armed and in armour. From the number alone, you would think we were already at war.

"Inzali's little trick just added fuel to the fire," I breathed. "I hope the council sends enough soldiers."

Rai looked troubled.

"What's the matter, my lord?" I said under my breath. "You've played *Hanza*. You make a move, your enemy counter-attacks. You're looking at Ozo and Yuebek's counter-attack. They've taken your lie and *used* it to bolster their claims. Don't forget. Together, the Oren-yaro and Yuebek's soldiers are a force to be reckoned with. All it takes is a province or two to lend their support and..."

He scowled. "Oren-yaro rule, at last. With you on the throne."

"And my son's corpse as the rug. No thank you, my lord." There was no sign of Qun, though I could see what appeared to be a group of Kibouri worshippers mingling outside one of the taverns. I decided to pay a visit to the one next door while I waited. The prospect of impending war didn't seem to dampen business one bit; if anything, it increased it. The tavern was so dark and so busy, nobody paid me or Rai a second glance.

Or perhaps I had overestimated the power of people's recollections. I ordered a draught of Oren-yaro beer straight from cellars chilled by the River Agos itself—which took forever to arrive—and barely caught news from the castle—nothing but snippets of what I already knew. Warlord Ozo had welcomed the Zarojo with open arms, designating Governor Qun as his personal guest. With so many Oren-yaro soldiers about, did that mean my son was safe from the Zarojo's clutches? Where did Ozo stand about my son's survival?

I sighed into my beer.

Rai opened his mouth to comment, but before he could get a word in edgewise, the door opened. Two Oren-yaro soldiers walked in. They were followed by two more men in civilian clothing. "A table for us," one said. The Zirano accent was undeniable.

I held my breath.

The owner seated them at the far end of the tavern. The lilt in the man's speech was enough to attract the other patrons' attentions, too, and I could feel the tension rise as they regarded the Zarojo with clear looks of disdain.

"Governor Qun is drafting the report as we speak," the man continued in Zirano, now to his companion. "Something about how the Jinsein folk see us." He glanced around the room, as if aware of the irony.

The other man gave a small grin. "Is he going to lie through his teeth?"

"I'd say yes, probably."

His companion giggled nervously. "I don't blame him. The Esteemed Prince Yuebek doesn't seem like the sort who takes *no* for an answer."

They called for an order. I glanced at Rai, who was observing the conversation as closely as I was. Fluency in Zirano was something mostly royals indulged in—Agos knew the basics, picked up after years of having to sit with me during my lessons with Arro, but I doubted their guards understood them half as well. They chatted freely about their work—as government officials accompanying Qun, they seemed to regard it as their civic duty to ensure the entire trip went as planned.

They were close enough that I could hear them without having to strain my ears too much, but the murmur of conversation from the other tables made it difficult to follow everything they said word for word. They lapsed into their personal lives—one had a child in some university in An Mozhi, another was trying to decide which of two women he wanted to marry. I didn't realize I was tapping my plate impatiently until I caught Rai giving me yet another look.

"Don't start anything rash," he grumbled.

I bit back my retort. He wasn't the object of my irritation, anyway. It was the very idea that I was in my own city, *in disguise*, while listening to two foreigners ramble on about affairs that were rightfully mine, that grated at me. What kind of queen was I supposed to be? I would steal my son away into the night—and then what?

"When Lady Talyien weds Prince Yuebek..." one of the Zarojo began, and I found myself standing.

Rai reached out to jerk me back down to my seat. I slipped from his grasp. The men turned as I walked towards them. But it was their guards that I addressed. *My* soldiers, once upon a time. "You let them utter such blasphemies in your presence?" I demanded.

The guards blinked in confusion. Now I turned to the Zarojo. It took plenty of effort not to run them through with my sword where they stood. "You speak openly of Lady Talyien renouncing her vows. Do neither of you understand Jin-Sayeng's laws? Divorce is impossible, and having the priests dissolve the marriage is going to be difficult without the right reasons, so either you are implying that her husband Lord Rayyel will have to be killed, *or* you are implying that we break our own laws to allow this... Prince Yuebek... to marry her. It is treason, either way."

The guards' hands strayed to their swords. One of the officials stopped them. "Let's entertain the madwoman," he said. "Her Zirano *is* impeccable."

"Not surprising," the other added. "There was a time when the Empire of Ziri-nar-Orxiaro was well-regarded in this backwater place. Your nation was prosperous, then."

"For Prince Yuebek to even consider marrying a woman—especially one as disgraced as Lady Talyien is at this moment—is high praise indeed."

"I've heard of this Prince Yuebek," I retorted in Jinan, so that the guards would understand. "Isn't he your Esteemed Emperor's *Fifth* Son? Your praise tastes like ashes. Like desperation."

"Prince Yuebek commands an army large enough to trample your warlords'," the official replied. "I'd hardly call that *desperate*."

"*Queen Talyien* at this point is no more," his friend continued for him, following my lead in speaking in Jinan. The entire tavern was looking up in interest, and he looked like he was frightened of the backlash. "Even the title of head of Oren-yaro has been taken from her by Warlord Ozo, and rightfully so. Her rule has been steeped in too much intrigue and she has lost standing with not just the other warlords, but her own people. That said, it cannot be denied that she is the rightful heir of the Orenar clan, one that the Oren-yaro people won't easily forget. Warlord Ozo will restore her title and her lands if she proves herself willing to work towards progress. In this case, her first and only available option is to marry our prince."

"Her marriage to Prince Rayyel can be annulled easily enough," the other man said. "He has not shown any interest in reclaiming his position as her husband, and their separation can be examined by both the council and the priests once both step out under the light once more. Her husband's allegations will play a big part in the proceeding trial. When the investigation is over, decisions can be made for the good of the realm."

"Decisions," I repeated icily. "So Lady Talyien must decide between staying married to her husband *or* marrying Prince Yuebek." Speaking his name so casually made me shudder.

"If you put it that way," the official replied.

"I wouldn't call it *treason*, in any case," said the other. "Lady Talyien brought this upon herself."

It wasn't their words anymore, then, that was unsettling. It was the fact that everyone in that room—most of them Oren-yaro—listened without a word of complaint. As if they understood. As if they agreed. I realized some were staring too much now, that they recognized me. Their tongues were at the edge of speaking my name.

I strode out of the restaurant feeling like the wind had been knocked out of me. Rai watched me gather my breath at the side of the street. "Your overconfidence will be the death of us. Those guards...they're following us now."

"While pretending they're not. I know them too well." I sniffed. "This is my city. I've been slinking about here since before I met you. But walk a little faster— I want to lead them straight to Agos before they realize what's happening."

He glanced nervously over his shoulder. "You think he can take that many?"

"Those were once his men. Two runts he trained, and two unarmed officials? Not a problem."

"Their conversation was upsetting to you, wasn't it? More than it upsets me. This is our marriage they were speaking of, too."

"Maybe it's because you never cared about the marriage."

He narrowed his eyes slightly. "You know that's not true."

I fell silent, allowing my steps to match his.

"Being used as a figurehead *and* a scapegoat..." he began. He cleared his throat again. "Let us just say it is not a privilege afforded only to you."

"Tell me, Rai. We've gone far too long keeping things from each other."

"My lady, there are guards behind us."

"We have to look like we're in conversation, anyway."

He sighed. "It is not how I made it sound. Only, if you have ever wondered about the lack of support from the Citadel with regard to this issue, then you have your answer. They argue about me. Have argued about me from the very beginning. Many of the Ikessar bannermen do not agree that I should have been put forward as the heir. They do not agree my mother should've led the war against your father in the first place. And so it goes."

We walked in silence for a length of time.

"Figureheads," I repeated. "Puppets. Was there a time when we were anything more?"

Rai shrugged. "There was a time, back then..." He paused, fishing for words. "When you told me you were with child. I liked the name Thanh, I said. For a boy."

"I remember." I remembered dreaming of it, too, back in Phurywa. I could still feel the snakes inside my belly.

"Thanh. The first Kibouri priest. A great man. Perhaps not to your people, but to mine. He stood for the very ideals that the Ikessars would later be known for. I had the misguided notion that perhaps my Thanh could lead the whole of Jin-Sayeng along such a path. A boy loved by both his parents, and not for what he could offer them—not like you, who was Warlord Yeshin's sword against my mother, or I, who was to be the dagger to his heart."

My Thanh. He was chewing his lip now, staring into the distance. For the first time, I understood exactly what I had done to him. Old enough to have known better, but far too young to look ahead, to peer into a future that held no meaning for me... I had cast doubt on the one thing he could ever truly call his, dragged it back into the shadows of titles and facades. What was the love for a child in the face of political maneuvering? There was no room for uncertainty in our world.

"You did jeopardize the succession," he continued in a low voice.

"I know."

"I couldn't just turn a blind eye. If another had learned of it first, you might not even get an investigation. You'd both be dead before you could deny the allegations."

"I know that, too. But Rai...we could've done better. I should've considered the weight of our actions. I should've told you about Agos. And you...you could've told me about Chiha."

Rai took a sharp breath before lowering his eyes. "My lady, I..." His voice dropped to a whisper. "I have no excuses. I was young. We were not yet married, and Lady Chiha had been...a friend."

"You knew that I knew."

He scratched his chin. "I had wanted to believe...that I was mistaken. That the rose...I fooled myself into thinking it must've been a servant who...but I always knew..." He fell silent. I realized that this was not something Rayyel knew how to talk about, not something he knew how to face. I wanted to lord it over him, wanted to gloat. Instead, I just felt a hollow weight. And so here we were in this sea of treachery and vipers and intentions too muddled to break apart, with nothing to show for it.

"She was saying her farewell," Rai continued.

"Some farewell," I grumbled.

He turned red and fell silent.

I sighed. I couldn't even muster the old anger anymore. "You *are* aware of the hypocrisy, in light of everything that happened."

I had to give him credit. He simply nodded. "I am aware that I did not act as honourably as I could have."

A part of me felt as if such a moment should've carried more weight than it did. Should've felt like a blade in my heart, that *thorn* Agos had mentioned, getting yanked out without a care for how it made me bleed after. But I didn't feel that way. It was as if I was looking at our lives from the bottom of a glass jar, the distortion becoming more apparent with every passing hour. If our lives had been a play, if we had been nothing but puppets to our parents' desires, then I was now at the applause, clapping as I was made aware of what was and wasn't real. "It's all in the past," I said. "You said it yourself. We have to live with what we created."

He gestured. "This, you mean?"

"This. We can put the blame on my father, who managed yet another underhanded trick on your mother from beyond the grave. Or Yuebek and his damn ambitions. Or we can understand the part we played in all of it, too. And we can try to fix it."

"I thought I was trying to do that," he grumbled. "But it seems that Yuebek has always been one step ahead of us. None of us would've anticipated such a brazen move from the Oren-yaro. No wonder they chose to accept your disgrace—Lord Ozo stood to benefit from it."

"Then Qun really needs to die. We have to save Thanh and somehow kill the bastard while we're at it.'"

He frowned. "I don't know what that will do. Yuebek will still be alive."

"Didn't you hear what those men were saying? If the Zarojo are seen as saviours, they can't very well be seen as invaders now, can they? They want the Jinsein people to cheer them through the streets. But without Qun, they'll be floundering. There's a reason *he's* here."

"Killing him will only add to your crimes."

I gritted my teeth. "Didn't you hear them, Rai? I'm beyond redemption. What do I have left to salvage?"

My words were ominous. As soon as they left my lips, I heard the heavy clop of boots behind me and realized the Zarojo officials and the soldiers had finally caught up to us. We were also within sight of the temple. Agos stood nearby, looking frustrated.

I turned around. "Yes?" I asked.

"Who are you?" the older Zarojo asked. "A commoner doesn't just speak out in public the way you did."

I smiled. "I suppose there was no point in hiding it. But why don't you ask them?" I nodded towards the soldiers.

"Lady Talyien," one of the soldiers offered.

"You were once my guards," I said. "Does that not count for something anymore?"

They hesitated. It wasn't much, but the fact that they didn't pounce on me immediately gave me a surge of hope, the first I had felt in months. But before I could do anything about it, they glanced at something—at someone—behind me, and their expressions verged on panic and fear.

"Suras, Nandro," Agos said, sauntering up to them like he didn't have a care in the world.

"Captain Agos," the guards said in unison. Their last words. Agos drew his sword, using the familiarity to his advantage, and cut them where they stood. They were dead before they hit the ground. I was still staring in shock when Agos stepped over their bodies and slid his sword into them a second time, just to make sure.

"I'm sorry, boys," he murmured. "A waste, really. Akaterru forgive me." He turned to the Zarojo officials, who were both staring with sheet-white faces.

"We'll call for more," one of the officials stammered.

Agos rubbed his wet brow. "You'll be dead, and us gone, by the time they get here."

The official pointed. "If she really is the lady of Oren-yaro, then she has nothing to fear. We're..."

Agos killed the man. He didn't even have time to shriek. But the other did, scrambling over the blood and bodies in an attempt to flee from us. It was Rai who tripped him. He didn't do more than that, but he didn't have to. Agos struck him from the back.

"No time to hide the bodies," Agos said, spitting on the side. "Let's get out of here before a patrol comes this way."

We ripped out their pockets as an afterthought, to make it look like a theft gone wrong, and then we left them to stiffen and stink on the empty street.

CHAPTER SEVEN

BY THE NAMELESS MAKER

ITQY

The first blood spilled is often the easiest simply because it happens so fast. After that, the inevitability of death settles in, and you begin to weigh your options. How many more must die before you accomplish what you set out to do? Do you stop because too many are killed?

I don't actually like killing. The thought is irresistible at times, but the act itself leaves me nauseous. A hard thing for people to understand and an even harder thing for me to accept. But then again, my father didn't like killing, either, and he handled it well enough. He used to tell me it got easier, that you stopped thinking about it after the first few. I remember going over those words after I killed that innkeeper six years ago while I vomited my guts into a bucket. I remember thinking that if I was going to act like this every time, then maybe I didn't belong on the throne. Maybe I was Oren-yaro by name alone.

I could, if I had to, mention every single death attributed to my name. Qun might be loath to believe it, but even Biala Chaen's death had caused me many a sleepless night. I've never said these things out loud. I had been taught that things left unsaid do not get the chance to fester in your mind. Khine—nosy, persistent Khine—had seen it as a mask. And as Yeshin's successor, I had thought to make the mask part of me, and so I said the things that needed to be heard and did the things that needed to be done. But wearing it hurt. I wanted to tear it from my face and break it under my heel.

We walked around the corner a street away from the temple, and saw nosy, persistent Khine following us from the shadows. He looked at Rai and Agos first before turning to me, a sheepish grin on his face. "I heard the fighting," he said. "Thought it had to be you."

"Hard to avoid it when you're Yeshin's daughter," I replied. Just as it was hard to lie to him, to pretend everything was all right. I couldn't even look into his eyes; I was afraid I would give too much away. To find myself in the presence of three men who claimed to love me seemed almost too cruel to consider. Troubles only a queen might ever have to worry about, some would say while rolling their eyes, as if love was a thing you could own and show off every chance you got. As if one alone wasn't complication enough to damn me.

Khine gestured to us, and we followed him through the alleys. "I've got one pesky assassin still trailing me," he said. "Thought I'd get rid of her hiding out with the priests and priestesses, but she's *good*. She pretended to sell boiled quail eggs last night and if I hadn't been really looking out for her she would've gotten me." He showed me a thin slice along his neck. A sliver higher and it would've struck his jugular.

"We think Kaggawa's sent them," I said. "Where is she now?"

"I don't know. Everywhere. Could be waiting for us in the sewers now for all I know. I feel a little better that you're here, but..." He turned to Rai. "You look well. Did you take all your medicine?"

"You have my thanks for that, Lamang."

"I assume Inzali is with you."

"She was. She's now finding a way to save our hides," Rai replied.

"I hope it won't get her killed."

"I hope so, too," Rai said.

Khine nodded. "You can explain everything to me along the way. In the meantime, watch out for the bitch."

"Hey," I said.

"You'd call her that, too, if she damn near took your head off," he grumbled, rubbing his neck. "Sneaky bitch, slinking about trying to kill me..."

We walked as I told him everything from the last few days. He half listened, half stared at the streets. Eventually, he cleared his throat. "I've presented myself to your high priestess as a devotee from the empire, come to serve Kibouri all the way here. It's a wonder no one's asked me about prayers yet but—I've kept them at bay by pretending I don't know Jinan. They've allowed me to stay inside the main compound until I can gather my bearings."

"Why is this important?" Agos asked, a flicker of impatience on his brow.

"Because their main compound borders Old Oren-yaro," Khine said. "It used to be part of the keep before your father granted it to their sect. There's tunnels going from the crypts to Old Oren-yaro, which is supposed to be connected to Oka Shto. You'll be able to sneak your son through there."

I took a deep breath. "Old Oren-yaro is . . . my brothers' tomb."

"So I've heard," Khine said.

"I've never been there. Not . . . inside."

"Is that a problem?" Rai asked.

I shook my head, trying to focus. "I suppose it isn't. But getting into the compound would be. They don't just allow anyone to walk in, do they?"

"No," Rai replied.

"Not unless you were a worshipper with explicit business to attend to," Khine added. "Say, you're planning a wedding—"

"I am *not* marrying him again," I murmured distractedly.

"—or a funeral."

I stared at Khine for a moment before turning to Rai. I tugged at his shirt collar. "How well-known are you over there?"

"I haven't been here in years. The acolyte recognized me, but I don't know who's working up there anymore." Rai coloured at the attention I was giving him. "What are you trying to get at?"

"If we shaved your beard and moustache, and passed you off for dead—"

He pulled away. "What?"

"Hold on," Agos broke in. "We're not *actually* going to kill him?"

"Of course not."

"Rats."

I smiled. "I'm wondering if there's anyone in the temple who can recognize your, er, corpse. Maybe not. We want to pretend you're someone else. An *aron dar* Ikessar—you've got the look, they're not going to question it. A poor young man who died from . . ."

"Some kind of rat-borne disease?"

"What is it with the rats, Agos?"

"Saw too many in the sewers earlier. Can't get them out of my mind now." He shuddered.

I held a finger up. "Actually, that's brilliant. It'll stop them from looking too closely at you. An infectious disease. Loose bowels. Didn't even have time to clean you up. Where can we get powder, Agos?"

"I am not letting you shave me," Rai bristled.

"Just like you to focus on the details. Come now, it's not like you're going to be doing much of anything else."

"I don't understand," Rai said. "You want me to pretend I'm dead?"

"Yes, we want you to pretend you're dead. You've got to pay closer attention, Rai."

He pursed his lips together. "This is insanity."

"Rai, let's be honest. You *can't* act. We can't dress you up in something and pretend you're... what's another way we can get in there, Lamang?"

"Confessing to some crime, maybe," Khine said. "Someone who wants to be shut away for years in a vow of silence. I saw a few people come in and out like that in the past day. I think they lead them somewhere in the country-side."

"And he's already done that. If we have him there walking around and talking, he'll give us away before we can blink."

"I have my doubts as to whether he'll make a good corpse, either," Agos said, balling his hands into fists. "Maybe we shouldn't take our chances."

"Stop scaring him, Agos."

"He does not scare me," Rai grumbled.

I held up a hand. "Clean clothes. Flour, to make his face all white. A coffin."

"Don't forget the shit," Khine said. "For the smell."

Rai looked horrified.

"Where by Akaterru's shiny tits do you expect me to find a coffin?" Agos thundered.

"Ask around, Agos. We have enough Kibouri worshippers in the city for someone to have set up shop. At worst, we'll have to make do. A box, a cart, some rushes..." I trailed off, letting him fill in the blanks.

I heard Rai give a deep sigh. "You are making me regret my decision to assist you."

Khine patted his shoulder. "Let's start with the clean clothes."

Khine went ahead to the compound, leaving us to carry on with our preparations for the fake funeral. Agos had found a coffin, surprisingly enough. A Kag had set up shop near an old friend's house, and Kags asked fewer questions when confronted with a bag of coin—or in Agos's case, credit. There were advantages to being honourably discharged as Captain of the Guard, and Agos still carried around the letter signed by General Ozo that allowed him whatever sort of assistance he needed in the city of Oren-yaro and beyond. He bragged about using the same letter to procure a rather nice rental house for his wife and children.

"Do you not want to see them, Agos?" I asked while we loaded up the cart. "We may not have the time when Thanh is with us."

He paused. Out of all the men I knew, he was the easiest to read. "Better not to stir the pot," he finally mumbled. "I made my choices a long time ago, Princess. Don't get me wrong. I'm grateful for them, for what they were to me when I needed them. But when all is said and done, you know where I belong. It's easier if they just take me for a drunken fool who ran off in the middle of the night and never returned. Hate and anger could be good. Wield them right, they'll make them strong. Did it for me with my father, the bastard I never knew. Did well enough for myself." He glanced at me, long enough that I found it unsettling.

"Your love is wasted on me," I said.

He smirked. "Perhaps." He turned to Rai's figure in the distance. "But I've always known that."

"I'm sorry," I murmured.

"Don't be," he replied, echoing words he had uttered a long time ago. His eyes twinkled. "I'm not."

And with that, without even giving me a chance to reply, he strode up to call Rai. We reached the temple before evening, right before the last prayers for the day. The wind was drenched with moisture, a clear sign of an impending storm. Just as the priest acknowledged our cargo at the gates, peering down at Rai's still form only for a moment before demanding we close the coffin, lightning cracked through the sky.

I cringed as the thunder rumbled right behind it, followed by drops of rain. I felt Agos's hand on my shoulder. I reached up to touch his fingers slightly—a soft brush, so faint you could've imagined I was simply wiping the moisture off them—and wished, not for the first time, that I had more to give.

Khine met us at the gates. He'd warned them about our arrival, under the guise that we were old friends. We carted the coffin all the way to the garden, where we placed it under the pouring rain. A priest came by with a lantern and a leather-bound tome I vaguely recognized as the texts of Kibouri.

"What's his name, eh?" the half-blind priest asked, prodding the coffin with the sort of toothless grin that didn't belong around the dead. I recognized him from my time as queen, but thankfully, the opposite didn't hold true—I think I had been too young the last time he was at the castle.

"R...ordan aron dar Ikessar," I said. "Struck down just two days since we arrived in the city. We didn't know where else to take him. They wanted to burn him. But his last wishes were to be taken back to the mountains someday, with a proper funeral in a coffin, not a jar. What else could we do?"

"I would've advised on the burning," the priest said, crossing his arms. "It would help with the spread of the disease. Who knows if you're both infected by now?"

"We're not," I replied.

"Did you handle the body properly?"

"Of course we did, old man."

"Respect—" the priest started. He seemed to change his mind about lecturing me and shook his head. "I'll tell them to get the crypt ready. You'll want to perform the rites over him, I suppose. I'll see if anyone can spare you the time."

"I can do them myself, if you'll just give me the prayer beads and one of your little booklets."

He sniffed. "You're Oren-yaro."

"I'm not."

"Do you know it's a crime to the Nameless Maker to lie to a priest, child?

I didn't spend years in this city just to get fooled by an accent that reeks of it. No—you'll just botch it. I think one of the younger priests may be able to do it."

"The infection will spread," I said. "We'll have to open the coffin up ourselves. I don't want my master's wife finding out I killed an entire temple of priests, even if you are Kibouri." I wrung my hands together.

The priest regarded me with a long look before giving a soft sigh. "Wait by the crypt."

I nodded at Agos and Khine. We rolled the cart as far as the path would take it before dragging the coffin down. It banged on the ground, and I thought I heard Rai give a soft groan, which I covered up with a cough.

"Some dead man," Agos murmured. "You should've just let me do it for real."

"I can still hear you," Rai hissed.

"Stop it, you two," Khine added.

"Idiots," I grumbled. I started to hum as I grabbed the end of the coffin. We slowly shuffled up to the crypt entrance. Various names were carved around the pillars, famous figures known for their contribution to the Kibouri religion. I noted that Rysaran the Uncrowned's name was on there, which was surprising—I figured my father would've had the power to have it removed if he had wanted to. I traced my fingers around the one that said *Thanh*. It was about the first priest, not my son, but the name filled me with a rush of warmth, and my heart skipped a beat at the thought of seeing my son tonight.

I saw a silhouette in the distance. A young priest arrived, stepping lightly towards us. He smiled at me and then at Agos before thrusting the string of prayer beads and a leather-bound booklet into my hands. I glanced down at these items while he busied himself with unlocking the crypt doors.

"The rooster crows at midnight," he said, just as he stepped away.

"What?" I asked.

But the priest was gone before he could answer my question. I turned to Agos, who shrugged.

"Who knows? Crazy bastards, these Kibouri worshippers."

We dragged the coffin all the way into the tomb. Agos shut the doors, dropping the bar in place. Khine draped a chain around it to ensure the locking mechanism wouldn't work from the outside. "They'll leave us alone the whole night if we're lucky," I said as I cranked the coffin open. "Damn Kibouri rites take hours, from what I remember. Not that I've ever had to do them myself, thank the gods. I'd sooner stab my eyes out." I set the lid aside. Rai gingerly stepped out, wiping his face.

"I hope the escape plan doesn't involve this again," he said wryly.

I grinned at him. "And here I was starting to enjoy your silence as a dead man."

He didn't look amused. "Has anyone ever told you how inappropriately morbid your jokes are?"

"It's unbecoming for a queen... yes, so you've said lots of times."

Agos pulled out shovels from the bottom of the coffin and handed them to me and Khine. He took out a pickaxe for himself. "I know you hate lightning, but it's a good thing we'll have that to drown out the noise."

"Since when did you hate lightning?" Rai asked.

"There's lots of things you don't know about me, Rai."

"So it seems."

"I really should admit to you that I've always found it entertaining to irritate you."

"I've always known that."

Agos cleared his throat. "I thought we were digging."

We reached the far end of the tunnel. I pulled up the lantern, noting the rows of stone likenesses that marked the tombs.

"That's a lot of Kibouri worshippers," Khine commented. "I'm surprised. I thought, since the Ikessars favoured Kibouri, and the Oren-yaro hated the Ikessars..."

"It's strange to me, too," I said. I glanced at Rai. "Do you know," I found myself saying, "that my father hated your mother so much that he never referred to her by name? At least, not in passing."

"I am aware of that as well," Rai replied.

"He called her the Hag. The Hag Princess. The Ikessar Witch. And a few other names I won't utter out of respect for these dead, who must've supported her at one time or another." I made a small, exaggerated bow.

"His hatred is one of the reasons I was not allowed to leave the Citadel until his death. My mother never fully trusted him."

"A wise woman," I said. I watched Agos press his hands on the wall, tapping it. "I'm surprised he allowed this temple to exist at all. You would think he'd just outright ban the worship of the Nameless Maker in his own city."

"I never really knew him, my lady. You are perhaps the best judge of his character."

I snorted. "No, I'm not. If I was, I could've figured out this whole Zarojo thing from the beginning."

I stood up just as Agos gave a small sound of exclamation. He was still tapping the wall. "Hollow. You hear that?" He lifted the pickaxe and struck it. The tip plunged into soft dirt.

I held the lantern while he dug into the wall, breaking out chunks of loose clay. When he had uncovered enough, Khine and I stepped in to help him out with our shovels. Sweat gathered around my neck as I dug. Minutes passed.

"Let me take over," Rai said.

"Are you sure?" I asked. "You'll get calluses on those soft Ikessar palms. They won't press quite right together in prayer."

He glared as he pulled his sleeves up.

"Scrawny arms," Agos whistled. "She's got more muscle than you."

Rai coloured. "Let's just get this over with." He grabbed the shovel and got to work.

The hole in the wall got larger, the pile of soil behind us higher. I wondered where Thanh was and what he would be doing at this time of the day. It was too late for his studies. By now, he would've probably had dinner and was somewhere in the libraries or in his room with a book. I regarded the men in front of me. They had fallen into a rhythm, their faces tightened from the physical strain. Neither paused longer than to wipe their brow or catch a breath.

All this effort for one child. Rai was right in that at the very least, Thanh was loved. It wasn't perfect—nothing ever was. But it became clear, more than ever, why we had to get him away from this. Perhaps we could live with what we created, but my child deserved a better world than this. And perhaps *deserved* wasn't quite the right word, but I at least owed it to him to make it right after everything I had done.

"There she goes," Agos said, stepping back. There was a creak as the last of the soil caved in, revealing a long, narrow tunnel.

The path was dark and dusty, but there was a fresh intake of air coming from somewhere, which stopped it from becoming too muggy. It smelled of the rain, too—when I held the lantern up high, I could see the flames dancing.

From one tomb, into another. We found ourselves standing in the courtyard of Old Oren-yaro, among the ghosts that still haunt Jin-Sayeng to this very day.

CHAPTER EIGHT

FOUR BROTHERS AND A CITY

ʋô˄ʈɾ

For a very long time, I said nothing. I just stared at the courtyard and the blanket of rain, and the way it drummed over the moss-covered stone. It was much larger than Oka Shto—perhaps three times the size. I could make out what looked like a temple in the distance amid the rubble. There was also an old dragon-tower at the far east, barely jutting out of a pile of its own stone. The pieces had broken off slowly over the years—I would imagine it once towered over the whole keep. Now there was barely enough for you to call it a tower at all.

I struggled to catch a glimpse of what life here must've looked like once. Of my father as a younger man, not bent by age and sorrow, surveying his domain with the bearing of any powerful lord: in full armour, sword in his belt, his hair tied away from his face, his eyes full of light. Of the four sons that were his might and pride. Of the Oren-yaro army that was feared and respected, but not yet hated. It was hard. I had nothing to compare the fantasy to. The days in Oka Shto, nestled in the mountain, were slow and quiet. Days of emptiness, of quiet halls and meetings stretched out over the years. Old Oren-yaro was my ancestors' city as it ought to be, the very heart and soul of it.

"What happened here?" Agos said, breaking the silence.

"You know what happened here," I replied.

He stepped onto the overgrowth, his shoulders heaving. "But I mean—what exactly? Everyone says something a little different. The Ikessars started it. War-lord Yeshin started it."

"*Someone* did," I said. "The only man who knows for sure died sixteen years ago."

As if the gods were listening, lightning flashed across the sky. I shut my eyes, waiting for the thunder, knowing it didn't matter. Tears leaked through my eyelids. It shouldn't matter. The moment of terror was over. Whatever happened here was supposed to be over. Why wasn't it?

"Watch out, Tali!" Khine screamed.

I forced my eyes open, just as a sword came bearing down on me. Instinct took over; I leaped back and drew my sword even before my mind could grasp what was happening. The woman didn't even falter; she lunged a second time and the tip of her sword went through my shirt, past my rib, as I side-stepped.

Now the thunder came.

I lifted my arm to protect my neck for a third strike. Agos came barrelling through the mud in the same instant. He yelled something I couldn't hear through the rumble; the woman ducked to avoid his sword swing, an easy thing to do given her small stature and his height. She fled, disappearing into the shadows of the ruins.

"It's her," Khine gasped as he and Rai caught up with us. "The assassin that's been tailing me. How the fuck did she get here?"

Agos spat. "She knows better than to try again."

Khine shook his head. "She'll try again. She—"

Another flash of lightning, turning my insides to jelly. I swore. Did it have to be now? She emerged from the shadows again, and my body reacted slowly, like I was covered in a layer of ice. I wanted to drop the sword and hide. When the thunder arrived, it crawled past my ears and into my bones, urging me to curl up in the mud and let her kill me because—

I wasn't her target. She went straight for Khine.

I *saw* it happen before it did. It was in the turn of her sword, the angle of her footwork. But I didn't do a damn thing. He was too far away, I reasoned. At least ten, maybe twenty paces. He was too far away and I knew there was going to be a third lightning strike and...

"Princess, what are you doing?" Agos roared. "Don't just stand there!"

He's right, I heard my father laugh. *When are you going to explain to him what you are—that you are just this broken piece masquerading as my daughter?*

Agos grabbed my arm, jolting me out of my senses. "Lamang!" he screamed, barely paying attention to me. He wouldn't reach him in time, either.

Khine responded by running. I realized he didn't have a sword. He wouldn't have, not when he'd been staying with priests. He ducked straight into one of the old houses before her sword could connect, and they both disappeared from sight.

"What's wrong with her?" Rai asked from behind.

"Nothing," Agos snapped. "We have to get out of here."

"Khine won't survive a minute with that woman," I managed.

"I disagree. He's lived all this time. He'll live a little longer."

"Go . . . go and help him, Agos."

He placed his hands on my shoulders and looked me squarely in the eye. "I'm not leaving you."

I pushed him away, stumbling forward, hands shaking. Not from the cold. But I willed myself to lift my sword, to raise my eyes. I spotted them heading towards the dragon-tower, beside the wall. Khine was running up the ramparts—a bad decision when faced with someone as agile as the woman behind him. If he slipped, it was over.

I forced my legs to move.

Agos roared. For a moment, I thought he would stop me. "Give this to him!" he said instead, tearing his sheathed sword from his belt and shoving it into my hands. I saw what he meant. The dragon-tower was closer to us. I could run faster than him, faster than any of them. Faster than Khine and the assassin behind him.

I dashed up the other set of stairs, hoping to meet Khine halfway. He saw me just as I reached the top and doubled his efforts to reach me. There was a massive gap in the ramparts, where the dragon-tower's crumbling stone had smashed through—he dashed to the edge and jumped.

He barely made it to the other side. I managed to pull him up to flat ground before he could fall. As he got to his feet, I shoved Agos's sword into his hands. In that same instant, I saw the woman crouched down at the crushed top of the dragon-tower, sweat dripping down her face. She took a moment to gather her bearings before jumping herself.

She rolled on the stone next to us, blade striking Khine in the leg before he could react. I caught her rib cage with my foot and slammed the side of her cheek with the hilt of my sword. She took it like nothing. I doubled back, my reflexes stunted by my anticipation of the next lightning strike. I felt like I was swimming in black water and I couldn't feel the bottom. Why wasn't the storm breaking?

She grabbed my shirt, pulled me up towards her, and laughed.

"For the Sougen." She spat on my face.

Khine slashed her from behind.

She shoved me to the side and turned to meet his charge. He managed to cut through her defenses at least twice—an effect of Agos's lessons, though I could tell he had yet to recover from his injuries—he was struggling to keep his fingers around the hilt. He twitched with every blow. "You're supposed to take me out first, remember?" he asked, gaining confidence. "Finish what you started. Come on."

She threw me aside and pressed on him, both arms bleeding from his strikes. She was still the superior fighter, the one who knew her way with a sword and hadn't been gnawed on by a dragon mere weeks ago. Khine didn't stand a chance.

I managed to scramble to my feet just as she lunged for the killing blow. Khine deflected it, barely. I went for her ankles. My blade never even connected; she jumped well out of reach, turned, and kicked me on the jaw hard enough that I dropped my sword. It slid across the ramparts and stopped at the very edge. To make a dash for it would be to leave myself open.

"Get it!" Khine cried, stepping between me and the assassin.

I took one step when another flash of lightning lit the sky. I froze, waiting for it to go away, for the rumble of thunder to break the tension. It didn't. One flash gave way to another, and then another, until the sky looked like it was falling apart and I realized we were in the middle of a lightning storm. The panic struck all thought out of my head; far from swimming, I was floating now, as if my spirit was trying to break away from the terrible burden of my body. I could see nothing beyond the fear and the shame that Yeshin's daughter would find herself cowering like a dog. *Queen of Jin-Sayeng? Look at you, Talyien! What kind of a queen near-pisses herself over mere lightning?*

Nothing, at least, except Khine's eyes. I found myself gazing into them and felt a moment of relief. I didn't know what he saw, but his face relaxed. "Get your sword, Tali," he said in a softer voice.

"I—"

"Don't worry about me. I got this. You go do what you have to."

Without waiting for my reply, he turned to meet the assassin, shoving her with his elbow. They both slid down the rubble, down to the base of the dragon-tower. They disappeared from sight.

I screamed to drown out the roaring thunder. The sound broke my stupor. I tore across the ramparts, grabbed the sword, and dashed down the steps after them. I reached the dragon-tower before I was out of breath, and tried to crawl up the loose stone to where I last saw Khine. As soon as I touched one, I felt something hot crawl up my hand. The rubble parted, revealing a dark figure of a creature with an open mouth. A flash of blue surrounded my senses as it attacked.

"Get out of the way!" a voice screamed.

I did, barely. I made a bad roll and struck my elbow at an awkward angle. Cursing, I tasted dry soil and grass. I spat it out. Behind me, someone laughed awkwardly. "That thing's chained," the man said, pulling me to my feet. He patted the dirt from my arms. "Come on, Taraji. Don't be so dramatic. What will your father say?"

Taraji. My brother's name.

My mouth opened against my will. "Who knows what the old man will say?" Taraji's voice asked, with a hint of a sneer. "It's not like I'm not a constant disappointment." The thing roared again and I flinched, jumping to the side.

The creature struck the end of its chains, its mouth opening to reveal a human-like mouth with rows of long, white teeth. Its single eye rolled in the middle of its socket, but it was looking right *at* me with a sort of maniacal grin. "I swear," I said, "that thing looks nothing like a dragon. Dragonlord Rysaran's report must be mistaken."

"Did you wet yourself, Taraji? You're the Oren-yaro heir!"

"Ah, leave me alone. I don't see *you* going up to it."

"Bet you'll be a little braver if Ozo's here. Come on, you can pretend till he gets back. Chin up. Chest out. That's the spirit."

I ignored his ribbing and kept my eyes on the creature, which was pacing back and forth. "I know we don't have dragons anymore, but I would've remembered if they looked like *that*."

"Maybe it's the best we've got," my companion said. "Still. I imagine your father seized it for *you*. You ready to ride that thing, *Dragonlord*?"

"Don't make such vile jokes."

"Oh, come on. You know it's inevitable. We're in Oren-yaro—I can scream about this at the top of my lungs! Dragonlord Rysaran is a weak ruler. Might will always prevail. We are swords first, servants—"

The chain snapped.

It happened so quickly that for a moment, it felt like a joke. In fact, the first thing I thought of was, *My father is testing me. He wants to see my reaction.* So I kept myself standing perfectly straight, even when the dragon tore through my guard, even as his guts flew right in front of my face.

Horns sounded from the ramparts just as the dragon took flight. Tearing myself from the nausea of the blood-stench, I found myself running for the safety of the temple, my heart pounding. As I dashed up the steps, I saw tall Lang making his way down. He was dressed in loose-fitting white ceremonial robes, probably for practice. The priestesses had asked him to lead the ceremony for Father's upcoming nameday. I screamed at him to run, to turn the other way. He stared back in confusion, his lips quirking to say my name.

The dragon appeared behind us, opening its mouth. A shot of flame blasted from its jaws, leaving ash where my brother once stood. Some of it drifted with the wind, catching on my face. I wiped a streak off and stared at the dust on my trembling fingers, my mind struggling to grasp what was happening. Lang. Lang was dead.

Arrows flew from the ramparts, striking the creature in mid-air. It crashed to the ground just as soldiers appeared to subdue it. It attacked another guard, snapping him in half and then tearing into the body like a falcon with a fish. Undeterred, the other guards pressed on with their spears, surrounding the frenzied beast. There was another figure with them—Senjo. He was too close to the snapping jaws.

I came running back to save him. I had already lost one brother—I wasn't about to lose another. Before I could reach the bottom of the courtyard, I heard a thin hiss inside my head, boring deep into the crevices of my skull. The soldiers turned on each other, the creature seemingly forgotten as their spears jabbed into their brothers' bellies.

My own went for my throat.

"Senjo!" I screamed as he tore after me with his sword. He was the second-born, but he was taller, bigger, stronger than I ever could be. "Snap out of it, Senjo!" He didn't stop. His face was grim, steady, silent, and his eyes...his eyes were blank.

I fell on my back as he bore down on me. "Senjo!" I screamed, one last time before I felt his blade sink into my neck. In almost the same breath, the dragon bent over him, jaws wide open. My last thought was that we were all doomed, and that I was glad I didn't have to see Shoen, the little one, die.

I woke up to the taste of rain in my mouth. I was on Agos's back, with arms and legs that felt like lead. "Senjo..." I repeated, remnants from the dream. It felt so real. The grief, the panic, the searing, red-hot pain of the blade digging into my flesh.

"You're awake," Agos said.

I struggled to form words as he carefully lowered me to the ground. Rai was standing right behind us. "What happened?" I asked. "Where's the creature?"

"What are you talking about? You slipped on a patch of mud."

"There was a creature, Agos," I said as I pulled myself up. "It came from the rubble. I saw it."

"You slipped and you passed out," Agos said. He turned to Rai.

"He's saying the truth," Rai said.

"But..."

"You were on the ruins of that dragon-tower. It flashed momentarily when you passed out. I thought that was lightning. We didn't see anything else."

"What about Khine? The assassin?" In my mind, I saw Khine smiling in the rain, and it was all I could do not to turn and go tearing back after him.

"They disappeared in the brush."

"And you just left them?"

"She wants to kill you, Princess," Agos said. "You were unconscious. It was either leave you on the ground while we went looking for them, or leave. We couldn't take the chance."

I turned around. We were deep inside a tunnel, lit only by the lantern in Agos's hand.

"We're too far away," he continued. "Priorities, Princess. We need to get to the prince. We're right under Oka Shto now."

"He is, unfortunately, right," Rai added. "Lamang's escaped her before. I have no doubt he will do that again, or finish the job. In the meantime…" He pointed to the end of the tunnel.

I hesitated before I followed them down, my feet dragging with every step. The rough cave walls finally gave way to a long, circular chamber with a winding staircase. We were right under the mountain, Agos said. I tore myself from my worries to gaze in awe at the stone walls, wondering how they were built. A fresh breeze drifted in from the windows underneath the ceiling, covered with plain glass that had cracked over time. I could see the torrent of rain and swaying branches outside.

"Your father had this built?" I heard Rai ask in wonder.

I turned to him. He was standing at the end of the staircase, gazing up at an etching that glowed blue. They were runes in a language I didn't know, written in a circle. I felt myself grow sick.

"The *agan*," I murmured. I couldn't even make myself touch the etchings. "It can't be. He hated everything about it, everything it stood for. Rysaran's dragon killed my brothers." I flinched, remembering the dream. Was it just a dream?

"You have here a clear indication that he used the *agan* to build your castle," Rai said. "He used mages."

"Zarojo mages." It wasn't even a question anymore.

"It seems their partnership runs deep," he said. "Longer than our betrothal— longer even than my own birth, if I remember correctly when Oka Shto was built."

"How could you be so factual about it?"

Rai shrugged. "It is a fact, nothing more."

"It speaks of a betrayal that continues," I whispered. "My father detested the *agan*. He had nothing but ill words for Dageian mages. He spoke of how we should continue with the old ways, how it was Rysaran's obsession with the *agan*-mad dragon that resulted in the war in the first place."

"You keep repeating these words as if you find it hard to believe that Warlord Yeshin, of all people, could be so treacherous. You've already seen how his mind worked."

"But..."

"How could he lie to you, you mean?" It was Agos, this time. "If you ask me, he was probably just doing it to protect you. The less you knew, the better."

"The presumptuous bastard," I whispered. "What would he have been trying to protect me from?"

"I don't know. Lots of things. Can't fault the intent, much as you may hate it. What are you staring at me like that for?" he asked, turning to Rai.

Rai shrugged. "I just didn't realize you could speak so eloquently given half the chance."

"Fuck you up the ass."

"And now it's gone."

I began to walk the length of the chamber, which was bigger than I first gave it credit for. I stopped before I could reach the far end. There, upturned on its side, was a rusted animal cage with wheels. It was the biggest cage I had ever seen—six horses could've fit in it, maybe even seven, and I imagined it must've taken a good number of beasts just to pull it. Some of the bars were bent, bowing outwards. There were more markings on the iron, all of which also glowed blue.

"Perhaps you have the answer you seek," Rai said, coming up from behind me.

I swallowed. "I don't know what I'm looking at."

He scratched his chin before replying. "There are rumours that Warlord Yeshin was the one who brought Rysaran's dragon to Oren-yaro in the first place."

His words had an eerie quality to them. *Your father seized it.* I wanted to believe it was just a dream, but...

Rai walked towards the cage to touch one bent wheel. It turned with a creaky sound. "Warlord Yeshin was said to have sent his men to intercept this...thing. The dragon didn't come from the wild—a Kag merchant was transporting it from Gaspar, moving through Jin-Sayeng. That much might be true—do you see the Kag characters? Rysaran knew of this dragon from his travels. It may be that he baited Warlord Yeshin into taking it for himself. Warlord Yeshin sent the men, and then hired mages to open the cage, which was sealed with powerful spells."

"He hired mages," I repeated. *Might will always prevail.*

"That's why I didn't pay attention to these rumours myself." Rai pointed at the glowing markings on the wall. "Perhaps I should have. This was Warlord Yeshin's castle. It's hard to deny a mage's handiwork when you see it."

"He hired Yuebek's mages," I murmured. "They helped build the walls in Zorheng City. I'm not an expert on their handiwork, but the coincidence is too much to deny."

"Or perhaps the mages are Yuebek's mother's," Rai said. "He must've been a very young child when this all happened, and my understanding is that he inherited his skills from his mother's line."

"You've been doing your research."

"You're surprised?"

"No, just—pleased, oddly enough. That some things remain as they should be." I stared at the cage, half-shadowed under the lantern light, at this shallow grave holding the bulk of my father's sins. He had sent the men, hired the mages. Opened the cage. Released the mad dragon into the world. His ambition destroyed his own city, and killed his sons.

I prodded myself for what I felt. There was more than I thought lay there. What I didn't expect was sympathy for my father. It must not have been easy to live with your mistakes, to swathe them with your lies and carry forward as if nothing ever happened. The true reason for the War of the Wolves lay in front of me: Yeshin's actions, and the bloodbath that ensued, were a reflection of his hate not for the Ikessars but for himself. He killed his own children.

Your brothers loved dogs.

I got up, trying to ignore my pounding headache. "No sense in dwelling in the past," I croaked, echoing our conversation from that morning.

Rai nodded. But as I went up the stairs, my brother Taraji's haunting music began to play inside my head once more.

Madness, it seemed, ran in the family after all.

CHAPTER NINE

THE LONE WOLF

ひびひ

The tunnels opened up into the kitchens. It was very late, and I knew that most of the servants slept early to make sure they had tea and coffee ready before the rest woke up. With a storm right outside, it was unlikely they would linger through the castle hallway for long. But as we took a turn around the pantry, past sacks of rice, flour, and mung beans, I caught sight of a familiar figure bent over the large kitchen table. A fat woman, with eyes that disappeared every time she smiled. She turned at the sound of our footsteps.

"Agos," she gasped, recoiling as if seeing a ghost. And then she turned to me, and her face grew whiter. "My queen."

"Ma," Agos breathed. He walked towards her.

She slapped him.

Agos's face was red, though it had nothing to do with the heat from the hearth or the slap itself. A man who took blows like a tree trunk would have hardly felt it. "You show up here after years, without a single word..." she began.

"The queen's orders," Agos said. He took his mother's hand, pressing it against his forehead. If there had been room to grovel, he would have.

Hessa shook her head. "She ordered you to leave and never speak to your mother again? I find that hard to believe."

"I—"

"Beloved Queen," she said, pushing Agos away to look at me. She patted my cheeks with both hands, leaving flour on my skin. "Ah, you look thin. Wherever you've been, they haven't been feeding you very well, have they?"

"Not half as well as you did, Ma Hessa," I replied.

She bowed a little before pulling me into an embrace. "We missed you around here, child," she said, and I felt a flush of embarrassment, because I never imagined anyone in the castle would ever feel that way about me.

"I went to fetch Lord Rayyel," I said. I glanced towards Rai, who looked like a drenched rat in the corner.

Hessa pulled away without comment—you would've thought that wayward princes showed up at her doorstep every week. Instead, she gestured at the stove. "There's fried milkfish and bean stew, if you'll give me a moment to get the stove going. Maybe I'll fry some eggs, too—that'll warm up the rice. And you'll want to see Prince Thanh while you wait, I suppose. That child—ah! Don't you worry. We took good care of him while you were away. He pined for you, dear child, but I told him—your mother is smart, and strong, and quick-witted. Nothing they do will hurt her. She'll be back home, you'll see—and here you are." She beamed, her cheeks deepening. The familiar sight of her, the scent of *sambong* tea that seemed to reek from her pores, and even the way her hair curled around the fringes of her hat told me I was home at last. I felt as if a dreaded weight had been lifted from me. I wanted to laugh and cry at the same time.

"Is he in his room?" I asked.

"The last time I checked. But hey—you're not supposed to be wandering around the castle this time of the night, are you?" She took me by the arm, pinching me. "Warlord Ozo, he calls himself now. The nerve. You watch out for that one, child."

"I think she knows—" Agos began.

She turned to him with a vicious glare. "Children," she huffed. "You know less than you ought to." She finally uttered a soft sigh, this time pulling him into her arms. It looked odd to see such a large man pressed against his mother's bosom, but she didn't seem to mind. "I may just be a servant, but I know where my loyalty lies. We're Oren-yaro, after all. Can't say the same for your soldiers. I don't know what came over them. I've been asking for months why they haven't found you, or saved you if you were in trouble, and they kept their silence. You best be careful, whatever it is you plan to do. You…" She pushed her son aside and wagged a finger at him. "Pay me a visit once in a while, eh? I'm getting old, and lonely. A woman my age shouldn't be alone."

"I don't know if I can after this, Ma."

"Always so honest. Can't even lie to make me feel better. So nothing like your father." She patted his cheek before reaching up to kiss it. "Go, with my love."

We drifted from the kitchens towards the empty dining hall. My father's table was gone, replaced by a rectangular monstrosity of Kag make, complete with thick-bodied, velvet-backed chairs similar to the arrangement in Shirrokaru. Tapestries hung from the wall. They bore the wolf emblem of the Orenyaro, but of the green-and-yellow pattern attributed to the Tasho clan instead of the Orenar. I longed to rip them out and set them on fire. Should I kill Ozo, on top of Qun? I didn't like killing, but what was one more death? I was keenly aware that my anger, at times, was stronger than my ideals.

Agos took one of the swords hanging from the wall—a royal's sword with a hooked blade and a hilt carved like a crocodile's mouth. "I hope Lamang's putting mine to good use," he said, hefting it with a grin. "In the meantime, I'm going to help myself to this. Sorry, General Ozo."

"Is Thanh's room still at the top floor of this wing?" Rai asked.

It felt strange to hear his voice again here, echoing through the castle. "Yes," I replied. "The one next to our... to my room."

Agos bade us to wait in the shadows of the dining hall while he went ahead to make sure the path was clear. It seemed to take forever for him to return; I stood with my back to the wall in silence, trying not to think about Khine or compare that with my husband's presence beside me. Did I ever really expect Rayyel would be back, after all this time? A part of me must have set my hopes on fire before the rest caught up. I certainly didn't think I would find myself here, staring at my husband from the corner of my eyes without feeling a damn thing.

Eventually, we heard Agos whistle. We made our way to the staircase, which went up three levels to the main chambers and the study. I instructed Agos to stay on the second landing to keep an eye out for anyone coming in from the guest rooms. He looked conflicted.

"Rai could do it, but I'm pretty sure you'll fare better if there's trouble," I said.

Agos scratched his cheek. "It's not that."

"Then what?"

He swallowed. "Nothing. Go get the prince."

I sprinted down the hall. Rai followed close behind. I reached the door and threw it open.

The bed was empty.

I felt my insides unbuckle. "Thanh," I croaked out. It was not a very large room and there was nowhere to hide. I looked behind the door, in the closet, and under the bed. As an afterthought, I tore the sheets from the mattress and yanked the curtains from the windows.

I felt Rai's hand on my shoulder. "The study," he said calmly.

My senses started to blur, but I found myself nodding. Of course. If not his room, then the study—he always finished at least a book a night. I tore myself away from Rai. My hands were shaking so much that I could barely get the door open. When it did, I felt the sob rise from my chest to my throat.

He had been there. There were two books on the table and a candle that was burning dangerously low around a pool of wax. The cushions were scattered, flung to every corner of the room past the rug, and one of the shelves was toppled over, spilling more books on the floor. As my eyes focused, I noticed blood on the rug. There was no sign of Thanh.

Rai walked up to the candle, pinching it with his fingers.

Through the haze of my thoughts, I heard the rain dripping from the roof eaves and the sound of the wind howling through the curtains. I realized the window was open. The shutters were broken in, as if someone had crashed through them from the outside.

"Someone else got here before us." It was as if another woman was speaking in my place.

Rai's face flickered. "An assassin?"

"Gods, Rai, don't start—"

"I'm just making suggestions. It looks like there was a struggle."

I allowed myself to look back at the blood. Too much, from a little boy? I could see streaks of it on the wall, and more gathered near the windowsill. But there was none on the bed and none on the books, which meant it came from someone who fought back. If this was my son, they could have killed him while he was sleeping or reading.

I pressed my fingers into the warm wax on the table and glanced down at the books. It was *Famous Wars of Jin-Sayeng* by Ichi rok Sagar, a magister who served in Rysaran's time. The other was a book on Dageian fairy tales, the sort of thing Rai wouldn't be caught dead with. "Who could've gotten here before us? The castle is impenetrable."

"*We* got here," Rai pointed out.

I frowned and stepped back into the hall. I went to check the room Rai and I had shared in our brief time together. It was cold and dark. Grey. Empty. There were no lanterns on the wall, no candles, and the mattress was stripped bare—a thin, white surface that looked like something you might lay a corpse on. The air smelled of damp and mothballs.

I felt him utter a deep breath, as if his mind was wandering down the same path. For one long moment, we both stared at this reflection of our marriage and our lives. And then, without another word, I closed the door and bade him to follow me back to the staircase.

Briefly, I wondered if Thanh might be in the other wing, where my father's quarters and study were. I had not touched either since his death. For a time, it was because I couldn't bear to move his things around—a part of me still expected to hear his booming voice telling me to leave his inks and brushes alone. And then later, it was simply because other things had occupied me... life moved on, even after the loss of a man like Yeshin.

But I didn't have time to say these thoughts out loud. Agos wasn't on the landing where I left him. I could hear movement down on the first floor, in the great hall that also served as the throne room during my reign. I felt my skin crawl and drew my sword, motioning for Rai to keep alert.

The lamps were still lit. I craned my head around the arch and saw Qun sitting on the throne—on *my* throne. I couldn't help myself. Before Rai could stop me, I stepped out into the light. "That's my spot, you bastard," I said.

"Merely keeping it warm," Qun replied. He remained seated.

"You've worn my patience thin. Where's my son?"

"*Where's my husband? Where's my son?* You need to take better care of your family, Beloved Queen."

I drew my sword and advanced towards him.

"A moment," Rai said in a raised voice.

Qun's eyes brightened. "Prince Rayyel!" he exclaimed. "Now, *this* is an even better surprise. You both should have sent word—I would've ordered a magnificent spread. None of this despicable peasant food you all seem to love."

"I intend to withdraw my accusations personally, in front of the entire council," Rai continued. "I hope you understand what she will do to you when she is queen again."

"Withdraw?" Qun pretended to look shocked. "But that would mean you *lied*. How awful! Because you can't expect us to believe she really *didn't* spread her legs for another man?"

It took all of my newfound patience not to launch myself at him.

Rai barely flinched. "Your insults will not go unpunished."

"Ah. And such crimes, I believe, are punishable by death, yes?" Qun laughed. "What good would *that* do? Even as we speak, Prince Yuebek is on his way with all the documents of her wrongdoings in the years since you so honourably—as is your right!—departed from her despicable, debased presence. Her nightly activities, her many lovers, which includes one or two lords you might be acquainted with, Prince Rayyel, in addition to her usual menu of guardsmen..."

"You're babbling. Dead men like to babble before I cut their heads off," I said through gritted teeth. "My son," I repeated. "Where is he?"

"Wandering around the castle halls no doubt, hiding in shame from his mother—"

I struck the throne. The blade sank into the wood below his thigh. I could see the sweat pouring from his face. Yet somehow, the fear wasn't enough to stop his mouth. "You need not worry so much, my dear," he gasped. "When Prince Yuebek is here, he'll set everything aright. He is a loving, generous man, as you well know, and he is still willing to take you on as his wife *despite* your many faults. The nation need not learn of your many depravities. With the prince's assistance, you can secure the throne and end this foolishness once and for all."

I managed to wrench the sword loose and struck the armrest. He jumped back—I had cut him on the shoulder, a small nick. I don't think the man had ever seen his own blood in his life. It was amazing how fast he went from a smug official to a doddering fool.

I heard footsteps behind me. Guards.

"Governor!"

Jinan. I turned to see five Oren-yaro bearing down towards me. My own men, once.

I couldn't stop myself from lashing out. "Why are you on the Zarojo's side?" I called.

They had the same expression as the guards in the city—a mix of resolution and shame, as if the same unseen hand that had forced me into Anzhao was now driving them. That same hand that wanted to drag me, kicking and screaming, to Yuebek's side. I laughed as they drew closer. If this was how the bastards wanted it, then so be it. Five against one wasn't fair, but when had it ever been? It was always me against a multitude.

I lunged at the nearest guard. He backed away, and I realized my advantage quickly—he needed me alive. I, on the other hand, had no such qualms. The narrow passageway between the wooden columns that decorated each side of the great hall meant that his companions couldn't get to me fast enough, and I had his back to the wall in no time. My sword managed to cut his belly. The poor boy didn't even have time to scream. As he dropped to his knees in an attempt to staunch the blood, I turned to the next.

"Talyien!" Rai warned. "The governor!"

I saw Qun's robes disappearing in a flash.

"He must be going for Thanh," I cried. "Where the fuck is Agos?" I struck at the next guard, who wasn't as careless as the last one.

"He—"

"Stop talking and go after him, Rai!"

He turned awkwardly on his heel before scampering after Qun, who was heading for the back door, the one leading to the gardens. I covered his path as my opponent pressed forward. Parried, lunged again. Caught his arm. Harder to fight someone you were tasked not to hurt. Did they all think I wouldn't take advantage? He struck me with his elbow in an attempt to pin me down and I rewarded him with a dagger in the throat.

I wondered what went through the bastard's mind as he died. Regret, possibly. I didn't want to blame him—to defy orders would be to face death, too—but I still felt a pang of anger. He could've defied the easy path and deferred back to me. Wolves? They were Akaterru-damned dogs. We all were.

His body dropped to the ground and I managed to squeeze into the next hall and then through the back door, slamming it shut before I jammed the dagger into the crack between the frame. I knew it wasn't much of a deterrence, but anything to delay them was good enough for me. I could see Qun at the fountain, that same one where I had killed that innkeeper a lifetime ago. Rayyel had his sword drawn a few feet away.

"My son, Qun," I said, spitting to the side. "I just killed two soldiers back there. How much easier would you be, I wonder?"

The nervous expression had left Qun's face. "Let's say I have him in the woods behind me," Qun said, reverting to that old grin.

"He's lying," Rai commented.

"Bound, gagged, with my master's mages standing over him," Qun continued, ignoring him. "Would you be so confident then, Beloved Queen? Knowing you have everything to lose? My master doesn't need the boy at all, as he must've told you once. A worthless piece of meat."

"You're talking about the crown prince of Jin-Sayeng," Rai said.

Qun held out a finger. "No. Not at the moment. You yourself made that clear."

"I fabricated the announcement. It wasn't approved by the council."

"And they'll readily admit that, the mostly Ikessar council, that *their* boy would go and do such things behind their back? No, no." He made a sound in the back of his throat, shaking his head. "You knew you were playing with fire, Prince Rayyel."

"You—" I started.

"The sword, Beloved Queen," Qun said. "Drop it."

I stared at him, breathing hard.

"He's lying," Rai repeated. "Don't fall for it, Talyien. He's not…"

I dropped the sword into the fountain. It sank with a splash.

Qun clapped his hands twice. "There. Easy enough, isn't it? Any other weapons?"

"See any?" I replied, holding my hands out.

He smiled. "Now let's go say hi to your boy. *You*," he added, pointing at Rayyel. "Stay here."

"Don't believe a word he says, Talyien," Rai said in a low voice. "Why would Thanh be with him? In the middle of the night, after tearing his room asunder—"

"Stop, Rai," I replied. "Just stop for once, for the love of the gods. I have to see this through."

"You're going to be at his mercy in there."

"I already am," I murmured. I stopped right in front of Qun. "My son, you bastard."

He dropped his head in a quick bow, gesturing. Together, we stepped into the dappled shadows of the Oka Shto woods.

No, of course I wasn't a damn idiot. I was busy ripping my sleeve as I walked behind him, because if it came down to strangling him with a piece of cloth in order to save my son, well…I was happy enough to do it. I didn't think he noticed. The moon was shining on the cliff to our right, peering out from behind the tall trees.

"You make it seem like marrying our prince would be such a chore," Qun said, folding his hands behind him.

"The way he looks these days?" I asked. "I can imagine. The servants would be forever tripping on bits of him in the hallways."

"He's recovering," Qun said. "If you see him now, I think you'll be pleasantly surprised."

"I really doubt that."

"He—"

"I'm bored, Qun," I drawled. "Nothing Yuebek offers can ever interest me. *Ever*. I don't know why my people are so enamoured with him or why they let you just walk into my palace with open arms, and at this moment, I don't think I care."

"Ah, I do suppose you wouldn't. You've never cared much outside of your sordid little affairs, did you? Your husband. Your lovers. Your despicable little brat. Did you think we haven't kept an eye on what's happening out here?" He pressed his lips together. "Your lords to the west are riding against peasants as we speak. To the south—after the mess in Kyo-orashi, your coastal lords are arguing amongst themselves. The east is silent, but of course they would be after the remarkable news your husband gifted your nation with. Who knows what will happen once the truth of *that* is revealed?"

I swallowed. "So be it," I said. "If I must abdicate—"

"Ah, but we can't let you do that. *They* won't let you. It's so very interesting to me as someone who has observed power his whole life to see how *you're* the center around which everything revolves. Why you, Queen Talyien, and not your husband?"

I smirked. "Everyone hates me, so it can't be my charming personality."

"No," Qun agreed. "Definitely not."

We found ourselves where the path met the side of the cliff.

"It's your father, I believe," Qun said, folding his arms together. "Such a brilliant man. Such faith in his young daughter. I think the story he painted for you—what you were, what you could *do*—was enough to set your path. Your husband's mother never did such a thing, you see? To her, he was weak, unworthy, and so he spent his whole life trying to prove her wrong. A big difference. *You* spent yours trying to prove your father right.

"The power you wield was never attached to your name. It lies in that steel heart, the red-hot blood that runs through your veins. I didn't really think you would *face* that dragon, let alone make it all the way out here on your own. I was expecting you to give up. You looked like you wanted to give up. We needed you down on the ground, on your knees. Instead, every blow that should've sent you crying into my prince's arms only seemed to strengthen your resolve. I'm not quite sure how you've done it all, to be honest."

I stared back at him in shock. Admiration coming from *this* man was the last thing I expected. He smiled, seeing the look on my face. "You shouldn't have killed my wife," Qun said with a sly grin. "I might've been more lenient. Perhaps I could have learned what I could from you before—well, before the inevitable. But you, with all this power, can never bring her back, and my master finds your eccentricities a touch too much for his tastes." He grew serious. "Jump, Queen Talyien."

"What?"

Qun gestured at the ravine. "If you want to see your son alive again, jump."

I remember telling Khine that this was what they had been trying to do all along. I didn't realize they would mean it literally. I struggled not to laugh as I glanced at the sharp rocks, and then back at him. "That fall will kill me."

"If it does, that's nothing to me," Qun said. "But I don't see it happening. It will break your bones, yes, and quite possibly more. I have mage-healers in the castle—they will set you back the way they set my prince back. It will then be a match made in heaven, you see?"

"You're insane," I hissed.

"No," Qun replied. "I'm perfectly fine. *You* might not be when we're done with you, but you know...such are the sacrifices of war, won't you agree? My prince wants you compliant. My prince wants you *chained* to him, held together by the *agan* and unable to function without the same spells *he* needs after what you did to him. And then you can never run from him again." He reached out to grab hold of my shoulder. "*Jump*," he repeated, his voice seething. "Or I will do things to your boy that will make you wish you were never born."

I pushed him away from me, reeling, the memory of the threats he had uttered that night on the ship intermingling with thoughts of Thanh. "You fucked-up bastard," I said, before I threw myself off the cliff.

CHAPTER TEN

THE COIN OF SORROW

ㄒㄈ♏

A steel heart, he said.

But the truth is I just wasn't as brave as Mei Lamang. It was easy enough to entertain death as an afterthought to despair, but once I got down to it, my reflexes did the rest. *A chipped sword still has an edge.*

And so I jumped with no intention of dying. There were bushes to my right, the leaves thick enough to cushion my fall. It wasn't a perfect plan. I felt a tearing pain as a piece of wood struck my arm, and there was suddenly blood everywhere—dripping from the gaping wound and down to the flap of skin, up my nose, inside my head.

I heard what sounded like Qun climbing down the cliff. I closed my eyes, forcing my senses to settle, and stayed motionless as he approached, though my hand—the one on the injured arm—scrabbled about in the dirt. I felt a sharp rock, small enough to fit in my palm. I forced my fingers around it.

"Amazing," Qun said as he reached me. "You're alive, I can see you breathing. What did I tell you? A little fall like this can't kill you. Not *you*. And all for your boy, eh? An unfortunate weakness. I'm glad Biala and I never had children. Look what you did, and for what? I didn't even have the brat at all!"

The anger pushed the pain away. I opened my eyes halfway to see him, arms still crossed, gazing up at the sky. "No. Someone else got to him this same night. There were noises and—well, you must've seen the mess his room was in. Those guards you were busy fighting had been looking for him." Qun laughed.

"So foolhardy, Beloved Queen. To think you wasted yourself for nothing. And now my prince is on his way, and there's nothing you could—"

I struck him across the throat with the rock, hard enough that I felt skin under my fingernails. I did it again until I drew blood and ripped it right above his clavicle. His thin fingers grabbed my wrist in an attempt to keep me from attacking him further. When he realized that wouldn't work, he tried to go for the open wound on my arm.

I twisted his own arm instead, hard enough that he fell to his knees.

"I am so tired of people like you," I said against his ear. "From my Ozo to every bloody Ikessar in the land, to my father."

"The father who made you into this?" he gasped.

"But you've made it clear enough," I continued with a snarl. "If I don't do a damn thing, you people will burn the whole place to the ground, crawl over whatever's left, and bicker over the ashes. I don't want to play your fucking games, but you said it yourself—somehow, despite everything you and your mad, fucking undead prince have tried to do, I'm not broken yet. You know what, Qun? I've decided—"

He tried to crawl away from me and I struck him with the rock. He fell to the ground.

"I've *decided*," I repeated, sitting on him, my knee on his belly, "that once I find my son, I'm going to make all of you dogs pay, right down to your master."

"You, and what army?" Qun hissed. "You've got nothing. The Oren-yaro bow to Prince Yuebek now, and so do your other warlords."

"Right. The ones with *agan*-afflicted children that you've blackmailed." I gave him a grin. "Do you see how easily I can turn this against you, Qun?"

"You have nothing."

"What was that other thing you said? Every blow against me only strengthens me. Don't ask me how. I wouldn't know. I'd certainly rather it didn't, because I'm tired of dealing with all this scheming and treachery. But you're the one who's going to die out here, Ino Qun, not I."

The gravity of the threat engulfed his expression. Somehow, he managed to wrench the dagger loose from his belt, and struck me in the leg. A small cut. The man was weak. Stripped to *his* core, he was the one who had nothing. Stripped to mine, I was still too much Yeshin's daughter. I knocked the dagger from his grasp; it flew out of reach, disappearing between the weeds.

I hammered him once more to repay the favour, again and again until his eyes glazed over and I couldn't tell anymore what was my blood and what was his. I didn't like killing, but after the things he had told me he would do to my boy, watching his life drain in front of me was the most satisfying thing in the world. After he stopped moving, I kicked him down the next slope and watched his robes flutter with the wind as he tumbled down the mountain.

"Talyien!"

Rai's voice. I wrapped my loose sleeve around the open wound on my arm and limped towards the base of the overhang. The blood drained from his face. "What happened?" he gasped.

"Took care of Qun like I promised," I whispered.

He reached down to help me up. My arm was burning, but my body was still on fire and the shaking had yet to begin. "He didn't have Thanh," I croaked out, once I was back on the path. "The idiot lied."

"I told you."

I shook my head. "I couldn't risk it."

There was something in my voice that stopped him from arguing further. We walked back to the palace. I was expecting to come face-to-face with the rest of the guards, but I noticed that the dagger on the door was still there. I retrieved it, awkwardly managing to slip it back into my belt.

Silently, we made our way to the great hall. Dead guards decorated the floor around the throne, the ragged wounds on their throats spilling what was left of their blood. I wondered for a moment if it was the Zarojo's doing, but then my thoughts turned to other things as I beheld Thanh at the foot of the throne. He was standing perfectly still in the midst of the carnage, a lamb wandering into a field of bloody wolves. Against all my fears, he was unharmed.

He turned at the sound of our footsteps.

"Mother—" he began, before his eyes fell on the man behind me. On Rayyel. Fear danced in his eyes. Did he recognize the man I claimed was his father? He would have seen the one painting of him in the Dragon Palace before, the one above the throne room we never used.

He ran before either of us could take another step. We sprinted after him down into the next corridor. "Your son is frightened of you, Rayyel," I swore as I paused to figure out which direction Thanh had gone. "I don't care what you think. I don't. You claim concern for him on the off chance he turns out to be a bastard just like you. Well, then you should know better. For the sake of a child you claimed to have loved once in his life, you should have considered what *he* feels about all of this."

I turned to face him, and realized he had never thought about Thanh in that manner at all. He was struggling to put on that calm, stony mask, and failing.

"The boy begged for you almost every day since you walked out on us," I said in a low voice. I had no pity for him on this matter. He *needed* to know what he'd left behind. "Every day, Rai. Do you know how hard it is to lie to your son? Especially when you're all he has left? I might have never gone to your ridiculous meeting if he didn't ask me to. If not for that child, Yuebek would have killed you and you'd be rotting back in Anzhao like poor Zheshan, and none of this . . . we'd all be . . ."

We heard a whimper coming from underneath the stairwell. I turned into the shadows and saw Thanh curled up in the corner, his arms wrapped around his knees.

My mind stopped working. Not one moment longer, and then I was limping straight for him, my arms reaching out to draw him into the light. I pull him to my bloodied chest. "Oh Thanh, oh, my love," I murmured into his wavy hair. He smelled of sweat and tears, and he was a lot taller, less round, than when I saw him last . . . but he was here, he was alive, and this wasn't like the many dreams that had kept me sleepless in the long months. I kissed his cheeks and his hair, and promised myself that even if the world split in half I would never leave him again.

An instant, stretched out. We think we own these moments—that we can will time to stand still while we drink in these loves awhile longer, convinced that the forces of the world will bend their knee to the strength of our emotions. The truth is they are but a ripple in an ocean, a sprinkle of sunlight in a dark world—not ours to contain, not ours to hold as we please. I realized Thanh wasn't speaking. I looked down and noticed that his eyes were very red. His face was pale, and there was a bruise on his chin.

"Mother," he croaked out once more.

"It's all right," I said, wiping the remnants of his tears with my thumbs. "I'm here now. I'm not going to let anything happen to you. *He* will never harm a hair on your head." I pointed at Rai, who lingered in the adjoining hall, as if he was afraid to come any closer.

Thanh took a deep breath, his fingers curled over my breast and the blood there.

"It's not mine," I managed, trying to give him a weak smile. It was all I had left. I was so exhausted.

He looked up, eyes watering. "Mother, they said we're to go with them."

"Them? What do you mean?"

"Us," a voice broke in.

I found myself staring at the edge of a drawn blade. I slowly got to my feet. "Beloved Queen," the man said, pushing the blade up to my throat. I recognized Torre, Kaggawa's man. "Come with us, and no one gets hurt." He drew Thanh to the side and whistled to his men, who dragged my son to the great hall. He nodded and pushed me right after them.

"You bastards," I said as we stumbled back in the throne room. "You've been trying to kill me since Kyo-orashi."

"We can help you fix this. You can have everything you want, and more. My master is willing to give you a second chance."

"Listen to him, Tali," Agos said, appearing from behind them.

I stared at him. "What is this?"

In the distance, a horn blared. Agos looked up and grimaced. "We don't have much time. The Ikessars are at the gates. Your husband's doing, remember?"

"He sent Namra and Inzali to Shirrokaru."

"Those are Ikessar soldiers. Not the Dragonthrone's. Their banners bear the Ikessar falcon."

"You double-crossed us," Rai put in. "You..."

"Me?" Agos snapped. "You're the one who called for your *mother*, you son of a bitch."

"You're using him to cover your lies, Agos."

"Think! Who *else* wanted to save you? Not the Oren-yaro, not your friends—the whole damn nation turned a blind eye to you when you needed them the most. Dai had the most reasonable offer."

"The man tried to have us killed!"

"Of course he did," Agos growled. "After the Sougen, he thought you were going to jeopardize his plans. I've been sending him letters since that morning—since we left Kyo-orashi." Since I slept with him. A decision that had completely snapped whatever I thought we were. He had decided to take matters in his own hands.

"You'd dare...behind my back?"

"It's not like he believed me. He sent the assassins anyway. If I didn't run into his men outside the Kibouri temple—"

"That's why you disappeared."

"I convinced them I could still turn it around and make you see reason. Fuck, Tali, if you weren't so gods-damn stubborn..."

"They still tried to kill us."

"*One* of them did. The one who went ahead to chase Lamang. She didn't know shit."

"You understand that this is exactly what *Yuebek* tried to do?" I asked. "They followed us through the tunnels, didn't they? Oh gods—Agos...they were right behind us this whole time. You let them get to Thanh first."

"Did I?" he asked. "Tell her, Torre."

"The Zarojo were there," Torre said. "They were about to kill your boy."

"The struggle in the room..." I began.

"We took care of them."

"You see, Tali?" Agos placed his hands on my shoulders, turning me so I could face him, so I could look into his eyes. I had a brief flash of how he liked to look at my face when we made love, followed by pain, an echo of Qun's accusations.

"You went behind my back," I repeated.

"I haven't forgotten who you are," Agos said, his eyes blazing. "And if you must have my head for it, then so be it. But we don't have time for this. Those soldiers—"

A banging sound came from outside the locked doors. I froze.

The closest Shadow turned to me. "We've killed all the guards in the castle. If we leave now, we can still get you away."

"One noose for another," I hissed.

"I won't let Dai hurt you," Agos said. He turned to Rai, lifting his sword. "Unfortunately, he wanted one other thing. He needed one death."

Rai looked down at his own sword, as if realizing what Agos meant. He gave a small, resigned sigh. "I suppose it's fitting."

Agos nodded. "I'm an honourable man. I'll give you time to get ready."

"Stop this at once," I snapped, stepping in front of Rai. "I'm not going any-where without him."

"Kaggawa drove a hard bargain, and he didn't want Rai alive at all."

"Did you even *try*?"

"Why the fuck should I? You knew it would someday come to this, Tali."

"He's right," Rai said. "This should've happened a long time ago."

"I'm not a piece of gristle to fight over like dogs," I hissed. "But I'm not unreasonable. I'll play along. We'll go with you back to Dai, Agos. Leave Rayyel out of this. Agos—"

He drew me aside easily, a sudden reflection of his strength and how much he had let me get away with over the years. I caught myself, doubling back to try to reach him, but by then he was already bearing down on my husband. I screamed.

The gods are cruel. I know that now.

Should I have guessed that Agos—loyal, faithful Agos—would ever become deaf to my cries?

I had seen what Agos could do to a man with his sword in seconds. I had relied on it for years. I never thought I would see that same sword attempting to cut my husband in half. Agos missed that first time, the blade sinking into the wooden floor. He tore out splinters as he lifted it again.

Rai met the attack. Agos struck Rai's sword with such force that it flew from his hands. I spotted a spray of blood streaming from his fingers.

"Pick it up," Agos raged.

Rai crawled after the blade.

"Get it over with," I heard one of the Shadows say behind his mask. "We don't have time for this."

"I won't murder him. The man deserves an honourable death."

But his mind was clouded over what *honour* truly meant. As soon as Rai's hands clasped around the hilt, Agos was on him again, kicking him across the floor, striking him with one hand while he tried to position his sword for a clean strike. The only way Rai would've been able to beat him was if they fought in a debate room. "You fool!" I heard one man utter. "You're wasting time!"

Rai managed to wrench himself loose and struck an underhanded blow. It was a weak strike, one that barely clipped the flesh, but I heard Agos laugh. "So, you've got some fight in you after all, little man. I was worried this would be *too* easy."

"Do you really think that killing me will make her love you?"

Agos spat. "You'll use that? You sicken me. She loved you, yes. I've known that from the start. And what did you do?" He slammed his fist into Rai's belly. "You wasted it, you son of a bitch."

"Wasted," Rai said, spitting out blood. "You would say this. *You*, who she trusted. *You*, who is betraying her as we speak."

"You're one to talk about betrayal," Agos said, his face contorting. "Enough talk. Let's finish this."

The doors creaked. I expected the soldiers would've begun trying to batter it. I didn't expect the solid *narra* wood to burst into flames.

I was at the far end of the great hall, closer to the throne. Agos and Rai stood right next to the entrance hall. I called to them one more time, begging them to stop.

The splintered doors fell forward. A man burst in—a mage, I realized with a start, Belfang. Flames hovered over his hands. And then the soldiers streamed behind him, a formation of six, three on each side—a pincer attack, bows drawn. They dropped to their knees. Six arrows flew and struck Agos from behind.

He turned. Six more arrows lodged straight into his belly and his heart.

"No!" I screamed. Inside my head, I heard the gods laugh.

The soldiers moved past him, racing after the Shadows and Thanh. I didn't know where to turn. But I saw the sword fall from Agos's fingers, clattering to the ground, saw the blood pouring from the arrow wounds in his body, and my heart shattered.

Khine caught him first.

The knowledge that he had somehow escaped his assassin, that he was alive and safe, did nothing to wipe the feeling of devastation seeping into my bones. One life cannot replace another. I heard that as clearly as if it was being whispered against my ear. This wasn't a game of *Hanza*, where the loss of a piece only meant another could be placed in its stead. A queen ought to know. I arrived a second later at Khine's heels, somehow hoping he could do what he'd done before. "Don't die on me now, you bastard," I whispered, dropping to my knees. Agos was still fighting, his eyes streaked with red. I turned to Khine. "You have to save him. Call the servants. They'll have bandages. They..."

Khine didn't even reply. The expression on his face—that look of dejection, of helplessness... I had seen it before with the Gasparian merchant and knew all was lost. Agos's eyes were flickering, losing light.

"Princess," he whispered, placing a bloody hand on my face.

I pressed my head over his. "I'm sorry, Agos. I'm sorry. Please don't leave me." He tried to smile, and then he grew still.

I screamed his name as I cradled him on that blood-drenched floor, the once powerful body now limp in my arms. The ache wrenched itself around the frantic tones and tears, as if my voice was enough, as if I could somehow call him back through the gates of the afterlife. Whispering into his ears did nothing; my own ragged breath did not stir his. Yet I knew he would have returned if he could. If he could, he would've torn his way through time itself.

But no man or woman, not even a queen, holds authority over death. I should've told him it was fruitless trying to carve a path outside this constructed world of ours. How could we dream of freedom with what we were and what was placed on us? Loyalty, love, the thought of love, even brief moments of what we were sure would always be ours... *burn me, drive a stake through my heart, just let me be with you.* We owned nothing, us pawns of the past. The shadows that pulled the strings came from within.

I held him, though, even as the soldiers thundered through the great hall and the servants came and I heard his mother's own anguished cry. I held him until they left me alone and his body grew cold in my arms. One's traitor, another's friend... I imagined that in another place and time, if I had not been betrothed to Rayyel, if I had never met Khine, we might've been happy together. Always, these thoughts, once it was over and done with. As if they could change a damn thing.

The Shadows escaped with my son.

The Ikessars searched Oka Shto from top to bottom, following the tunnels all the way to Old Oren-yaro and then back, but they had disappeared as if into thin air. As much as I hated their presence in what was rightfully my castle, they at least did me one favour—they pulled every Zarojo delegate out of their rooms to be brought back to Shirrokaru for questioning. The precision with which they dealt with things gave me a sinking feeling in the pit of my stomach. They didn't look at me, or acknowledge my presence at all; Rai might have lied about the council's involvement in his announcement, but they took it as law. A woman who declared herself a priestess under the service of Princess Ryia Ikessar stalked the halls with a sword in her hands and a look of contempt in her eyes. "Where is your son?" she asked me when she passed by. "Where is the false heir? You cannot hide him forever. The one true queen of Jin-Sayeng *will* have her say, Bitch Queen, and if we have to kill your son for her rule to begin uncontested..."

"What rule?" Rayyel broke in. "This is nonsense. We need a trial before anything can be decided. I've spoken to the council representative to set a date."

"Your mother will take this chaos as an opportunity," I whispered.

"Foolishness," Rai scoffed. "She knows better." But there was a look of fear on his face. "I brought a mage. He can clear up any confusion, and..."

The woman smiled at us—a cold, hard smile, sharp as the gleaming edge of a dagger. "*You brought a mage.* Listen to yourself. You brought a mage to Jin-Sayeng. If you had been anyone but Ryia's son you would be put to death for causing dissent. As it is, your name alone seems to be enough to make the council agree. But the boy—"

"Could still be my son," Rai said.

"Why does the boy's father matter? You think too highly of yourself, lord bastard. What you've started cannot be smoothed over with a few words; there is no turning back time. It is enough that *she* is his mother." She gave me a last glance before she left, leaving behind the stench of the truth: we had led the Shadows to Thanh just in time. Even if we had saved him from Qun, the Ikessar soldiers would have killed him anyway. Agos's sacrifice was not in vain. Was it apt that I, queen of nothing, would find salvation in betrayal? That it has been—from the very beginning—this lack of loyalty and dedication that has allowed me to slip through the cracks of my enemies' plans?

I still cannot say. My pen falters—my hand drifts from this piece of paper for a moment. Our lives are forced through this narrow chasm where we see little beyond our desires and our failure to fulfill them. To make sense of it all... is the domain of those wiser than I. The scribe might have words for me, but I would sooner die than show her these last few pages, these words she should never read. I have caused much sorrow in the short amount of time I have been alive. While I do not think it will ever end so long as I remain the Bitch Queen, I would like to abate harm where I can. I have learned too late, and now I will carry the memory of Agos's last moments all my life.

Khine went with his body when they took him away. It was the last I saw of him before representatives of the Ikessar clan approached me with soldiers and manacles for my wrists. Whatever thoughts I had about Khine, about us, turned to ice. I pushed them as far away as I could before I faced my new captors: my husband's clan, the same clan that my father hated so much, he was willing to tear the nation apart to destroy them. Their presence in my castle was very nearly an act of war, but in the wake of my disgrace, there was nothing anyone could do. As far as the Ikessars were concerned, I had ceded my rights. All that was left was for the rest of the council to arrive in Oren-yaro and prove what the entire nation already believed.

Warlord Ozo refused to even entertain the notion that I was still alive. Before I could get the chance to ask for him, I was escorted to my room in silence, a prisoner in my own castle while I awaited the judgment of the council. But the thought of their wagging tongues wasn't what frightened me. The War of the Wolves was nothing to what I knew we were about to face. My father was in everything, in every corner of this nation, in every gasp of air I took, and though his crimes were not mine, I knew I was doomed to pay for them for the rest of time. For if Yeshin's sons had not been killed and he had not been compelled to march to civil war, I wouldn't have been raised the way I was— the bearer of everything, his heir in every way, both sword arm and womb. I would have never been betrothed to Rayyel, never been born. I could deny my shackles, but they would always be a part of who I am. If I had known from the beginning, I would've let them smother me.

But I am not a seer. I am one woman, heart as bare as the sun and powerless against the pitfalls before me, the gaping maws of fate. Perhaps someday I could be forgiven for the blindness that had brought us thus far; for now, I knew it was up to me to dig through the ashes where Yeshin once stood and unravel the threads he had left behind. Who else could do it? Who else *would*? Qun was right—I had everything to lose. And maybe I wasn't strong enough, maybe I wasn't worthy, maybe a mere shadow was nothing to a man whose dying breath could shape an entire nation, but if it meant having to wear this shattered armour for the rest of my battles, then so be it.

Alone, I could still fight.

THE STORY CONTINUES IN ...

**CHRONICLES OF THE
BITCH QUEEN: BOOK 3**

ACKNOWLEDGMENTS

I continue to owe a debt of gratitude to my editor, Bradley Englert, and my agent, Hannah Bowman, who have both done wonders in their marvellous support of this series. I also want to thank the rest of the Orbit team for their fantastic, tireless work, and for all the little things they've done to see these books through—including Angela Man, Ellen Wright, Dominique Delmas, Nazia Khatun, Paola Crespo, Lauren Panepinto, Laura Fitzgerald, Bryn A. McDonald, Hillary Sames, and my UK editor, James Long. Thank you to Tim Paul for your marvellous work on the map. I am also forever grateful to Simon Goinard's genius, for giving life to Queen Talyien through the cover art. Truly, I couldn't have asked for a better team.

This series continues to put me in touch with some very generous souls, and I want to particularly thank Shealea Jenice Iral and Kate Heceta, and the passionate team of book bloggers and reviewers who helped #HailtheBitchQueen take off. Your advocacy in helping marginalized voices has truly been wonderful to watch.

To my Filipino writing group, thank you for listening to my ramblings and frustrations and for helping me feel not so alone! I am grateful for all of you, including Christine Liwag Dixon, Myta Santiago, Kess Costales, Pamelia Delupio, Kat Enwright, Stef Tran, Wilfred Capella, and Theresa Bazelli. The brilliant Filipino writing community on Twitter has also been a source of comfort and encouragement—there's too many of you to name, but know that I'm thinking of you.

And of course, it goes without saying...but the Terrible Ten writing group has been a tremendous help through all the stages of this project, and the fact that you're all just terribly fun to be with only makes things better. A particular shout out to Evan Winter for his wisdom and support as I navigated my way through debut pre-release nerves. I also want to thank all the generous authors who took their time to read my book and blurb it, offer advice, and lend their platform or share promotional content for my work—you have helped this new-comer feel very welcome and eager to pay it forward when I can.

To all my readers: thank you, thank you, thank you. (And also I am so, so sorry...)

And as always, my family, who remains my guiding light as I continue down this winding path.

extras

orbit

www.orbitbooks.net

about the author

K. S. Villoso began writing while growing up in the slums of Manila amongst tales of bloodthirsty ghouls, ethereal spirits, and mysteries under the shadows of the banyan trees—a world where fantasy meets the soiled reality of everyday. She immigrated to Canada in her teens and was briefly distracted working with civil and municipal infrastructure. When she isn't writing, she is off dragging her husband, dogs, kids, and anyone insane enough to say "Sure, let's go hiking—what could go wrong?" through the Canadian wilderness. She lives in Anmore, BC.

Find out more about K. S. Villoso and other Orbit authors by registering for the free monthly newsletter at www.orbitbooks.net.

if you enjoyed
IKESSAR FALCON
look out for

THERE WILL COME A DARKNESS
by
Katy Rose Pool

THE AGE OF DARKNESS APPROACHES.
FIVE LIVES STAND IN ITS WAY.

For generations, the Seven Prophets guided humanity – until they disappeared, one hundred years ago.

They left behind a secret prophecy, foretelling an Age of Darkness and the birth of a new Prophet who could be the world's salvation . . . or the cause of its destruction. As a dark new power rises, five souls are set on a collision course that will determine the fate of their world:

A prince exiled from his kingdom
A ruthless killer known as the Pale Hand
A once-faithful leader torn between his duty and his heart
A reckless gambler with the power to find anything or anyone
And a dying girl on the verge of giving up

One of them – or all of them – could break the world. Will they be saviour or destroyer?

if you enjoyed

IKESSAR FALCON

look out for

THERE WILL COME A DARKNESS

by

Katy Rose Pool

1

EPHYRA

IN THE MOONLIT ROOM OVERLOOKING THE CITY OF FAITH, A PRIEST KNELT before Ephyra and begged for his life.

"Please," he said. "I don't deserve to die. Please. I won't touch them anymore, I swear. Have mercy."

Around him, the lavish private room at the Thalassa Gardens taverna lay in disarray. A sumptuous feast spilled from overturned platters and filigreed pitchers. The white marble floor was littered with ripe berries and the smashed remains of a dozen tiny jewel-like bottles. A pool of blood-dark wine slowly spread toward the kneeling priest.

Ephyra crouched down, placing her palm upon the papery skin of his cheek.

"Oh, thank you!" the priest cried, tears springing into his eyes. "Thank you, blessed—"

"I wonder," Ephyra said. "Did your victims ever beg you for mercy? When you were leaving your bruises on their bodies, did they ever cry out in Behezda's name?"

He choked on a breath.

"They didn't, did they? You plied them with your monstrous potion to make them docile so you could hurt them without ever having to see their pain," she said. "But I want you to know that every mark you left on them left a mark on you, too."

"*Please.*"

A breeze rustled in from the open balcony doors behind Ephyra as she tilted the priest's chin toward her. "You've been marked for death. And death has come to collect."

His terror-struck eyes gazed up at Ephyra as she slid her hand to his throat, where she could feel the rapid tap-tap-tap of his pulse. She focused on the rush of blood beneath his flesh and drew the *esha* from his body.

The light drained from the priest's eyes as his lungs sputtered out their last breath. He collapsed to the floor. A handprint, as pale as the moon, glowed against the sallow skin of his throat. Dead, and only a single mark to show for it.

Drawing the dagger from her belt, Ephyra leaned over the corpse. The priest had not been alone when she'd found him. The two girls he'd had with him—hollow-eyed girls, their wrists mottled with green and purple bruises—had fled the moment Ephyra had told them to run, as if they couldn't help but obey.

Ephyra slid the tip of her blade into the flesh of the priest's throat, cutting a line of red through the pale handprint. As dark blood oozed out, she turned the dagger over and opened the compartment in its hilt to extract the vial within. She held it under the flow of his blood. The priest's desperate words had been a lie—he *did* deserve death. But that wasn't why she'd taken his life.

She had taken his life because she needed it.

The door burst open, startling Ephyra from her task. The vial slipped from her hand. She fumbled with it but caught it.

"Don't move!"

Three men spilled into the suite, one holding a crossbow, and the other two with sabers. Sentry. Ephyra wasn't surprised. Thalassa sat at the edge of Elea Square, just within the High City gates. She'd known from staking it out that the Sentry ran their foot patrols through the square every night. But they'd gotten here quicker than she'd expected.

The first Sentry through the door stopped short, staring at the priest's body, stunned. "He's dead!"

Ephyra sealed the vial of blood and hid it back within the dagger's hilt. She drew herself up, touching the black silk that covered the bottom of her face to make sure it was still in place.

"Come quietly," the first Sentry said slowly, "and you don't have to get hurt."

Ephyra's pulse hammered in her throat, but she made her voice calm. Fearless. "Take another step and there will be more than one body in this room."

The Sentry hesitated. "She's bluffing."

"No, she isn't," the one with the crossbow said nervously. He glanced down at the priest's corpse. "Look at the handprint. Just like the ones they found on the bodies in Tarsepolis."

"The Pale Hand," the third Sentry whispered, frozen as he stared at Ephyra.

"That's just street lore," the first Sentry said, but his voice was trembling slightly. "No one is so powerful that they can kill with only the Grace of Blood."

"What are you doing in Pallas Athos?" the third Sentry asked her. He stood with his chest out and his feet apart, as if staring down a beast. "Why have you come here?"

"You call this place the City of Faith," Ephyra said. "But corruption and evil fester behind these white walls. I will mark them the way

I mark my victims, so the rest of the world can see that the City of Faith is the city of the fallen."

This was a lie. Ephyra had not come to the City of Faith to stain it with blood. But only two other people in the world knew the real reason, and one of them was waiting for her.

She moved toward the window. The Sentry tensed, but none tried to go after her.

"You won't get away with killing a priest so easily," the first said. "When we tell the Conclave what you've done—"

"Tell them." She tugged her black hood over her head. "Tell them the Pale Hand came for the priest of Pallas. And tell them to pray that I don't come for them next."

She turned to the balcony, throwing open the satin drapes to the night and the moon that hung like a scythe in the sky.

The Sentry shouted after her, their blustering voices overlapping as Ephyra flew to the edge of the balcony and climbed over the marble balustrade. The world tipped—four stories below, the steps of Thalassa's entrance gleamed like ivory teeth in the moonlight. She gripped the edge of the balustrade and turned. To her left, the roof of the public baths sloped toward her.

Ephyra leapt, launching herself toward it. Squeezing her eyes shut, she tucked her knees and braced for impact. She hit the roof at a roll and waited for her own momentum to slow before picking herself up and racing across it, the voices of the Sentry and the lights of Thalassa fading into the night.

Ephyra moved through the mausoleum like a shadow. The sanctum was still and silent in the predawn darkness as she picked her way through broken marble and other rubble around the tiled scrying pool in the center, the only part of the shrine left unscorched. Above, the caved-in roof gave way to the sky.

The ruins of the mausoleum sat just outside the High City gates, close enough that Ephyra could easily sneak back into the Low City without drawing notice. She didn't know exactly when the mausoleum had been burned down, but it was all but abandoned now, making it the perfect hideout. She slipped through the scorched shrine into the crypt. The stairwell creaked and moaned as she climbed down and wrenched open the rotted wood door to the alcove that had served as her home for the past few weeks. Shedding her mask and hood, she crept inside.

The alcove used to be a storeroom for the acolyte caretakers who had tended to the shrine. Now it was abandoned, left for rats, rot, and for people like Ephyra who didn't mind the other two.

"You're late."

Ephyra peered through the darkened room to the bed that lay in the corner, shadowed by the tattered sheets that hung over it. Her sister's dark eyes peered back at her.

"I know," Ephyra said, folding the mask and hood over the back of the chair.

A book slid from Beru's chest as she sat up, its pages fluttering as it bounced onto the sheets. Her short, curly hair was raked up on one side. "Everything go all right?"

"Fine." No point telling how close her escape had been. It was done now. She forced a smile on her face. "Come on, Beru, you know my days of falling off slyhouse roofs are behind me. I'm better than that now."

When Ephyra had first assumed the mask of the Pale Hand, she hadn't been quite as good at sneaking around and climbing as she was now. Having the Grace of Blood didn't help her sneak into crime dens or scale rich merchants' balconies. She'd had to gain such skills the traditional way, spending countless nights honing her balance, reaction time, and strength, as well as gathering information necessary for specific targets. Beru had joined her, when she was well enough, racing Ephyra to see who could climb a fence faster or leap between rooftops more quietly. They'd spent many nights stealing through the shadows, tailing behind a potential mark to learn vices and habits. After years of training and close calls, Ephyra knew how to get in and out of the dangerous situations she courted as the Pale Hand.

Beru returned her sister's smile weakly.

Ephyra's own smile faded, seeing the pain in Beru's eyes. "Come on," she said softly.

Beru lifted the rough blanket away from her body. Beneath it, she was shivering, her brown skin ashen in the low light. Tired lines had etched themselves into the skin below her bloodshot eyes.

Ephyra frowned, turning to the crate beside Beru's bed, where a shallow bowl rested. She opened the compartment in her dagger's hilt and poured the contents of the vial into the bowl. "We let this go for too long."

"It's fine," Beru hissed through clenched teeth. "I'm fine." She unwrapped the cotton from her left wrist, revealing the black handprint that marred the skin beneath it.

Ephyra pressed her hand into the bowl, coating it with wet blood. Placing her bloody palm over the dark handprint on her sister's skin, she closed her eyes and focused on the blood, guiding the *esha* she'd taken from the priest and directing it into her sister.

The blood Ephyra collected from her victims acted as a conduit to the *esha* she drained from them. If she were a properly trained healer, she would have known the correct patterns of binding that would tether her victims' *esha* to Beru. She wouldn't need to use the binding of blood.

Then again, if Ephyra were properly trained, she wouldn't have been killing in the first place. Healers with the Grace of Blood took an oath that forbid drawing *esha* from another person.

But this was the only way to keep her sister alive.

"There," Ephyra said, pressing a finger into Beru's skin, which was starting to lose that worrying grayish tinge. "All better."

For now, Beru didn't say, but Ephyra could see the words in her sister's eyes. Beru reached over and opened the drawer of the table beside the bed, withdrawing a thin black stylus. With careful, practiced motions, she pressed the stylus against her wrist, drawing a small, straight line there. It joined the thirteen others, permanently etched in alchemical ink.

Fourteen people killed. Fourteen lives cut short so that Beru could live.

It wasn't lost on Ephyra, the way Beru marked her skin each time Ephyra marked another victim. She could see the way the guilt ate at her sister after every death. The people Ephyra killed were far from innocent, but that didn't seem to matter to Beru.

"This could be the last time we have to do this," Ephyra said quietly.

This was the real reason they'd come to Pallas Athos. Somewhere in this city of fallen faith and crumbling temples, there was a person who knew a way to heal Beru for good. It was the only thing Ephyra had hoped for in the last five years.

Beru looked away.

"I brought you something else," Ephyra said, making her voice light. She reached into the little bag that hung at her belt and held out a glass bottle stopper she'd picked off the ground in the priest's room. "I thought you could use it for the bracelet you're making."

Beru took the bottle stopper, turning it over in her hand. It looked like a little jewel.

"You know I'm not going to let anything happen to you," Ephyra said, covering her sister's hand with her own.

"I know." Beru swallowed. "You're always worrying about me. Sometimes I think that's all you do. But, you know, I worry about you, too. Every time you're out there."

Ephyra tapped her finger against Beru's cheek in reproach. "I won't get hurt."

Beru brushed her thumb across the fourteen ink lines on her wrist. "That's not what I mean."

Ephyra drew her hand away. "Go to sleep."

Beru rolled over, and Ephyra climbed into the bed beside her. She lay listening to her sister's even breaths, thinking about the worry that Beru would not give name to. Ephyra worried, too, on nights like tonight, when she felt her victims' pulse slow and then stop, when she pulled the last dregs of life from them. Their eyes went dark, and Ephyra felt a sweet, sated relief, and in equal measure, a deep, inescapable fear—that killing monsters was turning her into one.